WIZARD PRINCESS

MIXED BLOOD

MICHELLE BARLOW CASILLA

Wizard Princess: Mixed Blood

ISBN   978-1-953150-70-7   (Paperback)
ISBN   978-1-953150-71-4   (Digital)

Lettra Press books may be ordered through booksellers or by contacting:

Lettra Press LLC
30 N Gould St. Suite 4753
Sheridan, WY 82801
1 307-200-3414 | info@lettrapress.com
www.lettrapress.com

 TABLE OF CONTENTS

Book II

PREFACE

Early morning dawn, with one last shimmer of the a star seen through the window; One last moment of immense pressure.

"Emily Star, OK?" She requested. She has one last look at Caesar's face.

Caesar assured her. "Emily Star it is my love".

Only one look at a precious new daughter. There was no magic, no reason, no hope. Reyna softly stroked the new babies face. Closed her eyes, and took her last breath; A quiet soft death of a new mother. With Joy of the child and devastation at the death of his love, Caesar held his child close and wept.

Reyna knew that having this child could end her life. Her heart too weak, too damaged to live through the gestation and birth of a child. But Reyna would not terminate the life created by her and her true love, Caesar. She knew that this child was special; Not only to her kind but to others as well. She knew she was special, made from true love and gifted by the Lord.

Caesar held his wife's hand and held his daughter in his other arm. The nurses and the doctor allowing him time to morn Reyna's passing. How would he be able to raise this precious child alone? What about the chance of the child inheriting her mothers ills. Not her heart weakness but her other ills. Those belonging to a sorceress and soothsayer. Those abominations of God. How would he have the know how to curb and corral these ills. He would have to ask the family to help him because he had to work. If they do help, they will want assurances about the child and her abilities.

His family never approved of Reyna. They believe her life before they married, dammed her to Hell. When they fell in love, she had given up everything and everyone to be his wife; Her friends, her family, her way of life. She took on his beliefs and his way of life. She made such changes to be his wife. So many changes to her live and how she had learned to live and survive. She gave it all up, to stay with him and love only him.

There were those dreams that she stated came from her family. There were nightmares that predicted danger and death. He was never given the details but those dreams, those nightmares, that caused his wife to scream out in her sleep. Reyna would think about them during the day. And when he asked she would just say, "Its nothing but a dream, My Love. Just a silly dream."

Sometimes Reyna would just stop and stare and say she forgot what she was doing. But she never again used her ills; at least not that he knew. She became a preacher's wife, and lived with him in a righteous and Christian home. Not that his family would ever trust her as a Christian. She was too different, and mystical; Beautiful and quiet. Never having to say much and always able to communicate with ease and grace. She could never fit in to his world perfectly. How could she. She believed, but she was from a different world. A different existence. She did fit with him and he loved her; loved her more than life and breath.

A nurse with a calm voice came close "Could I take the baby now Pastor?"

Caesar looked up through his tearing eyes and handed the baby to the nurse. He said to the Doctor, "How do I do this? How do I walk away? How do I leave here alone?" Tears ran from his eyes "How do I live without her. She is my life."

Doctor Henning placed his hand on Caesar's shoulder. He looked at Caesar and said "Do you really believe that she is still in there; In that cold and hollow body? You of all people...you know where she is".

Caesar stood up and looked at Doctor Henning's and said in a baritone voice, "With my Lord, Jacob, with my Lord".

Jacob Henning gave a weak smile, "That's right Caesar. Now, go to your family and prepare for your wife's funeral,… and your daughters homecoming". He paused a moment and as Caesar began to walk out of the delivery room of Redding Community Hospital, he said, "Call Mandra, Caesar".

Pastor Menelli looked at his friend and gave a sarcastic grin and said "Oh. Sure."

Once the Pastor had left the room, Jacob Henning sat in the Pastors chair, put his head in his hands and wept. He wept for his friend, and his friends child. But mostly, he wept for Reyna. He wept for her heart, her soul, and her beauty.

As the Pastor entered the waiting room where he expected to see his family. They were there. He saw that they sat very close together with their mother at one end of the waiting room. His brother Jason and his sister Della. held hands with their mother; all praying together. At the other end, ***the witch***, Mandra. She was dressed in her usual garb of dark color red, black, and green silk that softly moved as she did. He knew no one would need to call her as Jacob had asked him. She would just know and be there. As he walked in he looked at his family and they knew by his face that something had gone wrong. Jason was up and at his side while his mother cried in her handkerchief. He announced that he now was the father of a beautiful baby girl. He then looked over at Mandra, who had tears running down her face. He knew she knew that Reyna was gone.

She asked "I would like to pay respects to my daughter."

Caesar nodded to her and she left to see Reyna. He looked to his mother and said "She with the Lord now. I will need your help raising my child".

His mother responded in her broken Italian accent, "Of course my son. For you, and for Reyna."

Della, the Pastors sister, came to her brother and hugged him. She pulled back holding his shoulders with tears on her face and with a little shake of those shoulders, "Oh brother, I am so sorry. I will help if I can"

She moved back from the hug and looked into her brothers tearing eyes. She then stated "Well we will have to take the baby home and

Baptize her immediately. You shouldn't let the witch to close to her. You don't know what will happen".

They all heard the voice from behind them. Mandra stated in her smooth and deep penetrating voice. "I believe I have a right to see my granddaughter"

Della moved from her brother and dogmatically told Mandra, "You have no rights!"

Pastor Mendez calmed his sister with a hand on her shoulder. Without turning to look at Mandra; the Pastor said "Come with me Mandra. We will all see the beautiful child that my wife has presented us with".

The pastor, with his mother holding his arm, led the way to the nursery window.

The group found the only girl in the nursery front and center. Mandra held her handkerchief to her nose taking in the bitter sweet moment. She bent in towards the window and looked close at the sleeping child.

Mandra said, "Hello Emily Star my love".

Della's eyes grew large, then narrowed as if angered beyond control and she immediately questioned Caesar. "You never told us her name brother".

Caesar looked at his sister and stumbled over the words "Well…. Her name… well… it is …..Emily… Star".

Della challenged Mandra, "Well how did you know her name?"

Mandra stood straight looked Della and said "My Daughter told me".

Della raised her voice "How could she tell you? She's dead". Della never saw how that remark sent unbelievable pain through her brother and Mandra. Mandra looked again at her granddaughter, then kissed her own middle and index finger, and blow the kiss to baby Emily Star.

She then looked at Della and said, "Read your Bible Della. My daughter is not dead, only transformed."

Della screamed back at Mandra, "That's not what the Bible says!

Mandra smiled at Pastor Menelli "She will call me when you need me. Don't wait too long. Remember, she is special." He nodded as she walked (or floated) down the hall.

Della yelled after her "That's not what the Bible says!" Mandra was far down the hall. She rounded the corner and disappeared.

Then Mandra's voice came back to them in a whisper "He who believes in me shall never die."

CHAPTER 1

"Emily Star! You evil child" my aunt screamed as I ran out of the door. I had no idea she was planning for me but I was not hanging around to find out. I ran straight for the church where I knew my father was in the office. I jumped up the steps as fast as my nine year olds legs could go. I was looking behind me to see if my aunt was coming after me. I was taken off guard when I was caught in my father's arms.

His cordless phone placed between his ear and shoulder "Yes I have her Della." My father looked down at me with frustration "No there is no need she will never have your dogs hair fall out again. Are you sure it was Em and not a diet change or something else?"

I had nothing to do but think while in time out. With Aunt Della I spent a lot of time in time out. I never did anything right as far as she was concerned.

Dad sighed and sat on the steps and put me down next to him. "Yes! No!" There was a pause for Aunt Della to complain more about me. "Della I will talk to her. Well that's all there is." He looked down at me again with a bit of humor in his eyes and then caught himself. His gaze turned stern and I was in trouble. "OK Della. OK Della. Well maybe I should" Another pause was taken. "What about Taylor?"

I cringed and thought, *Oops, that's not good.* I thought she would like it. She was saying that Taylor needed a hair cut for the summer.

"Taylor has no hair at all?" Dad look down at me then rolled his eyes. "Well I can't talk to her while I am listening to you. OK BYE!"

Dad hung up the phone and placed it behind us. He held both my arms and looked very stern, "Em, when are you going to stop this. You know the church teachings about sorcery and witchcraft, and yet you still keep doing these things. Your aunt thinks I should spank you."

Tears entered my eyes and I remember saying to him " But Daddy, . I'm always told not to, but no one *ever*showed me *how*not to. Besides, Taylor's only three. He isn't; going any where special where he would need his hair." Dad looked serious as he in his thoughts.

"Dad, Aunt Della is always vacuuming after that dog because his hair is always falling out. He was hot and I thought about it and all his hair fell out. I really didn't mean too! And Aunt Della was complaining about Taylor needing a hair cut and I only though about it".

Tears rolling down my face, my father looked at me in a strange way. "Daddy, I'm not as bad as Aunt Della thinks. I am trying to be good like they teach in Sunday school. It just not working,"

Nothing ever worked. I really did not try to do these things. They just happened. My father hoped for a new TV. I wanted him to have it. And it was there. Of course he said to send it back. But how? I didn't know where it came from. Aunt Della was cold when we came in the house and a fire started in the woodstove. My father would say he wanted a sandwich and a Dagwood would appear on the table. Then I called Dad through my mind, and he heard me as if I spoke right in his ear. Well that one was bad. He did not handle that well. He told me never to do that again. My father would talk about the church needing a new coat of paint. We had a pink Church for a week because I thought it would be prettier pink.

I really did not do anything as serious as it could have been but enough to cause my mortal father real concern. It was not easy for a Christian Pastor to raise his daughter who was a Natural Witch like her mother. My mother Reyna, his beautiful wife, who he loved completely. Who took his heart when she left this earth. I, her child, was all that was left of her; an exact image of her. I had green eyes that looked like a clear ocean. Long dark hair with red highlights spun through. I was his only child, but I was a child of a different world. Not intended to be raised by mortals. But looking back, I believe that God want me there first. God wanted me to know first, that I was his child.

Dad was thinking for very deeply as he held me on the steps of the church. He pulled me into a hug. "Your right baby, its time someone showed you *how not to*." He sighed and then spoke under his breath, "But then she will show you how to do it better."

I said "What?" Not because I did not hear him, but because I did not understand him. He was quite and still for a minute.

It looked as if my father said a little prayer and then asked me. "I need you to think of a name for me, OK?"

I dried my face with my sleeve and asked "What kind of name Daddy? A girls name or a boys name?"

He smiled at me with his big brown eyes, "It's a girl's name. But I need to give you the name and you just have to call her in your mind, OK?"

I looked at him confused "But Dad, you said not to do that."

He hugged me and said "I know baby but I think we need your grandmother and that's the only way we can find her… quickly."

Again I looked at him confused and said "Nana is at home, Dad."

My father looked at me with humor again and then with concern. "Not Nana, honey, you need to call your mothers mom. Can you do that?"

I look at him and said "OK but I don't know who she is. Can you tell me what she looks like? Oh and I need her name".

My Dad was quite a minute and seemed to be struggling with a problem. He looked down at me again and then he described my grandmother. "She looks a lot like your mom, *and you*. She always wore her hair very long and dark like yours. It also had that red that shines in the sun like yours. Her eyes are like yours in a way. They are a blue green instead of real green like yours. She was not very big but she filled a room and never says much. But on the day you were born, she said she would come when we called. Her name is Mandra."

Mandra, my grandmother. I never knew I had another grandmother. Of course, no one told me about my mom's family. I did not even have a picture of my mom. They thought if they removed any indicators of my other side, my *Ills* would go away.

I closed my eyes and thought about this woman with the long dark hair like mine; the blue green eyes. I saw her with her dark brown hair blowing in the wind with her silken white robes. She was on a cliff over looking the ocean standing regal. She had many other people with her, all in the same white robes. In my mind, she appeared with arms out starched and a smile on her face.

In my mind I called *"Mandra…. Grandmother we need you."*

I did not even try to hear but there was a voice. It was low and soft. *"I am coming to you my precious Star."*

I opened my eyes and Dad was looking at me. I smiled, "She called me her precious Star. She is coming."

Dad went white. "O my God. What have I done? I don't know if I can do this after all these years. Lord forgive me."

Remembering that I was there, Dad brought himself under control and said, "You know Em, your mother never used her *'ills'* when she and I were married. I hoped you would not have inherited these ills, but you did. I am not sure how to deal with this. I need to pray so go play and don't pester your Aunt or the animals." He started to get up and said, "And Em Star, watch that cat. I don't want him pestering your aunt's dog. Precious has been through enough today. I am sure that now that Precious has no hair, Zee can really hurt him."

Dad looked really troubled. With a weak little smile he said." Do you think you could, at least, picture your cousin Taylor with eye brows and lashes?"

I looked at him and raised my shoulders because I did know if I could do that. He kissed my check and smiled. Dad got to his feet and moved to the door of the church. "Em, don't go too far. I know Mandra, and she will not take long."

CHAPTER 2

We lived in a small village in Northern California called Hat Creek. My Dad was the local Preacher for the Assembly of Christ Church. He also would preach in Redding and Chico from time to time. Hat creek was a forested area in Lassen National Park. The creek was always running and provided for good trout fishing. There were a lot of campers and fisherman in the summer and only cold and snow in the winter. The pines smelled sweet and towered over our little town. Chipmunks ran free through the town and the forest. The town consisted of a small store that sold gas, beer and bait. It also had a small inventory of groceries. Attached to the store was a small garage for car repairs and tires. They also aided unprepared travelers with snow tires and chains. We usually went into Redding twice a month for our supplies.

Mr. And Mrs. Anderson ran the local restaurant and motel. There place also substituted for the town gathering place and bar. It was the only one for at least fifty miles. And though there were few homes in town, the church filled on Sunday and the park after church for a community picnic. Well that is when the weather held. Usually, from November to late March or early April, the snow would be deep. It would be cold and Highway 44 was very treacherous in the winter.. Dad had very few for church in those winter months so the donations were few and far between. Most of the residents would leave in the winter to find work elsewhere and then return in the spring. Only the Snow movers, Loggers and Mill workers remained. In those times the Baptist churches in Redding 80 miles away, and Chico would help with a small salary for Dad. He, of course, would reciptacate by covering the other preachers when they were sick or out of town. It was those times that I was left with my aunt Della.

I was home schooled primarily because of the ills and my Dad was afraid. But also, because I would have to be bused so far and be gone until dark. He also felt that he could control what I was exposed to if he home schooled me.

My Uncle, Jason lived in Chico and is a teacher. Aunt Della also lived in Chico for a while. She and her husband John had a religious store there. They lived in the apartment above the store. John made a monthly trip to Sacramento for inventory once a month. One day, when he was on one of these inventory missions, he never made it to Sacramento. He had a heart attach and died.

From that point, Aunt Della sold her building and moved in with us. Of course, she never liked my mother, and she never hid the fact. She helped my father in cleaning the home and cooking. She was also left in charge of me because Nana was too old now to watch me. My father spent a great deal of time protecting me from my aunt's rants and rages.

Nana, who had always lives with us, would also make her attempts to protect me from my aunt. She would quietly tell my aunt "Please Daughter, the child, is a child." My aunt looked at my Nana as an old woman without brains; A pest who interfered. I use to hate my aunt for that alone. Nana was a quiet angel. Watching, measuring and praying. I will never forget her chuckle at the bald kid and dog.

What I remember most about Nana is that she loved me. Even with my ills. She always told me I was blessed, and special. It didn't matter to me weather I was special or not. I was blessed with her quiet and deep love for me.

I walked over to the creek behind the house. Zee, my notorious cat, followed me close. A big Siamese that Dad allowed me to adopt from the Redding Human Society. I had eyed a little black kitten but Aunt Della refused to allow me to take a "Black Cat".

She probably regretted that move. Zee was not a bad cat. He never bothered the chipmunks or hurt the birds. He did stock them but that was instinct. He always held back and never touched the other animals;

none but not my aunts Precious. He found great enjoyment out of pestering and scratching Precious. Aunt Della could never get close to me when Zee was near. Aunt Della threw Zee out of the house for good about a year ago. But every night when I go to my room, he is there in the bed waiting for me. It wasn't me that wished it, he was just there. He was my best friend. My only friend since I was labeled a child of a Witch. The other kids that are in the area would have nothing to do with me. Not even in church or Sunday school.

I was a strange child. I knew that. I talked to animals like I knew what they were thinking and like they could understand me. Nana said it was a sensitivity I had for them. The birds often sat around me sing beautiful little tunes. And sometimes they would jump around and scream at me that something was wrong. The hawk would give the single screech of alls well with the world. And then the three screams of trouble and danger But there were the strange things too. Things I did not understand. I loved running free through the creek and the forests. I would sing hymns at the top of my lungs and not one would hear me. But I also I would hear whispers in the forests. I would run through trying to figure out who it was. I would hear things like "Princess." And "The Princess plays in the forests." I would search and never see or find any such princess. I would often hide in the field behind the long grove of pines. There no one could see me. I would dance and dance to music that was always playing there. That mystical, beautiful music that sent peace and happiness to me. Then I would hear the whispers "She dances." I would stop dancing and I would look and look and never find anyone there. But I would hear the music. The mystical and beautiful music I loved so much.

Then, one day I said out loud, "Who is the Princess and where does the music come from?"

Then I heard the Whisper of "You are the Princess and the music is from us."

I was astounded. "Who are you?"

And then I heard "The trees of the forest. We are your friends, Princess." I smiled to the reference that they were my friends. And they would ask "Will you dance for us Princess?" And of course I always did. I loved to dance. But of course no one could ever understand that the trees were my friends, or the clouds, or the wind. It was a real bad thing to tell my family anything that may not be normal in their mortal world.

In my dreams I would hear voices that I did not recognize and men in long dark robes. I thought they were preachers. But they scared me. I would wake up crying. I was often afraid to sleep. I was afraid of the robed men with the monster faces. Often Zee would look out the window and growl. I would go to the window and not see a thing. Only the wind would be moving the trees. And I would hear the wind. Yes, the wind would talk to me too. It was strange and Dad never would believe me. It would always greet me and a wish of good tidings. But sometimes it blow beware.

I often thought I was not an evil witch but a delayed child or had a brain malfunction. But the world of Mortals that I lived in, labeled me Witch. They offered no other explanations to why these things were with me. And other than punishment and prayer, no one was able to help me or cure me of my ills. Things just kept happening and punishment and prayer were the only answers. My fathers frustration and concern; My aunt's disapproval.

I sat on a fallen log and the tears fell off my cheeks.

"Zee, I wish I was what they want me to be. But I am not. I don't know what I am. Maybe Aunt Della is right and I am evil." Zee climbed on to my lap and nudged my tear filled face. I hugged him and really cried at that moment.

Then I heard her. "You are what God the creator has made you. You are not evil unless you chose to be." Nana had come up behind me without me hearing her or sensing her.

"Oh Nana, why does Aunt Della hate me?"

My grandmother sat with me as Zee jumped down. "Oh child, your aunt is afraid of you and for you. She loves you but she is afraid." Nana put her arm around me and hugged me close. "Mandra, your other grandmother is coming soon to take you, I am sure."

I looked surprised at Nana. "No Nana! I don't want to leave Daddy or you!"

My Grandmother patted my back as she held me, "Child, you have to learn to care for your special gifts or you could hurt yourself." I looked up at her again, and she continued "Mandra will teach you. She also needs to know her granddaughter."

My grandmother spoke of Mandra as if she held no malice toward her yet I have never been told of this other grandmother. Nana looked at the creek for a time. She then turned to me and said " I am close to 80 years old my child. If I have learned a lesson in life it is that we should never disrespect or condemn any of Gods creations or gifts. You, your mother and your grandmother, all have been chosen by God to have abilities beyond the normal person. It will take faith, love and responsibility to use those gifts from God. And you my child are especially gifted. You are chosen by the creator for special things."

With out looking at my grandmother I told her "Daddy calls my ...." I did not know what to call these abilities," These things, *Ill's*, and I must never use them."

She tilted her head and said "Your father is afraid you will be hurt." She then looked at me and smiled, "He needs to allow you to be who you are; to find your true self."

I lifted my mouth to one side and said "An evil creature".

Nana giggled "Never my love. You know that evil could never be as loved as you are. You mother and your father were never evil and you will never be evil. And my child, you have a great responsibility in the future." She looked at the creek rolling by and we listened to the trickled of the water.

"Nana, why haven't you told me about this other grandmother?"

Nana hugged be and said "It was wrong not to tell you about your other side. But your father did not want you to know. He insisted that he and God knew what was best for you. He refused to consider that you would need a different kind of teaching though I argued with him about that." She giggled and then said "You proved my point little one."

Nana got quite and then said "Your mother had a wonderful heart. She believed in God and she did what ever she had to in making your father happy; except when she became pregnant with you. She was not a strong person as you know, her heart was irregular. The Doctors told her that she may not survive pregnancy, but she could not bring herself to the thought of not having you. Your father was a mess. He begged her not to go through with it. But she only smiled at him and told him that you were the result of the love they shared. She stated that you would be special, and she was so right." Nana looked deep into my eyes, "You must not let fear of others make you less than a gift of God and Reyna. You must be strong and brave. You have much to do. Much to do so that you, and others, are free to be different."

CHAPTER 3

Later that evening, while we sat at the dinner table, I heard her voice, *"I am here little Star."* I dropped my fork, looked directly at Dad and jumped from the table. I had to see this woman; this creature for my self. My father called after me as my aunt made her usual complaint against me.

"Dad, she is here. She's here!"

I ran from the kitchen through the dinning and Living rooms to the front door. I opened it wide and as true as the voice in my head, a woman stood by her car at the front of the walkway to the house. Only able to go so far, I stood on the porch unable to move any further.

She was beautiful. She was an older woman, but not like Nana. She looked young somehow. She looked more alive. She wore a soft red skirt that blew in the breeze. She wore boots and a red hooded cape that surrounded her. She stood and stared at me with a faint smile. Her head tilted down her hands under the cape.

Soon Dad was behind me with his hands on my shoulders. "Mandra, how are you?"

At that, her smile increased and she moved forward slowly. The whole time she was looking into my eyes. Her greeting to my father was a simple. "Caesar."

She walked as though she was floating; graceful and elegant. She lowered her hood and I could see, as Dad had said; her hair was long like mine, dark with white streaks through it. Her eyes remained on mine as she approached the porch. She stopped when our eyes were even.

"Hello my little Star. I have waited many years to see you again; though I have watched." She was so pretty. Old but pretty. I was enchanted with her. I couldn't speak or respond. I could only stare.

My father shook my shoulders slightly. "Em, this is your grandmother, Mandra."

I was still frozen. I could not move or say a word. Mandra then moved up the stairs and kissed her gloved fingers and blow them at me. I felt the kiss. It was as if she had truly kissed my cheek.

"Come in out of the cold Mandra" Nana held the door for us.

Mandra's eyes looked to the door. "Maria. How are you my friend?"

Nana smiled and took Mandra's hand, "Good and better now that I have seen you again. Our little one is in need of your help."

We all walked into the house. Della walked into the parlor and stopped dead in her tracks when she saw Mandra. She shouted "This is you solution, Caesar?" She was really upset "This cant be it. She will never be saved by this being. You're the Preacher, Caesar! You know this is wrong."

Mandra looked at Della without any feeling in her eyes. "Well, hello Della."

Della turned to Mandra and spoke curtly "Mandra, you know this is not the way. She needs to be cured of these ills and we should not encourage them."

Mandra remained calm and spoke softly, "And has your way worked to 'cure' her, Della?"

Mandra looked at my father then back to Della. "Punishing the child for what comes natural? Criticizing and humiliating is not producing the desired result?"

Mandra then turned to my father, "You know what must happen. She needs instruction and acceptance for who and what she is. You can provide that now, or suffer consequences later. It should have begun by five years of age."

Della then indignantly said "How Dare you say such a thing. We are raising the child in the Lord."

Mandra then turned her head, her chin lowered, looking at Della "How dare you and the way you have treated a small child in the name of the Lord. For the Lord said that any one who harms a child would be like one thrown into the ocean with a milestone around his neck." Mandra threw her hand and Aunt Della then sat on the settee and was quiet.

"Emily Star?" My new found grandmother called in her silky soft voice. I looked up at her and heard in my head, *"Pack a bag for the summer. Grab that stinker of a cat. You will stay with me for the summer and back in time for school."*

I looked at Dad. He must have hear Grandmother as well. He smiled at me and said, "Go on Em, you need to go with her."

"But Daddy, what about you? I don't know where she will take me."

He grabbed me into one of his bear hugs "I love you Em. Mandra loves you though you don't know that yet. She will never let harm come to you."

I nodded and ran up to my room and packed. I knew I did not have to find Zee. He was most likely already in the car. I came down the stairs with my duffle bag in tow. At the bottom of the stairs was father who looked like he was lost in a fog.

"I will miss you my daughter." his voice went very low " I love you so much." I dropped my duffle and flew into his arms. Tears filled my eyes as I told my Dad that I loved him. He pulled away and said "Mandra… Your grandmother, will help you control these....*things*that get us into trouble. Be good and listen to her for me. I know she thinks the world of you and you will have fun"

I looked at him hurting to leave him, "Oh Daddy, I wish I was normal and you didn't have to worry about me so much. Then you wouldn't be sending me away."

My Dad went to his knees and said "I love you for who you are. I love everything about you. I know that you will know how much in years to come. But… I know that you need to learn about these things. I know that I cant teach you how **Not to.**"

I looked over at Nana who held her arms out to me and I ran to her embrace. "You remember are talk we had today. You remember that your Nana will always love you and will always be with you." I kissed her cheek and turned to Aunt Della. Taylor was sitting on the floor by his mother.

"Bye, Aunt Della. I will see you in the fall."

Mandra looked over to Della and waved her hand. As if released from a vice, Aunt Della stood up and walked to me. She bent over and kissed my head and said "We will miss you, Emily Star." She hugged me tightly. I went over to Taylor and kissed his bald head.

Turning to my grandmother Mandra, she closed her eyes and tilted her head. I heard Aunt Della's loud intake of breath. I turned around and Taylor had all of his hair back. Precious came from the kitchen running in his full white coat.

Mandra looked at Aunt Della "Your welcome. But next time remember, Emily Star will always aim to please those she loves. When you wish for something, she will try to grant the wish. She will do this without knowing she is doing it. You need to take some of the responsibility in those cases. And be careful in the future. Be careful for what you wish for" Della look straight at Mandra and nodded.

Dad, Mandra and I walked to my grandmother's car. The trunk popped open and though I though it was Mandra's powers but it was her keyless function. My dad opened my door and I got in. He bent down and kissed my cheek and told me. Learn all you can so that you can live without trouble." Zee jumped into my lap as Mandra started the car as she said, "You know Caesar, you could have called me without Emily Star's, what do you call it, her *Ills*? I do have a phone." They giggled together. I could see that my Dad did not hate Mandra and Mandra did not hate him. Mandra handed Dad a business card. Dad looked at Mandra and said "How did you get here so fast?" Catching himself he looked at her with a half smile and said "Never mind." He looked at me once more "Take care of my girl Mandra." She nodded and we were off.

CHAPTER 4

"Where are we going Grandmother?" She did not speak, but I saw a picture in my mind. It was a beautiful white cottage like house with a wrap around porch. There was a steep cliff and a beach with large tall boulders along the water line, and the waves crashing against the boulders with a dramatic impact. I asked her with my mind how long it would take to get there. I could see the corners of her mouth curl upward, and I heard in my mind, "*a few days.*" We would be normal and drive, whatever that meant. We would be stopping along the way and staying the night in Redding and then Roseburg tomorrow. We needed to catch up and I needed to be prepared when we arrived there. I would now be with others like me.

Like me? Like me! I was not an evil freak. I was like others. Others that I would get to know. Who could help me control my 'ills.' I can be normal and accepted and not have to worry about a kid's hair falling out or curtailing the milk, or the fire in the stove starting with out a match, and that sort of thing. I was so excited. Then I was very scared.

We arrived in Redding around nine o'clock. Mandra stopped at the Oxford Suites and got a Suite for us. They did not allow animals in the rooms so we left Zee in the car. By the time we entered the suit and I went to the room Mandra pointed out for me, Zee was there. "Good one Zee. Now how do I get you out without the guys at the desk seeing you". He only purred loudly and cleaned his coat. I dropped my bag on the floor and dug out my pajamas.

I looked out to the main room. "I am going to shower, Grandmother."

Before I could turn away, she looked over at me with a smile. "I am telling your father in his dreams that we are here and ok."

My heart stopped in my chest. "But grandmother, he will be upset by that. He doesn't like those things."

My grandmother smiled and said "Oh, I think he can handle it. He has told me about you a hundred times in his dreams." She sighed a little and continued "He will understand and be happy to know we are OK." I nodded and left her on the couch while I took my shower.

While toweling my hair, I left the bathroom to find that grandmother had some food and milkshakes but up. Grilled cheese and a chocolate shake. We sat at the table and grandmother looked at me softly. "You know Emily Star; you look like your mother."

I smiled, "I really do? I mean Dad told me I did but I was never sure. We don't have any pictures of her." Grandmother got up and went to her bag. She came back with a photo. It was my mother, Reyna. She was beautiful with her green eyes and her black hair.

I looked at my grandmother and stated "She is so beautiful, and I do see myself but I am not beautiful like she is."

Mandra took the picture and turned it to look better at it. "Well, she is about twenty years old there, and you, my little one, are only nine. How do you know how beautiful you will be at twenty? We will all have to wait and see."

I looked at her with skepticism, "You know grandmother, you could tell me. I really want to know."

She smiled and said "Some things, little Star, are not for us to know."

She took the empty plates and put them back on the cart. She then moved to the couch. She looked over at me and motioned for me to sit by her. I made my way over to her and sat sideways on the couch so that we were facing each other.

She took my hands in hers and continued to look at our hands entwined. "You must not believe all the horrible things you have heard from others about you powers." My powers? I was lost and confused. Powers is what she called them. No ills or evil. Grandmother smiled. "Powers, Emily Star. God gave them to you. They can't be evil unless you want them to be and then there is a price for that. Your powers do not only come from my side of the family or you would not be so strong. Maria, my dear Maria, is descended from the old county Gypsy witches. She too has a little bit of premonitions and sight." Mandra looked into my eyes that had filled with tears and the fight not to sob. "You are not evil. You are perfect, and powerful."

At that point, I cried openly. "I never wanted to believe that I was evil. But I kept doing these things that were not normal. No matter how I tried I always mess things up."

Mandra petted my hair. "Little Emily Star, you are not evil. As with the others who chose to call you evil, you are created by God, and he thinks you are perfect, just like I do."

She took her hanky and wiped my eyes and handed it to me to blow my nose. "You need to learn how to control your powers and not let the powers control you. It is much like…. your arm. You tell your arm to move not visa versa. Right?" I nodded that I understood.

"Am I really a Witch, Grandmother?"

She smiled and nodded "Yes; A very special witch."

I looked at her confused, "But Grandmother, Witches are evil and ugly."

She started to Laugh. "No my little Star, Witches are not evil and ugly." She hugged me and continued. "Over hundreds of years, it was laid out that Magical people were evil or servants of Satan. But in reality, Witches believe in God and Mother Earth. We are not evil and do not harm others. If a witch does harm another, the act will return three fold."

I looked at her then and asked "I believe in God and his laws." Mandra smiled and said "So do I, and I am a witch as you are." She giggled, "God created witches as well as mortals. He created several races. He had many worlds working in one. Most of the time, the worlds work together, one ignoring the other. And then they work together unaware that they are doing so. I know this is confusing. And it will be confusing for a while. But what you need to understand is that you, my dear, are special. You are chosen by God to be most powerful." I was confused. I wanted to know and learn but I was confused.

She smiled and then commented, "Zee has been a good little guardian for you." I was in shook again. Mandra giggled. "Yes. I sent him." At that moment Zee appeared on the couch and climbed into my lap.

"But I almost took a black kitten."

Zee looked up and made a soft mew. Mandra had a big smile, "No that would not have happened. He was sent and he is the only one that you could have chosen."

Scratching Zee's ears, I made the claim "I am so glad. He is my dear friend. I love him very much."

Mandra petted Zee and said "Then I made a good choice. Now, go to bed and we will talk again tomorrow." Zee leaped from my lap and as I stood I looked at Mandra. This woman, only hours old in my life, made me feel more loved, more normal than anyone in my life.

"Could I hug you good night?"

My newfound grandmother smiled and I could see her joy. "You never have to ask to hug me. I am always available for hugging."

I reached for her and hugged tightly. "Thank you grandmother. Thank you so much."

Zee and I crawled into the bed and I began my prayers. *Lord, thank you for my grandmother, Both of them, but my grandmother Mandra. I feel normal with her. I think I may fit with her. Take care of Daddy he really doesn't want to deal with the ills. He is a good Christian, Lord, and a good preacher. He doesn't want to do things that will make you mad or hurt you. It has been hard with me there. Well … God bless Daddy, Nana, Taylor, Aunt Della, and Zee. And now God bless my grandmother, Mandra. Amen.*

CHAPTER 5

I don't remember falling asleep, but more unusual was that I don't remember dreaming. I woke to the smell of bacon and eggs. I got out of bed and put on my robe. I walk to the doorway where the table was set and my grandmother sat reading a paper and drinking coffee. She never moved her eyes but smiled and said "Good morning my little Star. Breakfast is ready."

I smiled and felt wonderful, "Good Morning, Grandmother" I hurriedly made my way to the table and took the cover off the plate. I drank some juice, and then grabbed a piece of bacon. My grandmother put down the paper and gracefully began her meal. Not like me, just digging in. She was graceful; taking her napkin and putting on her lap, then removing the cover off her plate. Taking small bits and chewing quietly. It was so different from what I was used to that I became self conscious of my own eating habits. I watched her as she bit her toast and picked up her cup.

"You will learn many things with me, Emily Star" she looked up at me then "Many things. But for now, eat and we will be on our way." I felt so connected to her, so right being with her. And I did not know her.

Once the meal was over I washed up, brushed my teeth and changed my clothes. I put all my things back in the duffle bag. When I walked out of the room, Zee was having cream on the table.

"Oh no! Zee! How will I get him out with out the people seeing him?"

My grandmother smiled, waved her hand and he was gone. I stared at the spot where Zee was a second ago and then slowly turned to my grandmother.

"He's in the car waiting for us."

My grandmother stated nonchalantly as she picked up her bag. I was not expecting this but it was kind of cool, scary, but cool.

"Can I do that?"

My grandmother retorted "Not right now. So let's get on the road."

I followed her out of the hotel with a little grin. And sure enough, there was Zee waiting on my seat. It was a warm day. Redding can be as hot as Hat Creek can be cold. I was late May and the sun shined bright. So once in the car, grandmother pushed a button and the top of the car retracted. She handed me a hair scrunchy "Put you hair back so it isn't blowing everywhere." She put on a scarf and tied it around her head. I still thought she was so beautiful and somehow young.

We started out heading for Roseburg Oregon. The day was beautiful and warm. We drove for a few hours and got into Medford. The mountains fields were green and smelled heavenly. The clouds billowed across the sky leaving shadows across the ground as they passed. It was cooler here and when we stopped at the Dennies to eat, my grandmother put the top up on the car. I gave Zee some food and water. He was eating when we left him.

"Coffee, Please" my grandmother ordered as she looked over the menu.

"Could I have a coke, please?" I requested from our waitress.

The Waitress smiled at me and said "Sure. I will be back with your drinks and to take your order."

It was really a treat for me because I was never allowed out much. It was risky and I could make a mistake. I turn my attention to my grandmother as she put down her menu. She asked if I knew what I wanted and I told her "Yes." Then I asked "Grandmother, what do you want me to know before we get to Pacific City?"

She looked at me with some concern "You need to be prepared to see many things that you have not had in your home. Different people with different beliefs. Many who don't believe as I do, or as your father does. Your faith must be strong and you need to be prepared for the differences and how not to judge though they will judge you."

She continued to look concerned. Then I heard her in my head, "*They believe in nothing or the devil. They have bizarre rituals that are not our way. Many look for power they do not possess as you and I do. Beware not to entertain their life styles, and beware to be what God has made you and not their tool to be used; though you are obligated by our kind.*" She smiled then and continued "*In my group, we are what are known as Natural Witches; each witch with their own special little powers and talents. We keep to our selves and play by the rules of the normal mortal world.*"

The Waitress came back with our drinks and took our order. I took a sip of the coke and then looked at my grandmother with a serious expression. I asked in my mind, "*Are there kids in your group? I mean, kids like me?*" She was pleased with me. I could tell by the expression in her face that she was usually guarded.

She responded in kind "*Yes little Star. Yes there are many children. Not many have any powers, and yours are stronger and more extensive than most that do*".

Our order arrived and we ate speaking aloud and about the drive and all of the things we saw like the cattle and the red tailed hawk. I loved seeing the horses and the deer eating in the meadows. Once in the car, and Zee on my lap, we headed north to Roseburg.

CHAPTER 6

We made it to Roseburg around four O'clock. Grandmother insisted that we get a room before we did anything else. Once we had our rooms, which were connected by a door, we settled on my bed and watched a movie. When the movie ended, grandmother ordered a pizza at my request. We sat on my bed and are and talked. Of course, Zee was there too, though we left him in the car.

"Tomorrow we will be home." My Grandmother announced. Many of our family and friends will be there to meet us."

My mind went to the word "Family". I asked her "We have family there?"

My grandmother daintily cleaned her mouth with a paper napkin, "Well yes. I have two other children besides your mother. I have a son named Matt and another Daughter named Elena; she is 17."

I stopped chewing my mouth full of pizza and looked at my grandmother and said "A 17 year old Aunt?"

She nodded her head as she swallowed. "She is much like your mother. She does not have powers as your mother. She is intuitive though. But your mother was much more grounded. Elena has fewer patients; more …..adventurous."

I asked "Will she be there at your house?" Mandra looked at me and said she would be.

"Now, let's get down to business." My Grandmother moved the pizza box off the bed and on to the dresser. She came back to the bed and laid down next to me so we were face to face. She stoked my hair and moves a strand from my eyes. "You have to pay close attention to the things I am going to tell you know." I was more than agreeable. I really was so curious about it all. It was all about who I was. Not just that evil Emily Star Menelli, but someone with more to her. I had family like me.

"When we get settled, you will be spending time with Edith. She is my dear friend and a trainer for our kind. She is what we call a Master Witch."

Witch. There was that name again. That title; that label. I was so unsure. I wondered if I really could be a witch as she said? I looked at grandmother and asked again "Am I truly a Witch?"

My grandmother smiled and nodded. "A very special witch. One with great power, or so I am told. Edith will train you in several areas and soon you will be able to control your .....desires in working your powers. You will be left with her each day after breakfast until lunch. Then you will come to my store with me. I need you to be responsible for your self getting to the store." I answered her with a yes but could not understand why she would believe me unable to get to the store without issues arising.

"I have a shop in town where I sell candles, books, fragrances, art and such. There are also many things of the craft. Some of those in town are not so nice about my store. They believe that the store is against God. So be nice and don't be too hurt at some things they say. We just ignore the comments and they don't, for the most part, come into the store. But we do well in spite of it. While most leave us be, there are some that are not so nice. Don't use magic and don't be fresh." I nodded really not understanding the full warning.

"Now, I want you to try something for me. I want you to look at the light and imagine it turned off. Do you think you can do that?"

I became nervous, What if the light did something I did not intend. What if the light blow up or something. I looked at my grandmother. "Grandmother, I make things happen that are bad and not what I really want to happen."

She smiled at me. "I will walk you through it, OK?" I nodded and took a deep breath. "Now, close your eyes and imagine the room dark."

I closed my eyes and saw the room as dark. I opened them and the room was dark. But as I looked out the window, I could see the city completely dark. Not one light twinkled anywhere. With chagrin I bellowed "No, not again!"

Grandmother smiled and asked "Again?"

She then waved her hand and all the lights went back on. "OK. Lets try this a different way. Look at the light, direct all of your attention to the light and ask it to turn off."

I looked at her and asked "No closing my eyes?"

She was very direct and said "No. Look directly at the light and ask the light".

I looked up and then back at my grandmother, "Ask it?" She nodded sternly. So, I looked at the light and concentrated on the light. I asked the light "Turn off, Please." To my amazement, the light, and only the light, went out. The city was still lit. I leaped to my knees and bounced up and down. "Grandmother! Grandmother I did it. I did it!. I'm going to turn it back on. OK?"

She patted my hand and I looked at the light, and said "Turn on, please." nothing happened.

Grandmother said "You must concentrate."

I looked up directed all of my focus on the light. "Turn on, please." Once again I was taken back by the light illuminating the room once again.

I looked at Grandmother and she smiled at me and said "Very Good. If you practice that and master it, you are half way there." She hugged me tight. "Now, it is time for bed."

As she pulled back the blanket and sheet of the bed I asked her "Grandmother, tell me about my family?"

She smiled and began "Your uncle lives in Minnesota with his family and works as a engineer. No one there knows that he is able to read their minds. Your Aunt Elena lives with me. We enjoy gatherings on Saturdays with our friends at the house."

"Now that is enough of that. Sleep and we will be there tomorrow."

I said "OK. Thank you grandmother." I looked at her very thoughtfully. "Grandmother, you have always been near? Watching me?"

She pulled the sheet back for me and as I got under the sheets, she said "Yes. Always."

I laid my head on the pillow and asked "Why did you wait so long to come for me. I really needed to know this stuff before this." I held her eyes "I needed you before this."

She sat on the bed next to me. Looked down and said "I could not be there until your father was ready. I knew that your powers unbridled would cause problems, and that he and Della would be unable to deal with them. I did not expect your father to wait so long." She paused, "Maybe he wanted to hold on to you and not lose you as he did your mother. He did love her so." She was tucking me in. "But you will be home in the fall. He will have you back." she paused; looked into my eyes and said "and then I will miss you until you come back to me in the summer." She kissed my forehead and quietly said good night. As she left the room she said "Out light" and light was out.

CHAPTER 7

Through the trees and heading down the highway, a few hours and we arrived in Pacific City. We drove through a fishing area where the boats waited for the next days work. As we drove through the little village, grandmother showed me her store. It was a small store with a white front and two bay windows on either side of the entrance. "Dreams &Wishes" read the sign at the roof line. There were fancy bottles and candles in the front windows on display.

We went north of the town where I could see the sun on the ocean. Shortly we turned on a side road and there were houses scattered along. A left turn took us up a hill where at the top was the house I saw in my thoughts. It was a white cottage like home. It was a large house though, with two stories and third story of only a little room on top. There was a wraparound porch that was large and had chairs and a swing in front. There was a view of the Ocean but also a cliff. There was a fence around the cliff edge. There was trail to the beach. The yard was massive. Like a football field with the grass. Then over on the ocean side of the house was a gate with a garden. As we pulled up in the drive way, several people exited the home.

I looked at my grandmother and she said "I told you they would be waiting. You have been known to many and they have been waiting to meet you."

"Who are they grandmother?" I was so scared. I don't know exactly why. Maybe because some were dressed in suits and dresses like they were in church. There was this huge man. He must have been seven or eight feet tall. His hair was white and he was very intimidating. My Grandmother never answered my question only parked the car and told me to grab my bag and cat. I got out of the car went to the trunk and pulled out my duffle. I looked and Zee was still on the seat of the car.

"Come on. If I have to do this, so do you!"

He looked at me and leaped into the back seat. The next thing I knew, the really huge guy was standing on the other side of the car door. My heart stopped beating.

With a funny accent he said "Miss Emily Star. I am Lincon. I will take your bag."

My neck was bent straight back. His eyes were blue, but so light, they almost matched his white hair. I never said a word and only handed him the duffle bag. He turned sharply and walked back to the porch were the crowd was waiting. I stood there for a minute then looked at Mandra.

She was at the porch. In my head I heard *"Come now Emily Star. No one will harm you."* Normally, at home, efforts are made to limit my exposure to other people. This was so new and scary for me.

I reached into the car for Zee. He hissed in protest. I ignored his reluctance and repeated "If I have too, you have too! So we might as well do it together." I grabbed him off the back seat and look over to the porch again.

I walk slower that I normally do. All eyes were on me and that made me very uncomfortable. Then one of the many faces came forward with a smile. She was dressed much like my grandmother except she wore a heavy gray sweater.

"Hello Emily Star, I am Edith. The Master Witch. I will be your tutor. Is this your Grimalkin" Her attention was on Zee. I had no idea what she meant.

I said "This is Zee, my cat."

She and the group giggled and then she reached out and Zee accepted her pet. I decided that she must be alright if Zee accepted her touch. I stared up the steps to reach my grandmother who was waiting. But at each step another would introduce them selves to me. Benny was next. He was about my age, thank God. He lived down the road and was Edith's grandson. Next was Millie. She was younger than my grandmother but very much like her in that she spoke softly. Millie lived in town and worked at grandmother's store. Gordon was Millie's husband and he seemed really nice. He invited me over any time and then he introduced me to their daughter Mandy. She was dressed in a pink dress and had white ribbons in her hair. She said hello and I responded in kind.

Grandmother finally came to my rescue "OK Em, you can meet everyone later. For now I will show you your room." I followed after her but when I reached the door, there was a blond woman smiling down at me at me. Zee growled his warning and I moved fast through the door hurrying after Mandra. I looked back and the Blond woman was staring after me, but she was not smiling. She was then scowling.

There was a entry way with a dinning room to the left and a parlor to the right. There was a tall stairway to the second story of the house. Grandmother and I went up stairs and at the top were four bedrooms and a bathroom. The bedroom my grandmother lead me to was beautiful. The bed was big and had several pillows across the headboard. The headboard was rod iron and bedspread was white and matched the sheers that covered the windows and blow with the ocean breeze. There was also a cat tree for Zee. I let him go then and he went straight for the bed and not the cat tree. My duffle was on the chest at the foot of the bed. There was a huge fire place on one wall and then a staircase leading up to the little room.

I ran up the stairs to find the little room had a big overstuffed chair and a table and lamp. The windows were big overlooking the front of the house, drive way and Ocean.

Grandmother was behind me. "This is what is called a Widows Lookout. When men would go to sea, the wives would look out of these little rooms waiting for there husbands to return. Sometimes, a lot of time, they did not return. So these little rooms became know as the Widows Lookout or widow's towers."

Looking out over the Ocean, thinking of the lovely room and this little hideaway, I realized my grandmother had been expecting me for a long time. I turned around and she answered that for me. "This was one of your mother's special places to come and think, study and just be. So, I have changed things in the bedroom, but this room is all her.

But yes… I have been planning for you to come. Your father wanted and needed to try to contain your power. And because he is a man of God, he needed to teach you his world and of God. God is, after all, the creator of us all."

We went back down to "my" room. Grandmother instructed me to clean up and gave me a dress. I looked at her as I never wore dresses unless it was church. You can't run along the creek, fish or run through the trees and fields in a dress. "We are the guests of honor for dinner. This would be most appropriate." I looked at the dress with a little shrug and hung it on the freestanding closet. Grandmother smiled at me examining the dress. She then turned and went back down stairs.

I looked back at the dress and it looked kind of old fashion. It was white with short sleeves. It had a white sash around the waist, and was about mid calf. What was really pretty about it was the embroidery and the under slip that peaked out below the hem. Skipping my notice at first, were the white slippers placed on the chest were my duffle had been. They matched the dress with the same flowery embroidery.

The bathroom was big and old fashioned. I liked it a lot. I showered and washed my hair, which was a mistake because it would not be dry for dinner. I decided to pull the front back in a clip and let the chips fall where they may. Dressed and looking in the mirror, I felt different already. I was different already. It only took three days to change a life. I kind of felt like a princess in that dress.

"Hi. Wow, you look like a princess." A voice startled me out of my thoughts. I turned and there standing in the doorway was my mother. I must have gone completely white because she came and took my arm.

"Are you alright?" I'm your Aunt Elena!"

I took a breath then and walked to the bed and sat. Zee, on t the bed of course, looked at Elena and went back to his constant grooming. Elena was a High school senior.

"You look like my mother. Or at least like the picture that Grandmother showed me.

Elena joined me and dropped on the bed with me. "Well good, you should be reminded that your mother existed and that she was wonderful. I hope I do remind you of that." Elena was beautiful.

"I am so happy to meet you. I really want to know about my mother and my mother's family."

She grabbed me around the middle and I squealed. "Good because you are in for it here!" Grandmother came in and looked funny for a second. "Well, this reminds me of my girls." Elena got up and reached out for my hand. I grabbed it and she pulled me to my feet. We continued to smile at each other. "Are we ready now?" was grandmothers only remark as she left the room.

Elena called after her, "Em still has wet hair we will have to dry it." Mandra's voice came back in a whisper "No it isn't."

My hair was dry. Elena rolled her eyes and then said "Try growing up with that. Are you Ready to meet the mob?" Still smiling I nodded and we held hands down the stairs. I think I loved my Aunt Elena from that moment on.

Chapter 8

We walked down the stairs and entered the dinning room. There was a long straight table that was filled with a lot of people. There were people sitting at the window seats. There were people sitting in the living room and on the porch. Grandmother had two chairs on either side of her for Elena and I. We sat and I was served turkey and potatoes. There were these carrots that were so buttery and sweet that I had a second helping, though I was so full I thought I would burst. There were several conversations happening at once and Aunt Elena was keeping up with all of them. She laughed a lot and it made me smile as I thought her laugh was musical. Many questions came at me and I managed to answer "Yes." and "No."

While I sat I heard in my mind, *"You need to call your father. He is asking to hear from you."* I looked at grandmother and she said "Use the phone in my room."

I got up from the table and went to my grandmother room that was on the first floor. Her room was dark and decorated in red, black and purples. A fire burn slowly in her fireplace. I saw the phone on the desk and make my way there. There were large window in her room and French doors leading on to the porch. She had big canopy bed with different colored fabric draped over it. On the bed, a big red cat. His green eyes watched me but he did not seen to mind me in the room. To the right of the desk was a bathroom. I moved to the desk and sat in the leather chair. On the desk was a picture of my mother and Aunt Elena.

I was then bewildered as there was also a picture of me. I wondered how she got that picture.

I dialed my house and Aunt Della answered. "Hi Aunt Della, It's me." There was a pause and then she replied "It took you long enough to call your father. He and your grandmother have been wanting to hear from you."

But not you was what I wanted to say. "Is Dad home?" Aunt Della said "I happy you're safe Em. I hope you have a good time." And I heard her give the phone to Dad.

"Emily Star!" I smiled at his excitement.

"Yes it is. How are you Dad? How is Nana?" He told me that everyone there was fine and that Taylor has been calling for Zee. I laughed "I bet Aunt Della is having a fit over that."

He confirmed my thought and laughed. "Well how are you, and how is it going there?"

I told him that there were a lot of people here right now and that I met my Aunt Elena. I told him that Grandmother has taught me a little on the trip, but that I haven't really made any mistakes outside of the blackout in Roseburg. I also told him that it was real convenient to have grandmother there to fix it.

"I can't condone the ills Em. But I love you. You sound so good so happy. I do want you home. And Em, don't forget your Christian teachings."

I missed my Dad. But I really needed to be here. "Dad, I am confused. If I am a Christian, why did God make me this way?"

Dad then conceded "He made you with love and you are perfect in his eyes and in mine. That is why you are with your grandmother. You have to know … How did you say it…. How not to."

I giggled "I love you Daddy."

He retuned with "And I love you. Now be good and call me from time to time; OK?" We said our good bye's and I hung up. I started to tear up a little, because I really did miss my Dad.

I got up and went back out to the living room. Elena grabbed my hand and introduced me to several people that I could never remember. The blond lady was there still staring at me. When we got close to meeting her, Zee appeared next to me. He was bugging me and almost tripped me by rubbing against my legs. So I picked him up. He continued to grab me at my neck and cry.

While I continue to attempt to control Zee, Elena introduced to the woman with the blond hair. "Emily Star, this is Deana." Pulling Zee's claw out of my skin, I smiled "Hi. It is nice to meet you but I think my cat is hungry or something. I better go feed him."

Deana said "Of Course, another time then."

I took Zee into the kitchen, where there was a lady with gray hair cleaning up after dinner. "Hi, I am Emily Star. I need to feed this crazy cat before he really gets out of control."

She smiled at me "Hi Emily Star I am Molly. I work here for your grandmother. Lets see if we can find a nice can of cat food for this little guy." he went into the pantry and came out with a can of food and a dish for Zee.

"Thank you. I haven't feed him in a while"

She put the dish on the counter and Zee leaped off me on to the counter. "He will be fine here with me. Go ahead and enjoy the guests." She noticed my reluctance when I did not move and only petted Zee while he ate. She then asked, "How about a cup of tea?" I looked up at Molly and recognized the rescue.

Molly prepared the tea and put two cups on table. We sat together and drank the tea. She was familiar to my existence. And she is pleased that I have eased my grandmother's heart by coming here. I talked about all the people I met and that I would never remember everyone's name. I felt better after the tea and the calmness of Molly. "Thank you Molly. I think I can get back our there." She smiled "OK then I am happy"

I walked out of the kitchen and on to the wrap around porch. Mandra walked over to me with a smile. "Are you and your beast calm now?" I smiled back and said that I felt better. She and I walked along the porch and some of the guest were leaving. Mandra went out to the front yard to bid farewell to the ones going home. I stood at the rail of the porch watching.

Mandra looked over at me and I heard *"I am here watching and listening. Don't be afraid."*

At that, I heard, "At last, I am able to meet and speak with you."

I turned around and found that Deana was there. And right on cue, Zee sat on the rail next to me. A low and steady growl erupted from Zee. I understood then that Zee was warning me.

"So Emily Star, tell me, how do you find our little group?"

I felt nervous and said "I don't know yet."

She smiled and continued to make small talk and I answered politely. Then she said, "So, I understand that you possess strong abilities. Can you show me?" She moved in closer and closer with her eyes burning into mine I shook my head in a panic. Her blue eyes wide and wild burning into my eyes. I could see the bursting blood vessels spreading through the whites of her eyes, as she looked in to my eyes. I felt the panic coming up stronger and stronger. I felt the sense of danger coming up. Zee began to growled more loudly and threatening. I had to get away from her.

Something in her eyes made my heart stopped. I closed my eye's to sever her intense glare. All I wanted was to get away from her and be where it was quiet. And then there was a CLICK. I opened my eyes. Zee and I were in the widows watch room. "Oh, my God! How did that happen, Zee?" I grabbed Zee off the table and held him near. My body was shaking, I held my cat close, and I sat in the chair.

CHAPTER 9

I heard someone coming up the stairs. "Emily Star?" It was Elena. Her head appeared between the railings. She saw me and called down, "She's here, Mother." She looked back at me and asked "Baby, are you OK?" I looked at her and nodded not trusting my voice would be normal.

Grandmother came behind Elena. "Em it is OK. We are here for you. Your will find new things all the time and we are going to help you" Mandra then said "Emily Star, come down now so we can talk."

I did not know if I could but I stood up never releasing Zee. Out the windows I could see the cars leaving. With a little hesitation, I tested my legs to see if I could walk. Once I was sure I wouldn't fall, I headed down the stairs. Elena waited for me and looked concerned.

I made my way to the bed and sat down and release Zee. He moved to sit next to me but stayed very close. Grandmother sat on the other side of me and Elena knelt in front of me. I looked over to my grandmother who slowly put her arm around me. "OK" grandmother said. "Now I see you can transport. Have you never been able to do that before?" I shook my head. *Before?* If I knew I could do that I would have done that to get away from Aunt Della.

I heard my grandmother make a little giggle. "No my love. You needed to feel truly in danger to be able to do that the first time. Della can be cruel, but you know that she would never truly harm you. She does, in her own self righteous and odd way, love you." I looked at her as if to dispute that comment but she grabbed my hand and petted it.

"She does whether you believe it or not. You are loved by all of your family. But this is a situation that is not as it is with Della. This was true danger. And you did so well!"

My mind screamed. *Well? Oh my God. Oh my God! I NEED TO GO HOME.*

Grandmother said, "This is only one of the abilities you have power with. This is why you had come home."

My mind screaming again, *Home? No. Home is Hat Creek California. Home is with my Dad.*

"Calm down Em. You need to hear and learn from this. Can you calm down now?" I looked at her without answering.

Lincon came in with a glass. He said "For Miss Emily Star."

He handed me the glass of warm milk. Only Zee was interested in the milk. He then announced to Mandra "The guests have all gone and Molly and I will be cleaning up. We will be off after that."

Grandmother nodded. Lincon looked back at me and said, "Miss Star, you are safe here. I will watch out for you and will protect you. Even from yourself. That is my vow to you." I nodded at the big man. He then turned and left the room.

"Lincon has been with us for many years. He loved your mother and watched over her too. He has gone to Hat Creek to see you for himself."

I looked at grandmother and asked, "Is that how you got a picture of me?" My voice was soft but normal.

My grandmother smiled and nodded to my question. "Is he a Witch?"

Grandmother nodded again. Then, knowing that my voice was audible, "Grandmother, how did that happened? I don't think I like this. I'm scared of my self anyway, but now, I am really scared." I began to breath heavy and looked over to my aunt, and the tears began. "I don't think I can do this 'Power Thing'.

I continued to babble and Elena reached up and hugged me and petted my hair. "SHHH. It's ok. I know this really scared you." She giggled, "It scared all of us, believe it or not." She moved back and I saw the kindness in her beautiful green eyes. "You have to listen now. You have to learn. What if this should happen with the normals. You would be a threat to the public. They would have you in some lab somewhere in some remote area and do weird tests on you. We, your family, want you with us and happy not scared of anyone or yourself." I looked at her still shaking.

My grandmother rose from the bed and said, "OK. Lets all calm down. Let's get you ready for bed." She looked softly at me. "I'll stay home tomorrow and we will go over this in the morning. You drink your milk" She bent down and kissed my head.

I looked up at her, "Grandmother, I am really scared." She stroked my cheek and said "You are special and you will master these things. I will protect you with my body and soul until you have mastered your true being. Good night my love."

She left the room and Elena stood up. "Don't leave me. Please!" She went over to the closet and opened the drawer. She pulled out a simple pink night gown for me. She opened the closet door and pulled out a matching robe, She came back and help me change my clothes. She hung the dress and put the little slippers on the floor of the closet. Her quite soft movement aided in calming me. I did not understand why. But it did help me feel better. She pulled back the sheet of the bed and I got in bed.

"Stay with me please?"

She smiled at me. "Of course I will. Now relax and I will tell a story. OK?" She laid down next to me and stroked my hair. Looking down at me she began with "Once upon a time…" and I found that funny and giggled. She smiled and giggled too. "Once upon a time there were two girls born to a powerful witch. They grew up having little of their mother's powers, but each with their own abilities. One could move items and see the future. The other could speak with her mind and manipulate the present. Their brother, born normal, was unable to understand the female members of his family. Then one day it was discovered that he could also speak with his mind and read minds from time to time. It was easier with normals as they are comfortable thinking that no one knows what is happening in their minds. The sisters would have to block their brother's intrusions into their thoughts as the brother was the informer to our parents."

She slipped. It was about her and her brother and my mother. "It's about you and my mother."

Elena smiled. "Yes it is. It is about how we learned our powers and how we handled them as we grew up. We had it a little easier than you, because we had our mother to teach us."

I asked "What about your father? Did he have powers?"

"Our father? Well, he and my mother loved each other very much. They were very different though. My mother, of course, was a witch and from a family of witches. My father was normal or so it was believed. He was from a wealthy family in San Francisco. They met at a gathering of mutual friends in San Francisco and fell in love at first sight. They dated like normals. And as their relationship grew, my father asked my mother to marry. Which in the normal world….is normal. But my mother could no longer hide her true being. She knew she could only hide it for short periods of time. She told him no, she could not marry him. He was devastated and did not understand. My mother was broken hearted but believed that my father could not understand her true self. The more he questioned her as to why she wouldn't marry him, the more her defenses wavered. When it became impossible to avoid the truth any longer, my mother told my father that she was a witch. At first he did not believe her. And then she spoke to him in his mind. He wanted to dismiss her ability. Then she asked were he would like to be at that moment. He said he wanted to stand with her on a cliff over the ocean. She transported them both to this very spot. He was very scared. Much like you were a little bit ago. He was so scared that she sent him back to the spot in the park that they were before she transported them here. She stayed and had the house built and opened the store. After several months alone, my father came into the shop one day. My mother, ever the pillar of calm, stood and waited for him to speak. He told her that it has taken him some time to understand and get a handle on his fear. But he loved her and could not live without her. My father said that my mother lost a bit of that control then and ran into his arms. They married in San Francisco and my father moved to Pacific City with my mother. He would go back and forth from Pacific City and San Francisco for work at his father brokerage company. And they had us three, and appeared to be very happy."

I was much calmer and very interested in the history of this side of my family. But I was feeling my eye close. Before I allowed myself to sleep I asked "Where is my grandfather?"

Elena said, "He died of a heart attack several years before you were born" I felt sad for that. Aunt Elena then added, "But in the mitts of the funeral and wakes, my mother found that my father's grandmothers were witches. He was actually a witch and never knew."

I remember nothing more as sleep took over. My Elena spent many such times with me. She would just tell me stories about my mom. I loved her very much. When she moved to go to school, I was heart broken.

I dreamed that night. I was dancing in the field back home. I could hear this strange music, but I loved it. A mystical soothing sound and then a demanding drive. I danced and danced, twirling and jumping. I was free. I was not evil. I was just me happy and knowing that I was made by God.

CHAPTER 10

I woke to find the sun up and the birds sing outside my window. I found Zee curled up by my side. I stretched and he looked up at me. He looked peaceful and comfortable. I got our of the bed and visited the bathroom. I washed my face, brushed my teeth. I combed out my hair that was noted from sleep. I headed back to my room and heard laughter from down stairs. I grabbed the robe my aunt had laid across the bed last night. I went down the stairs and found Mandra, Elena, and Molly in the sunroom that was just off the kitchen. They were sitting having breakfast. My grandmother smiled brightly "Well, your up. Come on and have some breakfast."

"Good morning grandmother. Thank you"

I sat down and Molly brought me a glass of juice and a bowl of cereal. Elena pour her and her mother another cup of coffee.

"Feeling better today?" My aunt had a smile on her face and I felt close to her even though we only met yesterday.

"I am feeling better. Thank you."

Molly pointed out that I had manners. "Knowing her Aunt Della and her father, she had no choice." my grandmother said. Though I believed that my grandmothers manners we exquisite. We sat in the morning light and had our meal with happy light talk.

Soon Lincon entered announcing that Edith had arrived. "I'll go change my clothes." I jumped up and ran up the stairs to my room. Zee was in the window looking at the birds in the tree. I looked for my overall shorts and my blue T-shirt. Nothing was there. I called down to

Molly who came to the stairs and told me to look in the closet drawers. I looked and still no overall shorts. But there were several shirts of pink and white. All had little butterflies and ladybugs. I found a pair or white shorts in the drawers and some white socks. The looking for my tennis or boots was just as mysterious. I did find a pair of white tennis. I put my hair in a pony tail and headed down the stairs with Zee at my side. Molly had a bowl of cat food waiting for him.

"Grandmother, where are my clothes?"

My grandmother said "You are wearing your clothes." She smiled "While you are here, we will keep you as a girl and not a wild beast. I have taken the liberty in buying you a wardrobe"

I smiled at her "Thank you grandmother."

"Well" Edith began. "Shall we start with what we know about you and your abilities? Or would you like to start with the lesson plan?"

Mandra said "I believe that we should do an inventory of her power. At least of what we know is there. I believe her experience last night made it very clear that there is defiantly more."

I wanted to know a lot about what happen. "Grandmother, what made me feel so scared of that lady?"

My Grandmother, ever the rock, said. "Something in you powers made the decision to transport. I believe it was the transport it self that scared you most."

Edith the said, "OK. Mind communication, transport, familiar…"

I interrupted her, "What is a familiar?"

Edith informed me "Your beast."

Looking at the cat, I said "Zee?"

Edith looked over at the now attentive Zee. "Many natural witches have Grimalkin, they are part of their being and their companion." I liked that. Zee has always been my dearest companion.

Edith continued "OK.. Familiar and wish maker. Did I miss anything?"

Grandmother said "telekinesis; distance movement."

Edith added it to her list. "Any Alchemy or potions?"

Grandmother looked over to me "Have you made any cooking or potions?"

I looked at her like she was crazy "I'm not allowed to play in the kitchen."

They laughed in unison and I was still bewildered. I wondered, do I tell them about the trees? Or the wind? I thought that I better not; they may think was I nuts too.

Just as the lesson plans were being developed, a man in a dark suit entered the kitchen followed close behind by Lincon. The man was very tall and broad. He had white hair and a white mustache and beard neatly trimmed. He was a middle aged man, with beautiful hazel eyes. He looked very stern and proper.

Lincon announced to my grandmother "Mr. Marcus, Mistress."

My grandmother lit up like I have never seen. "Marcus, please come in. Can I offer you a cup of coffee?"

He responded with "No my dear, I have only come to meet the child."

He very kindly said "How do you do Princess, I am Marcus. I will be your guardian."

I looked at my grandmother, "My guard?"

My grandmother smiled at me "Yes your guard. But not like you believe a guard would be. But he is a little bigger than the cat, and he will be watching to insure your safety. If you had started out being raised by natural witches, you would have been assigned a guardian then. He will only be watching from afar."

I looked over to him and said "How do you do." I thought about it for a second and my past issues and said "I hope I am not too much trouble for you. I do have a habit of ….. Mistakes."

He smiled brilliantly. He was very handsome. "I am sure that I will enjoy my assignment for as long as it lasts. Should you need me, you only need to call out."

I smiled at him "Thank you."

Over several years and several 'Mistakes' Marcus and I became good friend. I truly loved him.

So things continued as my grandmother said. I was home with dad in the winter and with grandmother in the summer. I learned a great deal about my Powers. I mastered them quite easily with Edith's tutoring. I was less proficient with potions and alchemy. It was a clear irritation with Edith.

With my powers under control, I felt normal. It was hard to study and practice at home with Dad and Della. Della refused to allow my books in the house claiming that they were anti-Christ. It did not matter that so many of the books relied on the Bible and Gods word. I was not allowed to make candles and potions while with Dad which was no problem with me. I really hated potions and alchemy.

When I was ten, Nana died. I was with grandmother at the time, but I heard Nana say she loved me and good bye. I screamed and ran to grandmother and told her. She actually broke her regal posture and cried. I transported home which was against the rules. But, when my father saw me he held me and we cried together. Mandra and I stood at the funeral alone while the others gathered together away from us. My father was standing alone at the coffin. We only stopped at the house long enough to say good bye to my father. I was soon back at Mandra's studying.

I did have fun with Benny on the beach and pillaging through the forest. I heard the trees whisper "Ahh the Princess." And though I would always sent my kiss to them, I never mentioned the trees to Benny. We became good friends and on the weekends when I was paroled from lessons, we were off all day long. I loved Benny. Molly and grandmother enjoyed our relationship until one day, when I was with Benny, I forgot myself and I read his mind and answered back. I did it out of habit and not to scare him. He avoided me then. I seemed to scare even my own kind. I don't know why that would surprise me. I scare me. I thought it was a real good thing I didn't mention the trees.

CHAPTER 11

At eleven, I returned home to find my father had become engaged to a widow who recently moved to Hat Creek. He had been seeing her off and on for a few years but she had lived in Redding. I recall her and her son and daughter looking down at me as the evil child and looking so pitiful at my father who was stuck with me. I was unable to attend summer solstice with grandmother that year as the wedding was that weekend.

A few weeks prior to the wedding, there was a shower for the bride. Tina was a pretty little woman with light brown hair. She dress modestly and was a good Christian according to Aunt Della; who, of course, was the authority on Christianity. I dressed in a simple cotton dress and sandals. My hair pulled back with a clip.

The shower included everyone from the church and the town. It was pleasant affair and I did try to be happy for my father. After all, I think he remained alone for so long because of me. I remained quiet and stayed pretty much to my self. Zee and I hung back in the yard while the "garden party" went on.

At one point, my father called me over. "Come on Em. Come and eat with us."

I had not seen my father so happy in such a long time. I walked over to the table where my father, Tina and her children were sitting. Tina's daughter, Nora, was my age, and her son, Tom, who was a year younger than I. They looked like there mother, small and with brown hair.

As I walked to the table, I did not do so unnoticed by the guests. I felt their eyes and there disapproval. I was more hurt for my father. He should not have to endure the disapproval of his child by his family, friends and congregation. I heard the whispers and the title of 'Witch'. I also heard the phrase " Dammed to hell." I looked at that person at that time and she turned away quickly. I sat down with my father at my side. I really never talked with Tina and her children before that.

"Are you enjoying your self, Em?" Tina inquired with a fake sweet voice.

"Oh yes." is all I said.

Nora then asked "Where do you go to school?"

I answered looking at my father, "Here. My father home schools me."

Nora looked at her mother and asked "Will we be home schooled?"

Her mother said "Yes, Fall River and Chico are too far for you to attend school. I want you close to home."

Tom noticed Zee in my lap. "I never have seen a cat hang with someone like that one hangs with you." He thought for a moment and said "He's more like a dog."

Zee did not like that comment and gave a little growl. "He is very special." I decided to tell the story. Kind of an Ice breaker if you will. "Once when we were in Redding, I managed to get Dad to let me have a pet. So we went to the animal shelter." I petted Zee with love. "Dad was looking for a dog, but," I said sarcastically "Aunt Della was afraid that a dog might hurt her precious."

My Dad said "Em. Don't tell this story and don't be disrespectful to your aunt."

I saw Tom give smirk and get an elbow from his mother. Disregarding my father's request, I went on. "Well, I went into the area where the cats were. I wanted them all. They were in these cages and they were sticking their paws through the cages at me begging to be released. I hated it I couldn't stand seeing them and their pleas to be free." Dad got uncomfortable and dragged his hand through his hair and shifted in his seat.

I continued. "Well all at one time, all those cages opened. And the cats were running everywhere." My Dad groaned as I gave a giggle of enjoyment of telling this part of the story. "Aunt Dells was screaming and was holding Taylor." Tom was smiling big

"Taylor loved it, and was laughing and screaming with all the action. Dad and the attendants were running all over trying to recapture the cats and they were getting scratched and bit." Nora and Tom were laughing at the story and though Dad was mortified, but he allowed me to continue. "Well I picked up this little black kitten, but Aunt Della had refused for me to have it. She started yelling at me and my Dad. 'No, you can not have a black cat. Caesar, don't allow it. Dad asked me to pick another one. So throughout the mayhem, I looked over, and sitting in a cage next to me, Zee was waiting. He looked at me and I looked at him and it was love. He has been with me ever since."

Tom was still laughing "I wish I could have seen that." I smiled, at least my new brother like me.

Tom and Nora were eyeing me. I kept quite and waited, but was watching as they elbowed each other. I listened to their minds and knew they were curious of me. Nora glared at Tom so he would ask. He was fidgeting and looking for escape but found none. Tom looked at me strangely and asked "Are you really a witch?"

My father dropped his fork in his plate with a clutter. And his mother said "Tom! That is not a proper question."

I looked at my father and he looked at me as if to say 'Don't answer that.' I smiled then. After all weren't these kids becoming part of my family? My new brother and sister? Still eyeing my Dad, "Well, I have some abilities. I practice the craft only when with my own kind.

Dad then said "Em Please we are in a Christian community."

I smiled at my father and said "Well Dad, I am in a Christian community with Grandmother. I wish you would remember that."

Tom asked then. "I thought witches were ponds of the devil."

I giggled. "I believe in God. I have lived with a preacher my whole life. I have given my soul to Jesus and have been born again. But at the same time, God created me with abilities. Sometimes I am thankful and sometimes.." I looked at my Dad "Sometimes it feels like a curse."

Tom got very excited "What can you do? Can you get me a Porsche?"

His mother swatted his shoulder and I laughed. "It doesn't work that way, but if I could I would." The truth was, I could, but wouldn't.

CHAPTER 12

Dad could not wait to change the subject. "Let's talk about the honeymoon. Where do you think we should go? At that time, I handed him an envelope from my pocket. "Mandra said to give this to you." He took the envelope and opened it. He pulled out two tickets. "Hawaii; A full week." He read the note.

> *Dear Creaser,*
>
> *Please accept my wedding present to you and Tina. There is a full week at the Hilton waiting for you. Please enjoy this, I know Reyna would want it and she wants you happy. I also wish you all the happiness in the world.*
> *Mandra*

Tina looked flustered and said "Well we can't possibly accept. You will have send it back"

I looked at my father and asked, "Why can't you accept it?"

Tina answered before my father, "Because she is ......Well it is just too much."

I was hurt at the rejection of the gift from my grandmother. "She paid for with normal money. It is completely legit." I looked at my father and was stinging from the insult to my grandmother. "Are you sending it back?"

Dad said "Why don't we talk about this later. Let's enjoy the day." He put the envelop in his pocket. I knew he thought that I would make one of my mistakes if I was upset.

"I am in control of ….things now Dad. You know that."

He leaned over and kissed my cheek "I know Em. I am proud of you."

I sat there and did not speak anymore. Tom and Nora continued to stare at me; Nora with some kind of distain, and Tom with fun and amazement.

Della came over with her precious running at her feet. "Emily Star, that cat should not be at the table. You both know better."

Zee hissed at her but jump down. I apologized half heartedly. "Caesar, Em's dress for the wedding will be here tomorrow and I know I will need to make some adjustments. I need to set up the sewing machine in the back room. Will you assist me?"

Dad looked irritated and said "Della we don't have to worry about that now. Why don't you bring out the cake for the guests?"

She said "Good idea." She started for the back door when she turned around and said "Have you spoken to Em about the room change?"

My father's face went red and stern and he told her to go get the cake. "You're moving me out of my room?"

Nora was smirking. My Dad looked concern at my reaction "Well we… That is, Tina, and I thought since you lived at your grandmothers for five months out of the year, you could take the back room and Nora and Tom could have the upstairs rooms."

I could not believe what I was hearing. I refused to allow these people, these *Christians*,to have the better of me.

"That's fine Dad. I'll move my things." The hurt was deep. But I had a plan.

As the Party was winding down and not noticed, I ran over the creek and ran to the field. I was still hurting over the fact that my father would agree to remove me from my room. But right then all I wanted to dance. As I entered the field, deer's were enjoying the wild grass.

I looked to the Trees and they welcomed me with "Princess, you've come to dance for us." I smiled and said "Yes I have. Could I have your sweet music?" And it started softly. I began to dance and prance with the deer. I twirled and jumped. I need this so much. I needed to be unbound by the mortal and immortal ties. Ties that were in direct conflict with each other. Though I did not want to leave, I knew that I would be missed after a few hours. I sent my kiss to the breeze for the trees. And I headed back. Waking slowly and listening to the trees. "He comes Princess." I turned around and I asked "who?" And they did not answer and I shrouded it off.

The next day, the dress came and my aunt was already to do her adjusting so she could complain about my "Beanpole" shape. I put the dress on and *adjusted*it my self before she was able to start sticking it with pins.

Tina said "It is perfect. Now, Caesar, I and the children will be leaving for Redding for out fittings."

I should have known I would be sequestered at the house.

Della said "Have fun." then turned to me and said "You should start moving your things to the back room.

I could not resist. Besides my new step mother needed her introduction to my *ills*. "I've already moved everything." Della's eye became wide and Tina was dumbfounded. My aunt quickly stomped to the back room and let out a scream.

My father, Nora, Tom and Tina all ran to the back room. I sat down with Taylor on the floor and play with him. My little dank room now was the biggest in the house. It was a complete reproduction of my grandmother's room in Pacific City. However I added a TV and entertainment center. There were large windows facing the church and the creek. The bed was huge and draped in silks; a fireplace and a sitting area with a free standing closet. I did think about adding the bath too, but I wanted to wait and see if Mommy Dearest would prevent me from using the two in the house.

My father came back rushing Tina, who was white as a stone, out the door." Wait in the car Dear. I will be right there." Nora came in looking at me as if she was looking straight at the devil.

I could hear Tom from the back by my room. "This is so cool. Sooo Cool."

Aunt Della came in then breathing like she had just run a marathon. "Brother, this can not be tolerated. You must do something with her."

My father looked at me "Em, change it back."

I stood up and looked directly at my father and said "No."

He flushed red "You do not tell me No Em."

I looked at him with anger. "If I give up my room, a room that has been mine my all of life, then I should be able to decorate my new room how I wish."

I looked over to Aunt Della "Auntie how you could let them take my room?" She lifted her hands as if she had no choice.

Dad demanded again "Change it back."

I looked at him and tears fell. I ran away to my room. Tom was still standing there in amazement and smiling. I slammed the door. I heard Dad call Tom. I laid down on the bed and cried. I heard Della coming and as she approached the door, she witnessed boards and nails and chains and locks covering the door to prevent her entrance.

She screamed again and then said 'Emily Star, you will not perform that Devil work in this house!" Then, with my help, she lost her voice. If she couldn't protect my room she has not business deciding what I do.

As I laid there crying, I felt someone sit on the bed. I looked up and Marcus was there. "Hello Princess."

I jumped in his arms and cried even harder.

Petting my head he said "I take it, that this is a first sign of rebellion from you to your family." He chuckled. "Well it is a bit much. On the other hand, you have learned a great deal of your magic, and you are doing well."

Through my sobs I said "Dad hates me. He even gave away my room"

Marcus continued to pet me and said "Oh no, my lady. He is just weak and confused. He loves you very much, but he also doesn't know how to be a good Christian while raising a powerful witch. He loves you and he loves his beliefs. He has several influences that also are causing some of his confusion. You, Princess, must try to be more accommodating to him. Have patients."

I looked at him then "I can't change it back to that ugly little room. I can't even fit my bed in it."

He smiled and said, "Compromise. Let it be as they wish when you are not here. And change it back when you are"

I stopped crying and said "OK". And then I said, "I think once Dad and Tina are married, I will ask to live with grandmother full time. I know Aunt Della will like that. And Tina and her kids will be more comfortable not living with evil me."

Marcus said "There is nothing evil about you. And your father will miss you terribly. You believe his life would be easier without you. But he would never have survived the boredom; Not without all the *mistakes*." He sighed, "Since your growing up, I think a good talk with your father would help. I believe your grandmother is on her way. She will scold you for using magic"

I looked very excited "God answered my prayers, Marcus."

He laughed and said "Yes his did. But she will not be taking you home. You, Princess, must be more cautious with your magic. Be more tactful."

I smiled and said "Ok."

Marcus gave me on of his big hugs, "Until I see you again, my Lady."

I smiled. "Bye Marcus."

Marcus left. I took a nap and then watched some TV. Zee and I were comfortable in our "Room" and I refused to come out or let anyone in.

CHAPTER 13

I heard her commanding voice in my head. *"Emily Star, take off all these boards and locks from this door and give your aunt back her voice."*

I did as my grandmother demanded. She and my father came in the door. I heard Della coming and as soon as my father and grandmother were well in the room I waved my hand and the door slammed before she could reach it. Dad jumped and looked at me with exasperation.

My grandmother gave me a look of disappointment "This is not acceptable Em. You can not use power to be uncaring to others."

I looked then to my father. "I can't take this anymore." I cried. "Grandmother, when I am with you, I have others treat me just as mean as Tina and the others. But the difference is that you are there and you make me feel OK." I looked then to my father "Dad I need to live with grandmother all the time."

His 'No' was immediate. "You are my daughter Em. I want you home."

I became confused. "Dad, you gave away my room. You never even asked me."

He looked guilty and said "I know Em. I just thought that we could make the move easier for Nora and Tom. We…Tina and I, spoke and felt that you would be happier in here. He looked around and then corrected, "Or in the back room, where you could have privacy."

I stomped my foot and said "Dad! You didn't talk to me." He knew he was wrong. I could see that.

"Dad, I will compromise. I will only have my room this way when I am here. I will not use magic when I am here. And I will be respectful when I am here. But Dad, I need you to understand how I feel in this house. How I am treated in my own home." I came closer to him "If you can't find it in your heart to expect kindness for me, why would you ask me to be kind to others?"

He looked at me and said "I do try Em. I just don't know what to say some times. I try to keep the peace, but what do I say to these things?"

Mandra spoke up "Here are some words for you use, Caesar. My daughter is a good girl. My Daughter is most loved by me. My Daughter deserves respect. How's that sound Caesar?" She huffed, "I can't see how you could leave her here while you and the 'New" family went to town? Is she that big of a risk?"

Then my grandmother turned to me. "Emily Star, kindness if from the heart. You give kindness not because someone is kind to you. You are either kind or you are not."

My father walked to the bed and sat. I sat next to him. "Daddy, I love you, but I don't belong with you. I never have."

He looked so hurt and so lost "Em I can't lose you. I love you so much."

Mandra then said "Then compromise with the girl, Caesar."

He said "OK. I will …. Allow this room while you are here. I will rein in your aunt and talk to Tina. But you did cause a lot of frayed nerves today." He looked over at me and sighed. He hugged me and said "I only want you happy."

At that point I watch Mandra open the door and Della and Tina fell in the room. "Well ladies, did you hear everything?" Mandra said smiling at the two.

Della being defensive "I only was concerned for my brother."

Mandra giggled "Really?"

My Father stood up and looked over at Della and Tina "Em will have her room as she pleases while she is home." Both dropped there lower jaws. "She will be treated with as much respect and love and any one else in this home. If that is not possible for either of you, I will make other arrangements for *you*. Oh and Tina, we will be going to Hawaii for the honeymoon." He looked over to Mandra "Thank you for the gift. And thank you for today."

The look on my Aunt Della's face was one I will never forget. Tina said nothing and followed my father out of the room. Della stood for a moment with her mouth open and then left the room, behind my father and Tina.

Mandra looked over to me and I was up and in her arms. "Grandmother I have missed you. I missed you so much."

She squeezed me and said "You'll be home soon and we can be together. You be good and no magic."

I asked in my best little girl voice "Not even in my room when no one is around?"

She looked down at me "Only small magic." She smiled softer "I will miss you for the Solstice."

That day was one that set me in motion. I felt able to stand up and be noticed. That Sunday, in my father's sermon, he spoke of those in line of being judged for judging others.

Mandra left but I did not walk her out. I know that my Dad did. It was quite, at least I did not hear the harpy or Della. There was a knock at my door. "Em? Its Tom." Never leaving my bed I opened the door.

Tom stood there "That is so cool!" He looked like he was genuine in his enjoyment. "Em? Could I come in and play Video games with you?"

I smiled at his acceptance "Sure Tom."

As we played I left the door open. Soon Taylor had joined us and were really had a good time. I had not had fun with people close to my age in a long time. Dad came in to check on us and I could tell he liked the interaction. I looked at him and got up. "Take over for me Taylor." Taylor needed no prodding. He had the controller and was getting really into it. I walked over and hugged my dad. He kissed my head. "See Dad, I can be like normal kids if given a chance."

Soon Tina came in and called Tom. "Oh Mom. Now!" She was nervous and said "Now Tom. We need to go home." She looked over at me and said "Good night Em" I wished her a good night. Della came in and called Taylor. She stopped and brushed my cheek with her finger. "I know you were hurt. I am sorry" I was sure she did not want Taylor to have too much influence of the evil one, though. The boys got up and said good night to me. Tom looked over as he followed his mother out the door "Tomorrow I will kick your butt."

I laughed and said "Bring it on Tommy Boy."

That night the dreams came again. Dancing in the forest and then surrounded by the men in the black robes. The music already unusual, turned eerie and dark. I looked to the trees as they whispered "Run, Princess, Run." I wanted to run out of the field. I looked for an opening but found none. I dropped to the ground and cried. I woke to being held and told that it was OK. Marcus was there and he was rocking me. "Shh, Princess. You're Safe." I looked up and I smiled at him "I was dreaming." He smiled and nodded. "Yes you were." I closed my eyes and said "thank you" and fell back to sleep.

CHAPTER 14

The day of the wedding came. The next day was, June 25, the summer solstice which I would miss that year. All in all, it was a real pretty wedding. I and Nora were the bride's maids and Tom and Taylor were Ushers. Aunt Della was Maid of Honor and Dads friend Jacob Henning was the best man.

I was in my room getting ready when my aunt cam in. "I'm here to do your hair. We can't have it wild for the wedding."

I huffed "Why then did you forget to make my appointment with the hair dresser. I could have gone with you, Tina and Nora?"

She flustered "That was an honest mistake, Em. I told you Tina made the appointment but they did not write it down and then could not fit you in."

She stood there with her container of sprays and hair pins. In her other had was a crown of fresh flowers. I took the crown and said to her "No worries Auntie, I will do my hair and you will be pleasantly surprised."

She looked at me with narrow eyes. "You promised not to use magic."

I shot back, "I promised not to use magic outside of my room and not to use big magic."

I pinched my fingers together and said "My hair is little magic." I giggled. "I use a brush and clips." She huffed at me and left the room.

I used magic. My long dark hair was curled at the end and pulled up in the front. The crown fit perfectly at the top of my head. The ugly yellow organdy dress fit perfect and I used a little magic to acquire simple yellow slippers to match. I doubted that anyone would notice under the skirt. But I could not bring myself to where the hideous used white sandals Tina gave me to wear.

The back yard was full of chairs and tables adorn with flowers and ribbons; the cake and food galore. I was actually excited by it all. I was ready and looking in the mirror. I hated the dress but all in all, I looked very pretty *for me*.

"You are lovely my Lady" I turned

"Marcus! I am so happy to see you." I ran to his arms and he gave me a big hug and the push back quickly.

"We do not want your dress and hair crushed."

"I don't care. How are you and how is my grandmother. She is not allowing communication while I am here."

I was speaking so fast. He took his finger and put it to my mouth. "Shhh" He smiled "I hope my dear that today you will behave as a Princess. Do not be goaded by others and lower your self to there level. You are to behave, and be, as a royal Lady. After all, you are my princess."

My heart melted. I loved him so much. "I Promise, but only for you." He smiled and kissed my head. Then he was gone. I looked back at the mirror for one last look.

From the door I heard a whistle. Tom was standing there. "Wow, you clean up real nice. You almost look as good as me." He was dressed in his off white tux and looked very handsome.

I gave a fake curtsy and asked "Would you escort a lady sir?"

He laughed and said "Where's the lady?" I laughed too because I knew he was right. Just then Dad Appeared

"Oh she is a lady all right. One of the most beautiful the world has ever known."

I smiled at my Dad "Thank you Daddy. You look beautiful too."

Aunt Della came in then and looked at my hair. "I wanted that hair up Em."

I looked at her, "Vidal Sassoon was busy. I had to do it my self" My father not wanting to laugh turned away.

He then turned back and said "Don't be fresh Em. And Della, her hair is beautiful. I would not have it any other way."

Della conceded "She does look lovely, doesn't she?"

I thought I would Faint. "Aunt Della, you complemented me?"

She flustered and said "I do that often you just don't want to hear me." She left the room and Tom smiled and followed her.

Dad put out his arm for me to take, "Shall we Ms. Menelli?" I giggled and took his arm and headed for the door,

At the church, Jacob Henning appeared happy and was always very kind to me. "Em. My goodness, you are growing up, aren't you?"

I smiled. "Hi Doc."

He stared at me. "You are as beautiful as your mother." I was very complemented.

My father stated "Well she does have some of me you know"

Doc laughed "Very Little my man. Very little."

Aunt Della had every one in line and ready to go. Nora walked with little Taylor. Being only five, he was not as compliant as the rest. Nora dragged him a few times. But he did ok. Dad grabbed him at he front of the church where and Pastor Norman waited. Then Tom and I walked up the aisle. I heard the gasps and the whispers. "She did put that one in the wedding. The witch?" Tom Smiled and looked at me and I felt better. He at least, liked me for who I was. Aunt Della and Doc make it up the aisle. Then the music changed to the wedding march. Tina walked alone up the isle in her pink wedding dress. She actually looked pretty.

We stood while Pastor Norman read form the Bible and the honor to the wife and the devotion to the husband. I could see Aunt Della taking little looks a Doc. Then she would look away and then he would do the same. It was kind of cute.

Dad and Tina exchanged rings and kissed their first kiss as husband and wife. I though about how long my father remained alone and did not have an interest in another woman after my mother. But seeing his happiness now, I was sorry I interfered there. If I was normal, maybe he would have married sooner and I would have had a mother.

Before they walked back down the aisle, Dad looked over the congregation. He held Tina close to his right side and then pulled me by the hand to his other side. He waved in Nora and Tom.

As we stood there, he said. "May I, my wife and our children invite you all to our reception next door. He looked down at me and kissed my head. I could have cried. He showed his love for me in front of the whole church. It never stopped the rumors and whispers, but for a day, he let the world know I was loved by him.

I really had fun at the wedding. If it weren't for Tom, I think I would have been a miserable as always. We sat at the wedding table and laughed and joked. Nora was refusing to join us. No matter how much we tried to include her. Dad looked over and I could tell he was happy. He also was pleased at my relationship with Tom. I think at that moment, my father was content.

The first dance started and Dad and Tina danced gracefully across the cement patio. As I watched, Dad and Tina broke off and Dad took my hand and Tina took Toms hand and we danced with our parents. Others then joined the dance floor. A boy I did not know came over with Nora and Dad Smiled and we switched partners.

"Hello Em."

I looked at him and said "Hello,"

I was very self conscious and did not know what to say. He was tall and I only hit the middle of his chest with my height. He had black hair and hazel eyes and very familiarly handsome. I could tell there was something about this guy. But for some reason, at the time, I felt it was insignificant. But I did take notice that I could not read him. He was not a normal.

He looked at me and smiled knowing I had sensed his not a normal and said, "My name is Max. Marcus sent me to ensure you were behaving and that you had fun."

I smiled at the concern of my Guardian. "Why didn't Marcus come himself and dance with me?"

Max said, "He is busy getting ready for the Solstice today. He is with Mandra preparing.

Besides, he thought we could have fun and I could help you be…. What did he say?" He looked down at me mockingly "Oh yeah," then with emphasis "'Royal."

Something in his eyes made me shiver. But I giggled at his reference to Marcus and Royalty. Giggling, I said, "What ever that means."

When the music ended, he said "Would you like to get some punch and maybe we could sit by the creek and talk?"

I smiled and said "Yeah. I would like that."

When the music started again I saw Nora and Tom dancing together with the other guests. Tom looked over to me and had a great smile on his face. Max handed me a glass of punch. We walked over to the creek and I sat on a fallen log facing the party.

Max sat next to me facing the creek. "It must me hard living with normals that know your secrets?"

I did not look at him "Sometimes."

He said "Well if it any consolation, you do it well."

I smiled at him and looked into his eyes I felt somewhat proud of my self. "Thank you."

He then stated "I live with my own kind. It may sound strange, but Marcus said we have a lot of the same problems you have."

I could not believe that "I doubt that, you would have to be evil with no chance of redemption. In your home you are…. Normal."

We started laughing. "I doubt my foster parents would believe that. They seem to believe that I am evil."

Being a nosy kid, I asked, "You have foster parents? Where are your parents?"

He said, "Well, my Dad….. He's around but not steady. He has a lot of other responsibilities. My mom is a normal and could not get a handle on our kind. Not even as far as your Dad has." He looked down. "She now is strung out on drugs with a new husband. I never hear from her." I felt sorry for him.

"Wow, I am really sorry for that."

He smiled I think because I truly was sorry for him. "Don't feel sorry for me. I have a really good life. My *Parents* are like us and help me. I study with the masters like you, and I will do my best for my father. He does watch."

He then laughed "And shows up when I am really in trouble." I laughed with him.

I got nosy again "What kind of things do you get in trouble for?"

He looked at me like he was embarrassed. "Well, once I turned three of my foster brothers in to white rats because they called me a lab experiment." I started laughing and he joined me. "It wasn't funny when my foster mom saw one she screamed, and the maid called an exterminator." We continued to laugh "When they couldn't find my brothers, my foster father called my dad. He figured out what I did and changed them back."

I was laughing and realized I was having a conversation with someone like me. "How did they punish you?"

He stopped laughing and only smiled. "My fathers bond my powers and I was restricted to the library for a month."

I was shocked. "I do some really big things and never was left in a library for a month. But I am not allowed to use magic here at all. So most of the year, is magic free." I giggled "At least when they are around." He giggled then too.

"Well tell me some of your biggest "got in trouble things?"

I started to laugh again. "Oh my God! I'm in trouble everyday. I don't know which one to pick."

He started to laugh. "Oh Come on. I bet you have some really good ones."

I had to think of the newest little thing. "Well, I made a new room on the house for myself."

He looked at me weird "why?'

I sighed. "Well, my new step mother gave my room to my new step sister. The room they wanted me in was small and dark. So when they told me to move my things out of my room, I made my self a new room."

He started to laugh "In front of the normals?"

I giggled. "Yep… My step mother was white as snow. If it was not for Marcus and Mandra, I would have the dark little room in the back of the house."

We talk longer about transporting and manipulating material. We both hated alchemy and potions. "I hate them. What good are they?

Take this to love, take that to hate." Max agreed "Why not let emotions, destiny and *God* be the potions."

I smiled at him "Yes. Yes that's it. That is what I have been thinking." I asked him "How old are you?"

He said "Fourteen."

I raised my eye bows "I though you were older." He smiled with pride I think. He had a really nice smile.

"Em. Emily Star!" I looked over and Aunt Della was calling me. "It is time for the pictures. Come on!"

I stood up " I have to go. It was nice to meet you."

He stood up and said. "I suppose to tell you something."

Aunt Della now had her hands on her waist. I looked back at Max.

He said "Marcus told me to say, act as you are. Act as a princess." I smiled and he didn't. "Bye Max"

He smiled then and said "Bye Princess, Be seeing you."

He disappeared and Aunt Della looked over the crowd to see if anyone noticed besides her. No one had. I hear Max laugh in my mind. It made me smile. There was finally someone close to my age that related to me.

Life went on and I was at grandmothers more and more. But when I was twelve, Marcus, who had been counselor, friend and guardian, was being called away.

"Will I ever see you again?"

I was so upset at his leaving. "Have I will always been at your beckon call, my Princess?" I looked at him with is bag waiting at the drive.

He then hugged me and then said "Claim your thrown and protect it." with that he was gone. My guardian. My friend.

I walked back to the house and grandmother was unusually quite and staring off. I walked over and sat with her in the porch swing.

'I will miss him. I will miss knowing that I have a guardian."

My grandmother took my hand and patted it. "You have a new guardian. He will be about."

I sighed, "I don't want another guardian. They will never be what Marcus has been to me."

My grandmother then said "Yes, your right. Marcus is a remarkable Wizard, few are as he."

I looked over at her "Marcus is not a witch?" I was in shock. I had thought all this time that he was a witch.

She smiled and said "Oh no, he is a Wizard. A very wise and powerful Wizard. We were so fortunate to have him for so long."

I thought a moment and asked "Will my next guardian be a Wizard?"

Grandmother, slowly rocking the swing, looking older then I have ever seen her, patted my hand. "Yes my Love. All Guardians are Wizards. But this time, it will be a Wizard in training."

Then I asked "Why am I guarded and from what?"

She sighed. "The Wizards, as well as the witched, are well aware of your powers. As I have told you before, you have a great deal of power." She smiled and said "You are the chosen Wizard Princess and my most cherished granddaughter."

"Is that why Marcus called me Princess?" She nodded. "Don't the wizards have a girl Wizard for their princess?"

She giggled, "There are no female Wizards." Grandmother took my hand and said "You are their Chosen Princess because of your powers. You are also special to our kind for you powers. Because these things, the Wizards guard you."

She looked to me a little strangely. "I must tell you that the Wizards are not like us.

They have a different way of life. They have a way of putting some ahead of others and work only to the greater good and not to individual good. The greater good of Wizards and not the other races. Hopefully the gesture of the witches will bring about change in their attitudes."

She smiled "Marcus is kind. But not all Wizards are,… Much like normals and Witches have some that are not so kind. But Wizards are….. Different. Make no mistake; they will follow their rule blindly and without question. They prefer not to think beyond their rules."

I looked at her with concern "Will this next Wizard be mean?"

She laughed "No. Marcus would never allow that. He loves you so."

I spent the day studying my potions and spells. I walked out to the cliff rail and watched the wave's crash on the boulders in the ocean. I was board so I went to the windows tower. I looked at some of the books and sat in the chair. Then I thought of Dad. I looked in on him and could see he was being screamed at again by Tina the harpy. I was so sorry for my dad.

But nothing I could think of would fill the void of thought losing Marcus. He said his was available at call. I wondered if he would notice when I took advantage of that. Then I thought of the Princess stuff. I wondered why I was not a princess with my kind if I was a Princess. And why do I have a guardian now. Why did they all leave me so long with mortals Where were they when I got in trouble with my uncontrolled magic? Well I figured I was not much of a princess since I have never lived in a castle.

That evening, grandmother called me down to the parlor. She was there with a boy not much older than I. He looked to be in high school. She introduced him to me "This is Max. He has been assigned as your guardian." I looked at this boy who was supposed to be my guardian. Recognizing him immediately from the wedding and for some reason I did not mention the wedding meeting. "Max, this is Emily Star" I looked at him and said hello and he returned the greeting. He was tall with light hazel green eyes. He had thick black hair that he wore longer now. He was dressed in a suit and tie which he seemed to swim in. But he was handsome like Marcus.

I had to wonder if all Wizards had the same look. "Would you like something to drink?"

He smiled at me "Thanks but no. I will be going now."

I looked over at grandmother and she said "Thank you for coming to introducing your self. Marcus believes that you will be an exceptional Wizard.

He smiled a the complement. "I hope so madam. Now please enjoy your evening"

He looked over at me, knowing I recognized him and said ":I will be watching My Lady. And you need only to call." With that he was gone.

I looked at my grandmother "He doesn't seem old enough to be my Guardian. And he is too skinny."

My grandmother laughed and responded with "Oh my dear. Marcus would never send a man or boy that could not do the job."

I plopped down next to her and said "I don't know why I have to have a Guardian anyway. I can take care of my self."

She shook her head. "No, we can't take that chance. You are too precious… to me."

Over the next few weeks, months and years, I would be walking or in the park reading, or staring out the window of the store and would catch a glimpse of my guardian. He only acknowledged me with a nod. He was more visible than Marcus had ever been. Except when I did see Marcus, he would talk to me. He and I had many afternoons on the porch talking. He was not just my guardian but my friend. During that time, Max was like …. A shadow.

Marcus and I would talk about the title and Princess. He told me that I was chosen because of my powers. He said that I had powers that I had not even discovered. He said that I was born to have great power and that I would have to be very careful with that power. He said I needed to be guarded not only for my self but for others as well. He made me feel special and I believe that is why I loved him so. He was always kind to me.

So the summer went on and I studied in the morning with Edith and walk to the store where I worked with grandmother. One of those days, as I slowly walking down the road to grandmother's store, Deana pulled up in her convertible mustang. "Emily Star. How would you like a ride to the store?" I have never been able to be comfortable with this woman. I had to get out of the ride.

My heart started to beat rapidly. I though of a lie real quick. "Hi. No thanks I'm… meeting a friend up the road." I lied to have her go on but she continued to follow me in her car repeating the offer of a ride. She was relentless and there was another two miles to go. And then the call "EM!" I looked and Max was up the road a short way. He was dressed in jeans and a t-shirt. He looked like and average kid not a Wizard in training.

"Max!" I was so happy to see him. It was a great rescue.

I said "Thanks again Deana, I have to go."

I ran to Max then. "Thank you."

We started walking and Deana sped by. "No problem, that's why I am here"

I looked up at him "I should have called sooner I know. Marcus would have been upset with me for waiting so long. He never wanted me to wait. And that lady gives me the creeps." He looked straight ahead as he talked

"Well I do watch. But it would be nice if you let me know you are feeling unsafe." We chatted about the summer and things going on in town as we finished the walk to the store. When we got to the store he only looked at Mandra and smiled. "I'll see you"

I smile "Thanks Max. I'll see you." He was gone.

"Well Deana tried again did she" My grandmother worked the grinder a little harder. "I will have to bind her from you." Binding only meant that she could not work magic against me. Lincon came out of the back with more boxes of candles to restock the shelves.

"I will do all I can Madam. I will bring Ms Emily Star to the store everyday and she will be safe" I smiled at Lincon. He was so dedicated to grandmother and I.

"Well since Max will be gone, it would be best."

"Gone? He did not tell me he would be gone."

Mandra then said "He has his schooling as well. It is unknown when he will be replaced. We will have to look out for another guardian…but until then." Her anger being taken out on the grinder.

I smiled and said "It is OK grandmother, I can protect my self."

Summer Solstice was here. The next day would be the longest day of the year. I was thirteen now and able to participate in the dancing which is what I have been waiting to do. Grandmother had the yard with Arbors of garland and all the tables dressed in flowers. From my window, the after noon was beautiful and I was so excited. I could see everyone working in the yard preparing for sunset and sunrise. Lincon was busy at he barbeque while Molly checked the caterer's inventory.

Grandmother came in my room and had my robes. She had a flower wreath for my head and a belt of hemp and flowers hang from it. I put my robe on, that was really like a roman wrap, but the bodice was tight. My grandmother waved her hand and the bodice fit perfect.

"Well, I hate the thought of you growing up. That there was my reminder that it will happen."

I decided to play with her and said "You mean I getting boobs?"

She looked at me and said "Don't be crude. And yes that's what I mean."

I giggled and spun away from her. "I didn't get to have you little very long."

She smiled and said, "Marcus is here." I screamed with delight and ran down the stairs. Marcus was on the porch and I leaped into his embrace. "Well my Lady, you are beautiful."

He put me down and I never letting my smile go. "Marcus, I am so glad you came. Are you staying for the night?"

He said yes of course I am. I would not miss the dance especially now that you are joining."

I held his hand and asked "Will you dance Marcus?" he laughed "As long as my back will hold out."

I looked over and Max was there. "Max. You came too? Are you staying?" He did not look very happy.

He said "It appears so. I did have something else to do, but Marcus insisted."

I twirled down the stairs and said "Well I am glad. I really happy you both could come." I ran across the lawn with my hair flying behind me and in my bare feet. I ran over to Lincon who stood stout at his post.

"Isn't all so beautiful Lincon? I wish we did not have to wait all year for this."

He said "Yes Ms. Em, it is beautiful. But I don't believe that it would not be as special to you if you did this all the time."

I smiled as I ran to through the scattered arbors and said "You are right."

I ran past the large prepared bond fire and the fire that we leap across. I felt so happy and free. I ran to the cliff side and leaned against the railing. I looked over and saw the waves below breaking against the big rocks jetting out of the sea and felt on top of the world. I looked across the yard and could see grandmother on the porch with Marcus and Max. I ran back to the porch to join her. I knew that she would want me to great the guests with her.

"Em. Settle down now. The guests will be arriving in about a half hour. I would like you to be neat and clean when they arrive."

With her warning given I walked over to the swing and sat down pouting. My grandmother smiled "Sit up and don't pout. It will all start soon and we will be dancing by nine. OK?"

I sat up and smiled back and said "OK."

She joined Marcus on the other side of the stairs where that sat drinking Ice tea. Max was slouch in his chair.

"You really don't want to be here, Max?"

He sat up and looked over and shrugged his shoulders, "I had an invitation to a party with some friends. I really wanted to go. But my…. Marcus insisted that I come here instead"

He smiled at me, "Don't worry about it kid, I will have fun. I doubt you will tolerate anything else."

I smiled and jumped up and twirled around and stopping only to say "Absolutely right. No one is allowed to be miserable on this day. I will make sure you have fun!"

The next thing I heard was "Emily Star, Settle down." Grandmother was warning again and I sat back on the swing. Max laughed at me.

"Don't Laugh. I think you should be excited too." I said to the *too cool* teenager.

He looked at me like a little pest "I would rather be the first of the summer party, than sit on a porch with a pouty Princess."

I huffed and was quite for a minute. Then thinking of the night of dancing I became excited again and said "Don't worry Max. This will be a great party and we get to dance."

The guests arrived dinner was served and the sun was going down. The guest started to arrive; mostly the same crowd as always. But there were some more Wizards this time. In addition to the Wizards Marcus and Max, Marcus introduced me to the other Wizards.

Marcus said "This is our Princess Emily Star. Em. These are my fellow Elder Wizard Leonardo and William." Max stood with another younger man, both were watching us. Marcus waved them over to us.

"Mandra, Em, This young man is Edwin."

Max looked a little irritated with the introduction, but stood quietly stout. Edwin was shorter than Max, but I guess all Wizards are handsome. He was taller than me and had thick blond hair. His eyes were blue and he acted vain.

"He is a also a guardian wizard like Max."

Edwin then said his 'how do you do's' to grandmother and then to me he said "Well, it is nice to put a face to the name, I hear so much from Marcus on the Princess.""

"You are very charming Edwin." Marcus returned and Max moved Edwin away. While other came to great us.

Once free of the precession, I grabbed Max and Edwin and insisted that the be my partners in some of the games. They were terrible. They could not get the ring and stick game and we came in last. The three legged race they lost which really made me mad because they said I couldn't be a partner because I would get hurt. "you guys aren't very good at these games. If you had just let be show you how we could have won." Max started laughing and Edwin scowled at me. They were kind of strange. Always at attention; always in control; Always dressed correctly and never ready just to have fun. They acted as though they avoided fun. Just a strict arrogant control. And they always stared.

Except when you looked in Max's eyes. You could see the confusion, the curiosity, the struggle to stay in control and not break lose. Edwin was content in that controlled world. He was arrogant and very uppity. He looked board and irritated. It was clear from his stance and voice he felt games and enjoyment with the witches was beneath him. Though he never said it, but it was written all over his face.

By night fall the bond fires had started and the music was started. Everyone was laughing and waiting to jumping over the fire. People hung around the bar for beer and wine. And some enjoy the mead at the end of the bar. Midnight came and the celebration was well on its way. Grandmother handed me my mask. The maidens, all masked, began their dance. All girls thirteen and up who were unattached dance. At this time, we were about a dozen. It was a ancient fertility dance to attract mates. I did not care I loved the dance and to dance. In the middle of the dance each girl would grab a male and bring them into the dance and they would both jump over the fire. So once our leaping and jumping parts were over we all spread out to the available males to leap over the fire with.

The music stopped and the drums began signaling the maidens to find their mates. I ran straight to Marcus but Mandy beat me. Max who had been standing behind Marcus was my next target. He bulked at first, but after I said "Please, you have too. I need a partner." he complied. We went back to the bond fire and leaped over it, and finished the dance. I was out of breath but still donned my mask. I was laughing and Max was smiling. "See it wasn't so bad." He smiled and said, "No suppose it wasn't." We walked over to Mandra and Marcus who both looked somewhat concerned. I looked around and asked if there something wrong. They both smiled and said no. Marcus put his arm around Max and they walked off towards and bar. I was smiling and enjoying the event. I danced more through the night but Max was no where around or I would have invited him again. The sun began to come up and all were quite waiting for the sun. Along the horizon line was a special arbor to catch the first light of the sun. As I stood quite with the others, Max appeared at my side. On the other was Edwin. It was normal for Max to do this sometimes but the way he was not around and then appeared at the end was strange to me. And Edwin on the other side was just creepy.

Through the arbor, the first light came through hitting me in the face. The clouds were red and yellow as the full blaze of the sun rose. As the sun past the arbor everyone cheered. Everyone except, Max and Edwin. They stood in their arrogant staunch way. "You guys are supposed to be happy with the sun, lighten up."

They never looked at me or answered and then I realized Deana was staring at us. Under my breath and only to Max I asked "Why does that woman creep me out so much."

Max stiffened as she and her daughter Lori made her way towards us. She reminded me of the snake slithering through the Garden of Eden.

"Well Emily Star. Two guardians for the price of one? Nice dancing Max."

Max did not respond and only stared at her in his stern way. I did not understand her at all and she made my skin crawl.

I said "I 'm sorry I don't understand."

Deana only smiled took Lori's hand and went slithering to her car as Mandra and Marcus walked over to us.

"We need to truly watch that Mortal" Marcus said.

Mandra looked at me "Its time for you to sleep."

She had my arm and was leading me to the house. Max and Edwin walked with us to the house. "Grandmother what is she talking about, and why are you all acting this way."

She only said "That woman is trouble…; big trouble and a big gossip."

Max and Edwin never came in the house. And I obeyed grandmother and headed to my room. I changed my clothes and jumped into bed. My body was trembling from dancing all night, exhaustion, and excitement. I fell asleep immediately.

And though the sun shined while I slept, I dreamed of a huge dark room. It was stone with an long alter like bench. The Men in black robes were there. They were angry with me they were yelling things to me but I didn't understand their language. I looked around for an exit. But there wasn't one. No way in and no way out. I looked to transport but I was bound. I called for Marcus. And as on of the robed men came towards me I screamed.

"Princess wake up."

I opened my eyes that were tearing and found Max shaking my shoulders.

He looked at me "Awake now?"

I nodded "Yes thank you." Zee was under the bed growling. Mandra came running in then. Max looked over to her and smiled "Nightmare."

He got up and allowed my Grandmother to come over to me. "Em are you OK?"

I nodded and sat up. "I'm sorry" Grandmother hugged me.

Her heart was beating hard. "Em you screamed so loud that it was like you were being murdered." She kissed my head and said "We can talk later, go back to sleep." I smiled I looked over to Max and he smiled and nodded and was gone.

CHAPTER 15

As June ended, and July began, I found myself wanting to dance. I could go to the woods but they were so close together there was no room for dancing. I went outside and walked to the cliff rail and looked out to the ocean. I was so board. I was so lonely. I knew that there were things to do in town like going to the movies or shopping. But I always had to endure the whispers of the young witch. I also had to go alone which by it self is scary. Then, I wanted company. I could go to the store with Mandra, but I didn't want to walk and she would kill me if I transported in or use any magic to get there. So I decided to sing and dance in the yard. I sang and danced till out of breath looking to the heavens. I sent my kiss on the breeze. As I turned and still singing "Come Play in the forest, come dance in the field, and sing, sing to the glory of the lord."

As I was almost back to the front of the porch, I looked up to see Max and Edwin sitting on the porch staring at me. Devastated that they were watching me. I stopped and stared at them back. I could not understand their constant staring. Watching and giving no normal indication of what they were thinking.

They stayed staring and I finally, in frustration asked "What?"

Edwin looked at Max in a confused way. Max looked at me and asked "What are you doing?"

I was a little embarrassed but confessed "I was singing hymns and dancing." I turned and conjured hackie sack for something to fool with while trying to hid my embarrassment of them seeing me sing and dance in the yard. I then played at kicking around a hackie sack trying to ignore them so they would leave. They looked back to one another again.

Max then asked "Now, what are you doing?"

I looked at them skeptically. I tilted my head "playing with a Hackie sack?"

Max looked back at Edwin "She is playing with a Hackie sack." Edwin started to laugh.

I narrowed my eyes, "Let's see you do it."

Edwin shook his head "That is undignified."

I started to laugh at him. "You just can't do it."

Edwin stood up and said "How dare you challenge me." I smiled and held out the Hackie sack. Edwin disappeared. I looked to Max who had remained quiet. I held the Hackie sack to him and he smiled and got up.

"Leaving too?" I asked with a smile. He walked over to me and took the hackie Sack and began kicking it around. Not very well but he did it.

He stopped and said "My mortal mom gave me one when I was small. Edwin has never been exposed."

I looked at him suspiciously "Why are you guys here spying on me?"

He looked at me and laughed "We weren't spying exactly, Just checking."

I giggled "That is the same thing." More seriously I asked "Don't you guys have anything better to do. I wish I did."

He said, "We have to check in on you. Besides I always find you doing odd little things."

I pulled in my brows and said "Kicking around a hackie sack is not odd. It was a boredom breaker."

Max smiled and said "Ok. So let's play."

Max and did kick around the sack and talked while we did. We kicked the sack around and to each other and he got better as we went along.

"So why is playing undignified for Edwin?"

Max smiled "As Wizards we are expected to watch and collect information. We don't play normally."

I looked at him, "You know what they say about no playing?"

He shook his head and I smiled and said "All work and no play makes a wizard a dull boy."

He started to laugh. "Well I do play. And I do get in trouble for it." He looked at me and smiled and said "We are only supposed to play with magic. Not Hackie Sacks and other objects. I play with magic a lot so I can learn. But I also take off and will ride a bike through park now and then. And join mortals for a basketball games. All kinds of things like that." He laughed then "That's how I get in trouble."

I missed the hackie sack and looked at him like he was crazy "That's what you get in trouble for?" He nodded. I rolled my eyes "I wish. I get in trouble for doing magic."

He started to laugh. " The thing is, we aren't supposed to be with mortals without restraints and supervision. But when we are supervised and our power restrained, we still cant do anything like playing basket ball or ride a bike. So when I can, I take off and do what I want, but I don't use magic at those times. And when I take off, the Elders get really pissed. I usually end up in the Library for a while." He looked off and smiled and then said "Its price is worth it to me." It was a nice afternoon. At least I wasn't alone and board. I handed the hackie sack to Max and before he left. "Practice."

About a week after that, as I stood at the cliff rail and looked out at the ocean. The breeze blew threw my hair and I hear her whisper "All is well"

I sent my kiss on the breeze and when I turned around both Max and Edwin were there. They looked at each other like I was weird again then they looked back to me.

Edwin said "Princess."

I looked over at him and Max and they both held large black books. I stared at them expecting them to say something; anything. Like why they were there. But they stood their like ninnies. Nothing in their eyes. Just their stern and stout erect postures.

I raised my brows and asked "What?"

Max smiled and Edwin was again insulted.

Edwin said "We have come to check on you."

I giggled and asked "Why?"

Edwin looked at Max who had stopped smiling when Edwin looked to him. Max looked at Edwin and nodded.

Edwin looked back at me and said "Because we must."

I giggled at the game "Why?"

Edwin looked frustrated and said "Because we are Guardian Wizards and that's what we do."

I shook my head and pointed at Edwin's book. I asked "Are those the instructions on how to be a Guardian Wizard?"

Max produced another smile. Edwin lifted his head a little and said arrogantly

"These are our Grimours."

I nodded and said "And what is that?"

Edwin looked back at Max again then looked at me and said "These are where we write down what we learn about Magic."

I giggled "The instructions. That is what I said."

Edwin was red faced and arrogantly said "Good bye Princess." He disappeared.

I looked at Max and he was still smiling. I asked him "What is with that guy."

Max said "Well you sure frustrate him." Max moved over to the rail and looked over.

I asked him "Do you guys always work as a pair?"

Max started to laugh "He wants to come. But maybe he wont next time"

I reached and asked "Can I see your book." and Max sent it over the edge of the cliff and it disappeared.

"Why did you do that? All you had to say was no."

He looked at me and said "Those books are for the owners use alone. No one else is supposed to see them."

I smiled and teased him "So you don't share the instructions?"

He giggled and said "No. Wizards travel the worlds separately but we are all under the same rule. We all learn different things in different places, not every Wizard learns the same. Some are more magical than others. We write down what we learn."

He smiled again and said "Edwin is insulted, Princess. But I think he would like to be your friend."

And though he was attempting to have me cut Edwin a break, I could see that he really didn't want to. I looked at Max seriously. I thought Edwin was a snob. He also makes it clear that I did not meet his expectations, which were beyond me at that time.

"He looks down on me. Like there's something wrong with me. He treats me like he is better than me and my grandmother. I don't know how to be friends like that." Though he continued to hold his proper stance and was expressionless, I could see a bit of understanding when I looked into his eyes.

Mandra came out of the house and called "Em come in and eat now. And bring Max."

I looked at him "Come on. And don't take off or you'll hurt her feelings." Max charmingly smiled and we walked to the house.

After several weeks of no nightmares, I had a real good one. I was in a castle and was standing on a balcony and looking into a court yard. My hands were tied and my dress was torn and dirty. My hair was matted and sticky. The court yard was filled with black robed men and angry women screaming and yelling at me. They were calling me names like "wicked witch" and "ungrateful bitch." I was shaking and my heart beat like a drum. I saw the stake and the bond fire ready to be ignited. Two huge blacked robed men grabbed me and pulled me from the balcony. I was taken to the court yard and tied to the stake. I saw the torches coming closer. My heart was pounding and I screamed. "Princess! Wake up."

I looked up to find Max shaking me. I jumped up and grabbed him in a vice grip. I was breathing hard and tears falling. I was shaking and I was very scared. He had me at the shoulders but when I had him in the vice hug he released my shoulders and hugged me back.

"They were going to burn me. They were mad at me and I don't know why. I don't know what I did to make them want to hurt me."

He petted my hair and close to my cheek he said "I won't let anyone burn you."

Then I said "I didn't know if you would come." I stayed hugging Max still shaking and not willing to let go yet and he said:

Wizard Princess wake or slumber,

my vow to you I live here under.
Twirl and leap my happy dancer
Wake or sleep, your call I answer,
Till the worlds and life are done,
Be assured, I will come.

I must have fallen asleep just after his incantation.

Max came and did his "checks" more and more without Edwin. He was more real then.

Or maybe more normal. He joined me in games or just talked. When Edwin did come, he was curt and arrogant. Those visits did not last long. I always felt that they came to my home and I was not going to be treated as less when Edwin came. Max laughed a lot to himself at those times. I guess because I would purposely irritate Edwin till he left. I also did it so Max could relax. When Edwin was there, he was quieter. He was much more reserved when Edwin was there. I actually had conversations with Max. But not when Edwin showed up. Edwin made the "Checks" uncomfortable and intrusive. I felt like he could show up at anytime, even private moments. But when I made these concerns known to Marcus and Max, they assured me that would not happen. I still worried about it. Being watched by Wizards and Wizards popping in and out at various times was creepy.

One of those last joint checks by both Wizards, I was at the table and Zee sat in a chair next to me. As I sat down with the tuna sandwich, Max and Edwin appeared. Zee growled at them and they glanced at him in time for him to hiss, and then returned to staring at me as usual. Molly, being ever so gracious, placed a sandwich and juice in front of the Guardian Wizards. Max said thank you and Edwin looked at the sandwich and said nothing. They watched me and I watched them. It seemed that they were more curious than anything else. They always stared and didn't talk much. I didn't say anything to them and began to eat. I looked up from eating and watched them as they watched me. It was like a curious cat watching a couple of curious birds through a window. The Witch watching the Wizards watch the Witch. Completely bizarre.

Edwin looked at Max who without prodding, began to eat the sandwich. Edwin looked back at his sandwich and thought about it. I thought maybe he thinks it is bewitched. I giggled. He looked up at me with his suspicious blue eyes. I still did not say a word to them. I took a piece of tuna and put it on the table in front of Zee. From a sitting position in his chair, Zee, very politely, reached out and took the tuna and savored it. Edwin watched with a disgusted look. He squished his face like he just witnessed something really sickening. Max watch and his enjoyment of the situation was clear in his eyes though he remained quietly eating his sandwich. When I saw how disgusted Edwin was, I did it again. Zee took the tuna into his mouth from the table.

Edwin looked at me irritated and said "Stop that. That beast should not be at the table."

I looked back at him. He sounded like Aunt Della.

"My house Edwin. My rules. Zee is my friend and companion. He deserves to eat tuna at the table." Max stayed stout and only ate his sandwich quietly. Edwin looked at him and Max shrouded his shoulders.

Edwin looked back at me and said "Its unsanitary."

I smiled and said "No more than eating with you."

Edwin became upset at that and said "You are not to speak to me that way. You need to learn your place, Witch."

I leaned toward his side of the table with my eyes in a threatening and entertained expression and said, "And you, Wizard, need to learn yours while you sit at a Witches table."

He looked at me shout and angrily and left. I giggled and rewarded Zee with another piece of tuna. "He doesn't know how special you are my love."

I gave Zee a scratch behind the ear. I looked up to see that Max still watched me. I giggled and he smiled. Max reached over and took Edwin's sandwich and ate that one too.

CHAPTER 16

It was about a month latter, that grandmother told me at breakfast, that we were invited to a ceremony with the Wizards.

I looked at her and asked "What kind of ceremony?" She smiled as Marcus appeared in a chair.

Mandra smiled at him and said "I was telling Em about the Shamans Ritual."

He nodded "Yes it is a special coming of age ritual for our young wizards." He thanked Molly for his coffee she placed in front of him. "They are given a mixture of Fly Agarics. They then will be in the mystic worlds of the Wizard and will see and learn a great deal. They also find their animal spirit. Much like the Witches familiar but the animal is actually within them." He smiled at me. "Edwin and Max will be participating this year. Now that they are 16, it is time."

I smiled and said "When is it?"

Mandra said "This coming Friday night."

I became more excited "Where is it. Is it in a Castle?"

They started laughing and grandmother said "No Em. In a open field. Edith and I will be cooking the mixture."

Later that day I was throwing out my failed Alchemy test. Instead of making the gold material that Edith was demanding, it turned out looking like burnt oatmeal. I open the trash can and set the lid down on the ground. I dug and chipped at the failed expectation of my worthiness of Witch hood.

"Wow that looks bad." I looked up to see Max smiling at my mess.

As I chipped at the pot I said "I will never get this alchemy stuff."

He said "I hear you, Edith and Mandra are coming to the Shamans Ritual?" I nodded still stinging from Edith's disappointment.

"Promise me Princess."

I looked at him and his stupid smile "Promise you won't be involved in the mixture of the Fly Agarics. I want to live through it."

Still disappointed in myself, his insult open the wound fresh. I looked at him through narrow eyes "Pray you make it there at all Max." He left then and I could still hear him laughing at me. I threw the pot in the direction that he left.

That Friday, Edith was all a buzz running around and taking the flats of mushrooms and animal fat to the trunk of the car. She ran back in and headed to the pantry. She came rushing through with a canister of dried belladonna, St. Johns wart and several other herbs.

I looked to grandmother "She is excited isn't she."

My grandmother smiled and said "Witches are not normally invited to such a ritual. In fact I do need to speak to about our appearance there."

She took my hand and led me to the parlor. We sat on the couch and she put her arm around me and said "Remember when I first brought you home and I told you that not everyone will be kind." I looked at her with my brows inward and nodded. She said "Witches are looked at in a funny way with some Wizards as well. To be honest, most Wizards, though you are the chosen Wizard Princess. Marcus and Max are not the norm in their kindness to us."

I pulled back some and looked at her straight in the eye "Than why are we going at all. We don't need to be there. We are Witches."

She grabbed me and hugged me and said "Yes we are. But the Wizards counsel has asked that Edith and I prepare the mixture tonight. This is due to the fact that we are of only a few who can make the mixture to the required magic. And we are invited which is, in its self, a great honor."

I shrouded my shoulders and said "Fine."

She then told me "You must not leave my sight." She looked at me very seriously and I nodded.

Edith called from the porch "Mandra, Em. Time to go."

I stood and grandmother raised her hand and I was in my Solstice dress with a red cape and hood. She was dressed to match. As we exited the house, Edith stood dress exactly the same.

We got into the car and Grandmother looked at me and said "Remember, not out of my sight." I nodded.

We drove out of the drive but instead of being on the normal rode to town, we were on a highway somewhere very different then I was used to.

"Grandmother where are we?"

She turned from her driving and said "New England, we will be there soon." I looked out at the fern that grew under the canopy trees. I watched the sun begin its mid afternoon decent. Just then Grandmother turned off the highway onto a dirt road. We followed the dirt road into a valley and we could see tents set up and several cars. In the center of the field, there was a huge arena with large boulders bordering its circle. Stone bleachers surrounded the arena except at one end that was open for entry and exit. There was a huge bond fire far at the end of the arena prepared for lighting later. Grandmother parked and Edith was out and at the trunk. I slowly got out of the car and saw three Men in black robes and gold sashes walking to the car. My heart started to pound and I looked for my grandmother. Then I felt a hand on my arm. I turned and pulled to find Max standing there in a black robe and hood.

"What's wrong?"

I looked at him and then back at the black robed men. I shook my head. The men removed their hoods and I could see that it was Marcus, Leonardo and William. I took a breath, as my heart pounded like a drum. Max looked at me funny and gave me a mocking shove.

"Let us assist you Edith "Marcus offered and he took the flats of Mushrooms from the car. Max also helped her remove the pots of animal fat. He looked at me with a pinch face "Looks appealing. Think you would like some." I just shook my head. I felt wrong there. Something was coming out of this I don't think I want to know. Grandmother took my hand and we walked to a open tent equipped with a open fire and a big pot.

Edith made quick work and put the pot in position over the fire, and poured all of the animal fat, and several herbs into it. She and grandmother then sat at a table and begun to cut the mushrooms stems off and cut the caps into little pieces. I looked at to the rest of the group of tents and saw they were venders and many people moving threw them. Many of the venders were selling books and masks. Some had robes and wands.

"Grandmother, they have wands."

She looked up and nodded.

"Could I go look?"

She shook her head. "You don't need props Em."

I saw birds in cages, crystals and little metallic balls on velvet covered tables.

I saw many women and girls but they looked at us with distain as they walked by. Several men in robes walked by and looked at us with anger or suspicion. I could not understand how we were invited and then looked at in such a way.

I looked back at the venders and was surveying the items offered for sale. Then I saw cats in cages.

"Grandmother! The cats!"

The cats looked over at me and cried their pitiful cries of entrapment. They were begging me to release them. Grandmother jumped up and Max appeared out of no where and grabbed my arm. But it was too late. The cats were free and running out into the woods. Just like at the SPCA when I got Zee.

Max said "Oh shit." A clear violation of a reserved Wizard.

He took my arm and started walking me in the opposite direction from the proprietor. We could hear him screaming about the insolent heathen that turned the cats loose. He didn't know it was me thank God.

I looked at Max who looked a little upset. "I'm sorry. I really didn't intend to do it. It just happened."

He smiled "I know that Princess. But if finds out it was you…."

I didn't understand. I felt terrible. I needed to returned and apologize. Max grabbed my shoulders and looked very serious

"No you don't. Just close your mind to everyone but me."

I did what he said and asked *"Why. I want to apologize."*

He sent *"Princess, you need to keep a low profile here. Please! For Marcus and I"* I looked at him, still not understanding, I nodded.

He said "OK let's get back to your grandmother."

Max returned me to the tent and then pulled up his hood. He looked at me and smiled sweetly and said "No Worries." and was gone.

I looked at my grandmother and she only had to look at me for me to know that I was in trouble.

"I'm sorry."

She shook her head. Edith grabbed my hand and dragged me to the caldron. She then put the end of the huge spoon that stuck out of the mixture in my hands. "Stir and if you daydream and forget, I'll whack you a good one."

I dropped my mouth and was so completely insulted. I pouted and stirred the mixture like a good slave, while grandmother and Edith continued to cut the mushrooms.

A short time latter I saw Max, Edwin and several other Wizards in Training walked by. I continued to stir and Edwin looked over and started laughing at me. He pointed and insultingly said "Look at the *Princess*cook."

I narrowed my eyes and was thinking of sending him flying for a while and then I got "Em. STIR!" I continued my stirring.

Max turned and looked at Edith, "We want to live through this. Why is **SHE**cooking?" That was it. I took the spoon out of the caldron and was about to send like a missile at the two when Marcus stood in front of me. He looked sternly at me and I put the spoon back in and continued my slaving. He looked behind him and soon Max and Edwin were standing with their own spoons stirring. I started laughing so hard I dropped my spoon in the mix. Edith was up and fishing it out with some other spoon while Edwin and Max continued to stir. Then Marcus looked at me sternly again and once Edith was through wiping the mixture off the spoon. Marcus then put my hands back on the spoon handle and said sternly "Stir." There was a little still on the spoon and it got on my hands. I, without thinking, licked it off. I then thought about it effects and turned to look at grandmother but then decided that I was in enough trouble. I only licked off a drop.

I huffed and continued stirring not looking at the two stupid Wizards who started it anyway. Then Max kept bumping my spoon. I looked at him with my eyes warning him.

He started to laugh until Mandra looked at him with a clear discipline in mind. He looked back at the mixture and sent *"OK. I deserve to stir with you. I'm sorry for making fun of you. OK?"*

I looked up into his eyes to see if he was truly serious and he did look sincere. *"OK"*

I looked over to Edwin who had a scowl on his face and looking at me.

"What?"

He took a second and then said "I only laughed and stated the obvious."

I widened my eyes and tilted my head "And why did you laugh?"

He looked away then and wouldn't answer. He had closed his head and I couldn't pick. Mandra then said "No Talking. Just stirring" And then she said "Max. No transmissions."

I looked up at him and he looked at me and shrouded his shoulder and continued to stir. Grandmother always seem to know Max and his little deceptions.

After Edith and grandmother had all the mushrooms in the pot and the mixture was fully cooked to their expectations, we were released from our constant stirring. Edwin stomped off and Max gave me another mock shove and left. Mandra had a decanter of rum. She opened the top and added the belladonna.

I asked "What is that for?"

She smiled and said "Sometimes it is hard to come out of the Mystic world and back to the earth world. This helps the body and helps the mind relax so the Wizard or Witch can come back." She shook the decanter and looked up at me with a smiled and said "It is almost time to start.

Marcus came with four other Wizards. I could not see their faces under the hoods and they did not acknowledge us in any form. They put two long poles through the openings on the sides of the caldron and lifted it. Then they put the long poles on their shoulders and left with the caldron. Grandmother handed me my cloak and I put it on. When I did not pull the hood up she did it for me. Marcus put his arm out for me and grandmother. Edith walked behind with the decanter of rum and belladonna.

The row of vendors that was busy and noisy earlier was now still and quiet as we walked with Marcus through the isle. The people looked at us suspiciously and angrily. I looked to the chubby man that had the cats in the cages. He looked at me. I doubt he could see my face under the hood. But I turned away anyway. My heart started to beat rapidly and I felt scared and didn't know why.

Max, wherever he was, sent *"It's OK. You are with Marcus and will be with the other elders. Don't be afraid."*

I huffed *"Easy for you to say."*

Marcus led us to a boxed off area at the front of the stadium. We sat with Leonardo and William. The Stadium was dimly lit by the scattered torches. But the full moon offered the light for the ceremony. All of the bleaches were filed with Wizards and women. The reception towards us Witches remain cold and unwelcome. I could see the caldron and the bond fire. There were Wizards standing in the arena with burgundy robes.

I looked to Marcus and asked "Why are their robes different from the rest?"

He smiled and said "They are Master Wizard instructors. The teachers of the Wizards."

Then several men without shirts walked into the arena with drums. They stood at the perimeter of the circular stadium and started drumming. It was deafening and primal. Just a repeated thunder of the numerous drums rumbled the seats and the ears of the onlookers. A Wizard came into the stadium with a lit torch and lit the bond fire. He then exited. The drums stopped abruptly. As the bond fire was in full force, the stadium was in clear focus. Eight black robed Wizards in training walked in and stood in a line at the opposite end of the stadium. I could recognize Max immediately though they all had their hoods up. He stood in the middle of the row waiting for his turn. Edwin looked to be the first in line. But I wasn't sure it was Edwin. I started to feel somewhat woozy. I didn't understand it then but it had to be the small drop of the mixture. I was also still on the single wave length with Max. My mind was only open to him and visa versa.

The instructors then had the Wizards in training recite their creed.

God, Ancient ones, Guides and Powers
It is I, the one who seeks you this hour
In the sacred circle I make my vow
The vision I seek from you now
To learn and work the living Magic
Accept the wisdom, grace and logic
With every breath and action
I do so seeking your satisfaction
Truth and honor my actions take
For life, Elements and Natures sake
I shall seek the way of the Wizard

Each Wizard in training was led to the caldron and handed a gold challis of the mixture. Each drank the challis and was led to the bond fire. The instructors removed their robes and they were shirtless with only pants and shoes. They all sat Indian style before the fire. And the drums continued their primal thunder.

Three of the Wizards in training stood and began to wonder around the stadium slowly. Edwin laid on the ground and wiggled like a snake. Three others began to leap through the stadium like gazelles. But Max stayed still sitting Indian style. I tapped him to see what was happening to him. He then in his mind, as his physical body stayed in front of the fire, was flying. He was flying over the mountains, fields and the oceans. He was free. He felt it and could see it. He felt bliss. Happier than he had ever been. He then physically stood as he looked into the fire. He looked deeply into the fire and saw Green Cat Eyes. His heart fluttered with a strong feeling of fear and desire. He was staring into the fire at the cat eyes. His vision blurred and he also became woozy. There were several people in the fire and they were all taking to Max at one time. He was confused and fought with his mind to remove the voices. Max then had goose bumps sensing something threatening.

I stood up in preparation of what was coming. As I stood, Marcus and Mandra watched me closely. Max and I heard the mumbled talk of several voices. As other voices went quiet, A white robed Goddess with a golden aura appeared within the fire. She smiled to Max showing the her fangs within her cat like smile. Then She began to recite her incantation:

Lonely spirit panther child
Come share in the life of the untamed and wild
Teach us lessons we need to learn.
For Old ways will wither and burn
Dancing partners, you and I.
Together as one, till we die
To dance the Maiden dance of life
Through this path of pain and strife
Dance with me to your end
Thy true love I will send
For your reward, freedoms victory
To rein down throughout magic's history
Awaken now Panther Spirit
Courage so strong that others fear it
Your fate to go far
The panther, now you are

He then saw the Panther looming large in the fire; a large and powerful beast. I had my own goose bumps and the hair on my neck was standing. I was breathing heavier then I wanted to. The panther was dangerous, deadly and angry. A monster with a full snarled of fangs and roar of a demon. Screaming and growling and moving towards Max with want and power. Then panther jumped from the fire and entered Max and physically knocked him off his feet. And I screamed. I saw Max as the panther and his left paw bleeding. Then all went black.

Max's body lay on the ground. Then his body began to convulse and I screamed again. Marcus and Mandra were at his side with the Belladonna spiked rum. Edith held my arm as I stood breathing heavy and looked as Marcus and Mandra forced the rum down his throat. Mandra looked up at me and smiled. I tried to see through Max. I tried to see if he was awake but he wasn't. Soon, Wizards in Black robes came and picked him up. They took him out of the stadium with Marcus and Mandra following. Then I heard it "Mixed Blood what do you expect."

I looked and other wizards were making comments of Max being Mixed Blood and he couldn't handle the rituals like Pure Blood. I looked to Edith, "Let's go." She nodded and we left the stadium. We met grandmother outside of the tent.

She said "Let's get going home."

I grabbed her "Grandmother, what about Max? Is he OK?"

She smiled and said "He is fine. Marcus is with him. We will let his kind look after him."

We walked to the car and as soon as we were on the highway, we entered our driveway. I went up to my room and said a prayer for Max and went to bed.

As I slept I dreamed of the black robed wizards taking Max away. But in my dream, they were taking him away from me, not the ceremony. I cried as I was losing Max and his protection and he was being taken to his end. The wizards were taking him away from me and I wanted him back. He remain unconscious and did not respond to my calls to him. I screamed for him and he remained unconscious. He didn't come. I woke crying.

The next day, while I sat at the piano trying to do scales, Max appeared next to me. I smiled and gave him a quick side hug. "Max. I am so glad your well." He then started to play a Chopin Sonata.

He looked at me seriously "What did you see?"

I was taken back by his question. I said "Max. I saw what you saw."

He looked at the piano. "I need to know. I am not sure exactly. I mean, a lot of it was symbolic."

I looked at him as he played softly. I took a breath I said "I saw you fly over the mountains and the ocean. I could feel you being free. How you felt at being free. You know, happy."

He looked at me with recognition of that. He nodded looking back at the piano continuing to play "And?"

I continued. "Then I saw the cat eyes. You felt something in your heart; because it fluttered."

He turned and looked at me and missed a note and stop playing. He continued to look at me seriously, "Go on."

I shook my head "I saw people all talking all at once in the fire. You were confused" I continued "I heard her incantation and I saw the panther. I saw it jump into your body and knock you back. I know you saw the danger." He looked at me seriously.

"Max. What did it all mean?"

He shook his head and said "I don't know."

I think he did. He kept it locked in his mind somewhere where no one could see it. I don't know how he did that since my mind was never closed except when he asked me. He started to play again.

Then I remembered "Max I saw you as the panther and the paw of the panther was bleeding."

He looked confused "I don't remember that part."

I nodded "I do." I then told him, "Max, the panther scared me."

He looked at me seriously for a moment longer. Then he turned back to the piano "Well at least that's over and I don't have to do it again."

I smiled "I am glad."

At dinner, grandmother and I were joined by Edith, Marcus and Max. This was not always unusual, as grandmother fed anyone that was there at dinner time. But this was more. It was planed and Marcus was very serious, Edith is usually gone by two o'clock. But today she stayed around and watched Max. And Max, he usually came to dinner with Marcus but today he was at grandmothers before dinner. Marcus and grandmother ordered him to stay put. He just looked at me like I knew something. I raised my shoulders and shook my head.

He then transmitted *"Close your mind to all but me."* I did as he asked mostly because I knew something was up and we were the targets. I couldn't imagine what I or Max did wrong.

Marcus and Max sat across from Grandmother and me. Edith sat that the front of the table. I looked at Max as Marcus had that serious stout look on him. Mandra too was very regal and quiet. Max looked to me and shook his head slightly. Somehow there was something serious going on. We waited.

Marcus began "Princess, It did not escape your grandmother and I …and several others,… that you witnessed Max's vision." Stunned I looked to Max.

He sent *"I never told him or anyone."*

Marcus continued "You stood and you screamed before there was any indication that Max was in trouble coming back."

I looked back at Marcus "I didn't mean to. I wasn't trying to. I ….."

Marcus put up his hand to me, "Princess, we are sure that it was not intentional. And we will not ask that you divulge what you saw, any more than we would ask Max. But what was seen and felt was for Max alone."

I looked at Max he sent *"Its OK Em. Just don't tell them anything Promise?"*

I looked at his eyes, *"I promise. I am sorry."*

Marcus continued "But you had the rare and unanswered opportunity to witness the ritual vision without actually participating. Our question to you is how you did this."

I shook my head and said "I don't know."

Edith looked at me suspiciously "Em. You know something."

I looked at her and said "No Master Edith. I don't." She looked at me suspiciously. Then I remembered. "I did accidentally taste the potion." I looked at her and then to grandmother. "It was only a drop on spoon. I put it in my mouth without thinking. I didn't tell you because I was already in trouble for the cats and because of the Wizards teasing me. I had my mind only open to Max." Marcus started laughing his beautiful laugh.

Mandra smiled. "Well that answers that. Em did see the vision. With the mixture and her mind open to Max accounts for Em seeing." Then she looked to Max "I am sorry that Em intruded with such a special event of yours. Will you forgive her?" I looked at my grandmother as I already talked to him. I can do my own apologies. And besides, he could have locked his mind and then I wouldn't have been able to see anything.

Max looked at me and smiled and said "The Princess is always welcome to intrude. There is nothing to forgive." He sent *"Next time, don't let anyone know by screaming."* I smiled and said out loud "Thanks Max." And though I believed that was it and we could just eat, I was wrong. Master Edith began her interrogation of what I could tell her about Wizards and Witches oaths and motives.

She looked over to Max. "Well young Wizard, What is the most important rule of a wizard or witch?"

Max was taken off guard and looked at me. *"What is this?"* I looked at him and again had to shrug my shoulders.

He looked back at Edith "I believe that the most important rule would be to harm no one with magic." Edith nodded as Marcus smiled.

Master Edith then looked at me "And what would happen if you did harm someone with your Magic?"

I looked at grandmother and then to Max and then back to Master Edith. "I believe in the three fold rule, Harm to another comes back three times." Edith smiled at me and nodded in approval.

She then looked back at Max. "Young Wizard, I see that you have gained the trust of the princess and that you show trust in her. How will this affect the expectations of your fellow Wizards?"

Max looked at Marcus and then back to Edith. "I must have the trust of the Princess to properly protect her. And I have a vow that I took before all powers and God. The Wizard Counsel has appointed me Guardian and I will continue the vow regardless of the opinions of others. I am also following the ethics and morals of the Wizards in loyalty and honor." I smiled at him because he answered so easily and genuinely. It seemed that Marcus did too. He smiled broadly at the answer Max gave.

Edith looked to me "And you Em? Knowing that the Wizards and the Witches are not friends, can you truly trust these Wizards?"

I looked at Marcus and back at Max. Then I focused on Edith, and said "I can only look at the individual. Not the difference in Wizard or Witch. Marcus and Max have always been good to me and come when I call. I like Marcus and Max. I trust them. I don't know about other Wizards because I don't know them." She smiled and I looked at Marcus and Max. Marcus nodded in approval and Max smiled.

Max asked then "Why are we being asked these elementary questions?"

Marcus looked to Max and then me. "You both are talented and are not in full control of your talents. There has been this situation, though not intentional, that could have been somewhat uncomfortable in the event that Em had a different experience and open only to your transmissions. We may not have gotten you back and may have also lost the Princess as well."

I looked at Marcus and then Mandra "It is all my fault. If I hadn't made the mistake of the cats than my mind would not have been only open to Max. I did take the mixture but didn't think it effected me. Max only was doing what Guardians do."

Marcus looked to Mandra and she said "Regardless of the mistakes, you need to be honest with us Em. We could have intercepted the danger. These questions remind you of what is important. Honest and good. And though there was no malice intended, we could have lost Max. We could have lost you."

Edith smiled at me "Princess, while you seek your true self, you need to always be honest for you and others that may be affected." She looked at Max " Young Wizard, you should also discuss this with your Master. He too will have the same opinion of validating your magic with more experienced Wizards."

Max said "Yes mam."

Mandra said "Have we all an understanding? That you both check with us with rituals and potions. That your magic will be under your control and if not, don't do it. And that the trust here at this table is good." Everyone smiled and she then said "How about desert?"

After dinner, while Mandra, Edith and Marcus had their coffee, Max and I went out on the porch. "I am sorry Max. I would never purposely interfere or intrude."

He smiled "Yeah but if you hadn't than I couldn't ask you what happen." I laughed.

He laughed with me and said "Don't worry Princess; I knew you were there, I could have cut off my mind. I just didn't." He kissed my cheek and was gone.

Shortly after that, it was my turn. I was informed by my grandmother that I would be entering into the coven and would go through my own ritual at the autumn festival.

I looked at her and told her "Grandmother, you know that the coven does not really like me. I scare them as much as I scare myself."

She smiled "What better way to bring us together. They will hear you make your promise to God, Mother Earth and to them."

I looked at her seriously "Do I have to have a potion like the Wizards?"

She giggled and said "No. No. You have to come pure of heart and mind."

September came and with it Autumnal Equinox . It was time to say good bye to summer and the sun and hello to the fall and winter. It was just after my birthday and with it more darkness and me back with my dad and the harpy. But first, Grandmother said that I would be presented to the coven. She would send me home after that. I didn't want to go home. I loved my father and missed him so much, but I knew I didn't belong there. Everyone knew I didn't belong there. But I was still sent back every fall.

Of course, this was a ritual of the witches to farewell to the long days of summer and to the last of the harvest. In this celebration, I would be welcomed in to the coven. I can't say that I was real thrilled with this. I not only was on display, but naked part of the time. My grandmother told me that my body was Gods creation and therefore natural and beautiful. She told me not to be ashamed of the Lord's gift. Well that was easy for her. She wasn't just fourteen. She wasn't going to have both females and males look at her naked. I was mortified. My only shield would be my thigh length hair.

The yard was once again dressed in the season of pumpkins, gourds, and corn husks. There was holly and rosemary, Lavender and mistletoe. Tables were set up and the path to the ceremonial bath was lit by candles. There was the bond fire to light the night and food and refreshments galore. Grandmother had harp players and mandolin players spread out through the yard.

I looked out my window and saw the guest arriving and Lincon welcoming the coven. There was a high priest there by the name of Alfred. He was to oversee and finish the ritual with the five fold kiss. The yard was beautiful but I wanted an escape.

"Oh no you don't" my grandmother was behind me with a simple cotton dress. "Grandmother, why do I have to be naked. There are boys here."

"Em, we have been through this. They too have or will have their turn. She turned and smiled at me "Don't worry, your back will be to the audience and your hair will cover your rear." She had me slip the white cotton dress over my naked body and then put a wreath of dried maple leaves and husks. She looked at me and smiled "Lovely."

She then took my hand and we went down stairs. I walked slowly as I entered the kitchen where I was sequestered until Edith called me for the ritual. Molly smiled at me and said "Don't fret girl. Your are beautiful and no one could dare make fun."

I looked at her and said "Would you do it?"

She smiled and said "I have a few times."

I was shocked. "Molly why? I don't even want to do it once."

She giggled. "Each time you enter a coven, this is what is expected. The coven must accept you and you must make the promises to the coven."

I nodded wishing I was invisible and then I was. Molly laughed and called grandmother. My grandmother stood on the porch looking into through the kitchen doors.

"Em. Stop it. You materialize at once." I came back and sat shaking for what was about to happen. Grandmother's voice came back softer "Em. I will be right there with you." I looked at her and gave her a smile.

I watched the last of the light of the day fade away along with any hope to my modesty. Edith came to the kitchen door and said "Em. It is time." I didn't know if I could get up from the chair I sat in. Grandmother came to the door and Edith disappeared. I walked to my grandmother and went out on the porch. We walked to the front and I walked with Mandra to the path of the ritual. The harps and mandolins continued their soft delicate serenades. I did not look at anyone and walked to the first arbor were Edith stood waiting with the ceremonial sward.

Millie was there and she took the sward and asked "Who comes to the gate?"

I had rehearsed this over and over but knowing once I said the words Millie would cut my dress off I hesitated.

My grandmother then nudged me. "It is I, Emily Star, child of earth and starry heaven." Millie then said "Who speaks for you?"

Mandra at my side said "It is I, Mandra, who vouches for her."

Then Millie pointed the sward to my heart and said "You are about to enter a vortex of power, a place beyond imagining, where birth and death, Love and hate, dark and light, joy and pain, God and Mother Nature meet and make one. You are about to step between all the worlds, outside the realm of your life. For know it is better to fall on my blade and perish than to make the attempt with fear in thy heart!"

I gave my rehearsed answer "I enter this path with perfect love and perfect trust."

Millie then said "Prepare for death and rebirth." She then took the sward and cut my clothing away. My hair covering my rear somewhat, as my hair hung with some covering my breast and the rest my rear. Millie completed the ritual of cutting off my dress and then stuck the sward in the earth leaving in my mind the Cross of Christ.

Millie and Edith then took a blind fold and covered my eyes, a cord was tied around my wrists and one foot.

Then Edith said "And she was bound as all must who enter into the Kingdom of Life and Death. And her feet were neither bound nor free."

Edith, Led me to the tub. Then Edith, Millie, Molly, Lincon, Grandmother and several others came as I was in the tub and bathed me. I was removed from the tub and while surrounded by my coven, and dried.

I was then carried to the ceremonial circle where I was surrounded by the coven. Then Alfred the High Priest entered the circle with me.

He kissed me and said "Now you have been brought to this coven. He then said "Hail Guardians of the Watchtowers of the East, West, North and South. Behold Emily Star who will now be made Priestess and Witch."

Though still blind folded, I knew what was about to happen. "Blessed be thy feet, that have brought thee in these ways. Bless the knees that shall kneel at the sacred God and Mother Earth. "Blessed be thy womb, without which we would not be. Blessed be thy breasts, formed in beauty." Finally he kissed my lips, saying Blessed be thy lips, that shall utter the Sacred Names."

Alfred then said "Are you ready for the creed?"

I said "I am."

Alfred then removed my blindfold and looked to my eyes and said "Repeat after me."

I repeated the words Alfred said them;

To Know
To dare
To will
To keep silent
This is the law of our coven.
Dark night and shinning moon
Listen to our rhyming tune
East, West, South and North
Hear us as we call you forth
Earth, Wind, Fire, Water
Watch over us so we will not falter
Promises made to do our part
Hidden deep in the heart

Without the wisdom, truth and light
Our magic will have no might
That the art will be passed down.
As we hand over our crown
That the power of magic is never used for wrongful end.
For the three fold rule will surely mend
The craft will be used and held in honor.
Never in doubt and left to ponder
Betrayal to these words in trust
will find retribution a must.
In perfect faith and perfect trust, I make this creed
And look to God and Mother Earth to lead.
Bless it be

After I finish repeating the last, Alfred then said "Arise and be anointed" He then said "May your mind be free. May your heart be free. May your body be free." Then the coven picked me up and turned me three times. And they all laughed and cheered.

When they lowered me I looked to the Widows Tower and saw Max watching. I was mortified. Grandmother then put me in my solstice robe as I stared at Max and knew he saw me naked. I was furious. I narrowed my eyes and thought of all kinds of pain for him and let him see what I was thinking. Things like sticking red hot needles in his eyes and tearing him limb from limb. I slowly and reluctantly went back out to the yard and saw that Marcus, Leonardo and Edwin were there. So they too saw me Naked. I was mortified. This was not for Wizards. I found my grandmother and was so upset that she pulled me over to the cliff rail to talk.

"Em. Don't be like this. You should be celebrating."

I looked at her "Grandmother Edwin and Max saw me naked! Not to mention everyone else on Earth."

My grandmother hugged with a chuckle. "They would never dare mention it. They are probably more self conscious about it than you are. You know how those Wizards are." I looked at her and did agree that they were more conservative than Witches, but I was still upset.

Marcus came over to us and said "Well Princess, you now have your coven. How do you feel?"

I know I was red faced knowing that they saw me. "I am embarrassed that you all saw me."

He laughed "Princess, you have no reason to be ashamed or embarrassed."

I shrouded my shoulders and walked over to where the bath still stood. I looked around and with no one watching I transported back to my room. I did not want to face anyone else. It actually made me happy to go home where no one knows what I look like under my clothing. I could hear the party out side with the Season Celebration.

Then Max called down from the tower "If I talk to you will you hurt me?"

Mortified that he was still there, I knew that he could not resist teasing me. I fumed "Yes! Go away."

It was quiet for a minute and I watched the party from my window. "Em. I didn't see anything."

I seethed at him still being there and said through my clinched teeth "Liar! Go Away!" Max appeared next to me. I looked at him through narrow eyes. "GO AWAY." He stood there and smiled at me. I pushed him and ran to the tower and stood at the window. He was on the stairs keeping back knowing I had already intended to hurt him and was ready to send the molten needles.

"Then can I talk to you tomorrow?" He stood at the stairs looking threw the banister. I didn't answer him.

"How about the next day?" I rolled my eyes.

"Can I make an appointment?"

I was fuming and said "Max go away."

He laughed and then said "Really, I didn't see anything. I tried. But your hair was in the way."

I hung on 'he tried'. I narrowed my eyes and looked to the stairs "What do you mean you tried?"

Then he said "I didn't try… I looked but could not see anything because your hair covered you."

I still would not let him off the hook "You looked?"

He backtracked again and said "All I saw was your hair and legs. I didn't see anything that is normally covered. OK? Actually no one that was not in the circle saw anything." He giggled and said "You're too skinny to have anything to look at anyway."

I tapped him then and he closed his mind as soon as I did and I got nothing. I put my hands on my hips and glared "Why did you close me out Max?"

He came up the stairs and sat in the chair and said "Because I don't want you snooping right now."

I narrowed my eyes at him and said "That's because you are lying."

He laughed shaking his head. "Em your ceremony was no less embarrassing then mine. Why are you so upset?"

I still didn't feel that his was more embarrassing since he didn't know anything once he was out. I was stark naked. "How would you know Max. You were out cold. I was naked in front of God and the world." He giggled

I looked back at the party in the yard. "Why were Wizards here anyway? This is a Witches deal."

He shrouded and said "Mine was a Wizard Deal but you were there when I passed out. Besides, the Wizards have a vested interest." He looked over with his stupid smile "Em, really, no one saw anything."

I sat on the floor and looked at him "I don't want to talk about this night ever again."

He smiled and stared at me. I glared my best threatening look and said "Max I am serious."

He continued to smiled but said "OK." He smiled charmingly, "Let go back to the party and dance. OK?"

I smiled and waved my hand so that I was then dressed in jeans and a sweater. He grabbed my hand and pulled me down stairs. We reached the party and then we danced with everyone else.

CHAPTER 17

Christmas was always a strange time for me. I love the Christmas Story and the who ritual of Christian belief, after all, I was Christian. I loved the Christmas Tree and the smells from the kitchen when Aunt Bella made her goose. I turned fourteen this year and was looking forward to being at grandmothers even though it would be months till I could go back. We had an early snow so this year it is a white Christmas.

"Auntie, you know I love the smell of the goose. I love the smell of the gingerbread." Aunt Bella, in her traditional Christmas Cheer "Oh I know. That's how I felt when I was a girl with your grandparents."

I was happy to be home with Dad I just did not see him a whole lot during the Christmas Season.

"Did your father give a nice sermon?"

"Oh yeah. All the kids were great acting out the Christmas Story. Taylor is the perfect wise man."

Aunt Bella liked that and smiled. "Now I just have to get him to take off the robes and put down staff."

I giggled. I then went to the tree and came back with her gift from me. I handed it to her and she looked at me strangely. "Em you did not have to do this."

I smiled "Auntie I made it with my own two hands. No magic"

She looked relieved and took off the bow. She pulled off the paper and opened the box. There was the silk rag scarf I knitted for her. It had lots of colors and patterns and was wide and long.

"Oh Em. Its beautiful. Thank you" and she hugged me.

"I was hoping you would like it.

She looked at me and she had a tear. "Em. You know I really do love you, don't you? I smiled and said "Well I always hoped and keep I trying." She wiped her eye and smiled. "Well I do."

Zee and I walked out to the creek. Some of the snow was melting into the creek and I watched it as it melted into the water. I could hear the church and the community center were still busy with parishioners. And I knew Dad, Tina, Nora and Tom were there. I sat on the same old log, and stared off.

"Merry Christmas Em."

I turned around and Mandra was there . I stood up and hugged her

"Grandmother I am so happy to see you. " I stepped back and stated "I don't know why you block me when I am here."

She looked up and then at me "You know this is the time with your family. You need to be here." She petted my hair and said "I just wanted to make sure you knew that I was thinking of you and that I wanted you to think of me." She looked around and sighed, "this is the winter solstice. This is the perfect place for it." As we stood there, the snow started. Grandmother pulled up the hood of her cape. " I was hoping, through your winter break..... You would do some Bible study?" I looked at grandmother like she was off a little.

"Grandmother, I have studied the Bible since I was a little baby."

She smiled and said "I know, I just think it might bring you and the family a little closer if you studied with them."

I knew she was right. "OK what ever you say."

She smiled her brilliant smile. "Merry Christmas My Precious Star." She kissed my cheek and she was gone.

I saw Dad and the rest exit the church. I knew it would be time for the family. I looked down at Zee who had a nice little coat of snow and he was looking at me like I was crazy to stand there. "Go in then you silly beast." He was gone.

Then I heard "Its snowing here!" I turned and Max was picking up some snow. He looked up at me and threw a snow ball at me.

I laughed at him "don't you have snow?" He shook his head and looked over at the church where the congregation was talking and giving wishes of good cheer.

"That is a good size pack of Normals. How come your out here by your self? I shrouded my shoulders.

He then smiled and said "I came by to wish you a Merry Christmas from me and Marcus." He kissed my cheek .

I smiled at him and said "Merry Christmas Max. And tell Marcus the same." He smiled and was gone.

"Em. Em come on lets go in. Its time for presents."

Tom was yelling as he ran to the house. I laughed and Dad waved me in. I made my way to just in-between the house and the Church. Through the snow I saw a dark figure in the trees across the road. I figured it had to be Max. I called out Max!" but he did not answer. I started to walk across the road but the figure was gone.

Dad called "Em. Come in the house. You will be soaked." I looked over and went towards the front of the house looking back at the woods for Max. Nothing was there.

I spent the Holiday enjoying the family. Only Tina had to find someone and something to scream at. This time it was Tom. It seemed unfair, he was so excited, he never meant to knock over the lamp.

"You are so clumsy. Look at what you did."

I looked at Dad, 'Dad its Christmas. Make her stop. It was a cheap ugly lamp."

He looked over to Tina, "Tina Stop it. He did not mean it and its Christmas."

She then turned on Dad and said "What do you know. You can even raise your own daughter!"

Dad turned red. "I will not allow you to disrupt our Christmas. If you want to be this way go up stairs." She huffed and stomped up stairs.

"thanks Dad." Tom with tears in his eyes repeated me "Thanks Dad."

Dad hugged Tom and said "Its alright kid, why don't we all play the new video games." Tom perked up and Taylor yelled "All right!" The boys ran for the TV and I laughed. Nora stood up, flipped her hair and told my father "I hope you don't think I like you taking to my mother that way. And don't expect me to call you Dad." with that she stomp up the stairs to her mother. The boys and I looked at Dad, he looked at us and we all burst into laughter. Della came out of the kitchen laughing. It actually wasn't that funny, but the dramatics were priceless.

That night, After Tina an Nora forgave us, we ate dinner in the dinning room which was never used except for special occasions. Dad said the blessing and then it was on. Boys trying to out eat each other and Nora, Della and Tina gossiping about the new star on some show. I was sitting next to Dad who held my hand.

"Wow Em. Look at how our family has grown."

I smiled at him. "I think your happy aren't you Dad."

He smiled into my eyes. "When you were born my cup run-ith over. I should have married before so you had brother and sisters. I like that part of this."

I told him "I do to, Dad." Aunt Della was laughing and I thought. Aunt Della needs a husband. She young yet, and pretty. Her hair thick brown and brown eyes. Her skin was a light olive and her smile was captivating. Besides, Taylor needs a Dad of his own. I turned back to Dad and said low and soft "Dad, aren't their any friends of yours that would like to date auntie?"

He giggled and said "don't tell but I'm working on it." My next thought was for me. Maybe she would have a better disposition. Just then there was a knock at the door. Dad looked at me while Tom jumped to answer it.

Dad patted my hand, "Round one."

Jacob Henning entered the dinning room and all the adults raised there voices in his welcome.

"Please sit and eat with us. I will get you a plate." Auntie said as she was off to the kitchen for a plate.

"Thank you. It does smell delicious."

I smiled at Dad and he winked at me. Doc sat across from Della and she handed him a plate and silverware. He served himself a hefty portion and began to eat. He stopped in mid chew of the bite of goose and looked up. I could not imagine what could be wrong. He said, with a full mouth," this is delicious!"

He chewed and swallowed and looked at Della and said, "This is absolutely marvelous" Aunt Della beamed and her smile was radiant.

I looked at Dad and said "Knock out first round." Dad and I laughed then.

Once the night ended and the dishes were done, Auntie had a date with Doc, and everyone was full and happy. The boys were sent to bed and I listened to the bantering between Dad and the Doc. Tina and Della listened as well and joined in from time to time. Nora acted board and irritated as usual. Doc left, Nora and Tina had gone to bed. I looked over at Auntie with a big smile and said "What a wonderful match…. A Doctor." We all started laughing and she throw the dish towel at me.

She got up and said, " I am going to bed, Merry Christmas you two."

Half way to the hall she turned around and asked, "Em you wouldn't use magic would you?"

I looked at Dad as if I was being blamed for his Bad, "No Auntie, I don't do well at those potions and I don't believe in them. This magic was all your brother."

She made a full turn and stared at Dad. "Caesar you did not make look like a old spinster did you."

Dad looked at her "All I did was invite a friend over for Christmas. What happen from there is not the doing of Em or me. Only God."

She gave that same pretty smile and said "Good night."

I kissed my Dad and said "Merry Christmas Daddy."

He hugged me and Said "Merry Christmas Em." I went to my room.

I sat at the window looking to the back to the creek. The snow was falling softly and I wished that everyday here could be like today. Today, I was part of a family. I loved it. I knew though, that tomorrow would be back to the norm. Well not with Tom and Taylor. They were always nice to me. Dad too, but he was always holding off the shrew Tina.

The scene from my window was so peaceful. Like a post card or painting. The fallen log lay with a fresh coat of snow and the little creek drifted by. The trees on the other bank were snow covered and waved gently as a warm Christmas wish. It was one of my favorite place to pray and meditate since I was very little. Nana used to be there too. I hope she was watching the family tonight. I hope it made her happy.

Just as I intended to change into my night gown and turn on the TV, Marcus was there. He waved his hand and I was dressed in a beautiful red dress with white fur trim. "Would you do us an honor of having a cup of eggnog for Christmas My Lady?"

I was so surprised. "Marcus. I don't know what to say?"

He smiled "Though it is not proper not to tell your father, Mandra is with us and I thought you could have a cup and then return. Are you with us?"

I nodded and he pulled me into a hug and we were …. Someplace. It was a huge room with tickling little lights. There was a huge Christmas tree. It actually had real snow on it with hundreds of little candles. There was Christmas music being played on a harp somewhere out of sight. There were three over sized couches that looked like they were made for really big people. They were in a open square facing the huge fire place with flames as high as they could go. I looked over and Max was there sitting in front of the fire place.

He smiled at me. "Merry Christmas Princess."

I was led into the room by the arm of Marcus. As we reached the square of couches, I found my grandmother.

She smiled and I sat next to her and hugged her. "Merry Christmas my precious Star." Molly and Lincon were there and I got up and kissed them both. Elena was on another couch and I kissed her on the cheek.

"Merry Christmas everyone." they all said Merry Christmas. And I went over to Marcus and kissed his cheek. "Thank you for completing my Christmas, my true Guardian."

CHAPTER 18

The next day I went to the field behind the grove of pines. I looked to the blue sky and the snow covered ground. I then heard them "The Princess has come to dance." I giggled. I thought trees hibernated in winter, but I guess not these. And they played their music and I did dance. I stayed as long as I dared. One the sun started to set I ran back to the house.

My father was waiting for me. "Em where have you been"

I think he suspected that I had used magic.

"I was walking in the Trees."

He looked at me with skepticism. "I think you need to stay closer to the house."

I felt insulted. I have always been free to run wild in the forest and now he's worried? "I was walking Dad. I wasn't conjuring.'

I followed my grandmothers suggestion and joined Bible Study with Tom, Nora and some other the other kids in the local youth group. I was always put on the spot like I had never touch a Bible before. I continued this for weeks. Finally, at the last stupid question about Lazarus and Jesus at the tomb.

I said "Please… I am a Preachers Daughter."

Nora then said "But you're a Witch."

Her normal response to me in every conversation. Each time it graded my nerves and resolved.

I lost my tempter with her. "I am tried of your bagging on me Nora. You are a fool. I know my Bible. And I am a Christian"

She gave a smirk. "Your just using magic to know the answers to the questions. I'm surprised your hands don't burn off just touching the Bible. Your evil and an abomination in the eyes of God."

I got up as the group of seven kids watched. I looked over at them. "I am created by God just as you are. What makes you the expert on what God loves and doesn't. By the way, the devil knows the Bible; cover to cover. And my Dad told me that."

I started to leave and this kid, Sam got up and said, "Em. don't go."

I looked at him and asked him "Why should I stay? To be told at each meeting how evil I am. No thank you."

I left. I walk down the stairs and headed for the log with tears in my eyes.

I heard them coming "Em! Em wait, wait up!"

I turned and Tom and Sam were running in the snow after me. I screamed at them "Stop! Just leave me alone!"

They stopped and watch me head across the road for the woods. I had to be alone and the woods were the only place I could find were that would happen. I saw Tom running for the house and Sam still standing were he stopped.

I went deep in the forest so that I could cry alone. The trees whispered

"She weeps."

I got so mad and I did want to use magic and get revenge. But the three fold rule hung in the mist. I felt so hopeless. It was so unfair. I could fit in even in Gods house. In bible study. I just didn't fit anywhere or with anyone. I didn't get them and they didn't get me. Not just the Normals but Witches too. And Wizards for that matter. They just hung around that thought me weird like the Normals and Witches. Only the trees let me be me. Only the breeze and wind let me be me. But I was not a tree or the breeze. I was flesh and blood. And I was alone in this mix of the worlds where I didn't fit.

Then I heard "Em. Don't cry?"

I looked up and Sam was there. "I told you to leave me alone. Why did you follow me!" He came closer. "Em not all of us are like that. I happen to think your special not evil," I looked at him. "Really?"

He smiled and said "Yeah. And I am not the only one. There are a lot of us." He sat down next to me. He put his arm around me and said "I know that Leslie likes you. And Joanna doesn't understand what's wrong with you and she is looking for herself. " I wiped my eyes. "Come on back Em. I personally will keep Nora in check, OK?" I smiled at him and said "Thanks." We got up and of course our butts and legs were covered with the snow.

Then the trees whispered "Princess beware." I looked around and I didn't see anything and continued to leave with Sam. Just as we started to go back I could hear my father yelling for me and it was echoing through the canyon.

I yelled back "I'm OK Dad."

And followed Sam out of the woods. As we got to the road I heard something behind me and as I turned I saw a shadow.

I called back "Max?" But there was no answer.

Sam looked at me strangely. "Is someone there?"

I smiled "I thought I saw something but I guess not." and we continued out of the trees.

"Em are you OK'. My Dad was running in the snow to me.

"Oh Daddy I am fine."

He looked over to Sam, "Thanks Sam."

Sam smiled and said "No problem Pastor Minelli" Sam went back to the church and Bible study.

I looked at Dad and said "I'll go back now too."

He said are you sure "I said yeah, I'm OK"

As I walked to the Church he said "Nora is grounded by the way."

I started to laugh, "From what Dad. Were does she go." He looked like I blew the wind out of his sail.

Over the weeks and into the spring, I was in Bible study. Sam did as he promised, and shot Nora down every time she started and asked her some really intelligent questions that she could not understand or answer. Tom had a lot of enjoyment from that and she always ended up snapping at him. Tom always took those little attacks like a badge of honor.

Sam was sixteen and in Nora's eyes, an older man. She felt that I should be hang around with him. I did not look at him romantically...

at first. He was tall and had broad shoulder. I guess from snow boarding and skating and what ever else he did. His hair was blond and he had piercing blue eyes. Because of that one handy ability of mind reading, I knew he liked me. Even though he was mortal, he was cute, and he was nice to me.

I never used magic around him and we never spoke of magic or my Witch status. He wasn't like the Witch Boys that only looked at me like something less then them, but yet special. Or the Wizard boys who looked at me weird and beneath them. And then called me princess. Except for Max. He actually treated me as an equal. Sam treated me normal; average. Like he looked at *me* and liked *me*. Just ME. Witch and All.

Nora was pee green and made my time with Sam Hell. She never stopped her insults about me and interrupted us anytime we were alone. She would go to her mother and tell her that I bewitched Sam when he actually like her. I thought that if I could bewitch everyone into liking me I'd be a happy camper. Unfortunately, I did not have that talent. And if I did, that wouldn't be what I wanted. I wanted to have friends because they liked me for me.

The church had a social that spring and I was going with Sam. The weather had warmed up and I was wearing a simple button down cotton dress and matching sweater. I wore my white tennis and let my hair go. Aunt Della was going with Doc and Tom had the duty of baby sitting Taylor . He said he did not mind it because he at least got to go.

I left my room and walked into the kitchen. Aunt Della was there all made up and warring a dress. She looked beautiful.

She was stunning. "Auntie, you look beautiful."

She smiled and asked nervously 'So you thinks so?"

I smiled and nodded. Soon Doc came in and stopped in his tracks when he saw Della. I walked by Dad and he and I had a knowing look with a high five.

Just as I reached the living room and Tina was coming down the stairs, Sam knocked. He saw me through the screen door, and I smiled "Hi". He looked very cute in his jeans, cowboy shirt and boots.

He asked "Ready?"

I smiled and said "Ready." She then said "Oh no you don't"

Tina rushed down the remaining stairs at the moment. "Where do you think you are going."

I looked at her like she had lost it "To the Church Social. Like everyone else."

She came to the door and said "You aren't allowed to date,"

I looked at her with disbelief "I have planned this and have not hidden that I was going with Sam. Why are you saying this now." My father came in and asked what was happening.

"She going on a date!"

I looked over at my dad with my eyebrows together.

He looked at me and Sam. "Is it really a date?"

I became irritated and said "I am going to the Church Social with Sam. What difference does it make if it is a date or not. I will be under your supervision." Dad saw my logic, and relented.

As soon as he said he did not see the harm, I ran out the door. I hear the Banshee in the house at my Dad. She was livid that he did not back her up. Sam looked back at the house and said "Man, I hope Pastor Menilli is OK." I giggled "Me too."

As we walked to the community center on the other side of the Church, Doc Henning called us "Hey you two. Let us walk with you."

We smiled and waited while Doc and Della caught up.

I looked at Doc and asked "Well Doc, will my father live?"

He laughed and said "It is too soon to tell."

Even Aunt Della was Laughing with us. She has lighten up a lot since Doc has been around. We walked in and the music was already playing. People were dancing and laughing. "Well lets dance" Sam said while he led me to the floor. I had the most wonderful time. I danced and danced. Fist with Sam, then with Dad and then Doc. I even got a dance with Tom. I was having so much fun. I did not even notice or hear anyone call me a witch though I am sure they did.

It was all winding down and time to go home. I really did not want it to end. Sam walked me to my door. He bent and kiss me softly on my lips and said good night. I smile and told him good night and he walked off. I was in Heaven. I had a boyfriend. A cute one. I got to dance all night and I had my first kiss. What more could a fourteen year old girl want. I walked in the house and through the living room straight into my room and closed the door. A little magic sound proofing and I let out the biggest scream. I threw my self on the bed. And closed my eyes to relive my night of NORALNESS! I gave a great scream and laughed.

I got up intending to change into my night gown and I looked out the window. There by the creek was that same shadow. I ran to the window and yelled out "MAX!" I forgot about the sound proofing and called in my mind MAX. I pounded on the window and yet there was not response from the shadow.

"Its not me."

I whirled around to find Max. He went to the window and saw the shadow. The shadow witnessing Max at the window with me, left. I suddenly got Goosebumps.

"If it's not you, who is it."

When I looked in his eyes there were no answers. "I want you to stay here. I'm going to check it out."

With that he was gone. While he was gone. I though 'Stupid' it is just the replacement. Of course it's not Max.

"it's not my replacement."

I looked up to see Max. "Who ever it was took off. I'm not sure but, just the same, I think I should stay here with you for a while just in case."

I looked at him and asked "Where is the replacement"

Max shrugged his shoulders and said "They keep me on a 'on call' assignment with you.".

I was confused "There is no replacement." He shook his head.

"Just so you know, I have seen the shadow before since being home. I always though it was you."

He looked at me and rolled his eyes. "When was I a shadow?"

I thought about it and said "Well never but you checked in and out fast so I thought….." He just turned on the TV and started the play station. He moved the chair between the bed and the TV and started playing. He stopped talking to me. He seem irritated with me. I took off my shoes and laid on the bed and watched him play a video game till I fell asleep.

The next morning I woke to "Mom! There's a man in Em's room"

Tina came running in lead by the informant Nora. I opened my eyes and found that I had a blanket over me. Max was sleeping in the chair. And the Banshee and Nora were staring.

"Caesar! Come Quickly!

I heard Dad jump out of his bed on to the floor in his room and start running down the stairs.

I quickly reached out and grabbed Max by the shoulder. "Max wake up"

He opened his eyes, saw the women in the door of the room and he was gone. Dad came to the room and turned in a full circle. Still half asleep, he looked at his wife.

"What!"

Tina in true Harpy voice, stated "She had a man in her room!"

Dad Looked at me and then back at her," When?"

She was screaming again "Just now. He was sleeping in the chair and when I called you he disappeared."

He looked at her like she was really gone this time. "Nora saw him too!"

He looked back at me and said " Tina, go make coffee." She did not move and started to open her mouth again. He never gave her a chance. "GO MAKE COFFEE."

She left the room and he turn his attention to me. " What in the Lords name is going on here."

I looked past him at nosy Nora. He turned around and he walked over and shut the door. "Em was there a man in your room."

I sat up in the bed and was still in the dress I wore night before. "My guardian."

My dad looked at me confused. "Your what?"

I looked at him and just gave up . It was way too much to have to explain. I just didn't have it in me. "Yes but he's not a man yet he's only like 16 or 17."

He stood there red and angry. "I don't care how old he is. I cant believe you would bring a boy in your room. And allow him to stay the night."

I got up. 'Dad it is not like that….."

He put up his hand and said "I don't care what it was Em. Its over. No Boys."

He was really mad. I could not get out of this one. "You, Young lady are grounded indefinitely."

So my perfect night ruined by stupid Max. Ruin by princess protection crap. And some creep running around like a shadow. I know that I was only lashing out but Max did not have to let those two see him. Now, not only was I a witch dammed to hell, I was also a slut.

I got up and dressed my self in jeans and a T. I did not leave my room because I just did not feel up to it this morning. I felt a little queasy.

"Emily Star, come to breakfast."

It took all I could do to go in the kitchen and look at their faces. And just as I feared, all eyes watched me come in. No one said a word. There was the average table noise of clacking utensils against the plates and moving serving dishes and cups. But nothing else. Nora looking at me with her triumphant smile. Tina with total distain, Tom with concern. Aunt Della did not look at me at all. Dad was stern and angry as I have ever seen him. Dad filled my plate with eggs and bacon. It made me gag. The more I sat there, the worse I felt. I knew I was going to spew. Dad looked at me and asked what was wrong.

"I'm not feeling so well."

Tina butted in "She probably pregnant. That boy is probably a frequent flyer."

My Dad threw his fork in the plate and glared at Tina. I looked at her and saw her glass of juice levitate, come up and pour down her white blouse. She screamed. But did not move. Dad looked at me accusingly "Em!"

I shook my head in denial. "No dad I did not do it"

Nora piped in and said "I bet she did!"

Then her eggs ended up in her lap. Dad stood up sending his chair flying. Della got up and grabbed a towel for Tina.

Dad was still looking at me "Em how could you. You promised."

I was still shaking my head "But Dad…."

Then we heard "Sit back down Caesar. It was me!" Mandra was there.

I cried, and had no idea why. The tears just start without reason. I got up from the chair and ended up in my grandmothers arms.

Della asked "Coffee Mandra?"

"Yes thank you Della."

Tina screamed "You get out. You are not welcome in this house."

Dad looked at Tina. "This is my house, Mandra is welcome. Always has been. You can leave if you want." Tina was stunned and quiet.

"What has happened to my granddaughter?" Mandra had my face in her hands "This child has a fever"

She shot my father an angry glare and Aunt Della came over and felt my head. "Oh my, Em. You belong in bed. Doc will be coming over I'll let him know your sick OK?" I nodded and Aunt Della led me to my room. While Aunt Della helped me change into a night gown I heard my grandmother talking to my father.

"What are you doing to her?"

Tom piped in and said "She's grounded indefinitely." There was a short pause and I heard him say "Sorry."

Dad voice came in then "She had a boy in her room."

Grandmother then said, "That *boy*is her guardian" Dad voice was impassive " It makes no difference to me *who or what he is.* I will not allow her to have boys in her room. It is out of the question."

Mandra then softly said, "Not only was it perfectly innocent, she was sleeping and had no idea he would be there in the morning."

Dad returned with "Regardless, this rule will not be broken."

Mandra then said "OK. That's fair. I only ask that you understand, the children had no intention of this incident. He came to me immediately to apologized. He wont repeat this situation." She paused "He felt that Em was in worse trouble than he."

I stopped listening. I did not care. Stupid Max, He could have stayed and explained to Dad. I wondered why my Guardians never showed up when Nora and Tina were at me.

Aunt Della pulled my night gown over me. "There you go, That's more comfortable." She pulled back my covers and I got in.

"Aunt Della?" She was pulling the covers up, and looked at me. "Remember when I was little, and I got really sick and you stayed with me all day even though Uncle John needed you in the store?"

She smiled "Where else could I be." I hugged her and said "This reminds of that time. It always made me fell good, special to you. Thank you."

She hugged me back and then pulled away. "I need to get you some Tylenol and some broth."

She left the room and I closed my eyes. I could hear them all in the kitchen talking away. Tina again tried to label me evil. My grandmother told Tina that a wart would grow on her face every time she repeated that. Tina was quite then. Dad told Mandra how great things have been and that from Christmas on nothing has happened. Mandra told him that she knew. And she was happy for the family and me.

My eyes remained closed and Auntie brought the Tylenol and some water which I took immediately.

She said "I'll let you know when Doc gets here. OK".

I smiled and nodded. She left the room and I closed my eyes. I felt someone sit on the bed. I open my eyes and it was Max. He looked at me and touched my head.

"Wow. Hot!" I could not believe him.

My eyes filled with anger, I said "Are you crazy? Aren't I am in enough trouble because of you?"

He smile that brilliant smile. "I am sorry. I had to come back and tell you. And also I had to ask you why you just didn't deny it? You could have let them try to prove it" with a giggle he was gone.

I must have slept for a time but when I woke up Mandra was sitting in the chair next to the bed. "Well how do you feel?"

"Terrible" My voice was scratch and horse.

She smiled at me and said "Well I guess this is a good time be restricted."

I smiled at the reference of being punished and sick any way. "Max came and said he was sorry"

Grandmother looked shocked "He promised he would not. That little rouge. Wait till I speak to Marcus."

I put my hand on hers and said "Oh Grandmother let it go. There's no use in us both being punished."

I rolled on my side and looked at her from the side. "Did Max tell you about the shadow?"

She looked at the door to ensure no one was there. "Yes and I have put in a request for additional guardian's but I doubt we get them. I am sure Marcus and Max will be close. A least until you come home with me."

She looked concerned. "Don't worry grandmother. I will pay attention." She petted my head while I fell back asleep.

I next was in the dark, but in my room. Everyone must be asleep. My eyes were hot. Zee was growling. I looked over to the window and I saw the shadow at the window watching with red eyes. I couldn't move. I scream for Max. The Shadow walked through the wall and was coming towards me. All I could do is scream for Max. But he did not come. The shadow got closer and closer. I tried to transport but I couldn't find the click. All I could do as those red eyes came close was scream.

"Wake up Em. Wake up." I opened my eyes and Dad was there with Mandra. Aunt Della and Doc came running in. Dad grabbed me up in a hug. "Your Dreaming baby."

I laid back down and was so hurt and angry that Max never came. I opened my eyes again and asked for Zee. He was no where. I had to find Zee. I looked around but he wasn't there. I called out "Zee." Tears escaping and fear of sleep resting in my bones. I felt like I was asleep and my mind was going wild. And I was alone. No Zee and no Max to help me.

I had to close my eyes again. I heard Doc say that I was close to delirium. He said that I needed to be watched through the night so that the fever did not get high and that he hoped that it is as high as it was going to get. But, he warned, it needed to come down soon. Mandra told them that she would stay with me tonight. But I did not hear anymore.

I felt the cool cloth being dabbed across forehead and on my cheeks. I opened my eyes and saw Max. "Max?"

He smiled and said "You called my Lady?"

I looked to my side and Mandra was sleeping next to me. "I think you fever broke."

I really did not know what he was talking about. "What?"

He said "Your fever, you've been sick."

I thought back and remembered the dream. "You didn't come."

He stopped and defensively said, "You were dreaming."

He resumed his task of putting the cool cloth on my head. " I know I was dreaming now, but then I didn't. I needed you."

He stopped again and said "I believe that I am here, my Lady. And have been here for the whole of the day and night."

I still did not have Zee. "Where is Zee?"

He looked under the bed and I heard the growl. "He's OK. He's under the bed. He is jealous of me" I did not understand that at all.

"Max, you are not supposed to be here especially in Em's room." Mandra shot up out of the bed.

He smiled at her and said "I was summoned by the lady." He put the cloth back in the bowl.

Mandra said "You know that was in a dream." He was smiling and seemed to enjoy his banter with Mandra.

"Yes but when I was called it was by a scream. And a scream means I must respond. I had no idea it was a dream until I found all of you with her."

Grandmother then was irritated "So you just hung around?"

He started to back away and said "Well yes. Any way, I see I am not needed so I will be on my way"

Grandmother said "Good."

He smiled at me and said "Feel better Princess." and he was gone.

Doc checked my heart and my blood pressure. Checked my temperature, and looked down my throat. "Well young lady, it looks that the worst is over. You will be doing Cartwheels in the front yard soon enough."

I smiled at him but still felt really sick. Aunt Della came in and brought me soup and juice. I really wasn't hungry.

"I know you don't want to eat but at least drink the broth. OK?"

I nodded. "What was wrong with me?" I asked Doc.

He was packing his doctor bag and smiled. "The everyday flu." He tweaked my nose and said, "Couple of days and you'll feel fine. Until then young lady, you stay in bed." Aunt Della put the tray on the night stand and said she come back for it latter.

"Auntie, where's Dad?"

She looked at me a little concerned, "Well the other children were so concerned about you and would not leave the house. So he thought he would get them out for a while and took them to Redding for a movie. He will be back in a while."

I was hurt. Eight months a year I am here and he never takes me anywhere. Well, I though I was probably sensitive because of the flu.

That night, alone in my room, I heard something at the window. Then it was there again. The shadow with the red eyes. It was advancing again coming closer and closer. I screamed to my self "Wake up!" But I laid there paralyzed and stiff. I was unable to move any part of my body. I screamed as it came closer. I then called for Max. but he did not come. The shadow reached for me and I screamed again.

"Wake up. Em" "Em I here. Princess wake up!"

I opened my eye's breathing heavy. I was in the arms of Max.

"Oh my God. Could you Please come faster next time?"

He giggled and looked behind him. "Ops gotta go!" He was gone and I fell back against the pillows on the bed. Della ran in the door followed close behind by Dad and Tom.

"EM?"

I put up my hand and said "I had another dream. I am so sorry. Go back to bed."

Della had her hand on her chest. "Em. You screamed as if you were being murdered. Are you sure you are all right?"

I gave a half smile and nodded. Dad came over and felt my head. "Well your not hot. Are you sure your OK?"

"Yeah Dad. Go back to bed." I looked at them all and said "Everyone go back to bed. I'm already embarrassed enough." They all left the room with concern on their faces. I shut the door from the bed with a wave of my hand.

"OK. Good Job." I looked over and Max was in the chair.

"Max if they see you in here again, I am going to have to go through people praying over me and freaky things you could not believe."

He laughed low. "I have investigation to do and have to ask you questions."

I really did not want to go back to sleep for fear of the nightmare. "OK. Ask your questions."

"Where did you first see the Shadow?"

I didn't mind telling he when I saw the shadow just what was going on when I did. He saw and read my hesitation

"You cant tell me anything that would make you less important. Don't hold back."

I sat up in the bed and looked down.

"The first time I was coming around the house. I was in between the house the church, and I saw the shadow. I called your name out loud because I thought it was you. The next time I was …..really mad and I ran into the forest."

He looked stern "Are you crazy. Running into the forest alone?"

I sighed. Another worry wart. How was I ever going to get to dance with the trees. "Well I wasn't alone for long. My friend Sam showed up and when we left the forest, I heard something and when I turned around and I saw the Shadow."

He looked a little irritated and mocked "Out in the woods with the boyfriend. That is not safe." I ignored his jibe. I wasn't about to tell him that I dance for the trees. "Well, someone is watching you. I just have figure out who it is. You will have to stay close to home and I promise to come when you call."

He got up "And Em? Don't be out on your own OK?

I nodded, though I knew I would go dance with the trees without anyone knowing.

Then he said "I guess a mortal boy is better than no one at all." He smiled and then was gone.

After four days of illness, I felt much better. I was still restricted and not allowed outside. Actually I wasn't able to leave my room. Tom came to see me a lot and ended up delivering messages from Sam.

He came running in one day and said "Sam had been asking me about you. I told him you were better. He grabbed a pen and paper and wrote you a note."

He looked behind him and then brought out the note folded in half. I smiled and wave at the door of my room and it shut.

Tom shook his head "Man. That is so cool."

I looked up at him and said "Yeah well don't tell, I'm not suppose to use any magic." Tom came over and sat on the bed with me and read the note with me.

> *Dear Em*
>
> *I was happy to hear that you are better now. I wish you weren't grounded. I really wanted to invite you to the movies this weekend. I guess until you have paid you dept to the restriction gods, I will hold off on the movie date. But that doesn't mean that we cant write to each other. I will see Tom tomorrow. I hope he has a message for me. OK?*
> *See you soon*
> *Sam*

"Yes!" Is all I said.

I looked over at Tom. "Well are you into espionage?"

He smiled "Well I will feel less like a spy and more like that stupid angel with the arrow. But OK."

I jumped off the bed and jumped around. I stopped and seriously told Tom. "Nora cant find out Tom. She will rat us out for sure."

He smiled. "She hates me and never talks to me and never looks to see what I am doing. If I talk to her in front of people she tells me not to. Were safe."

I smiled and went to the night stand and get a piece of stationary and a pen. I penned a note to Sam saying that I had another week or so on restriction and would love to go to the movies. I also told him that Tom would be the mail carrier. I put it in an envelope and sealed it.

I handed it to Tom "You first mission, Mr. Bond?"

He dramatically snatched the letter and said "That's 007 to you." I laughed and couldn't wait for tomorrows note.

Tom turned out to be a great spy. I told him that he should think about it as a profession. He smoothly and successfully took notes back and forth for a week. I was so excited about that movie date. I counted every minute of restriction leading to that date. Sam and wrote back and forth about what was happening in our lives at the time and who was doing what. He wrote me about Nora's taunting about me on restriction because I was evil. She even told him that she would more his type because she never gets in trouble.

That Sunday, I had one more day on restriction. I did not go to church because I was not allowed out of my room by Tina. Even Aunt Della said I need to go to church, and Tina told her I needed to be alone with my sins. Dad was already at church, so there was no intervention from him.

I stomped back to my room and I slammed my door. Tina came in and told me "Don't you ever slam a door in this house again. I will not tolerate your poor behavior. I will ensure that you do not end up like your mother."

I narrowed my eyes at her and in a quiet but threatening tone said, "My mother has nothing to do with this. And if you say anything again about my mother, you will be a mouse and I will let Zee play with you!"

She really got mad then and said, "You get used to this room because you have earned yourself another week!"

I looked at her "You know you can't make me."

She walked out of the room "Don't bet on it."

Before she could get to the out of the house. I stood on the Church steps. I stood with my hands on my hips and was about to pay the three fold price for doing something dastardly to this wicked Christian bitch.

When she saw me she was livid. "You go back in your room." I stood there glaring at her in defiance.

My father heard the conflict as he had been at the door meeting parishioners. "What's going on we about to start church."

Tina started to complain about my behavior being disrespectful. As she went on, Della walk by us and looked at my father in that knowing way. She looked over at me in a assuring way. Dad told Tina to go in the church. Nora and she entered as Nora looked back with her smirk.

"Em..."

I put up my hand because there was no defense." I'll take my evil self back to my room now, but don't think I am going to stay there for ever." I started back to the house.

Dad called me "Em come back to church."

I just kept going. I stayed in my room through church.

My father came in to see me between church and the Church coffee hour. "Em you cant be disrespectful to Tina."

I looked at him "She band me from church and told me to was not getting off restriction." He nodded his head "Your Aunt told me what happened. And I will talk to Tina."

It was such a crock.

I turn over on the bed and looked away from him "Fine Dad whatever."

He then told me "If that is your attitude may be you should stay put." I did not respond. I ignored him then and he left.

Not long after that, Nora walked by my door. "To bad your restricted. We are all going to Redding today. Hope you like your room after all."

I so wanted to hurt her. But I remembered the three times three. I don't need help in rotten things happening. And the day was not done. Tom came in. He looked kind of funny. He handed me a note and left.

> *Dear Em,*
>
> *I am sorry but someone told my parents that you and I were friends. They have been talking to Nora I think. Anyway, they have forbidden me to talk to you. Not even in church or Bible Study. I am really sorry. I really think you are cool.*
> *Sam*

I was so mad, I open my night stand drawer and pulled out all of the notes from Sam and threw them all over the room. How could he be such a coward. How can they just assume that there is something wrong with me without knowing me. Dad came in a short time latter.

"What's all this?"

I was laying across the bed with my back to him. I never turned around to look at him. "I was taking the trash out of my drawer."

He then said "We are all going into Redding. I would ask you to go but it looks like you are not in the mood."

I did not answer him. What for. I knew they didn't want me to go. "Maybe you could clean up your room while we are gone OK?"

I still did not answer. I decided not to waist my breath. I heard him walk out of the room and shut the door. I listen while they all left the house and the van drive away.

"Wow what's all this?" I looked over and Max was there. I did not answer. He started to pick up the notes and read each one. I jumped up and stared to grab the notes off the floor before he could get to them. I waved at the fireplace and a roaring fire began. Max was laughing at me and I threw every note I could get in the fire place. He still had a handful and I tried to get them. He held them above his head and I jumped to get them but had no success. He was laughing at me and my attempts to retrieve the notes from his hands. When he would not give them to me I waved my hand and set them on fire. He then threw them into the fire place with the rest before he burned his hands.

I walked back to the bed and laid down across the bed propping my head on my hands and elbows. I still had not said a word to Max. Just did not feel like it. So he laid down on his back next to me so his face looked up into mine.

I looked down at him and his stupid grin. "I guess its over with lover boy huh?'

I only looked at him.

"Oh come on Em. Don't be like this."

I did not want to be teased so I stayed quiet.

"Lets not dwell on unpleasant things today. Lets go have fun."

I pulled my eyebrows close and reminded him, "I am restricted again. And may I remind you, the first time was your fault."

He smiled and said "Your fault for telling the truth. And now you restrict yourself. What a goody two shoes."

I opened my mouth to dispute that but he was right. I was laying there, and there was no one there to rat on me if I left. But I did promise that I would not use magic.

"I promised I would not use magic."

He laughed "I think it was magic when you attempted to burn my hands off. Besides, I didn't promise."

Looking down at him I asked him, "Why would you want to hang with me. Don't you have a party or some older guy thing to do? Why hang out with a moody fourteen year old?"

He laughed. "I do that stuff all the time. Besides that, what kind of guardian would I be if I left you depressed and alone?"

He knocked one of my elbows out form under me, and I laughed. I looked back over at him with a smile and said "OK let me change."

I stood up and waved and was changed into my low rider jeans and a crochet top.

I grabbed the brush and brushed my hair quickly. "OK. Where are you taking me.

He got up and asked "What do you like to do?

I lifted my palms and shoulders and reminded him "I live on restriction. I don't do anything."

He thought a minute and grabbed me and said "hold on." He picked me up and spun around and as I laughed.

I found us on a beach with roller coasters and other carnival rides. Screeching "Oh my God"

I ran to the boardwalk where the rides were. I looked back to see Max walking to me "Can we ride the roller coaster?

He laughed and asked "Which one?" and of course I pointed to the tallest. I had such a fun time. I loved it. We stayed for a few hours and then returned to my room. I brought back my stuffed lioness that Max won for me.

"Thank you Max. You know, I've never gone to a carnival or a amusement park. I had a really good time"

He sat in the chair and said "It was fun wasn't it."

I nodded. I didn't want to give up my day of play. I wanted to dance. I looked sweetly at Max and asked "Want to go to the open field with me?"

He looked at me like I was crazy "Why do you want to go there? Besides your family may come home while we are gone."

I tapped dad to see what they were doing. "There still in the markets. It will take a while for that and then another hour and a half drive. Come on, we wont stay long? I just need to be free for a little longer."

He looked at me like he understood. But continued to bulk and I said "Well I could go alone."

He shook his head "With the shadow out there? No."

I smiled and said "Please Max?" He huffed "OK".

I grabbed his hand and pulled him through the wall and headed in the direction of the field. I let go of his hand as I scaled the creek and ran into the woods. "Em. Princess. Wait up!" I knew he was right behind me. I ran through the trees and into the middle of the field. My arms and hands were in the air as I twirled with my freedom. I smiled when I heard the whispers of the trees as they welcomed me back "Princess." I looked to the sky and saw the clouds nodding in approval of my return to the field.

Max caught up with me "Princess, don't take off like that."

I smiled at him "Can you hear them whisper Max? They are happy to see me." He looked at me strangely. I laughed "The trees. They were the first to call me Princess."

He shook his head looking at me like I was nuts. "You talk to trees?"

I tilted my head "You can't hear them?" He laughed and shook his head. I watched him laugh as I moved away from him and said "Too bad. Then you can't hear their music; their song."

I heard it. I loved it. I began to dance to the music of the tress. I heard the whispers of the trees "She Dances for us. The Princess dances." My eyes were closed but I was free. I could feel the breeze whispering love to me and blowing my hair in swirls as I danced. And the trees music, that mystical heavenly music, set me free. I twirled and dipped and ran. I was free. I danced till I was breathless. I looked back at Max knowing that I had the biggest smile on my face. But Max looked stunned. He looked like he witness something mystical.

I started laughed at him. "It's a Witch thing." Then I thought "At least I think it is."

I looked in a circle at the trees and blow a kiss in the breeze. I savored the peace and freedom.

Max then called over to me "Time to get back."

I turned and looked at him and his still had that funny look on him. I stepped back while looking to heaven and turn to return to Max. I was breathing heavy and continued to smile at my audience of trees and clouds as I walked with Max back to the house, my room and my prison.

He didn't speak on the walk back. He came in to the room and sat in the chair. "Thank you, Max." He smiled as he flipped on the TV. We watched reruns of Beverly Hillbillies. I produced a Pizza and some coke.

"What about the promise of no Magic?" Max asked.

I giggled and said "I was hungry."

We were quietly watching TV and eating pizza. About an hour later, I heard the Van doors shut. I looked at Max and kissed him on the cheek and said "Go Max!" He was gone. I waved my hand and the room was clean including the pizza box. The only reminder of the day was the stuffed lion on my bed. I laid on the bed and continued to watch the TV.

As they filled into the house, I could hear them bringing in groceries. Dad came in and asked if I was hungry. I shook my head not talking or looking at him. He left the room. Nora walked by, which was her usual.

She notice the lion on my bed. "Where did you get that lion?"

I ignored her. I was sure she would be running to someone to rat me out. But I learned something today. Don't be a goody two shoes and lead your self to trouble.

Tina came in after Nora went an informed her that there was something new in my room. "Em where did you get that Lion?"

I ignored her too. But I also put up a barrier so they could not come any further into my room. Of course Tina tried and ran right into the barrier. She looked like she it a plate glass window. She called my Dad and I dropped the barrier when he arrived in my room. "She has something there where we cant get into the room. "She's using magic."

Dad looked at her and Nora. "Why do you want in her room?"

Tina reported that I had a stuffed lion that I did not have before.

Dad told them "Why don't you stop looking for problems and get out of Em's room." Aunt Della came in with a bag with a hamburger in it. She was able to walk right by Tina who was still stinging from her walk into the invisible wall and Dad's instructions.

Aunt Della handed me the bag and I said "No thank you Auntie, I ate a cheese sandwich while you guys ate…" and I looked into Nora's weak mind and found " at Black Baer Dinner."

That got my Dad. "Well we wont be going out to eat without you anymore" Tina huffed and left followed by Nora.

Della said "I wont go without you again." then she left the room.

Dad then asked "Em where did you get the lion."

I wanted to scream *"Max won it for me at the Boardwalk when you left me here."* But instead, I said "I got it when I was at grandmothers last year. A friend gave it to me."

I still watched the TV and did not address my dad. I thought he needed to know I felt. "Em. Don't be mad at me. I am only trying to keep peace in the house.

"Don't worry Dad, I leave for grandmothers soon. With me out of the way, there will be peace." He knew that there was no conversation with me tonight. He left the room as well.

I heard Max "Good Job."

CHAPTER 19

I finally made it back at grandmothers for summer solstice. Again Dancing all I could. I loved Solstice for the dancing and the party. Max had come as expected and agreed he would be my partner for the Maiden dance. Marcus asked me why I always chose Max. "Because you always disappear," he laughed. You could tell Max was in a mood. He was not unhappy but mischievous. He had on that up to something or find something look.

Before the Maiden Dance, Max said "Got an Idea."

I looked at him and asked "About what?"

He took my hand and we walked over to the cliff rail. "Lets have some fun this year"

I was insulted. "We always have fun." I looked at him accusingly.

He laughed "OK we have fun but lets stir it up a bit? I feel like spooking the Normals tonight. Are you with me?" I smiled, Yes. I wanted so bad to play with my powers and I nodded.

He said "Do you see the tallest bolder? " I nodded still waiting for the big Idea. "When we jump the fire this time, lets land on that rock."

I started laughing "I think the crowd will flip out." I had my doubts as to the consequences. I said "We'll get in trouble, Guardian."

He thought for a second and said "Little Ms goody two shoes, Of course will get in trouble. But we will have some fun first. And how much trouble do you think we could get in. Its not like we would leave completely. Just over to the rock. Besides, just to see the faces on the normals will be worth it."

I thought about it. Yeah it would be great just to break loose with this constant restriction of our powers. We needed the chance and excuse to flex our magic. Besides, if the normals did expect to see Magic then why hang around the Witches.

I did have to tell Max "You know I can't jump that far Max."

He smiled and said "Wow that's too bad." And the more arrogantly said " But I can. So what do you say?"

He nudged me then. "Come on Em? I got to do something or I'll burst. I have to be so controlled all the time. I just need to be a little crazy. You know, like you and the trees." I smiled and said "You better be able to jump that far."

He laughed at me and said "I can so you better hold on tight."

I started to laugh "So we are purposely getting into trouble?"

He laughed and nodded. "Well at this is different then not meaning to and getting there." I huffed "Wow this could really change my image?"

He shook his head, " What? Like not Ms. Goody two shoes." I laughed.

So the Maiden dance started and I dance near my aunt Elena. When the music stopped and the drum started, I ran to Max. Deana's daughter was hoping to get to him first but I was faster and Max and I had a plan. Max said "We go last." I nodded. So as we all danced and each couple leap over the fire Max said 'Once over hold on tight."

So we held hands and leaped over and when we were about to descend to the ground, Max grabbed me and I held on and we made it to rock. I looked up at Max and we both gave a "Whoo hoo."

We looked up at the cliff rail and grandmother, Marcus and about everyone else looked over at us. We smiled at each other and looked to the normals who all had their mouths open. I looked to Max and he was laughing. Then he stopped and looked really serious. Max said "Ohoh." and we were hit with a wave that almost knocked me off the rock but Max grabbed me and I held on to him

"OK. Let's get off the rock before we get hit again with a wave."

Max did not respond and when I looked at him, he was looking at all three Elders and they were looking at him.

He said, "We can't transport. We have to climb down. The Elders ordered it."

I looked at him as if he was crazy. "I can't climb down, because there is nothing to climb down on. It's a tall straight rock Genius."

He looked back up at the Elders as another wave hit us. Then he made a growl noise and then said "OK . Let's jump."

I shook my head but he ignored me. He grabbed me and over we went. Screaming all the way down we entered the freezing ocean.

In my long Maiden dress swimming was impossible and the mask floated out in the ocean. I floated as best I could. Then Max pulled me throw the water to the shore. I got on the sand coughing and shaking from the cold.

I looked over at Max smiling all proud of himself. "You Ass, you could have killed us both."

He started laughing. I picked up some wet sand and threw it at his head and he turned and ducked. He got some water and threw it at me and he and I had a wet sand fight. Though I tried to get away from his assault of water and sand, I was actually having a good time playing in the sand and surf. It was cold but I warmed up pretty fast and had a wonderful time just playing like normal kids.

When we walked up the cliff side. Pushing each other and laughing. "We need to avoid everyone so let's go to the back and then we transported to the tower." Once in the Tower I said "Max we are in big trouble from the looks on the Elders faces." He waved his hand and we were clean.

"Don't worry princess, I will take the heat. I must like it I think. At least that is what I tell my self when I am in trouble." I laughed with him.

Then Marcus called us from my room. "Em, Max, come done now."

I looked to Max and he sighed and said "Let's go. " Max took my hand and we went down.

Marcus looked at us both and shook his head. "You both need to come with me."

I looked at Max and he had closed his mind. He smiled and whispered "Its OK." We followed Marcus into the kitchen.

Mandra, and the Elders were already sitting at the Kitchen table. Marcus then sat with the others as Max and I stood at the front of the table and awaited our fate.

Marcus began "You both have shown disregard for your gifts and the consideration of those around you."

Max looked at Marcus and said "It's not Em's fault. I talked her into it."

I looked at him and shook my head "I wanted to do it."

Then I looked from grandmother to Marcus. "We just wanted to have some fun. We did not mean to disturb anyone this much."

Grandmother then repeated "This much?"

I looked back at her. I really didn't see such seriousness. I was getting up set at the over reaction of Grandmother and the Elders. "This is not as serious as it could have been. Just knowing what Max and I can do with our powers, we could have done much more." Leonardo said "That is true Princess. However, you must follow the teachings. Your power is not to cause disruption or harm. With great Power, comes responsibility. Cause no harm. Great Magic is not to boast but to do good. In addition, you are our chosen Princess, and you must not take such risks. Max is your Guardian and not your playmate. Max you will be in the Library for a week for this. You must not cross the line of your position or status. Marcus will fill in as the guardian." Max nodded and was gone.

Grandmother then said "Young lady, go to your room, you may not stay up for the rest of the Solstice and you are not to do anything like this again." I was so mad at Max's punishment. I stomped my way to my room and yelled at all of them as I walked up the stairs. "At least Max understands that I need to have fun sometimes." It must have been the Normal Blood in us both.

When I got to my room I slammed the door. I ran up to the tower and sat down pouting in the chair. I closed my eyes and then I heard

"You need a lot more fun than that."

I opened my eyes "Max if they think your here....."

He said "Close your mind and they won't." So I did.

"I'm sorry you have to go the library. I get to miss solstice. I told you we'd be in trouble. He smiled "But this time you aren't a goody two shoes."

I giggled "No not anymore thank you sir." He laughed.

I then mocked Leonardo "You are the Princess you can't take those kind of risks. " I showed a little frustration "Don't walk across the street Princess you might step in dog poo." Max laughed. I asked him "I wonder if I was not the Princess if I could then have fun with you?"

Max smiled and shook his head. "Probably not."

Then I asked him "Why did they choose me as Princess when I am a Witch anyway?"

He looked at me serious then. "I think that is a conversation for your Grandmother and Marcus."

I got a little mad at him. I narrowed my eyes at him and said through clinched teeth "Why don't you tell me."

He smiled and said "Because I have to go to the library. Now that you got me in trouble" I took in a breath to deny culpability and he was gone.

That night, I dreamed that I hung from a little tree growing out of the cliff side. At the bottom were thousand black crabs. They were running back and forth and looking up at me as I hung from the cliff. They were waiting for me to fall. As I looked down at the crabs they changed into the men the black robes. They had monster face and reached up for me. I screamed and screamed. I called to Max but he didn't come. I cried and screamed and begged for Max to help me.

I woke to "Princess wake up."

I opened my tear filled eyes to find Max was there. He held me as he normally did when I had a nightmare but I had him in a vice grip.

"You took so long to come. I thought you wouldn't come."

He petted my hair and spoke softly at my ear

Wizard Princess, Wake or slumber,
My vow to you I live here under.
Twirl and leap my happy dancer
Wake or sleep, your call I answer,
Till the worlds and life are done,
Be assured, I will come.

"I will always come when you call Princess. Even from the library" I don't remember anything else, and was back sleeping.

That summer, I received an invitation to Mandy's birthday party. I was hesitant because I have not been very welcomed by the local kids.. One way or another, I scare them away. I was sure that Millie forced Mandy in inviting me. I really was not in the mood. My Grandmother was full of hope while I was full of dread. She just didn't understand that I did not fit anywhere. Mixed Blood; normal and witch. It was like oil and vinegar. Shack it up and it mixes for about a minute and then separates.

I put on a summer dress and let my hair hang. I had picked up a CD of her favorite rock band. Lincon Drove me to the party and told me to call when I was ready to leave. I told him that I was ready to leave then but he only waited for me to get out of the car.

I walked up to the house and knocked. I could hear the party in the back yard. Millie answered and escorted me to the back where the party was. Millie, like grandmother was hopeful for a connection for me. I walked out into the patio where there were a few dozen teens were milling about. At first I was unnoticed. Then as I greeted Mandy and gave her gift, I could feel the eyes on me again. "Happy Birthday Mandy. I hope you are having fun today." She smiled at me warmly. "I am having fun and I glad you came. Can I introduced you to some of my friends?" I smiled and said "Sure."

She made her way through each group and introduced me to several of the kids she goes to school with. They all were nice but I heard the comments of me "The Witch" as I move away. There were some adults the too. Deana of course was there with her daughter Lori. Grandmothers binding must have worked as she never got near me. Millie offered me punch and a hot dog. I took the punch and declined the hot dog. There was this guy named Jeremy who came and sat with me. I thought he was being kind and had pity for me sitting alone. We talked a great deal about books and movies. He was nice to me. Then, the largest of the groups, lead by Lori, addressed me. "Hey Witch, how about showing us a trick." Lori laughed "That's why you were invited isn't it?' Mandy came over and said 'Stop it Lori!" Lori and her group laughed. "Come on Emily Star, show us a trick. " Millie came out of the house and stood in front of me. "Emily Star is a guest in this house as you are. You have no right to insult her." I stood up and walked out of the house.

"Em!" Jeremy called after me. "wait let me walk with you." He caught up with me though I was walking quickly. "Why would I want to stay there when they are always looking at me like I have something hanging out of my nose?" Jeremy smiled as we walked "They like you." I looked at him like he was crazy. "I doubt that is it." I looked at him and asked "Why are you walking me home? I always walk home alone and never have any problems." He said "I want to be your friend." I huffed "Why" He just smiled at me. "My house is on the way do you mind if we stop so I can get my wallet?" I said I did not mind. He stopped at the third house on Robin Street . We walked to the porch and as I went to the swing on the porch, he said," Come on in. I have some ice Cream." Someone was saying "No" in my mined. "I don't think I should. I really need to go home." He would not listen to that and said " Oh come on, what's five minutes?" He looked so sincere that I gave in. "OK. Five minutes.

We walked in and he lead the way to the kitchen. He was in the freezer and in my head a voice, more like a low growl, told me said *"Leave Now!"* I became suspicious of who or what I did not know. Was it Jeremy or was it the voice. I only know that there was something wrong.

Jeremy served the ice-cream in bowls. But instead of sitting across the table to face me he sat next to me. I did not eat the ice cream as I was feeling very cautions at that minute. Jeremy's hand reached out and grabbed me by my hair. When I screamed he covered the my mouth with his other hand. He said, "Be still Em. I am only playing a game. OK" I looked at him with my eyes unable to answer with my mouth. He moved his hand from my hair to my shoulder. He moved his hand to the strap of my dress; he ripped it off. I felt the click coming. I needed to get out. He had a funny look on him. I wasn't sure what was happening with him. I only know that the click was close. He put his hand on my leg and was moving it up. I saw a pot on the stove and levitate it and sent it flying at his head. He ducked but the Click came in and I transported. As I did, I heard a blood letting scream from Jeremy.

I was in my room and crying in my pillow. Zee nuzzled my hand. I looked up and grabbed him and cried into his fur. "Never again Zee, I will never trust another one of those people as long as I live." I heard my grandmother pull up to the house in a hurry. She came running in and called out to me. "Em…. Emily Star!" She appeared there in my room. "Oh Baby…." She grabbed me and held me. I cried and held her for safety. After a time, she let go of me. "Go ahead and clean up. Come down stairs and have some tea and we will talk." She was still looking at me with concern. "OK grandmother, I will be down in a minute." Not wanting to be a baby, I got to my feet and headed to the bathroom. I turned around and looked at my grandmother "I will never be alone with those people again. It is just not going to happen where I have friends and normal teen experiences Grandmother. So I don't want those people around me." Mandra nodded her head.

When I got down stairs, Grandmother was somewhat pale sitting in the kitchen. "Grandmother, what is it?"

She grabbed my hand and said

"It is just that you were so close to danger. I don't think I could have been able to live if that animal succeeded."

I assured her "You know I did get out of it. I transported before he got anywhere. My grandmother stood up and paced. " I know you have powers, Em. That is not in question." she stopped and looked at me. "Your are naive in many things. All the power in the world will not make up for that innocence." She was staring at me. "You and I will add new lessons to the day. We know will also study human nature and how to take precautions."

The next morning I arrived in the kitchen to find grandmother, Marcus and Max at the table. "Good Morning all" They all looked up at me all with concern. Grandmother told me to sit down. I was weary of their mood and feeling scared. Their minds closed and guarded. Molly brought me some juice. I thanked her never letting the three on the other side of the table free from my stare.

"What is going on?"

Marcus started "My Lady, there has been a situation that we feel that you should be aware of. After yesterdays events, we feel that a full time guardian is needed once more."

I huffed, "Marcus, I got away on my own."

My grandmother then said "No. No my love. You did transport on your own yes. But he would have tried again" She looked over to Marcus.

He continued "He could not have you telling anyone what he had attempted. He would have hunted you to continue and finish his plan." He looked over to Max who sat staunchly and said "As ordered by the Wizard Counsel, Max will not be your guardian. He has another assignment at this time." I was a little irritated. But they were holding back and not letting me in their minds. Taking Max from me and replacing him with a new Wizard. They behaved as if I was a weakling; behaving as if I was helpless.

Marcus called "Edwin" and, Tall and blond Edwin the wizard was there. He wasn't Max who was actually my friend. Edwin looked down on me and he was slimy. I did not like him. Marcus said. "Em, Edwin will be you Guardian now. I looked over at Edwin as if he was not there.

"First of all, I can defend my self." Max rolled his eyes and made a huff sound. I stared at him with malice at that moment but continued "Secondly, I think you should be telling me the rest of what's on your mind and stop blocking me" My grandmother held her cup and stared at it's content. " We need to tell you…..that Jeremy is dead."

I was stunned "How?" "When?"

Marcus looked at me. "He was found dead this morning. There is no one to confront for this act, as no one knows who did this. Deana is beside herself as Jeremy was one of her favorite normals. He was most loyal to her."

Grandmother said "She is unaware, as most are, that he attacked you."

I sat back in my chair and said "I am not going to live being afraid. Not from a pig like Jeremy and not from people like Deana." I waved my hand in Edwin's direction "You can send a hundred guardians, I will not need them. I will protect my self." I got up from the table and left my grandmother and Marcus looking at each other with concern and Max Smirking.

I needed a sign that said walking curse.

CHAPTER 20

I spent the rest of the summer avoiding Edwin who was sort of a pest. Max showed up off and on. But when he did he would talk and joke with me. Edwin was showing up just to be there. He was to sweet to my Aunt Elena and me. But on the other hand, he was uppity and arrogant towards us. We really disliked him immensely. Elena told me that he was like one of those sweet talkers that are only really looking after them selves. Grandmother addressed him as she did everyone. But when he would being to really brother me by his presents she would only say, "Good-by Edwin." and he would leave in a huff. There was something off about him. He was not real, he had something about him that was more than guarding me. He always made sure that I knew that he was Pure Blood. He also made a number of attempts to touch me. He would grab my hand, or arm. He would put his arm around my shoulder. I always moved away and told him to keep his hands to him self. He often violated my command to him not to touch me. Edwin made it out that he was above my command. I also notice that there was nothing he protected me from. I usually had to be protected against him and his attempts to touch me. And I really didn't need him as a guardian. If anything was going to happen, I had Max.

Edwin would always attempt to be next to me. Elena and I would band together and she would stay in between Edwin and I. But when she wasn't there, he was stick to me like glue. Lincon would call me away when he could. And Marcus did show up and tell him that his duties were completed and to leave. If he showed up when Max was around, he would insult Max and I demeaning Mix Blood. I often reminded Edwin that I was mixed blood and did not see the difference or our abilities compared with the Pure Bloods. But I did. Max and I seemed to be stronger in our powers with our normal blood. I don't know why.

Max did come over now and again just to see what I was up to. And he still rescued me from my dreams. I was always happier when Max came over. He even went to church with Grandmother and I. Marcus would come sometimes too. Max always made the mundane studying easier. And when he would visit, we would sometimes participate in the potions instructions together with Edith. He sucked at it. But so did I. He really hated me making fun of him. I especially enjoyed making fun of him in a flowered or girl apron. Max did cause trouble then. He would do things like having my potions fizzle in the jars. Or blow up. Edith would throw him out. Basically because I did not need help failing in potions. But he made things fun for me. He was my friend.

Beside tutoring me with calculus, Max did study myths and legends with me. Edith enjoyed giving us a reading list and expected that we could answer all of her questions when she asked about the old stories. I liked reading about the fabled Wizards and Witches. Not all were very good souls. But those Witches and Wizards that were good, used their magic to help Normal, and Immortals, together. What was good for one was good for the other.

Max said "you are such a goody two shoes aren't you?"

Looking at him like something was wrong with my thought processes. "Why?"

He said "That is so unrealistic."

I huffed and said "I believe how I chose."

He was infatuated with King Arthur and Merlin the Wizard. At one of our afternoons reading,

I reminded him " That story is mostly fiction. Merlin is a magician not a Wizard" and he disagreed with me.

"No there was a pagan named Merlin. He was a Wizard."

I would tease him "No if he was pagan, he was a Witch." He vigorously insisted that Merlin was a true Wizard.

"Well than, if he was a pagan Wizard, were are the pagan Witches?"

Max laughed "Dancing in the forest with the pixies." I really missed dancing in the forest.

Edith was obsessed with one fable. She insisted that Max and I read the fable and be able to tell her about it. The fable was about the Sapphire Witch. She was very powerful and beautiful. She seduced Wizards, Witches, and Normals. She used her power for the freedom of all Witches and Wizards. She stood with both races in wars against those that would restrict the worlds. She could have ruled over both worlds but chose to live a secretive existence. I said to Max "Wow, she was something. I wish I could be like her. She was so brave and so powerful. A true warrior and a beautiful She lived free, too."

Max said "But why would a Witch fight with Wizards or Wizards let a Witch fight with them. It all seems too unrealistic."

The summer moved on. One day that while sitting on a blanket by the cliff rail, Max was reading about a Fabled Wizard, Emil, that was able to be so elusive, that no one could tell were he was or when he would show up. Max was so fascinated that he forgot to read out loud and I had to tap his mind to keep up. I leaned up against one of the pillars of the cliff rail as the sun and breeze kissed my skin. I watch the ocean listing to the soft gentle voice of Max as he read in his mind. Max laid face down towards the book. He read the story of the Wizard being sought by the counsels and being able to live under their noses without detection. The Wizard Emil had some ungodly number of wives and children. As I listened I felt the intrusion, I looked back at Max who was already looking at me with a sarcastic grin on. I asked in mind *"Who is it?"* He sent *"Edwin. Close your mind."*

As soon as my mind clamed shut, Edwin was standing over us.

"Em. Max. What's going on here."

He looked suspicious and his jealousy and superiority pushed him to over reacted to an innocent situation. It wasn't like we were laying on the blanket together. I looked at him surprised at his accusation.

"We are reading."

Max couldn't help himself "What do you think is going on Edwin?" He deliberately moved over to the cross rail and leaned against was very close to me. I smiled at his deliberate antagonism of Edwin.

Edwin said "Don't you think you should keep a respectable distance between you and the princess?"

I looked at Max with a smile, and I joined his game and moved right up against Max and he put his arm around my shoulders. We looked at Edwin sarcastically. Edwin was red faced and angry. He verbally called out to Marcus.

Marcus arrived and Edwin pointed and said "Max is being inappropriate with the Princess." Max and I started to laugh.

I stood up and walked to Marcus and hugged him. "My true guardian. It is confirmed. Edwin has no sense of humor or manners."

Marcus looked at Edwin. "What is the problem?"

Edwin looked at me and I smiled as we waited. "I believe that the situation was inappropriate as they are un-chaperoned and Max deliberately move very close to the Princess."

I started to laugh again. Max stayed sitting against the rail and was chuckling in spite of Marcus being present. It did not get by Marcus who looked directly at Max. Max then stopped his chuckle and stood up at attention.

Marcus looked over at Edwin "Go Edwin." And Edwin nodded to Marcus and Me and was gone.

Marcus turned to Max "Propriety Max. Edwin will tell a very different story then the one I believe to be innocent."

I said "Marcus, we couldn't help it. He just so…weird. He is so easily played with." Max said "And intrusive. We were only reading. He made that out to be somehow inappropriate."

Marcus looked at us both "He is the guardian at this time. He needs to know that the Princess is safe. Even from you Max."

I began to get up set then Max said "I have not been released from my vow to protect the princess. I am loyal to that vow."

Marcus began to say something and Max, to my surprise as well as to Marcus, interrupted him "The vow was to protect her; even from herself and even me." Max stood quiet and Marcus said "Max, you interrupted me."

Max looked down and back as if he realized what he had done. He said "I did sir. I apologize."

Mandra then joined us. I looked to her for support for Max. He had done nothing wrong. Marcus then said to Max. "I do believe that the interactions here today were innocent. But I need you to return home Max. We will discuss the issues that have and could develop further. Including, learning to wait for the Elders to speak before you do."

Max nodded and looked to me and nodded and was gone. I was upset at the thought of stupid Edwin getting Max in trouble when we were doing nothing wrong.

I looked at Marcus. "It's Edwin that needs to be on a leash. And he needs to leave me alone." I stomped off to the house leaving Marcus and Mandra standing at the cliff rail.

The next day was a perfect example. I walked down the trial to the beach. I heard the wind whispering hello. There were no trees and I wanted so badly to hear their music. But the waves whispered to me to hear their song. "Listen Princess. Let us play our music for you." It was soft and whirling. The sea whispered "Dance for us Princess." I was able to dance to their song as I did for the trees whimsical song. I had my feet in the water though it was cold and wet the bottom of my skirt I danced to the song of the sea. I felt free again. Free as the waves as they caressed my legs. My eyes shut I twirled and drifted through the water. I drifted away with the music of the sea and the winds encouragement as it blew my long hair towards the shore. I was in that beautiful world of peace and love. I danced and danced. I was just being free.

Breathless, I stopped open my eyes to the sea. I blew a kiss in the wind and the sea, "Thank you for the music." As I turned to leave, I ran into Edwin's chest. He had my arms in his hands. He had a funny look on him.

He asked in that slimy way "What were you doing Princess?"

I narrowed my eyes "I was dancing"

He started to laugh. "To what?"

I pulled my arms way from him and started to walk back to the trail. He caught up with me and grabbed my arms again, but tighter. He was hurting me by digging his fingers into the skin of my arms. He pulled me close to his face as my hair was flying back to towards the cliff. My heart was pounding with anger and fear.

"Let me go." was my command. He laughed again looking at me in that funny way of his. Half superior, half something else. I though of throwing him out to sea.

Then I heard Max. "Edwin, Let her go." He let me go and I turned to see Max at entrance to the trail back to the house.

I walked slowly passed Max and watched him and his angry face never leaving Edwin's. I looked back at Edwin standing superior. As soon as I slowly pasted Max, I ran up the trail to the house. Marcus and Mandra were on the porch and watched as I walked through the door. I slamming the door as I entered the house. No use in their help. After all, Edwin was the Guardian. I walked into the kitchen and sat at the table. Not only did he make fun of my dancing to the sea he put his hands on me. I was sick to death of Edwin. A cup of tea was placed in front of me. I looked up to see Molly's soft smile. "That should help you in your deep thought." I smiled and said thank you.

Max then joined me at the table. I looked at him "Thanks Max. Isn't funny that he's my guardian and you have to protect me from him."

He smiled "Well I have my vow. I am not released from the vow. Plus I don't want anyone bothering you."

I smiled. "Thanks." He reached over and brushed the fingerprint bruises on my arms left by Edwin. And then they disappeared.

I looked at Max and asked "What is the deal Max. Why does he act so superior to us?" Marcus came in then with Grandmother. They too sat at the table. Concerned with my anger.

Max said "He is Pure Blood. One of the few of our generation. Mix Blood is beneath him or it is thought." I could see that it leaves a bitter taste with Max.

Marcus said "The Wizard world is different from the other races. Normal and Witch." Molly gave them all tea as we sat.

Marcus went on "The Wizards have laws that govern the Wizards and their behavior, their status, their freedom." Max looked off at that comment. Marcus continued "This protects the Wizards and the other races. Pure blood is desired for our children but it is a fact that many of the females produced by the Wizards are not in turn, producing Magical Wizards. Mix Blood Wizards now out number the pure bloods. That cause the Pure Bloods status to rise above the rest weather they deserve it or not."

I looked from Max to Marcus. " So the Pure Bloods could be without powers and still be higher ranking then the Mixed Blood?" They both nodded.

I looked at Max "So you are under Edwin?" He nodded.

I stared laughing "You know, I don't think I have ever seen Edwin do any magic other than transport."

I looked at Marcus "I have seen what Max can do. He is very talented. How can they believe that Max could be controlled by an ass like Edwin?"

Marcus said "We are military like in our ranking. Pure Bloods rule and the Mix Bloods serve." He looked serious, "Wizards are loosing their power and powerful Wizards. Many believe that the race will end in the near future."

I shook my head "You're a Pure Blood Marcus?" He nodded. "I'm glad of that. I would hate to see asses like Edwin be totally in charge." I shook my head "I Mixed Blood. And I am a Witch." I looked back at Marcus "Where does he get off looking down on me as a Witch."

Marcus looked over to Mandra, She continued for Marcus, "Witches are rival's to Wizards. We are much stronger in our true number because we did not attempt to control our production of offspring as the Wizards. We rested in the decisions of God and Mother Earth as to who had power and who didn't." She smiled "You are not beneath Edwin in any way. You are a Witch. But we have an understanding with the Wizards at this time. We are working together to preserve the magic and the races."

I looked at Max "You are a great Wizard Max. Nothing Edwin can do can change that fact. He can't take that from you." Max smiled.

Some weeks later, I sat on the steps of the porch. Zee was there with his constant grooming. I was practicing levitation with a small rock as instructed by Master Edith. It looked kind of like a turtle. I moved it up and down and up and down. Then right to left and left to right. Boring, boring, boring. I needed inspiration. I thought, I would push my self with a bigger rock. But there were none bigger. Until I look over the cliff rail and looked at the big tall straight rock Max and I landed on at the solstice. I walked to the cliff rail. I thought "I Wonder?" I concentrated and it shock but didn't move. I huffed. I pulled from that middle part in my body, and the rock shook. Not ready to give up, I stood with my arms out above my head and said out loud "Up Rock!" The rock went up but that big rock was a lot bigger under the water and sand. The rock that must have been as long as the tankers that sail by, maybe longer.

Edwin showed up at that time and panicked. "Em put it back!" He startled me and as I looked at him and dropped the rock in the ocean. I stared at the rock that I had pulled out of the shore and said "O My God!"

Edwin said "Em you have to get it back in there. The ships will know it is gone.

I looked out to the sea and could see no ships. I shrouded my shoulders "You put it back."

He looked at me and huffed "I can not fix your mistakes. You will have to do it your self."

I Huffed in return "Marcus would have fixed it."

He put on his superiority attitude "Witches just don't think before they act."

I looked at him with narrow eyes "Goodbye Edwin."

He left. I looked at my rock in the ocean as the waves crashed and moved over it. All I could think of was "O My God."

Edwin retuned with Max. Max said "Hi Princess. What's up."

I giggled "No its down."

He came over to the rail and laughed when he saw the rock "You did that?"

I nodded "I did. Now I have to put it back."

Max looked back to Edwin "Why didn't you just wait till she put it back."

Edwin looked Insulted "She can't and wanted me to clean up her mess."

I looked at Edwin, "Go away." He looked insulted again, but did as I said.

Max laughed "He gets so mad when you give him orders."

I waved my hand not wanting to think about that snake Edwin. "He panicked and I told him to put it back but he told me no. I think he went to get you so you could put it back. How come he can say no to me when he supposed to do what I say?"

Max just smiled "Pure Blood."

I looked over the rail. "OK let me try this." I held my hands in the air "Up rock" the rock lifted. I blow out. "OK so far." I started to laugh because I was doing nothing more than the Normals cranes do. I conjured a couple of those yellow hard hats for me and Max. He started laughing. I moved the rock into position. I lowered the Rock but it would not go back in. So I lifted the rock high and intended to drive it back into it original position. As it hit the surf and suffuse of the ground everything shook. It must have been a four pointer on the rector scale. Max and I fell back and I lost my hat. Max grabbed me and laid over me until the shaking stopped. When it stopped I looked up at Max and he had a huge smile on his face. We started to laugh. I pushed him off me and we got up and ran to the rail. The rock was back in place. I jumped with my arms in the air and screamed "Yes" Max and I laughed and when we turned around, Mandra and Marcus were there. Mandra looked a little upset. Marcus had his arms crossed. I looked at Max. "Ohoh." He said "Yep"

Marcus said "Well, causing earthquakes now children?"

I shook my head knowing that Max would get punish far worse than I. "Max didn't do anything. He wasn't even here." Marcus was skeptical.

I narrowed my eyes "What did that disobedient snake tell you?" Marcus who was always closed looked surprised at my intuition.

Mandra said "Em. Leave the rocks where God put them. Is that clear?" I nodded and said "Yes Mam." Marcus looked at Max and there was a silent communications.

Marcus laughed and looked at me. "Very impressive Princess."

I smiled at Max who smiled back. I then thought of Edwin "I still demand to know what Edwin said." Max reached over and threw his arm around my shoulder and said "I deserve a reward of Ice Cream for my moral support" and he started walking me to the house. Though I walked with him, I said "I still want to know? Being a Princess without people obeying is not being much of a princess at all."

CHAPTER 21

After my fifteenth birthday, I never went back to live in Hat Creek. We had one final blow up and I moved out. Dad was hurt but he was too weak, and always had been, to deal with what came with me. Not just my powers, but my undeserved reputation. Of course, Tina tried to control me and my father's relationship. Nora joining in with her informant role whenever she had the chance. Tom never really involved himself.

On that terrible day in May, just a few days before I was leaving for Grandmothers, Tina was doing her usual screaming at my Dad.

"Outside of normal business hours, those people should not have free rein to come to this house and disturb our home. They need to wait until the church is open." Dad was, as always, patient. "Caesar, are you listening?"

He would only answer "Yes Dear."

A local family lost a grandparent and then other ended up in the hospital when she collapsed at the death of her husband. Dad has had an open door since I can remember. Now, when this family was in need of the Pastor, his wife was sending them away. I couldn't help relating her voice to a screaming harpy.

I walked in the house with Zee at my heals. Of course, Nora - the informer- immediately notified the Harpy. "Em brought that cat in again."

Tina switched topics in mid shrill. "I will not have that cat in this house."

My father spoke up then and said "Zee does no harm, Dear. And he will be in Em's room only." He looked to me pleadingly. I walked to my room and we went in. Not far behind was Tina with a broom. She actually meant to hit Zee with a broom. She entered my room and I said "Get out."

"You can bully your father but you will not bully me missy."

She took a swing at Zee and he transported. I in turn turned her broom into a snake. She screamed and dropped the snake. She then ran from the room still screaming. My father was once again the intended victim. She was screaming at my father about my evil ways and how dare he spit in Gods face etc, etc.

The broom a broom again, I took it in the kitchen. Aunt Della and Taylor had just come in from Redding. Aunt Della asked what was happening and of course I was evil. Della came into the kitchen and started her usual of "Why do you do these things. You haven't learned a thing. You promised your father and here we are."

I leaned against the counter and told her "She tried to hurt Zee."

Taylor, my cousin who was then about nine, looked over to me and said "I wouldn't let her hurt Zee ether."

Aunt Della told him to mind his own business. I walked over and messed his hair. He and I always like one another and he was one of Zee's best friends.

My father was in the living room be plummeted with insults and remarks about me. I stayed away and allowed it to play out as usual. The harpy tirade about the evil one living under their roof continued on cue. And when was he going to rid the evil from his life. Dad would just zone out and never saying a word to her. Until I heard 'That Evil being you created with that Bitch." And that was it.

I walked to the living room and looked at my father who was sitting with his fingers at his temples. She spotted me and said "Look there's the little evil being now." Dad looked over and shook his head.

Tina walked over to me and said "How does it feel knowing that you mother is roasting in Hell"

In a very low and threatening voice "Why don't I send you there and so you can pick out your house."

She looked at me with more anger than I believed she could muster "You are an Evil hell bound bitch." She lifted her hand to hit me. I looked at her and said "Sit and be still" with that she was on the couch sitting very still and unable to talk. Nora screamed and then came at me to attack and she ended up sitting next to her mother. Tom looked over from the TV, smiled, and then turned back. He was probably thankful for the peace.

Dad looked at me and said "Em. Let them go."

I looked over at him. "No! Why don't you stand up and tell her not to say such things?" He went back to looking straight ahead. I was replacing the Harpy. I could no longer deal with this. I had to be were life did not include denigration in my home. I bent down and faced my father in the eye.

I said to him in a soft voice "I was willing to allow her to fight with you. I was willing to take her borage of insults to me." He looked stern but also surprised at my new found authority. I continued "I will not allow her to insult my mother who never caused her any harm. I will not allow her to hurt Zee."

I stood up and away as he stood up and said "Emily Star you promised me."

I retorted sternly "You promised me."

Della came out of the kitchen and looked on. I only turned my head to look her in the eye. She stopped dead in her tracks when she saw Tina and Nora. Tom giggled.

"This is it Dad. I am not welcomed in my own home any longer even though I never believed I ever was. And to tell you the truth, I am only here for you. But you…. You have never been there for me. You have always allowing others to condemn me. Condemn me when I never hurt anyone. I always tried my best to fit in and know now,…. that will never happen."

Dad looked at me and defended with "How can you say those things. You know I love you…" I gave a little smile, "Yes. I think you do. But you gave up on me Dad. You gave up on you. You never stand up and say "No, she is not evil. No she is not going to hell. For all the Christianity in this house, you being the homeowner, preacher, *my father* never have I heard you take a stand in my defense; at least one that would stick."

At that moment, Max was in the room. Della screamed and the boys turned from the TV then back. Though I had not seen him in a while, and I was thankful for his support. He was taller, handsomer and dressed all in black.

Dad looked at Max "Who the hell are you?'

Max smiled and I felt my heart jumped. "Max. I am the guardian wizard assigned to Em. I raised an eye brow knowing that was no longer true but I also notice that Edwin never showed up. "Pastor Manelli I presume?"

Dad only nodded. Dad looked at me and said "Wizards Em! Snakes? What is next?"

I shook my head and said "Nothings next Dad. I'm leaving."

He came back with "Until you're eighteen…."

I laughed. "I am only fifteen and I know that I don't belong here. You the adult and father can't see that. You can't see how horrible this is for me." A single tear ran from my eye "Daddy, if you love me let me go."

He shook his head "I will have to call the police and they will bring you back."

I did not wiped that tear then, but I was resolved. "Dad, I am leaving. You can know that I am safe with Mandra, or you will not know where I am." He continued to shake his head. I kissed the boys, I kiss my aunt on the cheek. Zee leaped into my arms My father refused to relent. Why, I will never know. I kissed my fingers and sent Dad a kiss. He felt it and closed his eyes. I turned my room back to the little dank room, and then released Tina and Nora. Both were breathing heavily from there experience. But nether moved. "By Daddy." He came at me to grab me but I was gone. I only went to the creek in the dark. It was kind of a good by to Nana.

Max was behind me and Zee. "Where to?' I looked at him and I shook my head.

"I can't go to Mandra's yet. She will make me go back to Dad. Her word means something." Max grabbed me in a hug. Next thing I knew we were at Mandra's. We were standing at the cliff side.

"Max! I told you not Mandra's. The cops, dad or Mandra will be here to take me back." He looked at me. "If any one tries to take you back I will intervene. OK?" I wanted to go in and go to my room. I wanted to be alone. I wanted to come to grips with reality- *my reality.*

"Mandra is not here. In fact there is no one here. They all went to a party. You will be alone and no one to bother you." He took a finger and wiped my tear.

I managed a "thank you."

And he gave his usual "No problem, that's what I do." He was gone then. So Zee and I transported to my room and I changed to my night gown. I laid down in bed and cried my self to sleep.

That nights dream was of Nana at the creek side. "You must find your true self." I was so happy to see her. And then she was gone and I was in the stone room with the men in robes. They came closer and closer and I ran but couldn't find the door. The walls were lumpy but I realized that the lumps were arms as they reached out for me. Unable to find escape I screamed for Max. And I woke in his arms once again. "OK Princess. You're OK." I said to him, "The arms were reaching for me." He laughed softly and just held me till I went back to sleep.

Mandra called Dad that morning. She and he talked for a long time. He was very hurt. But Mandra left the door open for him to have open communication and he would sent authorization for Mandra to put my in school. When she was sure he could talk to me calmly, she handed me the phone.

I said hello and heard Dad say "Em. I love you. I wanted you to know that this is your home and I failed to protect that fact. I understand wanting to be where you are accepted. And that's ok. I need you to be happy and feel like a whole person. But if you want to come back, you can be assured that nothing like that will ever happen again."

I was weepy but said "Daddy I love you too. But I can't be there feeling the way I do. I needed to be away from people who hate me. You deserve to be happy too Dad. You were so happy when you got married and I need you to feel happy like that again. And me not to get in the way by being there."

He was quiet for a minute. "Em you are my child. I will do anything for you."

I knew he would. "Then be happy Dad."

He sniffed " Aunt Della would like to say something to you, is that OK?"

I had nothing to fear. "Sure Dad." I heard him say something and had the phone to Auntie. "Em?"

I said "Hi Auntie."

She started to cry. "I want you to know that no matter what, I have loved you since you were born. I loved you as much as my own child. Which is why anything I have said or done to you is a bigger sin that anything you have ever done. If I made you feel that you had to leave, Please forgive me. Please?"

I cried too and said "Auntie, I don't blame you. I do love you and I could never not forgive you of anything." She said thank you and gave the phone to my dad.

"Em. I need you to check in all the time OK?" I said Ok. He then said "But Em,,, Use the phone OK? I giggled and we said good by.

I stayed with grandmother from that point. I was sent to the local high school as the Master Witches knew powers and potions, but not calculus. I started as a junior. I had never gone to mainstream school so this was a whole new world to me. My first morning in high school, I spent going from class looking like the new kid and feeling stared at. I stayed to my self and attempted to be invisible to the others. Not a immoral way but a mortal way. I just felt small. At lunch I went in the cafeteria and grabbed a juice and a apple. I paid for the items and when I turned, I faced a table with several cheerleads and a few guys. At middle of the table was Lori. She saw me and said loud enough for several tables to hear. "Oh My God! The Witch is at school!" I just looked at her and went to find a quite place to read. I heard her giggling at my expense. I heard the murmuring and the talk spread across cafeteria as I looked for a seat. I couldn't believe I had to go to school with all mortals anyway. Obviously there were no available seats. I left and headed to the grass by the classrooms.

I sat in an area unpopulated by the other kids. I leaned against a tree and closed my eyes. I knew there was no anonymity here. Big mouth Lori should have gotten a blow horn, it would have been faster to destroy my high school life.

"Wow so this is High School where the Normals go?"

Before I opened my eyes I said "Hi Max."

He was sitting next to me and looking as if he had never seen a school full of kids before. "This is wild." He was watching all the social interaction like he was watching a new TV show. I started laughing at him.

Then I made the obvious clear. "I am in hell so why would you want to visit me here?" He smiled and said "I went to a private all boys' school. All Wizards School. It was nothing like this." He used his shoulder to bump mine "Cheer up. You'll make friends soon."

I raised an eye brow "Max. My reputation precedes me. The cafeteria had the news spread as fast as a bullet when Lori saw me."

He smiled "I think Lori will be mortified when she discovers the huge pimple on the tip of her nose."

I started to laugh and told him "No don't do that."

He asked me why "Because it will come back three times three and she will think I did it. I'm just waiting for the milk in the cafeteria to curdle and see what happens. I'll probably be burned at the stake for their homecoming ritual"

Just as we made the last remarks, Lori and her *crew* (the other cheerleaders) walked up to us. I knew she had her eyes on Max, after all, he was a college boy and he was very good looking.

"Hi Max."

Max turned and leaned his back on my shoulder and looked up. I couldn't have plan this better. I wanted to laugh so hard and had to keep my self from the picture of a really gross oozing pimple on the tip of her nose.

Max was so cool he said "Hello. Do I know you?"

She looked a little flustered and said "Max you know me. I'm Deana's daughter."

He looked a second and said "Oh yeah that's right." He knew what she was up to and wasn't about to cooperate with her. He then turned on the charm and said "Oh and do you all know my dear friend Emily star. She's new this year. Maybe one of you girls would be nice enough to show her around? I would take it as a personal favor." Lori's friends looked confused and whispered to one another.

Lori started to become quite uncomfortable. "Well we have to go now, By Max."

They walked only a short distance and Max said "Watch this."

He jumped up and said "Oh Lori?" She turned and walked back to him believing that she had impressed him in some way.

"Yes Max?" He got close to her ear and said "You should see the nurse about that pimple on your nose. It looks like it may be infected."

Her hand went right to her nose only to find the largest pimple that could possibly fit on the tip of her nose. Of course, she looked right at me. She ran to the girls room. Max turned around laughing and hugging his middle. He dropped down next to me again laughing and I punched his arm.

"Max, it will come back to you now."

He kept laughing " I like high school girls. They are so much fun to play with." We were both laughing hard. Then the bell rang.

"Well here I go again." We stood up and he pushed me gently. "Thanks for the rescue Max."

He smiled and said "Oh no this was more than a pleasure." He kept his smile and said" I could walk you to class?"

I reached up and patted his shoulder. "Thank you but I have to do this on my own. Besides, there might be an epidemic of nose pimples." We laughed and I started off to my next class. I stopped and turned around, "Hey Max. Be careful, I think you've turned into an almost normal nice guy instead of a Wicked Wizard "He raised his chin, " I am nice to you Princess, but an evil pimple producer to mean high school girls."

I smiled and went to class reminding my self not to look at anyone to ensure that I did not picture them with a pimple on their noses. You have to ask, where was Edwin, my so called assigned Guardian.

Chapter 22

Edith spent a lot of time criticizing me continuously about my training. I was still having issues with Potions. She insisted that I pay more attention. I tried so hard. A simple love potion of Lavender, dove's blood and mandrake was not even easy for me.

I would tell her "Why do I have to know potions anyway. I don't plan on using them." She would then say things like "What if you needed to help a witch cure a broken heart or a broken mind. You would need this information to help them." Then she would good old fashion guilt "don't you want to help your kind in their time of need?"

Then I would remind her "Edith, I can't even boil water. How can I be expected to make these complex recipes?"

All she would say is, "Because you must."

Edith did praise my abilities to manifest items and transfer items of interest. She did become frustrated when she would ask me to do things that were not in my abilities, Or so I thought. That's when she would laugh at me. "Em. You will be surprised when you find your true self." But that was the problem. I didn't know how to find my true self. There was no true self. If I was with the normals, I was the odd one. If I was with my own kind I was the odd one. Even the Wizards and the stupid Princess crap, I was still mixed blood. Even if they never said it to me, they said it enough to Max for me to know it was undesirable. With my mixed blood I was something beneath them.

Once thing Edith and I had in common was the tree language. I had to tell her. I thought maybe my delay in Potions was because of my ability to hear trees. I was surprised when she said that she could hear them too. It really was something special between her and I. She and I went to my field late in August We went on a beautiful Tuesday Morning. It was warm and the butterflies spread the news that we have come to dance. Edith, who was old, smiled and only waved her hands to the beautiful mystical music of the tress. I heard the trees whisper "Princess has come to dance for us." I smiled at their welcome. I danced to the rhythm of the tress beautiful song. Twirling and dipping jumping and running. I was once again free.

I opened my eyes to Edith and saw Max with her. Max was looking at me mystified.

I ran to Max and took his hand. "Come and dance for the trees."

He shook his head said quietly "I can't hear them."

I said "Its ok, I will help you." I looked to the trees and softly requested "Let him hear." I looked to Max and he tuned his head to me quickly. He looked like he was hearing something wonderful. He looked to the trees like he was memorized. "Em… is that what you hear?

I nodded. "Now will you dance with me for the Trees?"

He nodded looking at the trees and being completely mystified. And Max and I danced to the song of the Trees. Once breathless, we returned to Edith. She was smiling which was rare when it came to Max and I. "Well children, I believe that the trees are pleased." I listened and heard the trees "Bless Princess and the Wizard." I looked to all the trees and sent my kiss in the breeze. Max bowed. He looked to me and was smiling. He was still under the spell of the trees. But then he became very serious. "Em. You can just come up her and not take precautions about the shadow." I smiled and said "They would tell me." He looked back at the trees and nodded that they would.

Yes dads house was just through the trees and over the creek, but I never went see him. To see him was to deal with the Harpy. I couldn't do that after my tree dance. I always made me happier after I danced. I was always more at peace. Closer to God than in the home of my father.

My Birthday came in September just as school started. Dad called me and asked me if I received his gift. It had come the day before. It was a CD player and a winter coat. I thanked him and we talked about church and if I was praying regularly. I assured him that I could not get through without my dependence on Gods Grace. I then heard the harpy saying something about having to get to Nora's Play. My father hesitantly said he had to go. I told him I loved him and we hung up. *Wow*, I thought, *how easily we are replaced and forgotten*. Grandmother raised her voice from the parlor, "You can never be replaced in any world, Young lady." That made me smiled.

Well, yes, grandmother gave a little party for my 16th birthday. However, she actually never understood the difference between a little party and a big party. Lincon barbequed stakes and fish. The yard was filled with flowers and a table with a cake. I felt stupid. I could care less as long as my family and Marcus and Max were there. And Marcus did come with Edwin and Max. I felt that was enough but grandmother had the whole coven there. You know, the whole 'sweet sixteen' thing. Grandmother wanted me to dress and but I put on white hip huggers and a white peasant blouse. I pulled my hair into a ponytail and it hung to the middle of my back. I decided not to wear shoes so I conjured my toenails painted with a shimmering pale pink. It was getting about that time and I knew that I would have to endure the birthday song and all that crap. But Molly entered my room and said "Em your grandmother would like you to come down now." I smiled at her and she said "Maybe some color Em." I looked back to the mirror and I did look a little washed out. She a wave and my make up was on and my skin tinted with color from the sun. Molly smiled and left the room.

I walked out on the porch and was greeted with well wishers on my birthday. I also knew that the coven was skeptical of me. Yes I had power, but I was mixed blood. How loyal could I be to the Witches? I always wanted to laugh at that. Between the worlds I seem only to be truly loyal to the trees and the sea. To their caressing music and love for me. Other than that, I played along. What else could I do. I had a purpose, my magic had a purpose. But what that purpose was, was beyond me. I only wanted to have fun and be free.

The party carried on as most of my grandmothers parties. Lots of laughing and talking. Music and dancing. Marcus and Max put on a magic show and performed the mirror trick or moving through mirrors and that kind of stuff. I watched the crowd more than I did them.

Those that were so superior in their pure blood, but never even able to do simple tricks. As they finished up I joined the crowd and clapped.

Then Edwin approached me. "Would you like to dance Princess?" I smiled and nodded. Edwin and I danced to the slow calming music provided by my grandmother.

"At least you have music here. Not like at the shore."

I looked at Edwin and said "I hear the music at the shore."

He laughed at me "Princess. There is no music. Its all in your head."

I was infuriated. Just because he was limited in all abilities did not mean that he could make fun of mine. "Edwin I am sorry for you."

He stopped dancing and looked at me insulted "You feel sorry for me?"

I nodded "You limit your self and demean others that don't limit themselves in possibilities."

He stated to laugh in that uppity way and said "I Pure Blood, Em. I am not limited in anything. You should remember that."

I pushed away from him and he grabbed my arm tight and pulled me back to face him and in a low ugly voice he said "Don't ever turn your back on me Witch."

I narrowed my eyes and demanded "Let me go!"

Max was there in a flash, "Release her Edwin."

Edwin continued to look at me in his angry snotty way. Ignoring my demand and Max's order.

By then Elena was there "Edwin what is wrong with you? Let Em go."

Max said it again "Release her and if you left one mark on her I will report it."

Edwin released my arm by pushing first. I looked to my grandmother and Marcus who were just then walking to us. How can this animal be my guardian? There was no reasoning with them. Once again it was not their decision. I threw my hands in the air and then ran down the trail. I stopped at the waters edge. I went from the frying pan into the fire. I left dads because I was and evil witch there. But here, I was nothing more than a mix blood. These choices really sucked. Then there was the Wizards. Why are they so interested? I could careless if I had a guardian or not. I didn't ask to be anyone's princess. I don't want to be either. I wanted out of it all together.

"Not happening."

I hear Max behind me "Max now is not a good time to be in my head. I might hurt your feelings."

He giggled "No I don't think you will. Besides I agree with you. Being Mix Blood really sucks."

I turned around and said "Thanks Max for earlier." He looked at me funny "What?" I turned around to see if there was something there.

I looked back at him and he had his head tilted. "You are a Princess whether it is proclaimed by the Wizards or God. You can get out of it." He smiled and said "Come on Em. Let's get you back to your cake."

He took my hand and we walked up the trail to the house. Half way up I stopped pulling Max to a stop. I took my free hand and sent a kiss to the sea. I turned to resume being towed up the trail by Max and saw the look in his eye again. Only this time it had a little smile with it.

CHAPTER 23

Later that fall, Mandra and Marcus called me to the dinning room for dinner. I sat down and Molly brought in soup. I started to eat and the next thing I knew, Max was there sitting next to Marcus. He handed Marcus a note, and looked over at me with a charming smile while Marcus read the note.

"Hi Em."

I smiled "Hi Max. Are you the mailman now?"

He laughed at me "You are funny."

Marcus handed the note to Grandmother who asked Molly to bring Max a plate and some soup. Max said "thank you." Mandra looked at the note and her head popped up and looked to Marcus. She then turned and looked at me. The look in her face was one of concern but she had already closed her mind. In fact, I believed that she lived closed.

Max looked at Marcus and Mandra as they stared and silently communicated. I looked at Max who had his brows squished in trying to intrude until Marcus turned and faced him. Then Max smiled and turned away. When he was prevent to get the info, I knew I couldn't get it from him.

I dropped my spoon in the soup and said "Stop that. What is going on?"

Marcus looked to me from across the table. "Well my Princess. It appears that you are being presented to the Wizards Counsel next week." Max looked at me with some concern.

My grandmother had yet looked me in the eye. "I am being What?"

Marcus then said "The Wizard Counsel will be here next week to see the Princess for them selves. There is a presentation banquette to host it all. It will be held at the Wizard Center." He then said "They will ask for demonstration of your power."

I laughed "How about I just don't go and my power will be a demonstration."

Max sent *"be careful Smart ass, you'll end up in the library for a week."* I giggled. Mandra then looked to me sternly. "You will go. And don't be sarcastic with Marcus."

I looked at Marcus and said "I am sorry Marcus. I just don't understand this stuff and really don't live it until you guys bring it up."

I looked at Max with a big smile "If I was a real Princess, I would dance for the trees everyday..." I looked back at Marcus "I would have servants and beautiful clothes. A new pair of shoes for everyday of the year. And every type of cat there is on earth, to curl up with me in my gigantic bed. I would eat lobster for every meal." I looked at my grandmother "I would have ladies in waiting and live in a castle. I would be entertained by all the heads of Europe and the President and his wife. I would summer in the Bahamas and winter in Aspen." Max was laughing until Marcus looked over at him and then he turned his attention back to his soup.

Marcus looked at me seriously "You are a ***Real Princess***. Extravagance has nothing to do with being Royal and noble." He looked softer then and said "Honor, heart and love is what makes a Royal. And you are those."

Mandra said "I am not comfortable with Em there alone."

Max piped in "I will be there. I'll look out for Em."

Marcus nodded "We will all be there. We will all look out for the Princess."

I looked at grandmother "Why do I need looking out for? What are you afraid of."

She looked to Marcus "If they feel that you have not advanced in your powers, they may request that you return to with them for proper training."

I huffed "Right and they actually think I would leave my grandmother and my people for their training?"

Max then said "It's actually a pretty big honor."

I drew my brows in "Maybe for a Wizard in Training." He nodded. "Well not me. I don't know these people. Besides, I am a Witch not a Wizard." My grandmother smiled at that. Marcus smiled "I think they are going to be surprised with what comes naturally, my Princess. No worries."

The next few days were stressful to my grandmother and to Lincon and Molly. They were very concerned for me though Edith laughed at them saying "I would like to see any Wizard the same age as Emily Star, be as powerful." I smiled at her and felt she gave me some approval after being frustrated with me for so long. She did always say I held my true self back. But then she said "But pray they don't ask for alchemy or potions." That deflated my confidence.

Elena asked "So do you know what you are going to do?"

I smiled "No. I think I just wait and see what happens. I think I can do what ever it is they want." Edith came to my mind "Well, everything but a love potion." She giggled knowing my delay in potions.

A couple of days before the big presentation, I was at the cliff rail and Max showed up. He kissed my cheek and said "Are you prepared for the tests?"

I laughed "I am not preparing." Shrouding my shoulders. "I am what I am."

He shook his head. "I will miss you then."

I opened my mouth and looked at him. "What are you talking about?"

He said "Well, when the Counsel takes you with them. You know, for proper training."

I laughed. "I won't go."

He said "You may not have a choice."

I looked him square in the eye "You may not have choices in the Wizard realm, But I, dear Wizard, have choices. I won't go."

He looked at me seriously. I think I hit a nerve but he seemed to shake it off. Then he smiled and said "I could help you?"

I smiled in curiosity "How?" His smile increased showing his handsomeness and the light in his eyes. I think that was most favorite look on Max.

He said "I know what they are going to ask."

I opened my eyes wide "Max. You devil you tapped them."

He nodded victoriously "Yep." He then said arrogantly as he turned and leaded against the rail "Will I be rewarded to share my secrets?"

I giggled "Of Course."

He turned back to face me and said "OK. First they will ask for simple stuff like moving items and mind transmissions. I think you should block them from your mind. Actually, if you ever want to see *me*again you will, so they don't know I warned you." I agreed. "Then they will ask for transport and for something to manifest."

I looked at him "Like what?"

He laughed "They don't know. It's like a free style; your choice. So here is a plan." He looked around "Give them a light show and then change to your solstice dress or something like it and add something dangerous."

I looked at him, "Dangerous? Like what?"

He thought "If it were me, I would conjure a dragon and be sitting on it; or some mythical animal to stand by me. I would look dangerous; be dangerous." He then said very seriously looking into my eyes "Let them know you are not a dumb little Witch easily dominated or manipulated." I nodded smiling. He went back to his handsome smile and said "And Now Princess. Where's my reward?" I kissed his cheek and he gave a toothy smiled and was gone.

The day came and grandmother was as nervous as a cat. I still hadn't really prepared. Most of what was being asked was simple. All I could think of was good thing they weren't asking for potions. Then I would probable fail the tests. I felt that there was more to fear being on display. I would be in the Wizard world and without the coven. Even if the coven didn't approve of me, I still relied on their presents of strength.

I looked in the mirror and thought about my light show Max suggested. I smiled and conjured a deep blue long gown. Very full at the bottom. The top as a medieval maidens dress. Square chest and sleeves off the shoulder. Half sleeves draping with fabric at the elbow. The over lay of the softest lightest tool boasted hundreds of little faint glittery stars that only showed when the skirt moved. Small at the top and larger as they moved down the skirt. Simple matching slippers and my hair held in a deep blue ribbon with stars scattered through it. Little stars framed my eyes and blood red lipstick to finish the look. I turned and was satisfied. I called Zee. He would go with me tonight. I had a plan.

Mandra called "Em time to go." I walked down the stairs with Zee at my heals. Marcus was there and smiled at my modest choice of dress. But what he didn't know would not hurt him in the end. Mandra in a lovely red dress with sequin's all over it. She snapped and she had a matching cape with hood. I waved my hand and copied her with mine deep blue with stars. Marcus was in an gold robe reflecting his Elder status. We both lifted our hoods and covered our hair and faces. Marcus pleased with the unity, put out both arms. "Shall we ladies?" Grandmother took one arm and I looked at them both, and thought how lovely they looked together. I closed my mind and I stepped up and took Marcus's other arm and we were there. I called to Zee and he appeared.

We were in an outside chamber before the centers main room. It was a castle; all stone and wood. The big oak doors were opened and I could see the counsel at the front of the room behind a long bench. The scene looked familiar but I wasn't sure if was something I read or watched on TV. As I faced the heavy wooden doors, there were two witness boxed areas that sat on the two sides of the Counsel. Both of the witness boxes held a number of Wizards. All wore the same black robes. I found Max immediately and open communication to him only. I sent *"Here we go."* He sent *"You'll be fine. Call me if you need me."* I sent *"Thanks Guardian."*

Marcus told me to stay put until I was announced. I looked down for Zee and then I huffed. And he and Mandra looked at me with concern. Marcus took Mandra's arm and they walked slowly to stand in front of the counsel. They bowed to the counsel. An Elder stood and acknowledged Mandra and Marcus as mentors of the Princess.

The spokesman said "Marcus you have done well with the reports on the princess. But it is time for us to come to our own opinion." The spokesman then turned to my grandmother and said "Thank you for indulging this Counsel, Madame." Mandra nodded. Then Marcus said "May we present Ms. Emily Star Minelli, Princess of the Wizards." I rolled my eyes and thought *"Great. Not that I need this crap."*

Max came back and said *"Em. Just play along. Have fun with it."* He giggled and said *"I can see what you have planned."* I smiled.

Marcus and Mandra looked back at me and called me with their eyes. I said "OK Zee, here we go. " I walked forward through the huge hall with Zee at my heals. I walked pensively at first, and then Max sent *"Be Royal Princess."* I lifted my head and walked more assuredly. People were on either sides of the isle that I had not seen till entering. There were whispers of the witch. Only thing that help me was my hood. I still felt exposed and uncomfortable. I looked over to my right and could see Max sitting behind other wizards in training. Three in front of him, including Edwin, wore red sashes across their chests over their black robes. I reached Marcus and Mandra, who also continued to wear her hood. I was a little nervous and did not feel comfortable with being the only two witches in the place. The whispers I heard coming from the audience was clear. Witches were not welcome.

Grandmother looked over to me and she snapped her fingers and her cloak was off and I did the same. I face the counsel. They all smiled and looked happy enough with them selves.

One stood "We have come to see the Princess and we are pleased."

I thought, *too bad I didn't think about adding warts.*

Max sent *"Em you are funny."*

I almost started to giggle.

The spokesman then announced "Now, we will have the testes prior to the feast." I looked around the hall and could see light laminating from unknown places in the room. I could see the audience staring at me and grandmother with skepticism. I looked to Marcus who only smiled at me. I smiled back.

The Elder at the Wizards bench said "I see you can block transmissions and inquire. I smiled and nodded, and was thankful for Max. "We would like to see levitation." I wanted to laugh. Well Max warned me to be intimidating. I thought about it and thought of what would be intimidating. So I levitated the entire Wizard Counsel; bench and all. Marcus moved to me quickly and grabbed my arm and shook his head but I had already done it. Max came in loud and clear. ***"No! Em. No not that!"***

I hear the crowd behind us clamber and become insulted. They were making comments of the insolent Witch. I was getting kind of mad. I did not even want to be there. I lowered the counsel and the one Elder stood smiling and told the crowd, "Please, our guest meant no harm. Please."

Marcus said to the counsel. "The Princess is unaware of our customs and traditions. She meant no disrespect." It was a good thing that Marcus apologized because it would take a direct order from God to make me apologize.

The counsel looked puzzled "She is to be a wife to a Wizard, Elder Marcus. She should be made accustom."

I wanted to walk out and tell them all to go to hell. I was breathing a little heavy in my anger. How dare they assume that I would marry anyone? I looked at Marcus with a look of irritation and again he smiled and moved back to my grandmother's side. She smiled and winked at me.

I looked to Max and he sent to my mind *"Em. When in Rome..."*

I smiled at him *"Rome?"* Athena! I sent to Max *"Max you have earned another reward."*

The Elder then asked "Princess, we would now like to see a transport."

I smiled sweetly, "I would be pleased to transport but if would give me all of the tasks you want to see I think we can make this display quick and easy."

He smiled "Easy?"

I raised a brow "If I can do all that you ask."

He smiled at my retraction and added respect to their request. "We are looking for transports, conjuring, and a basic display of power."

I Smiled "OK" I looked at Marcus "Marcus would you take Grandmother to the side please." He looked concerned but did as I asked. Grandmother looked at me and smiled. I looked to Max and he nodded and smiled.

I looked down for Zee and he looked up at me knowing. I waved gently over the air with both hands, darkening the room. My hands lowered gracefully and lightly brushed my Gown from top to bottom. The stars on the grown illuminated and began to dance; Soft at first and then working into a frenzy. The stars left the dress and then encircled me and Zee. The stars twirled in their frenzy around me and lit the whole hall. I held one of the stars in my hand and kissed it and released it into the others dancing stars. I raised my arms and hands and sent the stars to hover over the crowd in the high ceiling. I produced a large ball of blinding light and I produce explosion in the ears of the onlookers. I then stood in the dress of Athena, including her golden sward and bow. A short Roman dress with sandals tied up my legs. Leather straps crossed my chest and my hair, lose flew in the wind that was unfelt. My cat was then a lion in full mane. Standing close to me, Zee was a snarling and growling lion that faced the Wizards counsel. I swung the sward leaving a trail of golden light. I kept my eyes directly at the counsel. I then stood with the sward held high. I looked to the stars above and sent them falling to the crowd. With no one the wiser, the kissed star found its way to the cheek of Max. I transported as fast a possible to the front of the counsel and then to the back of the hall where I entered. At that moment, I thought that I should just keep going. But then Marcus would be hurt. So continued my display and I then transported to stand before the box that held Max and Edwin. Edwin only stared and Max smiled and nodded. Max sent *"Excellent Show. And thanks for the reward."* The crowd was clambering and whispering. Other Wizards looked at me with skepticism. And the women in the audience looked on like they felt I was unworthy.

I illuminated the room as it had been I turned to the Counsel, "Did I miss anything?" They looked to one another and the Spokesman said. "No My Lady, you have passed your tests."

I looked over to my grandmother who smiled within her regal stance. Marcus smiled and nodded. I waved my hand and was dress back in my original star covered dress. I looked at Zee still the ferocious lion, and waved my hand and he was back to my cat. He jumped into my arms and I hugged and petted him with a lot of love. "Home beast." And he was gone.

The Elder stood once again. He waved his hands and the hall was transformed to many tables and benches. There were musicians playing their mystical Wizard music. I loved it. "Princess. Please join us for banquette." I smiled and nodded. Still standing halfway between the front of the hall and the box with the Wizards in training, I looked to Marcus. He motioned for me to join him and Grandmother. I walked to them and could hear whispers of disapproval of the witches present. I turned to the table that was whispering about 'How dare the Witch disrespect the Wizard Elders with that display. And bring a cat to such an affair." I looked at them about to say something and Max had my arm directing me to Marcus.

I looked up at him with a scowl. "Max I only wanted to tell them to.."

He interrupted me "Don't go there. Be Royal."

Marcus took Mandra's arm and led her to a table as Max and I followed. I sat across from my grandmother. Marcus sat next to her and Max next to me. I looked over the crowd that took looks of disapproval at grandmother and me.

I looked over to Marcus "We are not welcomed here."

I looked at grandmother "Why are we staying?"

Max nudged me. "You are the guest of honor. You can't just leave."

I looked at him, "I feel like I am unwanted and I want to leave."

Grandmother said "Em. Let's have dinner meet with the counsel and we will leave. OK?" I looked at her still stinging over the 'to be a wife of a Wizard crap' I gave an impatient "Fine."

Marcus looked at me "Please Princess. Be noble and royal. There is much said when one says nothing at all."

I smiled at him. Max then sent *"There will be dancing."* I looked at him and smiled. Then I frowned. I said out loud "But will I get to dance?"

Max laughed "I would be honored thanks for asking." I smiled at him and giggled. Then he said "But no Maiden dancing. I sure that will send the crowd over the edge." Mandra even laughed at that.

Dinner was served but I was still stinging from the whispers and looks I was still getting. I looked at Max "Why don't they like us?"

He looked over the crowd, "They are ignorant. They don't know you like I do."

He changed the subject "Did I complement you on your performance tonight Princess?" I smiled at him knowing what he was up to.

"Yes you did."

He smiled then and said "Did I tell you how lovely you look?"

I giggled "That must have slipped your mind."

He shook his head, "No I only was not able to voice it." With his charming smile he said "You look lovely." I smiled and said "Thank you."

Elder Leonardo came to our table and nodded to me "Princess."

He looked to Max. "Why are you here? Shouldn't you be with your class mates?"

I shook my head, "I asked Max to eat with us. Is there an issue?"

He smiled and said "No My Lady."

He looked to Marcus, and said to grandmother "Please excuse us?" Grandmother, guarded, looked to Marcus and nodded. Marcus left with Leonardo. Grandmother and I looked to each other.

Max said "Its OK. Marcus and I will not let you be alone here." Grandmother smiled at Max.

At dessert, Edwin approach as Marcus returned. "Hello Princess. Are you enjoying your self?"

I said *not now* in my mind and smiled to Edwin "Yes thank you."

He looked to Max "How did you end up at the Princess's table?"

I looked to Edwin and said "I asked him to sit with us."

He put on his Pure Blood personality and said "I would think you would be more inclined to ask a Pure Blood to eat with you Princess. Besides I am your guardian not this Mixed Blood." I felt Max growl deep. I saw Marcus look at Max.

I said to Edwin "Exactly. I see you all the time. I wanted to see Max." Max then smiled. Marcus then said "Edwin, insulting Max is not honorable in the presents of the Witches. I would expect more from a Pure Blood." Edwin nodded and left. Marcus then laughed softly and looking at me. I joined him. Max was still growling as Edwin left the table. I nudged him again.

Music started and I wanted to dance so badly. But no one else was dancing.

I looked at Max. "No one is dancing."

He looked around and said "Give them a chance. Wizards are slow to hit the floor." He teased "Unlike Witches who don't even need music, just trees." I giggled. As we sat, the counsel filtered by the table. All looking at me and smiling. I was uncomfortable; on display. I was not sure what to make of all this. Yeah Wizard Princess, but I never took it seriously, but boy did they. I Sent to Max's mind *"What if I was hideous to look at, deformed or something?"*

He started to laugh out loud and Marcus and Mandra looked over at us. He said in voice "Then they would fix that." He then said in mind *"If I could get you out of being Princess, I would."* I looked at him then and his eyes were more than serious.

Then Max sent to my mind *"Edwin's coming to ask you to dance."*

I looked at Max wide eyed and sent *"Quick! Beat him to it."*

He laughed and stood, bowed and held out his hand. "Princess, May I dance with you?"

I stood smiling at Max and took his hand. I gave a little curtsey and said "Thank you Sir."

We passed Edwin on his way to the table. I did not miss the intakes of breath as I walked to the dance floor with Max. I heard the Whispers of the Witch dancing with a Mix Blood. I took it to mean that dancing with a Witch, or maybe dancing with a Mix Blood, was a bad thing. I was both so there was no avoiding it.

Others also rose to dance. I respectfully and gracefully danced with Max. No Maiden dance stuff although that dancing was freer and was more fun. As we danced I was greeted with scowls and sarcastic grins.

I looked up at Max and he sent *"Let it go EM."*

I huffed *"Look who is talking. Wasn't you who was growling a short time ago?"* He smiled and admittedly nodded. I was getting more irritated by the minute.

I looked and smiled sweetly at Max "I know you can jump far, but guess what I can do now?"

He looked at me with some curiosity "What?"

I raised us above the rest and said "I can float."

He started to laugh loud and look down. By the looks of the other Wizards, Max's reaction was completely in contrast to an always in control Wizard. He looked back at me with admiration. I could see the disgust and hear the grumbling of the crowd. I looked down at the counsel and nodded my farewell and slowly and gracefully dance with Max close to the ceiling. When we made to the doors of the Hall, I lowered us.

"Well thank you for the dance and I'll see you."

Max looked at me. "Don't leave Em. Lets dance some more."

I shook my head. "No. I am uncomfortable and I will dance with you another time." I smiled at him big "Maybe where we can dance the Maiden Dance." He smiled and kissed my hand. I transported home. Mandra was right behind me.

She looked at me "Arrogant fools. Funny how they need us." I smiled at her.

Grandmother and I sat at the kitchen table drinking tea. "How can I be a Princess to the Wizards when they hate me? The Witch?"

Grandmother said. "Em. I told you, they need us we don't need them. Maybe if they were more careful with pushing pure blood, they would not need to go outside of their race for magic children."

I rolled my eyes. "Is that all that they want from me; to have a baby?"

She smiled, "You are special in your own right and to your own kind. You don't have to do anything if you choose not to."

I smiled and then Marcus was there. "Princess, you have made a hit. The Counsel was very impressed."

Max showed up next and smiling "The Counsel loved the exit Princess. It was very classy in their eyes."

I looked at them both "I think you guys are the only Wizards that actually can stomach us Witches." They both looked at me with concern.

I had a dream that night, a nightmare. I was in the Wizard hall but I was dressed in a maiden dress of the solstice. I was all alone with strange Wizards walking around me in a circle. All whispering that I was unworthy and insolent. I said nothing back. I looked for Marcus and Mandra but they were not there. One came and slapped me and I fell to the ground. The circle moved closer and they all had monster faces. They had snarls and protruding foreheads. As they moved forward, I became more frightened. I could not transport no matter how hard I tried. Then above at the ceiling I could see the red eyes. I called for Max. Then I screamed for Max. I woke in the in his arms. I couldn't open my eyes yet but I was safe. I knew it was him and I held on to him with all my might. "Are you OK?" I heard Max say. I nodded "The Wizards were monsters." He kept holding me against his chest and said "I would never let Monster Wizards scare you. OK? "I nodded and said "OK. Just don't leave me; don't leave me alone with them." I fell back to sleep.

CHAPTER 24

I spent the winter in doors while the wind blow the rain against the windows. Rain, Rain and more Rain. On one of my rain stranded weekends, I was in the windows tower and I stared out to the ocean lapping up ever drop that fell from the sky. Wind blowing hard against the rain. The ocean was in a frenzy. I had studied until I could not look at one more word in one more book. There was nothing on TV and I could conjure the newest movies but didn't want to veg. There was no way I was spending my weekend working potions. Grandmother was at the store and Lincon and Molly were busy doing what ever it was that they did.

I decided that I could not sit still one more minute. I headed to my room grabbed my coat and headed outside. The wind about blew me over but I was not detoured. I headed down the trail to the shore. I was assaulted by the rain and wind as I made my way to the end of the trail. The waves were huge and angry. I watched and the sea reacted to the winds demands. And I hear the sea say "Not today Princess." I was hurt. I needed to dance. I needed to do something. The waves crashed violently against the infamous rock and its neighbors. I decided to dance anyway, Why not. The music was their. It was fiery tempting music. I threw off my shoes and coat. The wind again warned as the sea "Not today Princess." I stood soaked and cold but unwilling to relent to my need to dance. I stepped in to the surf and danced in the rain and wind. Wet but warmer with the dancing I closed my eyes and twirled, Jumped and pranced in the water.

It was then that I was hit with a violent wave. I was pulled under and was being twisted through the water uncontrollably. I reached for the surface but could not find it. I was not able to hold what little breath remained. I wanted to transport but found that my heart pounded too hard; desperately hard. As I was about to scream for Marcus, I was pulled from the water by Edwin. "Stupid Witch! What were you thinking?"

I was shaking from the cold and soaked to the skin. Coughing and choking the water out of my lungs. The wind and rain continuing as they had in that violent fury. My t-shirt and jeans offering no comfort in their present state. I pulled to get away from Edwin so I could get to my coat. Edwin holding me by my waist did not let go. I pushed him but he did not let go. I screamed at him "Let me loose." He turned me around and grabbed my hair. He had me immobile and kissed me forcibly.

I had enough of him at that point. I flung my hand and sent him flying down the beach. I walked to my coat and he was back.

"How dare you, Witch. Who do you think you are attacking a Pure Blood Wizard.?"

At that point I transported back to the house and waved my hand and I was dry.

Edwin appeared at my face and said "You will not use magic against me again if you know what's good for you, you silly Witch. There are consequences for that."

I narrowed my eyes and said "If you ever attack me again I will make you miserable for the rest of you Pure Blood Existence."

He raised his hand to strike me and I waved my hand and he was about three inches big and locked in a little golden box. I placed him nicely on the mantel of the fireplace in the parlor. And though he was screaming at me I couldn't make out what he was saying and I didn't care. I walked to the kitchen and made a PB&J and got a glass of milk.

I sat at the table and began to eat. Very soon after sitting, Max and Marcus appeared. Both looking stout and stern. I had closed my mind but I knew it was something about a Wizard rule I knew nothing about. Knew nothing about and cared nothing about. I would let Edwin and the rest know, I will not be manhandled. And any offender would be handled by me. I stared at them blankly and continued to eat my sandwich quietly. They continued to stare at me with their Wizard stout and stern faces insinuating that I have cross the line. I thought *"Huh like that's going to convince me of anything."* A short time later, Mandra came in the door and joined us at the table. I waited for them to speak. I had nothing to say. I would follow Marcus's words and make my point by saying nothing.

My grandmother started. "Em. You have to let Edwin lose." I looked unfazed as I took another bite of my sandwich.

Marcus then tried. "Princess, he is a Pure Blood Wizard. He can't be treated as such." My mind said *"Wrong approach; Witch here."*

I looked at Marcus "So what."

Grandmother became nervous "Em. Don't be fresh with Marcus."

Max sat quietly, stout and stern, as a good Wizard should. He was closed but I knew when I looked in his eyes he was having some fun with this.

Marcus said "His behavior will have consequence but he must be released."

I only looked blankly at Marcus. Marcus looked to Max pleading to have some influence with me.

Max looked me in the eye and said, in his best servant Wizard voice, "Princess, could you please release the Wizard in the box."

I couldn't help it. It just came up, milk exiting my nose and mouth. I began to laugh mercilessly. Max, with the inter fight to stay serious and stout couldn't hold it together either. He started to laugh harder than me. A truly deep and powerful laugh. He looked at Marcus who was completely serious. Marcus looked at Max sternly. Max raised his hands to Marcus, then winked back at me as he transported out laughing.

Mandra and Marcus remained impassive and stern. I wiped my face and the table as I continue to giggle. Max returned back in control, but when he looked at me, we started laughing again. He looked to Marcus and held up his hands and was laughing to hard to speak. He had to leave again.

I looked at my grandmother with my humor of the situation and transmitted to her *"At least we will know where the pest is."* My grandmother tried with all her might but lost it and started to laugh.

Marcus stared at her. "Mandra this is serious."

Grandmother nodded and through her laughter said "I agree Marcus."

Max came back and was really trying hard to be stout. I did not look at him purposely trying to help him from laughing so he did not get in trouble with Marcus. But when he saw Mandra laughing he lost it again and had to leave. Marcus sat back in his chair with his hands up and shook his head. And as he shook his head his smile appeared and he started to chuckle. Soon the chuckle became his beautiful baritone laugh. Max came back laughing safely and Marcus put his arm around him and said "Nice attempt Max."

Once we stopped laughing about the Wizard in the box, Marcus said "Em. He will be held accountable and admonished from his advances to you."

I looked at Marcus with a brow up. "If he ever attempts to raise a hand to me again, I will think of something far worse then being in a golden box."

Max looked up to the ceiling with a smiled. Marcus looked at me and nodded with full understanding. I waved my hand and the little golden box appeared on the table.

I looked at Marcus "Tell him so there is no misunderstanding."

Marcus looked at the box where Edwin was screaming something. Marcus in a baritone voice said "Edwin, your behavior has brought you to this. If you attempt these behaviors in the future, there will be no convincing of the Princess to release you. Do you understand?" The box was silent and then a small squeak. Marcus looked at me and said "He understands My Lady." I waved my hand and Edwin stood on the table. He looked over to me with a scowl and transported away.

Grandmother started to laugh again and got up from the table. She went over to make tea for her and Marcus. At that point I dared to look at Max and he shook his head smiling. "You need a reward, Princess. Let go to the movies." I looked at Mandra and Marcus and both nodded and I was up and had Max by the hand pulling him out of the house.

Max asked "Are we walking in the rain?" I smiled and waved my hand and there was a Yellow Diablo waiting for our use. He said "OK that will work. Lets go".

CHAPTER 14

That summer, had been boring for me. After the Solstice, there was nothing else happening. Lessons with Edith continued and Molly was nice to talk to. Lincon went around making sure every flower had a stem and tended the herb garden. Grandmother wanted me at the store but I could not take it everyday. I could only do that sweet smiling crap to the normal hypocrites who called us evil and dammed for so long. The whole time they are sticking their noses up their coming in for love potions and such.

I sat on the porch, nothing to do and pouting. "What are you up to?"

I smiled and never having to turn and look, I knew, in the chair behind me was Max. "As you can see I am doing nothing."

I looked at him as he mockingly said. "Why not?"

I pulled my brows together. "I have nothing to do."

He sighed and shook his head. "Em. It seems to me, that with your power, you could think of something to do." I was kind of shamed then. I could do anything I wanted, but no one to do it with. I just turned away from him and didn't say anything. I would go back to the Boardwalk or go to another park. But what fun is it alone.

Max moved over and sat next to me on the step. "You know, if you really want to do something and want company, I would be honored to be that company."

I looked over at him. "Max, you have your things to do. I would just be a pain in the ass kid you have to baby sit."

He looked at me like he was sizing me up. "How old are you?"

I knew, with him about 20, I was a kid. "I am about to turn 17 in a week."

He smiled. "Well then, I know that there is a really big party tonight in LA. Would consider accompanying me?"

I sat there and could not believe this. "My grandmother is not going to let me go; especially with you."

He attempted to be insulted. "And why not?"

I giggled. "Because I hear grandmother and Marcus talk about you and your parties." I laughed and waved my hand in the air "Max is sowing his wild oats. He is wild and undisciplined. He disappears for days… He bla bla bla. " I looked in his eyes that showed the enjoyment of the comments about him. "Max has his wild life and she would worry too much." And I looked out over the cliff at the Ocean, and thought what if, While Max had a good laugh. I turned back to Max to watch him laugh. When he stopped, he looked at me with his up to something smile.

"We can dance all night?"

I looked blankly at him but inside I was intrigued with his temptation of dancing. He then said "There might be others like us there?"

I must have had my wheels turning in my head. "Em won't be the same dull goody two shoes?"

I was insulted then. "I don't think I am dull."

He laughed "But a goody two shoes." He nudged my arm. "Em, what's the worst that can happen. You dance, you mingle and you come home all escorted and protected by yours truly?" I was ready to say yes, but then I thought Grandmother will not let me go. He grabbed my face and looked directly into my eyes. "She doesn't have to know."

I did not understand "Max I think she will notice me missing."

He giggled "No she wont." He moved his hand and sitting in the chair was the perfect replica of me. And full exact, animated imitation of me. I jumped up,

"Max! You are a genius. Do you really think it will fool her and everyone else?"

He assuredly nodded and said "Absolutely. I have used this same stunt several times and have never been caught. The image is there and we add a little Em essence." He put his hand on my face and pulled down gently. He had a sparkle in his hand and blew it on the imitation Em. He then pulled me close and we were in my room. He snapped his fingers and the imitation followed.

"Now, we will hide Ms Em 2 in the tower. At nine o'clock say good night to everyone and meet me here in your room. We will reactive number two and we will be Partying in LA." He looked at me straight on "You in?"

I looked at him and his devilish smile and leaped in to his arms and said "YES!"

I stepped back and turned to number 2 and snapped my fingers. She was in the tower waiting to be activated.

Max said "Em. Block all transmissions. Make sure no one is able to find out. Nine O'clock " He was gone.

Grandmother came home at six and Molly put dinner on the table. I ate quietly but inside my adrenalin was crazy. I blocked all transmissions in and out. "Did you have a nice day Em?" Mandra inquired. "It was peaceful grandmother, nothing special." Grandmother looked concerned about my dull little life.

"Maybe you should volunteer with a community service."

I thought about that and actually liked the idea. "That is a good idea. I will look into it tomorrow." Grandmother smiled. We ate and then Lincon, Molly, Grándmother and I sat on the porch talking. I did notice the owl warning me that trouble was near. But I also knew it was just Max. It was close to nine and I said "Grandmother, I think I will turn in." I kissed on the cheek and said good night to Molly and Lincon.

I took two steps at a time to get up the stairs. As I walked in the door, there was Max. He was holding a Glamour Magazine and opened it.

"OK, chose your weapon."

I looked through the Magazine and found a sort black dress with rhinestone accents twisting into swirls at the right side. It had a sweetheart neck outlined in rhinestones. The shoes were simple high healed sandals. I giggled and with a wave of my hand, I was in the dress with my make up done and my hair up. Max looked me over with his arms across his chest. He looked at me in the eye and shook his head. I was surprised. I thought I looked nice. At that, my hair fell down and was lose. "It needs to be as free as we are tonight."

He dropped his arms and there was something else there but as his instructions for the plan, his mind was closed. I huffed "What now Professor Higgins?" He smiled and then said "Nothing. You are beautiful." He waved his hand and Em 2 walked down from the tower in a night gown. I was shocked at the night gown because it was very skimpy. I glared at Max and snapped my fingers and the night gown was appropriate. Max smiled devilishly. "Be nice Max." He put out his arm for me to take. I took his arm and his grabbed me close and we were in LA.

The city lights were sparkling from the street in the Hollywood hills. People were filing into this huge pink Mediterranean mansion. Max was dressed in a white shirt opened at the neck with a black leather jacket. He wore black jeans and boots. His hair combed back. He looked very handsome. "Shall we?" he started to walk and I got scared.

"Max maybe I really wasn't prepared for this."

He laughed at me. "Em, you're shy. Let it go."

He put his hand on the middle of my back and started directing me forward. We got to the door and a man asked for out names. Max said, "Max Marshal and guest." The man looked at me and said "Must be eighteen. Got ID?" While he checked off Max's name, Max looked at me and I understood without his transmission. Out of the bodice of my dress from the breast, I pulled out an ID showing me as eighteen. The man's eyes went wide with shock at the holding place of my ID. He looked and nodded and handed it back to me. I put the card back into the holding spot. We walked in and Max said "You could have given that guy a heart attack." We walked into a house full of beautiful people. All milling about with glasses and cigarettes. Max held on to me and I was grateful. I was really out of my dull goody two shoes element. Several people greeted Max and smiled at me.

Out of the crowd came a female voice "Max!" I looked and a very beautiful tall slender Blond came out of the mob. Wearing (Or not) a very low cut, thin, very short, red dress. She walked up completely ignoring my presents and kissed Max on the lips and hung on him though he still had his arm around me. I was livid. How dare she. Then I thought, we maybe she can dare. I am the one that is never out.

"Max . Where have you been? We were waiting for you."

Uncomfortable at her nearness I tried to pull away from Max. He held me in place. Max was smiling in his board way

"Ashly? Did I not say I would be here?" She continued her flirt and Max pushed her back with his free arm. "Your are being rude to my companion." She looked over at me like I was a little bug to be squashed.

I looked at her with an eyebrow up. *I thought how she would like to spend the night as an ugly houseplant.*

Max gave me a squeeze, open transmission to me and transmitted, *"Be nice Em."*

Then he said in voice "This is Em. She is a very old friend of mine."

She laughed "she can't be more than eighteen so how long could you have known her." Max said "A long time."

Max, pulling me along, waked out to the patio with Ashley hanging on his other arm. At the pool side, a dark haired guy about the age of Max jumped up and waved Max over. Max nodded. As we walked to the table, the man was standing.

"Leave it to you Max to walk out here with two beautiful girls. I know Ashley but who is this enchanting creature?"

If only you knew is all I thought. But I had no Idea why I was being hostile to him.

"This is Em. Em this is Randy"

I smiled and said hello. He pulled a chair out for me and I moved from the protection of Max's arm. "Well Em, tell me about your self?"

Max sat next to me and Ashley was left standing. Before I could say a word, Max said "My lady is a sequestered Princess of the Wizard Realm. She will be answering no questions." I laughed at him as the rest, and he winked at me. He came close and in my ear he said, "Leave them guessing."

The pool had floating candles an there was little lights in the trees. Over on the side was a patio used as a dance floor but there was no music. There seemed to be hundreds of people there. A server came by and asked us what we would like to drink as she placed a plate of chocolate covered fruit. Max ordered a beer for us both. She looked at me, and no one else, and asked me for ID. I pulled the same stunt but showing that I had just turned 21. Max smiled knowing that his tutoring of manipulation was taking hold. She handed it back and I placed it back at my breast.

Randy who had watched the maneuver, came out with "Far out". He then made the comment, "I can't believe that your 21 I would not have guessed any more than eighteen." Max raised an eye brow, "Why would I introduce you to anyone under the age of 21. That would be contributing in its self."

The beer came and the conversation at the table was about Max and his brothers. Ashley had found a chair and brought it over. "Where are you brothers Max. I was sure at least Edwin would show up."

He smiled as I got nervous. Edwin would blow the whistle for sure. "Edwin is working tonight. And well the others got hung up."

I opened my mind only to him. *"We can't let Edwin see me here."* He came back with *"He is busy guarding you as you sleep. He has this notion that the shadow is hanging around. Marcus ordered him to stay close until dawn."*

I was uncomfortable because it would be difficult to get back in my room and get rid of number 2 without that slimy Edwin knowing. Max only patted my hand.

The music started and Max grabbed my hand and we headed to the dance floor. We danced and danced until we were out of breath. He grabbed me by the waist and we walk back to the table. Ashley had taken my chair. Max never hindered and grabbed his beer and drank it in one gulp. He looked over at me and I smiled.

He then told his friends "Well gotta go."

I am sure my mouth dropped open. I was disappointed. I wanted to dance some more. Randy looked confused "Max the party is just getting going, where are you going?"

Max smiled "I think we will enjoy the clubs on the strip."

Randy laughed "Max, you will never get in now." Max arrogantly said "Never underestimate me Randy, I have my ways."

I was not happy. I wanted to stay but Max had other Ideas. We walked through the house with many people acknowledging Max and staring at me.

"Why are they staring at me that way?"

Max smiled "Curiosity of the beautiful girl they've never seen before."

Just then another woman approached. This one was dark haired and strikingly beautiful with blue eyes. She stood directly in front of us. She was mortal but there was something there. I tilted my head and Max sent a transmission that she was a daughter of a Wizard.

She stood and stared at me. "Hanging with the **Witches**now Max?"

I took offence of her reference as witches beneath her. Max sent to my head *"Don't let her get to you."*

He then answered her "I am hanging with this one."

She looked over at me and looked me up and down "The Princess."

I looked her up and down "Whatever I am, I am a witch first and foremost."

Max squeezed my hand. "Julia, why do you care?"

She looked back over at Max "Can we say I'm mildly curious. Besides she young and doesn't know what type you are. I do."

I let Max take that since I had no idea what she was talking about. "And what type is that?"

She smiled at him and said "Mix Blood."

I laughed then and said to her "Well then we are good company for each other because I am also Mix Blood."

Her head snapped back in my direction, "You are nothing to him or me. Stop addressing me Witch."

I stepped back and was about to send her to hell when Max laughed and said "Julia, I would use caution." She started to say something else and I clipped the air with my fingers and took her voice. She looked at me and I smiled assuring her that it was me.

I said in a friendly witch voice, "If you can't say anything nice, don't say anything at all." The spell sent and she was allowed her voice back. "It was nice to see you Max." And then she touched her mouth knowing that was not what she was going to say. She looked to me and then Max. Max pulled me by the hand and we started for the door again.

I turned back and said with a sweet smile, "By Julia."

Max was laughing and he said in my ear, "I thought you like the mortals."

As we approached the door, there was a handsome dark haired guy with hazel eyes looking at Max with daggers in his eyes. He looked over at me with a nod. Then he sneered at Max "Max, we have been released."

Max smiled "Good." He kept moving to the door with me held tightly to his side. The dark haired man said "Max, are you crazy. Think about this Max."

Max and I made it out the door and there was a black convertible Porsche waiting for us. He opened my door and rushed me in. He quickly got into the drivers seat and we were gone.

I looked at him "Who was that?"

Max smiled and said "Some guy who blames me because he was tricked. I can't even remember his name."

I looked at him with narrow Eyes as he had blocked me out. "Liar."

He just laughed. He then said "You better give Julia control over her mouth. She is a nasty mean thing and people will know that she's been bewitched."

I thought about it and said. "Maybe they will think she turned over a new leaf and is being nice." He laughed and said a warning "Em?" I waved my hand and unbound the little demons mouth.

So true to his word, Max and I got into the clubs. Of course never waiting at the doors and begging for our turn in. Max and I were in and dancing and dancing. I had so much fun just dancing and laughing with Max. About three in the morning, we found ourselves walking along Santa Monica beach. I watched the waves and though they told me to take care, I only noticed the florescent color of the foam.

"This has been great. I love to dance. Thanks Max. Even if you are wild, undisciplined, and a Mix Blood, I would never see or do anything if not for you. I would only get to dance at the Solstice or my room alone."

He smiled very proud of him self. "Yes I am the boredom rescuer of the princess." He then gave a little laugh and said "it's a risky job." He looked off over the sea and said "Next week, let's go to the clubs in New York. There are a blasts."

He looked back at me and I gave him a smile and said "I'd love to."

He grabbed me up and twisted me around as I screamed with the feeling in my belly like I was falling. He then put me down and I held his hand and we walked slowly.

He talked about his life at Stanford and what he planned to do in the future, "I have no idea." he looked down at me "If I was to choose for my self? I think, I would like to teach. But not college, I would like to teach grammar school. I think I could make History exciting for the kids"

I was surprised at that. But he could make it exciting "I can see you doing that. I just don't know how the parents of your students would take your style." He looked over at me and I continued "You know, taking the class physically to Egypt or Gettysburg." He smiled.

Then after a few minutes he said "I am not sure what I will be allowed to do. Being trained as a Mastered Wizard has its obligations. And being Mixed Blood I am obligated to the others. I …..I could just chuck the Wizard stuff and be a Teacher, but something inside wont let me." He then asked me "And you My Lady, what do you think you would like to do?"

I thought about it. "I think I would like to work with kids in some way. May be like you, a teacher or couch of some kind."

He laughed "Oh no. You will be a professional Dancer." With that he twirled me in the sand. I laughed with him because he was right.

I loved to dance. "Yeah but I would want something more than my favorite pass time. I like having dancing as a something special and not a profession." He smiled and nodded.

Then Max waved his hand and there were beach chairs for us. We sat looking out over the Ocean. "Max how am I going to get back in my room, and get rid of number 2 without Edwin detecting."

He looked over at me. He then turned in his chair, reached out and petted my cheek with the back of his fingers. "Leave her and go with me."

I looked at him confused, "Where?"

He smile slightly "Everywhere. Anywhere." He dropped his hand to mine "Number 2 will go through the movements and act just like you. She can even take a test at school. No one would be the wiser."

I couldn't do that. I loved my grandmother and couldn't do that to her. One night, alright I did it but longer seemed to be really wrong. Then I giggled at the absurdness. "Max you know I can't. Besides, they would notice you gone and you have to finish college."

He looked sad then. He sighed and then said "They are used to me disappearing. We could take just a couple of days." He stopped and looked in my eyes "Two days EM. Then we can renegotiate.

I was intrigued. Think two days of just being free; Just being normal. But….He then was a little excited when he saw me thinking.

"Where do you want to go. Monte Carlo? Paris, London?…… You name it."

I looked at him then and with his most charming smile he said "You will never regret it." I thought,hum… We could do this. And it's not like I have a full calendar. I turned to him this time "OK. If I do this, you have to be on your best behavior Max." he nodded "No playing games with the morals. Just leave them alone." He nodded. "And its two days only and I go home" he looked at me with a little less enthusiasm.

He was thinking "Two days?" I nodded sternly. He said "Not for good?" I laughed and shook my head. He said "OK Fine. Two Days. But before we go back, I can try to talk you into more, OK."

I laughed and said "OK."

"Well where do you want to go?" I looked at that wicked Max. I knew he wanted something more sophisticated, but I have had so little travel and sightseeing. All I could say was "Disney Land." He started to laugh at me and I continued "Then Coney Island."

He kept laughing but then said "Today doesn't count"

I pulled my brows together, "Yes it does."

He shook his head though he kept smiling. "We need to sleep, tomorrow we will go to Disney Land" I was tired now and agreed.

We drove to Anaheim. Why? I don't know. Max got a room at he Disney Hotel. He even produced luggage. Max was good. He was great a deception and manipulations. Once in the room I waved my hand and was in a night gown and crawling into one of the two beds in the room. I was asleep as the sun shined in the sky. .

The next day we were up at the opening of the park. We spent the whole day and after the Pirates of the Caribbean, Max in his best Pirate voice said "Lets sail the Caribbean, My Lady. We will be a new and improved Pirate Crew. Pillaging all flags and taking all the riches just for fun." I laughed at him "Two Days, Max." We rode every ride and watched as many of the shows we could. After dinner, we went back to the room.

I jumped on the bed and was looking at the book on Walt Disney. Max turned on the TV and found that we could watch any Disney movie was wanted. He put on the Pirate movie and I moved over to the floor next to him leaning against the bed.

He moved closer to me and put his arm around me and said "Everyday could be a Disney land."

I looked over at him and smiled and said "It creeps me out knowing Number 2 is living my life, as sorry as it is."

He smiled "But today wasn't sorry. You had fun Ms. Goody two shoes."

He was right. I did. "Yeah how bout that." After a while I got up and got in bed. I fell asleep before the movie ended.

That morning, we checked out and got in the car. We were driving for a while.

"Where are you going?"

He looked over and said "Just driving a bit. We will transport soon."

I was quite and was confused why we did not just go. We ended out in an open desert. It was hot and there were no people or cars. He pulled over and we got out of the car. He waved his had and the car was gone.

He looked over and asked me. "You should see the sunset in the desert Em. The wind blows and the sun has so much red and gold. And if there are clouds they turn all kinds of colors. God's canvas; a gift of beauty. If you just sit and listen there is silence, freedom and peace."

I looked at him then and wondered what brought this on. "What's wrong Max?"

He gave a smile, but not a usual up to something smile though. "I am having a problem accepting growing up is all. I'm nineteen about to turn twenty and I feel like I will never have control over what happens to me." He looked over to me and he had his charming smile back " I guess it's the mix blood thing."

"Because we are Mixed Blood, do you think that there will be a time when that won't matter?"

He took a deep breath and said "I don't know."

He smiled at me full force then grabbed me and twirled around and we were in Coney Island. After a full day and several rides on the wooded roller coaster, Max transported us to LA again. He had the car on a street corner parked and we got in.

He looked over at me and I knew that it was because I followed his lead and did not balk. "OK. Now what are you up to, Max."

He drove as he smiled. "Their planning a surprise birthday party for you."

I could not believe he was ease dropping again. "Max. You said to close your mind to them. There going to find out and I never get out of the house again"

He looked over "Don't worry. They can't trace me. In fact, they are looking for me all over but not here."

I was shocked. "Who's looking for you?"

He had that wicked smile again "My Brothers. For some reason, they are upset with me." I turned in my seat "What did you do to them? And don't lie Max."

He only giggled. "How do you know I did anything to them? I could be innocent."

I looked at him and shook my head "No your not. So spill"

He laughed again "I knew that they would go to the party, and I did not want them to see you and talk. So I had to keep them away." He did not continue.

I said exasperated "Max?"

He shrugged "I tricked them. I took then to Paris to find the latest fashion for the most hip Wizards. "He laughed at his own little Joke. "While they were in the dressing rooms, I transported the dressing rooms to hang in a ice cavern in Antarctica. I knew it would take time to get out.."

I could not believe that "Max they are your brothers." He raised his brows and corrected "Foster Brothers. And they are nosey."

I shook my head in disapproval "I can only imagine what terrible fate I would face if you got mad at me."

He grabbed my hand and kissed it "Never will that happen."

Max drove up highway one along the Ocean. It was beautiful with the sun going down. "Its time for me to return home, Max."

He looked over from his driving and turned back. "I know."

I sat back and enjoyed the ride and the sunset. Max pulled over on a vista point lookout. He got out of the car and came to my side. He opened my door and held out his hand. I put my hand in his and we moved to the railing of the vista point. He held me in front of him and had his arms around me. I had butterflies. I wasn't sure what he was up to. Close to my ear he spoke "Em, I will take you back, but give me two more days?"

I was so unsure why he held me like this. Why he had been more serious today than I have seen him in a long while.

"Max, I have to go back you know that."

He spoke closer to my ear. "Two more days."

I knew there was something more here. "Max, tell me what's happening here. Why do you want to keep me away from home?"

He was quite for a second, and then said "I will tell you if you give me two more days. If you don't, I'll have to figure something else out." I really did not know how to answer. I need to go home, but I think my friend needed me to go along with him. And because he was my friend, I gave in.

"OK Max." I turned around "But I want the truth."

He smiled then and we walked back to the car. He stopped at a no name Motel where I had to pull out the fake ID again. But this time it was out of my back pocket. We walked down the walkway to room 12. There we entered and the room was not what I had hoped. I decided that I could change my room I could do this one. So I did. Then it was luxurious. Reds and gold's for Max and a big over sized bed with silks and satins draped over it. A huge TV, and a pizza for me. Max's looked at me with admiration. "Very good Em, but where are you going to sleep." I looked at him and said "I'll split the bed later."

I ran to the bed and jumped on it and grabbed the pizza. I watch Max come over and take a slice. He then laid down on his back opposite me so that we faced each other.

"You shouldn't eat laying on your back Max, you could choke." He rolled his eyes but turned over onto his elbows.

"Well, are you going to tell me why we need to be gone two more days?"

He chewed and swallowed and gave a smirk grin. "Why don't you just give in and take off with me forever."

I giggled "Spill."

He sighed, "Edwin." He looked at me "Do I have to say any more?"

I knew Edwin was an ass but what did that have to do with me not being home? "Max, keep going. I am not satisfied. Keep taking." He looked really uncomfortable. He put his pizza down and he looked me in the eye.

"Edwin had been telling my brothers that he would be forcing himself on you this week and claiming your ….. He will have two more assignments next week so he feels that time is now."

I could not believe what I was hearing. That little snake, if he thinks he would be able to attack me, he would have a sorry awakening. I threw my pizza back in the box

"I am going home and teach that slimy snake who he is dealing with. How dare he believe that I am so weak that he could dare over power me and take my….."

Max grabbed my hand. "He believes that he fulfills the Prophecy of producing a child."

I took an intake of breath and became angrier. "No way! I am only seventeen. What is he thinking?"

Then Max looked serious "OK princess, but now that you know, I need you not to let on to him or anyone that I have told you OK?"

I jumped from the bed. "I going to go kick his butt and then turn him into the pile of crap he is." I was so mad.

Max got up and came over and grabbed my shoulders. "Em Promise me." He started to laugh and said "But, Please include me when you kick his butt and turn him into crap." Then he looked straight at me. "Promise!"

I looked at Max. "Promise."

I went back and laid across the bed and put my face in my hands.

"Is that why you took me to the party?" He laid down next to me and separated my fingers at my eye.

"No. I have fun with you Em."

I felt he was just being nice. I picked up my head and rested it on a pillow.

"Max you had another reason; it wasn't to have fun with me."

He sighed. "I did not want to tell you and you need to have fun" He smiled "I was killing two birds with one stone. I stopped Edwin's little plan and I had the prettiest girl at the party." He threw in his charm "There were perks for me." I felt awful. I was actually having a wonderful time. Now I know it was a guardian move and had nothing to do with just having fun with me. I was hurt that once again, a Wizard screwed things up for me and what I thought was fun was not real.

Max, reading me again, looked over and said "No true. I have the most fun with you. Why would I ask you to leave with me forever if I didn't?"

I rolled my eyes "I have no idea."

I smiled at him and he said "Well… want to?"

I was confused. "Want to what?"

He said "Leave for ever."

I started laughing and "No. I have to go home."

I jumped and looked at Max. "What if he attacks Number 2."

Max gave the devil grin "He will be sorely surprised to discover that she does not have any …… Female parts."

I started to laugh imagining his surprise. "I wonder what he will think then. He will know it isn't really me." I yawned and said "He will rat as the rodent he is."

Max smiled as he turned on to his back. "He wont, He would have to tell how he knows or someone with read him and his little plot would also be known."

I then said "But they would know that I was out for days with you in addition to Scummy Edwin's little plot."

Max moved back to his side and looked really serious "I really don't think I would survive that consequence."

He turned over on his back and looked at the ceiling. "You know Em, if you would just take off with me all that stuff wouldn't matter," He turned over and looked at me "We could be free."

I brought my brows in "So far the only one who I am actually free with is you. I am sorry for that."

He looked over at me "Why?"

I smiled at him, "Max you have a life to live outside of me, my boredom, and my virtue. I hope you can be released from your vow someday. I hope you have happiness in your life."

He ticked my side, "I like my vow and I have fun with you. I am happy."

Then I asked him, "So if I had said no to two more days, what were you planning?" He smiled with his eyes shut "Oh, I would get the same punishment for kidnapping." I giggled.

We talked some more before I fell asleep. I woke up in the morning with Max sleeping close to me and his arm around my waist. I did not want to move. I actually liked it. It felt natural, safe, right. I went back to sleep. When I woke next I was alone in the room. Max was gone. I wondered where he had gone. I got up and showered. I changed into jeans and tank and a sweater. I came out and change the room back to its dreary self.

Max walked in with some egg burritos. We sat and eat and I asked. "Max, how am I going to know what gone on at home these last few days?" He looked and lifted his shoulders and said "I guess read the minds of the others in the house. Don't worry, I will read Edwin." He then smiled and said "Let's go to the water park today and forget the worlds." I joined his smile and nodded.

We drove a ways and stopped. He waved the car away. He grabbed me and we were in Sacramento at raging waters. But the bathing suit I was warring was for a grandmother. It was striped with long legs and had sleeves. I changed that quickly to a stylish black high hipped one piece. Max looked at me disapprovingly. "Leave it Max. I will not be ashamed of my self by wearing the rag you chose." I saw the first slid and started for it. Max caught up to me and said "That suit is a felony waiting to happen." I smiled at him and said "Get over it. Besides, aren't you a guardian?" We had a great time. But we were sunburned. I liked having color but this would be hard to explain at home. I waved hand over us both as were normal again.

Then Max said "Let's go to Vegas?" I got excited "Las Vegas?" He smiled knowing that he had my interest "Yeah Las Vegas." I nodded. He then said "We have to drive in though, when the sun goes down. There is no better way to see that town for the first time than in a convertible with all the lights on down the strip." And that is exactly what we did.

We transported near Vegas, in fact I could actually see the lights. Max conjured his little convertible porch. We got in and he drove slowly up the strip and then I begged him to do it again. We stayed at Creasers Palace and we gambled and danced until early morning. We walked into our room laughing and I had a little gold buck that I received for the thousand dollar winning at the slots, which happened with help from Max. I was dressed in the dress we went to dinner in. It was black with thin straps and short. Once in the room I threw my shoes off and jumped on the bed. Then, I realized, there was only one.

"Max? Where's your bed?"

He smiled and said "We can split it later."

I thought about that and realized that is what I had said the night before and never got to it. I brought my brows together being a little freaked over the mad rush for my virginity. Max laughed "I just like hugging you. Besides I'm the mix blood remember?" I wasn't sure but Max has always been my protector. He wouldn't hurt me. I insured it by spiting the bed and blankets. He looked a little irritated and changed it back.

"Max! You said you would behave."

He smiled and turned on TV and jumped in the bed next to me. He grabbed me and put my head on his chest. I actually like it. So I stayed there.

"See it isn't so bad. Besides you'll be sleeping soon." *I thought how does he know?* But I was asleep as soon as that thought left my head. I woke in the night to find my self dressed in PJs and a tank; And with Max asleep next to me with his arms around me. And I liked it. I was safe. I fell back to sleep.

We were home the next day but had to stay back in the trees while Edwin was trying his magic on Number 2. We were laughing at his boasting and bragging.

"I am pure blood you know. I will be a mastered wizard before long. I come from may long respected wizards and have a good future planed for me."

"Yeah, with a ring around his nose." Max spit.

Then it came. "It should please you to know that you have a pure wizard protecting you rather than a half wit mix blood." Max growled and was gone.

I said to his mind *"Max! What are you doing?"*

He sent back *"Just stay there."*

Max appeared on the porch. "Hello Edwin, did you call?"

Edwin stood up "What are you doing here Max. Em and I were having a lovely day without you."

Max walked over and said "Hi Em."

Number 2 got up and hugged Max. "Hi Max. Where have you been? I haven't seen you in so long."

Edwin became very upset. "You know what Max?' As he walked over to Max .

Max stood his ground and said "NO. What?"

Max and Edwin were almost touching noses. Mandra came out of the house then and said "Edwin, Max. I will not have this and I have no problem in calling the Elders regarding this behavior. Settle down."

Max said "Yes mam." Edwin nodded and was gone.

Mandra went back in the house looking at me, or number 2, with some concern. Number 2 stayed still through the whole argument. As soon as Mandra was inside, Max waved his hand and Number 2 was gone. I immediately transported to the porch.

"Max, why do you respond to his crap?"

Max shrouded. "I have to go home. I need to face the music for what I did to my brothers. Then I'm going to pound Edwin to a pulp."

I giggled and hugged him. "Max take the fact that I adore you and hate him. I would never..." I whispered to him "Spend four un-chaperoned days with him."

When I backed up he was smiling his self conscious smile. "Em you're going to make me soft going home and I will be a sitting duck." He kissed my cheek and was gone.

I did not see Max until my "Surprise Party". I was self conscious and felt silly listening to the Happy Birthday song. The usual group was there along with Marcus, Max and Edwin. I stood next to Max on purpose so that Edwin couldn't make any moves. We ate cake and played croquet. It was, all in all, boring. I stood over at the cliff rail and soon I was joined by Max.

He kissed my cheek and said "Happy Birthday Princess."

I smiled up at him and said "Thanks." I giggled "I hate to ask, but how bad was it when you went home the week of the party? I see Edwin is alive."

He smiled "Yeah he lived. He never figured out it was not you. My other brothers were somewhat mad, but one actually said that he couldn't blame me. The only good thing is that no one spilled the beans."

I waited "Did you get in trouble?"

He smiled again and said "Well Marcus was furious with me for disappearing again. I barely was able to get out of the library for your party. But the price paid was worth ever minute."

I smiled. "I have been waiting to go to the clubs in New York but I don't have a guardian to go with?"

I looked over at him as he smiled and then I said "I would hate to have to ask Edwin to take me."

Max dropped his smile and said "That's not funny Em."

I started laughing. He smiled looked back to see who was watching. "Five tomorrow night, close you mind." I nodded.

In that time, I rarely dreamed of anything but dancing with Max. I never dreamed of anything scary or hurtful. I contributed it to feeling safe with Max. I was having a really fun and peaceful time in life.

CHAPTER 25

It didn't stay that way for long. School had started and I studied a lot. But Edith said one day," Em would you make another trip to the trees tomorrow afternoon?" I was more than honor at her request. "Absolutely." Edith looked a little older these days. She was slowing up and I did worry about her. After all, without her, what would I know about anything? I did have a true affection for this Master Witch and my teacher. However, she remained disappointed in me with my potions skills.

As planned, I came home from school that afternoon. I even ditched my last class so that we could go and have more time dancing. I entered the kitchen and Edith was their waiting. She was dressed in a peasant blouse and skirt. I waved my hand and I was in a cotton dress that moved in the breeze. I let my hair free and looked over to my teacher and she smiled at my choices. Of course, neither of us wore shoes. I smiled at Molly who nodded knowingly and then I took Edith's hand and we were in the little field behind the creek and grove of pines. I watched Edith as she scanned the field. Too old now to dance.

She said "Oh princess, I can still hear the music."

I listen and could hear that heavenly music of the trees. Then I heard the trees whisper "The Princess has come to dance. Edith has come." I smiled at Edith as she sat on a stump. She smiled and waved her cane telling me to dance. I needed no prodding. I ran to the center of the field. I danced and danced. Once again peace and freedom.

While I danced I felt the breeze caress me and felt the love of the trees. I had a thought that maybe I should have been a tree. Then I thought, no then I couldn't dance in the field or in the sea. Then the warning came, The trees whispered, "Run Princess, Run." I stopped dancing and I turned to Edith at the far end of the field. She lay on the ground with the shadow standing with her. I screamed and dropped to my knees. The hawk sounded three times and I was unable to move. The shadow slowly began to move forward. I threw a fire ball to it and the shadow caught it like a rubber ball and sent to into nothingness. I stood not willing to die on my knees. I sent the call to Edwin. But as the shadow took another step towards me, I realized that it was unfazed at my call to Edwin. I called Marcus. But I could feel that the Shadow had no concerns of Marcus either as it slowly walked toward me. The shadow seemed to know that they could not hear me. I knew the only one who could hear me now was Max. I just knew he would hear me no matter what. In voice I screamed "MMMAAax!" The shadow rapidly picked up his advance and I lifted into the air. The next instant Max stood in the path of the shadow. Marcus arrived next to stand with Max. I dropped to the ground behind them. The shadow disappeared into hundreds of little shadows across the field as the sun began its decent behind the trees. I ran to Edith screaming her name "Edith, Master Edith." When I dropped next to her, I could see that she was dead. I screamed in agony, and Max grabbed me into his arms and Marcus examined Edith.

We then were in the Parlor at grandmothers. I still cried into Max's shoulder and shook over the experience. I refused to let go of Max. I had him in a vice grip. I was scared and didn't understand what was actually happening around me. The scene was played off as her collapsing at home. Paramedics and ambulance and cops. All saying her heart gave out. Grandmother speaking to the all with Marcus at her side. The story is that I found her on the floor. But that was the ruse. I knew the truth. She was murdered. I knew what happened. I saw that creature over her body. And now it is being played off in the Mortal world like it was natural. I refused to witness anymore of the lie. I felt sick and ran to my room. I ran up to the tower and sat in the chair and cried.

Some time later, Elena came up and held my hand. "I am so sorry Em."

I looked at her with my eyes swollen from crying. "Elena, why did that thing have to hurt her? After all she was an old lady. She was no threat to anyone."

Elena looked at me and said "Em. I have no answers." She then looked down stairs. "Come on Em? Mom, Marcus and Max are still in the kitchen. Come eat with us?"

I looked at her "I'm not hungry."

She shrouded her shoulders "So what. Come down anyway. Let's mourn this like a family. Like we should." I understood and smiled weakly and took her hand.

As we made it the bottom of the stairs, Edwin decided to show up. He looked at my face and said "Princess are you crying?"

I was so angry at him. "You are a very poor guardian."

He got all high and mighty " You are a very poor Princess. Very ungrateful and disrespectful."

I walked away from him and he followed me into the kitchen. Elena was behind him with her hands up. He saw that Grandmother had also been crying.

"What is all this about?"

I looked at him with disgust and said "You didn't come when you were called. So why do you care now?"

Marcus put his hand up to me but I was not finished.

Max jumped up and pulled my out to the porch. "He probably didn't hear you."

I pulled away from Max and went to the front and sat in the swing. Max sat down on the swing with me. I then remembered to thank him for showing up

"Thank you Max. At least you come when I call." He looked at me "Why do you always hear me. Even in my dreams you hear me and that snake cant?"

He shook his head. "Maybe the mix blood or something. I don't know." He put his arm around me and said "Let Edwin off the hook. You are hurting and I think you are just looking for someone to be mad at." I looked at him, agreed, smiled and said "Ok."

That night I did dream. I dreamed of what happened that day. Every second. Every moved in my dance. The caressing of the breeze. And the shadow over Edith's body. And finally, my scream for Max. And without fail he was there waking me. "Max" He had me in his arms and I cried. "Max, will I ever just be able to sleep? You know like when we took off. I never dreamed."

He giggled "That's because you were exhausted everyday." He pet my hair. "You were in different places and different climates. There were all sorts of reasons." He kissed my head. "This time, you had something really bad happen to you. I think that's why you had a bad dream."

I nodded. "Just the same, can you stay? I don't want to dream anymore tonight. Max, I'm really afraid of my dreams."

He giggled said "You really want me severely punished don't you?"

I lifted my head "No. I don't. I just need to sleep. I need you to hold me so I can sleep." He laid down next to me and pulled me into him. His arms around me and then said "Only till you go back to sleep." I nodded being satisfied just being in his arms. I woke early in the morning and he was still there with me in his arms. When I woke again, he was gone.

That day I stayed home from school I went to the kitchen still in my PJ bottoms and tank. I poured some juice and when I turned around, Edwin was there.

He stood close to me and said "I apologized for not responding when I should have. I really wasn't sure I heard you but next time I will respond even if I doubt you called. OK? Truce?"

I nodded "Truce."

He grabbed me and hugged me with his face in my hair which was unsettling to me.

He step back and with narrow eyes said "Why do you smell like Max."

I closed my mind. I pulled my brows in "How do I know. Most likely because he hugged me yesterday when we found Edith." He looked at me suspiciously. "What are you insinuating Edwin?"

Mandra came in at that point "Yes what are insinuating Edwin?" When he turned to grandmother I waved my hand to have the bed fresh.

Edwin said "That is a very strong sent. Not fading from yesterday as would be expected." I narrowed my eyes at him "Edwin, if you have him punish without cause I will personally see that you suffer immensely."

Marcus came then I was sure at the call of Edwin. "What is the problem?"

I looked at Marcus "Edwin is being weird again."

Edwin stood erect and stated "Marcus I smell the sent of Max on the Princess. In addition she is threatening me again."

Marcus looked at me "Yes I threatened him" I looked back at Edwin "and I mean every word."

Marcus looked at Mandra. She said "Edwin feels that Em smells *too*strongly like Max from yesterday."

I looked at Marcus "I have not washed my hair yet today."

Marcus disappeared and then returned. "Edwin, Stop looking for trouble where it does not exist." Edwin nodded and left.

Marcus looked at me and smelled my hair. "It does smell strongly like Max."

I rolled my eyes. "Fine I will take a shower. God knows I wouldn't want to smell like Max."

I left the kitchen shaking and praying that no one finds out Max stayed with me last night. I couldn't bare it if he was punished following my stupid request. I ran up stairs to my room and grabbed my clothes and headed to the bathroom. I got in the shower and heard "Good thinking Em" From outside the curtain. I poked my head out and he was sitting on the commode.

I looked at him as if he was crazy "Get out of here!"

He looked at me "If you hadn't freshened the bed I would be in the halls."

I looked at him "Max go." He smiled and was gone.

Life went on and I was doing well in school. I was pretty much left alone since Max's pimple producing incident, but there were still the remarks and the stares. I think there may have been a few new kids but they were quickly informed of the Witch and to stay away or she would put a pimple on their nose. Then some numskull came up with date the Witch contest. And since I really did not waste my time in empty minds, I was uninformed.

There was this bet that the first guy that got me to go out with him, and have sex with him, would be the winner. All of the sudden guys were smiling at me. I started to become self conscious like there must be a hole in the butt of my pants or a bugger hanging out of my nose. Then Billy De Wit walked over sat on the grass with me during lunch. I stared at him as he said Hi.

He smiled at me "I know that you are a little freaked out an all. You know; because we. My friends and I don't talk to you. But I thought maybe you would be willing to go out for a coke after school with me?"

Aha, got it. All he had in his head with his little attempt to trick me, and then ooh, sex. When it was said that teen boys think of sex at least twice an hour, the scientists were being kind.

Staring at him with a little witch smile I asked "Now why would I do that?"

He looked a little more cautions. "I thought we could get to know each other and then it would be fun for you."

I looked at him and said "Fun?" he nodded. Just past him, I could see others looking from behind the fence like there were not watching. They were lining up to chance that I would say yes.

There was a motorcycle coming but it did not stop in the parking lot. It drove up on the lawn and right to me. Max once again to the rescue. Decked out in black leather and hair slicked back by tons of jell.

"What's going on?"

I smiled and said as I stood up "Oh, Billy here was just asking me out for a coke after school,"

Max looked over to Billy "Dude, did you ask my girl for a coke after school?"

Billy was a little nervous; Max was pretty big and about twenty years old. "I didn't know she had a boyfriend. I'm sorry." Billy got up and took off as fast as he could. I started to laugh.

"You know Max, I think I could have taken care of this one on my own"

Still with his silly smile said "Yeah but I couldn't help my self." We were laughing and we looked over at the others who were rethinking there little joke. The fence lined with disillusioned boys and the cheerleaders, including Lori.

I looked at him in triumph. But he had that look in his eyes "Come on, lets ride."

I change my look so he knew I thought he was crazy. "I have three more classes."

He tilted his head "Come on Em, be bold, be wild, and don't be a goody two shoes" I caught sight of the security officer with the huge belly running as fast as his belly would let him. He was coming straight for us. I thought about it for a moment, and grabbed my bag and jumped on. Max spun the rear wheel throwing up the grass. I screamed a big "Ooh Hoo" and the student body watched as the Witch, with her hair flying behind us like a tail, take off with the Biker.

We rode for a while and we stopped at the beach. The waves were crashing against the rocks. Star fish and barnacles were scattered over the gigantic rocks. We left the bike, I walked right out into the surf with my arms spread and tangled hair flying. I was surprised when Max joined me. The sea welcomed me with "The Princess." I blew a kiss in the wind.

I looked over to Max "I don't know how I will be treated when I get to school tomorrow." I smiled at him then and said "I know that the plan has been squashed."

He giggled "Guys like that always get it in the end."

I thought he had another meaning and looked at him. "Max?" He smiled and walked back to the sand. I ran to catch him "Max!"

He smiled and "What?"

I shoved him in the sand as we walked "Did you do something to those kids?"

He produce a mock shocked face "Em, What do you take me for? I don't hurt little innocent kids."

Then he got real serious "Ho oh."

I looked at him, my heart dropped and then with horror asked. "Ho oh what?"

He smiled sheepishly this time. "We are in trouble. We have to go to Mandra's. The message was *immediately.*"

I stopped and looked at him "Who?"

He grabbed my arm and turned and headed back to the motorcycle. "Mandra and Marcus." Marcus too, I was mortified.

Then I hit him on his arm "You always get me in trouble!"

He started laughing "No I don't."

I started to walk without him. I stopped, turned and looked straight into his eyes, "Max, all worst trouble I have ever gotten into was because of you."

He laughed. "No. You just didn't plan properly." I huffed and walked towards the bike.

He caught up and grabbed me around the waist and spun. I started to laugh and told him "Stop messing around. We have to get back."

He stopped and grabbed my shoulders. He look directly in too my eyes. "Lets not!"

I open my eyes wide and said "Lets not what?"

He got that look. "Let's not go back. Let's see the world and climb mountains and float down rivers. Let go to New Orleans. Let's live wild."

I laughed "Not again. I don't want to hurt grandmother."

He took my arm and said" I guess your right. But can you imagine being free. Doing all the normal stuff"

I reminded him "I failed my driver's license test. That is normal enough for me right now. But I do wish sometimes I could just have the normal stuff. You know. Make friends who didn't care about my mixed blood, grow up, finish school, get a job, and have a family of my own. I wish sometimes."

He looked at me seriously for a second and then smiled and said "but as a witch and a wizard, we can have way more fun. We really could do some wild things" I agreed. He then was serious again and said, "Do me a favor. Lock everyone out of your head but me, OK?" My eyebrows pulled in but I nodded.

We rode the bike in slowly to the house. On the porch waited Mandra and Marcus. I hit my head purposefully hard against Max's back.

"You owe me."

He giggled, "Most likely my whole life after this."

I got off the bike and looked over at grandmother. Her eyes that never gave to much expression caused me to consider my appearance. My hand went to my hair which was completely tingled. And I had wet sand on the legs of my pants. We walked up the porch and stood side by side.

Marcus waved up to the opposite chairs from him and Mandra. I looked at Max but got nothing.

Then I heard in my head *"Just be quiet"*.

We sat down. Mandra did not move from her regal posture. Marcus on the other hand leaned on his elbows and looked at us both in the eye.

"I am surprised at you both." He shook his head. "I could see average teenagers showing such disregard, but a perspective mastered wizard and witch, with so much to expose and put in danger, leaves this situation appalling."

I bowed my head and then I receive a transmission from Max *"Nice touch"*.

I sent back *"It was real. Have some shame."*

Mandra then said "Lincon went to the school to pay for the grass that was ruined. The estimate was about five hundred dollars." I looked at her and she continued "You, my dear, will work that off in the store. And Max, you will only see Em here at home. Don't go back to the school. Am I understood?

Max nodded "Yes Mam."

Marcus said "Max, I will expect more responsible behavior in the future. You are fortunate that his can be handled at a lower level and this does not reach the Elders."

He nodded and said "Yes sir."

He then said "I understand that you are supposed to be looking for the shadow. Have you had any success?"

Max looked very serious "No sir. There have been no sightings in since Edith." He took a breath and looked at me. "Em had only seen the shadow while at her fathers and in her dreams." Marcus said "Vary well."

Mandra then said "Dinner is being served. Both of you clean up. Em, comb out your hair."

Seventeen was my senior year in High School. As May approached and it was almost over, I was questioned repeatedly by the community about two things. What college I was going to and who was I going to the Prom with. I had canned answers, I am going to Cal State

Sacramento and I am not going to the Prom. Every time I said that Mandra would slip in her reserve. Prom was only a week away.

She said "You'll be sorry if you don't go to the prom."

I looked at her "Grandmother, no one is going to ask me and I am not going alone." Elena was home and she said "I could find someone if you really want to go.?"

I looked at her "Aunt Elena, I am not going to go to the prom with some mercy date. I am not going. I am the witch of the school and not one boy there would dare walk into that prom with me."

I got up from the table and walked out to the cliff rail. I looked over at the ocean. I never could get anyone to understand I can't be a normal or an immortal. I am mixed and I have to live that way. And that way means that I am not going to have the perks of Normal. Prom included.

Mandra was real careful about the Prom thing over the next week I guess she could read that it did hurt in a way not to go. It just reminded me how different I really am. At school, the week was really long and all conversation was about Prom; Posters and signs announcing the Prom and where to get the tickets. The minds were on who is going with whom and who would spike the punch. It did really bother me. I wanted to go, but I knew the reality of it was not in my future. Who would want to go with the witch of the school?

The day of the prom came and I stayed by the cliff rail. I really did feel bad about the prom but did not want grandmother and Elena finding me a mercy date either. I had some pride. Elena came out of the house and walked over to me.

She said "Em. Marcus is here. He would like you to come in."

I looked at her and nodded and walked with her holding hands. As we went in the house Marcus was in the Parlor. I walked over to him and hugged him "Hi".

He looked at me and asked "Why are you so low today?"

I looked up at him "Oh it's nothing just another being mix blood thing."

He smiled "Is that all. How cane I help?"

I laughed softly "You already have by being here." He looked mischievous, but I let it go.

Mandra came in and handed Marcus a glass of tea. She looked over at me and said, "For some one who doesn't want to go to the Prom you have such a frown."

I did not want to talk about it in front of Marcus. "Grandmother, Please. Not in front of Marcus."

She smiled slightly. "Go clean up for dinner Em. It will help improve your mood." I could not believe I would have dress for dinner on this today. I did not even want dinner.

I went up stairs and waked over to my room. I looked to the bed for Zee, and there, lying across the bed was a sleek red Prom dress. On the chest red sandaled heals. I walked closer, gently picked up the strap of the dress and wondered what were they thinking.

"They thought you and I could cause trouble at the Prom." I turned and Max stood handsome in his tux, He held a lily. He looked at me like I might back out. "I will tell you, should you turn me down, I will pester you with out mercy for eternity."

I ran and hugged him. "You cad. How are you"

He smiled and said. "I will do better once someone else is dressed as funny as me. So hurry up."

I smiled. "I know that you were ordered to do this, and if you really don't want to go, I'll understand."

He turned on his charm, "I am honored to escort you My Lady. Now hurry up and get dressed so that your grandmother can take her pictures."

Elena came in and pushed Max out. She closed the door and said "It was his Idea."

I looked at her with eyebrows together. "I bet it was Marcus." She handed me the dress and help me put it over my head.

"No. I heard Marcus say that the Elders don't know and that Max insisted."

I was confused. "Why would the elders care? It is only a High School Prom not an exorcism? Well maybe it is." We laughed at that.

"No one expects me there. But I think with wicked Max, no one will mess with us"

Elena looked at me curious "Wicked Max? Who there knows Max? I had to giggle first "Well Lori does." I told her the pimple story.

I though she would stop breathing from laughing so hard. "What else?" Well the guys were trying to play a trick on me. Remember the Notorious Motorcycle incident? She nodded and she rolled her eyes. I explained the intensions of the guys at school.

"Well the next day, I was at my locker and I noticed all the guys in my class waking funny. And they were all staring at me with looks like I had done something to them. I over heard these girls saying that there was an out break of Jock itch and it was scorching."

Elena laughed breathless again. "You think Max did that."

I was laughing with her "I have no doubt Max was the outbreak."

Elena stood and looked at me, "What to do with all that hair" I looked in the mirror and my hair was on my head with ringlets and little crystals scattered through it. My make up light but dramatic with the glider that flared to each side of my eyes. I turned around and Elena said "You are gorgeous" I smiled. "Thanks" she opened the door, "Let's go"

I walked into the Parlor where my Grandmother, Marcus and Max were waiting. Mandra grabbed her camera, and made me feel silly. Then she had to remind my how I resisted dresses and skirts and now look at me. "OK grandmother, there is no need to bring up the past" She then maneuvered Max over and posed us in the usual Prom date pose. Marcus was giving her lighting ideas and she was snapping away. I elbowed Max, and he piped in and said "We have to go now." I turned quickly and wave goodbye. Mandra kept snapping her camera. Molly and Lincon stood with Elena, all smiling watching us as we left. We walked out and there was a limo waiting. Wanting nothing more than to get away from Mandra and Marcus, we got in as fast as possible.

Once in and the doors shut, I said "There very proud of themselves and there little scheme."

He smiled and said "There just excited."

I laughed "Mandra really wanted me to go and I guess that's how you got tapped. But if you want we could blow it off and do something else.. Maybe a new club or something?" He looked shocked "Em. I want to go. I asked to take you."

I looked at him not really understanding "Why?"

He grabbed the champagne and poured a glass and I repeated "Why, Max?" He drank his champagne and handed me a glass. "For a couple of reasons; first you should know that if I haven't gone to a prom before. My school had dances but I just didn't go to them as a mixed blood." He nudge my side, "Second and I needed an excuse to cause some trouble with you. Third …" He sighed "I could let you go with anyone else. When I caught a transmission between Mandra and Marcus discussing how you were going to miss something memorable, it bothered me. I interrupted and begged them to let me take you. After I got chewed out for being nosy, Mandra said it was a wonderful idea. M… Marcus almost chose Edwin because I was being overbearing again. But Mandra told him how you and your aunt think that Edwin is "Icky". It took some fast talking and" he cleared his throat "begging, one less Please Sir, and you would be here with Edwin."

I immediately said "Oh no. I would not."

I smiled at him and he became self conscious. "What? Go ahead make feel stupid before the dance."

I kissed his cheek. "You are my best friend in the world, Max." I had to add "well, you're my only friend…." And I added "but I wouldn't change that for anything."

The car door opened and we go out at the Town Auditorium. There was several couples entering the grand walkway to the entrance. Small lights had the entrance laminated. The there was a artistic sign over the door that read "Welcome to Enchantment." I stood at the beginning of the walkway and Max put out his arm for me to take. I was having second thoughts and thought about leaving.

"Oh no you don't. I put on this Tux for a reason. Now buck up and let's dazzle them." He smiled and he did dazzle for a second. Sparkles were flashing off him everywhere. I looked around to see if there was anyone looking.

"Stop it."

He smiled and said "Then take my arm." I did and we walked down the long entrance.

At the door, a man asked for the tickets. Max pulled the tickets out of his tux. We were escorted to a table that was for eight. I knew I was going to be uncomfortable. Another couple was lead to our table. They smiled and said hello. They had no Idea who I was. Max seemed to be thinking of what way he could play with this innocent couple.

I sent him a message *"Leave them alone."*

He sent back *"Thinking is not doing."*

Soon, two more couples were at our table and though they knew each other, they did not recognize me.

I started to suspect something and sent a transmission to Max interrupting his conversation with Aaron Storey.

"What have you done? Why don't any of these people recognize me?"

He waited for a lull in his conversation to return *"I haven't done anything."*

I was pulled into conversation with the couple next to me. Jenny Brawly and Ned Turner asked if we had to go through the parents taking picture scene. I smiled and nodded. They then told me their tale of the mother holding the lamp just so and the father with the movie camera while they left. They wee laughing because her parents tried to follow them out the door but the lamp cord was too short. I laughed at the story with them. Jenny then said "Who did your hair, I love the crystals." I lied "My Aunt, She is very talented with hair."

Dinner was served but no one ate the dried chicken breast and I think everyone was too excited. Jenny then became kind of uncomfortable when she looks towards the entrance. "Well there she is. We can only hope Billy keeps her occupied."

I looked over and there was Lori in her baby pink dress. It looked like a negligee. Her nipples were visible through the fabric. I smiled and looked at Max who had a devil smile on. He looked at me and in unison we said "Nasty!" The table erupted into laughter. Mia and Randy, the third couple at the table were nodding their heads and the fourth couple Connie and Josh, covered their mouths in laughter.

The girls at the table talked about how Lori would be trying to take over a college like she did high school. They talked about all the mean things that she had done to them and others. Then they talked about the pretty girl who was ostracized by her rumor that she was a witch. My face must have given everything away.

Jenny looked at me and said "Oh my God that's who you are." I could only nod. "You look so beautiful tonight I did not recognize you."

Max had my hand and squeezed it. Mia then said "Emily isn't it" I nodded again.

She then asked "well is it true? Are you a witch or a Lori Victim?"

Before I could answer Max was giggling "Her Dads a bible thumping Baptist Preacher." The table laughed again and then Mia said "Well I rather be a witch than that Bitch. You should have let people know Emily. Then she would have ousted for the liar she is." Then Max told the story of her pimple, of course, without the fact that he put it there. I think that made Mia and Jenny night.

I then told them "She thinks I put it there for flirting with Max."

Jenny said "Just let her keep thinking that Emily. She deserved it." Then the music started.

Max was the first guy up. He put out his hand "Will you dance with me Princess?" I smiled and put my hand in his. The girls at the table made an Ahh sound and we walked to the dance floor. I don't think I was prepared to be held so close to him because I lost my breath for a second.

"It isn't the maiden dance is it?"

I laughed and said "I think you are obsessed with the maidens dance and I think that would not be permitted here anymore than the Wizard Center" We danced and danced and I closed my eyes and when I did I found that it was only me and Max there dancing. Not reality but a little fantasy while we danced. I opened my eyes and he smiled down at me and I knew he was mind dropping.

"Max, is there anybody whose head you don't intrude upon?"

He was honest "Nope."

It was then that Lori recognized Max. She slithered over like her mother does.

"Hello Max."

Max kept his eyes on mine but I could see the devil emerging. He was just waiting to do something. Of course I was pleading with him not to.

He looked over to her and asked "Not dancing?"

In that stupid little girl pouty voice she said "I was hoping you would ask me to dance." He looked back at me and said "I'm already dancing."

She looked over at me and her eyes got really big and then narrowed. She huffed and returned to her entourage.

When we returned to the table, Aaron looked at Max and put out his hand. "I like to shake the hand of the Mastered Wizard." Max took his hand and looked at me with a devilish smile.

He looked at Aaron and asked "I don't understand."

Aaron and the table then laughed and said "Lori came by and told us that you were a Mastered Wizard. She said that we should have you show us some magic." Max laughed with the table while I was mortified.

He then said nodding "A Mastered Wizard in training."

After the laugh was winding down, Josh asked Max "So we know you aren't a student here, your older and well what do you do?"

Max put on his best big boy responsible man personality and reported that he was a student at Stanford. He was studying History and religions. And he would graduate with his masters at the end of the year.

Then he said "Along with Wizard training, I pretty busy." It was all true but the normals took the latter as a pun.

It wasn't long before Lori made her way over to our table trailed by Billy and another couple. "Hey Max, why don't you show everyone some magic, I bet the Prom will be the most legendary."

The other couple and Lori stood very close to one another because of the tables and chairs. "Lori, that's your name isn't. I knew we had met before." Max was planning something. Max put his arm around me and moved closer to me. I was begging Max not to do anything. The table was quiet, and listen to the banter.

"You know who I am Max!"

Max raised his palm and said "I think I said I remembered you. " He smiled and then said "I see you got rid of the pimple." The table was unable to hold back the snickers.

Lori was livid. "Why did you and that witch come here tonight when no one wants her here?"

He laughed at that, "I not so sure it's Em not wanted here, you should check yourself."

I knew he was not finished. He had been holding back and on his best behavior for too long. "And Lori, I have to ask, why would you ware your nightgown to the Prom?" She was mortified at his description of her dress that I am sure she spent weeks looking for. But before she could say a word, the glass of punch that the girl next to her had been holding ended up 'Spilling" on the bodice of her dress. The fabric became translucent completely exposing her breasts. Lori screamed and ran with her arms across her front. Billy and the other's trailing. The table was in a uproar as was the whole auditorium. I only stared at him.

Then I said out loud "Max you know she will blame me."

Aaron then said "Its OK Emily. Nothing could have been better than that. Whether you did it or not, that is what's going to put this Prom on the books."

The music started again and Max and I of course were on the dance floor. I just kept smiling at Max.

He looked self conscious again "OK what?"

I pulled his head down and kiss his cheek again and with out moving away I said "Thanks for a great Prom Night."

He picked me up in a big hug and twirled me around.

He put me down, and smiling he said "It has been my greatest honor, my lady." One last visit to the table and we said good night.

In the car on the way back home, Max and I did not talk for a while. I leaned against him with his arm around me I had my eyes closed reliving in the nights events. The free time we shared being normal people doing normal things.

He kissed my forehead "Get out of my head Max."

He giggled "But I love the thoughts that run through your head." He sighed "It was nice wasn't it. Almost like we were.....Normal." I made a hum sound.

Max then said "I wonder how it would be to be normal all the time. I would love a day that I don't have to listen to someone else. Follow my own instructions and expectations." He took a deep breath.

I said "Maybe when you are through with school."

He shook his head. "No. I still will have to follow the instructions of the Elders. I just don't know what they will expect. I can't see my self going my whole existence never being my own person. Like tonight."

I smiled "Are you your own person when we go out?"

He smiled and nodded "But I have to trick everyone on those little outings with you. I just want to wake up one day and say 'I wonder what the Princess would like to do today' and pick you up and go do it without hiding or asking someone." I thought about that myself. "You are right.

It would be something to be the ones in charge of our own lives. Then we could really have fun. We could also do some good things too." I looked up at him and he was smiling.

"Let's just do it. Let's go."

I laughed at him. "Max you are too funny."

We got out of the car and the limo left. We walked up on the porch and Max grabbed my arm and said "Oh oh."

I cringed inside "What?"

He looked at me and said "Edwin! Close your mind to everyone but me"

Max put me in a hug and the next thing I knew we were sitting on the couch; I was dressed in my pajama bottoms and a tank. He was in jeans and a T-shirt. We were sharing a bowl of popcorn and watching a old black and white movie.

"Hello, Em" Edwin was there on the other side of me. "Max."

I looked over at him and said "Hi Edwin, Why are you her so late?"

He looked at me trying to see what was inside of my head but unable to. He looked at Max, "Why are you here Max?"

Max pretended to have to pry his attention from the TV, "Marcus and I were invited to dinner."

Edwin then asked "Well I see you but I don't see Marcus"

Then Marcus's voice came from behind "I am behind you and you are in my seat." Edwin jumped off the couch and face Marcus. "I'm sorry sir." Marcus walked over and sat down next to me where Edwin had been.

"You are visiting late aren't you Edwin. I would think you would have done a check earlier."

He was nervous then and said "Yes Sir, I thought Em might have been at the Prom and I was Checking to see if she had made it home."

Marcus looked board and said "She has been here with us all night."

Edwin looked bewildered and said "Very good then Sir. I will be on my way. Good night, Em," He was gone.

"What a slimy pest." is all I could say. In my mind, I though he ruined the ending of a perfect evening.

Max said "He did put a damper on things."

Marcus looked stern at Max. "Propriety Max. And I am having an ethical issue." Max and I looked at each other and then over to Marcus. "Max, you and Em seem to have had practice at deception. But the skill displayed with Edwin tonight was Amazing." Max and I looked at each other and giggled. Marcus looked at us knowingly.

Over the next year Max I had a lot of time together. He showed up about every other weekend to take me to a party with him or dance at the newest clubs in LA. No one ever being the wiser that I was not at home, or so I thought. On one occasion, he showed up in the widow's tower where I was reading.

"What are you doing?"

I looked up then back to the book. "Reading."

He leaded against the window edge and said "Well I can see that every time I leave you for too long you fall back into that dull goody two shoes."

I looked up at him with a scowl. "Why do you think I only have fun with you?"

He put on his smart-alecky grin "Because I am the only one that takes you dancing." I smiled because it was true.

I lowered my book and smiled into his eyes. "And?"

He looked out the window "There's a new club opening tonight in Boston I thought you might like to go." He looked back at me and my book "But if you're too busy with your book…"

I jumped up as he disappeared. "Max…. How could you be such a tease?"

I heard him call back, Eight O'clock; activate number 2." Number 2 appeared in the chair reading a book. I giggled "Smart ass."

After dinner with Mandra, I said "I think I will go to my room and read. Good night grandmother."

Mandra giggled "Don't stay out too late with that Rouge Max."

I stopped and looked at her "Grandmother! You knew."

She looked up from her embroidery and said "I have known for quite a while. She is not really like you but she does throw off Edwin. That part I like." I giggled. She then said "If Edwin and the Masters find out, Max will be in hot water. He will suffer for it."

I sat next to her and kissed her "I sorry grandmother I lied to you. But we didn't want anyone to know. And if it weren't for Max, I never would have been out at all. No life at all."

She smiled "Why do you think I have allowed it. Now go before Edwin shows up on one of those fake checks of his. " I kissed her and ran up the stairs.

Waved my hand and was dressed in the latest club apparel, Red and glittery. My dress was short and backless and I had the shoes and bag to match. My hair was up in a pony tail that hung to my middle back showing glimpses of my bare back. I conjured the perfect make up and perfect red lipstick to match.

I was looking into the mirror and I smelled Edwin. I closed my mind immediately. I turned around and there he was. "What are you doing in my room?"

He smiled that slimy smile of his. "Wow going somewhere?"

I looked at him with a board expression. "I am going to a formal orientation when I get to Sacramento and I am trying on my dress. Why?"

He started to move in my direction. I put up my hand. He stopped; he smiled "why do you assume my intentions Princess?"

I rolled my eyes "Maybe because of the way you talk about how wonderful you are as a Pure Blood. Now get out of my room."

He stood there and looked at me thinking and trying to get in my head. " I waved my hand and was dressed for bed in PJ Bottoms and a Tank. I Looked at him and said "I am going to bed. Now get out of my room or I will call Marcus."

He only smiled and did not leave. He continued to stare. Then he began to move closer. And closer and reached for me. I stepped back and I called out to Marcus. And Max appeared.

Edwin was seething. In a loud voice he demanded "Why did you come. Who called you?" Max walked over to Edwin and I thought there would be blood.

Max returned with the same strength of voice "She told you to get out of her room. Since when do you ignore her orders?"

Edwin sneered and said "It's none of your business mix blood. You are not her guardian any longer."

Max replied "I have not been released from my vow to protect her. And you are her immediate danger."

Marcus and Mandra came running in "Max and Edwin. You are both out of order. Edwin this episode will be reported to the Elders. You are not to cause Em any discomfort or concern. What were you thinking?"

He nodded and then left Max's glare to face Marcus. "I apologize for my behavior. He looked at me "I apologize Em." and he was gone.

Marcus then looked to Max. "You have honor and showed that tonight. Thank you Max, you may go." Max nodded and was gone.

Marcus looked at me "Thank you for your patients and not retaliating with Edwin this time Princess. Thank you for allowing us Wizards to handle the situation."

Grandmother looked to Marcus "I want Edwin band from entering Ems room." Marcus nodded.

I went over and hugged Marcus. "I am sorry my true guardian. I told you I am trouble." He lifted my chin, "I would never choose it any other way Princess." He kissed my forehead. He went out the door and grandmother looked back at me with a wink.

I sat on my bed and figured that ruined my outing and then Max came back.

"You're not ready!"

I jumped up. "Where's Edwin?"

He smiled and said "He in his room practicing his excuse. He has decided that you had enticed him and then changed your mind." I gave a barfing sound. Max giggled and then said "I think he will keep trying."

I looked at Max seriously then. I really detested Edwin. Then I smiled and said "but not tonight." I snapped my fingers and was dressed again in the red dress.

Max pulled in his brows and said "Now I see why he didn't want to leave the room."

I waved my hand and down came Number 2, in a decent night gown and we watched as she got into bed. I turned to Max and he waved his hand and my hair was lose and draped over my right shoulder. "Yep. I know how you should ware your hair. Always free." I rolled my eyes and said "Let's go." He smiled and grabbed and we were gone.

When I was ending my eighteenth year, I had a house in Sacramento, where I lived as student of California University of California. I also had a job working as a day care Teacher. No one knew me there and I loved the fact. I had no friends but I was used to that. It was safer for all involved. I did feel sorry for my self because I would see so many girls at school and in the city with boyfriends or boys. I wanted a life mate, but normal's did not take to me well. It would be torturing another man like my father has been.

Max and I rarely went out since my move. He was busy as a Wizard somewhere and he was working as a substitute teacher. We did have fun when he did show up. But Edwin remained a pest and was pushy. He seemed to be showing up with all kinds of excuses. I saw your cat outside. I was looking for Marcus etc.

On morning, I came into my kitchen to make coffee. I was still in my night gown and had not washed the sleep from my face. As I turned from the counter and coffee maker, Edwin was standing in front of me. Standing very close; too close. He was blocking my escape to the other room.

"Get out of my way."

He looked at me funny and said "Princess, I was checking on you."

I looked irritated "You are checking too close. Let me by or I will call Marcus."

He stood his ground, and moved closer and grabbed my hair immobilizing my head and came close to my face. His pushed his body against mine. Because I was not going to wait for his intension to manifest any further, I called out in voice "Marcus!" And then screamed "Max!"

Edwin became angry pulling my head with my hair "How dare you witch. Why would you call that Mutt Wizard?"

From behind him came "Because I come when she calls and don't bother her when she doesn't."

Edwin released my hair and turned around and Max was about to hit him but Marcus appeared between them.

Marcus looked at Max and said "Thank you Max and next time remember yourself." Max looked at me and nodded and was gone.

Marcus turned to Edwin "What are you thinking? How can you excuse yourself for this behavior with the princess?"

Edwin said "I was out of line. I am attracted to the Princess. It will never happen again." Marcus said "Go now Edwin." Edwin left.

I hugged Marcus and said "He is such a pest."

Marcus giggled and said "He is your guardian. So be patient with him. He will be more careful once this is reported. Once again Princess, thank you for your patients in not retaliating." Marcus kissed my head and was gone.

Max came back and I hugged him. "Thank you, Max. I know I'm a pain to protect."

He giggled "No, you just don't take precautions."

He moved me back and held my shoulders. He looked at me, "Use a protection barrier over the house and keep him out." He spent that morning helping me prefect the protection barrier.

Since leaving Dad's, Aunt Della married Doc and she moved to Redding with him. Tina left Dad and Tom would not leave with her and Dad kept him. Each time I have spoken to Dad, he sounded happy and always says I was not the reason for the break up of his marriage. I don't know how I could have been since I never went back to the house. Tom told me that he was enjoying his last year in high school. He stated that he didn't mind driving to Fall River and that he was sure he was going to Chico State. He stated that he was thinking of Law Enforcement. I laughed because of the espionage we had played at as kids.

I loved school. I felt that college was a better learning environment than High School. I was happy with my classes and felt supported by the college in succeeding. I loved Sociology and felt that the more I learned, the more I would understand all social worlds. Even the three worlds in which I lived.

 Chapter 26

The summer solstice of my nineteenth year, was a turning point in my life. I was just as excited about the Solstice as always. This year though, I dressed in the priestess dress given to me by my grandmother. It was a short bodice with thin hemp straps. It had fringed hemp skirt fitting tight to my hips dipping in a V. The skirt was cut so that the right side was at my calf and the left side above the knee. The bodice and the skirt left my midriff bare. My mask now was only a half mask that covered from my eyes up. It curved to a crown like head piece with an arch of a half sun with beams shooting off of it. I had flowers and herbs dangling from the skirt, hair and off the bodice. Hemp with herbs tied to my wrist and ankles. My hair, held back only by the mask. I looked in the mirror, and I was taken back. I looked like something midlevel. Not a woman of today. I was feminine and feline at the same time. I felt something strange in that get up. I felt magic; I felt powerful. I knew something was about to happen and this outfit wasn't helping; it was inspiring. Magic was conjuring without solicitation. Inspired the Forest Priestess.

Aunt Elena walked in at that point. She stopped in mid stride and stared. She said "Maybe I am crazy, but you look so ancient. Kind of mystical; Beautiful but deadly." Her outfit was similar but there was something about mine. "You have a similar outfit, why would I look different." And though I played it off as her thought, I agreed with her. I could not name it. "Ready?" I looked out the window and the sun was almost down. I smile at Elena, "Ready." We walked down the stairs to be met by Joe, Elena's boyfriend. He wore a ring of flowers on his head. It brought a smile to us both. He was a normal, but willing to deal for Elena. I was jealous for my self but happy for her.

We walked out on the porch and took our places with grandmother to great the guests. The arbors were up and ready for the dancing. Both bond fires, one large and one small, were ready. We greeted everyone as they came in. I was pleased to see all the old faces. Then Deana came us the procession. My stomach jumped. Grandmother only greeted her shortly and I only nodded looking away from her eyes. She waked off in a huff. Elena giggled "She gets so hurt when she can get in your head." I smiled and agreed. Just as the last were through the precession, Marcus, Leonardo and William arrived.

I left the porch and launched into Marcus's embrace. "Oh My Princess, you look very royal tonight."

I giggled and said "I am so happy to see you." I looked over at the other Elder Wizards and said "Hello it is so nice to see you again." They gave their greeting and we started to walk to the porch to greet my grandmother. I could see she was happy to see Marcus.

Before making it to the porch with the Elder Wizards I heard, "Em?" I turned around and there was Max and Edwin.

"Max!" I ran over and hugged him. "I hoping you would be here earlier. I haven't seen you in so long. I hope you are ready to dance." He stood there without moving or speaking. Curtly I said "Edwin how are you?" Even though he irritated me, Edwin was more animated than Max, and he ignored Max non response that I, at first did not catch. Edwin commented "Em you look…. You look beautiful. Magical"

I smiled "Thanks" He went on talking and I took both their arms and walked to the porch.

Max was able to greet my grandmother and my aunt. That meeting, He was the most pleasant and mannered then any other guy I have ever seen. I stood watching him not understanding where his usual smile was. He was so serious; strangely serious. Not the normal Wizard serious and not the normal Max serious. The music started and Elena grabbed my hand and we went to dance. We danced and laughed. We twirled and jumped. Laughing and singing.

I looked back at where we left Joe and he was sitting with Edwin and Max. Edwin and Joe were in conversation and Max was staring at me. It made me feel funny but I continued to dance and laugh with Elena. I danced and danced. Jumping dipping and twirling. The power I felt that night, the magic. Something was building inside of me. I felt the spell of the Priestess. I liked it. It felt like freedom.

We stopped for a while to rest and wait for the maiden dance. We went to the table were Joe, Edwin and Max sat. They were drinking. Elena asked them what they were drinking. Joe said " I am told it is mead, a fermented honey."

Elena asked with a twisted face. "Do you guys like that?"

Joe said "It's not the wine we had last night, but I could get used to it." She shook her head. I looked at Max and Edwin and they seemed to like it. I reached out to Max's glass which he was still holding. "Can I taste it?" He looked for Mandra and Marcus. When he saw they were occupied with the Elders. he nodded his head and released the glass. Edwin acted as if he disapproved. I tasted the mixture and I thought I drank turpentine. "Ugh" is all I could say while my mouth, throat and stomach protested the toxic mixture. My face must have pinched but thanks for the mask, most was hidden. "That is nasty. How could you drink that?" The table was in laughter at my reaction. I handed Max his glass back and got up to get something else to drink.

He grabbed my hand and asked "Are you leaving?"

I smiled and said "You have to do more than laugh to get rid of me. I am going to find something else to drink."

He stood up and offered "No I'll go you sit down." I sat back down and was taken back by Max's gesture. Then I realized, he was finally talking and not staring.

He returned with a glass of punch. I was so disappointed.

I giggled "You know Max, I am not eleven anymore. I live alone and have a life as an adult. I can even Vote. I was hoping for an *Adult*Beverage."

He smirked "Taste it, it's spiked."

I took a drink and that same burn assaulted my senses. Once again my body reacted to the mixture. After the initial assault, my body gave a shiver. The table exploded in laughter.

I had to join them. "I think you spiked it with nail polish remover."

Still laughing, Max said "No, just vodka." Though the drink was strong, I found that if I only sipped it, it was ok. We sat at the table enjoying our selves for some time. Elena and Joe making a lot of the conversation an telling of parties they were recently at. Max talked about some of the clubs we had gone to but left out the fact that he took me with him.

Lincon came by and looked at my drink that was now about gone. He looked at the group and picked it up my cup and smelled it. His head shot up and he glared at all of us at the table. He staunchly walked away with the glass. I looked at Elena and we burst into laughter.

I looked over at Max "OHH your in trouble Guardian."

He was laughing as hard as the rest of us. "When I am around you, Princess, that is nothing new."

The maiden dance was about to start and the music was cueing the dancers. "Come on Em, lets go." Elena grabbed my hand and we went on to start the dance of the night.

"Almost Mid night girls" Millie warned. But my aunt and I were ready. We looked back at the table and saw Mandra and Marcus discussing something with Edwin and Max. We looked at each other, knowing it was about my drinking, and laughed unmercifully at their lecture. Max sent a *"Yeah, Ha ha ha."* I was glad I drank. I felt free and wild. Untamed, and dangerous as the priestess.

"OK girls lets start." Elena and I, along with a dozen other girls thirteen and older, began the twirling and leaping. Then jumping, and kneeling. I felt so wonderful; so beautiful, so free, and powerful. Something was being conjured in that dance. I felt it so strong and I liked what ever was happening to me. I liked the spell that was developing. I like this feeling of total beauty and power.

Elena and I moved closer together as we positioned our selves to claim our males to dance with. I saw Lori eyeing Max. I knew he would never dance with her though. It has always been an unspoken standing arrangement that Max would dance with me. The drum began to signal the mate find. Elena and I were off. Joe, Max and Edwin were standing. Neither of us ran wild as the others did to there intended mates for the dance. Elena went further than I, but Joe had no choice.

Calling Max with my eyes, I rolled out my arm and hand to Max. With his most charming smile, responded as expected and walked over and took my hand. Lori, made a face, and had to dance with Edwin who looked confused. I don't know what their problem was. Edwin was a really good looking guy; you would think Lori would like that.

Max and I twirled in each others arms and laughed. Max yelled out to me over the drum "Let's go last this time." I smile and nodded thinking he had another wicked Max plan. But it ended up my own plan. My own plan that changed my world and my life. Once every couple had jump the fire Max and I, holding hands, made a running leap over the fire.

As we landed Max picked me up and twirled me around and the crowd cheered and clapped for the last of the couples over the fire. Max had lifted me up and my hands were on his shoulders. I slid down his body only to be met with his eyes. Eyes that called me while he held me close. I kissed him. I boldly and intensely kissed him. And he kissed back. When the kiss ended, we were still looking at each other and never notice the hush over the crowd. Still in his arms and still looking in each others eyes, I heard my name 'Em!" I did not want to end that moment, but turned my head to see all eyes on us. Marcus and Grandmother were walking over to us. From the look in their eyes, I realized that I had done something wrong. I looked back at Max in a panic and I backed away from him. He looked confused at my moving away, his arms following my body as I left his embrace. "I'm sorry Max" Click.

In the widow's tower, I heard the crowd clamoring. They all acted as if no one has ever kissed before. Well maybe there clamoring because they've never seen someone transport before. I was still not breathing normal and stood at the window looking over the ocean. My head was against the window and my breath created condensation on the pane. Out loud I said "Oh my God, now what have I done…. that I don't know that I've done."

"You didn't do anything, Princess."

Max was behind me. I picked my head up straight and stared out the Ocean. Mortified at my pushy behavior towards him, but more mortified at the behavior of the crowd. "Obviously I did. Did you see the reaction? You can't tell me that is normal." He just stood behind me. "I can't be normal and I can't be immortal. One way or another, I am screwing up the worlds." Then I thought of Max. I am sure that he would be punished for my behavior. But I did not regret it. I loved that kiss. I turned just a little but did not look in his eyes again. "I'm sorry Max. I am sure you will have to pay something for this…. even though it was my doing."

He gave a huffed "My lady…" His voiced changed to husky and low. "I am willing to pay any price for that kiss."

That did it and my tears started. Not wanting him to see me cry. I kept quiet and kept my back to him. Though I knew my voice was nothing more than whisper, I said "me too."

He came closer, and from behind he removed my mask. From the reflection of the window he looked into my eyes. If I did not sense the intrusion I would have turned around and kissed him again. Marcus calm voice came up from my room. "Emily Star, Max, come down now." I turned around and faced him, and his finger traced the tail of my tears down my cheek. He looked worried and blocked my intrusion to his head. I thought that was a good Idea and followed suit for *everyone*. He took my hand and led the way down the stairs.

We were met with not only Marcus and Mandra, but also with Leonardo and William. Leonardo wave with his hand to us "Come children, sit down and listen." We walked over to the other side of the room that he indicated. We sat on the bed as ordered. They were all standing and then Mandra waved her hand producing chairs and they all sat

In a calm voice with his Italian accent Leonardo continued as he looked from me to Max. "The kiss was most beautiful. Given willingly by the most beautiful maiden; Accepted by the male. The pagans believed that once a couple jump the fire and kissed, they were bound to each other forever. However, we are convinced that is not the case now. We believe the kiss was innocent and with out meaning. And some of the elements of the ritual were missing." He looked at Max "But, as you know Max …the Princess is not for you. And there is an expectation of a Guardian or Master Wizard. Sexual attraction and display is not appropriate for a Master Wizard." He then looked over to me. "You cherished one; have yet to find your path. A path that is yours alone. One that only you can find." He smiled and went on "In years to come, as you both grow into your true selves, you will find that part of your life. You will have both your true beings, and loved ones. Much will happen between now and then. Happiness and heartache, but at the end of the path is the sun on the horizon." He then looked over to William and they got up to leave. Leonardo patted both Max and I on the cheek. William nodded his head to us and they went back to the festival.

When the door shut, I knew that Mandra and Marcus would have a whole lot more to say. And to tell the truth, I really did not want to hear it.

"Well transporting in front of practically the whole town was not a good idea Em." I looked at my grandmother and was sorry for that.

"I know grandmother. I did it before I thought of the consequences. I apologize."

"Oh Em, what were you thinking?"

I looked at her "Grandmother, I wanted to kiss Max. It wasn't planed or anything. I just did it."

I looked at Marcus "He did not do anything wrong."

Max squeezed my hand. Marcus looked at me and then Max "Max knows the rules and he will be facing the consequences. Unfortunately, part of those consequences is not seeing you again."

I looked at Marcus as if he cut out my heart. I Looked at Max and he nodded. "Don't do that Marcus. Max has been my friend; My only friend."

Marcus then said "You heard the elders, He must follow their instructions. He can not follow his path while he thinks of you. You can not follow your path while thinking of him."

I looked at Max, he said "Goodbye Princess. Remember what I said." They were gone.

I looked over to Mandra "This is wrong. This can't be happening." Mandra sat quite. "I need Max. I have always needed Max. He was always the one who came when I called. How can I live knowing he is not there?"

Mandra quietly said, "You just live. You find your path."

I let the tears flow. "I hurt him and I never meant to. I have always loved Max. Now I cant tell him."

Grandmother said "He knows you do Em. He has always known." I laid down on my pillow and stared at the stars in the sky.

After a few minutes, she asked "Are you coming back to the solstice?" I looked at her and shook my head. She stood waved her hand and the chairs were gone. She walk to the door and said "I do know how you feel. I hope in my heart, that you will do your best to handle this well." She left and closed the door.

I got up and locked my door. I did not want more visitors. I put on my night gown and put a soundproofing around my room so that I did not here the mob outside my window. I told the light out and laid on my side in my bed. Then I saw his arm come around me. The other above me head and I grabbed the one hand in front of me.

I cried and said "I am so sorry Max." I felt him move closer and felt his chest to my back. I felt His breath in my hair. I shivered. "Wont they know your here with me?" He whispered "No". We laid there for a while not saying anything. He held me close and I held on to his hand attempting to keep him there as long as I could. After a long time of just laying there with each other, Max spoke very softly and close to my ear.

"You have to understand what is expected. You mean a great deal to your kind and mine. Your powers, and who and what you are; Powerful witch to yours, Princess to mine. I have been told I am not worthy of you and I agree. I am not your future. I am a Mixed Blood Wizard and no better than a servant. You are destined to greater things. You're special. You are above me."

With a little sob, I turned around in his arms and said "The only real rules I know are in my heart. No one has given any rules about anything. I don't see the difference between Mix Blood and Pure Blood. How can I. I don't know anything about this princess crap. I don't care about it either." I looked deep into his eyes then "I chose you to love, I believe that makes you worthy."

Max kissed me with passion and love. He and I made love without any hindrance for hours; touching, kissing, exploring. His naked body moved over mine. My night gown now gathered at my waist.

At the end, he looked into my eyes, and said "Remember, Any price."

He kissed me again and then abruptly pulled back and said "Your Dreaming, My Love."

I opened my eyes and sat straight up. The morning light came in the windows. I looked down and my gown was still bunched at my waist. I looked over for Max and only his scent and lilies remained. I began to breath heavy shaky breathes and felt my body shake. I slipped out of the bed and my gown fell off my hips to the floor. I grabbed my robe and tied it on with shaky hands. I knew he was gone out of my life forever. It was like a death. A death I did not think I could live with. My friend, my protector; now my lover; gone all at once. With deep shaky breaths I could feel something begin to build up in side of me; something I was not going to be able to subdue.

It was the scream of the Priestess. It roared through the house like a wounded lioness. I dropped to the floor is sobs. It was very soon that the door, though locked, opened and Mandra, Elena and Joe ran through. Elena had me in her arms and Mandra looked to the bed. Joe stood confused at the scene of the sobbing girl on the floor and the rumpled bed. I heard Mandra call Marcus.

"No. Don't call Marcus!"

But before I got the words out, he was there. I looked at them both. With venom, I screamed at them

"No more. I can't take any more. I can't be normal and I can't be natural. I can't be a Christian, but I believe in Christ. I'm evil and I not. I can't be immortal and enjoy my powers. I can't go to school and be like normal kids. I can't have friends mortal or immortal because of Mixed Blood. Now I can't have him even though I always have. What are the rules?" I waited and they only looked at me. I asked again through my angry sobs "What are the rules. What happiness can I have?" I cried on my aunt's shoulder while my grandmother and Marcus watched the lilies where Max had been, wither and die at my command.

Elena then addressed them. "They have been separated now forever. She can't go through this any more. Let her go now. Let her find her way. Let her find her life; a life of her own. A life without others deciding who she loves or what she does. This is too far out of hand. How could any living and breathing soul live this way?"

Marcus move the sheet slightly as I stared at them they found the proof of the deed. They looked to each other in a concerned way. It took only a short minute and I stood up. Lifting my arm and pointing to the bed

"Is that it? Is that what you are all worried about? That the Witch lost her virginity to a mixed blood Wizard in training?"

They only looked at me. I snapped my fingers and was dressed in my jeans and top. I had my bag and purse. I looked back at my grandmother and Marcus.

"It means nothing. And don't think I plan on being lonely in the future; Max or no Max." I walked out of the room. Elena came after me.

"Em. Call me OK?" I looked back at her and went to her and hugged her. "I will." I jumped in the car where Zee waited, and drove home to Sacramento.

CHAPTER 27

By August grandmother and I had talked. She came to Sacramento and stayed with me. She was truly sorry that I my heart had been broken so badly. Nothing that had occurred was intended by anyone. I had to disagree. It has all been intended. Everything has been intended. My whole life has been intended to be controlled and designed for everyone's benefit but mine. Here I had all this power and could not use it for my self. I could only wait for a time that mix blood, Witches, Wizards and Normals could just be content. I often asked God when that would happen.

Elena had a wedding coming up. She and Joe were getting married in New York. I wanted to go but was in the middle of finals. I thought of Number 2 but couldn't bring myself to use the ruse. I seemed to find that I held back from a lot of things that reminded me of Max. Including magic.

My dreams still came in spurts. Some were happy memories with Max or Dad. Sometimes they were scary deadly dreams that woke me in screams or sweat. I often dreamed of Monster Wizards reaching for me, or holding me so I could not get away. I would scream for Max and wake to find myself in tears. I knew, Max couldn't come and sooth me. I had to endure the dreams. Or should I say nightmares, alone.

I mostly hung out at home; never really doing anything. I collected all the stray cats in the neighborhood and feed them daily. Though none ever came in the house, Zee was disgusted with the infidel cats. I went on a few dates but could muster enough enthusiasm for those guys. But ever so often, I catch a sense of Max. I look around but never seeing him. I would call to him but he never answered. And every now and then, I would catch a glimpse of a shadow.

Edwin was still assigned as my Guardian at that time. I held him at bay. He made great efforts for me to open my heart. He would check on me each day. I had to tell him he could not do that. I then had to tell him not to check on me at home, although he still did. He still attempted to touch me in little ways. Taking my arm or trying to hold hand. He never did try his little trapping me thing again. Of course, he couldn't surprise me anymore due to the protection barrier.

Marcus did come to see me. I think he felt it was safe now that time had passed. It was close to my birthday, I walked out of my kitchen as sitting on my couch was Marcus. I stopped and gave my most shame felt face.

He opened his arms and I was in them. "Oh Marcus I am sorry for everything."

He patted my back. "My Lady has nothing to sorry for." I looked at him and he continued. "It doesn't change anything. But you can't help falling in love."

I buried my head in his neck and shoulder "Please forgive me, just the same."

He then chuckled "OK Forgiven."

I looked back up and he was smiling. "I believe that Edwin has been ordered to stay away."

I huffed "I don't want him hang around so much. And he is too…. clingy"

Marcus giggled. "Well he does have his duties to perform. So don't be too hard on him." I huffed and said "I won't."

He was serious then "Have you seen….Max?"

I sat up surprised. "Why would I see Max, wasn't he *forbidden*to see me again?" He nodded. "Marcus, cant you just pop over to wherever he is?"

He looked concerned "He has blocked me. I don't hear from him at all." I felt for Marcus, I did believe that he cared about Max.

"Well he is still studying, couldn't speak to his master?"

Marcus then said very business like as he got up from the couch "Max had finished his studies by the last Solstice. He is a Master."

I found that surprising. "He never told me."

Marcus smiled "No. He wouldn't. Well My Lady, I'm off. Give an old man a hug." I got up and hugged him. He then said "I hope, that one day,….' He looked off, "we all find peace in our hearts. He was gone.

I spent Christmas with my father and Tom. Tina lives in Redding with Nora. They did come to Christmas and actually were pleasant. New Years was at my house with Mandra. Then Easter with Dad and Tom. Doc, Della and Taylor came and Auntie cooked a wonderful dinner. Tom told me that he likes being with Dad but he has to leave to go back to Chico State in a few days. He did not like seeing Dad alone. Of course Dad doesn't feel alone with his parishioners. While there, I cross the creek and went to the field. I had not returned since Edith's death. I knew I took a chance at the Shadow returning. But I couldn't help my self. The breezed kissed me a welcome and the trees whispered "The Princess has returned." I smiled at the tress and asked "Could I hear the music?" Then as the trees began to bend in the breeze, I heard the music. Then the trees asked "Will you dance Princess?" I smiled and ran to the center of the field. I danced for hours listening to the beautiful music of the trees.

I continued in studying Sociology thinking it would help me fit in. I took a few mastered level courses and continued working at the daycare. I walked a lot and read in the park. I kept to my self and was numb. Then every so often, I would feel Max was near. I would look around; I would call in my mind. But he never showed him self or answered me. It only made my heart ache more. I felt so split. Not full or actually an entity at all. Max had become such a part of me that the hole left by him would never be full again.

One day in late April, I pulled into my driveway and Edwin was sitting on the porch. I did not even want to get out of the car. I blocked him because he was just a little to much of a kiss up for my liking; Pushy at other times. There was a slimy quality about him. I just knew he was untrustworthy. I got out of the car and walked over to the porch. "Edwin."

He tried his most charming smile. "Em. I thought this was a good time to check in." I walked past him and unlocked the door.

I entered the house purposely not responding to him. He followed me in. I dropped the keys on the hall table and went to the kitchen.

"Em. Would you like to have dinner with me in Paris?"

In my mind I said "Yuck." but my face remained still; like stone. My answer was "No." He dropped his smile and then said "Why, because I'm not Max?"

I never changed my expressionless face. "Whatever the reason, the answer is no."

He was red faced and obviously stung by my simple response. He stood there and glared at me. "You know, Max is a rouge Wizard. He has a hard time with instruction."

I huffed as I open the fridge "Not from my perspective. He follows his instructions very well."

He gave a little laugh. "That because he has no chance. He is not from pure blood and…." He stopped.

I Looked back at him straight in the eye "And what?"

He seemed to become uncomfortable. "I am of pure blood. I am in consideration of…." I was not sure what I was hearing, but something was starting to piss me off. " Of What? What has pure blood have to with it?"

He looked trapped. "Edwin if you take off on me I swear to the Lord God, you will be hideous to every female you meet." I slammed the door of the refrigerator and had my hands on my hips. "What are you talking about? I want the truth. And I want it now! I demand it!" He shifted in his expression. I knew he would not be totally honest so I needed to direct the conversation. "What does pure blood have to do with anything? I don't have pure blood." I waited and he still had not responded "Talk!"

"The elders expect and have prophesized that you will marry a Powerful pure blood Wizard. You will produce a powerful wizard. There is a small group of pure blood wizard males. Of course there is me, and two others. We believe that you will marry one of the three of us and produce the child."

I eyed him with my head down, "Why would I marry any of you?"

His face was red and looking like he has said too much for the elders. But it was too little for me. He then threw in "You can rest assure, it will not be Mixed blood Mutt Max."

I kept my voice calm. "Tell the elders and any once else who believes in this pipe dream to......Forget it." He looked scared at that moment and needed to be. "Get out Edwin." I did not have to tell him again, He was gone.

So that was it; the plan for my life. Why Max is forbidden from me for a kiss. He is not pure blood. Well now we have it. It all started to come together and make sense. The anger at the design and the arrogance of the Elders. I wasn't only the mix blood. But the intent of the outcome of control. Their arrogance in twisting and turning the events and desires of my life. Why would they want this other than making me subservient to a pig like Edwin? And if I am subservient with my powers, my kind, witches, would be subservient. Normals would be subservient. My own children used against my kind, both my kind. In my anger and hurt, my disappointment and loneliness, I looked to the Lord. "*My Lord, give me the strength, and endurance. Let my magic be strong enough to do good and be upright. Bless those that I love who may not understand. Help me control my anger and pain. Amen.*

Again I had a plan.

The Summer Solstice of my twentieth year came. My mood was not what it had been in previous years. This year I was mad; so mad. Furious with the games the Elders played with the lives of others. Not just mine, not just Max's, everyone's; including that little snake, Edwin. What I have bottled up for so long in hurt and disappointment was at the surface as anger. The pain of not being normal; The pain of being held back as an immortal; The pain of having to mind my manners with my powers. I was not going to be lead along a path that was nothing but what others design for me. Keeping me from the one I loved. No more. This year, I would show my power. Screw the Wizards and their rules. It was a matter of physical, emotional and mental survival. The Priestess demanded it.

As usual, I greeted guests with my grandmother. As the Wizards arrived and came through the procession, I did notice that Max was not there. Not there and pushing my anger farther. I felt a surge of something stirring inside me; pushing me. Unlike all other times at the Solstice, I did not avoided Deana's eye's. And before my grandmother intervened, I looked directly in Deana's eyes to her enjoyment. She smiled until I, with a slow venomous voice, said "Deana, this is your only warning. If you ever try your little trick on me again, you will be blind. Blind not for just this life but for eternity." She backed away as fast as she could. Grandmother grabbed my arm "Was that necessary?" I looked at my grandmother and in a strong direct voice I said "Very necessary." Elena and Grandmother knew something was boiling up in me but I never told them. They did not ask and did not approach me. They watched me cautiously and with concern. They knew that there was something emerging that was immense and dangerous. My mind was blocked to all intruders even my grandmother. This much I can say was a precaution Max often had me use.

I did not sit with anyone. I did not eat. I did not drink. I wanted no conversation; no interaction what so ever. I could feel the power emerging from my middle. I stocked the crowd with my anger behind my mask but it was only clear to those closest to me; and of course the Wizards. I saw Marcus taking note as I prowled. Marcus watched me with caution. He noted the stalking stroll. He watched with interest. He also gave me a wide berth. As I stocked the perimeter of the gathering, Marcus turned with me and took note of the danger I was willing to produce to the Wizards.

Grandmother watched with concern but never hindered me. She was holding back noting the danger that was so close. Noting the anger, pain and disgust. Noting the power. Elena stood back looking to grandmother. Looking to find the answer to the creature that was stocking the Wizards. The creature that was once a gentle soul. Once gullible and pliable. Edwin watched but was too wrapped up in himself to understand the danger that was so close. So close to his demise.

I was dressed in full ancient garb of a priestess, but there was no dancing for me prior to the Maiden Dance. The power of the priestess dress encouraged my anger and possessed my soul. I saw Leonardo speaking to Edwin and looking at me. As I taped Edwin's mind, and the plan was reveled Edwin was to come to me when the mates were pick at the dance. Arrogant bastards believed me weak minded or fickle. With every breath I took, I knew this would not be. I would take back my life, and my free will. However, William, like Marcus, noted the danger. He could feel it. I wanted them all to feel it. To know that I could, at any time, end this charade. He only nodded with respect. Respect to the primal Priestess.

When the Maiden Dance begun, I joined the other Maidens to the delight of the Elders minds. In their minds the little plan to have me pick Edwin was developing. I danced with power and demand of the night. My movements more a command, hard and wanting. When the music ended, and before the drums to signal the maidens to find their mates, I found myself facing the bond fire, crouched down on one knee; Hands on the ground with one ahead of the other. My back stretched and lowered, my head level and menacing. the stance of a attacking feline. I looked at the fire and knew I could and would not jump the fire with any other than Max. No matter what happens. Never with any other than Max.

Like a cat, my head twisted with my body remain in its position. I looked back at the elders encouraging Edwin as the drums started. Never leaving the crouching cat stance, my hand shot back and locked Edwin in place. He could not pick up his feet. He and the elders, Marcus included, knew that it was me. They looked directly at me. I stared at the Elders with defiance behind my mask but with the fierce green feline eyes of the Priestess. Frozen in place, I never blinked as the others danced around me. The Elders looked to each other in confusion and concern. Edwin continued to try to free himself without success. He gave an ugly sneer in my direction. As the last couple crossed the fire, I rose pivoting on the balls of my feet to a standing position. I rose faced the Wizards. I must have looked like a lion about to attack. *Rouge?* I thought to myself. *I think I can do rouge.*

Standing was the priestess worrier and a voice of pure authority; I directed my command to the elders. My actions, my presentation, my command, encouraged and provided by the priestess. The Priestess in her death stance directed at the ones who stood in the way of her life, love and freewill. The priestess insulted by the Wizards goals and their arrogance to Witches. Their disregard to God and mother earth and the Priestess her self. Their disregard for the love that I had for a Mixed

Blood. The crowd had hushed at presents of the Priestess. After all, there was no ignoring her.

.

In the Witch voice of authority I projected
"Wizards! I stand in defiance. Defiance to you and your plans."

To prove my point, I threw my hand and Edwin was the caged in a metal bared cage, like an ape. The crowd made noises but remained still. All taking note of the demand of attention by the Priestess.

"At your instruction *My* chosen partner is not here. I won't replace him with one that you have decided is more appropriate partner for me." I continued to stare the elders down. Head down eyes up displaying the deadly Priestess. Anger and threat penetrating through my eyes. Eyes of an immortal feline.

"Only I will choose who and what is right for me and what is right for my kind."

Looking to my grandmother I could see that she was not going to make a move to stop me. She stood as regal as ever. I looked back at the elders.

"I have mixed blood, and am as powerful as you are. But only pure blood is what you have *planed*for me. Why? To keep me less than your chosen one? To have my offspring used for your end?"

I yelled a little louder. "To be second to that Wizard and thus my kind?" I hissed, "I will never be less and neither will my kind. Your plans needs to include my agreement, and that you will never receive. You make your laws and rules and I will follow them and respect them as long as they are to the benefit of Normals, Wizards and Witches alike. But leave free will alone." Then more deadly "Leave me alone."

I paused only a second looking back at the fire. My head turning to the Wizards in a deadly stare.

"I will jump the fire. But I jump alone. As alone as I live." And with an angry scream. "Alone as the life you have designed for me"

With that I ran at the fire and jumped over it, landing straight on my feet. I threw my arms up and back The bond fire shot a blue flame into the sky . The blue fire spread like a twenty foot wall across the yard to keep others back and away from me. Breathing heavily from emotion alone, I dropped to a knee with my head down, my arms still out holding the fire. Then I knew Max was there. I looked up and he bent down and kissed me.

He looked into my eyes and said, "Any Price Princess." and he was gone.

I stood and dropped the fire curtain and ran to the cliff rail. A panther crouched on the tallest rock looking back at me as waves crashed around him. I knew it was Max. I only whispered his name. And he was gone.

Elena reached me at the rail first. "Was he here?"

I looked at her and nodded my head. "Please don't tell them."

She had her arm around me "Not on my life."

I turned from the cliff rail and Mandra had come up to us but stayed back slightly. I waited for her to speak. "I was never as proud of you as I was just now."

She still had not given and expression. "Your fire trick will be explained as a trick." She then came forward and hugged me. "You looked and acted like the royal priestess of the forest. I never could have seen this. My granddaughter the Priestess."

Marcus came up then and was thoughtful in his opening line "My, what a power you have become, my Princess." He came closer and I saw the other elders hang back. "I believe you have hit a nerve with the elders though. I for one am in ah. And hope that I still am in your grace"

I hugged him. "You know how I love you Marcus. I just cant have my life played with like a pawn on a chess board"

He smiled at me "No My Lady. Nor can I". I hugged him again for his support.

When I stepped back from Marcus, the elders approached, and I released Edwin from his cage. I was aware that there could be consequences. As they got closer, I was flanked by grandmother and Elena. I stood as straight and as I could. I demanded my body be as regal as grandmothers. Leonardo approached with a smile on his face. William was unreadable and Edwin scowled.

Grandmother said under her breath, "We are Witches not Wizards. They rule their kind not ours. We are ruled by God and mother earth. Remember that in your response." I made a slight nod in acknowledgement.

"My Princess." Leonardo took my hand and kissed it, which almost threw me off guard. Then I remember the kiss of death was on the mouth. Continuing to hold my hand, "You have made a statement that we can not ignore. It is, after all, a command. We have decided that you are entitled to command your life. We will not interfere. As you know, we are wizards and you are Witches. "I nodded to him. Leonardo continued still holding my hand. "Though we have our prophesy and our desires, we will obey your wishes. We do understand that Edwin is not to your liking. We have decided to reassign him. You, my lady, will no longer have a guardian. We will as you requested, 'Leave you alone'. As far as Max goes, once again, he is our kind. A Master Wizard, and will not be released from his instructions. He is….. Somewhat difficult Yet. But we have great hopes for him." I pulled my hand from his and nodded. "May I give him a message, my lady?"

I said "Yes. Tell him… at any price."

He could not look into my mind as it was locked. And he only tilted his head. "As you wish my lady."

I stopped him by reaching for him "Master Leonardo, thank you." He smiled and bowed his head.

Edwin stood staring at me. When Leonardo and William turn to return to their table, he came closer to me. I could see Marcus was irritated by Edwin.

Edwin put on a sour face. "You will be sorry for this, Em. All for a mix blood criminal Wizard."

He gave a little laugh, "you'll never see him again. And I offered you my pure blood and you rejected it. That will not be forgotten, at least by me."

Marcus stepped up "Edwin. Am I to understand that Em should be looking for retaliation by her rejection of you?"

Edwin look back at me then "No. I will not retaliate. I don't have to. She threw everything away, for a mix blood nothing."

Marcus then ordered Edwin, 'Return to the others and mind your manners." Edwin nodded to Marcus and turned and glared at me as he walked away. Marcus, Mandra and Elena, stood with me at the cliff side. A group of like minded Immortals. The beginning of the force of change.

I never returned to the Solstice. It was over two years since my notorious Priestess appearance and I had no desire to return. I would not be in a position for the Elders to try their scheme again. I did not see Max or feel him close. He was gone. This time, really gone. I was really all alone now. Oh, I had my father, my grandmother and Marcus. But, I felt so alone. And I hated the Wizards.

I worked now for a community organization for families. It was basically my life. I mentored mothers overwhelmed by life, children, and poverty. I took some joy thinking that my organization made a different for the children. I could never be sure that it did. I never used magic anymore. I was really trying to be normal. Average. I attended church regularly and taught Sunday school. This delighted my father immensely. I think he was just pleased to see some of him come out in me. Dad and Tom remained in the mountains. Tom now a forest ranger and stationed close to home. Dad was pleased to have Tom with him. I was pleased that Dad was not alone. I had no social life to speak of. Once in a while I would go with friends from work to office parties and celebrations. Mostly I stayed by my self. I did find one night stands when I felt like it but never pursued or allowed a relationship. There was no reason. I would never allow that in my life again.

Elena and Joe had a baby boy. The named him Hunter. They send me pictures and we write back and forth. I don't have a lot to tell and have a hard time getting anything down on paper. How do I write about how I wish for that life. How do I write my envy for a family of my own. Mandra comes every few months to see me. I know it hurts her that I don't go home. Lincon often sends care packages. He sometimes accompanies my grandmother on the trips to see me. And then spends his time with us cleaning and cooking and catering to us.

Marcus comes from time to time. Often he is quite and distant. I never asked about Max. I felt that it was hurtful to Marcus and it was fruitless. He was gone out of my life and his name only hurt me. But, on one occasion, he had told me that Max was "occupied."

Marcus Said "Max has become very powerful, and very dangerous. Though he is a Mastered Wizard, he has become a threat with his anger to the restrictions of his station and the way of life of the Wizards;

To the Pure Blood Wizards. They can't have an undisciplined and dangerous Wizard lose in the world without controls."

I felt concern "Marcus, you are an elder are you afraid of Max?"

He looked at me with hurt in his eyes. "I care deeply for Max. I know Max's heart. I am not afraid of him."

Edwin showed up a few times. Mostly trying to be charming to melt my heart to him. I had no interest what so ever. I knew the plan for my life and had no intention of aiding these fools in their domination of me and my kind. Edwin even attempted to reason with me like "Princess this is prophesied. You will produce a Magic Heir. It must be with a Pure blood." I would only look at him and say "Edwin, why would you think I would help the Wizards dominate my kind." He would only stand with that stout look and try again "The Elders will have their heir. You must understand that that is your purpose." I would laugh at him. I even threatened with "I will have no children. Especially children to be used by your kind." He would leave and would not see him for a while. I did have a great deal of enjoyment at his insulted exits. Every time he did leave I always wished it would be the last time I would see him or any other Wizards except Marcus. I already knew I would never see Max again.

CHAPTER 28

After that meeting and continuing my life of so so normality. Days were getting shorter. And the wind was stronger. The sparrow called to me a let me know that there was a visitor coming. I believed it to be Mandra. The trees whispered to me to take care. Watch and take care. I believed that to be Edwin. I wasn't concerned with visitors or Edwin. I could take care of him. And I did miss my grandmother and wanted to see her often. Maybe it was Marcus who I would always love to see.

Then out of the blue, moving into the third year since our last kiss at the cliff side, Max was sitting in a lawn chair in my back yard. I stood motionless when I saw him.

We only stared at each other at first. I didn't really believe he was there. We looked into each others eyes for a long time. When I finally did believed it was really him. I opened the door and I ran to leap into his arms. But he stopped me by putting up his hands. In confusion, I stopped before reaching him. I looked at him closely and could see his pale pallor and dark circles. He wore all black. His hair was long and reaching to his shoulders. His face was unshaven. He looked so menacing, dangerous, and deadly. He stood up dominating the space, moving like the panther to his prey. I looked at him surprised by him being there, his appearance and his demeanor to me. He gave a wicked cat like smile that sent me goose bumps and my hair on my neck to stand on end. I actually felt danger; Danger from Max; my friend; my protector. I focused on keeping my breathing in check, though I was failing. I was breathing heavier than I wanted to. He began to circle me. I stayed still waiting; knowing that there was a true threat very close. He was towering over me, and proving his threat to me.

Never ending his circling; moving around and around me, he said in the most evil voice. "Well, Well, Well, Princess. You are even more beautiful then when I saw you last." He reached out taking a lock of my long hair and dragging his fingers down the length. I shivered but I did not give any other response. I only looked in his eyes as he past in front of me. His eyes were cold and empty. He eyes lost of the spirit of Max but not the angry panther. He spoke slowly in a deep angry snarl with his canines showing demonstrating how close the panther hovered. "I see you are denying your true self. Never using magic; never allowing others in." He paused, "You are not having fun are you?" He smiled and then laughed wickedly. He said in deeply ugly voice "except with your little trysts now and again. Poor mortal males." He was very close to my ear "They haven't got a clue. Bewitched, used and then forgotten" I mustered up some bravado, and I encased myself in a barrier of protection. He laughed an ugly little laugh, "Very smart Princess. Amazing you can do that knowing that you never practice."

I taunted him then "And what of you Max. I understand that you are a Wizard Criminal." He stopped at that and looked closely in my eyes. I started to regret my taunt, when his eyes were the yellow panther eyes. "Yes. I am a criminal of my own kind. My existence a threat to their very souls." He continued to looked into my eyes but I did not see my Max any longer. I saw only bitter anger. Only the panther. "I am a threat to the future is how they stated it' He paused but continued to look directly in my eyes. Then said "The price of sleeping with a Princess." He looked at me up and down and then he began his circling me again.

"But I am not here to discus my social Wizard status. I have come to see you. And see what has become of you." An evil laugh again "An immortal playing at being Normal. No real success at it. Alone with only the cat for true company. Hiding in this make- believe normal world where you don't belong." I stayed silent and closed my mind to him. "Well, I believe little Em has used more magic today than she has all year. And I see the priestess lays dormant."

My retort was simple "You sure know a lot about me for being band from me."

In mid circle he was back staring into my eyes with unnatural speed. I felt a little unnerved with that. In a soft yet dangerous voice he said, "Yes I do." He started his circling again. I closed my eyes only for a second. He was really frightening me. His towering form looming over me. His voice of full of anger, and threat. I prepared to defend my self. In disbelief, preparing to defend my self against Max. He continued "You hold on to things that are forbidden. I can't understand that. After all it was nothing more than a race you might say." Confused but not willing to ask, I remained silent. He did not stop though "I, of course, was the victor. However, that's were the trouble began. Am I right Princess?" He gave a little laugh "A pure blood was planned for your desire and to father your children. But when my foster brothers found no way in to impress you, and take your virginity, I was the victor of the game. I won … a mix blood Wizard could out wit a pure blood Wizard and …" causing my heart to stop he somehow moved past the barrier, close to my ear "…..Capture the maiden." I was beyond hurt. I was numb. I could not think of anything but that the ties are cut. I am free of him.

I asked in a angry sneer "So why did you come back the next year? Why bother?"

He stopped at my eyes again, I couldn't read him as he could not read me. "Oh, I suppose it was to rub salt in the wounds of Edwin. I could let him think he had a chance. He was so sure you could not resist him. He even attempted to enchant you but you do have those natural defenses." he paused. He looked deep into my eyes "But given some time and circumstances….?" He tilted his head waiting for an answer to that. I stayed quite and still. I refused to answer such a ridicules assumption. Only meeting his dangerous eyes with my own immortal green eyed feline glare. His evil smile appeared again. He gave acknowledgment saying "The Priestess is impressive."

He looked around and then back at me. "Now my love, you have the truth. I have come to tell you that. So I will be on my way and allow you to return to.." he said with disgust "Your existence." All I would do is stand still. I would not look at him again and did not respond to his taunts. "I will never see you again, Princess, So goodbye." Once again, somehow, he move past the protective barrier, and kissed me lightly. And he was gone. I wiped my mouth with the back of my hand. I stood there still as the night. I was there for a very long time. Not thinking, not feeling not moving. Then it happened, the repeated stabs of pain in my heart. The devastation of the lies that I have lived. The tricks. Even Max, who I thought was my friend, my love, was a lie.

I went through the months numb and uninterested in joy or human touch. The only interest was for the families I worked with. At least those kids could feel like someone cared how they felt. How they lived and how they ended up. I encouraged then to love and live. To dream for the imposable and work to achieve it. Discouraging them from allowing circumstance and social belief to control their lives. I worked with mothers and children during the day and taught Parenting Classes at night. I stayed very busy with work so that at night I would be in oblivion. So I could sleep and not dream. So I could look at my self in the mirror the next day. Bitter and alone was a nice way to put it.

Mandra talked with me her next visit. "Em. I think he was trying to help you live without him and him live without you. He knew he could not come back."

I look at her said "Then why not stay away. Leave things as they were. I had accepted the fact that he wasn't coming back."

Mandra poured more coffee in my cup. "Em he did love you. No matter what he said that day, no matter what you think now. I can tell you that he showed love."

I twisted my mouth "Grandmother, he never said he loved me. And the only promise was that he would protect me when charged with it."

She grabbed my hand "He showed love. He never had to say it or promise it."

I smiled at her "Well OK. But the ends have proven otherwise. If it were me ordered to stay away from him, I would have broken every order and rule to be with him anyway. I loved him that much."

My grandmother looked far away. I patted her hand. She smiled a little "Funny how our hearts have a mind of their own. How our social worlds interfere and make situations that break hearts. You were right that night at the Solstice. If they had left things alone, who knows what would have happened between you and Max. And ….. Other couples." We never spoke again about Max.

Late September, after my 23rd birthday, I saw the shadow again as I was walking along the rivers edge. I had no idea who or what it could be. I decided that I would chase it down if it returned. I continued walking and being aware of my surroundings. I knew I needed to leave the area and be home were I could protect my self without detection of the mortals. As I approached my car, Edwin and another guy were leaning against it blocking me from my car door.

I closed my mind immediately. "Get out of my way Edwin."

In his snobbery he was unfazed by my command, he asked "We're on the hunt for a cowardly wizard."

I laughed "Have you looked in the mirror?"

He stood straight and threatening "You will not address me in that manor, Witch. Not if you know what's good for you."

I laughed at him "Don't be so sure of yourself Edwin, you might discover what I have known all along. Your nothing more than a snake in the grass."

With that he was a snake. He slithered through the grass disoriented.

The other wizard stood smiling. "Very Good my lady. Couldn't do a better job my self." I looked at the tall man at my car. A year or two younger than Edwin.

"And you are?'

He smiled gracefully and made a slight bow, "Christopher my lady. At your service." I felt he was not evil as Edwin but I retained my caution. He was sandy haired and blue eyed. As handsome as Edwin… and Max.

"I'm a foster brother of Edwin and Max."

I was curious "Why are Max's brothers hunting him?"

He had less of a smile "Who knows him better?" I could think of some.

"Why haven't I met all of you before?"

He looked for the words "It was not my design my lady. I would have liked to have met you before. But my brothers kept you and your time to them selves. Jordan, our other brother, and I were not given an opportunity."

I did not want to hear about the Wizard race to my virginity again. I moved passed him and got in my car. "Well Christopher, I have no information for you and tell Edwin to stay away from me."

He laughed "As you wish my lady but I don't speak snake." As I began to pull away, I waved my hand and Edwin was once again a man but he stayed on his belly in the dirt trying to continue to slither.

"Reminds me of something Max would do." Marcus was in the passenger seat with a big smile.

I smiled and then we both end up laughing. "I am so happy to see you Marcus. How are you?"

He smiled but there was little joy, "I am fine. But I am afraid that Max has been detected. He will have to be careful not to be captured."

I was concerned for Max. And then I had to analyze why. Why do I care. He is no longer a part of my life. And then with a heart ache, I remembered, I loved him. Rather who I had thought he was. I was fighting it tooth and nail, but it was there. Marcus looked at me then knowing my inter struggle.

"Will you stay and have dinner with me Marcus?"

He smiled and said "As you wish, my lady"

We sat at the table and I asked "Why have I not met Christopher and Jordan?"

Marcus dabbed his whiskered face and said "I believe that Max and Edwin designed that. Max was your guardian at first and took his task seriously. Edwin was…encouraged and infatuated." I felt hurt that Max never expressed even infatuation for me. Then Marcus said "Oh no my dear, He cared for you very much and was very protective of you. He continued his vow even after he was reassigned."

I gave a little smile and said "I know he did.

"He often threaten Edwin in protecting your virtue."

I gave a sarcastic little laugh "Protecting my virtue? Why it ended up as a joke anyway." Marcus looked concerned. "I know what he has said to you. I am sorry that it has left such a bitter taste in your mouth." He held my hand "But he was of pure heart that night. Not the monster he has become."

I looked at Marcus concern "Is he truly a Monster Marcus?"

He looked into my eyes and I could see the pain of the thought of Max as a Monster. "I can't say. But we will pray for him. We will pray that he returns someday, happy and... free." Marcus than said "Em he has become very powerful. He is able to hide from the Elders and all others that seek him; even under their very noses." I thought of the fable Max was so fascinated with. "He is not to be challenged or baited, Em. Please remember that should he return."

I smiled at Marcus "He told me he would never see me again. And I don't plan on challenging him or baiting him. Besides, I do have my own powers." I continued "Why are Edwin and the other foster brothers hunting him? Christopher said it is because no one knows him better. I think that is not true."

Marcus smiled," I think you are right. I think I know him much better...."he then looked down, "but don't know anymore. He has been... he has changed a great deal."

I continued the conversation trying to directly avoid Max. "Christopher is not like Edwin is he?"

Marcus shook his head "No. He is much more grounded. He has not had the influences that Edwin has. Edwin believes himself as very entitled." I agreed with him.

"He sees himself as your chosen partner."

I rolled my eyes "I hope today made my feelings know where Edwin is concerned." Marcus laughed, "I understand but he has a hard head."

I asked "If Max is so powerful, what makes Edwin and the rest believe they can capture him?"

Marcus said on word "Arrogance ." And then "Ignorance. Max will recognized this as a deadly combination" Deadly? Max? I could not see it with the Max I know, but the one that I was last visited by... remembering his eyes...yes. Deadly.

I asked "Do you think he would kill them?"

Marcus looked weary. After a second, "If they attempt to capture him, he will kill them or have them kill him." My heart tore a little more.

CHAPTER 29

Life continued, I numbly continued. There was nothing of any consequence for months. But there were little changes in the sky. The colors of the sky changing from the deep blue to red and yellow at sunset. It tended to be more silver then more pink. The cats were more nervous and the scrub jays more devious. Meadow larks were singing a different tune. The moon stay larger than it should; lower than it should. The trees moved in the breeze in a subtle different way, whispering that change was coming, danger was coming. There were changes. There was nothing that pointed to any one thing. Just the changes that a Witch would take notice to. It was a Witches warning. I kept a watch.

In one of my many outings to find a mortal playmate for an evening, I sat at the local coffee shop. I was sitting at out on the outside tables. Eyeing my prey. This was the most fun part. Picking who I thought I would have the best time with. Which mortal would be the most fun to play with? I sat looking over the choices and this one guy stopped by my table and picked up my key's - my trap. I smiled as he handed them to me." I fond these on the floor here." I acted surprised, "Oh my, how did I not notice my key's. That was really sweet of you. Thank you." He shuffled a little and said "My name is Jim." I smiled and shook his out reached hand "Emily. Want to sit." I waved my hand at an empty chair. He sat down, and we chatted for some time. He was a teacher at a local grammar school. He was recently divorced and had two kids, Ben and Rose.

We continued to talk until the sparrows began their warning. Quietly at first. One here, another there. giving off a little short song of beware. Then more and more began to appear. The more that showed up, the louder the warning. In was close to the sun going down so for the birds not be in their nests, meant that the danger was greater than I first believed. I became very nervous. The trees were waving in their odd little way. The Oaks whispering "beware. Danger calls." I looked over at Jim and smiled. "I have to go but it was really nice to meet you." He said "Yes it was really nice to meet you. Do you think I could call you?" I smiled and gave him my business card. "I am normally there." he said "Great I call." As I rushed to cross the street I turned back and said "That will be great." I rushed across the street and walked across the capital lawn.

Walking down the street and heading home something was happening by the screaming of the elements. I surveyed the street and there, just outside a alley way, the shadow. Then as I was about to enter the chase, my mind received a transmission of *"Stay away from it."* I could have sworn it was Max. But thought that was impossible and I ignored the warning. I knew I had to see this shadow. Find out who it is. Why they follow me. I started to sprint towards the shadow and I received, *"I said stay back."* I stopped immediately. I froze. It was Max. I looked all over. I did not see him. Marcus's warning came to my mind. And then I closed off my head to all intruders. I started for home again. I wanted to get to the house and put up the protection but continued to survey the area. I was being cautious and aware. I had the immense feeling of danger. Was it Max or the shadow, I didn't know.

As I was passing the park Max stepped out from the trunk of a huge oak tree. Dressed all in black with a black hat. His black T-shirt showing the huge muscles on his arms and shoulders, but he did he looked thinner, angrier. "Em" I stopped in my tracks, and I kept a safe distance from him. "Max." He stood with his body not really forward, his head down and looking to the side at me. His eyes were filled with anger and danger. He turned forward and started to come closer. Moving like the panther advancing forward. I put my hand up.

"Stay away."

He stopped, still eyeing me in that evil stare. In a low and evil voice he asked "Why be freighted of me and not the shadow?"

I did not know how to answer that. "Let's just say I want you back away from me." He ignored me and moved forward. I placed a barrier that he stopped in front of. He smiled evilly with his hovering monster close.

"I can get through it you know."

I stood stone faced and ignored his taunt. "What do you want Max?"

He laughed "Do I need a reason to visit you?"

I raised an eyebrow "Yes." is all I would give him. He laughed his evil laugh again.

Continuing his evil smile, complete with the cat like fangs, he moved past the barrier. I instinctively placed the barrier around me and stood still with my head held erect and challenging. He may have his power under his control, but I was not willing to allow him to think that I could not care for my self. He slowly moved as close as he could before the barrier. Looking into my eyes and I worried he could get past that barrier as well. "What is it that you want?"

He increased his grin. "Only to see you."

I shook my head "Aren't you concerned that your brothers will find you? Aren't you banded from me by the Elders?"

He dropped his smile "I am not afraid of the buffoons finding me. And I don't answer to the Elders as you know."

I felt no fear, no threat but remembered his last visit. I remembered his threat the last time. "You said you would never see me again. Why are you here?"

He must have known what my thoughts were without reading me. "No I wasn't. And I know that I freighted you the last time I saw you." He returned to his evil grin with extended canines flashing. "I came to make peace."

I must have lost my straight face with a bewildered expression that caused him to laugh. At that point I snarled "Go to hell. Why would I want peace with you?"

His head tilted slightly to the side. "We used to be friends."

I slowly shook my head, "No… I thought you were my friend, but in reality, I was a Wizard joke." I looked around and he knew I was looking for Mortals intending to transport without detection.

He shook his head "No. I am not ready to end our meeting."

I looked directly into his eyes with my own evil glare of the immoral feline and the threatening voice of the Priestess I said "I am."

With that I was home with the protection barrier up.

He sent a evil laugh and said "I can get through that one too." He didn't though. He was gone. Shaking I sat in the kitchen chair and couldn't believe that he would risk being here. Especially after telling me the truth. What more could he want.

I continued to live in solitude; only work and home. I heard nothing more after seeing Max. I was hurt, and bewildered. I was on a yoyo and my heart ached with every pull of the string. I made myself work in the yard and scrub in the house. I needed to sleep without dreaming. I had to be exhausted. I had to sleep in oblivion. But the dreams would come regardless. I had dreams of Max and I dancing for the trees or Max and I at Coney Island. I would have dreams of his smile and talking with him for hours. But I also had the nightmares of the Shadow with the red eyes. Or the Monster Max. I wake up screaming or sweating. Sleep scared me more than any shadow or Wizard. I spent many nights refusing to sleep. Or I would use drinking to sleep. I had a Doctor prescribe pills for sleep. I even called grandmother for a potion. I did anything and everything to control my wild mind at night while I slept. Anything not to dream of Max.

I worked as much as possible. I was volunteering for any necessary activity that could take my mind from the Wizards and the shadow. Remove the thought of Max. My coworkers watched me with concern. They were concern over the shaking of my hands; the circles under my eyes; my quite distant mood. They watching me work like a demon and only to see me zone out at my desk in the middle of a conversation or written task. My coworker Lucy would often pat my shoulder and say "Earth to Emily. Are you OK?" I would smile and nod.

Over the next few weeks I saw and chased the shadow. I ignored Max's warning. I could not continue to up with it. This shadow demon watching and listening to my life was more than I could tolerate at that time. I had decided that I would start to make the changes I needed to. The changes that freed me, and freed my dreams, and freed my life. I would start with the shadow.

The first time was when I left work. It was dark but I could see it just across J Street. I took after it and it went through 7th street and I followed. Then it was gone. I heard Max laugh and sent '*I told you not to chase it. But it looks like your not equipped to catch it either.*" I sent back "*Why don't you catch it? Or is it you.*" He didn't answer.

The next time I was leaving home and got a glimpse of it and drove my car 45 miles an hour down the street chasing it but it got away. I heard monster Max laugh again. I sent to Max "*So you got away again.*" He returned "*You know it is not me.*" He continued to laughed with his monster voice "*your just too slow. And you forgot your magic.*" Maybe he was right. I have been in the normal world so long, I hadn't tried just magic.

The next time I was walking out of the super market. It was dusk and I could see it at the end of the parking lot. I left my bag on the trunk of my car and gave chase. As I followed around the corner I ran straight into Max. My heart dropped. He had me by my arms in a firm grip. Fear raced through me but I made the effort to hide it. I mustered a "Let go." He looked down and shook his head. "Do you know what you are chasing?" His eyes evil and his face the monster. Yellow eyed panther Monster. I did not answer him. I pulled to get lose from his grip and was not able to. Then as I was about to send him flying he bound my powers. I snarled at him "How dare you. Let me lose." He held my arm and we walked back to my car with groceries on the trunk. He grabbed the bag never turning lose of one of my arms. I knew, with him holding my arm and binding my powers, I was not getting away. But at the same time I couldn't bring myself to call for help and risk his life; or mine. He knew what I was thinking. True to form, Max always intruded. In his evil voice he made it clear "Good thinking Princess." He looked directly into my eyes and assuredly stated "We would die together." My heart stopped and I knew he was telling me the truth. He told the trunk to open and he put the bag in the trunk. He turned to me and waved his hand and I was dressed in a black dress and heels. I snarled "I am not playing your games Max. Let me go."

He smiled and said "Em. We are going to dinner." I shook my head. He returned by nodding his head sarcastically. He waved his hand and though my mind was unwilling, my body was lead by him. He opened the passenger door and I got in unwillingly in my mind and perfectly willing in body. In my mind, I was in a no win situation. Be his victim or be the reason he kills or is dead. He got in the drivers seat. He started the car without a key and made a comment about driving a sedan. He went through an alley and the car was a black corvette. I rolled my eyes, the only part of my being that I believed I had control over. I did not speak to him and did close my mind. But I decided to only focus on his confession of the race; for him to think about and me to remain angry.

He continued to drive with his monster face and said evilly "I can interrupt transmission and still get in your head even if you close it."

I found that my voice and words were mine to control "Why are you doing this. Why don't you just stay away?"

He gave his evil laugh "Because you chase shadows and because I wanted to see you. You know, break the rules."

I laughed at him. "You have no rules Max. Remember?"

We stopped at the Firehouse Restaurant. The valet came and took the car and we walked into the restaurant. The maitradee asked for the name on the reservation. And with no surprise he said "Yes Mr. Marshal, this way." Holding my hand against my will he led me to the table. The maitradee then pulled out my chair and I sat. I said thank you and he asked if we wanted to have something to drink. Max ordered a very expensive bottle wine. I had to remember that I was the only immortal that worked for a living. "Your choice." Was his remark to my thought. I noticed he dropped the Monster but in my mind, I could only see the Monster. He looked at me reading that thought and looked back at his menu. I did not look at the menu. I sat there like he planned but I didn't have to willingly play his game. When he noticed that I hadn't looked at the menu and he picked it up and put it in my hands. "Don't be a bitch. Find what you would like to eat or I will order for you." I wanted so badly to scream at him. I was not hungry. I only want loose and to go home free of him. He looked closely at me and said "Not sleeping?" I only huffed.

And as my curse would dictate, the director of my agency appeared at my table.

"Emily, what a nice surprise to see you enjoying your self out."

I looked over and smiled at him "Hi Don."

He had his wife there and introductions were made "This is my wife Pat." He looked to his wife "Emily is one of our most dedicated workers. She works very hard with our families. We are fortunate to have her with the agency."

If only he knew that I used my job to hide and drown. I smiled sweetly and said "Well thank you Don." He looked over to Max and then to me "Oh I am sorry." I was really trying to avoid introducing Max. "This is Max."

Max stood up and reintroduced himself "Max Marshal. I am an old friend of Emily's." I made a huh in my head but continued to smile sweetly at the director and his wife. Max still had his ability to deceive and manipulate. Don and Max shook hands.

Don smiled and said "Nice to meet you, Max. Enjoy your selves and try the fish it is delicious." I smiled and told Pat that it was nice to meet her and they moved away.

I stared away from Max. I was so mad and sad at the same time. I just had a wonderful complement and could not allow myself to take it. I used the job. I used it so that other kids (Mortal Kids) did not get sucked into the social crap that ruined lives. I knew the immortal kids were lost. And it hurt me so desperately, so deeply.

He took my hand that I wanted to pull away, but involuntarily allowed "Immortal kids need help too."

I looked at him and with sarcasm and said, "Yeah right. And how do you get by the Wizard bull shit to help them. Who helped us?" Then I thought about his complicity in the whole thing, I snarled through clinch teeth and looking directly in his eyes with all the hate I could find. "Who helped me?"

He looked sad, and he returned my comment with a soft remorseful voice "I thought we helped each other,"

The waiter came and poured the wine and left. Max did not let go of my hand. I drank the wine quickly. I intended to have more.

Max then said in my mind *"The shadow is dangerous. That much I can tell you. If you continue to follow and chase it, eventually, you will get hurt."*

I looked at him. And sent back to him, *"What do you care? I am not going have that thing hanging around. And I, when not prevented, can take care of myself."*

He took a frustrating intake of breath, "Just the same. It will be harmful to you."

I ordered the fish for my self not wanting him to have the pleasure of having control. I drank another glass of wine and did my best to take in the ambience of the restaurant. But interruption to my mind came *"So why are you living this way. With your power you could be anywhere doing anything."*

I looked at him and sent back *"I want my life to matter. I want to give back."*

He laughed "Give back what?" I looked directly into his eyes; Eyes I have missed; Eyes that lied. And I sent in my mind, *"That we all, immortal and mortal, matter. Our lives and freedom matter. Our knowledge of the truth matters. The knowledge and truth helps us make vital decisions in our lives and what we want out of our lives matters."* He looked down and then back to me and I continued in voice "Like being a teacher. But… that too could have been a lie."

He smiled and huffed "No just not practical as a Master." Then he corrected "A Criminal Master."

I asked him then in voice "why are you a criminal. It can't be just because of me."

He gave an evil smile "And what if it was?"

I laughed then. "That would be ridicules. What purpose would it serve?" And as I turned my eyes away, He squeezed my hand and I looked back.

He said "They still want their Pure Blood heir"

I stopped laughing and became very serious. I was so tiered of that "Your kind needs to get over it. Maybe find a gullible Princess instead of this bitter one. I am not, and will not be, a Wizard incubator." He squeezed my hand hard and said out loud in his evil deep voice "Not my kind." He sat back and the food came.

After a few minutes I asked him "With your power, you could be anywhere doing anything and from what I understand, no one could find you. Why stay around and risk it?"

He nodded and looked off. "Want to go with me?"

Added by the wine, I laughed "No."

He smiled, looked back at me and said "I have some unfinished business."

We did not speak anymore. I could have asked him what that business was but in reality, I did not care. I did not eat and only drank the wine. It was obvious that it affected me while we did talk. That was the most I have said to Max in years.

Once we left the restaurant, and got back in the car, Max put on the monster again. We were also quiet in the car. He drove around the city. We were just driving. I didn't ask where or why. I sat quietly and thought of mundane things like cleaning house and capturing a cat with a hurt back leg and taking that cat to the Vet. I think he must have become board with my normal thoughts. He started in the direction of my house.

He was driving up my street and I said "It's not safe for you here. I smell the other Wizards from time to time. I know they are looking for you." He did not say a word. He pulled into the driveway and I attempted to move and was unable to, he still had the spell over me. He got out of the car and came to my door and opened it. He held out his hand and I unwillingly put my hand in his. We walked up the porch and the door opened. We walked in and the door shut. Zee who had been waiting for me hissed at the sight of Max and ran to the bedroom.

Standing in the living room with him still holding my hand and his monster on, I said in voice "What now? Wait for the Wizards? Wait for hell to take us? What?" I looked up to find a smile on his face. He came close and I could not move still under his spell. He kissed me and I unwillingly kissed him back. I became so angry that I was screaming at him in my mind to let me lose. I couldn't do anything but comply with his will. Try as I might, I could not release my self. Tears of anger began to run and he let me go. He looked at me as I brought myself in to check. I wiped my mouth with the back of my hand discovering that I had my movements at my will. Then I screamed at him "Why would you do that? Is it just getting back at the Pure Bloods? Am I still that stupid pawn in the stupid Wizard games?" He stood there saying nothing. "Why don't you leave me alone?" In his eyes was a little of the old Max. "Bye Em." And he was gone. Waving my arms I put the protection barrier up full force and with all my might. I dropped to the floor Indian style and cried into my hands. All I could think of is getting free of the Wizards; all of them.

That night, I dreamed. I did everything in my power not to. But it came anyway. I was laying with Max at the cliff rail at grandmothers. I could smell the surf. Feel the wind. Hear the waves hit the rocks. I could hear the music of the sea. He brushed my cheek with the tips of his fingers. He looked like my Max. The Max I thought I loved. "Leave with me Em? Leave with me before it's too late." I did not answer. He pulled me into his embrace and I felt so relaxed, safe, loved. We kissed and looked into each others eyes. I felt his skin with mine. We made love in the sun. I thought to my self that it was a beautiful dream, where I could love Max freely. My Max. I laid in his arms content, never wanting to leave. For the first time in a long time, I was completely happy. He looked down at me with his most handsome smile. The smile I loved. But that smile faded and it manifested into the monster Max, and he said "Wake up."

I sat up with a start with my breath labored. The sun rising, and me naked. There was a Lillie lying with grass and sand in the bed. I was discussed with my own weakness, my own heart. More tricks. More lies. I screamed into the air "I hate you." My heart breaking all over again, and the tears starting to fall all over again.

I went through the week numb. Feeling so out of control of my emotions, my body, my will and my life. I had no control what so ever. Not even in my dreams. I refused to sleep. Work being the only release to me. But I did find myself on autopilot. Not having the passion that once drove me. Not being in body and mind. I watch the elements still scream danger. The oaks whispering that there was true danger coming. Sparrows and Jays bouncing and screaming that it was coming. And I thought, "I don't care anymore. Let it come. Let it end." I was tired of being alone in all of this with no say. No say as to how my life runs. Living in dreams and wishes. Destine to what others want from me, but the happiness in life was missing. You know, the part that makes it all worth it. All I knew is that my life was false like Max said that day in my backyard. I was living in a world I didn't belong in. Actually I didn't belong in any of the worlds. I had to face realities. abrupt and discouraging realities. I only wanted to hide from the worlds. All of them. I could continue to fight. But what am I fighting. Fate and destiny? Did they exist? I couldn't even tell when the next bump in the road was coming. What was there to fighting for? What made it all worth it. I prayed to God, but he has not answered me. That broke my heart. Broke my heart more than anything. I depended on his love.

Saturday, I sat in the park on the grass. Zee sat with me daring any dog to make a move towards him. They all seem to know, his mood was as mine. He would take care of him self. The tress whispered to run. Hide away. I watched the clouds move across the sky gracefully. They too said to take care. I was fed up with it all. Yes I had power to change everything. I just didn't know how. Didn't know how to change things. I mean I knew how but to what? What would make my past lie of a life change. My heart mend. For my life to mean more than nothing. And then again, maybe that was it. All the power and control means nothing when you are nothing. Nothing but an incubator for the wizards, some kind of status symbols to the Witches, and a pain in the ass to my family. Zee growled and he was gone.

"You are so much more than those things, Em."

Max sat close behind me. And hearing his words, in his voice, cause tears to fall though I didn't turn around.

Defeated I said "Go away Max. I really need you to go away."

I pulled my knees up and wrapped my arms around my legs. I laid my forehead against them and cried quietly.

He petted my hair and said "Can't."

I could not understand any of this. I couldn't understand my own heart. I stopped crying and wiped my eyes but laid my head back on my knees. I wanted to badly just to give everyone what they wanted from me. I thought then I would be free. Everyone would be happy and I would be free.

From my knees I asked "So Max, I know what the Wizards want from me, what the Witches want from me, what my family wants from me. What do you want from me?" He was still there petting my hair but didn't answer me. I shook my head at the lack of response. Typical for me. Anything that would help make sense, denied to the Mixed Blood Witch.

Then I smelled them. **Wizards**!

My head popped up. I looked back to Max who had already detected there approach. His monster on. I told him. "Max. Go!"

He shook his head, in his deadly monster voice he said "There not hear for me."

I looked at him confused. He looked into my eyes and said "There here to take you." I was still confused. He continued "They have become impatient for the heir."

I laughed "You know that I don't care." The jays bounced in front of me screaming. The oak warned to me hide. I said to Max "Leave or they will kill you." I turned my body to looked directly at him "I don't know why I should care, but go anyway."

He shook his head "Not without you."

I said, "Maybe its time to end this. Maybe its time I made a stand."

He said "That day will come, but not today." He rose like a tall tree and grabbed my hand. He had me standing and said "Maybe when you come back, you won't hate me so much." He had me in a bear hug and I found myself on a mountain, with mists hiding the lower valleys. I looked around and there was a little cabin. And Max was not there.

I attempted to transport home but nothing happened. I was bound. I sat down on the ground and cried again out of anger. Again in the power of another. No control over my life. Nothing. I called to Zee and he appeared. I grabbed my cat and walked over to the cabin. I looked around and found that the place was very isolated. In the cabin was a fire burning in the fireplace. A table and chairs and a bed. Holding my cat I walked to the over stuffed chair by the fire. I sat and stared into the fire and thought of nothing. I just stared. I must have been there for hours. Never moving, wondering or thinking. Just being. Being trapped in a Wizard game again. Maybe I was getting used to it.

Waking, and noting that there was no dreaming, I could smell the bacon cooking and found a blanket over me. I looked to see who was there. Mandra was at the stove and Marcus sat at the table. Mandra looked over at me. "Grandmother?"

She smiled and Marcus looked over at me "Well Princess. How are you?"

I huffed "Like most of the time, I am confused."

Grandmother put the bacon on the table and put eggs on a dish and handed it to Marcus. "Would you like to eat Em?"

I shook my head. "How did you know where I was?" I thought about it "Where am I?" Mandra handed me a cup of coffee. "Max told me where you where."

I was surprised "Max told you?"

Marcus then said "He made a rare appearance to your grandmother and explained the situation. He seems to have some honor left."

I did not respond to that. I had no Idea what Max was about anymore, only the monster and the dreams.

Grandmother said "Well he was in the dark and spoke in a voice I barely recognized. I think you are the only one to have seen him in full form in a long time"

Again I thought Max was still a mystery to me now.

Marcus knowing my thoughts smiled. He then said "The Pure Bloods are becoming bolder and more expectant of you. They believe the time is now for the heir."

I looked at him blankly. My depression overpowering, "I don't care anymore."

He looked concerned. "Em. You are the Princess. You are entitled your respect and your dignity."

I looked to Mandra. "Why can't I just be? Just be me. Not the Princess. Not the Witch." Mandra sat on the arm of the Chair. "You are you. You are Em. You are who we all love. The Princess and the Witch are parts of you but not the total you."

I thought about that. Yes. My family loved me. And I loved them.

Marcus looked off and then back. "The Wizards counsel has called off the Wizards. They have been admonished."

I looked at him "I hate the Wizards Marcus. I hate their assumptions; their intents."

He looked at me somewhat concerned. "We have to look to God in this Princess. We must pray." I nodded.

We walked out of the cabin and were about to leave when I smelled the Wizards. I looked to Marcus who stood stout and looked forward. Then Edwin and several other Wizards appeared. I readied my self though I had no idea if I could defend my self still being bound. Then I felt my power return full force.

Edwin smiled and said "Em, its time to come with us."

I laughed at him. It hit me so funny. I laughed so hard I could barley stay straight on my feet. Maybe because I had been in the Normal world so long that it sounded ridicules. Maybe because he couldn't make me do anything; maybe because it was time for all to stop.

Marcus stepped forward. "The counsel has spoken Edwin. The Princess is not to be accosted."

Edwin nodded to the Elder. "Yes, but what of the Heir. It is time for the Heir."

I felt Max then though he was not visible. I saw something in Edwin's eyes. I knew Edwin felt him too.

The Wizards stood without retreat. I looked to my grandmother and she nodded. In that moment she and I stood ready in witches war appeal of brown leather pants and shirts. Swords in our hands above our heads ready for battle.

Marcus walked in front of us and said to Edwin "You see. This is not the easy task you believed it to be. I suggest that you follow the orders of the counsel. In fact, I order it." At that moment, standing across from us on a rise above the Wizards was the monster Max. Dressed in his normal black, with black duster blowing back behind him.

Edwin turned to face Max. "Ah the Wicked half blood Wizard. I should have known you'd be about.' He sneered with hate "Ready to face your end?"

I looked to Max and back at the Wizards. Max the Monster laughed his ugly laugh at Edwin "And are you the Wizard that is able to do that Edwin? I am ready." And then he gave a little challenging bow.

Edwin was caught by his words as he knew he did not possess the power that Max did. He never has in spite of his pure blood. He looked to the other Wizards who, in reality were Mix Blood. He knew he stood at that moment the only Pure Blood.

He nodded to Marcus. "Another time then."

He and the other Wizards disappeared. The Max looked over to us.

Marcus held out his arms to Max "Please Max. Please"

But Max disappeared; again hidden from all who seek him. Marcus dropped his head. When he raised his head, his eyes looked to me.

He softly and sadly said "He continues his vow Princess."

I nodded. I knew Max protected me that day.

Mandra looked to me "Come home Em. Come home and heal." I looked at my grandmother straying from her ever regal pose, with pleading eyes. I weakly smiled to her and nodded.

We returned to Pacific City; to my grandmothers home. I was greeted by Lincon and Molly. They hugged me and Molly cried. We all had dinner, and I knew that my mood was depressive and quiet. Once everyone had gone, I said good night to grandmother and Marcus.

"Em. Being home will help."

I smiled at my grandmother and said "You have always helped me grandmother." I smiled at Marcus "And you too, my true Guardian." He smiled as I turned for the stairs.

CHAPTER 30

I went to my room to find that it was the same as when I left. I went to the widow's tower and looked over the ocean. Remembering the last time I had stood there. It was after the infamous maiden dance when I kissed Max.

I huffed and said out loud "I sure screwed things up that night." And from behind me I heard

"Why do you say that?"

I didn't have to turn. He was going to plague me. As the smart ass bitch he thought I was I said "Why do think?"

He laughed and said "But you loved me then."

I turned around with the priestess hovering. "And you won your capture the maiden crap." I started to walk down the stairs and thought about transporting home

"I'll only follow you."

I looked back at the Monster Max with the immortal feline eyes of the Priestess and with full truth and intent I snarled. "If you want that joint death wish Max, let's get on with it. I tired now. I want it over."

I walked down the stairs and he was sitting on the bed. I closed my eyes in frustration. I opened my eyes to find Max standing in front of me.

"Please go away."

He shook his head. "I want to call a truce."

I laughed "Why? What do you need a truce for? You do what you want anyway."

He shook his head. "No… I don't do everything I want."

I raised an eyebrow. "It appears so to me." I started to walk around him and he grabbed my arm. I stopped and didn't move or look at him. I didn't ask to be released I stood waiting for the next move.

"I am sorry Em. I can only reach you in your dreams. You close me out and push me away all other times." He wrapped his arms around me. "I never tricked you in those dreams. Everything that was said and everything we did, you had free will over."

I was going for the click when he pulled me closer to him. Well of course my heart beat like a drum and the click was far off. My face was at his and he gave a devilish smile "I am a Wizard. I can control you if I chose."

I narrowed my eyes, "don't go to sleep."

He laughed at that comment which was delivered with total commitment. He stopped his laughter and looked at me. The monster gone from his face and only Max remained.

In a soft voice he started "We should have consummated our relationship when we got back from the Prom." I looked into his eyes with pure hate. I hated the conversation. I was hurt and ashamed. I did not want to talk about this.

I pushed to get lose from his hold and in an angry threatening voice I said "Shut up Max." Then my powers were bound again, I tried to pull away and he held me to his chest. He kept on going "Things may have been different then. Maybe that day on the beach, if you had agreed to take off, we may have been free. Maybe there would have been a chance we…."

I was livid at that point, "A chance at what? It was just a game to see who could get to the witch first? It wasn't real, remember? So why talk about it. I know the truth. I live with it. You tricked me and I fell for it. There is nothing else to say." He just held me.

He continued in a soft voice." On that night of the infamous maiden dance, I had no choice. I was …bewitched. Under a spell that I was not able to overcome from the moment I saw you that night. You were the Priestess, and I was at your command." Again I snarled "Shut up! There is nothing more I want to hear about the past."

He ignored me and continued. "When you kissed me, it was a dream I carried for years. After the kiss, I was ordered home and sequestered. Not to leave the grounds. I left anyway to come back to you. Again, the spell I could not nullify. I had to be with you."

I tied for the click again. All I got was a Husky laugh. "Stop talking. I don't want to talk about it." Still ignoring me, "When I showed up the next year and kissed you at the fire, the elders knew. I was bound in the halls for years. No freedom, no magic and definitely no you. In the halls I could only look to see where you were and what you were doing. *And who you were doing it with.*"

I could not believe that he had actually been watching. Looking away from his face I sneered "Shut up."

He just kept going "What kinds of dangers were around you. My only chance at freedom was to cut ties with you forever as the Elders ordered. I had to hurt you so I could protect you. So I could be released to protect you." He nuzzled my neck. "It was my vow; to protect you even from me and from your self."

I pulled my head back to look directly at him. "So why now? You are free you can go any where and do anything you want. You don't have to hang around. I release you from your vow." Defeated I continued "I am tired of hurting Max. I lived a semi normal life. I don't want anymore heart ache. I've learned to live without you or anyone else. Why now? You have your rouge life and you stupid games. Why pull me back in when I don't care anymore."

His eyes breathlessly beautiful at that moment though his monster hovered close. "I have my vow. I have that left. Everything else faded away except you and that vow." He let go and I walked to the window and looked over the yard and garden.

He followed me and then stood next to me. He sighed "OK look. I was kind of messed up there for a while. You saw me. I was pretty insane." He nodded with acknowledgment "Still am in a way." He looked away and then back to me "Anyway, once I... left you... the Elders let me go. I guess they thought I would just go home. I didn't. I dropped off the radar so to speak." He looked at me. "I...well... I wasn't as discreet as a Mastered Wizard should be. " He laughed a little shook his head. "I don't know what I was thinking. I was stocking my brothers. I was stocking the Elders and I was…. watching you."

I interrupted "Stocking me."

Looking deep into my eyes he nodded. He looked back out the window "I sent messages that I was going to kill them all. I even caught Edwin." He smiled "Caught him at your house trying to figure out how to get in while you slept." He looked down. "I could have killed him. I wanted to. If Jordan had not stopped me……" He looked off. He looked back into my eyes "I was doing what I wanted; transporting in front of the Normals; Levitating in front of the Normals. Doing anything I wanted in front of and with the Normals. The Elders tried to reach me over and over. I knew they wanted me locked up again; under their control again. It didn't matter that I kept my part of the bargain and had not made contact with you again."

He look away and then back at me "The… Elders reported me to the Wizard Counsel as a wild mixed blood wizard; a Rouge Mastered Wizard. They reported that I was not following their instructions; Attacking and attempting to kill a Pure Blood Wizard; Killing a mortal." He paused for a second "I am the one who killed Jeremy." I stopped breathing for a second. I never would have thought it to be my Max. He was so young yet; still pure of heart. He looked at me and I did not give any expression. "I left him impaled on a stake in Deanna's patio." He was quiet for a second. He continued " They also accused me of showing a lack of discretion; Disrupting prophesies….." He slightly bent in his face to mine, and looked clearly into my eyes "I slept with the Witch chosen for pure blood to produce a magical Wizard Heir." He looked away again. "The Wizard Counsel sent a hunter after me. I knew he was there and actually dared him to find me. He did. He attempted to restrain me." He raised his brows looking back at me. "I was hoping he would kill me. Just to get it over with. I was pretty empty. I felt just the way you have been feeling." He looked off again. "But he said that I was being taken back to the halls. I released my self from his restraints. The 'Hunter' attacked me and I killed him. I just lost it. He came at me, not prepared in dealing with the powers I have picked up and perfected. When he came at me with the intent to kill me like I wanted, something happened in me and I thought of you. You left to deal with the Pure Bloods. I knew I couldn't let that happen. I killed him with a lighting bolt he never saw coming. I never meant to harm anyone in my whole life, but have found that I am good at it."

Max looked back at me, "After that, I couldn't stay away. Why? I worried about you. I wanted to be with you. I missed you." He pulled me into a hug "And I can't let you feel that empty hopeless way. I can't let *you* give up."

I felt for Max. I had to realize that he too paid a price. I gave in and wrapped my arms around his neck and hugged him. I said to him with all my heart "I am so sorry Max. I have been so self centered and never realized that you would be so punished. I never meant to hurt you." I let go and moved back out of his arms remembering him in my backyard and his words to me. I then said "But you meant to hurt me. And you did emotionally, but you meant to hurt me physically." I shook my head "I can't understand why?"

He nodded, "Because I could not allow them to take control over you. I wanted to die and dead I couldn't protect you. They want only to use you for their own ambitions. Once I was given my power back, I was ordered to break ties with you. I closed my mind so that the Elders would not know my plan as they watch to ensure that I had fulfilled the bargain of my release." He reached out and petted my cheek "I wanted to take you with me, whether it was hiding somewhere or death. I only knew I couldn't let them have you." Realizing that he would have killed me that day and remembering him as the monster, I shook my head and moved away from his touch. "Em, when I did see you, when I looked into your eyes, I knew I could never hurt you. It was a plan that I could not carry out for any price. Including their plan for you."

He stood and looked at me then, "That's why I came back and tried to talk to you. But you refused to listen."

I looked at him and snarled "What did you expect? I was nothing more that the race, remember? Nothing but the stupid little Witch bound to the Wizards by some stupid prediction." He stood where I had left him at the window. He looked so sad, yet as handsome as ever. He said "I was not apart of that. I'm a mixed blood remember. I could not be the one so I was never involved in that race. I spent my time protecting you from the race. I never would have believed I would ever be with you… though I dreamed of it since the day we met."

I stood in the middle of the room with my mind racing. Who do I trust, who was right who was wrong? What is the consequence with any of the decisions that I make. Where do I go from here? "Trust me Em." I looked at him. He was Max and he look sincere. And wanted so much to trust him. I wanted so much to be able to have that feeling of safety and love in my life again. To love Max again. But how? After everything over the years, how do we get back there?

There was a knock on my door. I looked to Max who faded but remained by the window. He was nothing more than a transparency in my sight alone. "Come in," Marcus opened my door and walked into the room. He looked at me and he could smell Max but could not see him. His look was of worry and pain.

He desperately asked "Is he well?"

I looked to Max who nodded "Yes. He is well."

Marcus then took a breath and gathered him self. He said "Princess, the Wizard Counsel has asked for a meeting. It will take place three weeks from Wednesday." He took my hand and looked weary and old. "Princess, forgive a silly old man. I am insulted and grieved at what is expected. I had no idea how much I would come to love you, and how much the agreement would harm you."

I hugged Marcus and said "Please, my True Guardian, I have only felt love and care from you. I have nothing to forgive you for. But I will request from you, your loyalty in the near future. I will not be used. By your kind or any other."

He smiled at me. "I am and always loyal to you, my Princess." He began to leave and turned to me, "Will you tell Max that I am, and always will be, loyal to him as well. I wait for the day he forgives me."

I smiled at him and nodded. He left the room quietly shutting the door. Max became full again and I asked him "Why hurt Marcus? Why does he need forgiving?"

He shook his head "It's a Wizard thing. He and I….well let's just say, can't agree."

Max then walked to me and he put me in a hug. We were in the field at Hat Creek. The sun was out and the trees moved in the warm breeze. I heard their whisper of "The Princess returns." I looked to Max who knew how I felt there; how special it was to me. He asked "Let me hear please?"

I looked to the Trees "Let him hear."

And I could see that Max could hear the trees welcome me back. They began their mystical and beautiful music. I closed my eyes and rocked to the sound. The peace entered my heart and soul.

"How long has it been since you danced Em?"

I looked over at Max "Since my last Solstice three years ago."

He took my hand "Than Dance with me now?"

I hear the trees saying "The Wizard will dance with the Princess." Max waved his hand and I wore a simple white dress that blew with the breeze. We danced as if at a ball. I raised us into the air and we floated as we danced. He held me in his arms and I laid my head on his shoulder. I relaxed in his safe arms. I felt the peace and freedom from the music of the trees. When the sun was moving down I lowered us to the ground. I looked to all the trees and blow a kiss. I said thank you to the trees and the breeze.

I looked to Max and smiled with warmth for his gesture. It made all the difference for me. It brought me back to Mother Earth and to Gods creations, Gods love. Max then said "Stay with me? Only for a while?" I dropped my smile. I did not know how to answer him. Yes or no. I was so lost and yet the trees and the breeze brought me some peace. Max said again "Stay with me. Just for a little while. Please." His same question that has been posed to me for years. Leave with him and now stay with him. I looked to the trees for help and received their whisper "He is like you." I could see then, that Max was as lost and alone as I was. I nodded and he pulled me into a hug.

I found that I was in a bed room in a castle. Everything was of stone and wood. There was a huge door and a sitting area around a fire place. There was a huge bed on top of a platform with stairs to the bed.

I looked and Max stood near me. "Where are we?"

He kept his eyes on me "It really isn't anywhere. But it's where I live in my heart."

I walked to the Window and looked out and there was a cliff side and ocean. There was also a field and trees like at hat creek.

I turned to Max, "You created this?"

He nodded. "I created it for you."

Then I remembered. The day at the table when I described what I thought a real princess would have. I walked back to Max and kissed him. I had to. I needed too.

I pulled away and asked "Am I safe here?"

He said "No one will find us."

I asked "And Zee, can he come?" Max nodded and said "If he chooses too."

I called Zee. He appeared and he hissed at Max but curled up on the bed. I looked at Max then. He no longer came to mind as the Monster Max. But my Max.

Max took my hand and we went out the door. We stood on the landing, and the bottom floor was open to the elements. Birds and butterflies flew and nested. There were thousands of Lilies, roses, lavender and rosemary. There were other herbs and other flowers I was not able to name. There were Willow trees, Apple trees, cherry trees and dogwood trees sprouting out over the room that was open to the sky. Max pulled me to the next door and opened it. There were ladies in waiting sitting in a room filled with thousands of gowns and shoes. I laughed. Max closed the door and he lead me down the stone stairs to the bottom floor where the birds met me with their sweet song. The dogwood, apple and cherry trees singing and dropping there blossoms to surround me. Max pulled me on to another area on the bottom floor. There was a huge dinning room and the table over flowed with Lobster. It ranged from whole lobsters to every dish made of lobster. I laughed and He took me out another door. There on a lawn were every kind of cat on earth. Lions, tigers, bobcats, cougars, leopards and many I could not name. All grooming, sleeping, or playing. I looked in disbelief and then I cried. I dropped to my knees and cried.

Max sat on the ground next to me. "I only wanted to make you happy Em."

I looked at him. "Max, this is wonderful. I cant believe you remembered a stupid little dream of a little girl" I looked deep into his eyes. " I am crying for us. For our childhood and our desires. Our lives as God made them." I looked back out at the felines spread out over the lawn. He said nothing and I continued "What we could have developed into if left to God and not the Wizards and Witches."

He nodded knowing he had the same thoughts. In fact they were very close to our first conversation at the creek side. And he said "Why not let God develop our destiny?"

I looked at him and nodded. "After all, he is the creator."

Max took my hand and stood taking me with him. He looked at me seriously. "Your grandmother calls for you."

I didn't hear her. "Why didn't I hear her?"

He smiled "That's part of my dream. You only hear me?" I smiled at him. He looked hesitant "Should we go back?"

I shook my head vigorously "No! I want to stay." He smiled and kissed me and we were once again in the bedroom in the bed and we made love for hours. I knew in my heart, Max was my life partner. No other could take his place. No other could understand.

I stayed with Max for days. Just being together. Sometime quiet, sometimes playing in the ocean and dancing with the trees. A lot of time loving. Making up for years separated. We talk for hours, like in my dreams of him over the last few years. In fact he said that he lived in my dreams. He often waited for me to open to him in my dreams so that we could be together. He said "I think that those dreams kept me from really going over the edge. You kept me from going over."

We were there about five days. One morning I woke to find Max not at my side. Only lilies. In panic, I looked over the room and he was not there. I jumped from the bed. I called out to him and he did not materialize. I looked out to the ocean and it was gone as was the grove of trees and field for dancing. I opened the door to the room and found that everything was gone. Only white nothingness. I sat in a chair next to the fireplace confused. And then I realized, I was losing my perfect world that Max had created for me. I screamed for Max at that point and he still did not come. I sat there with tears running down my face.

I looked at Zee, and said "I guess that is the end of it. His game is over." Anger filled me again and I screamed into the air "Bastard! I hate you" Max was gone again mocking my love for him. Zee and I transported to grandmothers.

I stood at the cliff rail and looked out over the sea. My heart once again breaking and I felt so alone again. And honesty was there too. I loved Max and would fall for his tricks because I wanted him to love me in return. I wanted to be with him, no matter the outcome. I looked to the sky *"Lord, be kind to Max. Please forgive him for all that is sinful in his life and world. Pleased grant him your grace."* I looked down and then back to the heavens and said *"And maybe some for me too."* I knew it was his game. I was once again a pawn in a Wizard game. But I loved him. Couldn't help my self.

As I stood at the cliff rail Marcus called to me from the porch of the house and then was next to me. "Princess, we have been worried. Where have you been?" I looked at him without answering and he nodded sadly and said "Oh…. with Max." I nodded. He looked over the Ocean and said "I fear that Max is lost to us all. He may never be able to return free. And I know he would rather die than be controlled."

I looked at Marcus "As would I."

Marcus nodded and said "I know that Princess."

I hugged him and said "Maybe it is that wild and undisciplined Normal Blood. Or maybe it is the creator."

I step back to see Mandra standing with tears in her eyes and I grabbed her in a hug. "I am sorry grandmother. I had to go with him."

When I stepped out of the hug she was smiling "I know Em. I know."

She looked into my eyes and then her smile faded and she looked concerned.

I drew my brows in and asked "What grandmother?"

She smiled and shook her head "Nothing. Come in and have some tea."

CHAPTER 31

I went back to my home in Sacramento. I had quit my job and just lived quietly with Zee and my stray cats. I missed Max and I could not feel him near. I didn't dream of him. And then in the next breath, I hated him for playing with my heart. I still heard from my coworkers from time to time. And I did go out with them every so often. But I was not really interested in the normal world or any world except for the one that Max created for me. Where I could dance and sing. Where I was free with Max.

Needless to say, I defied the Wizard Counsel. I did not make the demanded appearance. What for? To be disrespected by those that thought they were superior to me. To be ordered to produce a child that was going to be used and tortured for their survival. Grandmother was right, if they had only trusted in God, their Pure Blood race would not be in the shape it was in.

Marcus was so concerned with that. "Princess they will send hunters for you." I laughed "So what. I can take care of my self."

He would say things like "Do you want to live as Max. With no one and nothing." Though I was hurt with Max and felt hate for him, I also knew I loved him. I would always defend Max with "He has something. He has his freedom and my love."

A month went by and I was expected to stand as a brides made with a coworker, Tiffany. I dressed with the other bridesmaids and stood in the church as witness her marriage to her true love. It was lovely and festive. She looked so happy and I was happy for her. I had to say that the normals knew how to love. And express and celebrate their love.

At the reception, I sat quietly at my assigned seat. I watched as the bride and groom danced. I remembered my last dance was with Max in our little world that did not exist. But I did not regret it. I loved remembering it. But I also was hurt with it. Why give me that to take it back without a word. The reception went on and I got up to stretch my legs. I looked around at the mortals laughing and dancing. Celebrating love of two people. I realized that I would only have that make believe place. No where would I have what Tiffany and her new husband would embrace. With my mixed blood, I could never to have that.

I stood in my room that night brushing my hair dry. I was so tired of being different and the wedding today was a reminder of things that would not be for me. It was another reminder of how different I was. *Never*fitting in any of the worlds under God. Never having the average of life because the Mortal or Immortal blood lines offered me no path. Only playing with my life and my heart. I knew I would not have a life with Max. Only the make believe world. The reality was clear but it didn't mean that I didn't long for the normality of the average life. The one that Mortals and Immortals enjoyed. A job, a lover, a home, maybe a child. I had tears run out of my eyes at that thought. I could not understand why I was denied these simple and average things.

"Because you are special."

Max stood behind me Obviously breaking through the barrier "The Priestess and the Princess of the Wizards. The mother of the future of the Wizards. You have obligations to your heritage." He said it softly. But not coming to close. I wiped my eyes and stared out the window. "I wanted to tell you I am sorry Em. My games go to far sometimes."

In my head I commanded *"Get Out!"* I did not turn around. But began with a new round of tears, I remained in my broken heart at the window. I would not allow him to see me cry. When I did not turn around, he left.

A month went by and I had not seen or felt Max. I did see the Shadow, but it seemed to understand that I met to confront who ever it was. It stayed back far enough that I new that I could not catch it. Even transporting was fruitless as by the time I did the shadow would do the same ending up out of my reach. I told my self that I was not devious enough to capture it. I always looked for that direct confrontation instead of capture. But what would I do with it once captured? I was just not interested enough in it to live my life around it.

The last time I saw the shadow in Sacramento was on a dusky rainy evening. It stood down the street from the coffee house that I was headed to. It stood as bold as you please watching me. I knew that the mortals could not see it. But I stood looking at it ready for confrontation. My posture demanding confrontation. The priestess stirring. I made it Clear in my posture that I would bring this to an end now, regardless of the mortals that stirred about. Then it was gone. Cowardly gone. I went into the coffee house and grabbed a coffee and went back out to sit at a table under the awning while the rain water ran off of it.

As I sat I thought of who it could be. I knew it wasn't Max from the time he was in my room and he was standing with me when it was at the creek. I didn't think that it could be anyone I knew yet it knew me. It knew where and when I would be somewhere. I was frustrated and refuse to live with it.

As I sat there I felt Max near. I was about to leave when he appeared with his hand on my arm. "Let go, I am in no mood."

He had his evil smile but not the monster face. Maybe due to the mortals milling about. "Since when do I care about your mood when it comes to these little encounters?"

I huffed "Your right. Never."

I was uncomfortable with him.

I needed to get away from him. "You are not getting away until I allow it. Sit still and listen to me."

I had enough and got up "don't you dare try your crap with me. I am not allowing it."

He laughed never letting go of my arm. "Really? And how are you going to stop me?"

I looked at him and said " I will find a way."

He pulled me back in the chair. I was going to pull a mortal woman scream when he stood to see the shadow across the street. He let go of me for a moment to see it. As he was standing and watching, Click; I was gone.

I was in the mall. Around a lot of people. But he was then there walking next to me. "Princess, how rude to transport with out word."

I did not look at him but kept walking quickly. "Leave me alone" is all I could say to him. I walked right into the lady's room. He did not follow and I clicked to a dressing room in Sears. I walked out and he was standing there. I headed for the exit. He was next to me.

I stopped. "What are you doing here."

He gave a evil smiled "To see you. Way else."

I knew I could not tolerate being near him "You've seen me. Your mission is over. You can go now." He gave an evil laugh.

He grabbed my arm and I knew if he did not let go I could not transport at least not without him. "Let me go."

Without looking at me he said "Don't be a difficult bitch. Do what your told."

I turned from the exit and he looked back at it. I headed for the pillar in the middle of the walkway. With the store crowded, I was able to maneuver it so he was caught by the crowd and the pillar. He was forced to let me go. I was now in the middle of the court yard of the mall. He was right there next to me.

He had my arm again and spoke to my ear in a ugly, threatening tone. "You will not get away from me. Behave and do what you are told."

I looked in his eyes and my response was simple. "Go to Hell were you belong."

He gave his evil grin. I began walking towing him with me. But he had a good grip on my arm. I know he would not fall for the pillar thing again so I ran into a wall with my shoulder and pretended to react in pain. When he lighten his grip, I pulled away and click.

I was trying to loose my self in the crowd. I saw him looking at me from the second floor. I clicked again. I was in a movie and sat through it. I was hiding and I knew it. I was discussed with my self.

I entered the house completely exhausted after the events of the day. I throw my hands up and the protection barrier was up over the house. Zee was very happy to see me. I then showered and put on a simple night gown. I grabbed the cat who was waiting at the bathroom door and got into bed. I brushed my hair till it was semi dry. I did not even look at the mail or turn on the news. ZEE made him self comfortable.

I turned off the light and, closed my eyes being thankful for my bed and the peace. I can't believe that Max would dare come back after playing with my heart again. And he scared me. I did not know him anymore. But then I felt kind of bad. Maybe he needed help. I wish I could help him. Help him be the Max that I remember. The Max I fell in love with…..but, who knows, the monster could be the real Max.

Out of a dead sleep, I woke with the hair on my neck and arms standing up. I could smell him. I opened my eyes to the dark room. I sat up to scan the area. Though a light emulated from the kitchen, it was not enough to help me see. Zee growled low and steady. And then, in the very darkest corner of the room, he stood motionless. Before I could build my defenses, he was at me with incredible speed. The Monster Max! He held my arms down with his strength. His body on top of mine. And then I felt his magic holding me and binding my power. "What do you want, why are you in my room? How dare you bind my power." was all I could get out while fighting his successful attempts to immobilize me. Zee ran under the bed continuing to scream and howl. He pulled my hands above my head. Held my hands with only one of his. He then look down at me with a irritating wicked grin. He met my angry defiant eyes. I knew I had to get it together if I was to escape.

"My, my Emily Star… You are so easily captured. Isn't it fortunate that it was me" His voice was smooth and deep; almost sensual. I continued to glare at him while I sent out a call for help. "Oh no my Dear, there is no call to send. I will block all incoming and outgoing information. I need your full attention." He moved his head so that he was at the side of my head and was breathing in my hair. He then lifted his head and gave me a smooth but evil smile.

Though warned against it, I challenged him at that point not willing to give up without a fight. "I will kill you if you touch me. Besides, you've already gotten what you wanted from me."

He returned to his grin and with his finger trace my jaw and moved slowly down my neck while I angrily glared at him, my breath labored . He moved his head back but kissed my cheek and then continued down the side of my face and neck. I then bucked a jerked only causing him to laugh low and lusty. He moved over and only looked down into my face.

"If your not after …" I stumbled and could not come up with the word "… then what do you want?'

Looking directly into my eyes he said "Only you."

"What are you talking about? Make sense!" Though I tried to look away, that creep had my eyes with his, and I could not move or look away. He was making sure I knew his power and that he could over power me if he chose. I did note, his eyes were older, wiser and angrier.

"Why are you bewildered, my love. I only want you." His voice low and dark. He repeated the reticules.

"You're a pig. What is it you want? Let me go, I don't want to play in your games."

He smiled big again and then he moved his lips to my neck under my ear. That released his gaze. His eyes then moved back to mine. He was looking at me but his hand was caressing my neck. His smile continued as he said "As I have already made clear to you, I am here for you. After all, that is what I have been charged with since I was fourteen." He then returned to his evil smile as his fingers outlined my Collar bone.

"Guarding me Max. Not raping me." He only smiled big and continued his little game of touching me. I decided to challenge him again. I needed him to slip. I needed full power back. In a evil witches snarl I said "Why hold my power back, Max? Are you afraid?,"

He only laughed at me. Then He stopped, and so I understood clearly, He looked into my eyes with pure truth. he said with a low ugly voice "If I let you use those powers we would both be dead before it was all over."

I knew my heart was pounding and he could hear my blood pumping. He continued " Besides, in addition to guarding you, I have an…attraction to you." He then bent his head and began to kiss the lower part of my neck. I knew I had to get out of this before I was unable to go. I could not trust my self when it came to Max. I tried to think of something to retaliate with. I attempted to levitate the lamp and throw it him but it dropped to the floor. He laughed "What a shame. You broke your lamp." He then seriously said "I guess I should tell you, that I will thwart all of your efforts." It was true he had my power bond tight. I was not prepared which was my own undoing. The birds warned me.

All of the elements were screaming at me and I did not prepare. I was a fool to be in this position. He then moved back to kissing my neck.

"I don't believe that Mastered Wizards are to show sexual attraction to their charges or at all. So what are you up to."

He gave a low laugh and then said "Don't believe what others have told you about Wizards, Emily Star."

I hissed challenging him "The Elders said it Max, you were there."

He stopped and he moved so that we were face to face and eye to eye. The Monster face in focus, with the fangs clear. It was more frightening than I had ever felt with him. The panther so close with the heat of his breath on my face. He said in a angry whisper "I don't answer to those Elders, remember." He narrowed his yellowed eyed stare angrily "And neither do you from what I understand."

I started to become afraid again. Afraid of Max once again. But I would never let that monster know it.

"Get off me!"

He was laughing low again. "Really? I thought you might enjoy this with me." I was really getting mad now. I needed to be mad so I could get away. But it had to be when my heart slowed to get to the click. And until he slipped and let me go and the click happened, I was stuck. And as long as my heart pounded I could not get to the click. Then he said "It wont happen. I am not letting go." He knew my effort.

"Get off me Max!" I looked straight in to his eyes and matched his anger and added hate. He just gave a sigh and moved his hand to the little buttons of my night gown. My eyes got really big and my heart went nuts again. *Calm down, Emily Star, calm down. Get to that place.* He looked at me again and he knew what was happening in my head. He opened my gown and exposed my breast.

I was mortified. "You would not dare." I challenged him through clinched teeth. He attempted to move his mouth to mine and I turned my head. He pulled by arms tighter and my head locked in-between my arms. He only brushed his lips over mine and I got a chill up my back. He looked at me triumphant then. I only became angrier.

In a slow growl I told him "Let...Me.. GO!" Several tortures for him entered my head which I let him see clearly.

His head again moved kisses down my neck to my chest and over to the exposed breast. "STOP!"

His head came up and he gave a mock evil pout. "How do you know you would not like it."

Seeing red I stated "Let me go. I have had enough of this. I do not intend to be your victim"

He then stated. "Well, if I let you go you would only leave or set me on fire. So we will have to stay this way until your calm and rational. And I have to talk to you about something. And to prevent any interruptions, I need your heart beating hard so even if I do let go, you cant transport." How was I supposed to be rational?

"This is not a conversation starter, Max? You heard my demand. Follow it."

He laughed his evil laugh again and looked in my angry eyes, "Princess, I cant not acknowledge your demand. I am not that kind of Wizard any longer." He was having too much fun. Another game for him.

Without being able to stop my self I screamed in his face and said "I DON'T WANT YOU!" Again a laugh.

My breathing was still out of control. My heart still pounding. "Please Max, I will not set you on fire. Let me go?"

His eyebrow went up " Well, 'Please'. He was being wicked and he knew it. He was having so much fun with this. I decided that I would no longer allow him a reaction. So when he came close to my lips I stared at him without expression. I wanted only to concentrate on getting to the click. He returned my porcelain stare with a feather of a kiss. Again my spine shivered. He continued to kiss my lips softly and I refused to respond. He would not be ignored and as his kissed me again. Then he placed his hand on that same bare breast and I opened my mouth to protest. He took advantage of that as well. He kissed me with a little too much imitation of passion. When he was through with that kiss, I expected him to let go of my breast. But of course, the breast was reacting and he smiled.

With true death in my heart snarled "You son of a bitch. I am going to kill you when I get free."

He only retorted "Then I will never let you go."

Each time I had a plan to calm my self, he would do something else. I did not want him to go any father, and he knew it.

When he lifted up to uncover the other breast, I quickly asked." What did you have to talk to me about?"

In mid movement he stopped and looked back at me. Not continuing in his assault and not smiling. "May I say that I was hoping this could be stretched out a bit. But you are right, Em, we do need to talk." I thought this would be my chance to get away from him. "Then get off and we will have a cup of tea and talk." I tried to be convincing, but hiding ones nature from a immortal is not a power I possess. A ball of fire was in my head.

"I can see my self now, Locked in some stone crypt in Louisiana or in France should I let you go."

I giggled at that "Thanks Max… I never thought of that."

He smiled "If it is fire or the crypt, I should enjoy myself until that time." He looked at me with the same mocking evil grin as before. "Lets continue having fun. Shall we?" I gave in to the conversation so he would not go farther.

"OK! Lets talk."

He moved so quickly I had no time to react. He had sat up braced against the headboard and I was sitting between his legs my back to his chest, with his arms holding my arms in front of me. The blood started to run back into my arms. They still felt numb and tingled and I was still unable to move. His mouth at my ear, he started the conversation he should have begun from the beginning of my life. But my mind went to the voice in my ear and not the words.

"In my secret moves and eavesdropping I have discovered, Edwin and his cronies have plans my love. Unfortunately, you and *I* are the targets of his plan.. He seeks power transfer. Oh and me dead. You on the other hand… Well let just say, youth, beauty and power. And of course you dead. He never really had any power to talk about." He shifted to my other ear while his left hand held my arms and his right dared to hold my bare breast. "Max!" He continued while he held the traitor I called my breast began to react. "I believe that he will have successes in his little scheme because he has help from somewhere. And depending on his accomplice there could be further things that we don't know. " He then softly moved his finger around the nipple of the breast when it decided to stand up and take notice. I was still arguing with my heart, my breast and my breathing. "Max, Stop it *Please!*" I then asked "besides what about being immortal." He laughed "Yes well, being immortal has its perks. You get to stay young and live a very long time. But we can die. We can be killed."

His hand went back to hold the breast and not teasing it. "How can they do anything to us. You have your 'Ways" and I have mine to protect my self. And I may protect you too if you let me go."

He chuckled "I believe, as long as they know where we are at, there is a chance that they will devise a way." He kissed my neck and then said "And I cant let you go because I will, I'm sure, burst into flames."

I huffed, "No one has known where you have been. Why worry about it, Just keep being gone."

He only laughed at me. I was concerned with my reaction to him. He was molesting me and my body was reacting in his favor. The only solace was what he was telling me. "What can they do. They can make you assist them in changing someone's powers. Can They?"

He resumed his last stunt with the nipple and my heart began to pound hard "No, but I'm not the only wizard on the block. And the accomplice could be a Witch or Wizard with substantial powers. " Still continuing to prevent my click of escape he said "He needs to become a Vampire though, I think that is the change he will use. And change the others as well. It all has to happen at the right moment to achieve his desire. At least that is what I believe is his plan. Then you and I will have a very hard time remaining alive." He continued to nuzzle my ear and neck.

"Why are you doing this. Cant you see I hate you. Are you thick headed?"

He was smiling. I could feel it. "Oh no. Just enchanted." Trying to direct the conversation and ignore his touch I asked. "Why does he want you dead? You've been gone. What do you have to do with this?" He was quite for a minute and his hand on my breast had stopped. " Lets just say that I am not nor have I ever been his favorite person." Max laughed "Especially after I slept with you." I though of Edwin always trying to touch me and maneuver to attack me for the heir. But was Max any less evil for the same thoughts?

I challenged "What difference which Wizard? You all wanted the same thing."

Max grabbed my chin and turn my face to him. His monster face on and evil voice said "He did not care about you. His plan was to raped you, and take what he could from you. He did not care about you or what you represent." He took a breath, and said " I see you for who and what you are." He loosen his grip but I did not turn away this time.

"Why me, Max? Why would he be so obsessed with me? He is not the only Pure Blood." He remained serious. "Your powers, the heir, what else. He feels that he should father the future." He kissed my cheek and spoke against it while looking into my eye's. "You may deny your gifts. And what and who you are. But others are fully aware and are envious, or frightened." I continued to look into his eyes knowing he was not going to hurt me. I just knew. Maybe I could see it or maybe he allowed me to know it. I was safe.

He continued "I believe that Edwin is both envious and scared. Which causes him to desire control over your powers." After a moment of silence and eye to eye interaction, he resumed his teasing of my breast. I attempted to pull away and he held me in place..

"How do we protect ourselves?" I could hardly get the words out.

"We take a trip"

I turned my head away. "Go to Hell. I am not going any where. And especially with you." He laughed "Well maybe that grandmother of yours will make sense to you. We have to go see some…. Friends"

I huffed "I don't have friends."

He stopped and in a soft whisper in my ear he said " I am your friend Em."

I looked over at him and he looked sincere. He looked like my Max then. But what kind of friend takes over your mind and body against your will. Tricks you and teases you. He smiled and then began his little game again

"How else was I going to be able to talk to you and enjoy your company for so long."

I could not understand him anymore. He was so back and forth. One minute teasing and smiling like Max, the next the monster snarling and threatening. He allowed my beating heart to slow before I had a heart attack. He laid down next to me to the chagrin of Zee. As long as I was not as violent physically to him as I was in my mind, he did not make any more advances. He did continue to hold me down and block my transmissions.

"Who do you want to see and where are they?" I had to know.

Max who had me with my head on his chest, spoke softly "These are the High Wizard Counsel. The true elders; They are in Paris." With my head on his chest, I could hear his heart pounding as loud as mine. I asked him sarcastically,

"You mean the same Elders that ordered you never to see me again, *or touch me again?*" He was still for a moment only and said "No." His heart still beat as fast as mine, "They are the only ones to prevent a new creature being created out of a non worthy beings like Edwin. They will speak with the Vampire lords. We will have to also see some of your people in Italy. He sighed again in stupid arrogant way, "Though they have no rules to speak of."

I thought of one, "Harm to another comes back three fold" I was hoping he would take it personally.

He chuckled and cupped my breast again and held me so I could not move. " I will take my chances. And who knows I might like the consequences"

I was so tired. I had no fight in me anymore. And though he was still there, my eyes were heavy. I had to sleep. I didn't know if I was really that tired or if Max was doing it. "Max, I am going to sleep now. Don't touch me a whole lot. If you do, I will wake up and burst into flames with you."

He took a mock in take of breath. "Oh Em, What do you take me for. I like my victims coherent and attentive as you know."

I could not keep up with his bizarre bantering. "Just the same. FIRE Max."

When I opened my eyes the next morning, I was looking directly into the light hazel eyes of Max. "Why are you plaguing me?" To my chagrin, my arms and legs were entwined with his. I untangled my legs as quickly as I could, and started to get up.

He grabbed my arm, and was staring at me in a serious way. I tried to pull away and he continued to hold my arm. "You were very … active in your sleep." is all he said. He was not saying it in humor as expected. I didn't realized that I had dreamed. I did not remember. Of course, I did not have bad dreams when I was with Max.

I said "Max, let go. I need the bathroom." He did not let go at first. He just kept staring at me. "Max!" and he let go. I made my way to the bathroom and after a minute of wake, I realized I was free.

Then his evil mocking voice came through the door. "I will just follow you. Besides. Mandra is on her way."

I brushed my teeth, washed my face and combed my hair. I left the bathroom to the smell of coffee brewing. I walked to my closet and pulled out some jeans and a T-shirt. I heard Max go in the bathroom. I changed clothes quickly so I could have privacy. Of course, Max emerged from the bathroom fully groomed and dressed in slacks, shirt and jacket. His hair combed back.

He then stated boldly and proudly, " Just so you know Em, I can see through doors when I choose."

I stared at him with boredom as I left the room. I went into the kitchen and poured my self some coffee. He came out of the bedroom and I, out of good manners and because he made the coffee, poured him a cup. He was quiet, his mind locked and had that evil expression on his face. He grabbed the paper from the porch, and walked by me taking his coffee as he walked to the table. It had not escaped my attention, that the Beast did walk and move in the most astounding panther like way.

I hear Marcus warning again. "Don't Bait him." But I felt like testing the waters slightly. He was here for a reason and I wanted to know the reason. I need him to start to talk more clearly then want information he had given to me last night.

"I believe that *real* Wizards need no paper to tell what's happening in the world"

He continued to read and then sipped his coffee. He only looked up when he could tell I waited for the come back. "Everyone thinks they know the nature and the power of a Wizard because of Harry Potter. You have to know a Wizard to know a Wizard."

I drank my coffee at the counter not willing to be in his reach. " You are ignoring me to hide from something. You are afraid to tell me something." He continued to ignore me "Besides I have known Wizards, Including you. And I have read the collective works of Dr James Cohen who is an expert on Wizards."

He smiled from his paper and said " Dead Mortal"

I countered with "He was world renown in his expertise of the life of Wizards and Wizardry."

He smiled and sighed that stupid arrogant sigh. " He was killed for telling things about Wizards that was not true just to turn a buck." he looked over at me then "Mortal, greedy, dead." Frustrated by his nonchalant attitude I reminded him

"You know Max, I am mortal."

He stopped and looked at me for a second, "Only half."

He then said in a very sarcastic way. "You talk in your sleep."

I looked at him and said "So what."

He looked up in with his evil smile "I liked it."

I rolled my eyes "Cant imagine why. Besides, you were not invited to listen to me in my sleep or hang out in my bed." He gave his evil laugh.

The knock on the door saved me from the morning conversation that never went anywhere. I opened the door and Lincon and grandmother entered. Mandra entered the room and looked directly into my face.

She raised an eyebrow and half her mouth. Looking directly at Max she spoke in her low soft way "I told you to watch her not molester her. What part of 'don't touch her' did you not understand?"

Max smiled wickedly. "How can I watch her properly when she avoids me and transports everywhere? It was horrible the way she avoided me. I was quite hurt. I had to have her confined in one place. Besides, I like touching her."

Mandra glared at him "You should be set ablaze." Max dared to look hurt.

"You sent him after me; for what? I don't need to be watched like a five year old. Marcus would never have done what he has over the last 10 years." I was furious.

Max smiled "Has it been that long?"

Mandra shot him a evil glare. I continued my tirade, "How is that protecting me. Besides, he is being hunted. So how does that equate safety?".

Then she looked over at me. "I have to apologized for his behavior and understand, it will not be condoned by Marcus. ." She looked back at Max "Max, you will answer to Marcus." He only looked mildly concerned. When Mandra looked away from him, he dared to flash his evil smile .

I pointed out "Max is not in the Elders good graces . Reporting him is probably not a big concern of his."

Mandra looked over at me cautiously "Max is once again, under the control of Marcus." Max did not dispute the fact.

Mandra looked to me and began "This has been brewing for some time. Really ever since you where born. It actually started with your mother, though she was never as powerful as you." She moved to the kitchen and poured a cup of coffee for her and Lincon. She and Lincon moved to the table with Max. I was amazed that there could be something about me they did not tell me. I shouldn't have been. But I could not fathom what more I needed to know. I'm mixed blood, not normal and cursed.

"I need to know what is going on here and if I don't have all the information at once I believe that I will blow my top." I was furious. Mandra motioned for me to sit at the table with her, Lincon and the Beast. I shook my head knowing I would need a target for my anger and Max would be in flames. He know what I was thinking and said "Stand if you wish my love, I will stay over here un-chard."

Mandra and Lincon looked at each other for a moment. I piped in and also attacked Lincon, my so called protector. "Lincon, you're my friend. How could you allow this? How could you not have brought all of this to me a long time ago?"

He only bowed his head. He looked up at me "I was bound to secrecy. I had no intention to mislead you."

Seeing how hurt Lincon was soften my irritation with the people who I believed had my best interest at heart as I had theirs. "I am sorry Lincon. I know that you would never hurt me intentionally."

I moved to the table and sat down. I moved my chair away from Max and closer to Lincon. This caused Max a great deal of enjoyment until Mandra looked over to him. "Now. I want all of you to talk to me. I want the truth."

Mandra looked hurt then. She looked at me and for the first time, I saw tears in her eyes. "I never would have deceived you. We had always hoped that these rumors were rumors only." She looked away for a moment. "After so many years, I was informed by the governing witches, that your mothers death was deliberate and orchestrated." I was bewildered again. "She was killed for her powers. Though she was never as powerful as you and I, she was quite skilled. The plan was to catch her at a weak moment, Her heart never being strong, the deed could be done easily. The demon was able to use Reyna's labor and weakness to attempt to take the power. Casting spells that they were not talented for and resulted in nothing. But It was enough to killed Reyna. It was not your birth. To that disgusting devil groups dismay, Reyna's powers went to you and not to Deana."

I laughed "Deana? What does that irritating normal have to do with this."

Grandmother continued, "Deana and who ever is pushing her, wanted so badly to have the powers you have been given by God. They then could produce the Heir to their advantage and create a monster."

Max continued in place of Mandra who was horrified at her weakness with the pain over the death her daughter – my mother. "Deana was furious of course. She wanted so badly to be a powerful witch, like you . You the witch who denies her gifts" He continued to remind me. "She believes that is where she belongs; in some fable of a powerful witches." He was very serious and then said, "When their plan failed at your birth, Deana posed as a nurse, she took you from your father who was sick in grief. Her callousness and greed was so enmeshed in her being, that she could not admit defeat. She continued to attempt to take the powers but you, even as an infant, were able to protect your self. She even attempted a curse. It also failed."

I huffed and shook my head. I interrupted in a defeated tone "Are you sure?"

He smiled "You see, she is not a witch. She is clairvoyant, but not a natural witch."

I looked at him directly, "If she is clairvoyant, wont she know the outcome?"

Max sighed and took my hand in his. I tried to pull it back and gave him an angry stare. "She does see. But she is a fool in some respects. She is overly confident and arrogant in her simple powers. She is also lacking….. in education. She has never studied under the masters as you and I. She also has friends, a powerful friends, pushing her. And now somehow Edwin is in the mix." He released my hand "She may only be day dreaming ignoring her simple powers warnings. She reads what she wants and only what pertains to stealing others powers." He took a deep breath and continued. "The whole design is to take place on the summer solstice. While other celebrate creation and nature, she will be stealing your powers. Of course you will have to be there dying and she and her friends will have to make a change. She must make a physical change - thus Vampire." He looked at me so sincere like his story could really happen.

Still looking at Max, Mandra, through her tears, said "She has a Vampire in mind to commit the change. His name is Martin." Max snarled "Of Course." He shifted then and stated "Martin was never to be. He is an accident that was given mercy due to his innocents in the situation of his creation. He has spent century's proving his rulers wrong." He looked at Mandra "His own will be notified of his activities."

Mandra then looked at me with conviction "Em. You are the Princess of the wizards and you have the Priestess. You are chosen, to my dismay to have been chosen, for these roles." She looked off and then back. " With these roles you have a responsibility to preserve the races. That being said, I need you to care for your self and keep you somewhere in that mix." Each of her eyes shedding a tear.

I reached out and took her hand. "Why me. Don't I have a say. I don't even speak to any Wizards except Marcus." I thought about it and looked at Max. I had not really counting him as talking with a Wizard. "How can they still concerned me a Wizard princess?"

Max broke in "You were chosen at birth by the Wizard Counsel in Paris. You are not so easily replaced with a Witch with such power. In fact, there is no other Witch with your power. As far as the Priestess, I have no answer."

I looked over at him "Why can I just say no."

He laughed at me. Then he said quietly, defeated "Isn't it clear yet Em? It doesn't matter what anyone wants. It just is." He then said "And in addition, you are being sought by the hunters. We cant stay here long."

I rolled my eyes "What do they want?" He only looked at me. I said "They cant force me to have a child." He only remained quiet as did grandmother. I sneered "Let them try."

In frustration I asked 'Can we get back to this little plot that you all believe a simpleton can carry out? She is too old to have children now."

Mandra looked at me sternly "She is a normal, but not a simpleton. Be aware that she has a plan in motion she has had twenty four years to prefect. *She will* die trying to kill you and take the power from you. And there is someone powerful helping her and encouraging her. They may also have a plan to create the child."

I looked at her with more questions. "How can she do this? I am not going to lay down and die for her. How can they get near me to do this?" Grandmother looked away, and Max took over again.

"They already have several times. The shadow and some of your "Boyfriends. and" then he said more cautiously "Through those you love."

I was taken off guard. Mandra was here. Lincon, Molly…Max… .."Dad and Tom!" with my heart stopped and I was in Hat Creek. Standing at the creek side, I turned to the church where I heard the congregation singing.

Then Max was there. "Are you crazy!" He grabbed my arm. Mandra was there next and then Lincon. Max was angry but continued talking through his teeth. "This is what they have been looking for. You alone. Your brother and father as hostage or dead."

I pulled my arm from him and screamed at him then. "What do you care! I don't hear from you in years. Only to show up now and then to trick and deceive me" I threw up my hand and he fell back. I started to walk away He stood directly in front of my desired path.

"You have to leave here, Now." He with incredible speed took my arm, pulled me to him and we were back in my house in Sacramento.

I screamed at him "Why did you do that. I need to see them. Protect them."

Holding my arms, He said "Looked at me. I must have looked because he stated " that is not for you. They have a protection over them. They do not believe in the magic as you and I. Those that seek you don't realize that the belief is half the battle. The other is that they have not had our belief in God. There is the natural protection of God. And your father and brother have that. We also have place a barrier around them. It is from Marcus and some friends." He looked at me deeper and then said "We have to go." I could hardly believe my ears.

Mandra and Lincon were there then. "Be on your way.

Lincon reached into his inside coat pocket "Here are your ID's and passports."

Mandra said to me "I will not be in contact and you are not to contact me. That Vamp will be able to intercept."

I asked "Is he the shadow?" Max only gave a maybe.

I looked at my grandmother. "Wait what is happening here. I have a life here. As sorry as it is, it is my life." I looked at them all as if there you out of their minds. "How do I just take off?" I looked over at Max "And why with him?"

Mandra looked into my eyes. "This is more than your lives. This is existence for us all. Max will keep you safe."

I then thought about her safety. "Mandra, what about you." She gave a small laugh. "I still produce some fear in Deana. I think I will stay and have some fun. I will be looking to who is helping her. They will rue the day they played with my children. I love you my sweet Star" She looked over at Max "Go!" He nodded to her grabbed me in a hug and Mandra said "Max! Behave."

CHAPTER 32

e arrived in the middle of 5th Avenue New York. "Are you crazy! Do you want to sent the Normals running and be on the nightly news?" He looked at me and said "They only see what they want." I looked down and I was dressed in a White Jacket black pock-a-dot dress with matching bag and black pumps.

"Oh no… I look like a middle aged rich bitch." I looked at him in his Brown Sports Jacket and black pants.

"We have to blend and we have to stay off the radar. So, our plan is that you and I do this in the 'Normal way', so be nice and cooperate,"

I gave a little snort, "And how do you intend to make me?"

He look serious and in his evil voice said "This is not just about you. That's how." He was right. I had to think of Mandra, Dad and Tom…. and Max.

"OK. What next." He took my arm in his and began to stroll. We spent most of the day window shopping and having lunch in the park. But no speaking.

"Max are you going to tell me the plan here. Or do we just keep walking around aimlessly?.

He told me "Just shut up." He never looked at me. I was about to just leave when he grabbed my arm and started to walk again.

He gave me the silent treatment through out the afternoon. I would have enjoyed it for a little while longer but had no Idea where we were going. He hailed a cab and we were taken to the Harbor. We were ushered on to the Cruise liner and escorted to our cabin. It was huge. A living area and a bedroom. Very plush with a balcony over looking the ocean. I refused to break the silence until the valet said. "Mr. Goodman; Mrs. Goodman, please enjoy your voyage." With the evil face on Max, the valet was concern for me. He looked over to me and I gave him a little smile. Max put some bills in Valets hand as the valet back out of the door.

"Why in the world would we have to pretend to be Mr. And Mrs. Goodman and why are we sailing?" I then glared at him, He grabbed a flute and poured a Champaign all the time ignoring me. "Why do you enjoy these stupid antics?" He continued to ignored me which suited me just fine.

I left him with his Champaign and I pulled out a night gown. I entered the bathroom which was luxurious with a whirlpool bath and Italian tile through out. I started the bath and the jets. I poured in the bath beads provided by the liner. Bubbles started and I slipped in. The heat and the jets melting the tension away. I laid in the bath trying to imagine my self on a Caribbean alone. Once the water cooled, I put on a long night gown and put on the robe. I intended to go right to sleep.

Opening the bathroom door, I saw the flute of Champaign in front of my face and Max blocking the way. *Thank God I put in the bubbles or he would have a free show.*

He looked at me in that wicked way and said "If I can see through doors…."

I decided not to bite at his hook.

"By the way, there is a angry cat in the bed. I believe he is your familiar?"

I squeezed past him taking the glass and I sipped at the wine. I ignored him. If the cat hates him, so do I. I set the glass down on the dresser and I sat on the bed pet Zee. Ignoring his presents I took released the clip in my hair and began brushed out my hair. I just kept thinking if I ignored him completely he would go away. I only wanted to relax and go to bed. He pulled the brush out of my hand and sat down next to me and he began to brush my hair.

I got up and hissed "Go away!" he only smiled. "Max I refuse to do this again tonight" He continued to smile as he begin to get up and moved closer as I watched as a metal barrier encased the room. It covered the exit to the other room the walls, floors and ceiling. He was too close, and I shivered when he moved a stray strain of hair off my neck.

"I do find you very lovely."

I again sneered in his face "Marcus is going to have a lot to speak to you about. You know he loves me. He will take this as a direct insult to him"

He sighed that arrogant sigh of his and said "Yes, I suppose he will have that *Talk* with me. And I am sure your grandmother has already reported me as a sorry retch. However, I do have a reputation of being an undisciplined devil Wizard. I am under the radar and being hunted." He made his evil laugh " And now so are you. Now, It seems the I have broke the Wizards laws again and defied their orders. I am with the Princess. Besides, I need to keep my eyes on you. Not only to protect you but because I like looking at you. So until I am band from you again, I would like to have some fun."

I pushed him away and walked to the window. I refused to engage any further. I would ignore him regardless of what he did and click out.

"Never happen. No matter how hard you try."

That hit a nerve and I sent the champagne bottle at his head. He easily manipulated the bottle and moved it back to its place on the counter.

"Em, play nice." Play nice? He had no idea how he broke my heart. How much I hated him at that moment. When I was about to send a siren into his head he pulled be back against his chest and began to kiss my neck.

"Let go of me Max." My back on fire when it touched his bare skin. He went to my ear and softly said, "Don't hate me, Em."

Continuing my sneer I warned him "Get out of my head Max." He held me with his arms around my middle.

He and said "Fair enough. I will leave you to your empty window."

He let go and remove the barrier. He left the room and I remained at the window wondering how I get through this adventure without killing him or myself.

I woke to the sun coming in the window. His arm and leg draped over me insuring I did not get away. My heart still stinging. And his touch burning my skin. The I remembered that crummy motel room that I transformed and waking up in his arms. I remembered the world he created for us. How wonderful it was. Every morning waking just like this. How I felt then and how I feel now were worlds apart. How I wished this was a different situation. Where I could wake him with kisses. Make love all day. I move some stray hair from his forehead. Wishing and getting angry all over again at the lies and the tricks and my heart.

I slipped out of his hold and I got up and called for coffee. I put on my robe and went into the living are. Zee joined me and I scolded him and told him that the Valet could not see him. When the knock on the door occurred he disappeared.

The Valet entered with the coffee cart and I tipped him as he left. I poured a cup and dressed it properly. Moving to the Table and watching the sea. I could only think of how I got in this mess. How could this all be happening. I wanted to go home so badly. I wanted my family.

"Your not to think of them remember?"

Max walked to the cart and poured his own coffee. He joined me at the table uninvited. I sat back away from the table and stared out the window. He had no reason to have me speak to him. He only had to read my mind.

"But I like your voice." He kept staring at me which was uncomfortable and then pissing me off.

"what" I challenged.

He looked tired and serious. I think I like him better acting the buffoon. "We have to stick together, work together on this …Mission. You need to talk to me." He looked down and then back at my eyes. "You need to forgive me a little. You have to know I would not ever hurt you. I only want to protect you. Even from me, even from you."

I made a laugh sound "How does last nights incident and the other night in my room protect me? Or the castle in nowhere land protect me? I was left in the middle of your games and tricks." My intent resolved. "Don't presume that I need you to protect me, Max. You have made a vow to, but I can do it my self. I refused to be a simpering little coward that you all expect me to be. I am not living my life in fear and want. I will have my own way. I will have a life on my own terms."

He looked at me in his most serious stern way and through clinched teeth "You will follow the plan.

"Only if I chose to. And only if I have a say in my existence. Because if my life and happiness depended on everyone else, I will live in misery as history has proven."

He looked at me frustrated "There is no talking to you now. Why don't we take a walk on the deck and get some breakfast.?"

"Go to hell Max. Or should I say Mr. Goodman. I am not going anywhere with you and playing your little game." I stared at him in defiance and anger. Only softening when Zee jumped into my lap.

Max had anger in eyes and his voice low and dark. "I am not as patient as I once was, Em. There are things to do; Planning and safe guarding our lives and the future of all the races." He looked down at his ringing hands." You need to think a little more about broader things other than being Normal." He then roared at me "We are not Normal and never will be. Get over it."

He got up from the table and went in the bedroom. He emerged dressed and left the cabin. I was never more relieved. I needed alone time. I needed to be me. No pretence not magic. Just me. Maybe the mortal half needed to be released for a little while. I needed to think. I needed to pull my self together. Here I was I floating in the ocean heading to God knows where and hunted by Wizards. And to think, I used to think living with the normals was hard. Living with the Witches and Wizards has been just as hard. Hard because they knew things I didn't. Things about me. I came to a firm resolution for my self. Yes, I loved my grandmother, Marcus, and against my better judgment, Max. But I was not going to allow any more deception. I was going to have control over my self and no one else. I said a prayer to God *"Hold on Lord. It looks like a bumpy ride from here on out."*

I watched a sappy movie with Zee at my side. I had room service bring my lunch. I took a nap and then washed my hair. I was on the couch brushing my hair dry when he returned. I refused to acknowledge his presents. But he stood in front of me.

He voice without feeling. "You'll have to dress. We are invited to the captains table."

I looked up "And why is that?"

He hissed "How the hell do I know. They picked us out of the hat."

He reached down and dragged me up by my arm. I was on my feet. But my arm flew out and Max was locked against the wall and unable to move by leather straps holding him. I bond him so that his powers were minimal. He was able to get out and stand in front of me. I once again put him back but bound him tight. I softly laughed the witches devil laugh and slowly walked over to the wall where Max was imprisoned. My eyes, the priestess cat eyes, looked up while my head stayed level leaving the death threat visible.

No more would I hold back. And in a deadly tone "Don't you ever touch me like that again. If you do, I will have you at the bottom of the ocean in that exact condition." A leather strap across his mouth made it impossible to talk back. At least in voice.

His head was another story. "You Bitch. Let me lose."

I continued to laugh at the situation. "And how does it feel to have the tables turned? " I continued to stock along the wall were he was imprisoned never removing my eyes from his. "I believe that I need to have *your*complete and uninterrupted attention Max. I no longer am to be treated as anything less than your equal. Is that understood."

I waited for the transition. "I have not treated you as less."

I stopped. Laughed and said "May I remind you, the disrespect I have encountered over the last three days. Come to think of it, the last ten years." I continued my stocking my eyed on my prey

He transmitted "Em. I am not the same as when we were kids."

I tried his wicked smiled "Nor am I. In fact I think… I am a Bitch." The smile still on my face "Have I made my point?" He still watched me. "We will go through this adventure by and with an agreement. Mixed blood to Mixed blood. Equal. Witch and Wizard as Partners. That's the only agreement that releases you."

It took a few seconds but he transmitted "As you wish, My Lady."

I walked to the middle of the room, waved my hand and I was dressed for dinner at the captains table. I waved my hand again and Max dropped from the wall. He landed on his feet and stood up. I waved my had and he was dressed in his tux. I smiled sweetly "Shall we go?"

He smiled breathlessly and then said "Are you going to put me back on the wall if I take your arm?"

I walked to him and put my arm in his arm. "That depends on how you behave?"

At the Captains table I remained quiet while Max spun a tall take about his electronic business in California. Of course, he never said but the impression was that we were obscenely rich. "Mrs. Goodman, are you enjoying the cruise?" the Captain's wife inquired I responded with a smile," Yes thank you." she continued "And your cabin, is it to your liking?"

Max broke in "It is very comfortable for us. Thank you. But I would like to dance with Mrs. Goodman now that the music has started."

The Captain smiled "Of Course."

Max came over and put out his hand aided by his charming smile. "My Lady."

I put my hand in his and we walked to the dance floor. The music was slow and other couples join us. Max held my hand to his chest while his put his arm around my back. My other hand at his shoulder as I began to follow his lead. I looked up at him and said "You are a snob Mr. Goodman."

He giggled "No, I am afraid of disappointing Mrs. Goodman."

I smiled at the lesson learned.

He smiled too. "Just so you know, I will not fear your power any more than you fear mine. And mine come with a twist."

I tilted my head "What's that supposed to mean?"

He smiled at me and continued to dance. He put his mouth to my forehead and kissed me. And kept his chin to my forehead. And I hadn't notice he had held me closer.

He started to talk again "Remember the prom?"

I didn't want to talk about it. In a warning snarl said "I don't want to!"

He kept talking "I remember your little daydream. You know the one where you and me were dancing all alone. He sighed "I remember. I remember how... on the way home, how we felt."

I did not know where he was going with this. "I told you I don't want to talk about it."

He took his hand leaving mine on is chest an tipped my face to look at him. He looked softer than I had seen him in years. "I remember, you loved me then."

I stopped breathing. I pushed him away and walked back to the table. I said a quick good night to the Captain and his wife. I then walked out to the deck.

I was so angry at him. I knew my life was all a joke. He didn't have to remind me. My life is only for the Wizards whimsies. Nothing more than an incubator at best. I walked to the stern that was deserted and looked out over the Ocean. I was wishing I left him up on wall and thinking of putting him back. How could he use my own heart against me? My love for him used against me. Then I remembered his kind and how they orchestrated my life. Their plans for me. Their plans for my life. I had to keep in my mind, Max was a Wizard. Mixed Blood, but a Wizard just the same.

But the water turned a different shade of black. The sky was hinting to something. I started to back away from the railing when I heard.

"Princess Emily Star?"

I turned to find a devil. Six foot blond chalked skin Vampire. I set up a protection grid. Which he was aware of. He attempted to circle it and me. I walked to match him so he was in my line of sight. With narrow eyes and a commanding voice I asked, "Who are you?" I called in my head for Max.

The Vamp smiled complete with fangs. "So with Wicked Wizard is with you? Oh, and it is Martin by the way."

I closed my mind to him. But continued to call Max. "I don't know where he is. He shows when I need him."

He continued to speak softly. "Do you need him? I believe you must if you call for him?"

Something in me snapped. I felt her emerging. I felt her demanding and deadly. I tilted my head, in the voice of the witch priestess I asked "Are you sure Martin? Aren't I supposed to stay alive and....lets see, be subdued?" He made a wicked sound from his throat.

I continued "Besides the simpleton Deana, who else are you aiding."

He laughed at that with a fang smile "You are talented. You are beautiful. Your blood smells irresistible." He paused " Those cat like eyes. Why don't you and I come up with a different understanding that is more appealing to us both."

I gave a little witch laugh. "You mean appealing to you."

Martin continued to smile and circle the protection barrier. "My Lady, I could aid you in being more powerful than any Witch, Wizard or Vampire on Earth."

I gave the little witch laugh "I am already more powerful than you." He snarled at me then.

At that moment I went into defense mode. "Subdue me Martin. If you can?" The vampire hissed and moved at me with incredible speed. But he never made it through the barrier. He fell back but was up on his feet and tried again. I then with a wave of my hand sent him flying into the ocean. He returned with a vengeance hovering high in the sky preparing for his death decent. Flying directly at me. With speed I never would have thought to possess, I dropped the grid and waved my had and produce a wooden saber. I rose to in the sky and I waited for the impact from the ascending vampire. The saber impaled Martins heart with a brittle crunch. He fell to the deck. I watched as the creature decayed, shrivel and turned to dust. I waved my hand and the dust blow and saber fell into the Ocean. I lowered to the deck of the ship. I showed no mercy or option. I showed no feeling of another creatures demise. I, coldly killed another, vampire or not. Christian or Witch, to kill is a sin. It's morally wrong.

As the feeling of power eased, I started to shake. I was returning to me. But I am not a killer. I walked to a rail and held it for strength. I was not a killer. I became very cold and then hot. I couldn't breath. Who was I? How was I able to do that. Think that fast. Move that fast. Kill that fast. I needed to breath. Pray. I needed to pray. I dropped to the deck. I looked to the sky. I found a breath and began "Our Father, who are in heaven.." And I heard Max. He knelt down next to my shaking form. He prayed with me. He looked at me and said "You must live. If that means he dies, then let the devil have him. You must live. God wants and needs you to live."

I nodded and turned into Max and cried. He helped me up and we started to walked back to the room. "why didn't you come ?" he looked down at me "I did. You had already …taken care of yourself."

I shook my head "I don't think that was me."

CHAPTER 33

Sitting at the table with a very large bourbon with the decanter very close by. I watched Max write a note on a paper.

MM Inc@Witwiz.net
Los Angeles Ca.
Dear Mr. Marshal

Please be informed that the Princess line has demolished the Martin take over. Continue with original plan and keep eye on other stocks of interest. Further contact will be as necessary.
Yours Truly
Mr. Maxton Goodman

"What is that?"

Max smiled at me "Mortal Espionage."

I drank my very large glass of bourbon and reached for the decanter. Max grabbed it before I was able to . He walked over to the phone and asked that a Email be sent, to please send valet. As he was on the phone, I took the liquid from the decanter and it filled my glass. Max put the phone down and looked at the decanter his monster face returned.

"Em you need your wits. Drunk you are not prepared."

I looked at him. He was all business and I did not feel like business. I felt like drunk, and oblivion. I downed my second glass and waved my hand and the glass filled again. The valet arrived and took the message from Max and assured Max that he would have a confirmation by morning. He then lost his patients and took my glass. I glared at him then and thought of the wall. He laughed and I was in bed and held down again. He was still in the living room and I was alone with my self. Held down and bound when all I needed was another glass for a straight sleep of nothingness. Instead, the two large glasses it made me more weepy. More weak. More apt to think. More apt to dream.

I felt Max get into bed but didn't turn to look at him. He will never see me like he used to. But now, I am as dangerous as he is. The difference was that he controlled his devil. I was not in control of mine. He put his arm around me and pulled me close and it made me cry again. All I wanted was to cry in his arms till I went to sleep. I didn't want to hear anything from him. I only wanted his arms. So I turned around and buried my head into his shoulder and cried.

He started to talk again and I said "No Talking no transmissions, just let me be,"

He held me tight and petted me. I got my way and fell asleep.

I got up the next morning alone in the bed. My head felt like there was a basket ball game going on in it. I felt awful. I got up and stumbled to the bathroom. Came out and went right back to bed. I laid there not sleeping but feeling like crap. I got up, took a shower, then dressed in my PJ bottoms and a cotton tank. I walked back to the bed and laid down. Max came in with a glass with something green in it.

I looked at him and asked "What is that?

He asked "Can I talk now?" I nodded but regretted it. "You look awful."

I looked up at him and he was wickedly smiling.

He handed the glass to me "This, my lady, will make you feel much better."

I sat up and braced my self on the headboard. He sat down on the bed. While I took the glass. After drinking the concoction, I thought I was going to be sick. I can not describe the chalky vial tasting crap. I had to wait a second to see if it would stay down. I put the glass on the night stand.

I looked back at him. "what was that."

He shrouded his shoulders " Wizard hangover medicine." He patted my leg " The Captain and his wife came by and asked about you and your running out the way you did." I looked up at him and he said with the same smile "I told them you were seasick." He took a pause "they want us back at their table. But I told them today would be impossible and so tomorrow night we would join them. They agreed."

I looked at him with out anything to say. I know I have killed and nothing can take it back now. Max came over and got on the bed with me. He moved me to lean against him and I didn't care. I just leaned my head against his chest and stared out thinking.

"You know Em? Technically he was already dead." He put his hand on my arm. "He was truly a monster." I just shrouded. He pushed me up and said I've got something for you to see," He pulled me in-between his legs and I reclined against him. He waved his hand that there was a three foot by three foot book hovering in front of us. The title was memories of my minds eye. He waved his hand and there was a picture of him and me at the creek during my Dads wedding. I looked at us and we looked so young and so happy that day of our first meeting. We were laughing. I was amazed, almost honored that he would remember. He waved and turned the page and it was just me. In that ugly dress but I looked so pretty.

Reading my mind he said "You were... are pretty."

I smiled. He turned it again and he had a picture of me twirling before the Solstice. It had to be the first time I got to dance in maiden dance. He flipped it again and it was us at the Boardwalk. I remember that day. I really loved that day

I told him "I think I like this the best."

He paused, smiled, and then waved the page. The next was me at the cliff rail at grandmothers. I was about sixteen, with my hair blowing in the sea breeze. I looked so beautiful.

"I don't remember this Max. Where were you?"

He took in a deep breath "Just watching." I really looked beautiful.

"Did I really look that way to you?"

He did not answer.

Then he said "I'll show you my favorite." the pages flipped and stopped. It was me at the Solstice in my priestess outfit and mask. It was were I was addressing the Elders. I looked so intimidating and yet so mystical.

"You were there?"

He huffed "Of course. I thought no one saw me but you, but I was wrong."

I did not want to see anymore. Knowing that my life was a joke. The Wizards still had control.

"Put it away Max. I don't want to see anymore."

He waved his hand. The book was gone but some kind of holographic TV was in its place.

I looked at him "You don't have to hang in here and wait for my recovery.

He smiled "Vegging is what I do best."

I laid back down on his chest and watched The Ghost and Mr. Chicken. Max laughed at the most stupid stuff.

"You know, I've met Christopher."

Max huffed, "You met Jordan too… in a way."

I picked my head up and look at his face. "When?"

He smiled and said "Remember the party?" I nodded "He was the guy at the door yelling at me as we left."

I was surprised "He was Jordan?" Max smiled and nodded.

"I cant believe your brothers would hunt you."

Max laughed "Foster brothers and there is no love lost. They're pure blood and I mixed blood."

I thought I would be funny and said "Too bad I didn't meet everyone at the same time" Max moved the TV and Pushed me out of the way and got up. I was surprised at his reaction. He looked back at me with anger and the devil look. I could only shake my head and my palms up.

He looked at me angry. "I was joking."

With his evil on he glared at me. "Not funny."

"I'm Sorry for what ever meaning you got out of that."

Max came back and pulled me down on the bed with him. He looked down at me and said "They only want to use you for their own ends."

I looked up at him with confusion. "And you? Didn't you use me?"

He didn't answer my question he kissed me instead. A sweet kiss. Then a more powerful wanting kiss. My heart was pounding and there was that feeling in my middle. I moved my arms around him. I felt like this is what I had been missing.

He stopped the kiss and breathless he moved to my neck and ear. "No, I never used you." I attempted "But you …" But he kissed me again. Kissed me again without answering me. Then a there was knock at the door. We looked at each other and Max got up.

Following Max to the living room, He opened the door to find the valet with a return message. He took to message and sat on couch. I sat next to him and read.

> MM.inc
> Dear Mr. Goodman
>
> Be advised that investors who pursue to acquire desired numbers with the Princess line have found some success. To avoid hostile take over in England, avoid unnecessary exposure for this point forward. Brothers inc. has some information and are heading off the desired success of Princess and company.
> Sincerely
> M. Marshal

I looked at Max and he looked at me. "We need to get off the boat." I only said "Why not just transport. We are close enough to England.

He only shook his head. "Normals will know we are missing and it would end up being big news for Mr. And Mrs. Goodman to go missing at sea. Plus the Wizards will know we transported." He was slapping the paper against his hand while he thought.

"OK. We stay on the boat until it is about to dock. I don't think the pure bloods wont make a move till then. We will leave a note for the valet to forward the luggage to another hotel. We will go on to Paris by car."

I was confused "Why by car. This normal way of traveling is taking to long." He only stared forward with a worried look.

"If we stay low key and they can't intercept transmissions or transports, I think we can fool them. I'm pretty sure they know we are together." He looked over at me. "They will take care because of that fact. They know my power and they suspect yours. Individually they are unable to capture us, together, with enough in number and with the right plan and objective, they could."

I sat back on the couch and thought of how I could avoid the brothers and the car. And then if came to me. I jump up and said "Max! I got it." He looked at me. "Shape shift." He smiled at the Idea. Zee jumped in my lap and hissed at Max and I petted him. I went on "We stay on the boat till the last minute. We shape shift into gulls and fly to Paris." I gave a smart-alecky smile "We go undetected and we stay out of a car."

He said "They may pick it up?"

I immediate response was "By the time they figure out which gulls are us, we will be in Paris."

He smiled then whispered "It could work."

That Night I felt Max get in the bed. And as usual he threw his arm over my middle. I wanted so badly just to feel him, just love with him. But I was having an inter struggle. The I hate him, love him deal. I loved his kiss today and I thought we could make love when the knock on the door came. To feel his chest to my back his arm over me like it has always been there. I only want to touch him freely. How am I to change the way my body and heart feel, and still have dignity. I need to keep hating him. And then I thought it would only be sex. It didn't have to really mean anything.

"Stop thinking about that."

I sat straight up. "Get out of my head or the bed. I don't care which."

He started to laugh. So I decided I had to leave the bed. When I started to get up he grabbed me. Pulled me down on the pillow.

He looked in my eyes and said "You think this is easy for me when all my thoughts are about you?"

I only looked at him and said nothing. He kissed my cheek and spoke against it, "I live everyday wanting you." I petted his cheek and he kissed me and that was it. And for most of the night we made love.

The next day was the last day on the ship. We had breakfast in the room and then went out to the deck We ended back in the cabin because it was very cold and windy out.

"So once we get into Paris, do you know where we are going?"

He looked off a little. "That's were is gets dicey. I know where to go, but you have to understand…" He looked at me with a mock guilty expression, "I been a bad wizard."

I couldn't imagine what he could have possibly done. My brows pulled in I asked "How bad, Max?" He smiled his wicked smile turned on the music. He pulled me up and we started dancing.

"Max. I need that questioned answered." He pulled back and looked to the ceiling. "Lets see, how bad?" I stopped dancing and stared at him waiting for the answer. He huffed and stopped the music. He walked over to the bar and pulled out the bourbon. He got a glass and then motioned as if asking me if I want some. I shook my head still expecting my answer. He drank a little. And I sat on a stool waiting.

He took a breath and said "I've already told you. And now I am with you again and hiding you from the hunters. They may keep me or kill me when we get there." He looked back at me to meet my narrowed eyes.

"It will never happen."

He laughed at my bravado. I looked at him ready to prove my point. He put up his hands laughing "Wait! Think of what you are saying. You against twelve very old wise and powerful wizards."

I looked at him straight on "Watch me. I have enough anger and hate to do it."

He patted my fist laying on the bar. "We have no choices here princess. We must seek help from the counsel for your protection. You have to survive in one piece."

So frustrated with the image of me as the baby maker for the pure bloods.

"For what Max? To produce a child for the pure bloods." he only looked at me with concern. "I am my own living being. I am more than a baby maker, I have my own feelings; my own life."

He then looked down and said "A child is for the survival of the Wizards and the Witches. The power and way of life."

I was so insulted "Then why don't all those concern make their own children and leave my perspective children be?"

He leaned over the bar and put my face in his hands. "No one can produce a magical child as you. You and a Powerful Pure Blood Wizard. This can be a blessing to both races. A future." He looked down and back with his monster at the surface. "It can also be a curse. And I am not willing to think about which Pure Blood will have the honor. If I knew I would kill him and the races."

We went to dinner with the Captain and his wife again. The conversation was light and I said little. Until the Captains wife, Marie, asked "Are you sure you over your seasickness.?"

I giggled and said "I'm sure I am over it. Just in time for the boat to dock."

She continued to talk and told us about her family in Washington DC. She had two daughters and four grandchildren. The Captain and Max had their own conversation going. But I could feel something in the air, something about the way the ship moved. I looked over at Max and he looked up at me. He could feel it too. He stood up and said to the Captain and Marie, If you will excuse us, I think I will try and dance with my wife again. He took my hand and we went to the dance floor.

I looked up at him "Can you feel it?" He nodded being very alert.

Then I smelled him "Edwin!"

Max looked at me and nodded. Low and deep he quietly told me to keep dancing. Max moved up to the middle of the floor. He his lead turned us gracefully to survey the room. "Max, we have to go."

He was not listening. He was somewhere else. "Max?"

He looked at me but the Monster was back. "Shut up. Do as I say."

Confused, I watched and readied my self.

Max walk us back to the table and we said our good bys. He was dragging me behind him. As we started down the hall way I pulled back as the sent of the brothers was strong. Max stopped looked back at me. I pushed him against the wall and we moved into the wall becoming apart of it. We could see out. But they could not see us. We could see that Edwin, Christopher and two others were coming down the corridor. We watched as each walked by.

Edwin was saying "I cant wait for that mix blood to meet his end. I only hope he knows I had the witch before he dies."

Max made a growl and I had to nudge him. The last stopped as if he hear the growl. He looked around and sensed something. But I sent Zee to come around the corner. Once seeing the cat, he moved on.

Once alone in the corridor, we left the wall. I told Zee to go.

"Max. We have to go now. Leave them here searching.

He looked down the corridor and said "Lets go."

He grabbed me and twirled and we were in England on the docks. He grabbed my hand and we ran to find a taxi.

Once in the cab, I asked "Max, shape shift is the only answer."

He nodded "But not here. Wait." He had the cab take us to the airport. He was able to get on the next flight to La Rochelle. We got a cab to a local hotel. I was so tired by this point but so scared at the same time. We spoke very little on our journey. Max surmised that once they discovered we left the ship, they would look through London or go on to Paris.

CHAPTER 34

Once in the room, I went to shower. When I came out of the Shower I heard Max talking with another male. I waved my hand and dressed in jeans and a T. I slowly left the bathroom ready to fight. My protection up and intact. I came around the corner, and found Max and Jordan at the table talking.

As I walked into the room, Jordan stood up and I grabbed the air for a saber. Once in my hand I was ready to kill him.

"Em! Stop!" I looked over to Max. He was up and had his hands up.

"Em its OK. Jordan is not here to harm us."

I waited until I felt the truth for myself. I lowered the saber but continued to hold it in my hand. In a slow deadly witch growl I asked "Then why is he here?"

Max started to walk and I looked over at him and he stopped.

"Em? Look at me. Em?"

He smiled gently. I looked back over at Jordan. He stood perfectly still and I could smell his nerves.

"EM. Look at me." I looked again at Max. He said "Its OK." He started to walk to me and I let go of the saber and it disappeared. He moved his hands to my face and looked in my eyes,

"You OK?" I nodded.

He took a breath and put me in little a hug. "Oh my God, I will never get you mad at me again." He let go and walked with me back to the table. Jordan was still staring at me. Max looked over at Jordan.

"Go ahead and sit now." Jordan came over and before sitting he bowed slightly

"My Lady. You are the priestess. I will vouch for that." He shook his head "Those eyes of the priestess. Cat eyes."

I looked at his reaction to me. I said "I am sorry, but we've been under attack before. I thought you were here to hurt us."

He slowly sat down. I looked back at Max who was also a little nervous.

"What. I'm sorry "I threw my face into my hands. " What am I becoming."

Max took one of my hands from my face and moved a chair so I could sit down. "Its OK"

Jordan, more comfortable, said "I ….I can see why you are on this mission Max.

I looked up at Jordan, ready to cry, "I am not that way. I don't know how to control this." He said "No my lady, you are beautiful and magnificent."

I Looked over at Max "Max I need my grandmother, I need Mandra."

He looked serious at that point. "You are not supposed to think of them."

"If I am going to control this…. I need instruction. We are not like Wizards that have a book on everything."

They both had a laugh at that assumption. Max sat down and lightly rubbed his knuckles across my cheek.

"Your eyes are yours now. Are you Ok now?"

I felt normal just freaked over my behavior. I nodded. I looked over at Jordan.

"You will forgive me?"

He smiled very sweetly, he was very handsome like Max and Marcus. "More than forgiven." I thanked him.

Max then started "Jordan says that Edwin has solicited school chums to help him search for us. That's who that guy was in the corridor."

Jordan said "One is Red and on is Jeff. Both are mixed blood and Masters. Neither matching either one of you."

Max asked Jordan "Where are they?" Jordan laughed "They are still on the boat. They keep chasing a cat."

My heart dropped. "Zee!" I looked at Max. And then I heard Zee growling at Max as he jumped in my lap. I grabbed him and hugged him.

Jordan Laughed and said "Yeah that's the one."

I looked over to Jordan. "Why are you here and not with them?"

he smiled "My Lady, Max is a beast and a rouge, but only at the making of Edwin and the Elders. I am pure blood but I see that this mix blood Monster Wizard has more honor and dedication to his vows than Edwin could ever have. Max and I have our differences, and he has done things that I have issue with as we grew up, but right now in this situation, I am proud to call him brother." He and Max had some special hand shake.

Jordan looked back at me "As far as you, princess, no women of your power should be subjected to Edwin's and his plans. I see why Max has protected you so fiercely."

Then to both Max and Jordan "Where is Marcus? He loves Max why would he let this go on."

Max Said "Marcus had obligations and responsibilities. He is aware of things and is in communication with Mandra."

Jordan said "I have been aware of the Elders and Edwin's plans for years. And though it was a pure blood that was to have you according to the expectations of the Elders and the Wizards prophecy, All available pure bloods should have been presented to you. Your would choose the Wizard and produce the child. Edwin ensured that he would be the only one pure blood to meet you. He continued to thwart the rest of us from meeting you. So did Max but for his different reasons. Max tried to keep you from being hurt. Edwin feels that he is all powerful and is some what aware of your power. However, I believe he underestimates you. And over estimates himself. He is not the Master that Max has become. None of us are. Edwin has had influences from some of the Elders who tell him he will be the one chosen. He feels that a child, male of course, sired by him delivered by you, will be the greatest Wizard in the world. He believes that he could not only rule Wizards, but witches and mortals as well."

Jordan then started to laugh, I looked at him and then to Max. He said "Max, when you were off pouting,," Max look disturbed by that. "Edwin approached Em. Christopher was with him and was very taken with the lady."

Max looked at me and saw only the irritation I felt at that encounter. Max asked "Well what happened?"

I looked at him "That's when I met Christopher. I was walking at the river. Came back to my car to find Edwin and Christopher leaning on my car. Edwin asked if I had seen a cowardly wizard. I told him to look in the mirror. He threatened me. And I told him he was nothing more than a snake and I turned him into one."

Max and Jordan laughed together. Jordan then told Max that when she left and turned him back he was still in the dirt.

Jordan between laughter said "Christopher could not wait to tell the story. Edwin was furious." He got serious then. "I believe that you are both equipped to handle these fools. I am more worried about the counsel of Wizards."

Max nodded. "Jordan I did not know before. But I am sure now. It is a Wizard that has been stocking Em and partnering with Deana."

I looked at him. "Why did you not tell me? He shook his head. "I am really just now sure. It all adds up."

There was a knock at the door. I jumped and Max patted my arm. "Its the food I ordered." He went to the door and allowed the cart in. Once alone again with food in front of us we discussed a plan.

"Once in the hall of the counsel, there is no escape, Max." Jordan interjected. "They may kill you, but I suspect that they will imprison you instead."

Max only looked down and blocked his mind.

I said "I will go alone."

Max looked up and said "No. That would give Edwin the opening he is looking for. With me, you are guaranteed a audience immediately. We need their help now." I left the table and sat on the bed with Zee.

Jordan said "I will go as well. I think I can bring out what has been happening in the states. I think it will be in your best interest for me to be there. Maybe present as well. But I don't have any idea which way they will go. I am sure they are aware that we are coming and with Em."

Jordan then became uncomfortable. He looked from me to Max. "They will know that the Princess is no longer…. Intact."

I started to laugh. "I am a witch not a nun."

Both Max and Jordan laughed with me and Jordan nodded with the reality.

I asked "described the hall to me." Max grabbed a napkin and drew out the chamber. I looked like a garden open by walls that curved up like a dome but remained open to the sky. There was a long half moon counter or bench were the Elders assembled. I studied the drawing. "Could we go in and be unannounced?" Both Max and Jordan said no. "They have their protective barrier around the chamber."

I sat back on the bed. Petted Zee while they continued to discussed the presentation. And then it came to me.

"Number 2!"

Max and Jordan looked over confused as I jumped from the bed. "Max, number 2!" He remembered

"We can use a Number 2 for you."

Jordan was still confused. After Max explained it to him,

Jordan looked at Max "That's how you got out. That how you got out of punishments!" Max gave a little laugh "All but the big one."

Jordan smiled "Its brilliant."

Max sighed, "But I need to be close to Em. Edwin could show up or the shadow wizard."

I smiled again waved my hand and Max was the spiting image of Zee.

Jordan roared. "Yes. That is it." I waved my hand back. And Max was himself. "Don't do that!" he was serious.

Then I explained. "Max you shape shift to Zee. You come as my familiar.' I Smiled "Your could even have Max 2 on remote control so that you can speak and move." Jordan was very enthusiastic about the Idea. "Max. You have to admit this is a great plan."

Max said "The Wizard Counsel can smell deception. They will know any of these things before we walk in the door.

Then I became more serious. "I need you two to understand. I am a witch and am not bound to the Wizards." I looked directly at Max. "I have gone along with the Wizards for Mandra and Marcus and you." I took a breath "Because of this, I am vulnerable in a room full of Wizards. I knew that when I was presented to them as a girl. I would feel better if I see my people first. I would like to enter with Witch escorts along with Jordan."

Max Looked concerned. "I'll protect you, Em."

I smiled "As you always have. But in this case Max, I need my own kind."

Jordan then said "You know Max, that's not a bad Idea ether."

Max was thinking "We would be another week." He looked at both of us. Then directly at me "OK Em. What ever you say. It does give us more time."

Jordan got up "OK, I heading to my room. I will see you both in the morning.." He turned to me and nodded "My Lady." I said good night.

I got back on the bed and braced up against the headboard. I watched Max push the food cart out after Jordan's departure. I was sitting with on leg bent and had my arms and head resting on my knee. Max grabbed the napkins and papers they had been doodling plans on. He came over and sat in the bed next to me. He continued to study the notes. I turned my self to the side of him.

"Max?"

he said "Huh?"

I asked "If we had been normal, and maybe went to the same school, do you think you would have noticed me?"

He looked quickly and said "Of course." and went back to his notes.

I had to know what I was to him. Princess, Priestess, nothing or something. Not willing to let him off the hook, I asked "Outside of being the guardian, and the wizard, have ever just thought of me as flesh and blood not witch?"

He did not take his eyes off the notes he continued to write. "Of course I have, Em."

I did know if I wanted the next answer but I needed to know. "But did you only think of the vow you made or did you really ever just care for me? I mean is it all for the vow or is their any real feeling for me?"

He looked up as if slapped.

He looked at me seriously then "EM. How can you asked that"

I could help my self. I need a answer of what I was to him. "I guess I need to know that I am not just the vow or a bet." He dropped his pen and papers and held my face to his and said, "I have loved you since I danced with you at your fathers wedding. Love you with my whole heart and soul"

I kissed him with every inch of my being. I finally heard him say it. He loved me.

He then asked "Does that mean you don't hate me anymore?"

I smiled "It means that I don't have to make myself hate you any more and can just love you again." He and I made loved all night.

Sleeping late, Jordan appeared in the room. Still undressed but in a sheet Max jumped. "Jordan I could have killed you."

I stayed with my eyes closed and wanted to sleep more.

Jordan said "They have a good tracker with them. They are on there way here by car." "Em wake up."

I responded "I don't want to."

I received a kiss on my bare shoulder and Max said "We have to go. You need to get up." Max got out of the bed and the next thing I knew I was standing fully dressed hair combed and fresh breath.

Snarling I said "I told you I didn't want to."

He giggled. Zee jumped into my arms and I hugged him. "Zee, go find some food and catch up." He was gone.

Jordan Max and I left the hotel. There we got into a Mercedes C300. Max drove like the devil.

"Where are we going?" I had to ask since I was never told.

Jordan said from the back seat "Ancona. There we will meet with a priestess. He name is Anita" I turned and looked at him and he continued "Mandra has notified her that you were coming."

Zee appeared on my lap growling at Max. I turned back around. Just about to think of my grandmother and Max snapped into the monster. "I told you not to think of them. You not only in danger your life, but hers as well."

I glared at him for snapping so. And turned and watched the landscape. Then I waved and produced a coffee for me. I handed one to Jordan who said thank you. I did not give one to Max who had since dropped his monster.

Max noticed and patted my leg "I did not mean to snap at you. I'm just worried."

Then I gave him his coffee. Training is how I looked at it.

Jordan then asked "How far are you planning on driving today."

Max said "I think as far as we can. Maybe Lyon."

Jordan laughed " 250 miles? We couldn't go further?"

Max said "We will see. Do you have a fix on Edwin and Chris?"

Jordan answered " Their in Le Mans headed to La Rochelle."

I asked "Jordan, cant they 'get a fix' on you?"

Max smiled and Jordan said "Max gave me a tip and no they can not."

By late afternoon, we were in Lyon. We drove in traffic for an hour. We stopped for some food and stretch and went on to Genova. We got a room in a local hotel off the main areas of interest. Once in the room, I dropped in the bed. Max and Jordan went over there presentation and I called Zee.

Zee appeared and Max said "He might be getting used to me finally after all these years." I looked over at he and asked "How do you know?"

Max said "He slept with us last night. Usually when I around you he goes under the bed." I looked at Zee who was purring at my scratching of his ears. Max and Jordan gave up on their project and turned on the TV which was in French. Apparently they spoke French. I went to sleep.

CHAPTER 35

The next morning, I woke to find Max sleeping next to me and I was wearing a night gown. Jordan sleep in the bed next to us. Zee was curled up in-between Max's legs.

I stretched and Max said "I told you he was starting to like me. But I think he is still jealous."

I leaned over and petted Zee. I looked up to see Max looked at me surprised.

"What?"

He said "I though I was getting a kiss good morning and instead the cat gets petted" I giggled and kissed Max.

There was a knock at the door. We both jumped. Max went to the door in his PJ bottoms and shirtless. The valet gave him a note.

Max called "Jordan!" Jordan jumped up.

I looked and said "What does it say?"

Max looked over at me and read "Wake up and get dressed. We will arrived in 20 minutes. Marcus."

I Screamed "Yes!" I jumped out of the bed causing Zee irritation. Ran to the bathroom and jumped in the shower. Max came in and shoved me over while I washed my hair. "Hey!"

The shower was only made for one and he blocked all the water. So I enlarged it and added a shower head. He looked over at me and said "Show off." I only continued to shower. Once done I dressed in jeans and a T and produced a brush and began to brush out my hair. Jordan and I past at the bathroom door and I heard Max yell about not wanting to go from showering with me to showering with Jordan. Soon Max came out dressed in jeans and a white T shirt, hair combed back and looking very handsome to me that morning. Jordan came out dress as Max. Jordan then knocked Max over on to the bed. I was pacing as I waited. "He said we." I was thinking out loud.

Then the phone rang. I went to get and Max got it first. "Yes. Right away." He looked at me and said "He's in the restaurant down stairs." I ran out the door only to be grabbed by Max. "No. Don't take off like that." I looked at him. "I'm sorry." Jordan, Max and I walked into the restaurant. It was a small café But sitting at one of the table were Marcus, Lincon and Mandra. I ran to my grandmother and flew into her arms and cried like a baby.

"Oh my precious Star. My beautiful granddaughter" I Looked in her eyes and she smiled then dropped her smile. "Max will you ever stop molesting my granddaughter?"

Max looked embarrassed but then said "I don't think so. Any way, she likes it now." Grandmother looked back at me with concern and I shrouded my shoulders. I turn and kiss Lincon on the cheek and he turned red.

The I flung myself in to the bear hug of Marcus. "Oh my princess. I have missed you." I let go and moved back to grandmother and Marcus Grabbed Max into a great hug. "I am proud of you my son." My mouth dropped. "Son?"

Marcus moved away from Max, but I eyed Max who only raised his hands. Marcus moved to Jordan hugged him and said "I knew you would help your brother. I am proud of you as well my son."

"Son?" I looked at Marcus. "Marcus how could you not tell me they were your sons?' Marcus looked over gently. "It was a rule of the Wizard. None of our children were to know who their Wizard fathers were. Only that they were children of Wizards. Max knew because he was of Mixed blood. Jordan was told by me when I could. Max and Jordan are my sons." He smiled then "And I think you approve."

I was still surprised but I loved Marcus and Max. I smiled "Can everyone start telling me the truth from now on.?" Max put his arms up.

I looked at my grandmother. "Something has happened to me. I need your instruction." She smiled and took my arm. We left Marcus and the rest and walked in the hotel garden.

"Grandmother, I am becoming a monster. I feel it. I… killed Martin and almost killed Jordan." I looked at her and fought tears "Help me?"

She hugged me sideways. "Em. You only have to understand, when you and yours are in danger, you will become the Priestess."

I looked at her. "Grandmother, I am not the Priestess. How did this happened?"

She smiled and said " I not sure. I may have help. I did not mean for it to happen. But once it did I believed that God had answered my prayers. The Elders were getting to invasive and trying to move you to produce a Wizard. I hated them for that. So did Marcus." She stopped and looked off and then she stopped at a bench and we sat and faced each other. "I hid things from you so that you could feel some home and family. Some self worth. The Elders, infatuated with your powers and the Prophesy. They looked at you like brood mare; Their Princess.

I knew that you were worth so much more than that; …and now…" She took a breath and looked away like she was worried. She looked back at me "Your are so wonderful just being you. But you are special. Not only to our kind but theirs." She sighed "I gave you the priestess dress and ceremonial mask. I knew that it was the dress of the Warrior Priestess of the forest and special but it is only to…activate in certain situations. I knew you and Max were found of one another." She huffed " I have to say looking back, I knew you loved each other. I had no Idea that Max had drank the mead and that you had also drank from the same glass. Elena told me later." We still held hands and my grandmother still beautiful. "When you went last over the fire at the maiden dance, and you kissed your chosen mate, you sealed you love for each other. You also released the priestess."

I looked at her seriously "Did I, or the priestess, make Max love me? Or did he love me on his own?

Mandra smiled, "He has always loved you. Loved you before he was a Mastered Wizard and you were the priestess."

I asked "How are Dad and Tom?" She smiled "There fine and off the radar. Della and her family too. No one will dare get near them. I think God him self will take them out."

I looked at her. "Grandmother, I killed Martin."

She looked at me and said "I know. And he would have killed you or worse."

"Grandmother, I may hurt someone."

She shook her head. "No, the priestess will not go beyond your own will. She will use your heart and mind, but she is fierce and dangerous."

I shook my head. "Why now. Why is she coming now.?"

Grandmother laughed. "She has been there since the night of the confrontation with the elders. She has really always been there. If she was not in you at birth, she would not emerge now. She is the Witch. She is dangerous and she will protect the Witches."

We sat quietly for a moment. Then grandmother asked "Now, what is this between you and Max?"

I looked at her "You just said that I have always loved him."

She nodded "There is a chance of never seeing him again when we approach the Wizards Counsel."

I looked at her and smiled "I have a plan."

She nodded. "Yes I am sure you do. But he is not our kind and they have their own laws they follow. Don't you think that Marcus would have saved his son by now?"

I said very strongly "I will save him." I did not know how I would save him, but I was determined to die trying.

We spent the day with our parents and walked along the tourist areas. We had dinner and I noticed something between Mandra and Marcus. They have always been close but I was seeing something more now. Max came back and walked behind the group with me. "So do you think your grandmother will let me sleep with you tonight?"

I started laughing. "She will be OK." He put his arm around me and we walked behind the group. "Marcus is your dad?"

Max smiled "Yeah he is."

I shook my head. "He has known what has happen and did not help us."

Max looked down, "No. He has. He never condemn our relationship, he felt it was right. And he has always loved you." Max sighed "He had to work from a different path. He had to his vows as a Mastered Wizard."

I looked up at him "You're a Mastered Wizard and you were following your vows."

Max said "They were not the same. I am not an Elder. My Dad is and had to make a case for the Wizard Counsel. It was more diplomatic. He negotiated my release when I was held in the halls. He knew I could not stay away from you but he knew that I would think of something." He stopped and looked at me and then kissed me. "He knew that I would never stay away from you."

I stopped and let the group get father ahead of us. I then asked Max "Why did you stay away from him so long. It really hurt him"

He sighed "He wanted me to conform. To give in to the Wizards and be under the thumb of the Pure Bloods for the sake of Peace. I told him that I couldn't for all kinds of reasons. Mostly because of you." He looked at me with a smile "I would be forbidden to see or be near you. I couldn't live that way." He kissed my head and said "Even when you hated me. I couldn't stay away." He then said "And I like being free. Not being condemned for my normal blood" He giggled "And I like sleeping with the Princess. And I like …." I laughed and pushed him.

Max gave our room to Jordan and Lincon. Marcus and Mandra had rooms at another hotel. Max and I entered the Room which had only one bed. I changed to a night gown. And got in the bed. I felt so good with grandmother there. Max got in and laid down with me.

It occurred to me that he knew everything about me and my life at home. I knew nothing about him. "Where did you live when you were a kid. And how come you never took me there?"

He was quite. And then he said "I lived in LA." he stopped and then said "Well when I lived with my mom." He stopped and didn't continue.

"Max tell me about your home life. You know *everything* about me. I know nothing about you."

He huffed "You Princess know me better than anyone. I lived some where, I went to school somewhere. That's about it. But my life has been with you." I turned back around and leaned back against him and was quite. After a minute he started to tell me.

"When my mom couldn't deal with me levitating and being able to get out of punishments, she called my Dad. It was pretty clear that my mother could not raise me. She was….nervous." he laughed a little. "I was not a wanted child. My father and mother played at a relationship. I guess my mother liked the novelty of a Wizard as a lover. My father loved my mother but never intended remain in the relationship or produce a child with her." He sighed "My dad knew that she couldn't keep me and he wanted to ensure that I would be trained and educated. Don't get me wrong. My mom was a good mom. She took good care of me, hugged and kiss me a lot. She never called me names or anything. She screamed a few times when I made thing appear or disappear." I giggled with him I turned around and laid my head on his chest. "I would go to see her from time to time. She just didn't know how to talk to me. She tried, you know, in the normal way; How's school how's things. But when she started using drugs, I thought it was because of me. She told me later that it wasn't, but you never can be sure."

"My Dad had a lot of obligations and never was home. He couldn't take me home with him. Only on weekends sometimes and Holidays when I was older. I remember begging him to take me home. "But….. Well, like all Wizards, I was placed in a Wizard foster home. There were six of us. I was the only mix blood." He was quite and I asked "So how does one become a Pure Blood anyway. There are no women Wizards." He was talking against my temple, "Unlike witches with both sexes, There are no women Wizards. But Wizards do produce girls. Those girls are expected to be the mothers of Wizards. If they produce with a normal, they get a normal. If they produce with a Wizard, they produce a Wizard. If my mother and father had a girl, who would still be a mixed blood, she would have no powers but would have the potential to produce a wizard."

"My Dad has tried to be the best he could be for me. He use to tell me 'you are a Wizard regardless of the normal blood. How powerful you are and the respect you get is all up to you.' But that was not true. Mix Blood is lower status and I cant change my blood." He sighed and continued, "I had a really good education with him. I studied with him when he was home and, because of that, my powers always stronger than the pure bloods. That didn't stop them from letting me know that I was beneath them."

I giggled "Yeah right. Beneath them?"

He sighed "My kind is supposed to be subservient to the pure bloods. I have yet to master that and will probably die before it happens."

I huffed "I cant imagine you subservient to Edwin. He is such a slim."

Max laughed, "That he is." He laughed a little bit "He was so pissed when I was appointed you guardian. He felt that a Pure Blood should be appointed, after all, he believed that he was your future husband."

I got mad then "How dare they believe that I would marry any one of them."

He giggled. "After I killed Jeremy, the Elders felt I was too close to you. They reassigned me to a baby Wizard. But there was no challenge there." I mockingly hit him on the shoulder.

He was giggling. "Once I wasn't your guardian anymore, I guess I just became your friend. Edwin was mad as hell with that. You know, like when you left your dads. He never showed up and I waited for him to. He was too busy with this other girl in Aspen. So I took the job. Because we danced at the Solstice and because I visited you I was hindering his ability to impress you. Chris and Jordan were on his side. They felt that I was only interfering." He giggled again. "Just think if they knew how often we took off and left number 2" He paused "But when Edwin said he was going to force himself on you that summer, I think I lost it a little. That's why I did not want you to go home. That's why Number 2 was so important. But, I really wanted to be with you. I wanted you to go with me forever. Forever, so you did not become…beneath them." I stayed quite. " Once you kissed me at the maiden dance; once.. We made love, Edwin got his way with the Elders. And I was kept from you. But the next year, I defied them again and returned to kiss you again. Couldn't help it. Your spell was too strong to demanding for me not to be there and kiss you." He sighed "that's when they held me in the halls and left me there alone for years. All I had was images of you and books of Wizardry. I was left there pretty defeated. I had a yearly visit from Edwin, He loved telling me how he would take you and produce the Wizard with you. I believed it would most likely happen since no would stop him. No one but me. And I was bound and held. I was pretty messed up in the head. Even when they said that the Elder came up with a plan for my release, I did not comprehend it at first. When I did I still needed time to think. Think of where to go and what to do. Knowing that they would never let me near you again." He smiled and huffed "At least not legally." He snarled "The plan was to continue to push Edwin on you. Regardless of what you wanted. They didn't care about what you… or I felt. Only their plan to have you produce a powerful Wizard sired by a Pure Blood Mastered Wizard, Edwin." He growled " So I told you about the race. I let you think that I used you. I went under ground and looked on from afar. He smiled, "You took care of Edwin's little plans. You protection over your house at night was a big obstacle for him. Your attitude to him was more than apparent. I think that is why you were introduce to Chris." He kissed me. I looked back at him "You scared me that day. And I did put up my protection barrier. How did you get through to kiss me?"

He smiled "I studied how to get through barriers. I am able to get through most."

We laid there for a while quietly and then I asked "If we had left Max, you know, just left number 2 and took off. Don't you think they would have eventually found us?"

He giggled "Yeah but by the time they did, I be working at a factory and you would be home with two or three kids. Their plan would be demolished." We started laughing and then as I laid my head on his chest.

I pictured that simple life and said "I wish I had gone with you." He moved me over and looked down at me and said "We can pretend?" he kissed and we again spent most of the night making love.

CHAPTER 36

The next day, we all took off for Anacona. Grandmother has stated that the priestess is a cousin of my Nana. We entered the boarder and made our way through the Italian countryside. We made it all the way to Rimini. There we stayed the night. I still could not understand why we were driving. But Marcus and Mandra never made any comments. I finally asked "Why are we driving? Why cant we just go?" Mandra said "Transporting is one way to detect movement and location. We are forced to travel as normals."

By the third day, we finally made it to Anacona. We were cautious as we moved about. There was no doubt that this was a Witches haven. Many watched us move through the streets. Many taking note of the Wizards who accompanied us. Marcus and Mandra went to a hotel and got us rooms. Jordan and Max stayed very close to me. And Lincon walked just behind. It must have looked like what it was. A barricade. Max had his monster hovering. I prayed that he kept in control.

"Why are you walking with me like this?" Max and Jordan stone faced did not answer. I could see the Monster Max close. When we made it to the rooms, Mandra had everyone meet in her and ***Marcus's*** room. I eyed my grandmother and she transmitted *"We've decided that we could come out of the closet since you and Max have never been in a closet."* I giggled with her.

We gathered around the table. Marcus started with "With this icy welcome, it is apparent that the Wizards are not welcome here. It is also apparent that by our company, Mandra and Em are suspected of treason." He took Mandra's hand. "We must all attempt to be low key and follow the directions of the Witches." He looked at his sons "Be aware, we are not their kind and are a threat to their existence just by being Wizards. They have been insulted and harmed by Wizards." He looked at me in the eye "Your relationship with the Wizards,.. Max in particular, is not a secret here. Though you are powerful, you are not trusted."

Mandra took over "Here it is not safe as we witches would have thought. Many suspect the Wizards as evil and enemy of the witch. And from what we are attempting now, what has transpired, does not dispute that." She got up and waked to the middle of the room. "Its time to make contact. Close your minds. Only hear my voice."

Her hair blew though there was no wind. Her arms stretched out with a glow of the sun. She then recited "From the power of God and mother Earth, from the powers of the north, south, east and west. We call on Anita of Anacora." She lowered her arms and her hair stopped blowing. At that moment we heard Anita with a thick Italian accent. *"Come to my home. I will be waiting for the priestess. Do not bring Wizards."* Max stood up, Monster appearing and said "No" but Anita stated again *"Do not bring Wizards."*

Mandra and I looked to each other. I looked over to Max now with his fathers hand on his shoulder. "I will be fine. I will be with my grandmother and with our kind. Stay here and be safe." Max shook his head. "Don't go alone." Mandra looked over at Max and Marcus. "We are strong in our powers. We will transport should there be a need." She walked over to Max and lightly touched his monster cheek and smiled. "Have faith in us as we have faith in you." She looked over to Lincon "Stay with the Wizards." He nodded. She looked to Marcus for a moment. Turned and waved her hand. She and I were in long white cotton maiden dresses with brown hooded capes. She raised her hood over her hair and face and I followed suit. With that we walked out of the door.

We walked down the street feeling the direction by the breeze. Not speaking and keeping our minds locked. Many stopped and watched as we passed. None approached, None made a move to us in anyway. It seemed that all action ceased in the village. I linked my arm with my

Grandmothers as we walked. The suspicion on the faces of the residents was not ignored. We need to see Anita and get back to the Wizards quickly.

We came to a small villa on a bluff. There was a great deal of vegetation surrounding there. Lots of Hesperia and rosemary. As we approached the gate it opened. We walked through and it shut. In the courtyard, we caught the sent of the witch of the home. The door opened and she was there. Anita. Dressed in peasant blouse and skirt. Bare footed and a scarf tied on her head, much like a pirate. She was old, and her eyes were ancient. "This is my cousins granddaughter. The priestess?" Mandra spoke "Anita, thank you for seeing us. I am Mandra, this is my granddaughter, Emily Star." Anita smiled "Emily Star carries the Priestess." I looked at her with curiosity. She smiled as if she felt she knew everything about me. "The Mastered Wizard is nervous without you." I only nodded knowing that Max would feel anxious.

She motion for us to sit at the table in the court yard. She then said "He is the one you know. Regardless of the Wizard Elders desires." I looked at her and said "He is the one because I chose him." She smiled "Yes you did. And the Priestess agreed." She poured tea for us all. Mandra then said "We come because of the Wizards plans and the fact that my granddaughter is in danger of being killed for her powers. We have come for counsel and to ask for sentries." Anita sat back and smiled. "I know what you require. I have a gathering prepared for the Priestess. Tonight in the clearing east of town. I suspect all will gather at the eleventh hour."

She looked over at me. "The Wizards are welcome but will not be included in discussion. They are allowed only by their loyalty to the Priestess." She giggled at my thought of the haste in which we had to move. The other Wizards and demon Deana hot on our trail. My grandmother then spoke my thoughts. "We are being pursued." Anita said "Yes but not tonight. They have all been detained." She smiled, "The mortals are questioning all of you pursuers at the border." She sipped her cup. "There papers have been…. altered. And they have been seen by the mortals. To disappear would cause a great commotion and.." She laughed "That would cause the Wizard Counsel great displeasure." She also said, "this Demon Mortal who looks for the power, she is spirited on by another. That is the one who is the danger. That is the one, who will be your true enemy." She sipped her cup. "The mortal will be disposable. But there is another mortal working with this evil one. That one can, if she achieves your powers, produce a rival child to yours."

She looked at me then and asked "Should you have a child sired by a Wizard, how do you intend to raise a child of mixed blood?"

I looked at her "I am mixed blood. I can only offer any child my love and protection and Gods good grace."

She took my hand and I looked at Mandra who gave me a comforting smile. Anita looked in my eyes "There will be a child of the Priestess and the Mastered Wizard. Take head, as the Wizards will ask for your child. They will do all they can to have the child. And raise that child to rule over Witches and Wizards alike. They will make a monster from your love."

I looked back at grandmother who looked concerned. I then asked "How do I prevent this from happening?"

She patted my hand. "The priestess will know."

I then asked "When?"

She smiled, "Some thing's are Gods design and not ours to know."

OK. I thought, First things first. "We will meet at the Clearing as asked."

Anita smiled and we got up to leave. Anita then said "The priest and priestess of our counsel will expect you as the Priestess, Emily Star."

I looked at her "I will try." What more could I say. I cant snap and be the priestess. I never know when that part of me emerges.

We returned to the hotel room. We had the same response from the Village as we had on our walk to Anitas. "Grandmother, why do they stare."

She held my arm "They know why we are here and they know we are with the Wizards." I asked at her to stop for tea before we go back up. She nodded. We sat in the little café and had some more tea.

"Grandmother, what if there is a child?" I looked so concerned. After all, this is not a real good time to have a baby.

Mandra smiled "Em. There is a child. I saw a glimmer when you returned from your disappearance with Max last month. I saw it clearly when Marcus, Lincon and I met you and the other two at the restaurant. How you deal with this is up to you." She laughed a little. "You never took precautions where Max was concerned, but I thought is was only with magic."

I was so scared. " We have only been together a few times . How could you know?'

My grandmother looked into my eyes. "Em. Weather you chose to believe or not, you are pregnant."

I was so concerned with this new twist. "I cant tell him now. It would not be a good time." I laughed then and said "I don't even know how I will keep his big mouth shut tonight." I held my hands to my face. "I am not ready for this on top of everything else." Mandra then said "Eve wasn't ready, Mary wasn't ready; I wasn't ready; None are ever really ready. But you do it. You do for your child."

My concern "I cant let the Wizards know. I will never have peace." I looked at her "We keep this between us?" she smiled but I could see her concern "Yes. We keep it between us. If we can. But Em, Make no mistake. This is a child of Powerful Mastered Wizard."

I felt bad. If I was normal, I could be happy. I could tell my child's father. I could shout it to the world. One more piece of joy stolen by my mixed blood, by Wizards and by Witches.

When we entered Mandra's suite, all three Wizards jump to their feet. We walked in the room and took off out capes. Max was antsy, though his monster only hovered now,

"Well?"

Though he was expecting me to answer, Mandra stated "We have a meeting tonight. Its in a clearing east of the Village. They are willing to have all of you there, but you are not to speak or interject." She looked at Marcus "You are allowed only by your loyalty to the Priestess."

I looked at Max and Jordan. "Stay here tonight. Don't go."

Then simultaneously they said "Are you crazy?"

I then said "Lincon will be with us."

I closed my mind. And Max, unable to intrude asked "Em?"

I looked at him. "Please stay here."

Jordan voice Max's dissention. "How can you expect that. We need to be there for the Priestess and for you."

I looked from on to the other. "You must not speak and you must remain in the background." I looked directly at Max then and said quietly "Promise"

He looked concerned and irritated by my blocking my thoughts. He only nodded. I looked at Mandra and she knew I was concern for the Wizards.

That night, at eleven o'clock, the six of us walked into the clearing. Many torches light the meadow. Max and Jordan at my sides, Lincon and Marcus on each side of Mandra. As we walked in the clearing into the presents of the Priest and Priestess's, as a united group. But a sentry motioned the Wizards to sit off to the side. Max looked at me and I nodded. Mandra, Lincon and I walked to the center of the circle of witches.

Anita was flanked by two Priests. One stood. In a broke Italian accent He stated "I am David. I am one of the High Priest of this coven. You have met Anita who is the high Priestess. On her right is the High Priest Antonio. We have expected you. We had expected the Priestess."

I looked at him and said "I thank you for seeing us, but I do not chose when the Priestess appears."

The group looked to one another. Then David provided Mandra, Lincon and I tree stumps to sit on. And then he took his seat. I looked over to Max and could see his irritation of my mind being blocked.

The Anita spoke. "Our kind is under attack. Not by Mortals, but by Wizards. They have made many efforts to control mortals and efforts to control witches." She looked over to the Wizards. "The older Wizard is know by this counsel. He has made efforts to speak in defense of the Witches of the world. However, his lack of conviction has lead to your plight. If he had used his power to remove the wicked wizards we would not be here now."

I stood up "Marcus has been most loyal to me. He has, under the laws in which he lives, protected me."

She stood and then said "But his son has brought forth the Prophecy of the Wizards. He did not protect you from him."

I became upset "I have told you. I have chose him."

She stated "We now must take steps to protect our legacy. Protect our line from the Wizards." The three high priests rose and through their arms towards the three Wizards that stood to the side. All three were then bond arms and legs spread on tall stakes. Bond fires and sentries with torches stood ready. I recognized this. My dream but it was me being burned by the robed men not the Wizards being burned by the Witches.

In shock I looked to the High Priests "How could you reward the protectors of the Priestess in such a way." and then in the voice of the Priestess erupted "Release them!" I walked forward and in a flash of light, I stood in the priestess outfit, mask included and again demanded "Release them."

The high witches looked at me "How do we have assurances that the issue will not be corrupted?'

I stocked the group. "How do I know you will not corrupt the issue. I am here for help and counsel. I am not here for those who have been loyal to me, loved me and cared for me to be abused. I will have them released immediately."

Before the high witches made a move Max, with his monster on, was at my side. I looked over and Marcus and Jordan had joined Mandra and Lincon.

Max open his mouth. "How dare you." He spoke through his Cat teeth "How dare you disrespect a Elder Wizard and two Master Wizards. We came in peace and honorable intentions."

Antonio stood and looked at Max. "You are very powerful Wizard as proven by your ability to remove yourself from our restraints. However, you come here not as representatives of the Wizard Counsel, but as a wanted Criminal of that Counsel. Your allegiance to the Priestess is clear, but how does that protect witches. How does you relationship protect the witches?" All I could think was don't say it. "We have concerns with this relationship as do the Wizards."

Max stood his ground and said "My allegiance is to the Priestess and no one else. I protect her. Not Witch or Wizard comes before her."

I stepped in "I and of normal and witches blood. My companion is of Normal and Wizards blood. How is this a concern. We have not been a enemy to the Witches as the Wizards have been to us. As it turns out, my relationship with this Wizard has somewhat thwarted the Wizards plans. He is pure of heart not blood."

Antonio then said "No Priestess, he has followed the wishes of the Wizards. Yet we do believe, his heart is pure."

I warned then, " He is also very powerful as am I, we will not be toyed with."

Leaving Max with the our group, I walked the circle looking at each of the witches "I am here for your counsel. I am here as a respect and to acknowledge that my kind have a say in their future. Do not make me regret that choice."

I stood in front of the High Priests and Antonio asked "and the issue?"

I looked of full authority and quietly said "I will protect my child from all corruption from both sides. There is a guarantee from the priestess." I stepped back and said "I will require sentries for my appearance to the Wizards Counsel. I will require the Priest and Priestesses align with me in my demand of the Wizards Counsel for their protection from all those who would corrupt the priestess and all of her children. I asked for the protection from efforts that would endanger the authority and legitimacy of witches. Do I have what I ask?" I looked at the witches then all looking to one another.

As they did their closed communication, Anita stood. "Priestess, by your command, we will abide by your wishes and align with you. And we will provide you with sentries. However, you and your chosen Wizard will leave blood behind binding your promise to the Witches and their authority over our kind."

I looked to her and said "And how is that to be done? How is any issue protected from corruption of any kind?"

She looked blank, "you will be protected and thus all issues." She waved her hand and a gold challis was set on red velvet. The challis was surrounded by a green candle for earth, yellow for air, red candle fire and blue candle for water. Then a unlit white candle. White for the Goddess. Also Laying close was a ceremonial dagger.

Anita motioned both Max and I forward. We moved forward and Mandra, Marcus, Jordan and Lincon staying close behind us. Anita asked "May I have you left hands." I looked at Max and we held out our left hands. Anita took our hands and turned our palms up. She twisted a golden cord around our wrists, holding them together. She picked up the dagger she dragged the dagger across the heals of our hands. As the blood appeared she turned our hands over. As the our blood mingled it was collected in the challis. She then handed us a candle and said "you must both hold the candle with the wounded hands. Then you must make the creed." She look at us both "You must repeat these words." We agreed

God and Mother Earth, our prayer to you,
Enemies to the family rue
Pure of heart, pure in soul
Mingled blood, pay the magic toll
Strength for those who work their art
Facing evil with honest heart
Strength and power to protectors of our kind
Strength in body, in heart and in mind
Bless it be to the one just new
Blessings cover as morning due
Promises cherished through the night
Promises equal through the fight
Witch and Wizard live in kind
Blood for blood, ties that bind

She then had us light the white candle to the Goddess. After the candle light, Anita took the candle in our hands. She untied our hands. And she stated "This binds you to seek the truth and justice for our kind and the Wizards. It also insures that what happens to one happens to the other. Together, we believe you are more powerful than any other mortal or immortal; Witch or Wizard.

She then picked up the challis. Toss it in the air and it transformed into a golden dust that fell on Max and I. She turned to the sentries behind her. They came forward. Anita introduced them "This is Sal and this is Dino. They will accompany you to the Wizard Counsel." I eyed the two. Both large handsome men with black hair and dark eyes. Both joined our group.

At that point I looked at the witches and said "Thank you."

Marcus came forward and addressed Anita "My lady, as an Elder of the Wizards, I assure you, all will be done to ensure the authority and dignity of the Witches. This is my word." Anita smiled "We appreciate your commitment and ask you for your forgiveness of our earlier assumptions."

Marcus nodded and smiled "Of Course."

We started to leave and Antonio call after Mandra "Mandra. You have done well with your granddaughter. You have done well in your art." Mandra smiled and bowed and we left with Sal and Dino following.

We returned to the Hotel. Mandra retained a room for the Witch Sentries. But all of us met in Mandra's suit.

Marcus welcomed the Sentries. "We appreciate your help. We have some plans for this event. And ....Max may be taken at that time. Our Princess will need more security should that happen." He hesitated somewhat with worry. "We would appreciate any ideas you may have."

Sal Smiled. "It is an honor to work with you and the priestesses. My brother and I have volunteered for this assignment. We feel that the Priestess has much to offer us in honor."

I smiled "I hope she does."

We all sat and planned out how we would approach the Wizard Counsel. Marcus said "I believe that I can call the Counsel together at anytime we chose. I am concerned to their reaction to Max."

Max looked at his father "I must help Em first then the rest can be considered. We have to stop the Wizard Pure Bloods and Deana."

Dino spoke up and said "We will die for the priestess, Master Wizard, her safety will never be in question. And I believe that the Witches High Priests made it clear. With you and the Priestess together, no one can over power you."

I said it before Max "We heard it, but we don't know how to work it."

Max continued "They also said we had to be together. If we are separated....which is a concern, I don't know if we can find the key to that riddle."

Jordan spoke up. "Look, you've got me and Marcus, the sentry brothers, Lincon and Mandra all standing with you. We may not be the Wizard Counsel, but we are not a force to be ignored."

Mandra said "Your right Jordan. However, we need to avoid the fight. We need them not only to help us squash this Prophecy, but also find out who helping Deana."

Max said again "It is a Wizard. But I cant think of who. There are so few of us that the answer is right here."

Marcus stated "No Max, there are several other mixed bloods. They also are trained. We can't discount those Wizards."

Max smiled at his father. "No Dad, I know the Mix Blood. It has to be Pure Blood working with her. Mix blood follow but also look for freedom with honor."

I then said "OK. Max and I are not to be separated at any time. Marcus will call the Counsel together at a chosen time. We will plead our case and defend the actions of Max. If all goes well, no fight. But, be aware, I will not leave their with out Max."

Max laughed "You may have to. And you will do what you must do. That is survive for your kind and mine."

I shook my head "Don't argue with me on this."

Jordan said "we will do all that can be done for Max."

I repeated "I will not leave if Max is not with me."

Marcus said "Do you think any of us want Max taken? But Max has his alliance to his kind as well. He must obey the Counsel. He may have to stay behind."

I thought about his alliance to a child he knows nothing about. His alliance with me and my kind. I slammed my fist on the table. "I will bring that place down to rubble before that happens."

I got up and left to my room. I went in and fought with myself over the news of the child and the promise to the Witches. Then with the thought of Max being taken by the Counsel. I felt over whelmed and angry. I had to stay closed to Max from here on out. I could not even warn him of the prophesy coming true. He did not need this added pressure. He had his life to save. But how would I keep the promise and the child safe with out him?

There was a knock on the door. "Em its Mandra?" I opened the door to her. She came and I shut the door.

"They don't understand you short fuse but I do. You have to think only about the hear and now."

I looked at her. Then shook my head and looked away. "Grandmother, the prophecy has come true. I am having a child of a Mastered Wizard. No not a pure blood, but just the same it has come true. And what happens to our kind? What happens to my child. And what if Max wants the child for the Wizards?."

She walked over to the couch and patted it and I sat down on it next to her. "That was a powerful ceremony that the High Priests performed for both of you. They would not have done so if Max was not worthy." She held my hand, and patted it. "Do not start to distrust him now. He will do what he must for you and any children you may have."

I felt terrible. "Grandmother, I trust him. I am so scared now with this news, I think its making me crazy. Is it normal to start fighting for a child that is so new?"

She laughed "Yes, of course it is. And this child is going to change the world for both races."

I looked at her. "I have to keep it from him for now. I cant let him start worrying about one more thing. He is following blindly on a vow to me, in spite of the danger to his own life. His own future. But he is already trying to figure out why I have blocked him."

She hugged me "Don't worry, he will excuse it precaution. But make no mistake, he and the other Wizards may already know and are only waiting for your announcement." She got up then. "Get some rest now. We leave tomorrow morning." She kissed my cheek and left the room.

I decided that I would just calm down. I went in and took a shower. Got on my night gown and prayed to God to look out for Max. Not to make this potential child a fatherless child. To not allow my heart to break again. I laid down next to Zee and petted him as he purred. At some point I fell asleep.

I felt Max correct my position on the bed. I opened my eyes, and looked up at him. He said Hi and I moved over. I closed my eyes again and he wrapped his arm around me.

He said in my ear, "I wished you would have stayed. I needed your brain tonight. And I don't understand why you have blocked me."

I turned over and looked at him and said "I need to be private right now. And I think my brain is mush."

He kissed me and said "OK, I can wait to intrude." I feel back to sleep.

CHAPTER 37

We started off the next day exchanging the C300 for a van. Lincon drove with Jordan navigating. It was a nice change from Max frantic speed. I leaned against Max and tried to sleep some more. Dino sat on my other side. Just in front of us in the next seat was Marcus, Mandra and Sal. Max, Dino and Sal discussed different theories of magic, training techniques and the difference between Sentry Witches and Guardian Wizards. Marcus and Mandra remain quite but I new they were talking through transmissions. Jordan was instructing Lincon as to how to drive in Europe. It was so much noise and I could stand it. I told my self, quiet.

I could hear nothing. I slept. I dreamed of sitting on the log at Hat Creek. Watching the creek grow move and turn. The sun was bright, glowing through the trees with a gentle soft breeze. I looked to the side as saw the child playing close to wear I sat. He was about two, with dark haired with hazel eyes. He was smiling at me. Giggling and pulling up the wild flowers. Zee sitting near watching. I felt so at peace. Until I looked to the trees and saw the shadow. But this time it did not come for me. It was going for the child. I could not get off the log I was stuck and the water from the creek was rising up to my knees. I screamed as the shadow came closer to the child. I called for Max. I screamed for Max to stop the shadow from taking the child. But he never came. And just and the shadow reached for the child I was being shaken. I opened my eyes to see Max saying something but I could not hear him. I remembered and told myself hear. The noise came in with roar. Everyone looking at me and Max say "What did you dream? You were screaming again." I looked at him and shook my head. Put my head in my hands and gave a muffled "I don't know." I had to lie. Besides the dream was insignificant. I don't know why I had a nightmare. Especially since I was with Max.

We finally ended the day in Lyon. I was tired of being in the van. We found lodging and went to dinner. I stayed closed and quite. I felt that it was best considering that I was not my self. I was not the priestess ether. I don't know who I was. Or even if I was a legitimate entity. I asked God to guild me. I knew we would be in Paris tomorrow. I knew I may lose Max forever. I was not afraid of the Wizard Counsel I was afraid of living afterward. Living without Max and raising our child. Afraid of the Wizard talking my child.

Max kept looking over at me. I knew he knew I was not myself. I smiled at him to reassure him that I was ok. But I could tell he knew I was worried. I finished my meal, or what I decided to eat. And left the table and went out into the garden. I sat on the bench and just thought. Sal came and sat with me.

I smiled at him "Thank you and Dino for your help."

He shook his head. " I have already said, we are honored with the task." He looked in my eyes "Are you unwell?"

I smiled "No. I'm …. worried I guess."

He nodded. "As we all are." then after a minute he said "Will you raise the child as a witch or a Wizard?"

I looked at him in shock "You must say nothing about a child."

He looked confused. "The Witches already talked about the child. It is not a secret." I was hoping no one got the meaning. "Just don't say anything. I don't want to think about it right now. OK?"

He laughed "As you wish. But I still would like to know. *If* and *when* there is a child, will you raise the child as a witch or wizard?"

I looked at him, "As a mix blood immortal under the grace of God and Mother Earth." He thought for a moment and nodded approvingly "Very good answer. Diplomatic; While offering some satisfaction but still remaining vague and not answering the question at all."

I started to laugh and he did too. "How can I answer that and make everyone happy. I will raise the child in love."

He smiled and said "I like that answer best."

I could see that everyone was getting up from the table. I stood and Sal got up as well. He looked concerned at that moment. He grabbed my arm and we rushed in to the restaurant.

He walked directly to Max. "We have a visitor. A figure hovering near by."

Max grabbed Jordan and Dino. As his monster appeared, he looked over at Marcus. "Take Em and Mandra up stairs and wait. Lincon stay here and watch the doors."

I yelled "No. I going with you." He shook his head. And he, Jordan and the Sentries left out the door. Marcus looked over to me and Mandra and said "Shall we?"

I reluctantly followed Mandra and Marcus to their room. Furious at being left behind. I paced and thought. That's it and I opened my mind to Max. I looked in and found that it was Edwin and his cronies. I looked over to Marcus and Mandra. "Its Edwin." I watched and Edwin explained to Max that he had a Weapon to take him and return him to the Elders. I saw the others in battle with magical weapons arching as the are deflected. I turned to Marcus and Mandra "I have to go." with that I transported to Max as the Priestess. I saw the Sentries battling the unknown Mastered Wizards. Jordan was holding Chris back and trying to talk to him. Simple waves of the hands of the Priestess sent the attackers flying.

I appeared at Max's side and faced Edwin who was standing on the top of a statue platform. "Princess" Edwin greeted as Max sent a ball of flame directly at his face. Edwin spun and dodged the ball of flame, and sent the weapon towards Max. Max was taken to the ground and held by magical chains. He struggled as Edwin smiled pompously while he believed that Max was captured. Edwin had a sward and I could feel he meant to kill Max. I put out the protective grid around Max and with a wave Edwin was sent flying. He then came back to the spot I flung him from. Edwin sent a binding charm and I defected it with a simple wave of my hand. My head down and eyes looking up at Edwin as a cat ready to attack.

In a low Priestess voice "You better try harder Edwin. I am not easily taken."

He growled, "I have other means."

I looked at him in the most evil way and challenge "Show them."

I called in the sentries and Jordan. " Come my friends." They stood in a half circle behind where Max worked the restraints. I stood looking at Edwin with death in my heart. With the priestess voice I asked. "Edwin. What do you want? Death? I will do that for you."

He laughed as his followers returned to his side. " I have come to take Max to prison and you to bed."

The Priestess then laughed at Edwin "You will be dead before that happens."

Jordan challenged Edwin then "What is it brother. Jealousy and greed getting the better of you?"

Edwin snarled at Jordan "And what of you turn coat. Busy job watching the back of you Bastard mix blood Brother."

Jordan laughed "With honor. You have lost yours."

Jordan looked at Christopher "And you, you follow a mad wizard."

Chris said "I am following the instructions of the Elders."

I addressed Christopher with a little witches laugh "You follow death"

He looked to me "My Lady, we did not expect you to fight."

The Priestess replied "Oh, and what did you expect? Complicity?" I laughed that evil witch laugh "I will die before I allow Edwin and the Elders dominate my kind."

The Monster Max was then at my side then. Edwin looked confused and his followers only looked to one another. Chris looked with what only could be admiration.

Edwin started "How did you…" I laughed a evil witch laugh and watched as the four Mastered Wizards looked a little worried. "You must have understatement the power of the Mix Blood Mastered Wizard." With a smile "Do you not possess the same abilities with your pure blood?" I sent Max a message, while giving the intruders a death smile of the Priestess. "Lets find out." Max then sent magical chains to subdue our pursuers. They were doing their best to get out of the magic holding them. They struggled and struggled, but had no success.

The Monster Max taunted. "Are you willing to leave here on your own? Or would you like some help?"

Edwin snarled at Max "you will be charged again with harming Pure blood. Edwin looked at me then.

I gave another evil laugh and said "Or I could permanently curtail your activities. I can offer you death. My sentries and I are witches. We are not held to the same ridicules rules of the Wizards."

Edwin was red face. He did not know if he was scared or angry. "Don't speak any more witch, you are not worthy." The Sentries became defensive swinging their golden swards threw the air.

Sal said "You disrespect the Priestess."

Max laughed then "Obviously Edwin, you are not worthy. You depend on tricks to subdue me and my friends; My princess." The Monster Max walked to the four chained wizards. He moved between them as the panther. All standing still at that point in fear of the Wizard holding there fate. The chance that he panther would strike. He stood then in front of Edwin and Chris. "Your plan has failed. Take that back to the Elders in the states. Max walked back to our group. "Where do we send them?" He smiled "Bind them and send them to Death Valley. Let them see the sun set."

Edwin looked a little scared at that time. I bond the wizards. Edwin was livid. "Unbind my powers witch."

I laughed the evil witch laugh. "Tricks are not powers." Together Max and I with our hands held, sent them on their way.

Once the threat was over and the attackers gone, the Priestess subsided. I turned and hugged the Monster Max. I waved and change in to jeans and sweatshirt. After a second I looked up and he said "I thought I told you to stay with Marcus." I looked up and said "I tried." He dropped his Monster and all five of us walked back to the hotel.

As we walked to the corridor to our rooms, Dino asked "Priestess, will you unbind their powers?"

I looked at him in thought "I really shouldn't. But I am not afraid of the fools and I doubt you are."

He smiled "I would like to battle with them again in the future. I would like to for the honor of our kind." He stopped "I mean no disrespect to the Priestess. You are magnificent. I only would like to present that the witches are a force."

I smiled at him. "You bring honor to our kind with your heart and your devotion." I unbound the Wizards. He smiled and bowed his head. He and Sal went to their room. We checked in with Marcus and Mandra who were watching anyway. We said good night and Jordan walked down the hall with Lincon. Max and I went to our room.

Max went in to shower. I changed into PJ bottoms and a tank. I got on the bed and leaned up against the head board. Turned on the TV but everything was in French. When Max came out of the bathroom and I asked "Can you translate?" He got on the bed and took the controls and turned the TV off. He then put his head at my stomach facing away from my face. My heart dropped. He knows. He looked back I my face and said "Yeah he's there."

I closed my eyes as heard my heart beat into my ears. I took a deep breath and opened my eyes to his. "A premonition by old witches. I only slept with you a few times."

He shook his head. "I hear him. He is there and growing."

I drew my brows together worriedly. Max said softly. "Why would you think I did not know?"

I huffed "I was hoping you did not know."

He looked confused "Does that mean that you don't want to have ***my***baby?"

I shook my head "I don't want anyone else's. I keep thinking about you as that factory worker and me with the three or four kids at home."

He smiled "I think I said two or three." I giggled.

He stroked my cheek and asked "Why this reaction. Why are you unhappy about this. I am so happy. I want you to feel what I am feeling." I did not speak. Max asked "Tell me Em. Tell me."

I looked up at him, "I did not think. I did not prepare and now it has happened."

He looked at me "So what. We're having a baby. I love you and I make an honest woman of you if that's what's bothering you."

Through the tears I laughed. "I don't need marriage to love you." I looked down "Max, don't you realized what has happened. What this child means?" He looked confused. I looked directly in his eyes. "Max, the prophecy."

He shook his head in understanding "No. It is supposed to be pure blood."

I corrected him "The child sired by a Powerful Mastered Wizard." I let him think about it for a second. "Max, the Elders will want my... our child. They will try to take our child. And I will kill them or die first." He looked at me seriously then and I repeated my last statement "Anyone who tries to take him from me will die."

He kissed my lips softly and said, "I will kill them my self before that happens."

He kissed me again and said "What kind of Factory am I destined to?"

The next morning I woke alone. I was content to stay in bed and linger. I did not think that Max understood when I said I would kill **anyone** who tried to take my child. I meant him too. He is after all a Wizard. I felt that way for no race benefit. Not my Witches blood, Not his Wizard blood and not the normal blood. I felt this way for my child. I wish I could just disappear and live peaceably with the child in safety and contentment. I was already tired. Weary of all of this. And knowing that I need to face the counsel, for my life, the child's life and Max's life.

There was a knock on the door. I asked who it was and Mandra replied. "Marcus and I." I opened the door with a wave as I put on my robe. Mandra had a cup of coffee for me. She and Marcus looked to me. I motioned to them to sit at the table. I took the coffee and sat with them. "You looked worried Princess." Marcus begun.

I smiled "Its all right, I will be fine."

Mandra took my hand. "We have come to ask if you would like to be hidden instead of meeting the Elders. We would stand in your stead."

I looked at them confused. "Why?"

Mandra looked to Marcus. He looked as weary as I felt. "They will know of the child. Probably already do."

I got up from the table. "The child is not a child yet."

Mandra said "No but do you think they will let you go, let you out of their sight? You will be held and not released until after the child is born and they take control over that child. Be reasonable."

I looked to Marcus, and desperately asked "The father is not pure blood. Isn't that a consideration."

He shook his head while looking into my eyes. "The princess and a powerful Mastered Wizard. Max is much more powerful than any Wizard of his time. It makes the pureblood less important now."

I sat back down and put Marcus's hand in mine. "Will they let Max go?"

He looked somewhat worried. "He has served his purpose. I have no answer to that. If he is a threat to the plan or prophecy he will be eliminated. He must see them and make his case. As a Wizard, must follow their rule."

I gave a little laugh "So that's it. Max and I are nothing more than instruments of their plan. We are not living breathing beings, Gods children, Mortal or Immortal, just....objects of their plan." I put my head in my hands.

Max came in the door "Are we discussing futures here."

Mandra said "We are. All of our futures." I looked up then stood up and waked to the bed. I petted Zee. Then a thought crossed my mind. I would just not have the child. "No!" Max snarled.

I turned to look at him with his monster at the surface. I demanded "Stay out of my head."

I looked away from him then. Mortified at my own thoughts. I looked at the healing wound on my hand and touch it softly with my finger. I heard Max's intake of breath. I looked at him and he as he looked a his wound. He looked up at me with an understanding of what those wounds met. He looked at me knowing my thoughts. He stood his ground while Mandra and Marcus got up from their chairs.

"Princess think of what your doing? Don't be rash."

Mandra then said "This child is also important to the Witches, Em."

Numb and angry. Trapped like a rat on a sinking ship. "I can not make myself dam my, or any, child to this." I faced the three and in a quite and defeated voice "What Max and I have had to endure from childhood. Mix blood, Nothing of our own selves that mattered. Denied a normal or immortal existence because of the prophecy. Only lead about by a string until we created the child. Only bred to breed for their desired outcome. Like a prized bull"

They all look concerned but stayed still and quite. I took a breath and looked at Max. "No matter what we have done to have our own lives, our own behaviors and thoughts; Our freedom; our love for one another, have all been for not. We are now, unnecessary and disposable. " Looking at Max " For you, this child is your death sentence. For me worse. For me, emptiness and nothing." I gave a little laugh "Even if we hid, or stood up to the Wizards, or did everything possible, we would still be caught in the net. Our love for one another and what comes from that love tainted and corrupted. I have to, for my self, for my child, make a stand."

Max said softy "Don't Em. " Marcus looked deep in my eyes and they all could see, the helplessness and hopelessness that consumed me. Mandra lost a tear. I had to get away from them now. All of them. I waved my hand and was dressed in jeans and sweatshirt. I smiled at them and said "I love you all." and was gone.

CHAPTER 38

I found myself on a mountain somewhere. Snow still packed in little piles while the grass sprung up green and fragrant. Three tiered small lakes glistened in the warm peaceful sun. I put up by barriers. No transmissions. No indicators of where I was. No paths, no people. No Max. I sat in the grass and cried. Cried for my life, and for what could have been for Max and I. The pines whispered "The princess cries for her love."

I scanned the area and In a hidden out cove of the mountain, I put a small cottage. I would not be found. I would not be taken, nor my child. So for the next several months I lived alone. I did not want for anything, I had zee for company and I read a lot. What I needed I conjured but mostly grew my own food when I could. I pillaged the natural berries that grew close by and had many peaceful walks. I imprisoned my self in this place, but felt more free than ever. I dances everyday to the music of the trees and had them for my company. Though I did long for my family, my grandmother and father. I longed for Max more. I would touch the scar and knew he knew I thought of him. And every so often I would have the feeling of a kiss on that scar. Knowing he was thinking of me. But I had to remember he is a Wizard. He follows their rule.

The trees would play their music for me and I would dance. The would also talk to me and say things like "Wizards are looking for the Princess." and "The grandmother cries for the Princess." That broke my heart but the one that made me cry was "Your Wizard searches and worries. Your Wizards heart breaks." They stopped saying that about six months in. I had to wonder were Max was. For all I knew he was dead at the hands of the Wizard Counsel. I could bring my self to asked the trees.

Through the months, my belly grew stretching my skin. I could feel the baby moving and watched my belly ripple with his movements. The experience was more mystical to me then any magic. Then I had to remind myself that Gods mysteries are more powerful than anything else. That it is Gods great design and magic. He does control the universe. Then I remembered my Christian teachings. God allows free will. The creator allows free will and is still in control.

One day I walked through the forest as it began to snow. I felt a kiss on my scar. Max sent a kiss. Then I thought that Max could be dead. Maybe his spirit reaching out to me through the scar. Regardless, I just was not secure in his obligations to the Wizards and his kind, and his promise to me and my kind. My child's survival, his being, his freedom and life, meant more to me than anything. That being true, it did not end my love for Max.

The next day the snow continued. A hard blowing snow, that landed quietly against the window of the cottage. Zee curled on the bed and tea steaming from my cup, I felt the first pain. I began to feel a little scared. I put the cup down, and felt my pregnant belly. I talked to the child inside "OK so you want to come out. Well, we will follow God and natures will." I spent the day preparing for the birth by covering the bed with sheets and towels. I had the hot water on the stove. Why, I don't know. I just knew that there is always hot water when babies came in the movies. I had no idea what to expect as the pains got closer I was pulverized with pain. I looked to Zee. "I need a doctor." I felt so helpless and then thought, Jacob Henning's and Auntie. I could do it, but how would they react. Do I attempt a transmission. After all, the transmission would only be to mortals.

I was hit with a hard pain and dropped to the floor. I thought what if something is wrong. I could lose my child. My son.

I sent the call to Auntie. "I need you. I need Doc."

I heard her, "Em Where are you." She was desperate. "Emily Please Where are you."

I was hit with another pain. I waited for the pain to end and took a breath. I brought both Auntie and Doc to the cottage. Della screamed and grabbed her husband. He was still standing in shock of what he has experienced.

I held my hand out to my aunt. "Auntie, Help Me. I am so scared."

She came to grips instantly and ran to me taking my hand. "Oh Em. Where have you been. What have you done to your self." I looked at her while being hit again with pain.

Auntie turned around and shouted at Doc. "Jacob, Jake, Please."

He looked at me in my pain and moved into action. He was feeling my belly and taking my pulse.

He checked and said "OK Em. You are doing fine. Just hold on and breath. Make sure you breath."

Auntie held my hand through each pain. Hours later, Maxton Caesar Marshal made his first sounds. Just a little whimper. Soft and gentle. Doc checked him from head to toe. Looking at me with a smile. "He is beautiful and healthy." Auntie took the baby and bundled him while Doc took care of me.

Soon he was in my arms, and when I saw him and his eyes I could not imagine life without him. Perfect in everyway. Truly the love of my life. My life and soul.

I looked at Auntie "He is beautiful isn't he?"

she nodded. "You did well, he is very precious."

I smiled at her "Is this how you felt when you had Taylor?"

She giggled. "O yes. Nothing can describe that feeling. Nothing."

I took the babies hand and touched my scar of the promise.

Doc grabbed a cup of coffee and sat at the table. "Well I have delivered so many babies. But this experience takes the cake." He watched the snow out the window and asked "Where are we?"

I smiled "I don't really know. I know it is where no one has found me."

Aunt Della said "Including your father and I."

I felt so bad but I had to "Auntie If I could have let you and Dad know where I was I would have. We, this little one and I, are not safe. We have to hide right know." And then I giggled "No one will suspect you of knowing where we are or seeing me. I think they are afraid of you."

She then fussed over my covers and said "Well Em, I have power too. It is called the grace of God."

I smiled and said "Yes, you do have the grace of God."

She smile and took the baby. "You rest. When you wake this guy will be ready to eat." Before I Slept, I added a room for auntie and Doc to rest. I already had the cradle ready so my baby could have his sleep.

Later that day, I woke to the baby crying. I sat up and Auntie was there holding him. "He's hungry."

I took the baby and fed him. I was amazed that he and my body knew what to do. "So much God prepared for."

Auntie brought me a cup of tea and I could smell the soup. "Looks like he has protected and provided for you." I nodded.

"I can send you back now Auntie. You don't have to stay and baby me." She looked at me sweetly, "We else could I be. You need me. At least for a few days. I don't know how you think you can stay her alone."

I smiled "I have been doing it. I do miss all of you so."

Several days past and I had already sent Doc back. He said he would handle the trip back better that the first one. Auntie and I spent our time talking and caring Maxton.

She finally asked me. "The baby's father is that boy who came to the house the night you left. I can see him. Same eyes."

I smiled "Yes he is the dad."

She looked away from the sleeping baby in her arms and asked "Em. I don't live in your world. But where is he, why are you alone."

I had blocked everything about Max away. But now that Maxton is here, I yearned for him. " I don't know. I am hiding from him too. As you remember, Max is a Wizard. He…Well, I loved him very much. But the wizards want my baby. I am so scared that they will take him that I am hiding from him too. I cant take any chances." I looked at her. "And that was being hopeful that he is not dead by the hands of his own"

Auntie looked down at the sleeping baby. "Em. Come home." She looked up. "God will protect you and Maxton."

I smiled "God has kept me safe here. He allowed you to come when I needed you so. I believe that the peace I feel here is from God."

She then said "Your father deserves to see his grandson. To know him and teach him Gods will"

I thought a moment "Auntie, he needs to first know that God is the creator and who he is first."

I took her free hand, "I will teach him of God. After all, I am a preachers Daughter. And when I can, we will come home."

I spent the next year daring to send Della messages for her and Dad. I felt that so far, it was safe. The immortals would never suspect Gods servants as receivers of messages from me the Witch. Funny how life goes. Auntie who I thought would be the last person I would call in the world, has been my salvation. Maxton grew and I spent every waking moment with him. He was a delight. He smiled and had expressions much like his father. He was now walking a little now. We played in the snow and snuggled at night before bed. I said prayers with him and exposed him to God and Mother Earth. And every night, I would take his hand and touch the promise scar.

By spring my son was growing and learning to speak. He would call me and say "look Mama look." I think that was my favorite name "Mama." My aunt often sent messages about baptism and when would it be safe to go home. How could I answer that. I knew by five he would have most of who he was. And I guessed we would stay at least till then. And then there was the issue of living with the mortals with an immortal child. Maxton was already levitating and making things like blocks and frogs appear and disappear. I know dad, a normal, did it with me, but the whole wizard kingdom wasn't trying to find me and take me from him.

One sunny afternoon, Maxton and I went to the little shallow lake and we were playing in the water. We spent the whole afternoon out by the lakes. I had little sandwiches for us to eat and we laid on a blanket so Maxton could have his nap. It was so peaceful. I danced to the music of the trees and listen to their sweet whispers. I at one point closed my eyes to wake at Zee growling. I jump and found my child playing in the grass in between me the cottage. The tress whispered "Run Princess. Danger has arrived." I looked at the poppies bent oddly. The jays were pestering the sparrows. And then the hawk, soaring against the clouds, screeched three times the warning bell.

I jumped to my feet and ran to my child. I picked him up as I ran to the cottage. I threw up the protection and prayed to God to protect us. I sat and held my son tight. Shaking I dared to look out the window and saw nothing. But Zee continued to growl. I looked at him. "What is it?" He just walked in a circle and growled. Then his scent assaulted my nose.

Then his voice was there. "My Princess." Edwin. My heart stopped. I turned and there he was. Standing still and threatening. "Get out!" was all I could say and put a protection around Maxton and I. "We found you. And you know why we have come." Keeping the protection around Maxton, I and ran out the door. As I prepared to transport, a dozen Wizards surrounded me with only the protection barrier keeping them back. I held my child close and called to Marcus. In a panic I screamed for Max. I opened all communication and was screaming

"Help me Max their trying to take him. Please Max".

As I stood I felt her emerging. She was coming and she was angry. I looked at my son, I could not put him down. I could not fight with him. And yet she came.

The Priestess stood with Maxton wrapped on to her back. Sward ready and powerfully glowing.

"If you leave you will live. Stay and I will kill you all."

Edwin now joined the circle of Wizards. Edwin with a sour face said "We've come for the bastard child. You knew that this was expected."

My eyes deadly and ready for battle I raised the sward in my hand. "Take him if can take him. But you should be prepared to die."

One of the unknown Wizards made a move to take the child. I twirled about and I cut off his head. Others came forward to attack the Priestess but she injured or killed all that approached. The other wizards try as they might could not bind the priestess. Two other Wizards came to flank me and another coming straight on. Another lost his head and another his arm. The third moved before injury but left my side cut open and bleeding from his sward. Maxton remained quiet on the back of the priestess.

I stood again in the center of the Wizards, ready and wanting to kill each one of them. Then Monster Max appeared next to me and the priestess threw the sward but he had predicted this and had his protection up. We looked into each others eyes and the Priestess had recognition of her partner in the Promise, the two stood shoulder to shoulder. Then the Witch Sentry Brothers appeared with on in front and the other behind, swards ready. Then Jordan, Marcus and Lincon stood to form the protective circle.

The Wizards stood and waited for their instructions from the Mastered Wizard Edwin. He came forward "Princess, we have come for the child. You know this has been foretold and there is no escape."

The Priestess growl low and deadly "You all will die first."

He looked over to Max "Will you kill your own kind for this Witch?"

Max the monster stood. He gave a evil grin. "I will kill anyone who tries to take my child. But you I will kill for myself"

Edwin walked just outside of reach and with a quick escape close. "Oh Max, you are a fool. The Elders will have the child. And you will remain as a criminal. I doubt that your fate is promising. How do you suppose you will be able to play at fatherhood?" Max walked to face Edwin at a safe distance. "When you and this ' He waved his hand. "Rabble are dead, what will you care?" He looked at Edwin as the monster "The child is more normal blood than any. Leave him be."

Edwin laughed and said "No matter, Mix Blood. He is required. As is your death."

I then pointed my sward at Edwin. He could not mistake the death I intended for him. "No more talk. Leave or you, Edwin, will be the next to die." I saw the fear in his eyes as he backed into his circle of Wizards. My Sentries waved their swards and stood ready to follow my orders.

Max the Monster looked over to Edwin with his evil smile "Ready to die Edwin?" Edwin and the other remaining Wizards disappeared.

Max turned and began to walk back to me. Max only a mere yards from me, and I knew I could not take a chance. As He walked forward and I stared at the face of the Monster Max. With death in my heart instead of love. I raised the sward and with a sneer I said "Don't". Max stopped in his tracks but kept his monster on his face.

Marcus turned to me. He looked at me and softly said "No one here will harm you or your boy. No one will take him from you."

I loved him but could not drop my guard. "All of you move away!" they all waked behind Max confused. Hadn't they just stood against the Wizards with me? But the Priestess was not convinced of their intensions.

Mandra appeared close to Marcus "Em, Priestess, we are here to help you."

I looked at her and believed my grandmother but not the Wizards.

I sneered to all of them "Stay away"

The mother cat protecting her young, the Priestess stood threatening and deadly; ready for another battle. This one with her lover, and her family.

Max growled "Have we not been kept away from him long enough. You know any one of us would die for him." I stared at him in the same resolve to kill him should he attempt to take my child. "Why don't you trust me?" The Priestess only stared. He roared at me "EM!" I could see the monster. I did not see Max. He said it again "Why don't you trust me. Why do you keep me away.?"

The Priestess simply stated "You are a Wizard."

He laughed that evil laugh of the monster. He then said evilly soft "So is he."

Then confusion entered. The facts entered my mind. Yes, my son was a wizard. But first and foremost he was my baby.

The Priestess spit back "He's my baby."

Max looked at the priestess and loosened his monster "He is my baby too." The intent for death lightened but the sword held high for a death stroke. I stood still breathing heavy, bleeding and covered with blood of my victims.

He raised his hands with his palms up. He had a calm face now. He walked slowly never taking his eyes off mine. He held out his left palm so I saw the scare of the knife. The knife of the witches ceremony. He said softly "You have the scare, the promise. Look at it." He softly touched his scar with his other hand and my scar tingled. I lowered the sward and looked at my left hand. The scare was there.

I looked back at him. "You wont take him?" He shook his head. I asked "You swear on everything that is holy."

He said softly "I swear on everything that is Holy under God."

The Priestess began her decent. I felt her leaving. I released the sword. Took my son from my back and held him close. I felt the blood running from my side. But would not let loose of the child. Still not moving I looked to my grandmother.

She smiled and came to me. "Em shall we take care of your injuries.

I shook my head standing and not trusting just yet.

Sal approached and bowed. "Priestess we are once again at your command."

Then Dino came forward. He said "No fear, I will die before that child is ever taken by the Wizards. But you care for your self for the next battle that is sure to come."

I walked far around Max and the group as they watched and hurried into my cottage. I stood there for a minute. Thinking of what to do now. The group walked to the cottage. Maxton pointing at the new comers. Looking at me "Mama look." I nodded at him and kept him in my arms. I watched cautiously. Max standing back only watching Maxton. Maxton looking at him and giggling. Mandra came close and I looked in her eyes. My Grandmother with tears falling. I reached out and hugged her with Maxton still in my arms. She let go and looked at Maxton. "He is beautiful. What is his name?" I looked at Max "Maxton. Maxton Caesar Marshal." She smiled at Maxton and he looked to me as if to say "Look mama there are people here." Still bleeding and full of the blood of the Wizards, I still would not turn Maxton lose. Marcus came up then and I hugged him. He said "Well, a grandson. He looks like my side." I nodded. Jordan came in and met Maxton. When Max came and met him, Maxton smiled and reached for him. Still uncomfortable I was not turning him lose.

Max said, "Em Please?"

The baby corrected him "No. Mama."

Max giggled and then said "Mama Please?"

I whispered "Promise?"

Max looked at me and said "Promise." I let go and my heart dropped. But Maxton knew him. I don't know how, but he knew Max. He called him Da. Mandra had made a move to look at my wound. I jumped back and looked over to my son on the floor with Max playing with the blocks.

"Em come and sit with us." Grandmother and Marcus sat on the couch. I kept my eye on Max and Maxton as I moved to stand near the couch.

"I have to make Maxton his dinner."

Grandmother waved her hand and there was food across the table. Maxton gave a laugh and got off the floor and walked over to the table. Max followed him and picked him up so that he could grab a chicken leg. They stayed at the table and Max put the baby in his chair and they ate together.

"Em. Please calm down. None here will take him." Mandra had her hand out reached to mine. I took her hand but eyed Max and my baby.

Marcus asked "Why would you think Max would give up his own child?" I could not fathom "His child" Maxton was mine.

I said "He may take him for other reasons. I ….don't know."

Jordan smiled "Em you have to be so proud of that little one. He is fantastic. How old is he?" I smiled but kept my eye on my son.

"He is amazing and he will be two in December." I felt the injury sting. I knew I was bleeding still. I knew I was full of blood but could not leave my son.

Marcus said "What do you have planed now Em?"

Max called over from the table as Maxton put a olive in his mouth, "You cant stay here. They will be back."

Then I said "Then I will kill each one that sets foot on the clearing." I looked at my little cottage that I have come to love.

Mandra said "You have done so well. You have protect him all this time alone. Now let us help you?" I was feeling weak, shaky. I heard Max laughing and looked to see the baby levitating another piece of chicken.

The baby was saying "Look Da." I walked over to Max breathing heavily by anger and injury. "How does he know you?" Max looked up and then looked back at Maxton who put another Olive in his mouth. More insistent I asked again. "How does he know you." Max swallowed looked up at me and said, "He and I play in his dreams."

My expression was furious. He snarled at me then. "I couldn't reach you, but I found him. Just not his location."

He looked back at Maxton "We play in his dreams."

I couldn't believe it. I screamed at him "You lead them to him. Cant you see that? You lead them to him!" I took the baby out of the chair and walked away from Max.

He stood up and barked at me "No. If I cant get a location how do you think they could." I turned around "I don't know and I don't care." I stood in the living room breathing heavy and angry. We were so happy here. Now we had to leave.

Max came over and said "Em I didn't. I wouldn't"

I looked at him. And with my voice getting louder with every word I said "Any communication with him is potentially dangerous. You taught me that."

He was angry and he sneered through his teeth. "Em I only wanted to see him."

I rubbed my eyes which were getting blurry. "Now it starts all over." I looked at Max "But now, Maxton is here. Here, and is as hunted as his father." I held my son tight again. Maxton reached back for Max. I allowed the exchanged as my legs became shaky.

In complete desperation, I looked at Marcus and Mandra "Help me? Help me keep him safe? Please?" Marcus stood up and put me in one of his bear hugs. "With my last dying breath I will help you keep him safe." I went out then.

CHAPTER 39

I woke up in a strange room. It was bright with white curtains and a canopy bed with small crocheted curtains lining the top. I was clean and my side bandaged. Dressed in a tank and PJ bottom I could see the bandage covering my side. I felt weak and sick. I laid there for a minute disoriented and then I realized that my son is not there. I sat up quickly and had to lay back down from the dizziness and the pain in my side. I moved more slowly, and got out of the bed holding it for stability. I went to the door of the room and went out. I walked along the wall fighting the weakness and dizziness. The place was massive. I leaded against the wall for balance and came to a big stairway. And I went down the stairway half on my rear and half on my feet. It felt like it took hours with the pain in my side and dizziness. I made it to the bottom and sat on the bottom stair. I did not know which way to go. I had to rest for a minute so I leaned my head on the wooden banister and closed my eyes.

The next thing I knew I felt Max pick me up and started up the stairs. "No. I need to see Maxton." He did say anything and I was too weak to fight I only said Please. He said "Shut up Em. And stay in bed" I did not open my eyes because I was so dizzy. I felt him take the tape off my side and the pain there. He put a towel under me and left the room and I went back to sleep.

When I opened my eyes again, Mandra was sitting with me. "Grandmother?"

She smiled and said "Well your back"

I felt the same dizziness and pain but I had to see my baby. "Where is Maxton?"

She patted my hand and said "He is down stairs with Marcus and Jordan."

I looked at her in fear "You wouldn't let them take him would you?"

She giggled "No and they would never take him from you." I asked for some water and she gave me a glass and a pill.

"What is this?"

She smiled "Its for infection."

I looked at her and wondered about that. But took it and drank the water. I reached out and petted Zee at my side and I then slept again.

I knew I was dreaming. It couldn't be real. I was standing at the little lakes. Maxton played in the clearing. Zee was jumping at butterflies. I felt the sun warm on my face. I was so happy being home. I was free. Maxton was free. But then it got dark and I turned around to see Wizards walking towards me. I turned to get Maxton and Edwin was holding him up by one foot. Edwin had red eyes. I screamed and called for Max. I ran as fast as I could to the clearing but Edwin disappeared with my child. I could hear my baby crying. I sat up in the bed and with tears running down my face, I transported the child to me. He was crying "Mama" Max was right behind him with a scowl on face. I ignored Max and held my baby. He was crying and crying. And I matched his tears with mine. But I cooed to him and I rocked my crying son till he fell asleep. Mandra came in and looked at Max glaring and me with my child. She looked down at my side which I already knew was bleeding again. "Let me put him in bed Em. I looked at her and allowed her to take the baby due to my weakness. She then said," I will be back to take care of your side." I closed my eyes and my mind not feeling strong enough to deal with Max.

"You closed your mind because you are planning something, Like leaving again with Maxton, aren't you? . I shook my head but did not say a word. I looked at him. He still in his evil mood he sneered at me " You will never take him away again." I did not answer or remark. He began to become frustrated by my lack of response. "Are you going give me the silent treatment or are you going to talk to me?" I closed my eyes, feeling not strong enough to argue or excuse my behavior.

I said in a quiet voice. "I know your mad I left and I know you hate me for keeping him away. I don't know what else there is to talk about." Thinking that would be enough I though he would leave. I open my eyes and he remained in front of the bed where he first appeared.. He was staring at me. I was so tired and weak. I needed him to leave me alone. "What?" He very agitated but cautious.. In a very soft voice he said "Where do we go from here Em?"

I looked up into his eyes with dread and exhaustion "I don't know…., All I know is that our whole lives have led up to this wonderful little boy. Everything you and I did to foil the Prophecy, the love and protection we felt for each other, the more we fought for our freedom, have all created Maxton. I don't want him to ever feel the way we have felt when we were kids. I don't want him abandoned or taken from his parents. From me... Or you. I don't want him different or lonely. I don't want witches and Wizards taking him. I want him loved and free. That is all I ever wanted."

I couldn't look up anymore and closed my eyes. I was returning to sleep and I felt his soft kiss. I thought maybe he still loved me. Maybe I was only dreaming that he kissed me.

I woke in pain when someone was poking my side. I yelled a big EEEEE and looked over to see Doc. He looked up and smiled "Hi."

I smiled back "Hi Doc, do you mind not touching me there."

He giggled. "You have a good infection. You belong in a hospital but considering the cause of the injury, you would be in jail or the county mental ward." He got serious, "Em we have to drain the infection and pack the wound."

I looked at him like he was crazy. If examining me cause that pain, no way would I be able to sit through what ever he had in mind. I shook my head.

"I cant right now. I have to feel better first before I can sit through that"

He remained serious "You will not feel better with the injury like this, you will only get worse and possibly die. Now were would Maxton be if that happened."

I shook my head "Cant you do something else like give me antibiotics or something simple?"

He said "Well you will be taking antibiotics but they will not help much till the wound is cleaned and dressed."

He looked at me like he was going to start right then and there. I started to panic and began to get up and Max and Jordan appeared next to me and held me down. Not willing to give up, I started to send Lamps jars picture frames vases from all over the room right at them. "let me go you fools." Dodging the items sent right at their heads, Max bound my powers and used his power to keep me down.

Jordan looked at Max "You got it. Dam she gets mad." And he got off the bed and left the room.

I screamed at Max "Let me lose." He gave no expression only grabbed my arms and legs that were flaying. His powers held my side in position while his held my arm and legs. Doc started and I felt the ooze on my side and then Doc was manipulating the side and I grit my teeth and closed my eyes against the pain. I did whine a lot through the process. Then I felt a shot in my side and yelled a bit. Then I felt the push of the gazed enter the area and it was very painful. I remained stiff, eyes clamed shut and breathing through the pain. Doc said "Almost done." I opened my eyes and looked over at him as he placed a bandage on the wound. At that point, I was exhausted. Doc got up and patted my face. "I let your Aunt and Dad know that your awake.

"My Dad is here?" he nodded and I attempted to get up and was still held down. Doc smiled and said "Stay there." He left and I looked over at Max who had that evil grin on his face. I asked Him "Was that fun for you?"

He laughed "Of course it was."

I narrowed my eyes and told him "Let me go now."

He had his grin on still and said "If you get up, you will find yourself held down again." He released me from his hold, both magical and physical. But he kept me bound.

"Let go Max.!"

He shook his head. "No. Not yet."

I sat up and gave him a deadly sneer "You release my powers Now." He grabbed my shoulders and threatened "You will stay were you are, do what you are told and you will not transport the baby." And that was it, I pushed my face farther in his with out fear but total defiance.

"How dare prevent me from my child. He was calling me. He needed me."

Max pushed me back on the bed with a wave of his hand. He walked over to the window and snapped "Just do what you are told."

I was about to get up and walk over a slap him silly when my door opened and my Dad walked in. I was out of the bed and grabbed my father.

"Emily Star, my daughter." I looked at him and he was smiling while I cried. Then I felt Max grab me and pull me back to the bed. I looked over at the pompous ass with anger and looked back at my dad with a smile. Then Auntie came in and came right to me and hugged me. Dad reached over to Max and shook his hand.

"Did you meet Maxton Dad?"

He smiled big and said "All afternoon. He is a bundle of energy." He looked at me soft "He is wonderful and I like being grandpa."

Auntie giggled and said "He is as beautiful today as the day he was born." She looked over to the ass and said "I knew you were his father, He has your eyes." Max gave her a charming smile which made me sick.

Dad looked at me seriously then and asked "Why would you not come to me if you needed help. I would have moved heaven and earth for you and Maxton."

While shaking my head I started "Dad,,,"

But he stopped me "Em, I know that you have your thoughts and your beliefs in the magic. What happened to your belief in God and his power?"

I looked at him and told him "Who do you think protected us for so long. When we were at the cottage, I knew God was there. I felt the peace and the freedom. I believe it was God. I could feel him there."

Dad smiled at me and kissed my cheek. "Why don't you all come home. I will make sure you are comfortable and safe."

I giggled "Dad, I cant do that. I have to make sure your safe too." I then asked "Dad do you know where I am?"

He looked over to Max. I did not want to hear him but he answered.

"This is my family home. Marcus, Jordan and I live here. Now you and Maxton."

I could not believe how stupid this was to bring Maxton here. Before I could protest, I felt my self falling asleep again.

"Dad, don't leave, OK"

He hand my hand and said "I'll be here when you wake up."

When I woke next it was dark outside. I felt terrible but my side did feel better. I started to sit up and heard

"Stay put."

I looked over and my baby was next to me and Max on the other side of him. I bent over and kissed my child on his cheek while he slept. He was warm and looked comfortable. I looked over at Max who had on his evil face which was becoming normal. I began to get up anyway and he grabbed my arm.

He said again low and evil "Stay where you are."

I looked over at him with the same evil heart. "I have to use the bathroom. Let me go."

In stead he moved over to my side of the bed and secured the baby so he wouldn't fall out. All while holding my arm, he got out of the bed and helped me up but I got dizzy and sat back down.

He gave a huff. "See why I told you to stay put."

Not to allow him any superiority, I forced my self up. I had no idea where the bathroom was, but I wanted to find it on my own. I pulled my arm away from him and started to walk to the door.

He took my shoulders and pointed me to another door to the left of the main door. I walk through the door and found a big bathroom with a walked in shower. A huge tub and double sinks in granite. On the other side of the bathroom was another door. Once I finished with the bathroom, I opened the other door and found another bedroom with heavy wooden furniture and masculine looking. I figured it belong to Max. I made my way out of the bath with my side starting to ache more and more. I stopped just for a second, and found my self lifted up and carried back to the bed.

"I could have made it back on my own."

He did not say anything only got in on the other side of Maxton.

I turned to my son and was petting him and lifted his hand and kissed it.

"Your going to wake him up."

I ignored him.

He sighed and said, "He cried for an hour. No one could make him happy, not even Zee." Zee I wondered where he was.

"Under the bed."

He yawned and said "When I laid him next to you he snuggled in and went to sleep." I looked at Max and he said

"He wanted his Mama."

Max cupped my face with his hand which took me off guard. He looked less than the monster and Said "You must be a good mom." I smiled at the complement. I laid my head down on my pillow and left my hand on my son. Max laid his hand on my hand that laid at my sons side.

I looked at him and he said "We sure did make a good looking kid."

I gave a huff "Your only saying that because he looks like you."

Max giggles "Well your aunt thinks so."

He looked at the ceiling. "I cant get over those normals. They are really…tolerant aren't they?"

All I could say was "No."

He looked over at me "They laugh and have a good time when Maxy levitates things."

I was bewildered. "They called my powers Ills."

"Ills?"

I looked at him "To be prayed out of me." I looked at him "You know, you were around enough to see it."

He lifted his shoulders "They are more tolerant of Maxton then."

"Why did you bring us here to your home where they will look for us. Find us."

Max looked at me seriously "They can get in."

That's was it. He did not explain any further.

"Max they will find him."

He said "I am going to put in him his crib."

I shook my head and said "No leave him." But Max picked Maxton up and went threw another door at the end of the room. I closed my eyes and figured that was all he was going to say. And ran out so he did not have to answer my questions. Then I felt him get back in bed with me. Which to me was odd. He after all had his own bed.

"I came back to talk to you. And this way we don't wake him up."

He came close and I recoiled instinctively. I was not sure what was happening.

He propped his head on a hand and elbow.

"They know he is here." My heart stopped and I started to jump from the bed and Max grabbed me. I tried my powers and they were bound.

"Max Please we have to leave."

He shook his head. "No. we are safe here."

I shook my head, "No. And don't you think I need my powers to kill anyone that tries to talk my son. You turn me loose."

He smiled and I was held in the bed. I was desperate to get to my child and leave.

"I knew you would want to leave with *my son*, so that is why you will stay put until you listen to reason,"

I had death for him in my eyes "There is no reason to lay *my child* out like candy. He is not safe, they only need to take him. And you don't see any danger."

He looked at me amused and then said "I never said I did not see danger. I said he is safe here."

I was so angry and my head and side were throbbing. I look at him with daggers

"I am going to get out of this and I going to protect my son. You better get out of my way."

He giggled and said "I believe you but right now you need to heal. Maxy and me do just fine till he needs his mama fix. And I will protect him from all sources right by your side."

I looked at him still panic over my sons threats. "How can we be safe here. And where is here? I don't even know what part of the Earth I'm breathing in." He laughed again as if it was a big joke. I grit me teeth and sneered "Always have to control everything don't you. You learned well from the Elders." I regretted before I finished saying it. He got his Monster grin again and grabbed my chin hard. Slapped at his hand and he held my arms at my sides with magic.

He leered in to my angry eyes "Don't ever align me with those bustards."

Too much anger and to little patience caused me to spit out "Or what?"

He gave me that evil stare and I felt so irritated and tired of it all. I looked away from him and just wanted to ignore him now.

He then said in his evil voice "They know he is here and they will not take him but want a meeting with us." He turned my head to face him "They want to meet the Priestess who killed the Wizards." He smiled "And me the criminal."

I looked at him as if he was crazy "How can I protect my son and meet with them. It is impossible. And if you meet with them, they will kill you. They may kill us both. And then they will have achieved their goal of getting Maxton."

Max looked less evil but serious, "We will be meeting as a group in a few days when your better. Then we will cover all possibilities." He sighed and held his hand at the side of my face to ensure we were eye to eye "If we don't meet with them, there will never be peace or freedom for any of us. That includes Maxton."

I shook my head "If they attempt to kill you or me they will die."

He smiled and with a high girly voice "You mean you would protect me too?"

I rolled my eyes "Maybe."

He let me loose but did not unbind my powers. I moved to be more comfortable and said "Let go of my powers."

He shook his head "Can't."

I looked at him "Why?"

He came close and said "Because your going back to sleep." I started to protest but fell asleep before I could get it out.

A few days past and I woke up in the morning to see the sun just coming in the windows. I got out of bed and took a shower. The wound bandage smaller now. The shower felt so good and I lingered in the hot water. Once out of the shower, I combed out my hair and snapped and had on clean PJ bottoms and a tank. I walked back to my room and looked around. I walked to the door that Max had taken Maxton. I found my son awake and he squealed when he saw me. I went over and took him out of the crib and changed him. He pointed outside and said "Look Mama." and I could see the pines waving. They were saying that it was a peaceful time. I talked to my son softly. I told my son about the trees and their language.

"Witch stuff?"

I turned to see Max, in sweats and shirtless, in the door way of the other bedroom watching us. I nodded "Yeah, Witch stuff."

The baby looked at his Dad and pointed to the trees and said "Look Da." Max came over and took the baby from me and kissed him. "Good morning kid." The baby giggled and I smiled at the sweet scene.

I held my arms out and said "I'll take him and get him some breakfast."

Max shook his head. "No. I take him and show you where to go."

I lifted a brow, "You don't want me to have to much control over him."

He looked at me irritated "That is not true. But with the recent past, I should feel that way."

I did not want to ruin my day and just said "Fine" and then walked back to my room. He followed and went out the door. I followed like goody two shoes.

We got down the stairs with much less effort and time as it took the last time I tried. Max went to the back of the house. On either side of the staircase were rooms. One looked like a Library and the other like a grand meeting room. As I followed to the back of the house I noticed the high ceilings and a fresco at the center of the entry with a chandelier at the center of the fresco. I walked through wood double doors and found a large gathering room and a dinning room. The dinning room made for large gatherings and it took had a fresco of angels on the ceiling.

From the wall of windows in the gathering room was an immense patio with its own cooking area. It had a pool table, tables and chairs that looked more like they should be in the living room than a patio. I stood at the large windows and looked out over the patio and yard. There were mountains towering in the distance. I could see a large pool and spa. It looked like it was framed for cover in the winter months. There were roman pillars around the yard and what looked like a garden with a gate. It was very beautiful and I wanted to go see the garden.

"Mama?" I looked and Max and Maxton were waiting for me. I left the windows and began to follow again. We came to the biggest kitchen

I have ever seen in a house. I was only thankful that I was not expected to be the scullery maid. At least I was hoping.

Max walked to a sunroom where there was a highchair for Maxton at the dinning table. I looked around to find where the coffee was. I found the coffee machine and started looking for the coffee. As I began to look in the cupboards and then Max put the tin in my face. I took the coffee and went over and began to make coffee. I looked in at Maxton who was busy with a toy on a rug in the sunroom. I came back to the coffee and put in the water. Max leaning against the counter.

He just stared at me. "What?"

He looked blank and he was closed to intrusion. "You feel better."

I nodded. Then turn to the smart ass " Am I not allowed to get out of my room Mastered Wizard?"

He huffed "You shouldn't be, but since you made the coffee, we will let it go." I gave a fake little giggle. I went to the refrigerator and found the eggs. I looked at the huge kitchen and felt overwhelmed. My kitchen in my little cottage was just right.

"maybe we can take Maxton back there someday."

I looked at Max "Get out of my head." He moved pulled out a pan.

I asked "Make some toast please." And to my surprise he began to get bread. Only he used magic to toast the bread and butter it. I looked at him irritated knowing that my powers were still bound by his will.

I dropped the pan on the stove and told him "Might as well do the eggs too." And I walked in to the sunroom with my son.

Max was laughing as I left the kitchen. "I thought you liked doing things the normal way."

Soon there was a cup of coffee hovering in my face. I took the cup and could see that it was dressed appropriately. Maxton got up off the rug we were sitting on and walked over to Max who put him in his chair and gave him his eggs and toast and a sippy cup.. I got up and looked out the glass doors at the mountains in the distance.

"Where are we?" Max came over and stood next to me. "Jackson Hole Wyoming." I had to know "What mountains are those?"

He was serious "Those are the Grand Tetons."

They were beautiful and graceful. They were cliffs and rolls. There were still snow on the top and in the deep crevices.

"They are beautiful aren't they?" He just grunt "a huh" I walked over to where the baby was eating his eggs with his hands. He smiled at his meal and at me. He then offered me some eggs out of his hand and I giggled and said no. I took a dishtowel and cleaned his hands and face. He lifted his arms to indicate he was ready to get out of his chair.

Before I could move to pull him out Max had him in his arms. He held him high above his head with one hand. The baby giggled and laughed but I ran over to Max and told him "Don't. your going to drop him!"

Max smiled down at me and left go of Maxton. I screamed and reached for my child. And the baby floated down to my arms. I held him close and glared at Max.

"Don't take chances with him."

He shook his head and said "He's not going to break just because I play with him. He likes it."

Then he gave a smart alike smile "I still have my powers."

I replied quickly "GO to hell."

He mockingly said "Such language in front of the baby." I sat on the rug with the baby and we played. I ignored Max because I did not want him to ruin my day.

"Why would I ruin your day?"

I looked at him and said "Your breathing." He huffed.

I looked back at the baby as I heard Marcus and Mandra in the kitchen. Mandra walked into the sunroom. "Good Morning." I smiled at her and Maxton giggled and pointed to grandmother. "Good morning Grandmother." I got up and walked over and hugged her. "You look well today Em." I nodded.

Marcus walked in and I was in a big hug and Max barked "Watch her side Dad." Marcus put me down and looked at me to see if I was hurt. We looked at the bandage together and then looked at each other. I shrouded my shoulders because I felt no discomfort. I smiled back at Marcus

"Ignore him he is out to ruin everyone's day."

Mandra went back to the kitchen and commented that the coffee was made. She appeared with a cup for Marcus and herself. Not long after, Jordan walked in and said "Em. Princess, your up." I laughed and said "I am." He walked over and kissed my cheek. "Last time I saw you lamps and things were being thrown at my head." I smiled and said "I wanted lose. You were in the way." He laughed then and said "I promise not to be in the way again." He landed on the rug with Maxton and began to play with him.

Then I heard my Dad. "Em I so happy to see you awake and out of bed." I turned around and ran to my Dad's arms.

"Daddy. Your still here. I didn't know." He kissed me and hugged me. "I am still here." I looked up and Auntie and Doc walked in.

"Auntie, Doc. I so glad you're here still." I hugged both of them and Molly and Lincon were in the kitchen. I ran in there and greeted both with a kiss.

"Oh Em. You look so much better." I thanked Molly and kissed Lincon and watched as his face turned red.

Maxton and I spent the morning with our family. I enjoyed their company so much. Being alone for so long and missing all of them. And missing Max. I watched him converse with my father. I watched him be charming to my aunt and to Mandra and push Jordan for some reason. He laughed and talked and the whole time being nice to everyone, but me. Once Maxton had his lunch it was time for a nap. I decided to take him up and bath him. Once he was cleaned, I rocked him to sleep. I put him in his crib. I looked out and saw the garden. I decided to take a walk.

I left the family all conversing and the guys shooting pool out in the patio. I walked over to the gate of the garden. I went in and was taken back by the different plants and statues. There was a pond with frogs and little fish. There were arbors and benches. It was so peaceful in the afternoon sun. I knew that this was created by magic. These roses and lilies would never live for long in this clement. The breeze blew and I closed my eyes to it. I opened them and turned to walk back to the house.

I looked up and at the roof line by Maxton's window and there was the shadow. I attempted to transport to Maxton but Max still had my powers bound. I ran as fast as I could screaming to Max to get the baby.

"Max the baby Please."

He looked over at me and jumped into action. He transported back with Maxton crying from being awakened from his nap. I grabbed the baby

"The shadow was at his window." I screamed at him then "Release my powers."

Dad came over and looked up at he house while Max and Jordan transported out of sight. Marcus joined Dad and I dropped to the ground holding by baby while I shook. I had to get my baby to safety. I had to leave and couldn't because of Max.

Max and Jordan appeared at Marcus's side. Max looked over at me and I screamed at him "I want you to release my powers. Now!" My aunt came and took the baby confronting him as she walked back to Mandra and Molly. He stomped over to me and dragged me up by my arm.

"I warned you about that"

he laughed at me. I was so confused. This was not what he had said the other night. That we were safe; that they would not take Maxton as long as we met with them.

"Tell me what you saw."

I stared at him venomously. "I saw what you said we were safe from. I saw the shadow at my sons window."

He looked at me oddly and felt my head and I slapped his hand away. "Let my powers loose" I pulled away from him and looked to my family all looking at me as if I was crazy. I stormed into the house and went back to my *cell*. I paced and cried. No way could I stay here when they think I am crazy and I cant use my powers. I prayed to God to help me. To help protect my child. To help me raise my son to be a good man, Wizard/Witch.

Max went into his room and I heard him in the nursery. I looked and he was putting Maxton back down. I left the door way not wanting to speak to him ever again. If he thinks I need powers for my son and I to leave this house he was sorely mistaken.

"Try it."

I turned around and said "I can live normal. I have done it and can do it again. But if you think that I won't do what I have to in keeping Maxton safe think again."

I continued to pace and was so scared that they may succeed in taking Maxton.

"You need to calm down."

I looked at him with hate at that moment "Get away from me."

He stood there with his evil on. So I matched him. "Em, no shadow was there."

I couldn't not believe this "I saw it. It was there. And I didn't have my powers. If I did I could show you the dead body."

He gave his little evil smile. "No. there was no shadow. You imagined it."

I turned away from him "Get out."

He remained where he was, never moving. I stood looking at the ceiling infuriated and thankful that I did not have my powers because my child would lose his father. He started laughing at me. I walked out of the room and he was in front of me. I turned around and he was in front of me. I pushed him

"Leave me alone."

He would not move and I would not look at him. "Can you settle down enough to talk?" I shook my head. I decided not to respond in voice or thought. He stood there and I stood there and refuse to speak to him. Refused to have though process except the memory of my little cottage and the safety I felt there. Alone with Maxton.

"they found you there."

I refused to bite and continued with the sense of protection of God in the little three lake canyon. Max then had Maxton in his arms and I looked up at my son. Max grabbed me and then we were there. Home. The three little lakes and my cottage. I looked at Max and Maxton. Maxton squealed and wanted down so he could explore the clearing for rocks and frogs. Max let him go and he wobbled through the clearing. I looked and Max and said "Thank you."

He still did not release my powers and he still glared evil at me.

"You would rather be here then anywhere else? Why?"

I looked over to Maxton as he and Zee played in the clearing. "I felt safe and free here." He looked around and back at me. "You were alone."

I nodded "I had God."

He looked softer and said "But I didn't. I didn't have God, you or Maxy." That hurt, and I said "I wanted you. I missed you badly; like always. I was just so tired of the game. I was so sick of being held to their game." I looked at him with love then because I did love Max. "I couldn't be the cause of your death or the corruption of our child." I huffed without humor. "Without the Princess and the Mastered Wizards child, the game is over. You had a chance of not being killed and Maxton had a chance to be a normal kid." Max huffed "He will never be normal. He is like us."

I looked over to Maxton who walked after Zee. "You have your obligations as a Wizard." I looked back at him in the eye "I heard it all my life. The obedience of the Wizards. The instructions that must be followed. The blind obedience. And Marcus said you had you obligations as a Wizard and must face the counsels consequences of your behavior. He even said that once Maxton was created, it looked like you served your purpose. How would I know what purposed Maxton would serve? How could I put you against everything you know and were raised with?"

He looked away then back "Because an obedient Wizard would never take his ward to an amusement park. He would never kill when he was seventeen years old for someone attempting to harm his ward. He would never take his ward to the Prom or dancing. A obedient Mastered Wizard wouldn't go through hell waiting to see his ward again. He would never fall in love with his ward."

I hugged him then. I hugged him with all the love I had felt for him over our lives. It took a few seconds and he wrapped me in his arms and hugged me back.

"I never was the obedient kind anyway. You know, the mixed blood thing. And once you came into my life, I lived for you. And now Maxy. Please don't take him away from me again. Please."

I pulled away and looked over to check the baby who was sitting with Zee. "I will never take him from you. Ever. But you have to not take him from me. Never hand him over to the Wizards or the Witches. We need to be strong and solid in that promise to each other. And I need you to listen to me. Believe me when I tell you that the shadow was there." He looked deep and said "There was no sign, no scent. I don't know how we could come to any other conclusion."

I said "Because I told you it was so." He tilted his head and I said "I have never lied to you. Never." He seemed to have a revelation. He nodded. I said "Promise to each other. No one takes our son. Not Witches or Wizards"

He nodded and said "Promise" And then said "Want to stay a few days?"

I wanted nothing more. "No one will find us?"

he shook his head. "No we are covered." I nodded with a happy smile and walked over to my son and cat.

That night, after Maxton was asleep in his bed, and the fire burned in the fireplace, I sat with Max on the couch. "Isn't it peaceful."

He looked over at me from his thoughts, "Yeah, But the family is going nuts looking for us. I sent Marcus a message." I began to get scared with a transmission. He shook his head "Marcus and I have our own wave length. No one else can penetrate it." He put his arm around me "So lets examine this. You came here alone but missed me and wanted me?" I nodded. "So does that mean I can kiss you?"

I smiled and nodded. And he kissed me. This time I was sure I was not dreaming.

Waking in the morning with Max next to me. His arm was around me where I have been missing it. I stretched and rolled over to face him. He was looking at me. I smiled and he kissed me. "Zee is sleeping with us" I looked down and Zee was there between Max's legs again. I reached down and petted Zee and he purred. I looked back at Max and he said "he needs to move" And Max shifted and the cat jumped off the bed as Max and I made love again.

Later in the day while Maxton napped on a blanket. Max and I sat and looked over the lakes. "Do we have to go back?"

He laid his head in my lap and closed his eyes. "We Have to go back. We have to do this for Maxy." I did not understand why.

"Because, if we don't make a stand, if we don't stop them now, Maxy will be lost." I looked down at him and he opened his eyes and said "We cant run forever. Besides, the witches are also expecting us to stand for them." He looked deep in my eyes then. "Remember the promise. Our scars?" He brought his hand up and showed the palm with the scar. I brought mine to meet his. When the scars touched, there was a burst of bright energy. I pulled away.

Max jumped up. "Lets do that again.

I shook my head. "We don't know how to use it. It may be harmful."

Max was very excited. "No. We think of something safe. Something that will not hurt anyone."

I thought about it "Rainbows. Their only light and water particles."

He rolled his eyes "Leave it to a girl."

I laughed "would you rather have bunnies."

He shook his head. "Rainbows."

He looked at me and I looked at Maxton. I looked back at Max he said "OK think Rainbows, Ready?" I nodded. We put the scars together and I felt the energy flow through and everything rippled. The lakes and trees and every flower had a rainbow. The sky was filled with one huge rainbow. Max laughed and I was amazed. We let go and the rainbows were gone.

I looked at him and he was smiling. "Man, we could really do some damage with that weapon."

I looked over at him in his excitement. "Max did you feel the energy? The power?"

He was smiling still and nodded. He then gave a big "Ooh Hoo." Which echoed through the little canyon. Maxton sat up and laughed.

Max then said "OK. Now lets do something a little more impressive."

I looked at him with my brows pulled in. "Like what?"

He moved closer to me "See that rock down below the last lake?" I nodded. "OK. Lets blow it up."

I stood up and shook my head "No parts of it my hit the baby."

He threw a visible protection around Maxton. He stood up and had my left hand with his right. "Look at that the rock. Think blow up."

I looked at the Rock and he put left hand to left hand. The rock was obliterated. Max threw his hands up "Ooh hoo." He turned and grabbed me and hugged me. He look at me and said "Do you understand it now Em?" He kissed me "We have to do that again."

One last night, and Max and I loved again. I never could get enough of him. He was always my true love and I believed that God kept us coming together over the years. I prayed that he would keep us together forever. After the promise of a few days it was time to leave again. I looked at my little home and then at Max and Maxton. Then Max said something that made all the since in the world to me.

"Our Family. You, me and Maxton. We make the home."

I walked over to him and kissed him for that. He grabbed me and we were back in Jackson hole.

Walking into the sunroom we found Jordan watching TV. He jumped up and walked over and grabbed his nephew. He gave him a big hug and kissed him.

"You guys took my play mate and I had nothing to do."

I laughed at him "Is my Dad still here?" He put Maxton down and sat with him to play "Yeah, they all went to town for a while."

Then I asked both Max and Jordan "What ever happened to my sentries?"

They looked at each other and smiled. "Well?" Max walked over to the couch and sat down and Jordan said "I exposed them to some girls and we haven't seen them for about two weeks. Last time I saw them they were in LA."

I laughed but then said "How do I get them back?"

Max looked at me like I was losing it. "Call them."

I smirked at him "No Powers remember." He smiled and I felt the binding leave. And then I called the sentry brothers. About an hour later, Dino and Sal appeared.

"Priestess, we are pleased at your recovery."

I looked at them and smiled "I hope you enjoyed your time away?"

They smiled and greeted Jordan and Max. Max told them about the promise.

He said "Its wild Jordan. All we have to do is think together of what we want and put our hands together."

Jordan looked at me and then Max. "My God. What are the limits?"

Max shook his head "I don't know?"

Sal laughed "You heard the Priests. There are no limits as long as you are together." Dino then said "And what happens to one will happen to the other."

Max looked at me then and I said "Oh my God."

I walked over to Max and lifted his shirt and there it was. Faint, but there. A scare on his side exactly where my scar from the wizards blade was. We looked at each other with more concern then curiosity.

Sal then said "There is a top and bottom to everything. There are prices to pay." With that Max and I looked at each other more seriously.

At that moment Marcus, Mandra, Dad and Auntie and Doc came in.

Dad said "Well here you are. Just in time to bid us goodbye."

I shook my head "No Dad, don't go."

He smiled and said "We all have to go back to our mortal lives, jobs and so on."

I walked over to him "I am sorry Dad. We needed to reconnect."

He smiled "Get married. You will be connected for life."

I laughed. I hugged and kissed him and was sorry I had so little time with him. Auntie and Doc hugged me and Doc said "Take the antibiotics. And stay away from swards." I laughed and kissed his cheek. Max came over with Maxton and we walked out with them to the front of the house. I watched my family drive away.

I stood there. "We will see them soon. We will go to the creek." I looked at Max and knew he meant it.

We went back to the sunroom and I walked over and hugged my grandmother. She looked at me and she raised her eye brow. "Messing with Max again I see." I smiled and she looked over at Max and he said "She made me." I laughed. Marcus then said "Tomorrow we make our plans. Tomorrow we decide how to make our stand."

CHAPTER 40

The next afternoon while the baby napped in a near by playpen, Marcus call all if us to the gathering room. We all sat in a circle. Grandmother next to Marcus, Lincon next to Molly, the sentry brothers and I was in-between Max and Jordan.

Marcus started but I stopped him. "Wait. I need us to pray as a group, a family, for Gods protection, and his wisdom. Please?"

Marcus smiled at me. "I think that is a wonderful Idea." Marcus bowed his head and we all followed suit.

"Lord, guide us and protect us. Give us the wisdom needed to protect our children and our selves. In your name, we pray." We all said "Amen"

I looked up at Marcus and I smiled at him and he look at me knowing and offering comfort.

Marcus then started "We all see here the danger to both Em, Max and especially Maxton. Max is the Wizard they are most cautious of . But make no mistake. They are fully aware of the Priestess. She has complicated their plans." He looked over at me "If you had been a simple Witch with powers, they would have Maxton and his parents dead. However, the Priestess adds caution to their plans. They know that their task is impossible while the Priestess exists." Marcus looked over to Mandra.

She then began " Em. You should know, Deana is dead."

My heart dropped. "When? How?"

Mandra looked at Max and he took a deep breath. " She attempted to enter the house with an accomplice while you were sick."

I looked at Max and thought he killed her, but he shook his head "No I did not kill her, Her accomplice killed her when we caught her. We never saw him, but he sent the deadly bolt to her heart."

I began to get upset as this being proof of the shadow. I narrowed my eyes to Max and his deception of safety. He shook his head again.

"We are safe. I have covered the house and there are guardians surrounding the property now. No one can get in or out with out detection. Even your cat is in on the watch."

I asked "And what about the Shadow and the Accomplice? They got through."

Max looked over to Marcus. And he continued "The Accomplice is the Shadow. We don't know who it is. We do know that that individual has suffered some blows to their plans. One; the appearance of the Priestess. Two; demise of Martin and the lack of further cooperation from the Vampires. And lastly, a subject to attempt to take the powers." Marcus looked weary "I have to apologize Princes. I believe that the Shadow is a Mastered Wizard."

I looked over to Grandmother "And who is with us? Where are the Witches in this?" Grandmother smiled at that "They will never allow a meeting without them. Anita and the other high priests will appear at the meeting and demand the Wizards cooperation. We have arranged for a full coven and more if need be."

Marcus took grandmothers hand and kissed it.

Dino said "There are several Warrior Witches that would come if we call. No Wizard will dare risk their races existence. After all, Maxton is the one to replenish their kind." He smiled "Maybe with a different idea of the races."

Marcus looked at the group and asked "Do any of you have any Idea how we can keep Maxton out of here and safe?"

I shook my head. "Maxton can not be out of my sight."

Max huffed "Are you crazy. Maxton can not be anywhere around. He could be hurt or taken."

Jordan softy spoke as he took my hand "No one wants him in danger. But if he is here, he is vulnerable and so are you." He looked in my eyes, "Em. Think of the safest place for him. Who will keep him the safest in the world."

I knew. "With my Dad." They all looked at me. I looked at Max "You even said, they don't believe in the magic as we do, and have a natural protection of God." He nodded. "They do, But the Shadow got close to you. He watched you."

I nodded. "But never got real close. He watched but never came in the house. Never got close to the church." Max looked over to Marcus.

Marcus nodded "I believe that is a wonderful idea. I think we can also add a little protection as well and all bases will be covered." Mandra looked over at me and smile and transmitted *"Em. You are a good mother and daughter."*

Marcus then directed our attention to Max and Me. "Now the task of keeping you two alive. Max, my son, if I could keep you hidden and safe I would. Just as desperately as you have for you son. But you must address the Elders and state your case."

Max looked at his father "Dad, I am not afraid. I am more afraid for Em and Maxy." Marcus then agreed and said "I know that. I also have faith in you. Not just for your abilities, but for your intelligence. Your power is a barrier for them as well. None match your power and they know it. But together, I don't know. You will have to negotiate and be diplomatic."

Max laughed "Dad, I am not like you. You have an ability for diplomacy, that I don't have. You have a respect for the Elders I don't have. I want them all dead. I want them to pay for the pain in our lives and the arrogance in believing that I, the mix blood would hand over my child. And then want me dead whether I do or not."

Marcus noting the agitation in Max put up his hand "Max, the Elders will not be alone. The Wizard Counsel will be here as well. As you state your case, your attitude and your feelings of disloyalty, they will have to answer the counsel that will surely question their behavior and actions against you." Max then looked at me "And Em? Will they excuse her killing those Wizards?" Marcus looked over at me and Jordan squeezed my hand. Sal spoke up "No Wizard will pass judgment on the Priestess. Or a mother protecting her child." Marcus answered Sal

"She killed Wizards just the same. The law is clear; death for death. But again, diplomacy and negotiation will be the key."

I was getting upset, "So Max and I lay down and die if the Wizard Counsel decide that we are unworthy for life, and unworthy of our child?" I shook my head "I love you Marcus. I love you Jordan...." I looked at Max "And I love you. But you may be the only three Wizards left alive."

Max looked at me and said "Not all of the Wizards believe as the Elders. They follow instruction for survival. There are the Mixed Bloods that feel as I do but are unable to shed their chains and pay the price as I did. But given the chance to be respected as true Wizards with honor, I think they will take it."

I looked at Jordan and Marcus and I asked "And what of you two, after protecting and hiding us?"

Marcus looked at Jordan Mandra dropped her eyes. "We have a punishment I am sure. Jordan as a young Wizard can be rehabilitated, I on the other hand could be banished or killed."

Frustrated I said "My family is not going to be punished for living in the world that was created by these fools. I am not standing for it."

Marcus smiled. "Princess, we will all speak to that fact. And we will all offer our decisions as valid. But we are Wizards not Witches. We have our laws and rules."

I looked at him then "Then who are the Wizards to decide my fate or that of my child?" Mandra looked over at me "On your birth, an agreement with the Witches and the Wizards to look to your power and goodness. Your faith in God, your pure heart. Somehow, the Elders in our region twisted that to you producing the child. They did not account for the emergence of the Priestess."

Marcus continued, "Pure Bloods believed that once the child was produced by a pure blood, Witches claims would be nullified and the child would be more Wizard than Normal or Witch. Now this child is more normal than either."

Max huffed and raised his hands to his face and dropped them and said "Then why want my child? Why not leave him be?"

Marcus softly said "I think they'll take what they can get." Marcus shook his head "they may asked for a child of a pure blood by Em."

Max stood up Monster in tow, and said "I will killed them first."

I reached out and took Max by the hand and pulled him back down next to me. "If we are to meet the counsel and have the High Priests and Priestess here, I think we will have more support that to be insulted with that compromise. Besides, I am unwilling."

Marcus looked to the Sentry Brothers "We will need your protection and those who you will call to our defense."

Sal looked at Marcus with his head tilted "Would you consider living in the Witches world rather than the Wizards?"

Marcus said "I am a Wizard as are my sons and my grandson. We have lived among the witches our whole lives. But our true nature and our blood is Wizard. Our beings can not be altered."

Sal nodded " It is our honor. We will protect all of you.

Marcus then said "I suggest that we walk in as a united group. Lincon and Molly will escort the Wizards to the bench we will set up for them. We will request that the Witches be here before the Wizards. The Elders and the Counsel will be put on notice with their presents." We all agreed.

He then said "This is Sunday. We will have the group meet a week from Monday. Are we agreed." We all agreed. Marcus then said to Max "That will give you enough time to take Maxton to Caesar and place the protection barrier. Can you have it hold that far away?" Max nodded.

We were good in driving into Hat Creek instead of Popping in. Dad looked out the door and came running to grab the baby out of his car seat. He lifted Maxton and held him close. I walked over to my dad and gave him a hug. Max shook his hand.

"What are you doing here I did not expect you but what a wonderful surprise." Dad called to the house "Tom, Della. Em and Max and the baby are here." Tom came running out in his Ranger uniform and I hugged him.

"Hey Sis. Lets see the little guy." He went over to Dad holding Maxton. He smiled and turned to me "He's terrific Em." I smiled and said "Tom this is Max." and he and Max greeted one another and I wondered why I never introduced them before. Taylor came out of the house and I ran to hug my cousin. He was a man now and handsome as ever. "Taylor. You grew up." He laughed and I introduced him to Max.

Auntie appeared at the door with Doc and called over "Your just in time for dinner. Come in and eat."

We sat with the family and ate my aunts fantastic cooking. It was home. I loved the old house. Dad stated that we were invited to attend church with the family that night. He trying to do a service once a week at night for those that cant come on Sunday. We agreed though we, I, was no longer a faithful church goer. I changed my clothes from jeans to a respectable dress and snapped Max into slacks and a nice shirt.

He pulled his brows in and I said "My turn to be Mr. Higgins." We walked behind the family a little bit and I said "Max, bind the baby, OK?"

He looked insulted "No. I will not."

I stopped him. "You and he will hear the whispers, the insults. These are due to my magic without controls and unbound. He is little and will be excited about the church. I don't want anyone to say things about him." He looked confused. "Please. We are with the normals now." Max nodded and the baby was bound. Maxton whimpered a little knowing he was restricted.

We sat in the back and listen to my dads sermon of how important that we serve God. That God, Family and Community are the paths of our lives. That families united in God were blessed and powerful. We sang the hymns and prayed the Lords prayer at the end of the service. Dad invited to congregation to join in the community center for cake and coffee.

I walked with Max and Maxton into the community center and was met with whispers of 'Witch' and 'unholy union' and 'illegitimate child' and 'Poor Pastor Minelli'. I held my head high being proud of my family. Max looked evil at that time and I squeezed his had. "Just ignore it." Then Dad stood up and address the congregation present. "I would like to introduce my grandson. Maxton Marshal." He walked over with a proud smile and picked up Maxton. He turned and looked over at smiling faces and said "Isn't he beautiful and a wonderful gift from God." The room applauded and Dad looked back at me. "As wonderful a gift as my Daughter Emily Star." I waked over to him and hugged him. Dad then said "And this fine man is Max Marshal. Please welcome my family." Max looked at me with a knowing look that my fathers gesture met more to me that anything. He was proud of me and my family. He loved me for me.

Later that night I created my bedroom again. Of course Tom still loved the magic "God I wish I could do that." I put the baby to bed with Zee on guard. I walked back to the living room. Max was sitting with Tom teaching him some tricks that looked like magic. Dad watched as Tom fumbled. Auntie Doc and Taylor we preparing to leave.

"Don't go auntie. Cant you guys stay for a while longer?"

Doc smiled and kissed my cheek and said "I am due at the hospital for rounds first thing. And Taylor has classes."

Auntie hugged me "You stay in contact. I will be back to help your dad with Maxton. And I will stay till you return."

I looked at her and cried "Auntie, if we don't. Please help my son live happy. Don't ever let him out of your sight"

She looked worried. "No one will keep me from him. God will see to that."

I sat on the floor next to my Dad and his chair. He looked at me and said "Tells us Em. We need to understand."

I looked to Max and began "Dad, a lot of things I never expected have come about. I know that with out God in my life and his protection, I would not be here now or have Maxton." He looked at me then.

"I …." I looked to Max to explain. "Em is the chosen Princess of the Wizards. She is also the Priestess of the Witches. These things were not of her choice and she did not seek them out. But they exist just the same." He looked at me and I nodded for him to continue. "There is a prophecy with the Wizards that Em, the princess, would produce a child with a Pure Blood Mastered Wizard. That child is to represent the new generations of the Wizards and Witches. This prophecy was due to Em's power. She was to marry a Powerful Pure Blood Wizard."

Dad gave makes a suspicious look. "Are you a Mastered Wizard?"

Max nodded "I am a Mixed Blood Mastered Wizard. My mother was mortal. My father, Marcus, is a Wizard. An Elder of the Wizards." Dad was then confused. I continued. "The prophecy was reported as a Powerful Pure Blood Master, but when Marcus explained it, It never said pure blood only a Powerful Mastered Wizard. Max is very Powerful."

I looked back to Max. "They want Maxton and Em and I are fighting for that. We need him here with you." Dad looked as if it was without question where Maxton would be. He then asked "And what of you two. What happens from here.?"

I looked at Max and I began. "We need to face the Wizards counsel to state our case." I looked at my father and prayed to the lord he would understand. "Dad, I have loved Max….. Well forever. He has been my best friend growing up. He has been my protector growing up. But because of his mixed blood, he was band from me when we became more to each other. Max was imprisoned the whole time I was in Sacramento." Dad looked at Max "For loving Em?"

Max nodded. "I was a mixed blood. They needed her to mate with Pure blood to be able to dominate all races. Mortal and immortal. But because the pure bloods are less powerful than I, Maxton is now their target"

I pulled my father to my focus "Max was disobedient to the Wizard Elders. He has killed a Wizards who attempted to capture him." Dad looked at Max again and I reached up and gently pulled his face to look at me. "They have tried to take Maxton before. They have tried to take me before." I looked away and then back "Dad. I have killed." He stood up and paced in thought. "Dad they would have killed me and taken my son. And the Priestess is dominate in dangerous situations."

He stopped. "The priestess killed not you."

I was trying to think of how to explain. "Dad, it was me." He fell to his knees in front of me. Tom stood up and came over. "Daddy please forgive me. I have asked God and now I am asking you to understand. Please forgive me?' Max came over to the chair vacated by Dad. "They would have killed Em."

Dad looked at me. "Em they will want blood for blood. I know it in my soul."

I petted my fathers face, "Dad, I have to face them to protect my son. I have Witches backing and they have vowed to protect me. And I have Max."

He hugged me. " Oh Em. I could bare to lose you like your mother." I pulled back "You knew?"

He looked at me with tearful eyes. "She told me. In a dream. I knew you were special. I guess that is why it took me so long to call Mandra to help you. I couldn't bring my self to find out what was in store for you. I hoped that you could have a life of love and God."

I smiled at my father "Dad, without your teachings, and without your love, and without God, I would not have made it this far."

"We need you to protect our son, Please." Max looked desperate and Dad looked up at him "Of Course I will protect him with all the power of God." He looked to me and petted my face. He looked a little lost in his thoughts. But then he looked resolved.

Then Dad stood up and looked at Max.

"The sermon today, did you have any thoughts on it?"

Max looked at me confused and looked back at Dad "I was raised by my father to believe in God and family."

Dad looked at me and back at Max. "Get Married"

I was shocked at him "Dad."

Max laughed and said "OK"

I protested "Dad I can think of that now. God has already blessed us. And we have so much else to prepare for."

Dad shook his head and he closed his eyes and Mandra appeared.

Tom shook his head and said "Dam that is so cool."

Mandra looked at my father and smiled. "Good Idea Caesar."

I looked at her in shock. I was afraid to look at Max. I then asked "Is this like a shotgun thing?"

Marcus showed up and said "This is perfect. Cant you see?" I looked at him not understanding.

Mandra said "The Wizards marry for life. There are no second and third spouses."

I shrouded my shoulders "So What." I finally looked back at Max for explanation.

"They cant kill me and give you to another Wizard."

I huffed, "I wouldn't let them do that anyway, besides I am not a Wizard."

Marcus smiled and said "No; only the Wizard Princess who has made her choice and if there is marriage, another can not replace Max.

It may save his life. No other child can be produced by Pure Blood Wizard."

I looked down feeling upset again. Another stupid Wizard thing messing up what should be a happy thing. Max sat down on the floor with me. " After everything we have been through, I cant believe you don't want to Marry me?" I looked at him and sorrowfully said "I want to marry for other reasons than to thwart the Wizards. I want to marry you for love and Maxton, not them." He stood up and pulled me with him and we went out the door. Max pulled me along to the log by the creek.

He sat looking at the creek and I sat looking at the house.

He was angry and snarled "I said I would marry you when you were pregnant with Maxton."

I huffed and looked at him "Would and want are two different things. Besides, we do everything married people do; have sex; fight together and with each other; live together; have children together."

He looked at me and soften some. "then what is the issue."

I laid my forehead in my hand and said quietly "None I guess. My own mixed blood thing."

Max reach over and hugged me. "Em, I cant love you more, I already love more you than I love anything or anyone."

I did not say anything. I was disappointed about it all. He put his hand on my cheek and moved my face to his. "Please Marry me?"

I said before thinking "To save your life I will marry you ."

He let go of me and stood up and snarled. "Hey, don't do me any favors." He turned and as he stomped off to the house yelled "When will you get it in your head that we are not Normal." I sat there alone. Confused.

I sat for a while longer. Leaving the rest of the world to decide my next right of passage. No reason for me to think about any of it. All my life is already planed out in someone's little book somewhere. The same is true for Max. I knew that. I wonder what would have been if we where free and made our own decisions for our lives. Then I remembered his 'Lets not go back'.

I cried then. Why didn't I go when he asked? I thought maybe we would have had every happiness as we progressed through life. Naturally and Normally. I looked to the heavens and said "Lord why" I got up and ran across the creek and headed to the field. I knew the sun was already setting. But I couldn't help myself. I ran to the center of the field and I felt the breeze kiss my tear stained cheek. The trees announced "The Princess has returned. She cries." I asked "please play you music?" They played and I danced. I dances for peace and for my family. Then as the sun had its last bit of light, the trees whisper "Princess, he is your chosen one." and the music stopped. I walked back to the creek. Even the trees believed I should marry Max. I wanted to. But for NORMAL reasons not Wizard reasons.

I stayed at the creek a while longer and then snapped into my room and checked on Maxton. With the baby sound asleep, I changed to my Pjs and got into bed. I heard the talking for the living room. I had no desire to be reasoned with tonight by anyone. I wanted to be alone.

CHAPTER 41

I woke up alone and wasn't really surprised by it. Max is probably pouting at home. But then I realized Maxton did not wake me. I jumped up and went to the crib. He was gone. I hurried into the living room and found no one. I called for my father and Max. I screamed for Maxton and no one answered. I ran to the creek and it ran red with blood. And floating down the blood stained creek was Maxton's stuffed frog. I dropped to my knees and screamed in agony.

"Em. Wake up! Wake up." I opened my eyes and Max was taking the crying baby out of the crib. "You scared him."

Dad came running in and looked at me. I shook my head and said "Another dream Dad." Dad looked at Max trying to comfort the baby and I got out of the bed. I walked over and took the baby and talked to him calmly and said I was sorry.

Dad went to the door "I'll make some coffee."

I got back in bed and laid my crying baby next to me. Max snarled "You are going to make him a nervous kid. And eventually give me a heart attack." I looked over to him and did not answer him or apologize as he was in his mood. Soon Maxton was back asleep. The sky was just showing some color as the day was waking. I was with Max and I was confused as to why I had a nightmare.

I closed my eyes to sleep some more and felt the baby being lifted. I looked at Max put him back to bed and closed my eyes again. Max got back in bed. When I woke up again I was held tight by Max. Maxton was calling me "Mama" I looked over at the crib and he was standing and looking at me. I smiled at him and said "Good morning baby." I wiggled out of the grip of Max and I got out of bed and went to him and took him out of the crib. I hugged and kissed him and he giggled. He then said "Look Da." I tuned and Max was awake watching. I let the baby crawl on the bed to his dad. I then grabbed a diaper and clothing for Maxton. I turned back to the bed and Maxton was already changed and dressed. I looked at Max and said "Something's should be done normal for bonding and socialization of the child." Mandra opened the door a little and looked. She smiled "May I have Maxton for his breakfast?" I smiled at her and took Maxton to her. She left talking sweetly to him.

Next thing I knew, Max had me in the bed and I looked at him angrily.

"What are you doing?"

He put his head on my stomach and laughed. "She's growing."

My heart dropped. He sat back and I put my hand on my belly and looked at him "Another?"

He smiled at me and kissed me. He then said "A little girl,"

I smiled loving the thought of a little girl. I reached out and kissed Max and hugged him tight. I pulled away only to lay my hand on my belly. "How can you know, why cant I know."

He put his head back to my belly "I can hear her."

He looked up with a smile and then it was a evil snarl "I will bind you from this moment on if you try to take her away."

I smiled at him and shook my head. "I wont leave, I already promised you." He reached up and petted my cheek and said "Wow Em. This is almost normal." I didn't understand and only looked at him confused. He huffed "We just found out we are having a baby and we are happy about it, together. Almost normal."

I thought for a second and said "Yeah, I am happy." He came to my eyes and said "Did you ever think about the fact that we make babies the Normal way?" I giggled and we made love.

Max and I entered the kitchen with smiles on our faces. Dad, Mandra and Marcus sat with the baby at the table. "Ready for breakfast?" Dad got up and brought us some coffee."

I shook my head and said "No not now." He came back and look at us and our smiles. "What's happening with you two?" I looked at Max and he was smiling.

Mandra smiling looked over and said "They are having another baby."

I looked at her and she said "Yes I knew days ago."

Dad jumped up and hugged me and kissed me. "Another one?"

I nodded and said "A girl." Maxton was giggling in his chair. And Marcus hugged Max.

Then Dad stood back and said "Well Em. Then why not marry the man since you keep making babies with him?"

I dropped my smile "Dad let me be happy right now. I think about that later. I know that that it is an issue with you. But God has united us with or without a ceremony."

I turned and smiled at Max and he was still smiling. Max said "Come on Em. Lets just do it for us. For you and me and the kids?"

I dropped my smile and felt embarrassed. Instead of just being happy, I'm back in the design. But my daughter was not foretold. Something not designed and controlled by anyone but God.

Max said, "If I die, my kids are legit."

I looked at him seriously "Our kids are already legit."

He said "Do it for us. Do it because you love me." I looked deep in his eyes and smiled at the father of my children and knew, No matter what, I would always be drawn to him. I always have and knew I always would. "Ok."

Dad jumped up and said "I be at the church getting ready."

I looked at him and asked "Dad, don't we need a license or something? I did not say today"

Mandra handed Dad a paper I drew my brows together.

Dad said "Got it."

As he was leaving I yelled after him "Yeah by magic."

I looked over to my grandmother smiling and very pleased with her self. I asked her "Today?" she smiled and nodded.

She got up from the table and said "Its about time and we have to get it done before you change your mind again."

Jordan appeared and took me out of my chair and hugged me and twirled. I was laughing and he was smiling. He stopped and bent to kiss me quickly on the mouth. It was totally innocent and saponaceous but Max was there and pulled me away from his brother and pushed him. "Hey, go find your own woman and leave mine alone."

Jordan said "I have."

We all looked at him "She's getting ready for a Wedding."

I smiled "Yours?"

He smiled and said "No yours."

I thought about it "We are only having a ceremony. It isn't like a real wedding bash thing." I looked at Max "You know we are not *Normal.*" I walked over to my baby and took him out of his chair and Marcus said "But we would all like to be there."

I smiled at him "I would not allow it to take place without you." I went to my room with Maxton and put him down to play. I thought *What am I doing?* Max was there and pick me up into his arms and said "Marrying me because you love me." I looked at him and kissed him "I have always loved you and you have always known it."

Mandra and Elena appeared "Out Max. and take your child." Max moved at Mandra's command and grabbed the baby. He went out the door and looked at me with love. No smile, no snarl, nothing but love. It made my stomach lurch.

Elena and I ran to each others arms and I cried at seeing her. Then Auntie came in the door with tears in her eyes.

"Oh Em. I am so happy."

She then grabbed me. "Maxton deserves his parents united in God." I giggled at her. The there was something I never thought I would see. Auntie grabbed Mandra and they hugged and cried together. I looked at auntie with curiosity and Mandra said "God works in mysterious ways."

Grandmother waved her hand and Elena was dressed in a red dress. Compete with a veiled hat. I looked at my aunt and grandmother and found that they were both dressed in lovely dresses and Auntie only admired grandmothers taste. I looked at my self in the mirror and I wore a simple white gown with a sweet heart neck. It had a red sash around the waist. The sash tied in the back and its length matched a small train. I worn simple pumps. My hair was pulled up and a tiara with veil to cover my face.

"Grandmother, I thought I could just ware my jeans?"

They all Laughed. I looked out the window and could see that there was a food table and a bar. There was also a dance area and people to serve. I looked back at her, "Grandmother. What have you done?"

She smiled "There are others that would like to celebrate your day with you. So don't be selfish."

I looked at her and said "This was supposed to be simple."

Grandmother winked at me and Auntie said "I think it was simple for Mandra." Grandmother waked to me and hugged me. "Do this for us. Just do this because we deserve to have happiness and happy times as the normals do." And I understood. I never understood that grandmother felt like me. I only now knew that she tried to give me normal. She tried to mix the worlds for me. We lived in the three worlds and it was normal. She did that. I hugged her tighter then ever that day. I understood.

So My father, playing both father and preacher, walked me up the Isle. He put my hand in Max's hand and went to face the people there for the Wedding. The church was full of friends and family. Coven and selected Wizards, aunts and uncles, parents and grandparents and our child. Even the Andersons from the restaurant were there. We said our vows and kiss our kiss and we singed our names. Once Elena and Jordan signed as Matron of honor and Best Man, we were married in the eyes of the law and God. Then my father pulled another fast one. "Since we are here, I believe that Maxton should be baptized." I smiled at Dad and he had Jordan hold Maxton as he poured water over the child with made Maxton scream and laugh. He said his prayer and Maxton was baptized. "You got it all today didn't you Dad?" He smiled at me and Kissed me and said "They call that a Twofer. I have to have my magic too. I have God with me."

So we had a reception. And of course, Max and I danced. A lot. We hadn't really danced like that in a while. I missed it.

While we danced I asked him "So you don't seem to harmed by my family's rituals."

He laughed. "Em. You are not the only one who has been sent to Sunday school and baptized."

I smiled at him "Yeah but the only one who has in this family with Dad as a Preacher." He nodded with that. Then he kissed me and asked "So how do you like being married?" I looked at him with that ridicules question and said "Well for the two hours that I have been married I have dances a lot. So its is great."

He smiled and then said "Where do we go on our honeymoon."

I gave him a silly look. "No where. We have to stay with the baby."

Max stopped dancing and said "Mandra and Marcus will stay here with your dad and the baby. And we can have two days to ourselves." I thought about it "Come on Em. Two days and we will come back."

I laughed and said "Where have I heard that before."

He smiled remembering. "Yeah but this time we don't have to use Number 2 and we can have sex like I wanted to then."

I was shock "I was a little girl."

He shook his head "No you were almost seventeen and I was already wild about you."

"Where to?" I looked at my family sitting and enjoying on another and no doubt congratulating each other on their shotgun wedding. I looked back at Max "Six Flags." He started to laugh and we walked over to the family.

Well we didn't go to six flags, we went to New Orleans. We danced on Bourbon Street and drank Hurricanes. We had wonderful Cajun food. And of course had a lot of sex. Instead of two days, we took three. Max's negotiating skills once again. We were like kids again. Just happy and having fun together.

We laid in bed talking and laughing. I asked him "So you were also a threat to my virtue when I was seventeen?"

He had a devil smile and said "Of course I was."

I was taken back. "And here I thought you were protecting my virtue. And the whole time thinking about taking it."

He frowned and shook his head. "Thinking and doing are two entirely different things. Besides I wanted you because I loved you. Not for the other reasons." I sat on his lap as his back was propped by the headboard and said "And how about today?" He looked without expression and said "You don't have your virtue to save anymore. So we don't have to worry about that do we. We only have to worry about how many kids you plan to have." I started to laugh and said "Who plans?"

Friday morning we were back at Dads. Mandra and Marcus had already gone home. The baby was in aunties arms and waving to us and we pulled up. He must have sensed us coming. I grabbed my son and kissed and hugged him. I knew that today may be the last time I see him. Max took him from me and hugged and kiss him while I greeted my aunt and father. We spent the day with Maxton and Dad. Tom came home and we all talked and enjoyed the day together. Once Maxton was down for the night, Max and I stood over him and took the last look at our son before we left. I kissed my family with tears in my eyes.

"Dad, he does not have ills. He has gifts from God."

Dad looked at me and nodded. "I know that now Em. Forgive me for the stupid things I said or did. And remember I love you." He looked at me as if he was dinking in all he could before I left. I hugged my father and cried. I waked to the car that I knew we would leave at the first corner out of sight. Max put his hand out to Tom and then to Dad.

Dad grabbed Max in a hug and said "Watch my girl. Please." Max said "And you watch by boy OK?" Dad smiled and nodded.

We got back home and found everyone in the gathering room. I looked out the windows and could see the benches set up for the counsel. Marcus put me in a big hug and I hugged him back. "My Princess. How did you like your honeymoon.?" I smiled and said it was wonderful but to short. I hugged my grandmother and she looked worried, She looked older and less spry. "Grandmother, are you OK?" She nodded. "I am fine. I am worried." I nodded. Jordan grabbed me and swung me around and then with out letting me lose said "Well little sis, your having another baby?" I smiled and said "Well that's what I am told." He put me down and held his ear to my belly and popped up and said "She's there." I laughed with him and Max pushed him away. Jordan then said "You guys never met Mary. I shook my head "Is that who was suppose to come to the Wedding. He nodded. "She had to work. But she is coming to dinner tomorrow."

I had to ask "Witch, Wizard or Normal?"

Mandra said "Does it matter?" I shrouded my shoulders "Well I don't know since my son is all three."

Jordan smiled and said "Normal. So everyone be on your best behavior. Don't scar her away."

I looked at Max who had a devil smile on. I transmitted *"Don't you dare."* He laughed and said "I told you Thinking is not doing."

That night I went to my room and dressed for bed. I looked in the nursery and missed my son. I looked in at dads to see him asleep in his crib. Max came up behind me "It would be safer not to think about where he is, Not that I don't have protection around him but it just another safe guard." I nodded.

I turned in his arms and hugged him. " We still have a baby with us." He grunted. I told him "She is special. Just as special as Maxton."

He smiled at me "Because she's ours."

I nodded and then said "She wasn't prophesized. She is from God." He looked at me more serious. I continued. "She will be special in that they will have to worry about her. She will have powers of the Witches and wont be a Wizard. But could produce one."

He looked more worried then. I finished with "Be aware, Max, she will be special in her own right. She will be a threat to the Wizards and the Witches. She will not be their Princess." He looked at me more intensely. He said "That is something that will have to be discussed with the Witches. We will asked them not to deal with our daughter." I nodded.

He picked me up and took me to his bed rather than my bed. "This is your bed now." I looked at him and said "this room is too masculine. It doesn't show anything feminine." He laughed "The other room is too girly." He kissed me and said, "When the kids get older, we will give them these rooms and you can just add another." We laughed at that knowing that I was really into that as a kid.

CHAPTER 42

The next few days were a blur. We had dinner with Jordan and Mary. She was very nice. She had beautiful green eyes. Large striking eyes. Jordan look at her in a way that expressed pure desire. He saw me catching his look to her and transmitted. *'Is she not the most beautiful woman?'* I smiled at him and he transmitted *"Well not counting you princess."* I said "Yes she is and Good save."

Sunday was hard for me. I could feel the priestess pushing. I didn't know how not to worry and keep her at bay. I waked through the sunroom where the family gathered. I looked over to Max who seemed to know that he needed to give me room. I walked outside and decided to go to the garden. I wanted to calm down so the Priestess would submerge.

I walked through the garden and felt the Priestess. Not within me. But close. I kept looking and walking. Then I heard her deep and low; close and dangerous.

"Wizard Princess."

My heart stopped and I listened

"Wizard wife. Wizard mother."

I was breathing heavy.

"Witch of the forest."

I could not tell where she was and I answered "Yes, I am all of those."

The Priestess appeared translucent somewhat distorted, and floating. "My Princess, My Witch."

I looked at her. Her beauty and her presents. "Priestess"

She smiled yet looked so menacing. "You are my chosen child. And I have chosen well. For God has look favorable upon you" She smiled "And thus, on me."

I looked to her. "But the Prophecies and my children. How do these things become favorable?"

She laughed at me "You behave as a silly mortal. But you aren't." She came closer "You are a powerful and dangerous Witch. No one can touch your children or your Wizard."

I looked at her in confusion. "But I need you when I need to defend."

She shook her head "Its not me. My Princess." I did not understand "It is you. Always has been you." She moved back "I will be close, but you are the Priestess on your own. Trust in your self. Trust your Wizard. If you stand together, you will be victorious."

I was so confused. "Why did this only start at the Solstice. Wasn't it because I released you?"

She looked at me "No. you released you. You became your true being." She moved away, "Be strong Priestess. Your daughter is the gem. She is the future" she looked at me and became more clear, and I saw the face of my mother.

"My Mother?" she smiled and was gone. I fell to my knees. I looked to the stars. *Oh lord.*

As I left the garden, I felt the urge from within. I knew I was the priestess on my own. My true nature, and that of my mother. And that of her mother. I was not defenseless. I was not in power of anyone but me. I could do as I wanted and be what I wanted and go where I wanted. I was free and so is my family. I allowed the urge. I allowed myself to be my true nature. I felt the strength and the power. As the unfelt wind blew my hair and As I walked into the yard, I looked over the setting where the witches counsel would sit and laughed the witches laugh.

I turned and found Max there smiling. "You have the priestess eyes tonight."

I smiled at him "I am the Priestess."

He tilted his head. I laughed the witches laugh again and it echoes through the surrounding valley. Our group came out of the house and looked at me.

I looked over to my grandmother and in the priestess voice, my voice, I said "Show your true self Mandra. It is not another, it is who we are and are true nature." She started to breath hard and she released her true being. Cat eyed power of the Witches. I laughed the witches laugh again and was joined by her. The Wizards looked in ahh. The Witch Sentries were on a knee. I looked to Max who had a satisfactory smile. He had the look of amazement on his face. He said to me "My Princess."

I looked to my grandmother "There is no danger. There is only us and our family."

She looked over in a cat like grin "Granddaughter, who have you been taking to?"

I looked back at the garden and back at her "The priestess, My mother."

She faded back to normal and stared at me. She fell to her knees and looked over at Marcus.

She turned back "Em. What did she say?"

I grinned knowing that the fangs were there. Knowing that my feet where not on the ground. Knowing that the unfelt wind blew through my hair, I knew that my eyes were florescent cat eyes. "She gave me my true self. She told me I am the Priestess and not a vessel. I control my fate . I am not to be ruled by others. I know right now that is true. I am the priestess in my own right, so was my mother and so are you." Looking at Max "And so is my daughter." He looked at me seriously and nodded. Grandmother held her face in her hands and wept.

I dropped the priestess with ease. Never being able to do so in the past. I walked to my grandmother and sat down on the grass in front of her and put my arms around her. "We are special grandmother. We can be victorious."

She looked at me with a smile through the tears. "Then why Em. Why is she gone?" I looked at her with hurt in both our hearts. "God has his plans as we do."

That night while laying in bed Max looked over at me. "Now you know, we could have had such a blast as kids if we knew then what we know now." I laughed and said "Normals say the same thing." He grinned "But we could have done so much. Been more in the world. Really had the good of both worlds." I was quiet for a minute "We still can." He smiled weakly "Maybe" I faced him eye to eye. "We still can." He shook his head. "You are a force my love, but I am a Wizard. I have a true nature. I have my kind as well. My kind is also Marcus and Jordan. My kind is You, Maxy and…" He looked in my head "Lilly." I smiled at him "Lilly?" He smiled said "that's her name." But we what you need to understand, is that I will do what I have to so that our kids live free and happy. Don't be to quick on the draw. We need to be honorable and up right to win over the Counsel."

I looked at him and said "I do that only for you. I would rather just leave."

Max shook his head "Leaving is not the answer. An understanding and an agreement is what we need."

The witches arrived on schedule just ahead of the Wizard Counsel and the Elders. Marcus being the ever diplomatic host, provided food and drink. He even had musicians playing stings in the background. Touches lit the yard and there were tables and chairs for onlookers and, of course, the long counter for the Wizard Counsel and one for the Witches Counsel. The Witches were already seated when I made my appearance.

Dressed in the Priestess outfit including mask, I welcomed and thank them. I nodded to them never giving the impression that I was not powerful enough to do this my self. "I am pleased at you percents here tonight. Welcome."

Anita stood and addressed me "My Priestess, I see you have found your true self. It is with honor and appreciation that we are here." She smiled knowingly "And with joy of a daughter. A Witch."

I smiled back "Yes. A daughter not foretold. From the blood of all races." She nodded and sat back down.

Max came to my side. He wore black under the black and gold robe of the Mastered Wizards. Antonio stood then "Mastered Wizard. You are congratulated for the new child. You are congratulated on the holy union with you and the Priestess. We are most Pleased." Max nodded respectfully and said thank you.

Antonio sat and Anita Stood. "Mastered Wizard, will you be asking for the girl child to be a Wizard Princess?"

Max took my hand "No Lady, we ask that the Witches refuse any such deal. Our children must not be in any plan."

Anita smiled "We agree and will never enter in such a agreement again. It has proven to be a threat to our kind. Your children also have true beings to find. They have a purpose for the races and only God and Mother Earth should be in control." I smiled at Anita and then at Max. Max and I bowed to the Witches Counsel and walked to meet the family.

CHAPTER 43

We met the family in the front parlor and waited for the Wizards Counsel. Marcus and Mandra looking at each other and communicating without voice. Jordan paced and the Sentry brothers looked over to me.

Dino stood "Priestess, we are once again at your command. When and if you are in need of warriors, we will call upon them. In reality, they are yours at your command."

I smiled at him and nodded. We all sat quietly and I heard Max transmit *"My Princess, my heart is yours, my life is yours."*

I looked to him and returned *"Any Price my love."* He looked at me with the memory and smiled with the knowledge that it was true. We have paid so much for this moment. For each other. Now for our children.

Soon Lincon entered the Parlor. He looked to Mandra "My Lady, the guests have arrived. The Wizard Counsel sits." I looked at grandmother who at that moment was in Priestess warrior dress as I was.

She looked to me "Shall we stand as a family?" I looked to Max and Marcus who both smiled. Max trying to be stout, looked down for a moment.

He looked up at me with his charming smile and said "Shall we my Princess?"

Jordan broke the hesitant moment and looked to the Sentry Brothers and said "Well boys its time." We walked as a family, a group of change. A force not easily concord.

So there we were. Time for the reckoning. The confrontation of my life. Mine and my families. And for my un-foretold daughter, I was resigned. I would not accept anything but my families freedom. Including Max's freedom.

We entered the patio and yard as a united group. I could see the Wizard Counsel watching curiously and these Witched held the hands of their chosen Wizards. There eyes assessing me and Max as the fugitives of their justice. Max and I walked ahead of the others and stood in front of the Wizard and Witches Counsels. Unfazed at the fact that Leonardo and William sat at the closes table to the Wizard Counsel and with Edwin. Several other Mastered Wizards, I believed to be elders, sat at neighboring tables. All witches at one end and Wizards at the other. Max sent *"Closed to all but me."* I nodded. The Audience was Wizards and Witches watching the end of the Prophecy.

Max and I stood regal and unaffected. One of the Elders of the Counsel stood.

"Max Marshal, Mastered Wizard, I am Elder Thomas, we have been expecting to see you before this."

Max said "I am aware of that."

The Elder tall and handsome. Older than he appeared but soft spoken and clear eyed. He did not look accusingly at Max as Leonardo did. The Elder of the counsel said "And yet you defy this Counsel it satisfaction of you obedience?"

Max stood stout and answered clearly and without concern " I, We, have intended to meet before this but my wife and family needed me."

Leonardo stood in outrage as did Edwin. Elder Thomas only motioned for Leonardo and Edwin to sit. I looked into Edwin's mind and found that he expect to leave here with me in tow.

Elder Thomas looked over at me. "Princess we were looking forward to the last planed meeting. We were disappointed at not meeting with you then." I only nodded.

He looked back at Max "You have Married the Princess? Very intelligent thinking in your present condition."

Max responded "We married for our selves and our children. For our love for each other and our own freedom of will. Not for this counsel or any other reason." Max was making the effort to not be disrespectful but it was very hard on him when it came to dismissing our lives as easily as the Elder suggested.

Elder Thomas smiled and nodded. He looked over at me "And you my Princess, you are again pregnant?" I only nodded. Leaving the Counsel waiting for me to present my case when asked.

Max interrupted "A female child and no concern of the Wizards counsel."

Thomas looked back at Max "And what of the male child? Where is he."

At that I answered in the voice of the priestess. "It is only our concern where our child is."

Taken back by my bravado and retort, Thomas looked to the Counsel.

Leonardo stood and asked to be recognized. "My I have the floor Elder Thomas?"

Elder Thomas nodded and sat. Leonard walked toward me and I reached for my sward and stretched it out towards him as an extension of my arm. The Immortal feline eyes making it clear that I would, with out provocation, to end his life. He stopped and Max squeezed my hand.

"Princess, I mean no harm. I come to asked about the child."

I looked to him "And I do not have to answer you."

He said "My Lady, the child is foretold, the child is why we are here. He is our future."

I laughed in the Witches laugh "You sir, have no future. And the races will continue as the Lord sees fit. With or without my child."

Anita stood "The corruption of the prophecy is the question here not the child."

the crowd and counsels began to erupt into yells and chatter. A very old Elder Wizard stood. He put his has in the air and the crowd settled. He looked to me and smiled. "Princess, please indulge an old man. Remove your mask."

I stood still for a moment then looked to Max, He smiled and nodded. Leonardo walked back to his seat. I waved the sward away and removed my mask.

The old Wizard smiled and said "Ah, I can see the Masters efforts to protect you. He is most fortunate." He then looked to Max "We first must come to the decisions before the Counsel of the crimes that you and your Princess have committed."

Max said "My wife is not a Wizard. She is not held to our ways and laws."

The old Wizard looked to me "I am Maurice. I have been an Elder for one hundred years. I have lived with the prophecy much longer than most. And have waited for you and your child for all of that time."

He looked back at Max "Master Marshal, lets hear the charges against you and then we will hear your defense." Max nodded. I was mad. How dare they. But Max sent *"Quiet now. Listen. We will have our chance."*

A Herald appeared with a scroll. "Master Wizard Max Marshal, you are hear by charged with the following crimes against the Wizards and their laws of order;

Killing the Counsels Hunter who was to return you

Practicing magic in the presents of Mortals

Killing a Mortal

Disrupting prophecy by defiling the Princess intended for Pure Blood Wizard

Attacking and waging war against a Pure Blood Wizard

Ignoring and defying the Elders and the Counsels orders

Refusing to relinquish the child of the prophecy

Princess Emily Star Manelli, you are charged with the following crimes against the Wizards and their laws of order;

Disrupting prophecy

Ignoring the expectations of the Wizards Counsel

Killing several Wizards

Waging war against a Pure Blood Wizard

Refusing to relinquish the child of the prophecy

I laughed at them. Laughed as if I heard the funniest joke ever. "I am not a Wizard and will not be held to these charges. They are ridicules."

The Wizards all clamored as the Witches waited. Maurice again put his hands in the air. "Quiet down please." He waited and again stated louder "Quiet!" He looked me smiling "You are right my Princess. You are not a Wizard but your husband is and under our laws is responsible for your actions. Your charges are his to take responsibility for"

I shook my head "He was not present when I killed those Wizards. I was alone with my child when those cowards surrounded me."

Edwin stood and with venom stated "No one surrounded her. She is lying."

I looked at him and he knew the truth was out. I looked to him and transmitted *"I will kill you if Max should be killed for those I killed in self defense."*

He looked to me then and said "Don't threaten me Witch."

I laughed at him. "Sit down Pure Blood. You and your tricks make me sick."

He began to retort and Maurice said "Master Edwin, the Princess has given the command."

I looked at Murices, "How could this counsel be so blind as to what has transpired over all these years. How could you have sat idly by and watched the injustices and say to those tortured, stocked and threatened that we are charged with crimes?"

Maurice looked to Max "Tells us Master Marshal? You need to tell us in your words what has transpired?' Max began with the fact that he knew that he was not worthy of my affections due to his Mixed Blood. He told the Counsel that he had loved me from first sight and that the counsel had never released him from his vow to protect me. He told the counsel of our closeness over the years. Our closeness' by the loneliness of being mixed blood and shun by others. He explained that he did kill the mortal Jeremy for molesting me. He explained that we did deceive others to escape and enjoy dancing and amusement parks. He explained that if we had left when we were younger, as he wanted, he believes that would have been the only crime we would be guilty of. He continued and explained about the maiden dance and how he, already in love with me, was bewitched. He explained that he did return the next year for my kiss willingly and deliberately against instructions of the Elders. He then explained that his loyalty to me was more real than to the elders. He continued to explained that he was in the halls for three years for his love for me. He explained that he did study while their. He did learn much of his own power. He explained that he followed their instructions to end the relationship with me. And his plan that he almost carried out of killing me and himself to save us from the fate of being under the Pure Blood Wizards. He explained the threat to me with Deana and her Wizard accomplice whose name is unknown to us. He explained the wizards on the ship and in the town square attempting to kill him and take me. He stated that the original plan was to see them but when I learned of the child, and felt that the child would be taken and corrupted, I left. He looked for me for close to two years. He stated that he found me, injured and surrounded by the Wizards. "My child tied to her back while her side bled from the attack of the Wizards." He looked at me "My wife has her own story of the designs made for her life and how she felt. I cant speak for the princess."

When Max was quiet, and I only looked into his eyes, he smiled at me. He felt that there was some acknowledgement of justice. Maurice then looked to me.

"Tell me princess. What happened when you killed the Wizards?"

I looked directly at Edwin. "Fearing that My child would be taken, I sequester my self away from everyone, including my husband." I turned and smiled at Max "After all, he is a Wizard." I looked back at Maurice. "I saw the warnings of the elements. I grabbed my child and ran in the house and place protection around us. But Edwin was already in my house." Maurice looked to Edwin who looked uncomfortable. "I ran to the clearing with my son. The Wizards surrounded me. I called for Max and Marcus. I became the priestess and told them to leave or that they would die." I looked at Max who sent me a *"Its OK. Tell them."* I looked back at Maurice "Before Max and Marcus came, the Wizards came at me and I killed them." The crowd again erupted in clamor. Edwin calling me a liar and the Witches standing in protest at the disrespect to the Priestess.

Several Witch Sentries appeared at the wishes of the Witches Counsel. All in position and Anita stood "No disrespect to the Priestess will be tolerated. Nor disrespect to our kind. We have come as we too have interest in the child and the prophecy of the Wizards. But do not mistake our curiosity with weakness. We are not weak in strength and number. We know what has happened and what must happen for both races." With that the Wizards sat and looked to her.

"The Priestess and her Wizard are most powerful and can easily remove them selves as well as their children from any threat It is with respect to you that they stand here tonight. Nothing that has transpired has been at their doing or wish. They and their children are innocent to the corruption of a chosen few Wizards."

Leonardo stood and said "That is untrue. How can we be accused by witches who have no stake in our future.'?"

I looked directly at Leonardo " How can we be accused when we have only acted in our own defense?"

Leonardo stated "Everything said here has been a lie. There is no defense for the rouge wizard and a ungrateful Princess." I looked to Maurice. Then it came to me I looked at Max and then back to Maurice. And in a sweet witch voice I said "Elder Maurice? Can I make a suggestion?" He looked to me and smiled "Of Course, Princess." I looked back at Max who was confused. "Max has a "In his mind Scrap book thing. He could show that. It will tell you what has happened. ?"

Max looked at me concerned "Em that's private."

I looked at him seriously "But true." He nodded.

Maurice looked to Max "Bring it forward Master Marshal."

Max walk to the Counsel table and looked back at me. He was hesitant in giving his book up. He waved his hand and the book appeared. He stepped back and only the Wizard Counsel was able to see. They looked interested and then laughed at something and continued to flip through the pages. At one point they looked to each other with concern. After a short time they closed the book.

Elder Thomas stood he looked at Max "We have determined that the book is of truths and is innocent and pure. We have seen enough to pass judgment for you Master Marshal. You may have your book back." Max waved his hand to remove the book. Thomas looked at Max with a big smile. " A teacher?" Max looked a little rattled from his stout stance. "Yes Sir"

Elder Thomas asked "Who has evidence to the guilt of Max Marshal by witness and fact. Edwin stood up and said "I am a witness and victim to the assault of Max Marshal to me. There are also witnesses of Max Marshal threatening me and others."

I looked at Edwin and thought of dispatching him then and there. Max transmitted *"Stop it. Let him sink him self."*

I watched as Edwin made his way to face the Counsel. " I have been a victim of this Mix Blood Wizard. I have been assaulted by him and bring charge against him." Elder Thomas nodded.

But before Edwin could begin, Marcus came forward. "Elder Thomas could I be recognized?" Elder Thomas looked over to Marcus and nodded "Of Course Elder Marcus." Marcus came forward.

"I asked that the counsel read for the book of Wizard and disclose the wording of the prophecy."

Elder Thomas waved his hand and opened the book to the prophecy.

"these are the words of the book of Wizards. 'A powerful Witch will be produced from true love, purity and God. This Witch will be most powerful and will be the mother of the future of the Wizard and Witches of the world. The Witch will produce a child with a Powerful Mastered Wizard. The Powerful Mastered Wizard shall be a leader and *teacher*" he then looked up at Max " of the Wizards and bring great honor to his race.' this is the prophecy." Elder Thomas looked at Max and smiled. I smiled. Edwin looked confused. He continued to stand before the counsel. "It makes no matter what the prophecy says. Max attacked me and attempted to kill me. The Witch continues to threaten me with death."

Elder Thomas then looked to Edwin "State your case Master Edwin."

Edwin began "While looking in on the Princess, while Max Marshal was forbidden to be near her and being hunted for his past crimes, he attacked me. He bound my powers and hit me in the face." He was breathing heavy and said "I was then held in place while he put his hands around my neck and attempted to strangle me. If not for another Pure Blood Wizard, I would be dead at his hands."

Thomas looked at Max and asked "Is this true? Did you attempt to kill Master Edwin?" and to my surprise Max smiled broadly and said "Yes Sir. It is true."

Elder Thomas asked "Who is the Pure Blood Wizard that witnessed the act?"

Jordan step forward "I witnessed the act and have my own statement to the events of that night."

Jordan walked to the other side of Max.

Edwin stated "Master Jordan is the true brother of Max Marshal. He will twist the events to his brothers benefit."

Elder Thomas looked at Edwin "I believe that Master Max has admitted what he did. I believe that the witness account, since he saved your life as you say, will be honest. And we know who is honest and who is not."

Edwin shifted and looked somewhat concerned. Jordan then said "I was there that night. So was Master Christopher. Max, Christopher, Edwin and I are foster brothers. Max and I are Brothers by Blood and honor." He looked at Max and then back at the Counsel. "My brother is a rogue and a Mix Blood. However, I have only seen him act to protect the princess and his child. The night in question, Edwin was attempting to enter the home of the princess against her wishes. While she slept, he was working to subdue her protection that she had instinctively place to surrounded home and keep out Edwin and any one else interested in entering without her knowledge."

He looked at Edwin and said "Edwin had made advances before to subdue and take the Princess." Elder Thomas looked at me and smiled. Jordan continued "Edwin was trying different incantations to weaken the barrier. As he did so, Max appeared and hit him. Max did bound him and attempted to strangle Edwin. But what the counsel must understand, Max acted out of love for the Princess and to the vow he was never released from. Edwin was without honor as a Wizard that night, but I was able to talk since to Max. Max released Edwin at that time."

Elder Thomas looked at Edwin "Again Master Edwin, we know who is truthful and who is not. Can you dispute this account of Master Jordan?"

Edwin shook his head and quietly said "No."

Elder Thomas then said "I will remove the charge of attempting to kill a pure blood from the charges as this is a case of honor on behalf of Master Wizard Max." Marcus stood and stated "Since the prophecy does not stated that the Mastered Wizard who produces the child is a

Pure Blood, I believe that the charge of defiling the Princess and not producing the child should also be removed from both Master Max and the Princess." Thomas looked to the Counsel and they all nodded. Elder Thomas stated "Charges against the Princess and the Mastered Wizard for defying prophecy and not producing the child to the Wizards is hear by stricken." He gave a chuckle "Shall we visit the waging war against a pure blood?" Edwin stated "Master Max and the Princess waged war against other Wizards and my self, a pure blood."

I step forward "Edwin has made it his business to take me or my child. The only time I "waged war" with him was to protect Max, my child and my self. Edwin was very close to death at my hand. I willingly admit that to this counsel. At no time did Max ever harm Edwin or any other Wizard in my presents." The counsel looked over to Max. He stated "I did bind Master Edwin, chain him and sent him to Death Valley. I could have killed him easily but did not. I did not for the sake of my kind not for him." Elder Thomas asked "Why Death Valley?" Max smiled at me and looked back at the Elders "So he could be still and watch the sunset."

Edwin was angry "And what of the Witch killing the Wizards. She is still guilty." Max broke in "She killed protecting her child. She killed because she was attacked."

Elder Thomas asked "Who was witness to this event." Jordan raised his hand. Marcus followed and Mandra walked to the front. The Sentry Brothers walked forward and out of no where, Christopher came into the circle.

I said "None of my family was present at the time that I killed the wizards. Only other wizards that accompanied Edwin." Elder Thomas looked to Marcus "What did you see?"

Marcus stated "As the Princess has said. We were not present at the killing of the Wizards. We heard her call and were locating her. Once we appeared at the scene, the wizards were dead and one injured. The princess was also injured."

Elder Thomas then asked "Anyone there that can substantiate ether version of events?" Christopher came forward "I was there." I looked and did not remember him there. He stated "I had told Edwin that his plan to take the child was immoral. He told me to leave if I had no Honor. I saw the princess with the child. I saw Edwin enter her home."

He looked to Max and Jordan "I believed that it was wrong that we should take Max's child. That we take the Princess for Edwin as instructed. And though he told me to leave, I looked on from a short distance. I watched as the Wizards surrounded the Princess. I saw the Priestess take over and kill the Wizards that attempted to attack. I watched Max, Jordan and Marcus appear and stand with the Princess. I was ashamed of myself for lack of honor and loyalty to Max and Jordan when they only acted out of love of the child and the Princess." Elder Thomas looked at the counsel and looked back at me "The charge of killing the Wizards is now stricken."

Elder Thomas then asked "Master Max, can you tell us about the Mortal killed." Max looked at Elder Thomas "I killed him for attempting to rape and kill the Princess. I was young and impulsive. But I doubt that I would not do the same today." Elder Thomas looked to me "Is this true?" I looked at him and nodded. He looked to the others on the counsel and stated "The charge of killing a mortal is stricken." Elder Thomas looked to Max "That leaves practicing Magic in the presents of the mortals, ignoring the Elders orders and killing our hunter." Max stood stout and said "I will obey the Wizards Counsel in all things. But the actions of the Elders of our coven have been disloyal to me. They have twisted the prophecy to benefit only themselves at the sake of the Princess and other Wizards and Witches. Their attempts were to make the Princess subservient to Edwin and to all Pure Bloods. They intended to rule over Mortal and Immortal. I did defy the Elders not the Counsel." Elder Thomas stated "But when we sent the Hunter, you killed him." Max nodded "I spent three years in the Halls for the actions of my heart. When the hunter found me, he had no intent to end my life. I was ready for that. But to return me to the halls. I did kill him when he attacked me." Thomas looked to the Counsel who nodded to one another. Elder Thomas asked "And Magic in front of the mortals?" Max said "I did do that sir."

Thomas sat down and Maurice stood. "Master Max Marshal, this counsel has found that you are guilty of killing the hunter and defying the Elders. You do admit to using Magic in the presents of the mortal and that is clear. However, Defying the Elders and killing the Hunter, under the circumstances, we feel that it was justifiable. So that being said, we will take a break and discus your commitment for these crimes that you have been found guilty of."

Maurice then looked to me. "My Princess, you are without guilt and are free to go."

I looked as regal as possible "I stand with Max."

He smiled and nodded. I then asked "And what of Marcus and Jordan? They have only protected me and looked after my best interest. I would like to know their fate." Maurice looked over to Marcus and Jordan. "We feel their actions were of honor. We find no wrong doing." He looked to Marcus "However, the counsel is curious as to why you have disclosed that you are the father of these two Wizards"

Marcus smiled and bowed. "I did tell my sons that I was their father. My son Max knew I was his father as he was a mix blood and raised partially by his mother. Jordan was then informed when he was older. I wanted my family in my old age."

Then Maurice smiled and said "As do we all."

As Maurice turned back to confer with the counsel, Leonardo and William approached Max and I. Leonardo smiled and said "Princess, you are to be congratulated on your marriage to Max. And for the children of course." I gave him only a blank stare. He continued his smile "I would like to met the male child and give him a blessing." I did not respond. Max was holding my hand tightly and was growling inside. I looked at William "And you Elder William, would you like to met my child and give him a blessing?" William, whose voice I have never heard, only smiled at me knowing I wanted to see if his words and voice match his eyes.

I looked back at Leonardo, "You will not have the opportunity to see my son. He is protected by his parents and God." Leonardo then said "I demand to see the child. As an Elder, it is a command to the Master Wizard." I smiled as evil as the priestess could "I am his mother, The Priestess and the Wizard Princess, and I command that your efforts to corrupt my child cease." With that, Leonardo bowed and turned to leave, William followed but looked back to me and smiled warmly I looked over to Max who was seething.

At that point, Antonio stood from the Witches Counsel and addressed the Wizards. "Wizards!" The counsel and all others turned to his commanding voice. "The Witches have a demand of the Wizards." Many of the Wizards stood yelling about the Witches demanding anything. Many brought out arms to fight. Witches match the Wizards with weapons and -barking threats. The Wizard Counsel lost control of the crowd. I looked at Max "Can you think of a blinding light and a loud noise?" He smiled and I raised my left hand high above my head and Max took my hand in his left hand and the area was blinded by light and a bomb like noise. We let go and all were on the ground and holding their heads. Once the crowd was quiet and back in their seats, Max and I smiled to each other.

I looked at the crowd, turning my back to the counsel. "Standing before you is the result of the joining of the Witch and the Wizard. We are one, and what happens to one happens to the other. How dare you attempt to place one under the other." Max then made his voice heard by the crowd. "Wizards have a odd why of displaying courage and honor. Something that is most cherished in our realm. Tonight, my kind shows no honor. No honor of what is right and what is just." He looked back at his father and then the Wizard Counsel. "What are we afraid of? What can the Witches demand that makes any of us less than Wizard?" Thomas stood "What we have witnessed is most extraordinary." He looked from me to Max. "Your power surpasses the rumors." Maurice stood and announced "We will hear the demand of the Witches without bias. We will attempt to comply with the demand within our laws."

Antonio stood once again "We, the Witches, demand that the children of the Priestess and the Wizard are not labeled as Wizard..... Or Witch. We demand that the daughter is not declared the Princess of the Wizards. We Demand that the children of this couple live as Normals which is the dominate blood." The crowd clamored but remained in control. Maurice looked to Max and I "An you, the parents, what do you want?" Leonardo stood and protested "How can this be? The children are foretold and are to benefit our race." Max stepped forward "My daughter is not foretold. And My son deserves to live free. I stand here today to live free. The Princess is here to live free. Our whole lives have been played with and manipulated by others. It has caused so much heart ache and disappointment." He looked at me "If not for the Priestess, the Princess, I would be dead. Dead because I am a Mixed Blood, Normal and Wizard. Because my inner being can not live under a thumb. I believe it was that Normal Blood that allowed the Princess and I to fight for that freedom and equality." He looked back at the counsel. "My power is of my father, my determination to be free is my mortal mother. I can not separate the two." He turned and looked deadly at Leonardo and William. His monster in full focus "I am a man as well as a Wizard. And with the instincts that God has granted me, I will protect and shelter my children with any means necessary. Their lives will not be played with and manipulated. And neither will mine.

Leonardo spit "What insolents is this. You will not speak to Elders in such a way. You are a mixed blood and will abide to pure blood authority."

The Monster Max looked at him and smiled in with his evil panther smile "Elder Leonardo, How do you supposed to control my power and that of the Princess? There are none in your little group of Pure Bloods that can over power me should I chose not to bow down to you and yours." Leonardo only looked at Max with hate. Max looked back at the Counsel. "My wife and I are here out of respect and loyalty. But make no mistake, we don't have to be here and we don't have to let you find us. We can easily eliminate all threats to our freedom and threat to our lives and children. We are that powerful together." He looked back at Leonardo, William and Edwin, "None of the tricks and schemes worked to subdue the Witches or the Princess. Because God had a greater plan. I leave my families existence in his hands and not yours."

Elder Maurice stood "We have seen what has transpired. We have found that many of the issues that Master Max has been charged with would not be have come to pass if he was not push on that path." He looked directly at Max "On the other hand, you did make decisions that cause destruction and possible detection of the Wizards. And though we have empathy to you and your family, we must impose the following commitment" Max and my hands held tightly. He pulled out a scroll:

"Master Wizard Max Marshal, you are hear by found guilty of the following. One practicing magic in the presents of Mortals; Two, Killing the hunter sent to bring you to the Elders; Three, not following the instructions and expectation of this counsel" Elder Maurice then looked at Max with a smile "As a commitment to atone for these crimes, this Counsel finds that you will serve…" My heart stopped and I was about to whisk Max away when Elder Maurice continued "Service as a teacher of young Wizards, Mixed and Pure Blood, for no less than five years. You will be rewarded as any other teacher. In addition, you will be advising this counsel on historical facts with in the archives including all prophecy and its true meaning until this counsel releases you from that duty." I looked to Max and knew I had tears. Max was in shock. He did not move or say a word. Elder Maurice said "Class begins next week." Max smiled then.

Elder Maurice then looked to the Witches. "We agree with your demand. No race should dominate another, especially in these circumstances. We are honored to be brothers in kind with the Witches." Antonio Stood and said "We are honored to be called brother."

Leonardo and Edwin stood up. Edwin sneered "How can this be. Since when are Withes equal to us. How can you call that sentence to the rouge Wizard as just." Elder Leonardo stood and said "I am insulted. How can this Notorious Criminal be rewarded for his misdeeds. He should be, at least, in the halls for life."

Elder Thomas stood. "We do see things in truth and spirit. We do bring the following charges against Master Edwin and Elder Leonardo. One attempting to disrupt prophecy for your own gains. Two interfering in the roles and lives of others. And Three, threatening the virtue and life of the Princess and her child. Four harming another wizard, regardless of mix blood. Five for the attempts to take the princess and her child against her will ." Leonardo laughed "These charges are not accurate. How can you accuse an Elder of such disparaging charges? " William stood and spoke "I have been witnessed and have reported all of these charges in writing to the counsel. I have been watching at their request." Leonardo looked to William and sat back in his chair knowing what had been reported. Edwin stood and looked to the counsel. "I have only followed the instructions of the Elders. How am I guilty of any crime?" William then stated "Edwin followed the instructions of his true father." Edwin looked over to William with a sneer "Why are you not mute." William only smiled.

William looked over to Max and then to the Wizard Counsel " Leonardo and Edwin acted with disregard to the decency of Wizards, and Mortals. They devised plans that would do nothing but bring the princess unwillingly in to their web. All for the sack of power and greed. What would make a lesser Wizard kill and harm unjustly, Master Max was true to his Wizard Blood. He followed his vow and risked his life and freedom for that vow. I am a witness to these facts."

Elder Maurice stood "Elder Leonardo, you are hear by striped of the title of Elder. For your crimes you will serve in the halls for no less than five years. Master Edwin for your participation in these crimes, you will serve in the Halls for five years." With that both were placed in magical chains and Wizards appeared and took them away.

I looked to William, "Why did you not stop them before?" He looked softly, "I couldn't. I was to gather evidence. But to you Princess, " and he looked at Max "and to you Master Wizard, I do beg your pardon. Please be happy." He shook Max's hand and kissed my cheek. He bowed and walked to the Counsel. Maurice stood again and addressed the crowd. "No Wizard is to look upon another Wizard, Pure or Mixed blood, as beneath them. No Wizard will wage war against the Witches and will look at them as kindred." He looked to Marcus " I believe our host has provided food, drink and entertainment. Shall we all indulge." The elders left their bench and moved to the witches and warm greetings. Max and I only stared at each other until Jordan grabbed Max in a big bear hug. "You did it brother." Jordan released Max and kissed my cheek "You too Princess."

Christ walked to his foster brothers and they turned to face him. He looked at Max "I am humbled. I am sorry Max. I guess I'm thick headed and it took a while. But I would never harm your Princess or your child. Please forgive me?" Max smiled and put his hand out to Chris who took it readily. Chris turned to me and said "He was a snake in the grass. You were right my lady. I am sorry I was taken in. But I would never take your child or you for Edwin's plans. Please believe me?" I smiled and nodded.

Elder Maurice approached me. "My Lady. I hope you are pleased with the outcome?" I smiled and said "Oh yes. I am very Pleased." He smiled "And no regrets married to a teacher of wizards?" I looked at

Max and shook my head "No. Non at all." He smiled at Max too. Max placed put his hand in mine. Elder Maurice then said "As I have said. I have waited many years, a century, to see the child. I ask you both, with the assurance that nothing and no one will being any harm to the child, to allow the counsel to see him." I was taken back. My mind screamed no. but Max looked at me and transmitted. *"They cant take him now. They would never risk it."* I continued to look at Max. "I will fetch him and return shortly." With a touch of my hand on his arm I stopped Max. "Elder Maurice, I have spent the last two years hiding my son from the Wizards. I need your word on the lives of all wizards, that no one will take him or harm him. No magic, no taunts." He took my free left hand and touched the scar of the promise and said "I promise." I took my hand off Max and he left.

While he was gone, Elder Maurice said "We know the trials of what Master Max has had to endure over the years. We have not been insensitive to his predicament. Please forgive us for our slow response." I smiled and then asked "And what of the Shadow?" He smiled and said "I believe that the Shadow has been removed." I looked at him and he smiled "The shadow was Leonardo." I was shocked "Oh my God. Leonardo?" He nodded. I had to ask "Was he also Deana's accomplice?" He smiled and said "He and Edwin." I shook my head in disbelief. How could they go to such lengths. "Because of greed and a false sense of authority. Rest your mind, they are now were they will be rehabilitated. They are removed as a threat."

Max appeared and said "Your Dad wanted to shoot me!" I looked at him wide eyed "What, my Dad?" He smiled "He did not know it was me." He held our son in his arms and Maxton continued to sleep. Maurice looked a the child and said "Ah, the child." He then Conjured a bell and rang the bell softly for everyone to be quiet and still. All eyes, Witch and Wizard looked to the Elder. He smiled and put his arms out to Max. Max willingly allowed Maurice to take the child from him. Max and I looked at each other with some reservation. Elder Maurice said to the crowd "The child. Magic's future. The future of the races." Master Thomas and the other Elders approached and looked at our sleeping child. The Priestess and Priests of the witches also made their way to see Maxton. I looked over to Mandra and Marcus, who stood back smiling at the interest in their grandchild. Sal and Dino smiled at me and I knew they watched with intent to act should there be an attempt to take Maxton.

The next day we returned to my fathers home. Maxton was already calling him Gramps or something like that. We stayed for a few more days and family dinners being more comfortable and safer that we have in years. We participated in church and laughed with my Dad, Tom, Aunt and Doc. We felt Free. Free to make our own decisions and life choices. Free to love each other and our children.

Once home, Maxton asleep in his crib and laying in the arms of Max, I asked "Where do you go Monday?" He took a breath and said "it's a school of Wizards. Its hidden away in the Rockies. No mortal can detect it." I stayed quite for a minute. "When will you come home?" He said "I'll come home on weekends, at least I hope so." I was a little upset by it. Now that we are free of the plots, I still have to live without Max. At least during the week. "Don't worry Em. It isn't like before. I be home as often as possible." I looked up at him from where my head rested on his shoulder, "Maxton needs his father as much as his mother." He huffed "I will visit his dreams every night." He gave a devil smile "and yours too."

BOOK II

CHAPTER 1

December 5th, brought Maxton to two years old. Wyoming was cold and snowy. Max was home from his instructing the young Wizards in training. The whole family was there and we were making plans to visit Dad at Christmas. Maxton was in his wild twos and it was difficult to get him to behave and not do things that were dangerous. I often bound his abilities so that I could direct him appropriately. Max was able to not bind him and direct him but he too found our child strong willed and difficult. Though we should have been better prepared to raise a magical child, we found that it was not as easy as we would have believed. Now I know what my father went through.

My belly stretched as far as you would think it could be, I still had another month till our daughter was due. I was often made fun of by Max and his brothers about waddling and looking funny when I sat down. But Maxton and I would walk out to the forest and listen to the trees and the music. He and I would dance and laugh together at the whispers of good will by the tress.

January 15th, Lillianna Reyna Marshal appeared. She was so beautiful and sweet. Perfect in everyway. Though her eyes were blue as all babies, But later became clear green. Her hair was dark like mine. She resembled her father but she was more like my grandmother and I. Her father never taking his eyes off of her. I asked "Can I hold my child?" He would only shake his head. "Not yet. Let me hold her." I finally started to get out of the bed to take the child from him and he said "Ok." he handed her to me and said "She is so small. So beautiful."

He was totally amazed. I smiled at my daughter and agreed. "She is beautiful." As I looked into her eyes, the bond sealed forever, I was at peace. I had not remembered that Max did not see Maxton at birth. And though she was in my arms, Max stood next to me and stared at Lillie. He kissed my cheek and said "We really do make pretty babies." I giggled.

Time went on, and we lived a semi normal life. He still was gone a lot with teaching and interrupting manuscripts for the Wizard Counsel. He even began to write the new orders and laws for the Counsel. At five, Maxton was calmer and under control of his powers which to everyone's surprise were limited to conjuring and levitation. Max was not concerned and said he would grow into his powers.

As my son grew he became as proper a Wizard as there could be. Don't get me wrong, he has his father's wild side. But he did respond well to the Wizards stern and stout mannerisms when on display. He made his grandfather and father very proud. But when no one is around or intruding, Maxton still will cuddle with his mother and be my little boy. He was still my baby. He was very bright and energetic. His father enrolled him in Wizard school and he stayed with Max during the week for classes. He was assigned a master by the name of Ennis. Ennis, though proficient in his craft, was challenged by Maxton. One part of Maxton that was a challenge by the Wizards, Maxton was mouthy like me. Ennis often had to remind Maxton to remain still and often sent transmissions to Max reporting that Maxton was too verbal and not listening. Max would be frustrated and take Maxton's voice. I often had to remind him "He is my son too. I could never be so quiet as you Wizards. My son is like me." Max would shake his head and say "He is a Wizard and must learn their ways." He would smile and say "No matter that his mother is the undisciplined Princess."

Lillianna was more of a challenge. At three, she was able to transport early. Many times, I had to, call everyone from every where to help me find her. I finally had to bind her transporting powers. She then would be levitating everything in the house. Including me. Max would only laugh and enjoy my struggle to control the little witches powers. But even he resorted to binding her powers when she got out of control. Zee, old now, continued to follow Maxton around. But avoided Lillie. Lillie had a familiar of her own. Prince. He was a big black cat. He was part Siamese and very protective of her. He growled at all Wizards, including Max and Maxton. Lillie was head strong and did everything she could to do exactly what she wanted. Often when punished she would conjure something to lessen the punishment. She would sit in timeout and conjure a TV or a doll. I would have to bind her each time she attempted to get out of her punishments. She reminded me of Max in that area.

When the children decided though, their combined powers were amazing. Any time they held their hands together above their heads you could see the energy. That concerned even Max. Max who was thrilled with his magical children. We had not told them how to use the weapon. I hoped that they would not discover it till they were in their true selves.

When Lillie was Seven, and Maxton Nine, grandmother asked that we come to the Solstice Celebration that year. I had not returned since addressing the elders when I was twenty. Max laughed and said because I was not eligible to dance the maiden dance anymore, it should be safe. We did feel that the children needed to know their witch roots. It appeared that the whole family including the Sentry Brothers made plans to go. I was proud to have my family go with me. Needless to say, my grandmother was thrilled.

The whole family arrived a few days early. Elena, Joe and Hunter and their daughter Hanna; Jordan and Mary came. And Mary was now aware of her husbands Wizardry. Chris and his wife Jenny. Sal and Dino were right on time. Marcus of course already there. And then there was my family. Isn't that neet. *My family.* Me Max, Maxton and Lillie. We made it. We were finally there as a whole happy family. It was so average and NORMAL.

Dinner that night was filled with laughter and joy of being together. Of course Lincon and Molly were there. The whole thing could not have been accomplished if not for them. How do you feed all these people with such ease as Molly? Dinner did not go without problems. Lilly rejected the lovely roast and conjured her self a hot dog. Of course her father intervened and convinced her to eat what was served.

She told him "But Daddy, I don't think I like that food."

He calmly said "You have to try it. If you don't try, you might miss out on something wonderful." She looked at him and took a piece of meat and tasted it. She smiled and there was no more talk not liking the food. But then she conjured a milk shake.

The evening went on with lots of laughter and joking. I took the children to my room and conjured two beds for them and I looked up and extended the widows tower to a bedroom for Max and I. I had Lillianna in bed asleep with Prince at her side. Maxton watching TV with Zee curled up next to him. I helped with the dishes and joined the group on the porch. I sat with my grandmother who's hair was nearly all white by then.

"Em. I am so happy to see you here for Solstice. I remember you never could wait for it each year." I smiled at her and she went on, "It looks to me that God has answered all your prayers Em. He has given you NORMAL."

I leaned my head on her shoulder "He did and so did you." I patted her hand "When Max said he would leave the lives of his family in Gods hands, it seem to be the best decision."

She hugged me then. "I love that you are here again. You know that. I love having you home."

I smiled and thought about it. I had not been home in many years. Not since I got back from my fairytale land with Max. I looked at him and he was smiling at me knowing my thoughts. "Get out of my head." He only laughed and turned his attention back to the conversation with his brothers and Marcus. But I would never give up my life then for the fairy tale land. I was happy.

It was then I heard it. Then pines whispering to me. "Princess, beware."

I got up and walked away from the house and porch. I walked over to the forest door. "Why beware?"

The pines whispered "The Wizards watch. The Wizards wait." I turned to the house where my family, Witches and Wizards talked and laughed.

I looked back at the pines "Wait for what?"

The pines said "For the right time. Time to seek revenge."

I took a deep breath and I remembered. Edwin and Leonardo would be free now. I blew my kiss to the trees and walked to the cliff rail. I listened to the sea.

"Beware Princess, the Wizards come." I blew my kiss though my heart pounded with this threat. All I could think of was how do I keep my children safe. Max appeared next to me. "What is it?"

"The trees and the sea say that we need to take care. A warning that the Wizards are watching and waiting. That the Wizards are coming." I looked at him "Edwin and Leonardo are free by now." I grabbed his arm "The kids Max. What about the kids?"

He looked concerned "We will stay at the school. The children will be safe there."

I shook my head. "How do we really know that? And you forget that Lillie is a Witch. I will not have her looked down upon."

Max shook his head "No one would dare." He took my hand and we started to walk back to the porch and the family looked to us seriously. Marcus stood at the top of the stairs. "What is it?"

I looked at Max and he said "Em has been told that "The Wizards" are watching and waiting. She is concerned for the children."

I looked to the family "I can't let this happen again. There has to be a way to stop it. There has to be a way to keep them away from us." I started to shake. Just Max and I was one thing, but the children. Protecting the children was a whole new thing. How was I going to do this?

Marcus took my hand and pulled me up the stairs. He had me in his bear hug and said "Princess, no worries. This is a new time; New attitudes; New family." He took my shoulders, "We are strong and we are with God grace." I nodded and went to check on the children.

Once in bed, I looked out the window and watched the sea. I have been spoiled over these few years. I had only focused on the children and Max and I. I cared more about mixing the worlds for the children. Making sure that they were able to be accepted for themselves and accept themselves. Now the net begins to tighten again.

Max pulled me into his arms "We will be alright Em. You'll see." He kissed my head "You always worried too much."

I huffed "I was always right too." I turned around "Max, do you think that we really could be ok at the school?"

He smiled and said "Sure we will. There is natural security and Guardian Wizards."

I could believe what I was about to ask. "Do you think there should be Guardians for the kids? Maybe both Witch and Wizard for both kids?"

He giggled "Well that would be a sight on the campus. Witch and Wizard guarding the same child." He got serious. "How about we get through Solstice and go from there?"

I nodded, "OK. But just so you know, it wont stop me from worrying."

Solstice began and we all stood in the procession and welcomed the guest. Lillie was dressed in her little robes and I had my Priestess dress on. Max was in jeans as was Maxton. Neither wearing a suit as good Wizards should. And not warring robes like the Witches. They looked normal.

To my surprise, William and Maurice came. They were gracious and presented grandmother with roses. Also in the guest line was Lori. She slithered much like her mother. She even looked more like her mother now that she was in her thirties. As she approached Max and I she smiled and said "Hello Em. Haven't seen you at the Solstice in years."

I smiled back and said "No but I came at grandmothers request."

She nodded and move to Max "Well Max, I see you are still watching out for the Princess."

Max smiled at me "Yeah. How about that." She moved on at that point.

I looked to Max "A normal trying to be a Witch." I laughed "Wasn't it she that condemned me for being a Witch?"

Max laughed "She has always wanted to be you. You just couldn't see it." I never thought that Lori would want to be me.

Once the precession was over, we joined Sal and Dino, Jordan and Mary, Chris and Jenny and Elena and Joe at a table. We were all talking and enjoying the festival. The children joined the games and were enjoying them selves. That was until Lillie decided that another kid was mean and he found himself in a hole during one of the races. Max grabbed her while I apologized profusely to the parents of the child. I walked back to the table where Lillie pouted and Max looked concerned.

I knelt down to Lillie and said "Lillie, you must never use magic to harm another. The mean magic will come back to you."

She looked at me with angry tears "Then why does Daddy get to use magic to take my magic?"

I turned to see Max look to the sky hiding his grin. I looked back at my little girl, doing my best not to giggle "Daddy is punishing you for doing something you shouldn't. You could have hurt that child."

She shook her head "No. I didn't make him fall in like I wanted to. I only put him there. That wouldn't hurt him."

I remain straight faced though I wanted to laugh. "Lillie, why don't you and I dance?" She smiled "OK. Can I have my magic back?"

Max clearly and sternly said "No!"

Lillie looked at her dad with tears "Daddy please. I promise I will be good."

He wanted to melt so bad, I could see it clearly. He smiled and said "Dance with your Mom and will see about it after that."

I grabbed her hand and looked to Elena and Hanna. "Shall we ladies?"

We watched the Maiden dance with nostalgia and I looked over to Max "Well there is your dance of obsession."

He started to laugh. "Yeah, till you got us in trouble."

Lillie was pulling my hand "Momma lets dance."

I smiled at her "That dance is not for us. I am already married and you are too young."

Mandra came and took Lillie's hand "Come little one, let me tell you the story of the maiden dance." Lillie took grandmothers hand and she walked to the porch and sat with Marcus and grandmother and listen to the story. Soon I saw Maxton join them and I looked over at Max.

"Maybe we did have wonderful parents and never really noticed because they were labeled something else?" He nodded.

The children never made it to the sun rise. They were asleep soon after grandmother told them the story of the Maiden dance. So Max and I, in the same place we watched as kids, saw the sun make its way through the wreath. Molly and Lincon watched the children while we slept. Max had not unbound Lillie, so every one was safe from her tantrums.

CHAPTER 2

When I woke, I was staring into the eyes of Max. "Hi"

He smiled "I can hear *your* daughter yelling at someone."

I giggled "Well go take care of it."

He shook his head "Your turn. I can only thank God that I did not release her powers."

The yelling came up the stairs to assault our ears and it was clear that Maxton was her victim. I got up and put on my robe. I looked over as Max put a pillow over his head. Another scream and screech came from our daughter.

I walked to the bed and pulled the pillow off his head "Why didn't you take her voice as well?"

He giggled and I went to see what was going on. I found my son transporting to every available safe spot to avoid his hostile sister who was swinging and throwing her teddy bear at him. "Stop this. Your going to wake the house."

Maxton quickly said "She trying to hit me with her teddy bear. She is mad that I found the last of the cookies. She wanted me to conjure more and when I wouldn't she started to came after me to hit me. I think if she had her magic, she would have really hurt me."

"Lillie! You are not to hit your brother!" I looked at her sternly. "Go out on the porch and sit in the big chair until I call you." She started to cry being sent to time out. She dragged her teddy bear out the door being followed by Prince. But she did as I asked thank God. Who knows how long that will last.

"You were such a sweet child Em. Where did that wild one come from?" I looked to find grandmother smiling.

"I don't know what I am going to do with her. I need advice" I walked over and hugged her.

Grandmother hugged me back and was giggling. "She is going to be something. I admire her. No Witch or Wizard will ever get the best of her."

Max came down the stairs and smiled "Its quiet."

I giggled "*Your* daughter is in time out on the porch."

Max laughed and grabbed Maxton in a big hug "I am proud of you son, you survived."

Maxton looked at his dad seriously and said "Barely. Lillie needs Wizards school so she can learn re… re…restraint."

Max stated laughing "Lilly would spend her whole childhood in the library." He then headed out the door to check on *His Daughter.*

"EM? Where did you say she was?" My heart dropped and I ran out the door. And sure enough, Lillie was gone and only her bear remained. I panicked and ran to the tail to the ocean.

I looked down for her. "LILLIE!" she didn't answer. I looked to the sea "My daughter, do you have her?" The sea whispered back "No Princess, she is with the wizards." My breath caught in my throat. I backed away and ran to the trees "Have you seen her, my daughter?" The Trees whispered "The young maiden is with the Wizards." I started to shake and panic. I dropped to my knees and screamed "NO!"

Max was at my side. "Em?"

I could hardly get the words out. I couldn't breath "Wizards… have… her! My…Fault!"

Soon we were joined by the family but Maxton was not with them. I looked at everyone and jumped up barley breathing and ran to where I last seen my son. I ran in the house where he stood motionless. "Maxton!" I grabbed him and was crying.

Max was there and had his hand on his son.

Marcus appeared "I have called on the Wizards Counsel for help." I was in shock and couldn't breath. "Mandra stood at my side and called my name and though I heard her I did comprehend. I passed out.

I woke up on the floor with Max and Grandmother kneeling by me. Both calling my name. I realized what had happened and why. Now breathing I jump to a sitting position. "Max! Release her powers."

Max looked at me like I was crazy "Em. That might be the worse thing we could do."

I shook my head "She will be able to call us. She will be able to protect herself." He looked at me concerned "Max have faith in her. If she can capture an innocent kid, think what she would do to those who scare her. She is hostile to her brother even without magic."

Max looked concerned "She may be powerful, but she is only seven. They may hurt her."

Mandra looked at Max "They may hurt her anyway. They maybe are trying to take her powers for another."

I looked a Maxton crying for his sister in the arms of Jordan. Max fallowed my eyes then said "Jordan, please take Maxton back to the school. Tell the head Master what has happened and assign a Guardian to Maxton." Jordan nodded and he and Maxton disappeared.

Mary knelt down and hugged me "I will be praying until her return." She was gone then at the desire of Jordan.

Elder Maurice, Elder Thomas and Elder William appeared. Then Anita, David and Antonio appeared. They look to me and Max.

Elder Maurice said "We are dismayed that any Wizard would be so evil as to take a small child from her mother. We are at your service."

Max nodded and said "Thank you for your response. We will need your advise and security for our son." Max looked to the Witches and said "We also thank you for your concern and response. Lillie is a skillful Witch ."

I looked to the Witches Counsel "Please. Can you see her? Can you find her?"

Anita looked to me with sorrow "No Priestess though I continue to try." Then it occurred to me. Prince was also gone. I looked to Max "Prince." He looked not understanding "Prince is her familiar. He is with her. They may not understand that he too could be tracked."

Max jumped up and called "Prince?" but there was no response.

I huffed as I looked at him I stood up. "Prince would never respond to you." I looked into the air "Prince. Prince come here." We all waited quietly for a moment and as we gave up on his response, Prince appeared. I let out a loud sound of relief and joy. I knelt down "Prince is Lillie alright?" He rubbed my hand. I took it to mean that she was. I looked at Max " I will follow Prince. And Come back and tell you where she is."

Max looked at me with anger "No you wont. They will have you then too."

I looked at him with the full form of the priestess "No one will keep me from her. I will return with her or her location." I reached down and picked up the black cat to the chagrin of Zee who was too old for the adventure. I smiled to him "Please stay with Maxton Zee." He left at that time. I kissed Max and said "Take me to her Prince."

I found myself in a castle. I don't know where it was. I looked about and heard and saw no one. I put down Prince and followed him. The next thing I knew, someone had my arm. I turned and found Max. "I could have killed you!"

He pulled me to the side and said "this is the Wizards Center. It is where they congregate. The Wizards Hall where you were presented. Do you remember?" I nodded. "There is security here that you can not hide from. But I can." I looked down the hall and saw Prince looking back at us. I motioned to Max to look at he cat. He looked and said "Stay here." I shook my head and shaped shifted to Zee. I ran to meet the other cat and only could sense that Max was near.

Prince went down the long hall and came to a door at the end. I could hear my daughter threatening someone "Wait till my Dad finds us. He will take your magic and make you sorry." The laugh that followed was that of Edwin. I popped in and sat next to Lillie. "Zee!" She was sitting on a settee and was bond with invisible bindings. The room was small and there was a desk. Edwin stood at the window expecting something. He turned when Lillie announced Zee. Prince followed suit and sat on the opposite side of her. "Prince." simultaneously Prince and I growled at Edwin.

Lilly smugly challenged Edwin "My Mom is here and you're in trouble." When I tapped Edwin he was sending out a call of caution that the Princess was near. He then looked at Lillie "Your mother fails to teach you manners. She fails to teach you your station. That's why you are bound now."

Lillie looked at him "I only treated you like you treated me. You are mean and I will figure out how to get those horns on your head yet."

He looked back at Lillie "Be still little witch or there will be consequences for you." Lillie who either had no common sense or fear said "You cant do anything to me. You have no real magic." He began to move forward and I arched my back in preparation to attack. "If you do anything to me my mom will hurt you."

Edwin stood stern and stout. "Where is your Mother."

Lillie giggled with a glint in her eye, and said "I wont tell you." I took that to mean that she knew I was Zee.

Then he snarled "You will tell me or you will suffer a great deal of pain."

Lillie smiled and said "No, I won't." She giggled "My Dad won't let you hurt me."

Edwin had fear in his eyes with that. He then called for security. Then Edwin was hanging outside of the window screaming and held up by invisible rope. Max appeared and with an incantation released Lillie. I manifested back and Max grabbed us both and we were at the Wizard Campus with Wizards all staring at Max and his two witches. He still carried his monster face close. I grabbed my daughter in my arms and cried. "Oh Lillie I am so sorry. Did they hurt you?"

She giggled "No Mamma. They were afraid of me. They were afraid of Dad."

Max had dropped the monster and took her into a big hug. "Oh babe. My little girl." He looked at her in his arms "What do you mean they were afraid of you? You didn't have your magic."

Lillie tilted her head "Dad. They didn't know that. They said that they were going to trick mom into coming to get me. And they were going to do something. I told them that I would knock down their castle if they tried." Max started to laugh at his daughters bravado. Prince appeared and stood waiting for Lillie. Max put her down to reassure her familiar.

Maxton came running at that moment and he hugged me and his Dad and then hugged his little sister. "Lil you are such a trouble maker."

She giggled. And looked back at her father "Daddy, Can I have my magic back now?"

He looked at me with a smile and gave her back the powers. He said "Lillie, don't use your magic against others is that clear?"

Lilly smiled sweetly and lied "I won't."

CHAPTER 3

That evening we found our selves in the Wizard School Counsel Center. We sat at a huge table with the Elders and the Witches Counsel. Dino and Sal appeared and took the responsibility of watching Lillie. I don't think they realized what they were in for. Maxton sat with his Guardian Wizard, Nathan. Nathan was young like Max was when he became my Guardian. Nathan however, was a pure blood. Marcus and Mandra were there and Jordan and Chris. Elder Thomas called for tea for the adults and milk and cookies for the children.

Elder Thomas began "There is a division within the Wizard world. Some have decided that they are unable to conform to the new laws and expectations. We believe that there is at least a third that has left the mainstream." He looked over to me "Never has any Wizard been expected to be less than honorable and work only to educate and do good works. The most important being to do no harm with our magic." He took a breath "The harm intended to your family and to you Princess is not the way of the Wizard and never has been."

Maurice then said "Leonardo and Edwin believe that they can begin to start a new race of Wizards. One that fits their way of thinking." He looked at Max "You and your family will be safest here. But be fully aware. War is coming."

Max nodded. He looked at me and transmitted *"War against us and our children."* Max looked back at the Elders "We are grateful for your offer. But I think maybe that my family should disappear. Many can be saved if we are gone. We are the targets and no one wins in War."

Maurice then said "The son will suffer the sins of the father. You will stand now Master, or your son and daughter will later." Max took a deep breath and thought about what the Elder was saying.

I broke the silence "My daughter and I are Witches. And though we are a family with Wizards, we are not like you. How will the others feel about us here."

Elder Thomas answered with "They will adjust." He smiled "They will however, be most curious. Please be patient."

I looked to the Witches Counsel. "Are you in agreement? Do you have any other suggestions that we should consider?" Davis and Antonio looked to Anita.

She smiled at me "Priestess, you know the rule. No Wizard or Witch is stronger than you and your Mate. What happens to one happens to the other." She looked deeply "You are strong and others are close to aid you. But like your mother has said, you think too much like a mortal." She smiled at my shock of her knowing about what my mother told me. "You have the power to keep all safe. And She is close."

I asked "And my children, what about them?"

Anita said "Your children are as strong as their parents. Teach them, watch them, and love them. They have a great destiny."

I then asked her while looking into her eyes "And when will this war come?"

She stared at first not wanting to answer "Soon."

Elder Thomas then asked Max "Have you decided Master. We would suggest that you take up our offer of sanctuary here on this campus." Max looked at me and turned to the Wizards and said "We will stay. And thank you."

Master Thomas then said "As we all adjust to the new ways, we still have to adhere to our creed of good and honor. And though we often wish harmful things to those who harm us or threaten us, we must not harm them." I thought he was going to say something to Max and I when he looked to Lillie "Young Witch. You must remove the horns from Edwin's forehead. We must never use Magic to harm another."

Max started to giggle until I nudged him and he transported out. I looked at Lillie "You will do as Elder Thomas has asked, right now."

Lillie shook her head "He said he was going to hurt me and he made it so I couldn't move. He reminded me of the demons that Gramps preaches about in church. He looks like them too." All of us were in shock by this little one.

Grandmother spoke to Lillie "Sweetheart, one must never use magic to harm someone."

Lillie was impassive then grandmother in her quiet stern way "Young lady, you will do as you are told or you will lose your powers for a week."

Lillie sat up and said "But grandmother….

Grandmother said "Now Lillie." and the little Witch waved her hand.

"There are you happy." Elder Thomas looked at me in disbelief of the child's mouth. I looked at him and said "We are trying with her. She is very headstrong." He smiled and nodded.

Maxton said "I told my Dad that she needs to go to school here so she can learn…. Tolerant and Re..Re.. restrains." I looked to Lillie and then to Mandra "Could you watch her for me while I find Max?" she agreed.

I transported to his locations under a tree by the next building. He was still laughing. I started to as well. "Max you can just pop out when these things happen. You have to find some of that Wizard restraint, as your son says, and teach that girl."

Max had such a smile "She is wonderful. Maxton is a great Wizard, but Lillie is a Witch with an attitude. She reminds me of….. me."

We stayed in a little house I conjured just outside of the main hall. Over the years, the house grew as our family grew with new members. Max and I spent a lot of energy trying to devise a plan to protect the children. I thought we should sent the children to Anita, but Max refused to send the children away. "If this becomes the end, I want to be with them as much as possible. I want them to remember that there are different ways to live. And God to depend on."

Max and Maxton attended classes each day and Lilly and I studied at home. This went on for a couple of years. No war had occurred and I wanted to leave the campus. I wanted to go home. I called in reinforcements to instruct her in Alchemy and potions. And to my surprise knowing the deficits of Max and I in those areas, Lillie was a natural. Anita sent a Master Witch by the name of Mehgan. She was a lovely young lady with golden hair and an angle face. Her eyes a beautiful aqua color and she was truly sweet and good hearted. Mehgan could not have been more that twenty her self. It seemed that Lillie responded to Mehgan better then most. Mehgan had a ferret as her familiar, and its name was Trick. He seemed to like Max and Maxton more than the cats. Mehgan stayed with us while we lived on the Wizards campus.

Mehgan and I would be very cautious when out of the house amongst the Wizards. They watched us and we watched them. Lillie never had any fear though we all continuously warn her. She would walk across a campus filled with Wizards and Wizards in training as if they did not pose any threat or thought of her at all. Most moved away and stay back away from her. All would watch her as she walked assuredly to her father's office. All standing stern and stout, and would back away from the little witch. I was convinced that they heard about Edwin's horns. I often thought that it should have been Lilly as the Wizard Princess. What a joke it would have become. She was just too much her own person for the Wizards. I had to blame the Normal Blood.

On one sunny afternoon, while Mehgan and I prepared dinner, there was a knock at the door. Lilly jump up and said "I'll get it." I barely reached her to stop her. "No you won't. Go back to the kitchen." She stomped back to the kitchen and I was thankful to God she obeyed me.

I open the door to find a young Wizard in Training. Tall with brown hair and blue eyes. He must have been about twelve or thirteen. He had a formal letter closed with a golden seal. "Madam Marshal, I am to deliver this invitation to you directly." I smiled at the very proper Wizard. I heard Lilly giggling from the kitchen door. The proper Wizard said "I am to take back your response, Madam."

I nodded and said "come in young Wizard. What is your name?" He was taken back and chances a sideways look and said "Michael, Mam." I smiled again "Thank you Michael. Please sit down." Michael was uncomfortable and shook his head "Thank you I will stand." I opened the letter and it said

Dear Madam Marshal

The Wizard Counsel request your assistance in preparing and developing the festival of the harvest this October. We would provide all that is required including all food, drink, entertainment and decorations. A ball is expected the evening prior as our traditions dictate. We would also be delighted to have all Witches on campus and any others invited by you to attend.

Your immediate response is appreciated.

Elder Maurice

My God. How could they ask this of me? I was so … so … non creative. Plus we never participated in any of the Wizard Festivals. This request to do a ball and festival was so out of my league, I would have to call on grandmother. I looked at Michael not really knowing what to say. Max came in then and looked at the Wizard who nodded in respect of the purple robed instructor. Max walked over and read the letter over my shoulder and started to laugh. "Better call Mandra."

I glared at him "No need to be insulting."

Mehgan came in wiping her hands on a dish cloth. I handed the letter to her and she smiled. "Really? I have never seen Wizards invite Witches for anything." She looked to me "You are going to accept aren't you?" I stood and though for a moment.

Lilly came in and hugged her Dad. "Daddy!"

Max hugged Lilly and kissed her head. "Hi Baby." The young Wizard watched the family scene as if completely foreign to his world. He also took note of Lilly being near. Max looked up to see his curiosity. "Michael, it is not as unusual as you would think. Many Wizards live in families."

I smiled at Michael "OK. Let the Counsel know that I have accepted their invitation." He smiled and nodded and said "Thank you Madam. I will be leaving now." Max winked at me "Michael." Michael turned to as he made his way to the door. "Stay for supper. I am sure it will be more appealing then the cafeteria." Michael was taken back and stood in that stern and stout wizard pose. Then he said "I should take the answer to the Counsel Master Marshal." Max smiled and said "They will not expect it till after supper I am sure. Please be our guest." Michael nodded to the Master Wizard. As with grandmothers home, everyone in the house at supper was fed.

Maxton came in and was greeted by his sister "Maxton! What did you learn today?" Maxton smiled at his sister "What did you learn? I hope it was how to stay quiet and control your self." Lillie giggled "No I didn't learn that." Maxton laughed. Maxton nodded at Michael in recognition and Lillie announced to her brother "Michael is staying for supper." Maxton smiled at Lillie and looked at Michael and nodded.

Once the dinning room table was set and the food was on the table, Mehgan call the family to the table. Of course, Lillie said that she didn't like pasta and conjured a hot dog. Max took the hot dog "Lillianna, eat what you have been served." She started to open her mouth and Max looked at her in that disciplined way and she sat quietly. She just couldn't abide by her powers bound anymore. She would do anything to prevent it.

Max looked to Michael and asked "Where are you in your studies?" Michael looked up from his plate and said "I am in my third year in training and I am going into my freshman year. When I graduate, I will apply to Princeton.

Max looked confused "Is Princeton the only College that you plan on applying to?"

Michael said "Yes sir."

Max continued "Why?"

Michael remained quiet. But I could see the unspoken communication go on. Maxton squinted attempting to intrude but was unable to. Lillie… well she was amazing.

Lillie, as she was swirling her fork in her uneaten food said "I wouldn't care where my ancestors went to school. I would go where I could have fun and study what I wanted." Maxton dropped his fork and said "Why can she do that and I cant?"

Max looked at Lillie "Don't intrude Lillie. It is impolite to Michael. Apologize."

Lillie sat up in her chair insulted. "I didn't know I wasn't supposed to listen? Why do I have to apologize?"

Max looked at her sternly and she said "I apologize Michael. But I didn't know I wasn't supposed to listen." She looked at Michael. He nodded and looked at Max and smiled.

Max said "She is attempting to be more respectful. Because she has some abilities that she is unable to control as of yet, she has" Max looked at me "Mistakes." I giggled.

Maxton still insistent "I still would like it explained to me why I can't do that."

Lillianna said "Why talk about me like I am not here."

I spoke up and said "Children eat your supper."

Mehgan then spoke to Maxton "Wait young Wizard Maxton. Your time is coming." She looked to Lillie "You young Witch, you need control. I believe that will be on our lesson plan for tomorrow." Lillie nodded and continued to play with her food and Maxton giggled. Lillie looked up at him with intent do harm to Maxton. She had intended to have his supper on his head. The intent clear, Max bound her without notice. She looked at her father in surprise "Daddy!"

Max looked at her and said "Lillie, dinner is over for you. Go to your room." Lillie got up from the table and stomped her way up the stairs to her room. She then slammed her door. Max and I looked at each other as if to say 'What next.' And then we laughed at the amazement of Michael who looked as if he had witnessed a true demon. Max looked at Michael "Lighten up. Your headed to the normal world and you will see a lot of girls with worse attitudes." Michael smiled still stunned with the display of angry behavior of the nine year old witch. Supper ended with Michael and Maxton talking about classes and different instructors.

The next day, as Lillie and I went to see Max in his office, and as the Wizards all stood back and watched Us. As Lillie and I walked, Lillie spotted Michael. She took off before I could grab her. She ran right to him and the other six or seven Wizards he stood with. All of the young wizards were stout and stern at her approach. It was obvious that they were very cautious of her. "Hello Michael." Michael only nodded sternly surprised at the little witches approach. All eyes of the Wizards in training look directly at Lillie as if expecting her to do something.

Lilly smiled sweetly "I want to tell you that I was sorry again for being nosy. I won't do it again if you come back to dinner." He looked at her and then me. He looked back down at her and smiled "Thank you."

Lillie smiled and I grabbed her hand and was headed for Max's office. "Lillie don't run up on the Wizards. I am not sure how they will take that. They are not sure about us and I am not sure how they will react."

She looked up at me with her brows pulled inward "Mom, aren't I part Wizard?"

I smiled "Yes but there are no girl Wizards. Only boy Wizards. You are a Witch."

She looked at me "Mom. Maxton is a Wizard and Dad is a Wizard. How come I am not?"

I smiled and stopped walking. I took her to a near by bench thankful for the Wizards going back to classes.

"Lillie, you have Wizard Blood, Witches Blood and Normal Blood. But girls don't become Wizards. Only boys become Wizards. Your magic is from the Witches Blood. But don't make the mistake to think that you aren't just a powerful as any Wizard. OK?" Lillie smiled and said "I know that Mom. I just don't know why the Wizards act so funny. You know, so sad."

I smiled "Well I think some are. But most are following their teachings to be still and watch."

Lillie smiled and said "Well I watch too. But I see inside them. A lot of them are waiting and hoping to do something else and still have their magic. They are afraid to leave and not have their magic. I don't understand them. How could they have magic here and not somewhere else."

I smiled "They have their magic wherever they go. But they, like you and Maxton, need lessons. They need to learn how to use the magic." Lillie appeared to be satisfied with that.

We got up and started for Max's office once again and then I smelled Edwin. My heart started to pound. I screamed for Max not wanting to wait too long. Max appeared and I could see that he too could smell Edwin. Lillie giggled, "That mean Wizard is here." Dino and Sal appeared.

"Max what about Maxton?" Max had Lillie in his arms. "He is with his guardian. He's in a class with a friend of mine. A Mixed blood that will protect him." Max and I scanned for Edwin without success.

I looked at Max "Where is he?" Max shook his head.

Lillie said "Look Dad, he's over there by the big tree."

Max and I looked over to the big oak, but could not see anything. Max looked at me and I shook my head.

Max looked to Lillie "Lil, we can't see him."

She tilted her head and smiled "I can show you." She threw her hand toward the tree and a glow of Edwin was there. He did not know we could see him. He looked around and was watching the campus. He looked over to us and stared at us. Then Lillie twisted her hand and Edwin stood with horns and now a pointed tail. He turned around in a circle looking at he pointed tail and realized, Lillie could see him, but he didn't realize that the whole campus could see him. Edwin disappeared at that point.

I looked at Lillie "Stop that. Remove that tail and horns now."

Lillie shook her head "No. He was here to hurt us. He was looking for Maxton."

Max looked down at her and looked at her sternly "Lillie, we have told you before. No magic to hurt others."

Lillie had her hands on her hips "I did not hurt him. I gave him his true shape."

I looked at Dino and Sal with fear "The whole campus saw Edwin. They know she what she did to him. This is a violation in their world."

Dino said "No worries, Priestess. We will watch."

Max focus on Lillie "Do as you are told."

Lillie was impassive "No. He deserves it."

Max looked at her and said "You are about to lose your powers for the week." Lillie looked at her father and though she was about to cry she shook her head and began to run back to the house. Dino and Sal began to give chase but before they caught her, Michael had her by her arm and she was kicking him to get lose. He ignored the kicks and brought her back to Max.

Max grabbed her "Say your sorry to Michael."

Lillie in tears yelled at Michael "You should have let me go." Michael stayed stout and quiet and watched the Lillie being defiant.

Max had her magic and her arm. He gave her arm a shake "Lillie, now."

Lillie's face was in tears and she quietly said "I'm sorry I kicked you when you wouldn't let me go." Michael smiled and said "your forgiven." She glared at him with anger and he nodded with a smile.

Mehgan came up at that point. She looked at Lillie and then to Michael. "I will try to have her apologize appropriately tomorrow, Wizard. I am sure she is just feeling restricted right now."

Max handed Lillie's arm to Mehgan "She is bound." Mehgan nodded to Max and turned and walked Lillie to the house.

All I could do was say "Thank you Michael for you aid. I am sorry Lillie was so hostile." Michael smiled and nodded and walked to his class.

Max looked to the Sentry brothers "Well you guys volunteered. Good luck with that." Dino and Sal smiled and disappeared.

I looked at Max and took a deep breath. He smiled at me. "Don't worry Mom, we will find a way."

I shook my head "But the Elders will know about Edwin's horns and tail. How do we get her to take it back."

He smiled and then started to laugh, "I know I should laugh Em. But I think Edwin never expected Lillie." He looked in my eyes and said "We never expected Lillie, but God that girl is something."

I giggled because he was right. I was so proud of that girl. She new her own mind and desires. She knew who and what she was.

Max looked more serious "We need to see the Elders. We all need to discus how Edwin got on campus undetected. We may need to leave or have better detection system outside of Lillie."

That night, Max sat reading with Maxton and I went upstairs to see Lillie in her room. I found her sitting on her bed with Prince. Her eyes red and swollen from crying. When I came in she looked at me like I was coming up with another problem for her. I Jumped on her bed and grabbed her up in a hug.

"Don't cry anymore OK?"

Lillie looked up at me and said "Mamma, why don't I fit in. I try, but everyone is so different from me.? Everyone thinks differently than I do." Well, where have I heard that before.

"You do fit in. You fit with me and your Dad and Maxton."

Lilly said "But all I do is make mistakes and do bad things without meaning to. I feel like I am so different that no one understands me."

I smiled "I used to feel like that too. And then I was given my grandmother, my Master Instructor and I found a friend who understood me. I looked deep into her eyes "Lillie, it is true that you need to learn how to behave in different worlds. One way in the normal world, and the Witch world, and then another in the Wizard world. There are lots of twists and turns and a lot of things no one can explain." I petted her hair and kissed her cheek, "But through all of those different things that you must learn, remember, I think you are perfect the way you are. And your Dad is very proud of you. He also thinks you are wonderful and no matter what happens, you are special. You are so loved."

Lillie looked at me "But Momma, I am bad."

I giggled "Never. You are strong in mind and power, not bad. And it is the rest of us that need to learn you too. We need to help you in the way you handle things." I put her in a big hug. "OK my beautiful daughter, you get ready for bed." She smiled and put on her night gown.

I tucked her in bed and Max came in. He came over and kissed Lillie on the forehead "Sweet dreams my little one." She smiled at her Dad and I turned off the lamp. As I did I looked out the window and Mehgan was sitting on a bench by her self. I wasn't sure why.

CHAPTER 4

Saturday, Maxton wanted Mehgan to make pancakes for him. "Please Meg. I liked how you make them."

She smiled sweetly at him and said "Aren't you a charmer. And it is a good thing I like to cook." She put on her apron and began.

I poured coffee for me and Mehgan. The TV and cartoons started in the family room and I called out "Good morning Lillie" She ran in still in her night gown and no robe and hugged and kissed me. She then grabbed her brother and they returned to the family room.

Mehgan turned to me from the counter "She is a wonderful child. I know she is challenging, and if I was her mother I would be concerned as you are. But, she will show her true self. And be good hearted and honorable to her magic." She smiled and turned back to the counter and continued "And I have to say to you, Maxton is just as powerful and doesn't know it." She looked over her shoulder at me. "He is much more reserved and is unsure of himself, but the day is coming when he will show how powerful he is."

I looked at my coffee and back to her back "How do you know these things?"

She turned and smiled "I see."

I planned a picnic in the clearing behind the house. I wanted to dance for the trees but it was hard to do with so many Wizards around. I decided to hind us with a row of thick pines so that we could have privacy. We had a couple of blankets on the grass and a big area to dance and play. Meg, Maxton and Lilly ran through the field playing tag. Max was laying on one of the blanket correcting papers and looked up at me. "You always manage to work your way back to the trees." He put down his papers, stood up and put his hand out to me "My Lady, shall we?" I smiled at him and took his hand. He asked "Let me hear?"

I looked to the trees and asked "Let him hear?" He smiled at the mystical wonderful music of the trees. He and I began to dance in each others arms. I lifted us above the others and laid my head on Max's shoulder. We watched the children and Mehgan.

I heard Maxton say "What are they doing."

Lillie said "They are dancing to the music."

Maxton said "What music?"

Lillie turned her head as she asked the trees to let her brother hear. She said "let him hear."

Mehgan asked her "Could I also hear."

Lillie still was watching the perimeter of the trees and said "Let her hear." Maxton bowed politely as good Wizard should, and asked Mehgan "Would you dance with me Meg?" She smiled and began to dance with him. The next thing we knew, Maxton had lifted himself and Meg to the air matching Max and I.

I looked at Max who was already laughing. He looked at me and said "Well that he got from you." And though we enjoyed the music and the scene, no one was watching Lillie. When we descended, we all were giggling and still listening to the trees when we heard "The maiden has captured him." I looked at Max in a panic. I ran to the blanket with Max following in my rush. There Lillie sat with a rat in a cage.

Max was exasperated. "Lillie where did you get the rat?" he and I knew there was more here and that the rat was a person.

Lillie looked up at her father and said "He was spying on us through the trees. He was being nosy."

Max looked to me and walked away to do his laughing. "Lillie, remember our talk last night." She smiled and nodded. "Well part of that is to learn that you may not change a being into something else because you don't like what they do. We will ask this person what he wants. OK?" She looked at me and waved her hand and their was a boy about 12 years old. Tall and thin, with dark brown hair and hazel green eyes.

He looked as if he was about to flee when Lillie said "if you run and I will make you a toad." The boy looked to me and I smiled and patted his hand. "Hi, I am Emily. Who are you?"

Before I got the response, Max had the child up standing by his collar "Joseph! What are you up to?" I jumped up "Max! Let him loose." Max shook his head and held the child staring at him. The boy shook his head in fear of Max and Lillie. "Master, I was only watching. I meant no harm." Max was not going to let the child off the hook.

"What have you been told about intruding on others?" The boy looked over at Lillie and then to me "I wasn't listening only watching. I beg your pardon Master Marshall." Max let his collar go and soften somewhat.

I pulled the boy away from Max angry at the rough treatment Max displayed to the child. I looked to Lillie "Apologize to the young Wizard." Lillie giggled "OK. I am sorry you were spying and I changed you into a sneaky rat." Maxton started to laugh until his father looked at him sternly. He then stopped laughing and walked over to the other blanket and sat down. I looked at Lillie and was just satisfied this was not another argument for an apology.

I glared at Max and then looked to the boy "Joseph, would you like to join our picnic?" Max looked irritated "No he does not."

I angrily looked at Max "He will answer for himself Master Wizard."

Joseph looked to Max "I will be on my way than." I glared at Max with narrow eyes. How could he be this way to this child.

Max sighed at my disapproval. "Stay Joe. Have a sandwich and enjoy the day with us."

Joseph looked over to Lillie and Max smiled "Lillie will not change your form again." I thought *Huh, like you can be sure of that.*

It turned out that Joseph was a resident of the School. He lived in the dorms. He was a problem Wizard. Though Pure Blood, he was unable to conform in the foster homes. As he joined Meg, and the children in a two on two soccer game, Max explained Joe. He had been in several foster homes and none could control his behavior and his intrusions. He had strong magic that he was not able to control like Lillie.

Max said "He requires a strong hand and strong expectation. He is in the library a great deal." Max looked at me softly "Forgive me for being hard on him. I know you were mad about it."

I huffed "I would never tolerate that treatment for Maxton. I am sure that Josephs mother would not allow it either."

Max shook his head "He is a typical Wizard Child. He does not know his mother and father. We don't know his mother and father. Only that he is Pure Blood." I was angry at that.

I looked at Max "Did anyone ever think that he is alone in the worlds. That maybe why he looks and watches how others find their place? He has no foundation."

Max said "The Wizard way is his foundation."

I shook my head. I looked at Max remembering how alone he and I felt "He's lonely Max." Max snapped his head back to me and looked me in the eye. He thought deeply about it and I know he then understood. He got up and joined the game with the children and Meg. I did notice him being more personable with Joe.

On Monday, I received communication from Max. *"There has been a meeting called by the Wizard Counsel for this afternoon at 3:00 O'clock. Please be there. We need to decide things together."* I sent *"I will always come when you call."* I received a kiss on the promise scar. I then made a call to my grandmother. *"Grandmother I need you."* She then stood before me.

"Em? Is there something wrong?" I smiled at her.

"No, I have to ask for you help in planning the October Festival and Ball. I also would ask that you stay this afternoon and for dinner. I would like you to look after Lillie and give Meg a break. Would you be willing?"

Grandmother smiled "I will always be available for my little Lillie. Where is she?"

I pointed out to the garden and said "She is in lesson with Meg." I looked to my grandmother "Meg is very young and very intelligent. But she is also very sad. She is often alone."

Grandmother said "She has not found her true path yet. She misses her mother."

I nodded "Like I miss you." She hugged me then and went to the garden to see the girls. I did let Meg off for the day and told her to go see her mother.

At Three o'clock I was with Max in the Counsel Chambers. Marcus Jordan, Chris and the sentry brothers we present along with a dozen Wizards and the Counsel. I looked at Max and the rest of our group in their minds for an answer. But none had any information. Max came through "*Close to all but me.*" I nodded.

Elder Maurice said "Now it is time that we prepare. Edwin's appearance has made it clear that the oppositions moves are becoming bolder and less concerned." He looked to Max. "Master Max, you and the Princess need to know that we have no idea how he was able to enter the campus undetected." He smiled and then said "Outside of the child. However, it is inappropriate and undesirable to have the child be the only security against such intrusion." He looked to me "We cant be sure that another attempted will not be made."

Marcus asked "Is it more appropriate for my family to leave the campus in lue of the security issues. After all there are the wixard children to be concerned with."

Elder Thomas said "Master Marcus, it is the belief of this counsel that the family remain on campus. We will know that should there be an attack, are forces are greater with the purity of the children."

Elder William spoke then "We believe that the forces aligned with Leonardo and Edwin are becoming disillusioned. Their inability to reach the Princess and Young Wizard Maxton, has somewhat proven that they are undeserving." He looked to me and Max "at this table are a number of loyal and trustworthy Wizards. Both Pure and Mixed Blood. All here to make an oath to protect the campus and your family. These Wizards are guardians of us all. They will be watching at all times." I looked at Max and sent "*We cant only think of our selves. We must think of the others that will be affect by our staying. We can leave and they will be safe.*"

Max said out loud " I don't think so. Leonardo and Edwin have declared disloyalty to the Wizards Counsel and to all other Wizards following the Counsel. No one here is without threat." He looked to Elder Maurice, "We will stay and fight any threat to the children, the school and our family."

Elder Maurice then said "Stand Wizards." All of the Wizards stood, even Marcus, Max and his brothers. Then I felt the intrusion. It was Joseph under the table. He seem not to be notice by anyone else, or at least by the Wizards, until Max read my mind. Max bent down and pulled Joseph out from under the table. He had him by the arm and gave him a shake "Joe. What are you doing there?" Joseph knowing he was in big trouble said nothing but dared a look at me.

I stood and pulled the child from Max. "Leave him be."

Max shook his head "Em. He can not be allowed to get away with this one. It is serious." All of the Wizard were clamoring at the boy.

The Elders were livid. "Joseph!" Bellowed Elder Thomas. It made me quake and I was not even in trouble. "Explain your self!"

I had the child behind me "Leave him be!"

Elder Maurice said "Princess, he has violated a serious law of our kind. He must not intrude on the private Counsel Sessions. He must be punished so that he understand his crime."

My mouth dropped. "Crime?" The Wizards all looked at me like I was the one who was crazy. I tilted my head and narrowed my eyes "And what is the punishment of such a *crime*?"

Elder William had a slight smile and Elder Thomas said "Three strikes with the lash and a week in the library." I could not believe it. What did he hear that he would not be informed of anyway.

I looked at Max with the Priestess hovering "Were you hit with a lash?" He knew I was resolved and didn't answer me and closed his mind. I looked at Jordan and Chris who also closed their minds. I then looked at Marcus, he looked at me in the eye and I did not have to read his mind to know that Max and his brothers were hit with the lash. I shook my head and in voice of the priestess said "Over my dead body."

The Sentry Brothers stood next to me as we shelter Joseph from his intended fate. The Wizards looked to one another and then Joseph stood in front of me. "Thank you Princess, but I knew what would happen if I was caught. I will take my punishment." I narrowed my eyes at the Wizards "Don't touch him."

Elder William smiled at me "And what would suggest as a *just* punishment for such a child?" I looked at them and was at a loss. Merciless hit with a lash and a week in the library with no interaction or human touch was a torture not punishment. He was feral, he wasn't bad. He just needed a purpose. Then it came to me.

"Have him take the oath with the others." They all started to laugh including Max. Only William remain without laughter. I huffed and stood behind Joseph. I knew he was scared as his heart beat a thousand times a minute. The Priestess, then with the immortal feline eyes and in full armor, stood looking dangerously at the room filled with Wizards. They realized that I had not made a joke and that I was serious. They stopped laughing and looked at me in their stout and stern manner.

Max seriously said "He is not in control of himself yet. He is not ready for such an oath."

Marcus smiled at me "Princess, would Maxton be able to take such an oath at his age? The boy must grow into himself first."

The Priestess the said "What you say may be true. But this child is brave and honorable in his willingness to take responsibility. He is crafty and intelligent." I looked at Max "How old were you when you were made a Guardian Wizard, Master Wizard? I believe you were not much older than he is now." The priestess not willing to relent said "He needs a purpose and a belonging. You will help him in his quest to find his true self, or you will have another Edwin." I looked at the Elders "Let him take the oath."

The Elders looked to one another, and then Elder Maurice said "We will have a vote of the Wizards to determine if Joseph should be allow to take the oath. He looked at Joseph. "Joseph, the Princess believes in you. Do you believe that you can take the oath with truth and honor in your heart?" Joseph looked up at Max. He looked him in the eye and nodded. "Yes sir." Max looked over to me and I knew he did not approve.

Each Wizard was polled and I looked to each in the eye as they were called by name. "Master Max. Yea or Nay?" Max looked at me and said "Nay." He knew that hurt that I did not have his support. "Master Jordan, Yea or Nay?" Jordan looked to Max and then to me "Yea." and that is how it went all the way through. Half and Half until they got to William. He looked to the Wizards " I have faith in the Princess and believe that she is correct in her determination that this boy needs purpose and belonging. My vote is Yea." I knew Max was not happy with the out come. He only looked at me disappointed and then returned to his Wizard expressionless stout and stern posture.

Elder Thomas asked that all Wizards repeat after him. The Sentry Brothers and I stood back and watched and they made their vows to the Counsel.

We vow to keep our world and home safe from all that would destroy or corrupt it

We vow to protect all that dwell in the Wizard world that is loyal and devout

I watched Joseph make his vow and knew that it was heart felt. More than any other in the room. He was proud and happy. I think he then truly felt like he was apart of the Wizard world at that moment.

We Vow to follow the wizard creed and use our magic for good and just

We vow to look to all wizards as brother and attempt to always find the solution to the dispute.

We vow to defend the righteous and just.

We make this vow with pure heart and mind.

Once the vow was made all the Wizards sat. Dino, Sal and I stay back and standing as we witnessed the Wizards conference. I dropped the priestess and remained normal for the remainder of the meeting. I was pleased to see Max have Joseph sit next to him for the final outcome of the meeting.

Elder Thomas said "We all must be watchful and aware at all times. Make no mistakes, we are under attack and there will be more breaches in our security. We need to be watchful of the Princess and young Wizard Maxton. Please station your selves for the most optimal surveillance. Be open for communication from on another. We will work in shifts. I would prefer that there be a stationary position at the home of Master Max."

They decided on the schedules and positions. Each wizard having a four hour surveillance shift. I watched and listened to the plotting out of the campus and new where each position would be. The meeting ended and the Wizards disbanded.

Elder Thomas, William, Maurice and Marcus stayed seated. Elder Thomas asked "Master Max, Princess, we would like you to remain afterwards?" Max nodded to them. I looked at him, and he sent *I have no idea what more there could be. Unless they are upset with your outburst.*" I raised my chin "*I am a witch. I will not apologize.*" He only shook his head. He smiled at me then "*Why did Lillie come to mind?*" I giggled. Then Elder Thomas said to Joseph "Young Wizard. You will remain as well."

Joseph who was still standing next to Max, nodded.

As the Wizards began to leave, I stood with my sentries and waited. Max brought Wizards over to meet me. "Princess, this is Ben, He is a assistant with the school. He is intending to begin teaching soon." I smiled at him and said hello. He was tall and handsome as most Wizards. He had light brown hair and blue green eyes. He smiled brilliantly. "It is an honor Princes." I smiled. Then Max introduced me to Simon. Simon was sandy haired and blue eyed. He was Mixed Blood. I could tell because his eyes were more telling. "Simon is a fellow teacher and a friend from school." I said hello and he bowed and nodded "Princess. It is my pleasure."

Soon only the four Elders, Max, Joseph and I remained at the table. Elder Thomas said "We have an issue with the Young Witch and this Young Wizard." The Elders looked at me. "Princess, we recognized that punishment of the children is not your strong suit." I looked at them with my brows pulled together. At that moment Grandmother was there holding Lillie's hand.

Lillie looked at the counsel and at us "What?" She noticed Joe and said "Hi Joe." He nodded knowing now is not the time to open his mouth. Max looked at Lillie sternly "Be still Lillie." She looked at her dad and nodded.

Elder Thomas then said "Joseph is going to be punished for his intrusion. He will be in the library for three days. We would suggest that the Young Witch also be there for three days."

I stood up and shook my head "What is this. Joseph took the oath and I thought that would be enough. And what has Lillie done now that she should be held in the library?"

Lillie looked at her father in horror. "Daddy what did I do?" Max only told her sternly "Be still."

Elder Thomas looked at us sternly "Edwin still carries his horns and he now has a tail."

I looked at Max because I thought she reversed it by now. I looked at Lillie "Weren't you told to change him back?" She had tears and nodded. "Well did you change him back?" She shook her head. I looked back at Max as my stomach lurched. I looked back at the Elders "She will change him back but she can not be in the library. I will have her bound and in her room."

Elder Maurice said "Princess, with this child so head strong, we feel that if she sees a true punishment, she my think more before she acts. In these precarious times, it will be necessary for her to understand that everything she does affects another." I looked to Marcus her grandfather who would not look me in the eye. "Marcus" He believed it too. Mandra looked worried and surprised at something.

"She is a Witch not a Wizard. She has never been out of my sight. How can you expect me to agree with this." I looked at Max.

He looked me in the eye and said "She will be in the library as requested. We have to get a handle on her." Lillie looked at her father with panic and horror.

I was in shock, He made this decision without me. "Max! How could you."

He put his hand up to me "Em. We cant let this go on and nothing we have tried has worked. She continues to do what ever she pleased and ignores our instruction. She will be a teenager soon. I don't think we will be able to control her at all then."

He must have seen the anger in my eyes and I was bound "How dare you. Release my powers." I looked to Mandra and she too was bound by the expression on her face.

He shook his head. "Em. This time I am making the decision."

Lillie ran to my arms and cried and I seethed. "I will not have it!"

Then two robed covered Wizards appeared and one took Joseph and the other made his way to Lillie who tried with all her might to transport but had already been bound like me. The Robed Wizard took my daughters arm and they were gone. I screamed "No" I looked at Max with more hate and anger I had ever felt for him in my life.

I walked out of the counsel room and stormed out to the courtyard and started for home. I was walking across the lawn and Max was in front of me. I turned and walked the other way. He appeared in front of me.

I looked at him straight in the eye with many thoughts of pain for him "Get away from me."

He stood there stout and stern "She needs to learn Em."

I screamed at him then "This is not teaching her or any child anything, Nothing but resentment and anger." Then seethed "What did it teach you?"

He quietly said "It taught me there were consequences to my actions."

I laughed at him "You then had your little price list of what price you were willing to pay. The price to play, the price to be with me, the price to be free." I shook my head "You are no better than the Wizards that designed our lives. You have become them." I turned and started for the house.

Max stood in front of me and had my arms in his hands. Monster in full view, "Don't ever label me like them." I pulled my arms free and stood in defiance and said "Then don't act like them." I walked around him and started to walk home. "You better stay in the dorms. It will only be your family in the house. Witch and Wizard." I stormed to the house and slammed the door. I slid down the door and cried for my daughter.

Maxton ran down the stairs and stopped at my weeping. "Mom?" He walked to me knelt down, "Mom? What's wrong?" I could not even look at him. How could I tell him that his sister was taken to the Library.

But he sensed something and asked "Where's Lillie? Where's Dad?"

I couldn't even speak with the new break in my heart. I hugged my son and then regained some composure. I knew Max was listening and I transmitted *"You tell him Wizard. You tell him where his sister is."* Maxton pulled back with a red face. He had some type of communication with his father. He got up and ran back to his room.

There was a knock on the door. I opened and Mandra came in. "How dare they. Who do they thing they are."

I looked at her "As soon as Lillie is out, we are leaving this place. I will not have my children be punished this way." She hugged me and I cried more.

Of course there was no sleeping for me. I just sat in the dark and waited for Lillie's time in the Library to be up. All I could think of, and made sure that Max read that thought, was if they lay a hand on her it would be the end for all of them. I swore it before God.

CHAPTER 5

Maxton came down stairs that morning. "Mom, should I stay home from school today?" I looked at him and didn't know what to say. Did they have a Library punishment for not going to school. "Will you get in any trouble?"

He looked at me and didn't know either. Then he got red faced and said "Dad said I have to go."

I nodded and said "Better go then."

Maxton looked at me "Mom, I don't know how I will be able to study knowing that Lillie is in the Library. And you know they post on the bulletin board who is there each day." He shook his head "Why would Dad do this?" I looked at my son. And could not answer him. I kissed him and he went back up stairs to get ready.

Mehgan enter then and looked at me. "Em?" I explained to her what had happened. She sat down with her hands on her face. "I cant believe this. I would never believe that Master Max would go along with this." She looked directly at me then "Em I still have my powers. I could try to locate Lillie." I sat up. "YES. Please Meg. Find her." Then there was a knock at the door. Mandra had just got to the bottom of the stairs. She looked at me and I did not move. Maxton came down and he walked to the door. He opened it and Master Wizard Ben stood there.

He stood erect and stout as his eyes found me "Princess. Could I have a word?"

I looked at Mandra and Meg. I looked back to him and said "You are welcome to speak in the presents of my companions." I looked at my son "Maxton go on to school. Let you father know you did not have breakfast."

He smiled and said "No problem Mom." and he produced an Egg Mc Muffin. He kissed me and grandmother and left. I motioned for Ben to sit down and he did.

Meg got up "I'll make coffee." She looked at me "I will hear all that is said and unsaid." She looked at Ben insuring that he understood and left for the kitchen.

Wizard Ben began "Princess….I know that with the young witch in the library you are angry with us. I have come to ask for your patients and forgiveness."

I pulled in my brows and looked at my grandmother and then to him "Forgiveness? Patients?" He looked at me with some concern especially when I said "You all can go to hell. I will be calling on the Witches Counsel and I will have my daughter before the day is out. I demand it!"

Ben looked at me and smiled "She is very much like you. She has also threatened everyone she has encountered." He took a breath "Except of course her father who she refuses to see or speak to."

I huffed "Good girl"

Ben continued "There are two Witch sentries with her and though we have asked them to leave they say they only obey the orders of the Priestess. There is also a large angry black cat. The request is that you accompany me back to the Library and aid in getting control back. It is disrupting the other children who have been committed to the library.

I laughed at him with that. And then in the sweetest witches voice I said "No."

Meg came in with a tray of coffee for herself, Mandra and me. Not Ben. She smiled her sweetest smiled "We will demand that our Kind be returned to us and we will give the appropriate punishment under our norms and culture." I looked at her with her eloquence and authority. I loved that girl. Ben stared at her and was taken back. He looked to me and Mandra, we only smiled.

He got up and stood for a moment and then said "I will take your request back to the Counsel at once."

I looked at him eye to eye and with a sneer I said "It was a command."

Mandra then stated "We will also be unbound, for it will only be a matter of time that we will reverse the spell. We will be more apt to be "forgiving" and "patient" if that occurs as soon as possible. I believe that Elder Marcus will be able to vouch for that."

Ben looked to Mandra and said "Yes Mam." He nodded to us and walked out the door.

I started to giggle and looked at Mandra who started to laugh and all three of us were in a roar of laughter. Mandra said "I told you that any witch or wizard would have their hands full with that girl. Even her father." I nodded in tears through the laughter.

Mandra then got up "OK ladies. Let get the cleansing spell going over the house and get the protection circle going. No need to take any chances." Meg and I got up and headed to the garden and panty for the needed herbs and Candles. Grandmother prepared the alter.

As soon as the protection circle was up, I felt my powers return. I looked to Mandra. She continued her clean up from our spell work and smiled at me "I knew Marcus would understand that little threat." I understood that Marcus would give grandmother back her powers but I don't know why Max gave me mine. He knew I wanted to leave. I thought maybe he just didn't care.

We sat in the patio having coffee when I heard the door slam. I jumped and looked through the kitchen to see who came in. I put my cup down and around the wall came Lillie. I jumped up and grabbed my daughter in my arms. "Oh Lillie. Baby are you OK."

"They let me go, Mom." She said smiling "And I never did take the horns and tail off the mean Wizard like they told me too." I laughed. She turned to Mandra "Grandmother, I'm home." and she ran to Mandra.

With a big hug and kiss Mandra said "Yes you are my love. And you don't look any worse for wear. I hear that Dino and Sal were with you."

Lillie giggled. "Yep. They wouldn't let anyone near me. So when I left I had them stay with Joe. He needed a friend so Prince stayed with him too. They were mean to him but now they wont be." I looked at Mandra wondering if that was a good Idea. Then decided I didn't care.

Lillie ran to Mehgan and leaped into her arms. "Master Meg, you should see that place. It is in a castle and it has all these little rooms with bars on them. All the rooms have a desk and a bed. You sit in these rooms and all you can do is read and do what they tell you. Like sleep or eat or read or be quiet. And they don't answer questions either. One Wizard was standing staring at me. I was singing the hymns that we sing with gramps. I told him to go away and he told me no that I had to stop singing. I told him that I was going to sing and he couldn't stop me. He sent a spell and Sal swung his sword and the spell was sent away. So then the wizard told me I would have to stay longer if I kept singing." She giggled "So I told him, If I stayed longer because of him, I would make sure that he had boils for the same length of time." Meg started to laugh with her.

I tried again "Lillie, remember not to use magic for bad purposes."

Lillie looked at me with a smiled "Thinking about doing something and doing something are not the same thing, Mom." I was taken back. That is a thinking pattern like Max.

I grabbed my girl in a hug and said "Go upstairs and shower. Put on clean clothes and come down as fast as you can. OK?" She smiled and ran up the stairs.

I looked at my grandmother, "I think we need to leave. I don't believe that this will be the only culture issue that comes up. I cant take those chances with my children."

Grandmother looked at me seriously "You will be leaving Max."

I really hadn't thought that Max would not be coming with us. "Well that will be his decision. I have to be a mother first."

Mandra said "Yes you do. And think of the protection that the Wizards are providing those children at this time. We wont have the same assurances if you leave." Mandra then said "And what of Maxton. He needs his instruction. I doubt that any Witch Master understands the Wizards learning styles."

I reminded her "Edith taught Max potions and Alchemy."

Mandra put up her hand "Only once in a while and they were the Witches way. Not Wizard."

Mandra moved closer to the table and looked at me. "Give it a few days. Stay home and don't address any of the Wizards. Meg, me and the sentry brothers will stay." Her eyes had a little florescent green flash "Let see how they handle that." Then she giggled "Besides, you are still

the Princess. Their Royal Highness. They are to follow your command."
She and Meg laughed.

Meg looked at us, "We also have to plan the October Harvest
Celebration. I believe we need to start the shopping list and *guest*list."
We all giggled with the thought of several well armed Witch warriors
at the ball. So I felt a little better. At least, I had my kind with me. For
Maxton, I would try to stay. But would never allow a situation like this
again. Besides, what did they care if Edwin had a tail.

That afternoon, Maxton came in with a black eye and his clothing
dirty and ripped. He looked at Lillie, went to her and hugged her. She
looked at her brother "Maxy? What happen?" I walked over to my son
and he looked at me, "No one says anything about my sister. I will go to
the Library for the rest of my life before that happens." He then ran to
his room. Lillie looked at me sadly. Maxton was not sent to the Library
for fighting. He was seen as to be with honor for defending his sister.
Funny that only Lil could see Edwin who got past their security and
was still sent to the Library.

CHAPTER 6

Days past and we all stayed close to the house. Never venturing further than the garden and the yards. Through the windows I could see the Guardian Wizards watching the house as ordered by the counsel. I sent a request to the Wizard Counsel that Joe be sent to me as a foster child. I assured his behavior and school attendance. He arrived a short time later.

Maxton went to school each day and continued to defend his sister. He had more than a few scuffles. Each afternoon he played with his sister after he finish with homework that no one could help him with. That hurt a little. He needed his dad. But I refuse to relent. I knew that my daughter was a handful. But that did not mean I would allow her to be mistreated. And obviously, she wont allow it either. I had a real issue with my self. Stay for my son; stay for Joe or leave for my daughter. No where in the mix did Max or I become the issue. It didn't mean I didn't miss him. It just meant that my children had to be thought of first.

On a beautiful Saturday afternoon, we were all playing in the field with the grove of trees as a cover. Dressed in simple cotton dresses for the dance to the music of the trees. Maxton and Joe, of course, were dressed in proper Wizard pants shirt and jacket. But they still danced and played ball. We made flowered wreaths for our heads and reveled in a day of sunshine and Mother earth. The children ran from one end to the other. Laughing and screeching. Meg and I sat on the blanket and watched the kids and grandmother kick the ball.

The trees then said "He is here Princess." I looked towards the house and Max stood there with Marcus and Ben. I watched them but never moved. I looked over to Meg and she looked at me cautiously. "Em we need to listen and not react. We need to be closed." I closed my mind, but knew Max could get through if he chose. We watched and the proper Mastered Wizards walked towards us. Lillie spotting her Dad, grabbed her grandmothers hand and stayed still in the middle of the field. Prince immediately appeared and stood with Lillie. Maxton ran to his Dad and greeted him with a hug and he and Joe walked with him towards us. Max looked at Lillie who only watched as her father walked to me. Meg stood up and prepared for confrontation if necessary and I joined her. Grandmother watched with interest while she held Lillie close. We hadn't spoken to Wizards in two weeks. Of course, Maxton and Joe didn't count.

As they approached, Marcus nodded to Mandra who returned his nod. Max turned from Lillie's cautious glare and looked to me but was met with a blank expression and closed mind. He stood very prim and proper and I tilted my head. He said "I would like to speak to you." I strengthen my head and asked "If it is about Lillie, I don't want to." I watched as Marcus walked to Mandra. As Marcus approached her, Lillie and Prince ran for the house. Mandra and Marcus watched the child's escape with concern. I found that Max was watching Lillie too. He turned back to me and said "Could you help me with her. I have tried to apologize to her and she blocks me." I looked at him blankly and didn't answer. *He did it. He needs to fix it.* He took my arm and we walked away from the others at the blanket. "Em...I ... We...live here. We have to at least try to get along." I still did not say a word.

He stopped and faced me. "There are reports that Edwin and the others are close and breaking through the protection barrier. I would feel better knowing that I can communicate with you and with Lillie. Please try to understand that I only wanted do what is best for her."

I looked at him and he knew that was not what he should have said. He put up his hand and said "Ok. I made a bad decision. Maybe I was hoping it would help with her controlling her anger." He huffed "I think you were right. It made it worse." He looked toward the house

"I don't know when she will forgive me." Then he asked "And you? Are you ever going to forgive me?"

I touched the promise and he looked down at his hand. "You promised that you would not give our baby to the Wizards or the Witches. I took that promise to mean our children. Both Maxton and Lillie. You broke your promise."

He looked at me and shook his head "No Em. I did not give her to them. I punished her. Maybe it was the wrong punishment, but I did not give her to anyone." He looked down "Having her avoid me and not talking to me is breaking my heart more than anything. I really adore that kid." He looked back at me and said "If you want me punished… Well you and Lillie are doing a good job of it."

I looked at him and said "We need time to understand what has happen to us in this situation. I feel tricked as usual when it comes to the Wizards. But Lillie…, Lillie has learned something I have never learned and probably never will because of you." I looked deep in his eyes "Never trust a Wizard."

He glared at me then. "How can you say that to me. I would die for you and her. I may have tricked you in the past Em, but since the kids, I have never given you reason not to trust me."

I nodded and said "Until recently. And you are not the only Wizard."

He looked angry now, his monster hovered close and he said "I think I should leave now. Please tell Lillie that I love her and that I am sorry." I nodded. He started to walk away, then stopped and looked back at me. He turned around and grabbed me in his arms and kissed me. Very passionately and I responded as usual.

He kissed my cheek and held me and I said "I hate you, Max."

He kissed me again and then said "Its that thin line." He turned and walked away. I looked up to the house and Lillie watched her father leave. Ben jogging to catch up with him.

So we went on this way through July and August. No witch ventured beyond the house yards and gardens. Maxton and Joe attended school as scheduled and Max stayed living in the Dorms. Lillie stayed clear of her father and would not speak of him. Or any of the Wizards. I tried several times to talk with her and explain her father but she refused to listen to me and would run off. I never believed that Lillie would hold such a grudge.

True to form, my dreams began. I was dancing in the field with Lillie. She and I jumped and dipped and twirled. Then Lillie Twirled and she didn't stop but sped up and moved beyond the field. I chased after her screaming her name. When I found her she was unconscious in the arms of horned and tailed Edwin. I screamed and dropped to my knees. I screamed for Max and as normal for me, he was there waking me up. "Wake up Princess. I am here." I held on to Max without opening my eyes. "He had Lillie." Max petted my hair and said "Never will happen, my love." I then said "I didn't know if you would still come." And he recited his vow to me.

Wizard Princess Wake or slumber,

my vow to you I live here under.

Twirl and leap my happy dancer

Wake or sleep, your call I answer,

Till the worlds and life are done,

Be assured, I will come.

I slept after that. Alone, but I slept.

October was approaching and Meg, Mandra and I were busy planning the October Harvest Festival. They had already ordered and received the orange and beige table cloths and napkins for the ball. They had every pumpkin, gourd and Indian corn cob that God has created. We sat stringing dried leaves and holly. The food all arranged and in massive amounts for the ball. The Elders, in writing only, assured that the bond fire would be massive. And that the Festival would include games and venders. I remembered how I was treated at the Shamians Ritual and was dreading it.

We sat in the kitchen chatting and stringing the dried leaves. There was a knock on the door. Lilly got up to get it and then stopped and said, "Mom can you get it?" I nodded knowing that she was being cautious. I walked to the door and there was Joseph.

"Hi Joseph." He looked stern and proper but smiled at my greeting.

"Hello Princess. I have a note for you." He held up the note with a lily. I took both and smiled. Joseph then said "Bye now, and tell Lillie hello for me OK?" I smiled back and nodded. I thought it was strange that Lillie did not want to even say hello to Joseph.

I opened the note and in Calligraphy style writing it said

My Princess,
The time has come for the Harvest Ball. I am formally requesting that you allow me to be your escort to the Ball and festival. I recognize that I am a lowly scoundrel and unworthy, but would be most honored with you on my arm.
I will await your answer every minute until it arrives.
My heart has always been with you
Your Wizard Husband

I giggled and felt such softness for Max then. He could be so charming when he wanted. And such an Ass when he wanted. And then there was Lillie. I had no Idea if she would go to the Ball and the festival with us. I looked at her and she was staring at me.

"What is it Lil?"

She left the working table and came over to the kitchen with me. "Mom. I don't want to be with the Wizards. I don't want to go to the Ball or the festival. If I do something wrong, they will try to hurt me."

I petted her face "No Lillie. No one will hurt you as long as I am around. No one will ever hurt you as long as your Dad is around."

She looked at me "Dad will hurt me too. Dad is a Wizard."

I tilted my head to her "Lillie, will you ever forgive your Dad? He has been punished too."

She looked at me and couldn't answer. She looked off and said "I don't know. I am afraid of my Dad." I was so surprised at that. She has never been afraid of her Dad. Or anyone else for that matter.

"Lillie? Why?"

She looked at me in the eye "He is a Wizard. Wizards hate Witches. They hate us."

I shook my head "No Lillie. You Dad loves you. He could never hate you."

She got a little teary, and yelled at me "Mom, I hate the Wizards. I hate that they want to make us do. I hate them because they want to hurt us. I hate them because they want to hurt me." I shook my head and my heart began to beat hard. "No Lillie. Your Dad and Grandfather would never hurt you."

She shook her head and in full tears "They are Wizards and Wizards hate me."

Max was there at that point, I am sure due to my heart pounding so. Lillie took one look at him and darted for the stairs.

I looked at Max and he shook his head and said "This has gone on long enough."

He started for the stairs and I jumped in front of him "No Max. She's afraid."

He shook his head "I need to talk to her. So she knows I wont hurt her?"

I shook my head "No. I will talk to her."

As Max and looked to each other Lillie gave out a blood curtailing scream. Max was gone transporting immediately to his daughter. I was close behind as were Mandra and Meg. Lillie was in the corner with her knees up and her head down on her knees. And in the bed, was Zee. My Zee. His throat cut. On the sheets, with the blood of Zee, there was a drawing of a wizard with horns and a tail. I screamed and dropped to my knees and cried for my companion. My Zee. My friend for all of my life. And through my devastation, I looked to Lillie. I jumped and ram to Lillie and gathered her into my arms and we cried together. Lillie through her sobs said "See Mom. The Wizards are going to hurt us. They hurt Zee."

Soon the room was filled with Wizards. Marcus, Maurice Thomas and William stood looking at the dead cat in the little witches bed. Soon other guardian wizards filled the room. Lillie looked up and went white at the Wizards in her room. She looked at me and I said "Lets go to my room. OK?" She nodded and we transported to my room.

Lillie and I stayed in bed crying together never having to say a word. I held my daughter and petted her hair and remembered my familiar. My Zee. Max was soon there and sat on the bed. Lillie jumped up and was about to transport.

Max grabbed her arm and he look so broken hearted and so desperate. "Please Lillie. Please don't leave." Lillie shook her head and was breathing heavily and cried. She stood up on the bed with Max never let go of her arm. She pulled as she cried. She was terrified. "Let me go. Let me go."

I jumped in to action and tried to get Lillie out of his grasp but Max sent his magic and I was held back in the bed. That sent Lillie over the edge. She looked at me and then her Dad and screamed "Let my mom go! Let her go!" She started to hit her fathers hand so he would let her loose. She was actually thinking of how to get me loose when Max had her held down with his magic. She screamed and fought the binding that held her down. Max looked at Lillie and quietly asked her "Why do you think I would hurt you?"

Lillie snarled through her tears at Max "Because you are."

Max shook his head "No. I only want to talk to you."

I yelled at Max "This is not the way to do this. Stop traumatizing her."

Max never acknowledge my words. He only looked at Lillie fight her bindings. "Lil, don't be mad at me anymore. I will never let you be in the Library again." Lillie only looked at her father with determination to release herself. "Lillie, are you going to talk to me?"

Lillie, through her fear, sneered like a cat at her father "You want to hurt me. You and all of the Wizards." Her heavy breathing and total fear was clear that the child knew something but was closed to everyone. At that point Max looked at me with concern.

He looked back at Lillie and quietly said "No Lillie, I would die for you."

Lillie wasn't buying it. As she continued to wildly fight the bindings she screamed at her Dad through her tears. "I see you in my dreams. You are the big black cat with yellow eyes. In my dreams you try to bite me and hurt me. The angel tells me you and the Wizards are going to hurt me and my mom. He tells me about your lies and what you will do to us." Max looked more concerned and looked directly in my eyes with fear.

I looked over at Lillie "You see an angel Baby?

She stopped fighting and looked at me "I hear him all the time Mom. He said he was sent to watch me. He said that he would protect me from the Wizards."

My heart was pounding again. "Lillie, what does he tell you?"

Lillie looked at her Dad with narrow eyes. Continuing her anger she said "He said that Dad would be the cat and rip my arms off. He would bite me and make me dead. He said that the Wizards would take your Magic and make you dead. They want to take Maxy and make him help."

Max shook his head and softly said "No Lillie. No. I wouldn't hurt you or your mom for anything. No Wizard here would hurt you."

Lillie was convinced that he would and said "He said you would say that. He said you are a good liar." She went back to trying to get out of her bindings.

I asked Lillie "Baby, what does the angel look like?"

She looked over at me continuing her attempts to release herself and said "I don't know. He is a voice that talks to me. He has a funny accent and sings songs to me."

Max asked her "Does he have a name?"

Lillie looked at her father skeptically "He told me not to tell."

I said to her "Lillie, we cant fix things if you don't tell us what has been going on with you and the angel." She looked at me, no longer crying, but still angry and frightened. Max let me go and I pulled her into my arms and kissed her head. "Don't you know how much you are loved by me and Dad?"

She looked at her Dad "You love me Mom. Dad lies."

Then Max touched his promise scar and I looked up into his eyes. I nodded and he looked back at Lillie. "Lillie, I have a story for you." He held up his left hand and pulled mine up and showed Lillie the promise scars. She looked at the identical scars and looked back at her Dad. " Before you and Maxy were born, your Mom and I went on an adventure. We went to see the Witches high Counsel and they were like you. They were afraid of me and my kind. But I loved your Mom and they could see that. So, there was a spell sent and prayer to God and Mother Earth. We have these scars as a Promise to each other, to the Witches and to the Wizards. The scars reminds us of that." He looked at me "It means that we are strongest together. It also means that what happens to one, happens to the other." He looked back at Lillie "So you see, if I harmed you or your Mom, I harm me and my kind." He petted her cheek "I would die before I would hurt you because I love you. You are my little girl."

Lillie looked to me and I nodded. "Its true. What happens to one happens to the other." I showed her my scar on my side and she reached out and pulled her fathers shirt up and saw the faint scar.

Lillie looked closely at her father and asked "You wont hurt us?" Max shook his head. Realizing that she was no longer bound, out of reaction, she jumped into the arms of Max. He looked like he was in heaven. He revealed in the embrace of his daughter. Lillie had new tears "I'm sorry Dad. I love you and it hurt so bad to think you would hurt me. But I was so afraid."

Max kissed her cheek and said "Don't believe it Lil. Don't believe that I could hurt you or don't love you. I think of you all the time. I have missed you so much."

Lillie pulled away from her father and looked him in the eye "His name is Leo." Max snapped his head towards me and looked deep in my eyes *"How do we keep him out. He is transmitting not appearing."* He held his daughter and petted her hair. I returned *"Max. I don't know we need Mandra and Marcus in this."*

He nodded. Then to test Lillie tolerance to others he asked her "Lil, we need to meet with your grandparents. Can you do that?"

Lillie pulled back and looked at her father "Will Grandfather hurt me?"

Max smiled and shook his head "Grandfather would never hurt you."

She looked back at me and then to her Dad "Will you be with me?" Max melted and nodded "Forever, my little love. Forever."

Lillie was watched all day by Meg. That evening we had Marcus come to the house. Lillie watched him cautiously. Joe and Maxton tried to engage with Lillie and keep her occupied but Lillie stay very close to her Master. She looked to me several times for assurance and I smiled at her with a nod. It killed my soul to see her so frightened. Frighten of Max and her Grandfather. Frighten of Joe and Maxton as they tried to get her to join them in a board game. Max watched her as much as I did. She did make amends with him but she still was watching him with caution and fear. I knew his heart broke with that. I knew in my heart he loved his daughter.

Max and I sat with Marcus and Mandra at the kitchen table. Marcus looked at me with sorrow in his eyes. "I am so grieved that my granddaughter has been affected and tainted by Leonardo. We will do what we can to end the communication." Mandra said "I believe that the coven is needed for this spell." She looked to me and Max "Maybe we should see the Witches Counsel for the spell." Max looked at me and then looked back at Lillie. He turned to his father "Would it be appropriate for there to be a joint counsel meeting and go from there?" Marcus looked at me and then Max "Yes. But what do we do until that meeting. There is still a communication going on with her and Leonardo.

Mehgan stood at that table then with Lillie behind her holding on for dear life. "I will bind her communication. But it is for all not only the demon Wizards. It would be until the counsels meet."

I looked at Max and he shook his head "What if she need us. She would not be able to call out."

Mandra said "We could have someone with her at all times Max. She would never be alone. But the communication with Leonardo must stop."

Max looked at me and I nodded. He nodded to Mehgan and she pulled Lillie from behind her. Meg bent down and looked into her eyes. Lillie looked over to me and Meg shook her so she would look into her eyes. Meg then said

I bind the mind to save her soul
I bind the mind to be dark as coal
Nothing they will find
the intruders to her mind
All communication must cease
To this child bring peace
Bless it be

Mandra and I also repeated Bless it be. Max put his hand out to Lillie "My lady?" She looked cautiously at the hand and thought about it for a second and then put her hand in his. He pulled her into a hug and she hugged him back. He let go "Can you try to believe that no one is going to hurt you?" She looked at him but didn't answer. How could she . She was only nine. She didn't know what was happening in her world. Lillie, who was always so sure of herself. Lillie who had the heart of a lion, and strength beyond all others, stood in fear.

Marcus looked to his granddaughter "Lillianna, I do love you child. I am now, and always, at your call." She actually gave him a slight smile.

Maxton came over to the table and asked Lillie "Are you even afraid of me?"

She looked at her brother, "I am…..a little afraid of all Wizards."

He looked at me and I knew he was hurt. He looked his sister in the eye and said. "Well Lil, I am still your brother. Wizard or not. Weather you like it or not." He walked back to the living room and left Joseph looking on to the group at the Table. Joe looked at Lillie and he was thinking and she was looking into his eyes. He bowed to her and smiled and went back to the living room with Maxton.

Meg stayed in Lillie's room that night. And when the house was quiet, I conjured a beautiful carved oak box lined in red velvet and satin. I laid my dear friend Zee in it. Tears running from my eyes as I gave a last pet to his coat. "Good bye my love. You were so true and so loved." I closed the box. I laid over the box and sobbed for my cat. I felt Max and he petted my hair. "He was my friend before you. He always loved me." Max pulled me into a hug. I left his embrace and took the box to the Jasmine tree where I conjured a hole. I stood there unable to put the box in the hole. How do I bury him. He was a part of me. Max took the box and laid it in the hole and then waved his hand and the hole was covered. I continued to sob. Then he waved his hand again and there was a stone that read "Loyal and beloved Zee." I hugged him then. He said "Even though he hated me, I knew he loved you just as much as I do." I nodded.

Then Max had conjured a swing for us and I sat with him. He had his arm around me and I just looked off into space. I mourned for my friend Zee. I said "You know he protected Maxton too. He never left his side since he has been born." Max said "I know. It was kind of strange how he hated all Wizards but love Maxton." Max giggled and huffed "When I think of Zee, I remember that day at your grandmothers when you gave him Tuna at the table." He laughed then "Edwin was so mad." I giggled then too. "He was." I sat with Max there for a long time and must have fallen asleep. I woke up in my bed in Pjs and alone.

Maxton and Joe were off to school and Lillie in the garden with Meg, Mandra and I stood at the doors to the garden and drank our coffee. Then I felt it. I looked to Mandra who looked at me with the same feeling. Meg stood up and grabbed Lillie and ran to the house. She looked at me "Wizards are approaching. The Demon Wizards." In voice I screamed for Max and Marcus. Grandmother called the Sentry Brothers.

I looked to Meg as Max and Marcus appeared. "Take Lillie. I don't care where just as long as she is safe." Max reached for his daughter who backed away from him. He then only brushed her cheek with his fingers and gave her a warm smiled. She and Meg were then gone. Jordan and Chris appeared then. Then Simon and Ben. I looked at Max "Where is Maxton." He looked at me and I transported my son to my side not needing to wait for his answer.

"Mom what are you doing?"

I looked at my son and grabbed him in a hug. I looked at Sal "Take him Sal." Nathan appeared and looked confused. I looked at Sal "Take him to safety."

Max hugged his son and looked to Sal and nodded. Sal grabbed Maxton by the arm and they were gone. Nathan looked to Max and Max said "We need you here."

We looked out to the garden and there stood Edwin, Horns and tail intact. He had two dozed Wizards with him. I instinctively was the Priestess as was Mandra. The immortal cat eyes surveying the battle ground. Max had his monster on full force. Max's colleges who had never seen the Monster stepped back away from him. I stepped forward as several dozen Witch Warriors flanked Edwin and his group. Dino at my side. I swung my golden sward as did the other Witches prepared for battle.

Max came forward "Edwin, come to end this."

Edwin stood with his army and said "We will have what is needed to preserve our race. We will have the Princess and the young wizard."

Elder Thomas and William appeared "Edwin, you intrude where you are not wanted. You use your magic for evils end."

Edwin sneered at Thomas and William "You sold out our race to the Witches. Lowering our kind to nothing more than undisciplined animals."

With a laugh the Priestess said "And you Edwin. You look more like and act more like an animal than any here."

Edwin said "You have not taught the little witch Princess. She is as disrespectful and undisciplined as you are. But we are pleased that the Young Wizard is being trained appropriately"

Max the Monster then asked "Where is the coward Leonardo. He and I need to have a conversation."

Edwin looked at Max and smiled mockingly "Brilliant infuriation wasn't it Max. My Idea. The little witch was so gullible. It was easy to twist her mind and have her hate all Wizards. To have her hate.. *you*."

With that Max leaped at Edwin and the battle began. Edwin, true to form, disappeared as the coward he has always been. Witch on Wizard and Wizard on Wizard. Flashes of glowing swards hitting each other and dead and dying covered the ground. I stood in battle with Wizards and killing them without thought. Blood covered my body as I continued to defect magic and magical weapons. My only thought were for my children. These Wizards were the threat to my children. And I killed them for it. I found my self back to back with Max battling the defecting demon Wizards. Then as quickly as they had come they were gone. Only leaving their injured and dead.

Breathing heavy and covered in my victims blood, I looked back at the monster Max "One day, you and I will use that weapon of ours. And their will be no fighting or death." He looked at me confused. I was too, but I knew we could do it if we could find a thought that could work. I dropped the priestess at that time.

Dino approached us. I looked to Dino "Our injured and dead?"

He looked at me and then to Max "Five dead. Seven injured."

Then I asked him "Their dead and injured?"

Dino reported "They have nine dead and there are four injured." I asked

"The children at the school. Are they safe."

Dino nodded, "They were surrounded by both Guardian Wizard and Witch Warriors. They are well." He looked back at Max. " Master

Wizard……Master Chris is among the dead. Elder Marcus and Master Jordan with the injured."

Max roared the in the monster panther and drove his sward into the ground, still grasping the handle and knelt against it.

I looked at Dino "Mandra?"

He said "She is with Elder Marcus. She is well."

I knelt down with Max. His monster yellow eyes staring blankly. As we knelt there Meg and Lillie appeared. Max looked at Lillie, But when Lillie saw her father as the monster panther she panicked and ran. At that, the big cat look over to me and shed a tear.

Chapter 7

We all stood with Jenny at the lake side for our farewell to Chris. As the pallet was pushed off and Guardian Wizards lit the pallet with their torches. Fireworks were lit and we stood and watched until the pallet sink in to the lake and extinguishing the flames. It was so Arthurian like. And though Maxton and Lillie stood with me and Max, Lillie was careful to be on my left side away from her father. We all walked to give are heart felt condolences to Jenny. She looked at Max "He always saw you as a true brother." Max hugged her.

Jordan was recovering from his injured arms and leg. Mary aiding him and watching his recovery with a trained eye. The other Wizards injured were also kept in the Infirmary. Even the Pure Bloods that waged war on us. Marcus remained in guarded condition with a stab wound to his middle. Though I believed the Wizard Doctors were able to handle it, I had such an urge to being Doc in. I would go see him every day breaking the rule of staying away from the campus. Mandra never left his side. I sat with Mandra and watched as my true guardian sleep. She stroked his cheek and look to him in a worried way. I asked "Marcus is your true love, isn't he?"

She looked over at me and smiled "My truest Love."

I often wondered why she and he were never married. "Why did you not marry. Why did you not marry him instead of my grandfather?"

She looked up and took my hand. "If we could have married, we would have. But in those days, Witch and Wizard were sworn enemies. We met in the normal world. He was young then as was I. We knew each others nature and knew our relationship was doomed before it happened. So we stopped seeing each other. It was several years later that I met and married your grandfather." She patted my hand "Make no mistake. I loved that man and built a life with him. But on my wedding day, Marcus came to me. He told me that he loved me beyond this life. And he would wait for me and a time when we could love each other freely. When your grandfather died, I mourned him like a wife. He was the father of my children. I was devoted to him. After all, I could not have a life with Marcus. But… I never stopped loving Marcus. I would have dreams of him and knew he was there. So once I was a widow, he began to show up more. He was an Elder then." She paused and gave a little laugh. "He brought me the news that you had been chosen the Wizard Princess. I was so mad. I knew that the Wizards would try control your heart; and your freedom. Marcus and I had a serious falling out then. I don't think I spoke to him in two years. But my heart and soul has always been with him. I could never be away from him long. He and I have been together since. And the man can still make me weak in the knees when he chooses." She and giggled.

Marcus open his eyes and said "I practice." We started to laugh and he held his belly where he had been stabbed. He then said "How is Jordan?"

I smiled and said "Fine. Mary is with him and he goes home tomorrow."

He looked at seriously "And Max?"

I said "He is sad over Chris. Over Lillie. Lillie saw his Monster and she has hidden away from him since."

Marcus nodded "He will have to be consistent with her. And Patient." I nodded.

I walked from the infirmary and started up the walk way that would lead to the house. I thought of Max. I knew he was my true love. Always has been. I looked to the dorms where he remained living. Wishing for a time of peace for us. Wishing he would come home soon. But I had to think of Lillie too. I had to think of her well being and feeling safety and security in her home. I shook my head and thought about how happy my little family was until Edwin and Leonardo started in again. I really hated them.

I looked to the Wizards milling about and watching me, *The Witch and Princess,* as they headed off to class. None really understanding or trusting. All fully aware of the Priestess in battle. I no longer would be looked at as only the Mastered Wizards Witch Wife. But the Priestess. The Priestess that killed Wizards.

"So I am your true love?" Max was walking next to me.

I giggled and said "Stay out of my head. And Of course you are." He continued to walk with me down the path in his purple robes. "Don't you have a class?"

Max Smiled at me and said "We'll let Ben handle that for me." He grabbed me in a big hug twirled around and we were sitting in beach chairs on the beach in Santa Monica. I was dressed again in a bathing suit from hell with long sleeves and legs. I snapped my fingers and was again in the suit that I wore for the water slides.

He said "You know I don't like that suit."

I only rolled my eyes and asked "So what is this about?"

He put on his charming smile "I haven't received and answer to my invitation to be the Princess's escort for the ball. I thought if I could get you away I might get my answer."

I smiled and said "Well, I have had so many invitations to be my escort, I don't know who to chose."

Max looked angry and said "Who else has asked you?"

I started to laugh "No one else would dare. Of course I am going with you."

He smiled then and held my hand as I closed my eyes and listen to the music of the sea. We stayed the afternoon and it was peaceful for us both. As we were leaving, I blew my kiss to the sea and said "Thank you." and we were back home. Max walked me to the house and looked up. He was thinking of Lillie. He pulled me into his arms and kissed me. I really missed kissing Max. And then said "Tell Lillie I love her and miss her OK?" I nodded and he disappeared.

I walked in the house and Lillie stood with her hands on her hips. "You were with Dad."

I looked at her confused "Yes I was. He told me to tell you that he loves you and misses you."

Lillie shook her head and said "Mom. He is a monster."

I smiled at her and took her hand. I sat on the couch and said "Sometimes he is a monster. Sometimes so am I. We have our true selves. And you will have your true self one day. It is only when we are defending what we love. It is only when we defend you and Maxton."

"But mom. I saw him as the big cat. I saw his eyes. That's when he is going to hurt me?" I looked at her, "Lillie, who told you that?"

She looked at me "Mom I told you. The angel."

"Lillie, the angel is not an angel. The angel is a mean Wizard like Edwin." She looked at me confused. "But he told me…" I interrupted her "Lillie we know who Leonardo or Leo is. He tried to take Maxton from us before. He tried to have your Dad imprisoned or killed. He is the one who sends Edwin to do things to us." I looked in her eyes "And when you saw your Dad the Monster, he had just been in a battle to protect us from the bad Wizards." I hugged her "Just think about things you know Lillie. Think hard about those who love you and who you love. You will find your answers."

The Ball was a few days away. I had not decided on a dress yet and was unsure if Lillie would consider going. I looked in the mirror and thought a moment. Then I wore a beautiful white gown that flowed with every movement. It had a round neck line and a low hanging back. The accents were in gold as well at the sash. I conjured simple gold heals to match. I had my hair up and had gold glitter through it. My make up was perfect and I added gold glitter to the sides of my eyes for the effect of a feline.

As I looked to make sure this was the look I wanted, Lillie came in "Oh Momma. You look so pretty."

I thought then and waved my hand and Lillie had a similar little girl dress and glider through her hair. She wore gold slippers. She looked in the mirror and I said "You are beautiful." I smiled at my princess as she admired herself in the mirror. "Shame that the Wizards wont see how beautiful we witches can be."

She looked at me "Why?"

I smiled "Well since we won't be going to the ball."

She looked at me sadly "I want to go to a Ball but just not with so many wizards."

I said "Well, I was asked to go. I do so love to dance. But I can't leave you here all alone."

She looked at me "Dad asked you. I know."

I looked at her and said "How do you know it was Dad?"

She giggled "Cus he would turn into the monster and kill anyone else that tried to take you."

I laughed. I twirled her in the dress so she saw how it moved so gracefully. She looked into the mirror and had a wishful look. I petted her cheek and said "How about this. Dino and Sal can take you and be your escorts."

She watched the dress and she smiled "OK."

I hugged her "Now those Wizards will see true beauty when my daughter walks in to the room." She giggled.

CHAPTER 8

The big night came and Mandra was dressed in a flowing black gown with rhinestones scattered through. Her hair up and a diamond necklace complemented her look. "Grandmother, you look so beautiful."

She smiled "Well I doubt I will get much dancing in with Marcus still recovering, but who knows." She looked at me and Lillie in our semi matching dresses and look and smiled. "Well, it is clear that the Princess and her daughter will not be missed. You are both beautiful." Lillie smiled and twirled for her grandmother.

Just then Maxton and Joe came running down the stairs in their tux's. My little boy, now eleven, was growing up. He stopped in his tracts at the sight of the women he lived with and said "Wow, I bet the Wizard women are going to want beauty tips." Joe stood by and then said "WOW."

I started to laugh as they headed to the door. "Maxton. Aren't you going with us?"

He stopped with his hand on the door and turned and said "Mom, we need to go with the other Wizard guys or we'll be made fun of." He came back and gave me a kiss "Save me a dance." He twirled his sister to her delight and he and Joe left. I looked to Mandra and she smiled.

I said "Well he has that Marshall Charm doesn't he?" She nodded in agreement.

Then she looked to Lillie "Little one. Should you need me, you only have to call me and I will be there. OK?" Lillie nodded with a smiled at her grandmother.

Meg came down the stairs in a beautiful blue dress that swept the floor as she walked. It had thin straps and a square neck line. Her hair up and sapphire earrings finished the look. Lillie looked to her Master and said "Oh Meg, you are beautiful." Mehgan gave a beautiful smile. "Thank you, Lillie."

There was a knock on the door and Lillie looked at me a little panicked. I started to go to the door when out of the kitchen came Lincon.

I smiled "Lincon."

He nodded "Ms Em. You are still a lovely as ever." I kissed his cheek and as with all other times he turned red. Lillie said hello and he bowed to her "Ms. Lillie. I am at your service." She smiled and looked at me with a smiled. When Lincon open the door, Mastered Wizard Ben Stood staring at us or should I say Meg. Lillie grabbed my hand and I patted it reassuringly.

Ben continued to stand there staring until Mandra said "Yes Master Wizard, how can we help you."

He smiled and said "I am Ms. Mehgan's escort."

I looked to Meg and she walked to the door where Ben put out his arm. Meg looked back at me and Lillie and smiled. Lincon then shut the door.

I looked at grandmother "Did you see how he looked at her?" Grandmother nodded.

Lillie said suspiciously "How did he look at her."

Grandmother said "He looked at how beautiful she is."

Lillie said "Oh"

Then the Sentry Brother appeared. Both in brown tuxes with orange bow ties. Their tuxes had a bit a witch to them. The lapels were sharp and their hair a little spiky. They bowed simultaneously and Sal said "We have come to escort Ms. Lillie to the Ball." Lillie giggled at their performance and they both bent to hold their arms out to her. She took both arms and they were gone.

Marcus appeared next to Mandra. He looked pale and thinner but he had a smiled on his face. He slightly bowed to me and looked to Mandra. He put out his arm and said "My lady, my I have the honor." Mandra lit up and they were gone.

Then the knock came to the Door. Lincon opened the door to Max. He looked very handsome in his tux which boasted a purple sash. Lincon said "Master Max it is good to see you again."

Max smiled at Lincon and shook his hand. "Lincon. It is good to see you as well."

Then Max looked to me and smiled. "My Lady, you are…. lovely." He walked to me and took my hand and kissed it. " My Princess." He looked at me in the eyes and like the day when we married, he had true love there. My stomach felt butterflies and he put out his arm. I took his arm and we were gone.

We waited on the open balcony for each couple to be announced. I could see that Maxton was with a group of boys already in the ball room. I then heard the Harold "Elder Marcus Marshall and Lady Mandra." I watched as they descended the steps slowly for the sake of Marcus. Then we saw Lillie and the Sentry Brothers. I looked at Max but he had his eye on Lillie. "Witch Sentry Sal, Witch Sentry Dino and Lady Lillianna." Lillie looked beautiful walking down the stairs. She was scared but she walked more noble and royal then I ever could. Her head was high and her body straight and graceful. Both of her white gloved hands rest on each arm of the Sentry Brothers. She went down the staircase with ease and confidence. Max looked at me "My God Em. She is facing room full of Wizards. What she is most afraid of, and stared them in the face." He looked back at her standing regal and he smiled proudly.

The herald announced "Master Wizard Ben Thompson and Lady Mehgan." I watched as Ben and Meg walked the long stair case.

I asked Max "So how did Ben end up being Megs escort?"

He shook his head "I had nothing to do with it." I tried to tap him and he smiled when I couldn't.

We finally made it through the line and I was ready to dance. But then I though, dam, I have to be announced. All I could think of was that the dancing better be good. Max sent *"Try to be as royal as your daughter."* I returned *"If only."* The herald took the invitation and read "Master Wizard Max Marshal and Princess of the Wizards, Emily Star" I could not fathom why I would still be announced as Princess of the Wizards. Max sent *"Because that is who and what you are."*

We made it to the bottom of the staircase without me tripping or throwing up. It did not escape my attention that all eyes were on us as we went down the staircase. I tried to immolate my daughter and Meg but I doubt I was as graceful. I did see the looks on some of the faces of the Wizards and the women. I knew we were not to their liking. I decided that I was there to dance and not worry about it. We met Ben and Mehgan at the bottom and I looked over to Lillie who stood regal with her Sentries. Max looked to Lillie but she would not look at him. He let out a breath and we walked to the main Ball room. Lillie and the Sentry Brothers followed.

We all sat with Jordan and Mary. Maxton was sitting with the Other Wizards in Training at a table near by. He and Joe were joined Michael. Maxton seemed to have a good relationship with both boys. Maxton looked over to me and smiled. All I could think of was at least my son was able to fit in. Lillie watched the crowd with suspicion and concern. She stayed between Sal and Dino. She did look over to me and smiled. The Ball room was massive and it was perfectly dressed in the orange, yellow and gold's of the harvest. Mandra and Meg had done a beautiful job. They should have been proud.

The music started and, of course, Max was up and put his hand out to me. "My Lady, may I have the honor?" I looked around and no one else looked to be getting up to Dance. I looked at Max and he smiled "Lets set the pace." I took his hand and we walked to the middle of the dance floor. I danced close with my husband but respectable. As we danced, I saw Mandra and Marcus head to the dance floor. They held each other but did not move very much. Max said "Look at Maxton." I looked over to Maxton and he was asking his sister to dance. Maxton bowed and put out his hand. She looked at her brother cautiously but took his hand. They too, walked to the dance floor and Lillie held her head high. I looked at Max and smiled. I looked at the crowd all watching but I heard no comments at that time. Soon, others joined us and the dance floor was full. I noticed Maxton talking with his sister and her looking at him with a bit of concern.

Then they moved to us and Maxton offered "May we switch partners?" Max looked and me with a bit of surprise, and I nodded.

Max kissed my cheek and then put his hand to his daughter "My lady, shall we?" She looked at me and I smiled and though the concern was in her face, she took his hand and they moved away with the dance.

Maxton bowed and looked to me. He held out his hand and said " My Mother and My Princess? Shall we dance?" I giggled and began to dance with my son. He certainly was learning to be charming. I noticed that he was now as tall as I was. My son was growing up.

The music came to an end and I looked to Max and Lillie. They stopped and Max took Lillie's hand, bowed to her and kissed her hand. Lillie smiled but then moved quickly off the floor to the Sentry Brothers. I walked to Max and took his arm. He looked at me with a smiled and we returned to the table.

I looked to Marcus and he looked somewhat fatigued. "Are you well Marcus?"

He smiled and said "I am recovering, My Lady. I doubt that I can last the full evening but am please to be here for the beginning."

Mandra looked to Max "I see my little Witch consented to dancing with her father."

Max smiled and said "She did. It was not real comfortable for her but she was gracious." The music started again but Max and I stayed with Marcus and Mandra. Jordan and Mary were there but Jordan still had a cast on his leg. We all talked and laughed with each other enjoying a lovely event.

Then Maxton came to our table and asked Mary "Lady Mary, would you honor me?" He put out his hand and she smiled brilliantly.

She looked at Jordan "Your nephew is out doing you in the charm department." She took Maxton hand and we all watched them head for the dance floor. At that moment, we saw Lillie dancing with Joe. She watched him and he watched her. She was suspicious and looked regal but guarded. Max looked at me and I shrouded. Lillie continued dancing with Joe and looked to be ready to flee. The music ended and he bowed to Lillie. He stood back up and smiled at her and she ran back to the Sentry Brothers.

Max and I dance. Again, Max and I were enjoying to be dancing with one another, and just loving being together. As we danced, Maxton whirled by us with a lovely little girl with red curls. Max smiled and said

"Look at Don Juan." I giggled. The next dance Maxton was dancing with another young lady. Lillie danced with Sal. Then she danced with Dino. She smiled and giggled while with the Sentry Witches. Then we saw her dancing with Michael. She eyed him with caution and he was stout and proper. Her head was up and body stiff and straight. She was watching her surroundings with a jaundice eye. As they danced near the tables I saw Lillie look back at a table and then stop. She stared at the table and I stopped and watched. Max looked and said "Ohoh." I said "Yep"

I started to walk across the dance floor and Michael, who held Lillie's hand, was speaking to her. He tried to pull her away and she was not budging. The Wizards and Women at the table looked at her like she was a bug. Max walked right behind me and when I reached our daughter; One of the Wizards said "It is our own fault; The Elders electing a Witch as the Princess. We should have known she would choose a Mix Blood." An older women at the table said "Obviously they have not taught these mutt children their status or manners." Lillie stood defiant. Michael was pulling her and saying "Lillie. Let's just dance." I looked at Lillie "Lil, lets go." She only stared at the table. The table stared back at her. Max called to her "Lillie. Listen to your mother." Lillie never took her eyes off the table of Wizards and women. Max looked at me and I shrouded my shoulders. We did not want to cause a scene but I knew that Lillie would do something if we did not get her to move.

Michael looked at me and must have read my mind. He grabbed Lillie in a dance twirled and tried to get her to dance. But she pulled away from him and resumed her staring. Max said "I'll just take her out of the hall." I put my hand on him and shook my head. "You can't do any more to scare her. I will do it." As I went to pick her up she moved out of my reach. She looked at the table and pointed her finger and I yelled "Lillie no!" But before she could do a thing, Max had her bound and Michael grabbed her by the arm and waist and dragged her back towards the sentry brothers. She fought against his hold and was hitting and kicking him. She screamed at him "Let me loose Wizard." I stood there and watched Lillie being dragged away and heard "You see, nothing more than animals."

I don't know what happened to me in that second. I knew that my children were the more wonderful and lovely people in all of existence, and that my husband has shown loyalty and honor his whole life. And now, after everything we have had to endure, I was not going to allow my family judged and insulted on blood line alone.

My eyes narrowed and I turned to the table. I followed Lillie's lead and looked them all in the eye. In the commanding voice of the Priestess I said "How dare you." The hall stopped its action and the audience watched being drawn by the powerful voice of the Priestess. Max remained in control, but I could see the Monster hovering. Max looked at the Table and said in his monsters evil voice "Where is it in the Wizard world that you should lose all honor to cause harm to a child." He sneered at them in a challenge "You disgust me." One woman, dressed elegantly and obviously very high standing in the Wizard world said "As a Mix Blood should not question Pure Bloods or their actions." I stood there allowing the Immortal feline eyes to shine. Marcus appeared at my side and said "Princess. Please be Royal." Elder Thomas appeared as well as Elder Maurice.

I walked closer to the table. "I will not tolerate my children being demeaned by bigots. Nor my Honorable Wizard Husband. Prove your selves better than my family. Prove yourself before God and nature." The table sat quiet and cautious. With the eyes of the priestess I turned and glared at all of the Wizards. I made sure that I was not tolerating disrespect to my family. I finished with "As the Wizard Princess, *I demand* that there is never a reason to harm a child, Normal, Pure Blood or Mixed Blood, with words or deed." I turned back to the table that had insulted Lillie "And that it is considered a Crime. The punishment being no less then what the young wizards would face for lesser crimes." I looked back at the crowd "Three lashes and a week in the library." I looked back at the Table and the group sat with their mouths open. The crowed was clamoring and I turned away from the Elders toward my daughter. She stood at the table with the sentry brothers, Michael held her arm. She no longer fought against Michael and stared at me. Maxton stood regal and stout. Both stood watching me closely. I stood glaring and threatening at the crowd and took one last look at the insulting table. The crowd quieted and watched the Priestess. I looked to the Elders and said "I demand it!" Max took my arm and I dropped the Priestess.

Max and I walked to our daughter. She began to pull away from Michael so that she could run, but he held her in place. Lillie had tears on her face and looked at me funny. I bent to look her in the eye and wiped her tears, "Mom was that your Monster?" My stomach dropped. I looked her in the eye, with my eyes my own, and nodded. She looked up at her Dad seeing that he was not the monster but only her Dad. She looked at me again and said quietly "Do I have a monster?" I stood straight and held my hand out to my daughter. She looked at my hand and back at Michael who only look at her stout and stern. She then took my hand. My children, Max and I walked up the stairs and left the now silent Ball.

CHAPTER 9

We transported home and sat in the living room together. It had been a very long time since we had all been together alone. I looked at Lillie and she still was shedding tears, though not openly crying. I looked at Maxton and he looked straight ahead and displayed no emotion like a good Wizard. I think I was angrier about that then anything. Joe went to his room and left us to speak with Lillie and Maxton. When I looked at Max he was watching me, waiting for me to address the children. I turned my head to look at Lillie directly. "Lillie? Did I scare you?" Lillie stared straight ahead and did not respond. I took her hand, which she did not reject and asked again "Did I scare you?" She lowered her head and nodded.

She said "The angel said that you would have the big green eyes. He said that you were a demon." I lifted her chin and asked "Lillie, have I ever done anything to you or anyone around you to make you fear me?" She looked in my eye and said "No."

Maxton asked "Why have Lillie and I not been told about these….. monsters." Max looked at Maxton "We have our true selves. When we or ours are threatened we will choose to use our full abilities. When that happens, we do have some physical changes." He looked at Lillie "But we are in control. We know when and where to use these powers. And it doesn't change our love for our children."

Maxton looked at me "I feel like I have been lied to. I heard the rumors of the beings that exist in you and Dad. I could never believe that it could be true. I have never seen it until Lillie was taken. Then

I saw it in Dad." Maxton looked down "It sort of bothers me to think that my parents could be so….. Dangerous."

I looked to Maxton and Lillie "Don't you think that when these things happened to us that it didn't frighten us. Do you think we want to look like we do when that happens. I keep my….Priestess hidden unless I need her. Your father keeps his beast at bay until he needs it. Never do we use our 'Monsters' to harm others unjustly. We only use them to defend our love ones."

Lillie looked to her father and then to me "Will we have monsters?" I looked at Max and then back to Lillie and then to Maxton. "Yes." Lillie shook her head "I don't know if I want a monster. I am afraid of the monsters." She looked at her father and said "The angle said that the monsters will kill all of the Witches. That they will kill me and Mom. That they will take Maxton." Max said quietly and gently "No Lillie. Remember the Promise." She nodded and he continued "The promise has a rule like the three fold rule of the Witches. It says that what happens to one, happens to the other. If we harmed the Witches, you or Maxton, it would harm us in the same why." He put his hand out to Lillie and after thinking about it for a second she took her fathers hand and he pulled her into a hug "I have vowed that I would protect your mother for her whole life. I made a vow to love your mother her whole life. You and Maxton are that love. Why would you think I would want to hurt you, your mom or Maxy?" She only looked at him. He smiled and looked at me. He looked back into her eyes

Precious child, this vow I make,
To your will, for my hearts sake.
Protect and love to my own end
Your life and soul I will defend
My reward is my daughters love
Her life and freedom I hold above
Never will she have to fear
For her heart I hold dear
Never ending love for you
There is nothing I won't do
That love never will sever

I am yours now and forever.

I smiled at his vow to her. He so easily made his spells. Lillie then hugged her father full force.

I then said "Lillie. Go get ready for bed. We will talk again." She looked back at me and smiled. She kissed her fathers cheek and he straighten with a smiled and said "A reward." Lillie giggled and she when up stairs.

I looked over to my stern and proper Wizard son. "Maxton. No one ever lied to you. There has never been a reason to burden you with these things." I looked at Max "But it is a fact, we are not normal in any of the worlds." I looked back at Maxton "We have to adjust and depend on each other for *our normal.*"

He looked at me and I knew my son was confused. "When will we….I know, what kind of Monster I will be?"

Max then took over. "I learned at the shamian ritual. I don't know why I was given this. I don't know that you will be given a spirit animal. I assume that you will. But how you decide to live your life, Maxy; how seriously you believe the things we have taught you of God and Family; will determine what kind of man and Wizard you will be. And these things are very important for especially you."

Maxton then huffed "Yeah, Magic's future. What a load of …."

Max interrupted him and said "Maxton. Propriety at all times."

I looked at Max irritated. I moved to sit by my son. "You know, when they told me I was the Wizard Princess, I thought it was … "I looked at Max "a lode of Crap." He looked at me as I undermined the Wizard Propriety. "I was a young girl and never took it seriously. But it was there. It felt so confining and unfair. But I found out that God was stronger in his promise to love me. He gave me things I thought I would never have in my life. He gave me you." I petted my sons head and smiled at him "You are wonderful in your own right. Nothing about you makes you less than your own person and a wonderful person." I looked up at Max and then back to Maxton "Regardless of your Wizards Blood." He giggled and Max rolled his eyes. I hugged my son and said "Go on up Maxton. If you need to find out more and talk, your Dad and I will be here for you." He smiled and got up started to leave and turned and hugged his Dad. He smiled back at me "Don't worry Dad. I will work hard to be a proper Wizard; Regardless of my Witch Blood." We all three laughed as Maxton headed up the stairs.

Mandra and Marcus appeared just as Maxton started up the stairs. He looked back at his grandparents and said "I hope I see my self as respected as my father and grandfather." He continued up. Marcus looked as if he just received the greatest compliment. He looked back at Max with a smiled.

Mandra looked at me "Lillie?"

I nodded with a smiled "I think she may be on her way back."

She said "I think I will go up and say good night to her." I nodded. Mandra headed up the stairs.

Marcus said "Princess, I am here as a representative of the Counsel. We send our sincere apology for the events this evening. We have agreed to follow your command with some alterations." I looked at him for him to finish "We will make a written creed that no Wizard is to harm a child and we will use biblical wording. Max will write the new law and present it to the counsel. Of course it must fall in line with the standing laws of order." I nodded.

Max said "I am willing to research and write the law, but when will the counsel work to eliminate the bias in our world. Especially since the majority of the Wizards are Mixed Blood."

Marcus sat in the chair and looked to Max. "They have made the announcement but to write the law is another issue." He closed his eyes and I knew Marcus was weakening due to his recovery. He opened his eyes and said "I will attempt to push for the Elders to set that intent in motion. But we are not democratic in our law making. It is more authoritarian in its make up, for reasons that you yourself realize, Max. Wizards without conscious and control would threaten all the worlds"

"One issue that is not being taken seriously here Dad, is what I continually am reminding you and the other Elders. Mix Bloods have a different drive. A different make up. Pure Blood follow blindly and accept their lot. Mix Bloods look for possibilities and freedom."

"Freedom from what, Max. Freedom of our world, and how we have lived for centuries?"

"Freedom to choose a way of life for them selves. Freedom to think outside the box. To change and evolve to the benefit of all in our world." Max looked at his father with concern. "Look Dad, we have had this debate over and over. You are not well yet and I really don't want to tax you further." With that Max got up and poured his father a brandy and handed it to him.

Marcus took the Brandy and began to drink it. "Thank you, Son. I believe this will help."

I became concern "Are you in pain Marcus?"

He smiled at me "No my lady, just tired."

Mandra came down stairs and looked at me and Max "Your daughter is requesting that her parents come and say good night." She looked over at Marcus and said "And you need your rest, sir." Marcus smiled at Mandra and they transported to, I assume, was Mandra's room.

Max got up and put his hand out to me "Our Little Lady awaits." I smiled and took his hand. We transported to Lillie's room and Prince immediately growled at Max. Trick ran over Lillie's legs and jumped under the bed in a playful act. Lillie looked at us and smiled. I kissed Lillie and hugged her and then Max kissed her and she said "Good night Daddy." We closed her door and Max grabbed me and we were in our room.

Max looked at me and smiled "So My Princess, can I stay home tonight?" I smiled at him and kissed him. "Of course." He and I loved each other like when we were kids. We had missed each other and it was obvious.

CHAPTER 10

I laid in his arms and felt that same feeling of completeness once again. He asked "Well we have been saints for some time now, do you think we will return to that anytime soon?'

I giggled, "Absolutely not."

He let out a contented sigh "Good. I don't think I would have lasted much longer. And I don't want to upset Lillie and have her seen me sneaking in the house for you." He then said "I wonder how the kids are feeling. I think they feel supported by us, but I worry that they might feel alone in some way."

I said "I think that Lillie will have to work through some of her fears and suspicion. But Maxton holds things in and hides his emotions and questions, like a good Wizard. You will have to break through that."

"He does open to you more. I think he forgets that I am his father first and Instructor second." He looked at me "I do try to make sure he knows that he is my son first. But he sees me as superior while at school; which is appropriate. I do think sometimes it does blends into home too."

I said "He may need you to take him out like you took me out. Get him away from the regiment."

He shook his head "Cant. He is vulnerable off the campus. We could be attacked. He could be taken."

"No, I doubt that you would allow that. And I am only a call away." Max bent and kiss my head.

"We will see. Maybe a family thing? What do you think?"

I thought about that and said "That would be nice."

The next morning Max and I stayed in bed. We had been missing each other for so long. It was just nice being together. I didn't want to move. I just want to stay there with Max as long as I could. But the knock on our door soon came. It was part of parenthood.

"Mom?" Maxton inquired. He opened the door slowly and I covered up quickly. "Mom. Joe and I are going to meet Mike at the coffee shop. We are going to see the set up of the Festival. I wanted to tell you before we left." He looked in and smiled at his dad there with me. "Hi Dad."

Max giggled and said "Go on and go Maxy." Manton smiled and closed the door. Max held me closer to him and said "So much for adult time."

I giggled "It won't belong before the next one gets curious. And Maxton has already spread the word that your home." And sure enough the door swung opened and Lilly stood there staring at us.

"Lillie?"

She shook her head. She looked confused and upset and ran leaving the door open. I looked at Max, "Well that didn't go over well." He looked hurt again "Maybe she wasn't ready for me to be home. Maybe I should go back to the Dorms."

I looked sternly at him and said "No. We need to live our lives too. And as we make adjustments for her, she needs to adjust to us as well. We are either going to be married and live as a family or we are not."

He thought about and looked down "I don't want her to hurt or be scared Em. I will do all I can to help her through this."

I got out of the bed and grabbed my robe. "This is our home and family. You leave if you want to. I will not stand in your way. But I want my family together."

He just looked at the still open door and nodded.

I went down stairs and found Mandra and Meg sitting on the patio watching my little witch sit on the swing. Mandra looked over at me "She is concerned. She is still scared of the Wizards and it is not Leonardo this time."

I asked her "Then what is it?"

Meg looked at very strangely "She sees. She sees things that could happen and is afraid. She is afraid of losing you and Master Max. She doesn't want to be alone."

I looked at Meg and nodded.

Meg joined Lillie and worked in the garden. Max handed me a cup of coffee. "Is she OK?"

I smiled "She is. She is trying."

Just then, Lillie came to the patio and looked at her Dad "I am sorry Dad. I am going to try not to be afraid. OK?"

He smiled at her and said "As you wish my little Lady." She smiled and walked back to Meg. Max looked over to me and was smiling.

Marcus appeared and looked to us and said "We have the counsels meeting tomorrow. Maurice believes that since Leonardo was unable to continue to contact Lillianna, that may have push Edwin to start the last scrimmage." He shook his head. "I am surprised they didn't try with Maxton." My stomach lurched again.

Meg appeared to us. She looked at me concern. "Maxton has been approached, Em. He is unaware of the individual's intensions. And that individual is unaware of his possession of the demon Wizards." She turned to Max "Your son is a great Wizard and will be the Leader of the Wizards Armies. He will be a true Wizard equal to Merlin." Meg looked at me "There will be efforts to corrupt his mind and heart. There will be tricks and schemes. He will need to be strong and forthright."

I looked at Max. "We need to speak to him right away. We need to help him be safe. To guild him"

Meg moved to come into our focus and interrupted me "Maxton is the future of Magic." We all turned to her to listen. "But make no mistake, Lillie is also magic's future. She can produce both Witch and Wizard as her mother has, as Maxton will." She looked from me to Max "She is the gem." My mother's words; She is the gem.

I looked at Meg "Meg, what does that mean." I took a deep breath "For Lillie? What does that mean?"

Meg reached out and took my hand "She is the warrior to bring the magic worlds to working order again. She and Maxton will work together and use their magic for that end. She is the mother to Witch and Wizard, but the Warrior Priestess first. She is the Sapphire Witch; 'The Blue Witch.'"

I looked back at Max who knew, as I did, the fable of the Sapphire witch. The Fable that Master Edith was so forceful in having us read. The Blue Witch would be free but alone; She would be feared and powerful; A seductress and of great beauty; She would be hated and loved to the extremes by all.

I shook my head "No. She can't have a label. She can't. Not that one."

I looked back at Max who looked angry. He shook his head and walked out of the house. I looked at Marcus whose eyes stared at the front door that Max had just slammed.

I turned back to Mehgan "How do you know?"

She looked down "I see as she does. She knows as I do."

I looked out at the garden were my daughter stood staring at us. I watched as her hair blew in the breeze. She stood looking straight at me. Her stark green eyes looking deep into mine. Her head was high and her body straight. She was a true beauty and strong in her powers. She was noble and fierce. She has always fought to be free and do as she pleased. She was free by nature. Strong and brave by God. She could be no other. She was the Blue Witch.

She continued to look at me. She was looking for a sign from me of understanding. I smiled and nodded to her. Letting her know that I knew and accepted who and what she is. But my heart once again broke. I also had to accept that my daughter would never have normal.

I turned to Marcus and Mandra stood with him. She looked in my eyes and transmitted *"How could I tell you? How could I?"* I walked to her and hugged her.

"Two more souls for the sake of Magic and the Wizards." I laughed sadly then "And all I ever wanted for myself and my family was normal."

I smiled at Meg, "OK. I need to speak to Max. Will you watch Lillie?" She smiled and nodded. I kissed both Mandra and Marcus and walked out to my daughter. She looked up at me and I could see that she felt insecure at my acceptance. I looked her in the eye and said "Nothing can remove the fact that you are my baby; My Daughter. And what ever the future may bring, I am your mother and I love you, Forever." I kissed her head. She looked back up at me "Now you see why the Wizards hate me." I stared into her eyes "There is that fine line Lillie. They can't truly hate you if they don't truly love you first."

I sensed where Max was and I transported to him. He sat Indian style in the middle of the open field. I walked to him and sat behind him and put my head and hand one his back. We sat that way for a little while. Not speaking because all that could be said would be that our hearts are breaking for our children's futures. They will never be any more free than we are or ever where.

Max turned and laid me down on the grass and looked into my eyes. "Well, I guess we should have thought more about having kids. What it would mean and how it would affect them."

I looked deep in his eyes "Does this information really change our thrill and love for them. If we had not had the kids, we may have missed two of the most beautiful souls on earth." I smiled "Besides, it wasn't like we actually planned to have kids. They just sort of showed up. You know, we were too busy with each other to worry about having kids."

Max giggled and said "I know. And I love you. I loved you desperately then too. I thought every time I touched you it might be the last."

I raised a brow, "And Now?"

He kissed me and said "I can't exist with out you." He petted my face with his fingers "can't breath or bleed without you. I can't walk or talk without you. I can't feel or think without you." He kissed me again and said "You are my life."

I looked into his eyes "I love you, Max." And that was a beautiful morning for us. One of the last for Max and I.

CHAPTER 11

illy and I did not attend the October festival. We stayed at home together. Was watched as the sunset and celebrated the Samhain alone. We let the Wizards celebrate on their own. We read a book and then I showed her a embroidery stitch. Lilly sat quietly for a time and then said "you know Mom. I am more afraid of me then anything. I hope that I can be a good Witch."

I smiled at her. "I was afraid of my self too when I was your age. I had a lot to learn. I didn't have a Master until I was your age."

Lillie looked at me surprised. "Why?"

I giggled "I was being raised by the normals. They believed that my magic was a bad thing. They didn't understand that God gave the magic to me."

"Gosh, it must have been hard not to do some really bad things."

I smiled "Well, it was. But I love gramps and I hated being separated from him. But once grandmother took me, it seemed like it was real fast for me to learn controls. And gramps has his world. He deserves to be able to live in his world without thinking of ours."

Lillie sat next to me, "I wish that we could live in gramps world. It would be so much easier."

I started to laugh "Well, you might think so. But I have found, that what ever world I lived in, I had some problems. I was lonely and I was afraid. But you and me have each other. We don't have to be lonely or afraid."

She looked at me with something in her mind, but due to Mehgan's incantation, I was not able to read it. "Mom, the war is coming. I think it might change things." She looked away "I know it will."

I hugged her and said "War always changes things. So we will pray to God that we are able to get through it."

I sat in the family room and waited for Max and Maxton to return from the festival. And with a great deal of noise, Max, Maxton, Joe, Michael, Jordan, Nathan, Simon and Ben all appeared. They were laughing and talking all at once.

"Hi Mom." Maxton came over and hugged me. He handed me a wood wand with ribbons and crystals dangling off of it. I giggled and hugged him at the thought. He also had a rainbow ribbon head wreath and it also had crystals that hung down the back. "Where is Lillie?" And as he asked she stood in the entry of the room. She was holding back but not as she has been. Maxton smiled and said "Hey Lil. Look what I brought you." He walked over and put it on her head. She smiled at her brother and said "Thanks Maxy." Max then walked over to Lillie and kissed her head as he went to the kitchen. He seemed to be enjoying having Jordan, Ben and Simon over. Lillie did not shy from her brother or father. I believed she truly was trying not to be scared.

Jordan gave me a hug "Hi little Sis." I giggled and he moved to Lillie. She looked up at him and there was some concern but he petted her cheek with his finger tips and said "Hello My Lady." She smiled at her uncle and said "Hi." I was trying to move over to her so she and I could go up stairs and leave the boys to them selves. But before I got there, Meg was there. Ben looked over and smiled. Mehgan smiled and nodded to him.

I sat down instead and watched Ben and Mehgan. It was obvious that there was something there. Mandra appeared next to me. "Well I guess we are not the only Witches that have had their hearts stolen by these handsome sweet talking Wizards." I giggled with her. Max came back with beer for the men and soda for the children. He, Simon and Jordan sat at the game table. Marcus appeared then and looked somewhat better. Though I wondered if he would ever fully recover. He nodded "My Ladies." He looked over at Lillie. He nodded and smiled at her "My Lady Lillianna."

Lillie stayed in the doorway watching the interaction in the room. I looked over to Meg and Ben and saw that they were in their own world. Then Mandra nudged me. She nodded her head in Lillie's direction. Michael had move toward Lillie, slowly, which was probably a good idea. She was in position of defense. She was ready for anything if need be. Maxton, Nathan and Joe paid more attention to the video game they were attempting to play. Ben and Meg were in conversation. But rest of is watched to see how Lillie would reacted. As Michael slowly got closer to Lillie, she eyed him suspiciously. Michael move gently with his head tilted slightly and looking into Lillie's eyes. Lillie stood stout and watchful. Her eyes consistently reassessing the interaction as Michael approached. When he was close enough, he held out his hand and in it was a lily. Max started to get up and I grabbed his arm and he sat back down. Lillie looked at the flower and looked back up at Michael. Though he stopped a arms length away, he moved the lily closer to her so that she would take it. Lillie started to move her arm up to take the flower and hesitated. She quickly looked back at Michaels eyes and then looked back at the flower. She took the flower and then looked back up to Michael. Michael smiled and then turned and walked back to where the other boys played with the video game. Lillie eyed the flower and looked over at me. She then smiled. She walked over to Mandra and I. She looked back at the boys and then to us.

"He gave me a flower."

Mandra said "That is a Lily." Lillie look back at the flower and smiled again.

I looked over to Max who looked at me concerned. I transmitted "*it is not the same as when you left Lilies. It is no where close to your meaning of a Lily.*"

He looked somewhat irritated "*I always came back.*" I smiled at him.

The next day, Max came home to get me for the counsel meeting. I looked over to Meg and asked "Lillie is in her room. Could you look after her for me?" Meg smiled and said she would. It was then that Maxton, Nathan, Joe and Michael appeared in the family room to play video games again.

Max walked in to the room and asked if they had finished their studies. "All of you have finished your homework?" The boys looked at him guilty. He looked at them as the instructor and said "Homework first." They sat at the game table and began their homework.

He looked at Meg with a smile. "Watch those boys, they have a habit of trying to manipulate.

She smiled "I have my way to manipulate as well, Master Wizard." Max smiled and nodded. He then took my hand and we left for the counsel Meeting.

In the chamber, we found that both Counsels sat at opposite benches. Anita stood and greeted Max and I "Priestess, Master Wizard, we are pleased to meet with you. We understand that the young witch has had contact with the demon Wizards." I nodded and she said "This is concerning."

I smiled at the Witches counsel and replied "Yes. It has caused her a great deal of heart ache and pain. She is distrusting of the Wizards and of her father as a Wizard."

Antonio stood and nodded to both Max and I "We will be addressing the young Witch. We feel that she needs to be exposed to the Witches as much as the Wizards." He looked to Max "We have all agreed that the children would not be looked at as Witch or Wizard. Unfortunately, because of the threat to the children, the arrangement here is appropriate. But the young witch is not exposed to other young witches. She is in a group of Wizards and where only her Mother, Grandmother and Master are witch." He smiled "Oh and her Sentries. They are very found of the little one." I smiled. "However, it is our suggestion to you to have the young witch be more exposed to other young witches." I looked to Max and he gave no response or expression. He was only the quintessential Wizard showing no emotion and standing stout and stern.

Elder Marcus stood and addressed the Witches Counsel. "Priestess Anita, Priests Antonio and David, we welcome you." The Witches nodded to the Wizard Elder. "We must continue to contain this family here where there is security for them all. However, the infiltration of the child's mind is inconceivable to our Kind. The tricks and schemes that are being used are despicable and we all must come to a agreement to thwart these devil tactics. We would also thank you in your quick response to send your warriors at the last attack. We thank you for protecting our young."

Anita stood "You are most welcome. But there are other battles coming. There is war coming. And we all need to be aware and ready." She looked to Max "Master Wizard. You will need to be ready. And you will need to prepare your son."

Max asked "Why my son. I would hope to have him safely away from any battles or fighting."

Anita looked at me and back at Max "He will not be kept from the battles and the War. He will be strong and fierce. But to be so, he will require training and trust."

I shook my head "No. I do not want my son there."

Anita looked at me sadly "But he will be. He will be at his own design and his own heart and his own will. You will not be able to deter this." I forgot to breath at that moment.

Elder Thomas stood and addressed the counsels. "This collaborative of magic must work to preserve the magic of the future. The young Wizard must be kept from harm as well and the young Witch; for all of our sakes. And this is why we are here today. What can this group design to keep the Demon Wizard armies away?"

Priest Davis stood "It is our belief, that for the group effort to preserve magic and the children of magic's future, we will need to continue to combine forces." He looked to the Elder Wizards "And what we would propose may be unwelcome by your society, but needed for the protection of all the young Wizards and Witches."

Marcus who had been quiet stood "We have, to every extent, protected the children of magic's future," He looked at Max and I "My grandchildren." He looked at both the witches and the wizards "We have been successful, but also have suffered some defeat with death of love ones and Lillianna's infiltration. The latter being so painful to endure as a grandparent." He looked down "To see the fear in the child's eye at your presents is intolerable." He looked back at Anita "We will welcome all suggestions."

Anita stood "We purpose that we place a school and village of witches next door. Just over the ridge. Many of our young are in schools now and some should be." She looked at me and smiled "Like some should have been. With a village close and with a defense grid and Witch warriors, we believe that all will be protected. In addition, we would have weekly meetings to see if this arrangement is helping the situation or hurting it."

Elder Marcus and the other Elders looked surprised at the Witches Counsels offer and the fact that Witches would be so close. He stood "As you know, there has been much animosity between the races that the reaction of the Wizards is unpredictable. Most are willing to do their part in preserving Magic and protecting our world. We would like to agree at this moment, but will need to bring this to the Wizards as a full group. Will you allow us a few hours?"

Anita stood and smiled "Of Course."

CHAPTER 12

The meeting was postponed and the Wizards called far and wide for Wizards to gather in the Main Counsel room. In a short time, there were a few hundred adult wizards seated and waiting for the announcement of the counsel. Max joined Jordan, Ben and Nathan as well as the other Purple Robed Instructors. I stayed to the side and attempted to be inconspicuous. Unfortunately, I stood out as the only women there; the only woman and a Witch. Many of the Wizards eyed me suspiciously or with curiosity. I looked at Max and he sent *"Its ok Em. Just be still and listen."*

Elder Thomas hit the gavel and quieted down the room. "Could we come to order?" The wizards all quieted down and looked to the Counsel for the reason they were called. I could see some of the Wizards losing some of their Wizard posture and taking side glances at me.

Elder Thomas then began "We have called all of you to this counsel to inform you of issues that have occurred and a solution purposed by the Witches Counsel." There was some rumblings in the crowd of Wizards. "As most of you know, we have been recently attacked on campus by Leonardo and Edwin and their army. We lost fourteen Wizards that day; Five from our end and nine from theirs. If not for the Witches Warriors, more would have been lost." There was more rumbling. "The children could have been harmed as well as the children of magic's future. One was harmed through transmissions causing the child to learn to hate Wizards." He looked through the crowd "This is the totality of Wizard adult population. We have one hundred and fifty in the school as Wizards in training. Leo and Edwin command One hundred and thirty Wizards. Here at this meeting are 160 of full Mastered Wizards. In other words, our numbers are waning. For those wizards with exceptional powers, the numbers are much, much less. Warring against each other will lower our numbers more." He looked to the crown from left to right "Witches have offered to create a village and school over the neighboring ravine. They are offering to provide added protections and services to our young and to Wizards in general. This counsel is inclining to accept their offer."

The crowd began to yell and bark. Many pointed toward me and were screaming insults like "This is what comes from declaring a Witch the Wizard Princess. " Another saying "Our Pure Bloods must retain their status." and "Witches are nothing but animals." I looked at the crowd and then to Max. I so wanted not to shame him but I couldn't stand there and take that. The Priestess emerged. Max looked over but gave nothing in expression. Nor did he transmit anything. He only looked into the eyes of the Priestess.

I stood in the front of the hall to the side of the counsel. The Priestess was in full armor. The mask of the priestess replaced with a helmet that allowed the onlooker full view of the Immortal Feline eyes. Dino and Sal appeared next to me as half of the crowd sat quietly staring and the other became more incised. Elder Maurice and Thomas were asking for order. Marcus was asking me to be patient and noble. I once more looked at the Wizard I claimed as Husband. He looked straight ahead and gave no indication of his thoughts. I transmitted to him *"Wizard do you have any further suggestions?"* I received nothing in return.

At that point, I sent a siren through the hall and a blinding flash of light. All of the Wizards quieted and looked to me. In the commanding voice of the Priestess I snarled "Sit and be still. Sit and listen for what could be the existence of pure and good magic. The pure magic of the Wizard." I walked to the center to look at the Wizards in the eyes. "What are you upset about? There has been a well intended offer to aid you in preserving your race. To protect your young. Offered not ordered or demanded. It has been offered in good faith." I moved back to the side with my sentries. I looked over at Max who still did not look at me. I then looked to Elder Maurice.

He nodded and stood "As the Princess has said, this has been offered and we would like debate and vote on this most generous and genuine offer."

A distinguish Wizard from the middle of the crowd stood. "Elder Maurice my I have the floor?"

Elder Maurice nodded and recognized the Wizard. "Master Harris has the floor."

Master Harris stated "We have for many years held animosity for the Witches and their way of life. That being said, I personally have no grudges to the Witches and in fact, found those that I have met very honorable. I believe that we could have our own safe guards to protect any deception that could exist by the witches. But in this situation, at least with the information that I have, the child of magic is Mixed Blood with Witch. It seems to me that this situation would make sense." Elder Harris sat.

Elder Maurice stood "That is correct. The child is Mixed Blood." Elder looked at Max but Max stay stern and stout.

Another Wizard that stood at the back began to walk down to the counsel table. He was a tall man and as handsome as a Wizard could be. He had dark hair with white at the temples. He had blue eyes that seemed to look right into your soul.

In a deep voice as smooth as silk he asked "Elder Maurice, could I be recognized?"

Elder Maurice looked at the Wizard as he walked down to the counsel. "Master Robert you are recognized." Master Robert looked me in the eye with a charming smile. I had closed my mind and took on the Stern and Stout Wizard expression.

Master Robert spoke as he stared at me. "I believe that this offer is influenced by our lovely Princess." He walked closer, though staying a safe distance from my sward and the sentry brothers. Continuing his smile he said "I would like to know what is in it for her kind." He continued his smiled and said "Maybe to control all Wizards?"

I looked at him without emotion or hint of my thoughts. In the Witch voice of the Priestess I countered "I have a stake in my children and my Wizard husband. I have no desire to control Wizards or their world and never did. Being a Witch and Wizard Princess means little to me. My son and my daughter are my only concern"

Master Robert then said "Than why is the girl not a recognized Princess?"

Finally Max stood "May I be recognized Elder Maurice?"

Elder Maurice said "You are recognized Master Marshall"

Max walked to my side and looked at Master Robert "Our children are not pure bloods. Our request to both Witch and Wizard Counsels was not to label our daughter Princess."

Master Robert in his silken voice looked at Max and said "In a gesture of good faith, I believe that the young Witch should be recognized as Princess."

I snarled at him "Never."

Max shook his head "Leave them innocent of the games and plans."

Master Robert then said "Master Marshall, all of us here know of you and the Princess. Your exploits and powers are not a secret. We were not expecting the Princess to be married to a Mix Blood in the first place. In some options, you sir, have single handedly brought the race to its present condition. It would be in our interest to have a iron in the fire so to speak. The young witch with ties to the Wizards would show some good faith."

Max said "No. As a Master and the father of the child I say no. My son is already in this world and a Wizard. My daughter is free."

Max started to laugh which sent the other wizards into another soft clamor at his departure of the wizards stout and still posture. "We Wizards would never be able to control her. She is already too strong and free." Max became serious again "You only have to ask Edwin him self. After all, did you not recently speak to him?"

Master Robert dropped his smile "Yes I have. He is ….impressed with the little Witches abilities and the fact that she has not removed her spell."

Max said "The answer is no. But now that we know that you have seen Edwin and Leonardo, I would have to ask you where your allegiance lies?"

Master Robert regained his charming smiled "Yes…Well.. I am undecided you might say. As a pure blood, I must decide if I want to be equal to the Mix Bloods and Witches or fight for superior status. It is a dilemma. I am…weighing my options." Master Robert, staying a safe distance from us, continued to stare at me.

Jordan Stood up "May I be recognized?" Master Maurice said "Master Jordan Marshall is now recognized.

Jordan walked to face Master Robert. "If you are not loyal to the counsel and this body of Wizards, how can you make these ridicules demands."

Master Robert never moved his eyes from the immortal green eyes "As I said, I am weighing my options. And am looking for some assurances to our kind."

Marcus stood "We are all here to decide the fate of our kind. Our kind and those that are in support of our kind. If any of you choose not to stand and vow to stand with this counsel, it would be better that you leave. As I will asked that this forum vow there allegiance once again."

Max walked to the front of the counsel and looked to the crowd. "My children have come up more often than I am comfortable with. Edwin and other Pure Bloods.." He pointed to Master Robert "want control over these magical children. And Yet the children are Mix Blood. Wizard, Witch, and Normal." He paused and looked to me and then back to the crowd of Wizards "If Mix Bloods are to be respected and ever be recognized as full Wizards; as more than servants; to have freewill; then now is the time to make those changes." He looked at the Counsel "The majority of the Wizards here tonight are mix blood. Most have some form of Magic and more than the pure bloods. We can stand with others to defend our world. We don't have the same stakes that a Pure Blood would consider valuable. We only ask for our freedom of will and respect."

Several in the crowd stood clapping and cheering. I could see that what Max said was what he has been working with for years. His own reckoning of his existence. It was obvious that the other Mix Blood Wizards agreed.

Elder Maurice stood " It is clear to this counsel that the our numbers are made up of Mix Bloods. We are aware of their powers and strength are above the Pure Bloods. It is clear by the joining of the Princess and a Mix Blood, that producing very powerful children is possible through the Mix Bloods. Magical Children. Mix Blood Magical children. And the Pure Bloods have failed to produce magical children." He looked over the Wizards in the audience. "There is an effort by this counsel to change our laws to recognize all Wizards as equal. We have made efforts to treat all Wizards as equal. That being said, we need to focus on the question at hand. Do we accept the Witches offer?"

Master Robert still keeping his eyes on mine said "Why not. Let give it a try."

Jordan said "I make the motion that we, Wizards, accept the offer by the Witches."

Master Harris said "I second the motion."

Elder Thomas said "All those in favor? The crowd roared "Yea." This included Master Robert.

"All those opposed" It was quiet.

Elder Thomas then said "The Motion has passed. Now we will asked that this body of Wizards make this vow:

We Wizards are one body

We Wizards look to the other as brother

No Wizard shall disrespect another

We Wizards will be loyal and honorable to the Wizards Counsel

We Wizards will be honorable in our dealings with the Witches and others who aid our cause.

All of the Wizards took the Vow including Master Robert who continued to stare at me. I looked to Max and sent *"I will be with my kind."* I looked to the Sentry Brothers and we transported out.

Once back with the Witches Counsel, I informed them of the vote and the vow. Anita then asked "Priestess, we will need to see and speak to your daughter. As you are aware, she is the Sapphire Witch of the age. She will need additional instruction." Sill in the form of the Priestess, I only stared at the Witches Counsel. Anita then said "You can not change her stars. But you can make it easier on her. Help her find her true self." I nodded and dropped the priestess. I then Transported Lillie to me.

"Mom?" She looked at the counsel and became excited and said "What now? I haven't done anything."

I smiled and said "No you haven't. This is the Witches Counsel. They wanted to speak to you."

She calmed down and said "Oh."

Antonio stood and smiled "Hello little one. We are pleased to meet with you."

Lillie smiled "Hello."

David stood "Young one, we would like to have you attend a witches school. Would you be agreeable?"

Lillie pulled her brows together "I don't want to leave my Mom and Dad."

David said "You would not have to. We will be just over the hill."

Lillie shrouded her shoulders and smiled "Oh. OK."

Anita stood "We will be very interested in you, Blue Witch." Lillie was very still at that title as was I. "We will be at your call." Lillie nodded but remained quiet.

I took her hand and said "Go home now Lillie. I will be there soon." Lillie nodded to the Counsel and transported out.

I looked at Anita "Do we have to entertain this label. Could it be a mistake?"

At that point the Wizard Counsel appeared at their bench and Max and Jordan stood behind me. The Elders and Witches Counsel nodded to one another.

Anita still standing addressed me "Yes. The child knows who she is . We know who she is. It would be better to live in the reality of that. Let her develop into her true self with honesty and expectation. Not like you had to discover the Priestess."

I felt so scared for my child "I don't want her to live that way. I want her to have happiness in her life."

Anita looked at me softly and said "Priestess, you have happiness in your life and rarely recognize it . Who are you to decide what makes the Blue Witch happy?" I was taken back. I did have happiness in moments and short periods but little for long term.

Anita smiled "Oh, my Priestess, it has been long term. You have been given your hearts desires by God and Mother Earth. Because it is not in the Normal world does not mean that it is any less real." I nodded and looked back at Max. He looked me in the eye and nodded.

Antonio stood and looked to Max "We would expect that the young wizard be given the same opportunity to be aided to his true self. He is very powerful."

Max looked at the Witches "We have our rituals that lead our young to their true selves. He is too young yet to participate."

Antonio looked to Max, then to the Wizard Counsel and back to Max "Master Wizard, the young wizard does possess the Witches Blood. His being may not wait for the age of the rituals. Be aware, he is coming into his own as is the Blue Witch." Max nodded and Antonio turned his attention to the Wizards Counsel. "The Priestess has delivered the agreement of the Wizards. We will have the Witches Village and School constructed and inhabited within the week. No Witch will venture to your land without invitation. Other than the Priestess, her Wizard, her Wizard Son, and the Blue Witch will be allowed in our Village without invitation. We feel that will keep peace with between the neighboring races."

Elder Maurice Stood "We agree but will need to have a area of common ground to meet and train our forces."

Antonio nodded "We agree. We will also construct a Military center for such activities."

The Counsels agreed and the Meeting was ended.

Anita said to me "School for the young Witch will being at the next moon." I nodded. Max took my arm and we were home.

I looked in his eyes and asked "Have we been happy? Have you been happy?"

He put his arms around me and smiled "As long as I have been with you, I have been happy. I thought we were happy together."

I nodded "I have been happy with you. I guess I just wanted the normal happy. I just wanted to live without worrying all the time.

Max huffed "Em. Normals worry all the time. They have to earn money to pay bills and pay for the houses the food and clothing. You create your house whenever and where ever you want. Normals have kids that do far worse than ours. And we love as true and honest as any Normal. Always have." He kissed me "I am and have been happy with you."

Then I though about his attitude at the counsel meeting. "Why did you just sit there for so long. Why did you disapprove of my being the Priestess while suffering the insults. And why didn't you tell that creep Robert to get lost?"

Max looked at me with a grin "I knew you would be a force. And you would take care of things your way." He giggled "Robert believes himself a Casanova. And you are a beautiful and strong female. Witch or not." He kissed me "I knew what he was up too and knew from the look in your eye that he was not getting anywhere. But he will try again."

I shook my head "Why, he knows that I am your wife?"

"Yes he does. And feels it is a great tragedy. But on the other hand, he feels that he will prove something about the witches and the Mix Bloods by wooing you. He is testing the commitment."

I huffed "Well let him test away. He has already proven to be untrustworthy."

Max pushed me back and held my shoulders. He looked at me in the eye "And if he was loyal would you consider him?"

I was in shock "I am married to you! What are you talking about?"

He smiled and hugged me "Just being sure."

CHAPTER 13

Max was right. The next day as Lillie and I walked to Max's office, Robert appeared on the walkway in front of us. "Ah, Princess, how fortunate could this Wizard be." Lillie looked at the Wizard with suspicion.

"Master Robert." I greeted as I moved Lillie to walk around him. He then turned and began to join walking with us. Lillie watched this new Wizard and was prepared to take action against him.

"Princess I was hoping that I would have the opportunity to speak with you."

"Why?"

"I was hoping that we could get to know each other better. I have not had the opportunity to meet you before."

"And why is that?"

"Well, I was occupied."

I gigged "Oh you were in the Halls."

He laughed and shook his head "Actually no. I was sent on assignments in Paris. I would have met you then but you failed to show up."

I did not respond to that. He looked at Lillie and said "Hello little one." Lillie looked at him and nodded. She was not saying a word to him. I could not see what she was thinking as she was still closed by Mehgans spell.

"So, this is the daughter of Master Wizard Marshall. She is beautiful like her mother."

I looked forward and said "Thank you."

"The same little Witch that bestowed Edwin with the horns and tail?"

I said arrogantly "The same."

He looked at Lillie "Very creative and very skillful for one so young."

We walked to the building door and Master Robert open the door for us. I sent Lillie in first and said "Thank you Master Robert. Have a nice day."

Before I made it through the door way he asked "Would you like to join me this afternoon for a coffee at the coffee shop?"

I turned and looked him in the eye "I am busy with my family. I would not be able to join you."

Master Robert smiled broadly and with his silky voice asked "I wish you would reconsider."

I shook my head "I have my children to care for. Thank you Master Robert." I turned and walked down the long hall to Max's office.

Max was unfazed by the behavior of Master Robert. He said "I told you. He feels more worthy than a Mix Blood."

Lillie told her Dad "Why don't you use your magic on him."

Max looked at Lillie with a smiled "Because that is not using my magic wisely. I don't use my magic in a wasteful manner. I don't use it to harm others."

Lillie looked at her father and understood his reasoning. I thought it was a wonderful answer. One that he could have used with her a hundred times.

But Lillie said "Your have a good heart and you are a good Wizard, Dad." She sighed "But I would have him turn into a pig every time he looked at Mom." Max turned his head in shock at his daughter and we both had to turn away for a second. "Lilly, go wait for Maxton in the Lobby. As soon as she left, we laughed.

Through laughter Max said "I think she is on her way back."

I nodded "She is still watchful and suspicious, but that statement was a clear indication that she is. She is not hiding her thoughts."

As we calmed down from the laughter, Lillie came running back in "Dad!" Maxton is fighting." Max jumped off the desk were he was sitting and ran out the door followed by Lillie. I followed Lillie. We ran down the hall to the main lobby. Out in the court yard was my son and another boy rolling in the grass and hitting each other. Other Wizards in training were crowded around and watching. Max grabbed Maxton and Ben appeared and grabbed the other boy.

Max had both boys by the shirt collars. In a stern and stout voice he asked "what is this about."

"Maxton said "Tony said something about Lil." I looked at Lillie as she stood with her mouth open at her brother's behavior. Michael and Joe were standing with Lillie and me.

Max looked at Maxton and said "Go home. Tomorrow you and Tony will have detention." Maxton transported home.

Max looked at Tony "You need to speak to Master Bed." Max released the child to Ben. Max sent *"Take Lillie home Em"*

I took Lillie's hand and we transported home. Maxton sat in the kitchen with Mehgan toweling the blood from his nose. She looked at me concerned and I said "Lillie, go up stairs. OK?" She looked and nodded and walked up stairs. I looked over at Maxton and saw the flash in his eyes. Red, deep flashes. Mehgan looked at me and said "Call for Elder Marcus and Master Max. He will need them for the transformation." Maxton looked at me and I could see. His monster was coming.

"Mom what is happening to me?" His voice was deep and ugly. His eyes flashed more red,

I ran to my son "Maxton?" He looked at me with the red eyes and his look was deadly and threatening.

Meg yelled at me "Em! Call them now!"

I screamed for Max and Marcus. And with in a second both stood with me watching my son transform to his Monster. His face changed to look more like a wolf. His jowls shaped into canine. His eyes brown but flashing red. He looked at his father and his grandfather and in a deep ugly voice he said "What is happening to me?"

Marcus jumped into action. "Maxton you are changing to your animal spirit. You will have to let it lose. Once it is out and you calm down it will become dormant again." We could see Maxton continue to fight the transformation. Max talked to him calmly. "Maxy, Listen to us. Let the spirit out. Let it be. Learn from it."

Meg and I stood back holding hands while my son went through some kind of Wizard right of passage. He heard his father and allowed the monster out. He stood with the red eyes and full canine jaw and teeth. He growled and drooled. He looked angry and threatening. And Deadly as his fathers monster. Max and Marcus stayed close to him. Speaking softly to Maxton yet the monster continued to hold steady. Max looked back at me. I knew it was for me to speak to Maxton. I was so in shook. And admittedly frighten,. Frighten of my son. I stared into the eyes of Max.

He sent *"EM! He needs your calm. He needs your voice."*

I left Megs embrace and walked slowly to my son. He watched me as I approached. His eyes angry and deadly staring straight at me. As calmly and softly as I could I spoke to the monster. "Maxton? Son you need to calm down now. I need you. I need to speak to you." He made a noise in his throat. And I continued to walk to him "Baby, I need you to calm down and talk with me. OK?"

In his deep and ugly monster voice, Maxton said "Mom?"

I smiled and nodded. "I know Maxton. It is frightening and strange. But we are here with you." Maxton sat back in the chair and he looked up. His monster came in full force again and when we followed his eyes, we saw Lillie watching from the stairs.

Maxton then roared in his beast voice "No!"

I stood in front of the monster and looked in his eyes again and said calmly "Maxton, calm your self down. We need you to calm down so that we can sort things out. Please son."

He looked me in the eye and the Monster Wolf shed tears. "Lil saw me."

I nodded "Yes she did. But she needs to know and be able to help you as you will need to help her." He looked more calm with that and the monster slowly subsided. Maxton him self launched off the chair into the arms of Max.

"Dad, Help me." Max hugged Maxton

"I will son. We all will." I could see the pain Max felt for his son. I wondered who was with Max when he transform the first time.

Marcus took my arm and said "Lillie needs you now. I understand you want to help your son. But this is a Wizard issue and Lillie needs to understand." I looked at him and nodded and headed for the stairs where I last saw my daughter. I grabbed Meg by the hand and took her with me.

Meg and I found Lillie looking out the window in her room. She stood stern and stout and did not turn around though I knew she knew we were there.

"Lillie, Meg and I are here to talk with you."

She quietly said "I know Mom. I saw Maxy."

I looked at Meg. Meg asked "Well what are you thinking?"

"I am sorry for my brother. He looked scared." I looked at Meg. I did not see scared from the beast. I asked her "Scared Lil?"

She turned around "I saw inside of him. He was scared. The monster was scared too." She walked over to us "When he is calm down, maybe he will talk to me." She then looked at me seriously "When will my monster come?"

I looked at her and said "If you have the Priestess and are the Blue Witch, you already have the ability. She will appear when you need her."

Lillie then smiled at me "I hope it isn't for a long time." We giggled.

Later that evening, Max and I sat with our son. He looked straight ahead and was calm. Max said "I know that it is unnerving to have this happen so suddenly. The first time it happened to me, I couldn't calm down for hours. I thought that I would be the monster for life."

Maxton asked "Didn't grandfather help you?"

Max looked at Maxton and said "I was kept from grandfather for a while. I was alone." I had no idea that happened to him. So many things Max never told me.

Maxton said "I don't think I could have handled it alone. I didn't think I could handle it with all of you." Max ruffled his head and said "It will take some time to get a handle on the appearance of the beast. It will happen when you are angry or feel threat from others. The important thing right now is that you understand that once you feel the lift. The lift in your chest, go home or somewhere where you and others are safe."

Maxton nodded and said "I will. But I also want a handle on this fast. I don't want to freak out into the beast in front of the other Wizards."

I smiled "No. No other twelve year old boy would. But should it happen. Just come home."

Maxton looked at his Dad "What if the Monster doesn't do what I want."

Max giggled "Maxy, it is you. The same mind and heart. Just a physical change and abilities." He hugged his child "We will work on it everyday until you got it down. OK?"

Maxton nodded and quietly said "OK." He looked at us both "What about Lil?"

I smiled "Lillie is fine. She understands and is waiting for you to be able to talk to her. She knows your heart. Even when you were the beast."

He smiled then "I think I will go up and talk with her." Max nodded and Maxton got up from the couch and walked up stairs to see his sister.

I leaned up against Max "What happen at the school today?"

Max took a breath "Tony is pure blood. He is being raised to be superior to mix bloods and witches. He made a crake about Maxton's Witch Sister."

I giggled "Maxton should have let Lillie handle it"

Max laughed "Your right. But then Maxton would have to call on her all the time." Max pulled my face to him "Well here we are and dealing with our children and their coming of age stages. We are sitting on our couch and its calm." He smiled "Are you happy Em?"

I giggled and said "This is our normal. And I am Happy."

Max threw up a arm and said "Finally."

CHAPTER 14

Things went on and the Witches were over the next ridge. Lillie started school and actually was happy about it. Maxton and Max worked every night on controlling the monster. We were happy. We or I, accepted our world and existence.

Christmas came and the Yule celebration that Lillie, Meg and I attended with the Witches. We returned to find a Christmas tree in the living room and the house decorated in Christmas fare. We hung up our capes and looked into the family room to find Max and Maxton watching TV. I walked over to Max and Kissed him. "Thank you."

Maxton asked "Are we going to gramps for Christmas Day?" I shook my head.

"No babe. Gramps is going to Tina's this year. But maybe next time. OK?"

He nodded and asked "Well than, can we open our gifts tonight?"

I shook my head "No. you have to wait until morning."

Max nudged me and looked in my eyes "One gift each. And save the rest till tomorrow."

I smiled and said "OK. Just one." The kids ran to the tree and grabbed a gift. We walked in to see them open them and giggled when Maxton found new pajama bottoms. He said "That one doesn't count."

I laughed and said "Yes it does."

Joe found a new black jacket and gave an "Aw man."

Lillie open hers and found a box of hair clips and bows. She looked at me "I hope there are better ones for the morning."

I looked at her "Lillie, be thankful for all that you have." She only rolled her eyes.

As I looked at the children picking up the wrapping paper, Max sat a good sized box on the floor. He looked at me and said "For you my Love."

I shook my head "I will wait till morning."

Max smiled up from the floor "You may be able to wait but the gift cant wait. Please open it."

It was so pretty wrapped in gold wrapping and white ribbon. I sat next to Max and opened the paper. I lifted the lid of the box and there was a beautiful Siamese Kitten. No more than a few months old. It looked at me with its beautiful blue eyes and I was in love. I took the kitten out of the box and it purred immediately. The kitten seemed to know me. I snuggled the kitten and lifted it to look in its eyes. I was thrilled. I looked at Max and he was smiling.

"Oh Max. He is beautiful. He is perfect."

Max nodded with a smiled on "He's for you alright. He growls at me and even tried to scratch me when I put him in the box. Obviously he is already in love with you."

I smiled "I already love him. Thank you Max. Thank you." I held the kitten and hugged Max. But the Kitten growled angrily at Max and I had to move away." Lilly came to us and took the kitten. The kitten also growled at Maxton and Joe. Obviously this kitten was a true witches cat. I turned and kissed my husband for the gift.

Max asked "What will you name him?"

I shook my head and Lillie said "Oz. That is his name."

I smiled "Sounds like a good one. But isn't it the Wizard of Oz?"

Lillie shook her head "No. Just Oz."

After that we had a long period of peace and normal life. Well a normal life for a Witch and Wizard household. Leonardo and Edwin were still at it but they could not find a way to get back into the campus. The Witches proving their worth in their protection for all of the children. Several of the Mix Bloods that had followed them blindly came back to the Wizard Counsel and some were in the halls for rehabilitation. And Others were committed to the Wizard and Witch military Compound.

Lillie and Maxton grew and both made friends at school. Lillie was still her own person. She was often sent home from school for her stubbornness or behavior. Maxton stop fighting but was still irritated. He knew what the others didn't. He had a Monster. And Lillie if need be.

Max was finally successful in the Counsels decree that Mix Bloods were full Wizards and not below the Pure Blood. And they also pass the law that the children were no longer strapped. But they would not relent on the Library.

By the time that Maxton was 16, it was time for the Samhian ritual. I was not happy. The counsel asked that Mandra, Meg and I prepare the Mixture. I preyed that I did not see any cats in cages. Well there was no cats in cages and the four witches brewed the mixture. We watched the ceremony and with the drums thumping. Mandra was ready with her belladonna spiked rum. All of the Wizards were concerned with the Witches there but more so with Lillie there. As with the ceremony was much like the one Max and Edwin went through. Several boys wondered over the ground and others were on the ground. Maxton of course turned into the monster to the amazement of the crowd. Max took his son out of the arena and went home. Maxton mortified that now his world knew he had his monster.

Lillie was never linked to a coven. She never had to be presented or make any promises. I doubt she would honestly give a promise. She would sweetly lie and do what she wanted.

The children now teens meant more challenges for Max and I. Both children more in control of their magic and Maxton able to control his Monster. Michael and Joe were very aware of the monster and were cautious when it did appear. Which it did when he and Lillie were insulted by a Witch or a Wizard. Lillie seem to be unfazed as she did the first time she saw her brothers monster. She always said "I see in his heart."

She was not one to be insulted or threaten either. She often was called before both counsels and ordered to release or restore Wizards to their former selves. And though ordered never to retaliate, Lillie would always smiled sweetly and lie as she agreed. But she did make a name for herself besides the Blue Witch. It was well know with both Witch and Wizard students that Lillie would not tolerate insults to her and her brother and their Mixed Blood.

One issue that was hard for both Max and I was that Maxton was a "Chick Magnet." He not only was pursued by the lovely Wizard girls, but several of the Witches. Lillie had several friends at school and they all looked at her handsome brother with stars in their eyes. His hazel eyes were like a mirror that looked through you. He was the proper Wizard and played the part to the hilt. Except with me and Lillie. He knew we knew better. He and Max relax at home and enjoyed life with us *undisciplined* Witches. He and Joe dated and I was always concerned that they showed no concern in taking a Witch to parties and the coffee shop with the Wizards. They took Wizard girls to functions with the Witches. Maxton and Joe would say, "No one would dare bother us. We have a secret weapon." Max and I thought they meant Maxton's monster till they corrected our thinking and said "Lillie."

Make no mistake, Lillie was a beauty. Her clear green eyes were mesmerizing. Her very long dark brown hair had red highlights in the sun like my grandmother and I. She was willowy but had all the right curves. When she moved it was like a graceful swan. When she was angry, it was fast and ridged. Max was very concerned with Lillie growing up. He often was overly protective and watched all the boys around her. But Lillie had other ideas. She liked the attention. She only had to give her beautiful smiled to a boy and he was her slave. She found that power more intriguing than any magic she possessed. Joe was often used and abused by Lillie. She never actually encouraged a relationship beyond her brother, but couldn't help flexing her female power over him. Michael was a different story. He would stay back and watch. It was clear that there was a internal fight within him. He wanted so much to respond to her calling eyes and requests, but could not allow himself to do so. Nathan, though in college and not around as much, fell all over him self to appease the fifteen year old girl.

Of Course, Mandra insisted that their be a sweet sixteen birthday for Lillie. She had that party planed six months ahead of time. Of course both witch and wizard would be invited. She had tables set up in the open field and Maxton insisted that the music be the latest Wizard Rock Band. Mandra agree but with the stipulation that other music also be provided for us "Old Folks." Mandra of course invited the coven and Lincon and Molly were there to aid in the function. Max and I looked over the scene and I asked "Well how much of a problem is it going to be mixing the worlds?" Max smiled "I think that the kids will be fine, I worry about a the adults." I didn't believe that. I knew that the pure blood attitudes of both races continued to be strong in their opinion of condemning the mixed bloods.

The party started and it looked like everyone was enjoying them selves. Lillie, the birthday girl, with her caution and fear of all Wizards and Witches, seemed to be enjoying herself. Maxton stayed close to her with Joe and Michael. They were like a troop of body guards but in reality, they looked to her for protection. We all danced and ate and sang happy birthday. Maxton had his wish and the Rock Band played for an hour and all the kids seemed to appreciate it.

Max and I danced together as much as possible. We loved that time dancing. It always seemed that was the thing that we did together when ever possible. Old habits and love of dancing kept love for each other in our focus. I loved being in his arms and looking into his eyes. I loved him passionately even after all these years. He was older as was I, but being immortal has its perks. The aging process eliminated, he looked as handsome as ever.

We watched Lillie dancing with several boys. Maxton and Joe mostly but she did dance with Wizards and Witches with some caution. We did see her dancing with a very handsome Witch by the name of Samuel. He was tall and handsome. He had brown eyes and hair. He looked at Lillie with passion which sent Max into protective father mode. He left me and cut in on Lillie and Samuel. Lillie laughed at her father and said "Oh Daddy, you are so funny."

As the party was winding down, and we bid our guests good bye, I watched as Lilly and Michael dance. He was proper and stern. She was serious and cautious. There was a quiet talk going on. Lillie tilted her head several times obviously listening and questioning. When they stopped, Michael bowed and kissed her hand. Lillie eyed him and he turned and walked away. She watched him like she was confused by him. When she sensed me she turned to me and smiled.

Lincon and Molly began to clean up. Mostly waving their hands and snapping fingers. Maxton and his friends began to gather at one end of the field. Lillie and her friends were all saying good bye at the end of the field, by the house. Then it happened. Samuel Kissed Lillie. I was in shook at his boldness. Max growled and I grabbed his arm before he could move. But Michael transported immediately to Lillie and Samuel. He grabbed Samuel and pulled him away from Lillie. Of course the fight was on. Ben and Max were on the scene in a flash and Lillie was then standing with me. Both boys bleeding from noses and mouths and being bound and restrained by the Mastered Wizards and a Mastered Witch by the name of Timothy. I could thank only God, that they did not use magic to harm one another.

Lillie giggled "Wow."

I turned to my daughter and said "Lil, this is not OK." She only smiled at her feminine power.

Meg and Mandra stood with Lillie and I and Mandra cautioned Lillie "It is wonderful to have the eye of every boy on earth Lillie. Its another to cause harm of another's heart." Lillie looked concern at our grandmother.

"I never asked him to kiss me. And I don't plan on not ever being kissed."

Meg asked "Do you want him as your boyfriend?"

Lillie giggled "NO. I don't want a boyfriend. I just want to be kissed." Mandra, Meg and I all looked at Lillie in shock.

I said "Lillie, you cant go around kissing all the boys. You'll have a poor reputation."

Lillie started to laugh "Mother, I have a poor reputation just being me. Kissing all the boys will not cause anymore harm."

Marcus was there then and spoke to his granddaughter with authority "Lillianna, your behavior not only harms you but your family as well. Your father, mother and your grandmother and I. Your brother will suffer from you antics. Have concern for Maxton at least."

Lillie looked at Marcus and understood clearly what he was saying. She hugged her grandfather and said "You are right grandfather. I will be good for him." Then she pulled back and said "But I still want to be kissed."

Marcus giggled "Of Course you do. We all do. But be more discrete." Lillie nodded.

We looked back at the fight scene and saw Ben and Timothy walk Samuel to the house and Meg went with them. Max had given Michael a handkerchief for his bleeding mouth. Maxton and Joe stood by their friend. Michael listen to Max speak to him calmly but then looked directly at Lillie and I felt her heart flutter. I looked right at her. "Lillie. You like Michael."

She smiled "Well I do. But I don't want to limit my self yet. I only sixteen. Besides he is leaving for college."

I looked back at Max and he stood as the proper and stout Mastered Wizard but transmitted *"She is going to be more trouble."*

I smiled and nodded and sent sarcastically *"Do you think?"*

Maxton walked over to Lillie smiling he said "You are such a trouble maker, Lil."

Lillie giggled "They are foolish."

Maxton looked back at his friend still dabbing his mouth. "Well at least he is protective, instead of afraid." Maxton comment hit home. Michael was not afraid of Lillie. I wondered if Samuel had any fear of Lillie. He obviously wasn't afraid to kiss her.

Marcus and Mandra walked towards the house and Max walked to Lillie Maxton and I. He looked at Lillie with a brow up "My dear daughter, please don't make situations that endanger the lives of the boys?" Lillie giggled.

Later that night, Lillie and her friend Bonita, were in her room. Maxton Joe and Michael were in the family room. Max and I sat on the swing in the garden. I leaned against him and closed my eyes with the peace. Max petted my hair. He then said "So you are aware, my love, Michael is madly in love with our daughter."

I laughed. "She's too young for love. She just a baby."

"Regardless, He loves her."

"Max, she is not ready and has already said she is not limiting her self. And Michael will be leaving for college."

Max huffed "I went to college and still returned to you every chance I got." I kissed his cheek because it was true. He did come and see me a lot while he was in college. We even had our little get a way during that time.

"Well, it is a different time. She is not ready for a hot and heavy relationship. She even said that she wants to kiss all the boys." Max jumped up and looked at me with his concerned father look, and I laughed. "Don't worry, Marcus has spoken to her."

Max looked angry "Don't tease me about this Em. I don't like it. She is still my little girl."

I sat up and said "She is still my little girl but I recognize her being a girl and not a Wizard."

"I will not have my child running around kissing all the boys. She needs to be proper."

I leaned back against him "I think we were too proper. I think we should have been together earlier and then I would have probably left with you when you asked."

He turned to face me and smiled "I wish we had too." Then he said "Well, what to?"

I looked at him confused "What to what?"

He smiled brilliantly "Take off."

I started Laughing "In a few years when the kids are in college, we can."

He then leaned back and said "You mean I have to wait again. What….Another two or three years before Lil's in college."

I shrouded "Yeah. How about that." The I remembered "And then there is the war that is coming."

Max was quiet for a moment then said "Maybe it wont come. Maybe we can all avoid it."

"But the counsels and others have predicted it. They believe it is coming."

Max said in a hopeful tone "But they also said soon. And it has been years since they first said it."

"Remember Max. They predicted Maxton years before he was conceived."

"Yeah, but they got it all wrong." He smiled "And they did not predict Lil."

I nodded and said "God sent her for a reason. God gave her that 'do what I please' attitude. I pray that the label of the Blue witch is also wrong and God has another plan."

Max kissed my head "Me Too. Maybe she can be a nun." We started to laugh at the thought.

Maxton left for college with Joe and Michael. All attending Princeton together. Lillie continued at the Witches School and gave no thought to college. Max and I pushed her to think of where she would like to go. But she was uninterested. She went on dates with both Wizard and Witch. Never having a preference. Samuel spent a lot of time trying to convince her to be his girlfriend but Lillie always put him off.

At Christmas Break, Maxton, Joe and Michael came home for the holiday. They all stayed with us in the house which made Max crazy knowing how Michael felt about Lillie. We created an extra bedroom for Michael. Max and I did see that Michael was a proper Wizard and never made any overtures to Lillie. He would stay stout and stern and ever watchful. But the holiday went off without any problems until new years eve.

In a tradition that has been occurring since the Witches moved next to the Wizards, There was a New Years Masked Ball. It was held in the common Military grounds Formal Hall. We all went and watched the Races try to mixed it up. They actually were getting along better and were, at least, cordial to each other. This did not mean that Pure Bloods, Wizard and Witch, were still looking down on the Mix Bloods. Still looking down on us.

Lillie, flamboyant young witch, went with a cat mask. It was black like Prince and cut so that only her mouth and jaw were exposed. Her dress was sleek black satin. She wore a emerald dangling from a gold chain as the only piece of jewelry. Mandra was a swan. Wearing a White gown with a feathered train. Her white feather Mask only covered from her upper face. Meg and I were plainer. We only wore basic Masks. Her gown was mint green and her mask matched the color. The dress was mid café and was of soft silk. My dress was red with rhinestones. My Mask though basic, was red with the rhinestones outlining the eyes. My dress was full length with a train that swept the floor. Once we all gathered into the living room, Mandra put on her Mask. "Shall we ladies?" We all held hands and transported to the hall.

Max of course, knew me right off. He and the rest of the men were all in tuxes. All with plain masks. Max walked to me with his charming smile. I looked at him with a slight smiled and he took my hand. As the music was playing he asked "Will you dance with me Princess?" I never had no choice but to dance with Max. Even when I hated him. I loved dancing in his arms. I loved Max.

The night was pleasant and calm. No insults were heard, but of course, Lillie would be before the counsels if there were. Maxton paid a lot of attention to one girl in particular. She was a slight girl with light brown hair. She had beautiful blue eyes and a dazzling smiled. He looked at her with desire. It so clear to everyone, including Lillie. Lillie nudged me "Look Mom. Maxy likes her a lot." I nodded and smiled. Maxton danced most of the dances with this girl. She looked up at him with her beautiful smiled and he would melt. Her name was Angel and she was a pure blood.

Lillie danced and danced. Witch or Wizard made no difference. She only wanted to dance and flirt. She did it so well. Joe and Samuel competed for her attention all night. Michael stood back and watched. He watched Lillie for hours. He watched her dance. He watched her laugh and sweetly smile at the other boys vying for her attention. He watcher her flirt and tease. And Lillie ignored him.

She laughed and smiled and danced and flirted as much as any seventeen year old with her self esteem. By the time the Ball was winding down, Max and I told Lillie it was time to go. She shook her head "Not yet. Let me go home with Maxton."

Max looked at me with concern and I sent *"You answer. I don't know what to say."*

Max looked at Maxton "One hour and you and your sister are home."

Maxton smiled at his father "Of course Dad. No problem."

I looked at Max as he took my hand. He pulled me to him and we were home. I asked him "I hope she doesn't kiss too many boys."

Max looked at me irritated "I don't want to know."

I giggled "Don't worry, you wont."

He grabbed me and we were in bed. We kissed and hugged and loved.

CHAPTER 15

In the middle of the night, Max and I were awaken by Maxton's monster voice "Mom! Dad! Get up we need you." Max was up in a flash. I waved my hand and was dressed and ready to move.

Max walked over to Maxton who was in full monster "What?"

"Lillie is gone. We've been searching for hours and cant find her. She has blocked us."

I jumped out of the Bed and tried to find her scent or fell where she was. I had no success. I screamed for Mehgan.

Mehgan, and Ben, appeared in the room "Meg. Lillie. Can you find her?"

Meg looked off and looked at me "No."

I started to space. I went down stairs and looked out and called on Anita.

Anita appeared "Yes Priestess?"

Its Lillie. She is missing. We cant smell her or feel her. I was hoping you could."

Anita look at me for a moment. She shook her head. Max and the family, including Joe stood with me.

Then Max had his monster on and growled suspiciously "Where is Michael?"

Maxton looked at Joe who shook his head and shrouded his shoulders.

Then we heard her screaming and threatening "Take your hands off me Wizard. I am going to kill you when I get loose." We all ran to the front of the house.

Lillie made more threats "Bastard Wizard its none of your business what I do. Let go."

Through the fog we could only see the outline of figures moving toward us.

Lillie continued her tirade "Unbind my powers coward. Let me go."

The figures became clearer and we could see Michael being plummeted with kicks and punches. Both Michael and Lillie falling to the ground as Lillie attempted to get away. She tried to crawl on the ground out of Michaels reach but he had her leg. He pulled her back for a better grip and she continued to plummet his with kicks and punches. Michael was up and dragging Lillie up and pulled her along to the house. "I swear you are in for it. I will have my revenge." Michael continued to drag Lillie to the house never saying a word or acknowledging the physical assault he was being subjected to.

As they came into focus, we could see that Michael had on *his monster*. Puma eyes and facial features of the wild elusive cat. I looked at Max who only looked back at me just as surprised. Monster Michael walked to the monster Max and handed Lillie's arm to him. She continued to attempt to hit and kick him, but Michael stood a safe distance from her assault then.

Max looked at his daughter "Lillianna? Where were you. Why were we unable to locate you?"

Lillie calmed some and stood breathing heavy from her physical attempts to hurt Michael. Her dress covered in mud and grass. Her hair and face smudged with dirt. She looked up at her Dad. "I was at the Witches Village with my friends." She glared at Michael "This Wizard Beast made me leave."

Max loosen his monster. He looked sternly at Lillie "Go in and clean up. You and I will have a talk."

She glared again at Michael "Tell that bastard Wizard to give me back my powers."

Max looked at her and shook his head.

Lillie looked at her Dad in disbelief "Dad!"

Max only looked stern and stout. Lillie looked to me "Mom?"

I was so upset with her that I refused to answer her. She looked angry and stomped her way into the house and up the stairs. We all heard the her door slam.

Michael let his monster loose as did Maxton. Michael looked at Max and said "Lillie was in the Witches Village with friends but …….There was a lot of booze and she and Samuel were …very close to being ….intimate. I think I may have hurt Samuel."

I looked to Anita and she nodded "I will see to Sam." She looked off and smiled "He is well. He will be very sore and have a black eye. But he will be fine." She left then.

Max said "Thank you Michael. I apologize for Lillie. And as you know, she will not apologize."

Michael smiled and said "I know."

Max looked at Michael with his up to something smiled "Unless you are as smart a Wizard as I think you are."

Michael smiled broadly with the permission from Max to force Lillie into an apology.

The next day Lillie came down stairs and grabbed an apple and walked out to the garden. She was not speaking to any of us. No one really cared. We all sat and eat breakfast with out her and enjoyed our conversation.

Meg sent to me *"Do you think she will apologize to Michael for her powers back?"*

I giggled *"I cant say. But I know she can go on too long without them."*

Later that day, as Meg, Mandra and I were putting the dry herbs in containers, Lillie came in the kitchen. "Mom. Would you please asked Michael to give me back my powers?" She asked so sweetly. Like Lillie always did when she wanted something.

I smiled at her "Sincerely apologize to him and I am sure he will give them back."

Lillie stood there and I could tell that she was about to have a yelling fit. Meg knew too and began the count down "Three, two and One."

Right on cue, Lillie began *"I will never apologized to that slimy Wizard Beast. He is intrusive and I hate him. I would rather spend my life as a normal than apologize to that Monster."* She continued her tantrum as all of the house came to watch including Michael. He stood back and laughed.

When Lillie saw him laugh she picked up a mallet and threw it at his head. Of course he still had his powers and the mallet stopped and moved back to the counter. Lillie walked to the door of the kitchen and as she passed Michael she pushed him into the wall and snarled up at him. "You will be sorry." He only smiled broadly at her. Once her door slammed again we all laughed.

That night Lillie tried again. We were all in the family room watching a movie and the boys were playing cards with Max, Ben and Marcus. She came in dressed in jeans and a pretty pink blouse. Her hair was beautifully combed and her face clean and sweet looking. Meg smiled at me as did Mandra. Lillie surveyed the room before entering completely. We continued our activities as she walked over to Michael.

Lillie softly and sweetly said "OK, I am sorry." I knew she was lying. We all knew she was lying.

Michael looked up at her with a smiled and he asked "For what?" We all saw her face go livid.

With a break from the soft sweet voice she had intended for her ruse she snapped "what do you think. For beating on you."

Michael continued to smiled as did Max. "Is that all?"

Lillie huffed and stiffly said "I sorry for calling you names."

Michael played his card hand and looked back at her with the same smile "And" Lillie's face went two shades of red and three shades of green. Meg gave the count down "Three, two, one."

Lillie screamed at him at the top of her lungs. "I knew it. You are a son of a bitch Wizard. You never intended to give me my powers back. I swear before all that is holy, I will have my revenge. You cant hold my powers forever and when I have them back, you know you are going to be regretting this night." She turned and headed for the stairs and stomped to her room and slammed the door.

The Wizards at the table looked at Michael and then they all started to laugh. Mandra said "She has met her match. She maybe ready tomorrow. But I wouldn't count on it. This will most likely go on till the boys return to school."

I shook my head "I don't think I can take another screaming fit."

Max still giggling "Well think how the target feels. He still has to protect himself once he does give them back." He smiled broadly at Michael "Most likely have to protect your self forever. She will never give up."

Michael was giggling and nodding "I know."

We were all enjoying this game of teaching Lillie a lesson, until later that night.

As Max and I were going to bed, we stopped at Lillie's door and knocked. She did not answer. I opened her door and she was not there. But on the wall was a picture in blood of a horned and tailed Wizard. I started to drop to the floor and Max caught me.

I Screamed "Max! Find her. Find her now."

Max transported us to the Counsel Hall. All the counsel members, Witch and Wizard, appeared one after another. Maxton and his friends appeared as well as Mandra and Marcus. As the group came to order there was a laugh. It was Edwin's ugly and disgusting laugh. He hovered high at the back of the hall. He looked directly at Max. "Missing something Mix Blood."

Max, Maxton and Michael had on their Monsters and Joe stood ready with Jordan.

"Where is my daughter Edwin?"

Edwin smiled his wicked smiled "With us of course. She is occupied right now but healthy so far."

Max glared at Edwin "You will die this time Edwin."

Edwin laughed "Then how will you find that harpy you call your daughter. And where is her magic. She uses it as a threat and uses the most foul language." He looked at me and said "Very poor parenting Princess."

As the Priestess I said "Edwin, I will not ever stop killing you and yours should you touch one hair on her head."

He again had his arrogant grin "Oh Princess. She is valuable to us too. As you know, you failed in your commitment, but maybe your daughter wont." At that Michael growled and was gone. Max sent a spell and Edwin fell to the ground. He stood and began to run but Max had him before he could. He was bound and in the death grip of Max.

Max snarled deadly "Where is she Edwin?"

Edwin knew he was about to die "Why should I tell you. You will only kill me anyway."

Marcus spoke to Max and Edwin. "This is not the way of the Wizard. You both will face this counsel."

Edwin laughed "I no longer face that counsel in anything. It turned its back on me a long time ago for a Mix Blood and a Witch."

At that moment several of Edwin's Wizards appeared and one swung his sward at Max. But before the blow hit, Maxton had the Wizard against the wall. The wizards own sward impaling him to the wall. Several Witch Warriors appeared including Dino and Sal.

And the fight began. Maxton and Joe both joining the fight and I and the sentry brothers fought side by side. More Guardian Wizards appeared and the wicked Wizards stood back in surrender at being out numbered. None moving to avoid the instant death that awaited them. Max still held Edwin. Bound and unable to get free, Edwin stood frozen.

Elder Maurice stood and said "Take these Wizards to the Halls and hold them there." He looked at Edwin "You will turn over the young witch or you will not die. But wish you could." Edwin stood stout and quiet. Elder Maurice called on a Master Wizard from the halls.

"Take this Wizard and asked him where Master Wizard Marshall's daughter is. Up the anti each refusal or non response." The Hall Wizard nodded and took Edwin. The other evil wizards were also taken to the Halls.

Then Michael appeared with Lillie. Both covered in blood and Lillie crying. She held on to Michael and screamed "Help him." Max ran to Michael as he dropped to the ground. I had Lillie in my arms and asked her "Are you hurt?" She shook her head and dropped to Michaels side as he lay on the ground. She cried out to us all "Help him Please!"

CHAPTER 16

Michael lay in bed with a head wound and several stab wounds. According to the Wizard Doctors he would need time to heal and would need to be watched for infection. For a week and a half, Meg, Mandra and I took shifts to ensure that he was OK. Lillie hovered and walked in and out. She watched Michael sleep and but never got to close to him. She stood back and only watched. Lillie had her Magic back but never spoke of revenge on Michael. She looked worried and sad. Her lack of sleep and continuous crying had her eyes swollen and red.

When we spoke to her about what had happened she cried. She said "They wanted my magic but I didn't have it. I was still bound. They were angry. The voice of the angel was with the old one. He said that he was going to kill us. Our whole family." She looked at me in her tears "He said that because you failed to produce a child with a Pure Blood that I would have to do it for you." I could see the Monster hovering in Max. I took his hand so that he could calm down while Lillie continued her story. "It was a stone room. They held me with magical chains and they walked around me like I was an animal. I told them that I would kill them. I threaten them with every torture I could think of. They only laughed at me." She stopped and looked back and up the stairs "Michael appeared as his Monster Cat. He killed the wizards closest to me and released my powers. I got out of the chains as they were attacking Michael. They kept swing their swards at him. He fought and fought their attack." She looked at Max with a sob "I didn't know what to do. I dint know what to do." She put her face in her hands and cried for a second. "They were going to kill him." She looked at me "I couldn't let them do that. I finally decided to send bolts of energy at them. I only wanted to help Michael. But when the bolts hit them, they exploded" She shook her head. "I didn't mean to kill them like that. I didn't mean to kill." She looked at us and said "Then Michael grabbed me and we got back to the Counsels chamber." She looked at Max and I "Its my fault that he is hurt. He was very close to being killed and it would have been my fault." She looked from her father and I and said "You know he truly loves me." She laid in my lap and cried while I petted her hair. I looked to Max and he still had his Monster hovering.

Maxton and Joe stayed close and quiet. I asked Max if they were OK, because when I asked them they would nod like good Wizards. Never giving me any indication as to their true state of being. Max said "First real battle. It takes a toll and it takes time to come to grips with it." He looked down "This was their first kill." Marcus spent a lot of time with the boys then. Speaking to them about honor in defense of love ones and weaker beings. I killed many in the past. I still seek forgiveness though I felt no choice in the killing I did."

Late one night after the house had gone to bed. I was napping on the settee in Michaels room fulfilling my shift of watching him. I opened my eyes to see my daughter at the door. I closed my eyes and allowed myself to see through my eye lids. I know it was deceitful but I wanted to see what she was up to. She looked over at me and satisfied that I was asleep, she walked to the bed where Michael slept. She sat down on the bed and lightly touched the cuts and bruising over his stomach and chest. She followed to his shoulders and neck and finally his bruised face and head. Once she touched the bruise at his forehead, Michaels hand grabbed her wrist and he sat up out of a dead sleep. His face to hers. He and Lillie eye to eye. Michael looked at her sternly and growled "What are you doing"

Lillie teary and her voice chocked "I beg you Michael. Please forgive me for everything. Please." She took her other hand and stroked his cheek. "I can't live without your love and forgiveness. I just can't." She sobbed and said "I know I say horrible things to you. I have done horrible things to you. But I still need you. I still want you to love me.

Please forgive me?" Michael stayed stern but his inter struggle of control was weak.

He said in a quiet and soft voice "I love you My Lady. I love you with my whole heart and soul and always have. And to the detriment to my heart, I will always forgive you." Lillie gave a little sob and kissed Michael gently and nuzzled his cheek. Michael put his arms around her and they held each other. She then kissed his cheek and got up and left. Michael stared at the door where Lillie had exited. His heart breaking at that moment. He looked over at me sleeping and laid back down to sleep. All I could think of was that this was true love. True love with the Blue Witch. I don't know how it would ever be possible. She could not be faithful. And maybe that is why he said it was to the detriment of his heart. He knew she could not be his alone.

Days past and word from the counsel was that Leonardo survived Lillie's attack. Edwin remained in the halls defiant and angry. He made several demands to see Max but Max refused to see him. Finally Edwin asked to see Max and Jordan as his brothers from the past. Jordan told Max "He was once our brother. I know he was cruel and unjust to you and Em. But he was young and jealous of you." Max only looked at Jordan. Jordan then said "We are better than that Max. We have compassion, even for our enemies." Max nodded and they went to see him.

Mandra, Mehgan, Ben and I waited for their return. Maxton and Joe were with Marcus at the counsel discussing strategies and defenses. Nathan had returned and came to see Michael. And of course Lillie. She greeted him politely but did not flirt as she had in the past. Her mind still on Michael and the killing of the evil Wizards. Nathan join the boys at the counsels chambers.

Max and Jordan returned and we all met in the family room. Max looked at me with concern. He began "Edwin will not relent. He is willing to die for a life that no longer exists. He believes that the pure blood with rise again. In fact he is sure of it. He is bitter and angry. He is ultimately evil in his heart."

Max then looked down "He said he was heartbroken about Chris and asked for Jordan and I to forgive him for his death." He looked back in my eye "I forgave him in words but I don't know if it is in my heart."

He looked at Jordan "We offered him brotherhood liked when we were little kids. I could see a piece of him wanted to. But he has his loyalty to his father. He has a passion to have his fathers wish that he lead the Wizards come true. He can't let it go."

Jordan said "He wants a pure blood magical child. He believes that is what will convince the others to back down. We told him that we could not help him there, but he believes that Lillie should produce the Pure Blood Heir."

I gave a mock laugh "She is Mix Blood. More so than Max and I. What is he thinking?"

Max took my hand "He is stuck Em. Stuck with a promise of his father to be the Leader of the Wizards. He doesn't realize that Lillie will never be under a thumb. He doesn't know that she is the Blue Witch and I doubt he would understand that. We tried to reason with him. But he can't change his thinking. He only demanded Lillie."

We heard a growl and looked up to see Michael standing with Lillie's help at the doorway. Lillie looked at us with a devious smile ignoring Michaels growl.

She giggled "I could infiltrate and bring them down."

Max, Michael and Jordan simultaneously said "No."

Lillie walked Michael to the couch and helped him sit. She stood back up and looked at us "Listen to me. I am not weak as they are in their magic. In fact their magic barley keeps them alive." She looked back at Michael "I have my magic and I can end this." She looked over to Max "Dad I am able to do this. I can destroy their foundation. I think if I can get in there, the Mix Bloods will listen to me. They are the only real numbers in their Army. That army is low in number and support."

Michael growled "No."

Max shook his head "We cant take that kind of chance Lillie. They may be able to pool their magic and hurt you."

Lillie laughed "No Dad. They cant. I see what they think and what's in their hearts. Most of them just want to come home but stay out of fear and threat to those they love."

I knew Lillie was saying was true. I wanted to end this so badly that I to tried to devise a way to do this. Then it came to me.

"I will go as Lillie."

Max gave an immediate No. I looked at him "Listen, Lillie has a good idea. We need their numbers down and if we can convince the others that their love ones and they could be safe on campus, they may come back."

Max shook his head "Em. All they ever wanted was you. And I haven't spent my whole life and heart fighting to keep you safe to have you in their hands now. I cant do that."

I petted my Husbands cheek with a smiled "I am not a little girl anymore Guardian. I am older and wiser. This will work and I can not be overpowered by them. Lillie will be safe and we maybe able to live free."

Mandra looked at me "Priestess, you are able to do as you say, but Leonardo will never give up."

I looked to Max and then Mandra "I will kill him then. I have all the anger and rage from the heart ache that he has caused my family built up in me. I think I have turned my cheek enough times that God can see the justice in it."

Lillie said "We could go together Mom."

I looked at Lilly "No Lil. I have to do this one alone."

Max looked at me with concern "I could go with you. I could go as Prince or Oz.?"

I thought about it and he said "I can reach some of them too. Some had been friends at one time." We could go together. "Em, if anything, we have the promise." He was right. We still had our weapon.

Lillie looked confused "But what does the Promise have to do with this."

I looked at Max for his approval. We knew that once Maxton and Lillie knew of the weapon that we believed they inherited, there would be their curiosity and someone may get hurt.

Max smiled at me "They need to know."

I smiled weakly and looked at Lillie "When Maxton comes back, we will talk with you abut it."

"I want to know now."

Max said "It involves him too. He needs to be here when we discuses it."

Mandra grabbed my hand and looked in my eyes. I saw her pain and fear.

"Grandmother what is it?"

"I am fearful of what may happen. Please be careful and know that you are so loved by me."

I looked at her and could see that she saw something she was not saying but I wasn't going to worry about it then. I needed Lillie and Maxton safe.

Max said "Ok we will inform the counsels about this plan tomorrow. We will need their support and the Warriors ready just in case." He looked to Jordan "It may only set off the war." Jordan nodded.

That night, with all in the family room Max and I demonstrated the Promise Weapon. We stood at the doors to the yard. We blew up a rock the size of a bowling ball by holding are promise scars together. All looked in amazement. Maxton stood up "And you think Lillie and I can do that?"

Max looked at his son and nodded. "We have seen the energy when you were little. You held hands and put them above your head. If it isn't the promise, we don't know what it is."

Maxton looked at Lillie "Come on Lil. Lets see." Lillie walked over to her brother and as they were about to grab each others hands in air Max step in between them.

"Stop. You need to have a target and the same exact thought of what you want from that object. You can also conjure. If you think of something together, it will be."

Lillie giggled "Lets just say this will work. I would like to send a pack of pixies on the Evil Wizards."

Marcus stood up and said "No. Don't disrupt others worlds for vengeance in ours."

Lillie looked up and reluctantly agreed. "OK." She smiled at her brother "But what about wasps."

Maxton laughed "You are so wicked Lil. Lets do it."

They threw their hands together and we all saw the energy emitting from the grasp of their hands. They looked at each other and they were smiling at the power. I looked over at Max and he looked at me with concern.

Max demanded "Stop. Let go."

They let go. Maxton and Lillie then looked at each other with smiles on. Maxton grabbed Lillie and they were gone. I looked at Max in a panic "You don't think they went to see do you."

He had his monster on as did Michael and as it looked like they were going to find the two when they appeared laughing hysterically. They were hugging each other.

Maxton looked down at his still laughing sister "That is fantastic. We have to do that again. What else does your wicked mind want to see."

Lillie started with "Well we could …."

Max roared "No. Nothing else. This is a weapon comes with a cost. Don't abuse it. Don't waist it."

They looked at their father and Maxton said "Dad, we've had this all our lives and never have used it before. We aren't wasting it." He started Laughing "If it never works again, what we witnessed was worth it."

Joe asked "What did you see, Maxy."

Maxton had his arm around Lillie and looked to Joe and Michael "We went to the Wizards Center where they have been headquartered. They were all running with their arms swinging at the wasps wildly. They had no idea where they came from."

Lillie said "Even Leo was jumping around." Then she shrouded her shoulders and said "The wasps disappeared though. I guess the magic only works while are hands are together."

Joe asked "What are the limits? Where does the magic end?"

Jordan said "I asked the same thing when Max and Em discovered it. I was told by the Witch Sentries that everything has a top and a bottom. Everything has a price. So take care to use it with caution and acceptance of the consequences."

Maxton looked at his sister in the eye and they understood.

CHAPTER 17

After meeting with the Counsels and discussing our plans, Max and I returned home. Maxton and Joe were in the family room and Meg, Ben, Lillie and Michael were in the kitchen. When we walked in Jordan, and Marcus appeared. Jordan looked to Max "Well?"

Max nodded "it's a go." He huffed "Be ready. Have all the warriors ready." Maxton, Joe and Michael stood looking at Max. "You boys go back to school."

Maxton turned red. "No. I am not going anywhere until you've come back. And I will fight if I must."

Joe who was normally quiet and did what Max or Maxton told him stood stout and stern. He was ready for any consequence "I have only this family to call my own. I will not leave now that I am needed. I will not follow that directive Master." Max looked at Joe with admiration and nodded to him.

Michael only looked at Max without saying anything. Max asked "And you Michael?

Michael quietly said "You know I have to stay." Max nodded knowing that Michael would never leave Lillie unprotected and he would follow Maxton in any situation.

Jordan looked to the boys "Once Em and Max return, you three are to return to school. Agreed?" All three agreed.

Marcus looked old at that point "Could there be another way, Max? I fear for you both in that Center without more arms with you."

Max smiled "This has always been about me and Em. Its always been the Mix Blood and the Princess. I think it is time for us to stop hiding and running. We don't have to. Never did have to. But we did for the benefit of the Wizard Race." He look at me and smiled "For us to." He took my hand "We should have killed Edwin at the three lakes. It may have ended then."

I looked at Jordan "I… have to… ask. Should we not return, you will watch out for the kids?" I looked at Marcus then as well.

My son lost his wizard composure "Mom!"

I looked at him "Maxton, I could drive to the market and be killed in a car wreck. I want to make sure that you and your sister are not alone."

Marcus said "No worries Princess. They are our treasures as well." He had me in his big bear hug.

From behind us Lillie asked softly "When will you go?"

I smiled at her and said "In a few days."

She looked at her Dad "Its my idea. Why cant I just do it."

He only looked at her softly. And Lillie let out a breath of frustration.

Over the next few days, the house was nervous and quiet. I wanted more activity and interaction. Mandra knew what I wanted. She always knew. So she planned a big dinner and invited the counsels and the sentry brothers. Lillie would be thrilled to see them. They have been busy training warriors. She decided to set up the yard with flowers and tables. Of course the Madeline and harp music was playing. Before the dinner party began, I decided to go to the field and dance for the trees.

I ran to the center and listen to the music that they always greeted me with. Their whispers of greetings "The Princess has returned. The Princess will dance for us." I ran and jumped. I twirled and dipped. I dance and danced and danced. It was my peace. It was my own world.

As I danced the trees whispered "A stranger watches." I stopped and looked. There at the opposite tree line was Master Robert. I stared at him as he stood nonchalant. Not a Wizards normal at attention posture. I blew my kiss to the trees but I made no move to address him. I stood and watched. He smiled arrogantly as he began his approach. I remain regal.

"My Lady. You were enjoying your self. I wish I could have provided music for you."

I didn't answer him. I only waited for what he wanted.

"I must admit My Lady, I was enchanted." I tilted my head. He continued to walk towards me. "I am a guest for dinner and was walking around the grounds. I had no Idea I would find an angel dancing."

I remained quiet. I had no intention of entertaining this man. When he was a few feet away I flashed the priestess feline eyes. He stopped in his tracks. He smiled and in his velvet voice said "I mean no harm, My Lady. I only would liked to greet my hostess."

I nodded but kept the feline eyes. He stood smiling at me and I was becoming uncomfortable. He then said "I understand that you and Master Max will be leaving on a mission to speak to the Mix Bloods of Leonardo." I nodded. He continued "It is a very risky endeavor for such a lovely lady. I would think that Max would take another Wizard with him."

I challenged "Are you volunteering?"

He smiled broadly "Well, I am sure that Max would want a more skilled Wizard. I am pure blood and I am limited in my powers as you must know."

"I have no idea who has what powers. I am not concerned."

Never dropping his smile "No you wouldn't be. As I understand you, my lady, are very powerful." I did not acknowledge weather I did or not. I only continued to stare at him with the eyes of the Priestess.

He looked back towards the house "May I escort you back to the house and the party?"

He put out his arm. I looked at it and walked without taking it. He laughed as if I had made a joke. He walked with me. "I feel as though you don't like me Princess."

I looked at him and said "I don't know you."

"That is true. But once again, I would like to change that."

Fed up I said "Master Robert, I feel like you are stepping over proper boundaries. I am married to Max. And you speak to me as if I was a single woman."

He smiled broadly again "Well, it is our custom to respect marriage, and that respect is beyond the grave. However, there are many Wizard wives that are board or unsatisfied…emotionally by their husbands. I see my self as a service to them, not a rival of marriage."

I smiled and said "I assure you, I am neither board or unsatisfied in my marriage. I am happy."

He giggled "Wonderful. So now we can just be platonic friends." He put his hand on my arm and I looked at him "And I would like to be friends."

I moved my arm from his grasp and asked "Why?"

"My Lady, because we all need friends."

We walked in to the party area not unnoticed by Max. I sent *"He is a pest isn't he?"* Max smiled and sent *"I warned you. He will not give up. It's a matter of principle."*

Grandmothers dinner party went off without a hitch. The food was delicious thanks to Mandra and Molly. Seems that Lincon and Molly love coming for the parties. The remain living at grandmothers home in Pacific City.

The family had a wonderful time eating and talking. All of us were joking and laughing. Even the Elders joined the crowd. Elder Maurice was bantering with Maxton who was nervous about this interaction with an Elder. He finally gave up to the Elder to make himself more comfortable. Elder Maurice patted his shoulder "Never give up Maxton. There will be a day that you will be addressing the Counsel and will need that wit and charm." Maxton smiled at the complement.

Nathan was in conversation with Meg and Ben. Joe and Maxton continued to talk with the Elders. Max nudged my arm and when I looked at him, he nodded to the swing. Lillie and Michael sat there talking.

Max said "He is in for it."

I giggled "Well, at least she has some feeling for him. What it is I don't know." I looked at Max "She did apologized to him you know."

Max looked at me surprised "She did? When did that happen?"

"When he was healing. She came in and thought I was asleep." I took a deep breath "He told her that he loved her."

Max growled and I giggled "I believe that I was much younger than she when you say you fell in love with me. She is beautiful." I rolled my eyes "Wild, but beautiful."

After a few minutes I said "He said that it was to the determent to his heart. If she is the blue witch, you know as well as I do, she will never be faithful."

Max looked upset "I don't want to think about it Em. I don't even want her with Michael who I know loves her. I just want her my little girl again."

I giggled "Me too."

The next night, Max and I sat with Mandra and Marcus at the dinning table. Mandra looked old and worn. She looked at me and in a very worried voice she said "I wont lie to you or hide things from you Em. There is a chance that you and Max will be taken." I smiled at her "I know that grandmother. But you also know that I will die before that happens." She smiled weakly at me and looked out to the garden and said quietly "I know that too."

Marcus said "Princess, again your courage and heart out way all the magic. I pray that you take care and not be to hasty."

I smiled at Marcus reassuringly "I also have the grace of God. Along with all the magic and all the tricks and schemes, Gods good grace has been with me." I looked at Max "If not for Gods grace and protection, I believe that I would have missed out on the greatest love of my life."

Max kissed my cheek and said "We must finally take this stand." He looked directly at his father "All my life I have hung back, avoiding the fights and the battles. I did this for you, and then for Em, and for my children. But if my children have a chance to live without this rivalry and threat, I will do what I must." He looked to Mandra and then back to Marcus "Em and I have had happiness and love in our lives, and we know that now. We see it now." He looked at me "And we made this decision for the betterment of everyone. We are more powerful than any of the wizards we will be encountering. We have decided to use that power for peace."

I looked at them both "Lillie can not be used for their plots and schemes. Maxton can not be used for their ugliness and to rule over others. These children were not given to us by God for an evil purpose. They are our gifts from him to be cherished and to do what me must to make sure that they live happy and good lives."

Jordan and Mary appeared. Jordan looked at us and said "We will be ready for anything that follows you. The counsel has suggested that you transport to the ravine. It would be best since both compounds have access. We have a good size Military, and your children are insisting on being apart of the defense."

I shook my head "No. I would like them to wait at grandmothers house."

Jordan huffed a little Laugh "Good luck with that Em."

Meg and Ben arrived Ben looked excited and upset "Max. Edwin is gone."

Max jumped up and with a rare departure from the Wizard propriety said "How the hell did that happen."

Meg said "It is the one that has had Maxton's ear. It was Nathan. The Pure Blood."

Max called out "Maxton!"

Maxton, Lillie, Michael and Joe all appeared. Maxton, knowing his fathers emotional voice looked concerned and asked "Dad? What is it?"

Max looked at Maxton "What has Nathan been telling you?"

Maxton looked over the group "He said that he had sight. He said that I would lead all Wizards."

Meg said "It is true. You will."

Maxton looked uncomfortable and looked a his grandmother "Grandmother, you can see. What is it you see?"

Mandra looked at Maxton "You will lead, but who and what you lead, you have not decided."

Lillie stood like a Wizard. She was quietly listening and was stout and stern. Max walked over to Maxton and asked quietly, "Maxton. Tell us what Nathan has told you?

Maxton looked at his Dad without emotion "He said that it has all been a lie. Lillie and I are more Wizard than any other blood. He would tell me that we would be the parents of the new Wizards. The new pure bloods." Maxton tilted his head "I listened but I did not think about it. It bothered me. It didn't feel right."

Max then told Maxton and the others "Edwin has escaped and Nathan help him."

Maxton's face feel. "He was my guardian! He took a vow!" At that moment, It all came clear to Maxton. He had been used and who he thought was his friend and protector, was a liar and fiend. He was angrier than I had ever seen my son. I looked into his eyes "Maxton?" But he did not see or hear me through his anger. He shook his head and then transported out. Lillie looked at us in a panic "He's gone to the Wizard Center! He's gone to kill Nathan!" Lillie then was gone to her brother.

Max and I looked at each other and we too, transported to Maxton and Lillie.

CHAPTER 18

As we appeared to Maxton and Lillie, we found Maxton had indeed killed Nathan. He stood over his body seething with anger. Lillie was as the priestess. Full armor and her own immoral feline eyes. Max and I looked to one another.

Max walked to his son "Maxton. Go back before you cant."

Maxton looked at his father and said "I cant. I wont. I will not live this way any longer. I will make sure they all know that I will not be their puppet."

Lillie walked to her bother and stood next to him "Nor will I."

At that moment, Joe appeared to Maxton "What ever you decided, my brother, I will follow you." Maxton hugged Joe and they looked to Max in defiance.

Joe looked to me and Max "I want you to know, I have always considered you my parents. I will fight along side of you till my last dying breath." I shook my head in disbelief as Max hugged Joe. I walked over and petted his cheek with a smile.

Michael had Lillie's arm. "Go back Lil. We will take care of this." He showed no surprise at Lillie's Priestess.

She looked at him and Laughed in her Priestess voice. "Not happening." He was frustrated and scared for her "Lillie Please." She only laughed that witch laugh of hers and shook her head while she looked in his eyes. He knew he could do nothing to convince her to return home.

I looked at Max "Well lets get to it." I looked down at Nathan's body. Torn and twisted from the anger of Maxton. I looked at my son "Don't let them make you a true monster Maxton." He looked back at Nathan's body and back to me. He nodded.

Maxton looked at Max "Where are we in the Center?"

"In the cells… the wizards rooms." Max looked at the group. "There is security here that will detect all of you. I can get through undetected. I will go out and look around. All of you stay here+ and I will call you as soon as I take out the security."

I began to protest and Maxton put his hand on my arm and nodded to his father. Max was transparent and only I could see him. He kissed me softly and left the room.

We stood waiting for word from Max to come. I was nervous and scared for my family. But determined as they were to bring this to a head. To stop the hiding and give up our freedom for their evil beliefs. It seems like hours for Max to call.

Then I received the transmission *"Em. Security is out. But there are guards walking the halls. Have the group transport to central hall that is where I am."*

I knew that the kids had never been to the central hall. I looked at my son. "Follow me." He looked at the group and we all transported to the Central Hall where Max stood by on of the witness boxes. Lillie moved her hands over the center of the hall and looked at me. "Mother, you were wonderful." I giggled at the memory. She then said "They are planning a ceremony on the Solstice. Power transfer." She looked at us strangely. She asked "Who is Lori?"

Max and I looked to each other and I said "A silly mortal. No threat."

Lilly grinned and said "Oh but desperate for your power."

Maxton broke in "Where are they father?"

Max said "In the court yard." He looked to me "They have reserves. There are at least a couple of hundred standing ready in the court yard. They were expecting this breach. They believe it is only your mother and I. I want them to continue that thought."

I looked at the children "Go back. Let us do this alone."

None made a move. Standing in the Wizard stout posture, including Lillie. I looked to Max "What now. What is the plan now."

"Max said we go to the tower. We will take out the guards there and attempt to reach the Mix bloods through transmission." He took a breath "If they respond as I hope, they will transport to the military base." He looked at me in the eye "If they don't, they will raise the alarm." I nodded to him.

Max looked at the group and we all prepared to kill and remove the guards. We transported and found four guards watching all directions. All monsters on, Max, Maxton and Michael took three without issue Joe had a little more trouble but completed the job. All four lay on the ground. Lillie looked unfazed as she stepped over one of the dead bodies. We looked out over the court yard and as Max had told us. All the Wizards were in formation prepared for battle. Hundreds stood at Wizard attention. They all faced forward listening to Leonardo.

Leonardo stood on a platform with Edwin and Lori. He said "Victory of our cause is close. The ancient ways of our ancestors is at hand. We will take the magic back from the mutts that have been produce by the treacherous Princess and trader Mix Blood Wizard. Take back the magic that rightfully belongs to the Pure Wizards. We will have a magical child for the sake of the Wizard Magic." The group cheered.

I looked at Max as the crowd settled and Leonardo continued his rhetoric and propaganda. "I have a plan Max. I would pull your trick and be transparent and speak to the Wizards in the ear."

Lillie smiled "Oh let me. Let me do it. I know I can convince them." I knew my seductress daughter could if anyone could, convince their most staunch supporter.

I looked to Max "Let us try. You and the boys focus on Edwin and Leonardo." I smiled at him "I will take care of Lori." I giggled "of course she has that pimple on her nose back at this moment."

Max moved to the window and saw Edwin looking disgustingly at Lori. He started to laugh. "Ok Em. You and Lillie do your thing." He looked at Lillie who stood with her smile "And please use propriety. Any thing else will convince them otherwise." Lilly gigged and Michael growled without meaning to.

Lillie smiled at me and I said "Do not be visible to more than one Wizards at any one time. Speak softly in their ear and be convincing to the intended death of these wicked men. Let them know that there is no victory but that the counsel welcomes them back with their loved ones. That the Mix Blood had been made full status wizards." She smiled at me "Mom I know what to say." I pulled my brows together "Lilly follow your fathers advise. Be proper." She nodded and lied.

Lillie and I transported as transparencies to the wizards. We, both as priestess, floated invisibly through the ranks of the Wizards. Lilly stopped at the ear of a fairly young wizard. She tapped his name and in the most seductive voice I have ever heard began "Marc?" The young wizard stood stout but it was clear he heard. "Marc beware the death speech of Leo. He only cares for himself. But I care for you. With me you have a real life. With me you have freedom and love." His eyes moved to look towards his ear. " Go Marc. Take your family and met me at the Wizard compound. I will reward you." She kissed his cheek and he took a breath. He closed his eyes and was gone. I almost forgot what I was doing. She was so …magical.

I stood at a Wizard with graying hair. He was mixed blood. He was mixed with Witch. I was surprised at that. His name was Andrean. I spoke softly in his ear "Andrean, mix blood." He stood stout "Witch and Wizard. Listen to your Princess and your Priestess. Find your freedom and acceptance with me. Be who you are, my love. Meet with us on the compound." His mouth moved slightly and then a transmission *"You lie."* I spoke again as I saw another Wizard disappear as Lillie did her job. "Andrean, I am mix blood. My family is mix blood. Your magic will not aid you in respect with Leo. He uses you. We offer freedom. We offer acceptance." He looked unnerved. He knew he would never be but a servant to Leo. I continued "See your self as a true Wizard. See your Magic used for the righteous and good. Be loyal to your kind." He was breathing heavy and disappeared.

We moved in and out of the ranks and convinces about two dozed wizards and then one that I approached became irritated. His name was Arlo. I spoke to him with the same soft voice. "Arlo. Be free with us. Leave the lies of Leo and Edwin. Be free and accepted." He began to lose that proper Wizard stare and posture. He looked around but did not see me or Lillie. I look over at Lillie and she knew. Before he could send out the alarm. He lay dead by the invisible bolt of energy of Lillie.

The jig was up. All of the Wizards around Arlo moved to his body while Lillie and I moved to the platform. Lillie looked to me and I bound Edwin and stood full form to the Crowd. All of the Wizards stood clamoring. I looked at Lillie and sent to her to stay invisible. She nodded.

Leonardo stood looking at me in shock. "Princess. I have expected infiltration, but not by you."

I looked at the crown of Wizards in their ranks. In the commanding voice of the Priestess I ordered "Be Still!" They all quieted and stood still. I looked to Edwin seething at my appearance and my binding him. Lori stood in fear.

I looked at Edwin "Nathan lays dead in his cell. Maxton, the child of your desire, now knows the complete truth of your deceptions. Your lies." I looked at Leonardo "Make a move and you will be dead." He smiled at me "Princess, why would I want to harm you. I only wanted what was best for my kind." I sneered at him "No. You lie to me and these wizards. You only care about yourself. Even to the destruction of your son."

Lori began to move to escape. To my surprise, she was lifted into the air and held screaming. "Edwin help me. Help me." I laughed "He is unable to . He has never been able to you silly mortal." I looked her in the eye "You know it was Leonardo was the one who killed your mother?" she looked down at me "It was Max and you know it." I shook my head with a smile "No Lori. I was Leonardo." She looked at him, and the silly mortal could see the truth.

I Looked to the Crowd. "What has been promised to you? A life of servitude to Edwin and his mortal who planed to take our powers?" I laughed. " Make no mistake, you are used. Your Magic used for evil. You are offered amnesty and freedom from the true Wizards Counsel. Those that follow this mad man are doomed." They all looked at Leonardo who put up his hands and said "No. Listen to me." But many had already left. Max appeared as did the boys. All had on their monsters including Joe who was a phoenix looking beast. I had no time to marvel at him.

Max moved forward and Edwin made a move to him. Lillie had him stacked in the middle of the court yard with many Wizards moving away quickly. She giggled and became full form.

Max looked at Leonardo "It ends today Leonardo. It ends or you end."

Leo lifted his hand, and Maxton had him in a death grip of the teeth of the monster wolf.

Max addressed the crowd "Go Home. Be free. Love your families and live a life." He looked at me "Or die." He looked over the crowd "Many of you know me from childhood. A Mix blood. A mix blood who followed his heart and vow. You need to follow yours."

Max looked at me and looked over to Leonardo. Maxton let Leonardo go. I walked to my family and husband. Leonard was livid and pulled out his sward. But before he could swing, my sward swung and his head hit the ground. Max grabbed me and screamed at the kids "Go!" we were at the ravine.

As we arrived we saw the Witch and Wizards loyal to us dressed in red surrounding the ravine. Max barked at the kids "Move! get to the perimeter." Maxton looked at in our eyes deeply. Lillie nodded and they joined Marcus on the perimeter. We stood in the center looking up at the Wizards and Witches who came to battle. The battle that would be the one to set us all free. It was finally going to end.

Max looked to me and pulled me in his arms. "My lady, My princess. What ever happens, I have loved you beyond time and matter. I wish we had never left our dream world. I often see us there again." I kissed him with passion "That is where I will always be to love you." as we stood looking into each others eyes the Wicked Wizards appeared and the battle was on. Max and I swinging swards and magic at the attacking Wizards. Witch and wizards in red battling at the perimeter. Edwin appeared on a winged giant lizard. He flew at Maxton who threw a spear at the flying beast and it exploded. Edwin fell to the ground. As Max and I were being plummeted by the Wizards. Edwin moved toward us. As he did, he shot a golden arrow and it hit Max in the side by his heart. I felt the pain and dropped to the ground. Max in the same pain reached for me. I pulled my self up with the help of his arm. Max and I knew the wound was mortal. He recognized our precarious situation in the numbers we were battling. Edwin moved over to us and we fought the on slot of Wizards. They moved away bleeding and injured as he approached. We stood breathing heavy, in pain and on guard at the wizards that remained. All of Edwin's Followers moved to the center of the ravine and surrounded us.

Max look up to the parameter and order all to say back. "Remain in position." He looked at Marcus and then to Jordan. He then looked to his children he sent *"Be brave and honorable. Use magic for the good and just. Look for the lords good grace and be thankful for the love and happiness in your lives."* Lillie screamed down at him "Daddy!" I blew my kiss to my children. Lillie whispered to me "Mamma?" I sent a kiss to Marcus and Mandra. This was the end. But when I looked at Max. My guardian, friend and true love, I would have never change a thing. He was my life.

As Edwin approach he had that slimy smile on. "Its done Max. You are done."

Max smiled at Edwin "Maybe...Only God knows." Max looked at me and I knew what to do. He looked at Edwin and the monster cat leaped at him and with one tare to the neck, Edwin was dead. I jumped to Max as the other Wizards moved forward. I lifted my left hand. Max lifted his. He pulled me to him and we kissed. As our promises came together. All went to white nothingness.

www.ingramcontent.com/pod-product-compliance
Lightning Source LLC
Chambersburg PA
CBHW060742210726
48292CB00012B/61